Burn the Sea

Book 3 of the
Blood Wild Chronicles

Tamara A. Brigham

❧❀❧

For Eva and Willis...
...for the memories.

❧❀❧

Chapter 1

The weakest members of the group were thrown off their feet as the concussive force blew backward through the room. Shards of metal, bits of concrete, dust from the unswept edges and the ground outside, burst outward into the open air but those inside were not entirely spared. Refusing to leave anyone behind, Vance yanked the nearest woman up and began the charge through the seared, curled-open wound in the sheet metal the explosive force created. Under Jia's direction, words Vance did not hear, the others did the same, helping those who needed it to make a stumbling dash towards the perimeter of razor wire. Jia came last, the pack alpha seeing to the safety of the rest as Kato and Wist led the way.

The barrage of distant gunfire temporarily ceased on the side of the building where the hunters had breached. But the shouts grew louder as new commands were uttered in response to the explosion some of them could not see. They heard and felt the shuddering of the facility's grounds, however, the shaking of the walls, shifting the focus of their assault from the entry to the point of escape. Cries spidered through adjacent streets, a cluster of them following Helena and the Fela sisters as they endeavored to lead as many assailants away from the explosion as they could.

It did not take the four long to conclude that those in pursuit had given up following them in favor of doubling back to the focal point of activity.

Helena howled a warning.

Jia snarled in frustration.

They would run faster as Cana, as Fela, as Ursa. But some of those with her, including Liam, would never make a change in their weakened condition and she would not risk anyone else witnessing a revelation of her nature.

Nor would she leave Vance behind.

Halfway across no man's land, without the protection of the metal containers once used for transport but now used for storage and housing by people who could get to them, the next obstacle loomed.

Another spray of preciously rare bullets scattered.

The runners instinctively flinched and ducked.

The woman Vance dragged along screamed and lurched, causing him to stumble. Jia, the only one not dragging the ailing, caught the woman up by her other side, despite the blood spreading from the woman's upper shoulder and down her naked chest.

The shooters erupted around the corner of the building into the open where they could be seen, wraiths in black without visible faces. Wraiths that dredged the memories of another night, another flight to freedom, another hunt. Fighting against the pounding in her chest that strangled her efforts to breathe as the burden between them went slack and stopped moving, Jia glanced back to gauge the distance of the threats behind and before.

A gun was raised.

Vance, recognizing the unavoidable, let the limp woman drop to the cracked pavement after several more dragging steps. Jia lurched, unprepared for the shifting weight, but recovered her footing in time for a twisting motion that threw her body onto Vance's so both crashed to the ground as the bullet's buzz whined overhead.

Someone screamed.

Another fell.

"Wist! Do it!"

There was no need for Jia's instruction as she and Vance fought to their feet. The dead weight of those drained of life was left behind. The rest, limping as fast as long unused limbs could manage, would never make it over the fence. Wist recognized it too. Without breaking his stride, he popped the pin of the orb clutched in his hand and lobbed it forward.

Nothing happened.

"Shart…"

Directly behind him, shifting her brother's weight, Zen pulled the pin of her orb with her teeth and threw it too.

Its explosion, when it came, the second orb landing near enough to the first to set it off, felt twice as bright, twice as intense, as the first inside the complex. It blew Zen, Liam, and Wist into those behind, creating a domino effect as others collided with them or tried not to. Kato, at the front, dodged when the orb was thrown and avoided the worst of the blast's blowback, though he winced at the pricking sting of debris biting into his thighs and arms.

Somewhere beyond the fence, Helena howled again, announcing the arriving rumble of thundering hooves, clattering wagon wheels, additional shouts, and running boots.

"Keep going!"

Chapter 2

Lowell's incoherent wail ripped Oasis from the shadows where she had watched the argument between the Laedan and Thomas Quentin, the sound pulling her into the entrance hall in the hopes of learning what had happened, in the hopes that there was something she could do to help.

The possibility that the man's grief came at the loss of Donn made her heart trip with expectation.

He was on his knees, clutching the dangling female hand of the body covered with a canvas and borne on a pallet between two Protectors, while Chief Ernest, white-faced and grief-stricken, in range of both Laedan and victim, looked to draw further away from both with each screeching sob the kneeling man uttered.

Oasis could not see the woman's face.

She did not need to.

There was only one woman Lowell would grieve with such intensity. Whatever identifier he used to know her, he did.

Oasis' eyes lifted to meet Thomas' shifty, panicked gaze as he cautiously backed towards the door where the chief had just entered, taking advantage of Lowell's distraction to remove himself from any act of retaliation born of this new trauma.

"What…?" she began, her voice barely audible above the wailing. Thomas was not going to answer the question, not after the command to leave the Fortress he had been given. Lowell was unable to form words or thoughts or anything more than the wounded animal squalls echoing in the vast chamber, rattling the glass. Someone needed to be the rational one, the one to do the talking, the one to take action.

Oasis did not believe it should be her but there was no one else.

The closer she came to the heart of the grief storm, to Lowell's pain, the more keenly she felt it wrap around her until she was on her knees beside him, an arm around his shoulders, tears on her cheeks.

Lowell did not appear to notice she was there.

Ernest's mouth opened to speak as Lowell keened again.

Oasis swallowed hard and closed her eyes against the horror.

She had done this.

∾*∾

The Cana leaped from the dark places, using the wall of a crumbling building as a point of leverage to launch onto the back of one of the arriving horses and off into the face of the wagon's driver. The horse, gouged by canine claws, screeched its fear and reared, tipping the cart, throwing both driver and Cana onto the muddy street.

She was prepared for it.

He was not.

The driver, face bloody from the slashing fangs, screamed and flailed at the empty air to get free of his assailant, his distress greater than that of the bolting horse trying to charge away with the upturned wagon bouncing behind it.

Those nearest, men and women in mud-brown uniforms, scrambled out of the way, some trying to catch the reins of the errant animal while others rushed to retrieve the goods the tipped cart scattered into the street.

The beast, wolf or Cana, disappeared into the shadows from which it had come, unfazed by the commotion or the tranq shots taken. In the turmoil, perhaps the shots had missed their target.

The Cana howled.

Others before and aft pressed towards the sound of gunfire.

On another street, nearer to their original outlook point, three tawny Fela wove a braided path around the predators streaming towards the compound where their brother had gone. Hunting as one, they picked off one wraith, then another, until the solitary howl splintered the night.

The signal announced what their sensitive ears had already detected. The arrival of others.

There was no speaking, no argument or dissent between them. The howl had come nearer to the point of detonation and those they hunted had either already breached the compound or were running on the outer perimeter towards the explosion. Towards where they hoped their brother was. With the enemy approaching on both sides, the logical choice was to join the Cana, follow the sounds of chaos, rejoin their brother, save his life.

They would not abandon their own.

The Fela ran north along the razor wire fence. The bodies of the dead were left behind.

❧*❧

The uproar from below punctured Nik's dreamless reverie with the sort of terror recognized from too many drug-induced nightmares. He recognized his father's voice although he had never heard such wailing, not even after Jonni's death. It could only mean one thing.

Another Channon brother lost.

Bleary-eyed, he pealed from his bed, wrapped his threadbare robe around his shoulders, and stumbled barefoot to the lobby stairs. He was the sole witness, before his gaze landed on the tableau in the room's center, to the figure squeaking through barely open doors into the Fortress courtyard. The stride, the posture of the fugitive, identified him as he skulked away, but Nik's focus on the receding shadow was preempted by another of his father's piercing cries.

The form beneath the shroud was female. Not Donn.

Yiva.

Mother.

The realization pulled Nik's legs out from under him; he tumbled down the remaining four steps.

How could his mother be dead?

It did not make sense.

Despite the knot in his chest closing around his heart, steadily squeezing as if it would halt its beating in a painfully rhythmic fashion, Nik forced himself to his feet, forced himself closer. No one spoke. The stricken Protectors appeared not to know what to do, whether to set the pallet on the floor or continue to bear it as they were. Oasis, sincere in her mourning as she offered comfort to Lowell in his, seemed an odd addition to the room, but with Quentin's departure, maybe there had been some business between the three Nik was not privy to when the chief arrived.

Ernest looked as horrified and grief-stricken as Lowell though he bore his emotions in silence. Somehow, the man's grief did not surprise Nik. None of the others noticed.

"Chief…?" He haltingly stopped at the man's side, beyond his father's reach as though expecting to be blamed for what had happened. He could be liable. Sometimes he did things in his drug stupors he did not remember. To Nik's awareness, however, he had never killed anyone. He would never have killed his mother.

Besides, he was clean. Or as clean as he had been in too many years to count.

"I don't know." Ernest's voice was small, choked and reedy as though his lungs were not getting enough air. "Patrol found her in…"

"She was out there alone?"

"I…" From the chief's expression, this was not the sort of tale to tell in the Fortress lobby with Lowell wailing in the background. "We don't know; we don't know how long she was…"

Nik nodded. He understood what the chief alluded to. Unless he had slept for days, as sometimes happened when sleep finally overtook him, Yiva had only been gone from the Fortress for a handful of hours. The change to grubber could not be accurately predicted. Sometimes it took days. Sometimes only hours. If she would be affected by the strange condition. They could not keep her in the lobby.

Doing so was a risk to all of them.

Reaching to pull back the shroud, to see his mother's face one more time, possibly the last, Nik chokingly began, "Yes…we should spose of her before she…"

He had to say it. No one else would.

Ernest blanched.

Lowell yowled and yanked Nik's arm back before he could touch the shroud as if his touch would defile the woman beneath it. "We'll do no such thing!" Grip tight, he glowered at his son, mouth twisted in a grimace of fury and remorse, his face and nose wet with the expression of grief, daring Nik or Ernest or anyone else to contradict his decree.

Facing his father's wrath was nothing new. Nik had faced it hundreds of times, an occasionally preferred response to the resigned apathy that had developed in the face of Nik's host of addictions. He did not fear his father's opinions the way Jonni had, nor did he fight against him the way Donn perpetually did. Nik stood his ground against his father's glare, aware of who and what he was and knowing he would never be anything but who he was, no matter what his father thought, wished, or tried to make him into.

Lowell's anger this time, however, was enough to give him pause. Knowing what needed to be done did not mean this was the time or place to do it, to discuss it. That would come later, when the shock and horror had bled into the ache of daily reminders, and the need for burial set in.

"In the storage…where Jonni…" His murmur trailed off, his even tone cutting through his father's fury enough to temper Lowell into releasing Nik's wrist and wave dismissively in the direction of the door into the basement.

"Get Segara in here! Find out who did…"

"Segara's not…" started Ernest.

Lowell snarled, cutting him off. "Someone else then! I want the head of the man who did this! I want to see him bleed! Find him! I don't care how, just do it!"

He turned and stumbled towards the basement stairs, leading the Protectors and their precious cargo to a place where she would be safe from anyone else's attempts to harm her.

He would rather place her to rest upon their marriage bed until the inevitable final arrangements were made. For all of his bluster, for all of his grief, however, he knew it would be a mistake.

Arm around his shoulders, a gesture Lowell continued not to acknowledge, Oasis looked sympathetically at Nik.

Nik's closed eyes were set into an expression of defeat. He did not see her gaze. He did not watch them go.

✿*✿

By the time Jia herded the beleaguered group through the blasted fence and Helena's Cana form charged into their midst, they were caught in the crossfire between the enemy behind and those in the brown uniforms immediately recognized as Kennedy Guard. The Hallister soldiers did not aim at those pathetic few squeezing one by one through the fence opening. Rather they picked off the black-clad shapes rushing their flanks, dropping them with sleep darts and a few precious bullets from the refuge of the razor wire perimeter.

She did not know how many were behind them, how many the Fela sisters had chased out of the side streets into the path of the nearly three dozen Kennedy Guard.

Those chasing them were fewer than the Kennedy Guards.

"Come on!"

A man in a wool cloak stood on the driver's seat of the other upright wagon, waving the survivors closer as Kennedy Guards filled the gap behind them, a shield against attackers who chose to risk the outnumbering odds.

Kato and Wist faltered. Vance held Jia's arm to retard her charge.

The familiarity of the voice presented as many questions as it answered, but it was one Jia was willing to take a chance on trusting.

"Let's get you out of here!"

Did he recognize her, Jia wondered as she freed her arm from the mage's grip.

In the dark, how could he?

The Guards advanced through the hole in the fence, covering one another against enemy fire but the night, the battle, was not over. The odds of finding shelter, of making it across the border to the Bunker with Liam and the others, pursued by this unknown enemy, paled in the face of offered succor.

The decision was made.

"Go."

Kato narrowed his eyes and growled.

Wist was the first to obey.

"He tries anything…" Vance muttered under his breath as he followed and wincingly hoisted the weak and ailing into the wagon.

Jia's nod of agreement to his tacit threat was mollifying.

Kennedy Laedan or not, against so many Cana, Geary Hallister would not stand a chance…so long as the Guard remained behind.

❧*❧

"I'm sorry."

To Ernest's ears, the words were inadequate, barely befitting the woman brutally deprived of life. Hours earlier she had sat beside him, a frightened shell who insisted on leaving the Protectorate alone.

He should not have let her go.

"You didn't…"

"No, but maybe I could have prevented it." The older man staggered to the nearest bench and sank onto it with a groan. "She came to me, afraid; I thought…" He shook his head at Nik's curious expression. "I thought she was afraid of Jonni's killer, I suppose…"

Voicing his suspicion, repeating his unverified assessment that Yiva had been most terrified of her son, was an unwise card to play to Donnovan's twin. For now.

It might matter to the new Channon bride, but that, Ernest thought with a shivering sigh, was trouble for another day.

"Is Donn…?"

Nik shrugged, acutely aware Ernest was hiding something but understanding it was the chief's job to do so when engrossed in an active investigation. Nik was as viable a suspect as any other until proven otherwise. "Dunno; haven't seen him." He could not remember the exact hour when he had last seen his brother. Donn was no doubt far away from the Fortress tonight. If he were here, the commotion would have drawn him in as it had drawn Nik.

"I should have sent someone with her when she left…I believed she had an escort. Streets aren't safe for someone like her…at night." Coughing on choking bile he whispered, "Strangled, beaten…raped. Left in the alley where they had…"

"They?" Nik croaked. "You think there's more than one…?"

"Conjecture." The thought of many attackers was as sickening a thought as a single one. The number did not matter. The deed was done and Yiva was gone.

"Is there another mage…since Segara's not…?"

"Not in my crew." Given the discomfort tracker-mages endured in the line of duty, given the rarity of that particular mutation in the post-Undoing population, LaGuardia's Protectorate headquarters was lucky to have Segara. At the rate things were going, Ernest imagined LaGuardia would be luckier still if the mage stayed on when this was over. "Can't say when he'll be available, if she'll keep that long."

His words faded into an uncomfortable whisper. The dead did not keep indefinitely. By the time Segara came back from the windmill-chasing endeavor he had undertaken, the corpse would already be processed and any existing evidence would be in the ground.

Unless Lowell had other plans for her.

"I'll take care of that…of her." Looking up from hands clasped between his knees, Nik untangled his fingers to put a hand over Ernest's and muttered, "I know she could be…this isn't your fault." Her death was no more Ernest's fault than it was Nik's…or his father's. LaGuardia was rife with random acts of violence and not enough good men and women to prevent such things. The killer could be anyone, the cause anything. "You find who did this…and I'll see to things here…let you know when she…"

For several moments their gazes held, Ernest acknowledging the unusual, unfamiliar clarity in the young man's eyes. While he rarely trusted unreliable addicts, he believed he could trust Nik with his mother's care, at least until grief dragged him into using one more time.

꙳Burn the Sea꙳

Chapter 3

No one spoke as the wagon jostled along and the sounds of the laboratory battle grew distant. The clop-clop of hooves on ancient, grass-cut pavement and the clatter of the wood and metal wheels filled the void with each turn made onto seemingly random side streets. Those huddling in the wagon's bed stared at Liam, at Jia, seeking guidance and reassurance, hoping for answers as Kato, Wist, and Beren kept watch at the rear, orbs in hand, looking for an indication they were being followed, hunted. Near the front of the bed, Zen and Helena watched the decayed humps of collapsing buildings ahead of them and those flickering light sources behind inadequate window coverings with the ever-present concern that they would be ambushed, that they were being escorted somewhere as dangerous as the location they were leaving behind.

The Fela sisters reached the wagon moments before it began its retreat. Those who had traveled to this place with Jia were safe. Liam and some of those held captive with him were too. She had accomplished what she had come to do. With Kennedy Guard running behind and beside them and the sounds of fighting growing fainter, it seemed those in the wagon would be protected.

Vance's frown, however, as he nursed his injured hand on his lap and stared narrow-eyed at the back of Laedan Hallister's head, suggested the tracker-mage believed something was off.

Jia thought so too, though she did not think Hallister was aware of their identities yet or knew who, or what, Vance was.

This was not the time to talk about it.

She covered his bloody hand with hers, intending comfort, only to be reminded in his flinching that such contact for a mage could be torture. When she began to withdraw, he put his other hand over hers to keep it there. He did not look at her so Jia satisfied herself with glances at her twin and Liam who wearily leaned his head on his sister's shoulder as if to sleep. His unfocused eyes, however, remained on Jia as though he also had something he wanted to say.

The risk of being overheard by Hallister over the other noises of the rescue was not worth an attempt at conversation. Instead, she shuffled out of her jacket and draped it over the shoulders of the nearest nude, shivering form.

Others followed her example as snow continued to drift in large, lazy flakes from the deepening gray sky.

The echo of gunfire ceased. The shouts of combat thinned.

The wagon rolled on.

❧*❧

Lowell neither looked up nor spoke when Nik, still barefoot in his robe, trudged into the sitting room where, hours earlier, there had been a discussion about a family meal that had not come to pass. Only the staff seemed to have noticed Yiva's failure to appear at a table eventually cleared of platters and bowls when no one arrived to eat.

The absence of one or more of the Channon men was not unusual, as borough business, and addiction in Nik's case, often kept them away or delayed their attendance.

Yiva, however, had never missed dinner at the family table unless she was unwell.

Someone should have checked her room. Asked questions.

No one had.

Nik had noted, in the faces of staff members he passed, the same 'should have done' remorse dogging him.

His father reached back absently with a glass of whiskey he had poured, a second glass, Nik assumed, in preparation for someone to join him in his misery. The lure to numb the screaming grief pounding in the back of his skull, grief Nik had thus far refused to vent, was exquisitely real. Real enough to force him into this room, into his father's company, instead of allowing the opportunity to find refuge in his usual haunts and vices.

He did not expect sitting with his father to be pleasant, but it had to be done. It was better than using. As the number of living Channons shrank, pulling together as a family, as father and son, was more important than a pill, a needle, or a piped balm. Those things were absent in the Fortress.

Alcohol was plentiful.

The uncomfortable decision to remain sober made him shake his head before shuffling to an empty chair and wilting into it. Lowell did not see the headshake, but Nik moving away, not taking the glass, was answer enough to the offer.

Lowell drained the glass's contents and set it on the long, low table between them.

There were lip rouge stains on the clear surface.

Nik knew who had been with Lowell last.

"What did he say?" Lowell lifted his downcast gaze enough to interpret Nik's perplexed expression and muttered, "He brought her home. What did he say?"

Chief Ernest. Nik shrugged. "She'd gone to see him…he thinks she knew something about who…about what happened to Jonni…that she was afraid of whoever…but she wouldn't admit it. When she arrived, when she left, he believed she had an escort to…"

"Take stock of the Guard. Find out who…"

"Already have Captain Ortega on it." If any of the LaGuardia Guards were unaccounted for, Arlo Ortega would know soon enough.

If any of them were dead or guilty of murder or negligence, they would know that too. Captain Ortega was dependable, and firm enough with his troops when he had to be to maintain their loyalty, their service, in line with the Laedans' needs.

"Good," Lowell snorted.

Nik read a hint of pride in the sound that might not have been present. Eyeing the whiskey bottle, contemplating the previously offered drink as the next sentence formed at the back of his throat, he continued, "She'd been beaten…strangled…" He hesitated to say the next word and finally finished with, "abused. Maybe robbed. No one's gone through her pockets yet…"

"No one's gonna touch her." The snarled command was both protective and burdened with grief hinging on the realization that Lowell, too was included in the statement.

Rather than express the necessity of sposing that would prompt an argument Nik was not emotionally ready to have, he instead said, "They're asking for witnesses, trying to find an available mage…"

"Think he did this?" Lowell clutched the hanker balled in his hands between his thighs and then wiped his nose with it. He was no longer screaming, no longer blubbering and weeping, but the redness of his eyes and nose and the damp stains on the hemp cloth square proved he had been until recently.

"Chief?"

"Quentin."

Nik blinked. "I…don't…"

Having witnessed his father's aide slinking out of the Fortress as the others in the lobby gathered, Nik could, at first, think of no rational reason for the deductive leap. Nik had not seen Quentin in days, did not know where he had been before his departure, if he had been coming in or going out when Yiva was brought home.

If Yiva, like Nik, had an inkling Quentin was responsible for Jonni's death, and Quentin knew it, it gave the aide motive. It gave her a reason for the fear Ernest suspected. Other than a mad act of random opportunistic violence, it was the only motive that made sense.

It framed Lowell's aide as the prime suspect for her death too, regardless of how prized and cherished Lowell had held Quentin to be.

"I do." Another drink was poured and swallowed in a hasty gulp. "Find Donnovan. Have him redirect every resource we have into finding Thomas…bring him to me."

"Haven't seen Donn, but I'll find him." He would find them both. His father's faith in Donn getting these orders in place was telling, as was his unvoiced lack of faith in Nik's ability to do likewise. Nik was not offended.

He had brought his father's doubts upon himself.

"What about Jia and her friend?"

"The Fela?" Lowell grunted again. He had not seen evidence that Kato was Fela, had only Quentin's claims as evidence…the same claims that had condemned Roland and covered up Quentin's identity. Quentin had lied to him. The assertions against Jia's friend were likely to be more lies.

"No need to find them. We know who killed Roland and…" He coughed.

"Should I ask her to come back…help us find…?"

"She'll come back on her own. She's a Marrock; she belongs here."

The Marrocks belonged in LaGuardia's Fortress as surely as the Channons did. He believed she would come back.

Nik, however, did not. Not after the loss of her father. He masked his relief for his father's reversal of outrage with a feigned yawn and glanced towards the window at the night beyond. "I'll see to everything…when the sun's up. I'll take care of it."

His father's head half bobbed in acknowledgment. Sunrise was a few hours away. Less, perhaps. Another hour. Two or three. The orders could wait that long. A few hours would not make a difference.

In another hour or three, Yiva would still be dead.

Finding Quentin would only make a difference by giving them answers and peace of mind.

As the alcohol burned a knot in his belly, dulling his fury, Lowell could not claim he cared about those results either. At this moment, he did not care about anything.

❧*❧

The horse and wagon bumped to a stop in front of a narrow, multi-leveled building with windows boarded with weather-worn planks and the general collapse of the upper-most walls so common to the world after the Undoing. Nature showed little mercy to the works of humanity, and without the manpower, resources, and expertise to maintain what had once been, the natural world was gradually winning the battle. This was not part of Kennedy Fortress, a structure Jia had visited a handful of times with her father, but she would have been more surprised if Hallister had brought a wagon full of strangers there.

He might not have recognized her, might not know the truth about the Marrocks, but the odds were he knew the facts, or suspected them, about a number of those shivering in the wagon bed.

Bringing anthro into Kennedy Fortress was dangerous to all of them, Hallister included.

Whatever this place was, a makeshift chimney pipe sealed into the front façade belched a stream of steaming smoke into the pre-dawn cold, meaning warmth waited within. Mixed with the smell of burning wood was the scent of something equally valuable.

Food.

The driver, a likewise familiar face recognized as he climbed from the seat and came around to drop the wagon's rear gate, offered his hand to any who wanted to take it. The three men who had held watch at the rear of the wagon snorted or sneered at him as they jumped into the light snow cover on the muddy street. The others, the naked clutch of gaunt, sickly forms, accepted the aid offered by those on the ground and those still in the wagon behind them.

The cluster did not move towards the open door where Hallister waited, until Liam was with them, until Liam followed Jia and Zen to the cracked cement steps and waited for them to achingly ascend.

Vance brought up the rear, exchanging a look with the driver to express everything he needed to say.

He recognized Aman Fenway, as Fenway surely recognized him.

"Safehouse," Hallister said to Jia in a low voice when she reached him. "I use it for a variety of things" The last was added in an evasive tone but his gaze was steady and his demeanor, though formal and firm, was polite and sympathetic.

Though the woodstove inside burned, casting a faint amber glow about the room, the open main area was empty of life except for the rats scurrying away from the influx of intruders to take shelter beneath the wooden stairs built to replace the access of an unusable elevator. That room was open, filled from floor to ceiling with a collection of timber scraps for burning. On the wall on both sides of the door, bookshelves were filled with an array of tools, cooking utensils and pots, numerous blankets, a few locked trunks, and boxes of various sizes. A plank of wood siding propped on cement blocks served as a table surrounded by a dozen mismatched but sturdy-looking chairs.

"Beds upstairs." Hallister scrutinized the group casually before adding, "though not enough for all of you. There's extra bedding though…and Aman'll bring you anything you need."

"Food, bandages, medical kits would be a good start," Addi muttered, helping the woman he had assisted into the building onto one of the chairs before pulling his pack from his back to rummage through his supplies for anything he could use to help her.

"Yes, of course. There's staples in the pantry, water, food. Use what you need." Hallister ignored Addi's tone and Fenway, if he was put off by the responsibility dumped onto his shoulders, expressed nothing but the same cool apathy his face generally wore.

Jia did not think she had ever seen the man smile or frown.

"Miss Marrock…a word? There is much to discuss…"

"Laedan." So he did recognize her. She cleared her throat, looking away from her ongoing assessment of those settling as near to the fire as they could. "It's late…or too early…" She shrugged. "I've got people to tend to, exhausted and hungry and…"

Hallister scowled but nodded as his expression reverted to neutral sympathy. "Later today then. This evening. I'll leave men in case you need them…send one of them to me if you need anything sooner."

Looks of panic, fear, and disbelief circled the room. Guards left at the door suggested they might be prisoners as much as it suggested they would serve as protection against the hunters. Few trusted the Laedan's offer, but Jia presented her hand to respectfully seal the agreement. "Thank you for this," she gestured at the room, "and for what you did back there."

Her expressed gratitude and respect pleased him. "That was nothing…something that needed to be done. We will discuss it more this evening."

"We will," she agreed. She looked forward to the discussion…and to scouring every room in this place in search of potential traps and exits. If Hallister thought to trap them, they would vacate this shelter as soon as they were able.

As soon as each of them had a meal in their bellies, medical care for those who needed it, and a night of long, uninterrupted sleep.

❧*❧

Having fled the Fortress unprepared for snow, Quentin snaked through littered alleys and empty buildings for what felt like hours, doubling back often to lose any potential tails he may have picked up upon his departure. The snow exacerbated the ill gnawing in his belly as he replayed first the argument with Lowell and the final moments in the lobby before turning his back on the dream that had given him a purpose for the past several years.

The dream was abandoned for now but he was hopeful he could pick it up one day.

He had earned expulsion for his ill-timed, ill-prepared excuses for departure, but that was the least of his problems. Jonni's death had been an unfortunate accident, but whether Lowell believed the other Fela was to blame, whether he suspected the truth, the Laedan's words were accurate enough.

Quentin did not care about the brothers. They were obstacles, nothing more. He had nothing in common with them beyond sharing Donn's thirst for power. He did not wish them dead, but he did not care if they died. He only regretted that one death had come at his hands.

He regretted, too, without knowing the cause, that the Channon matriarch had died.

Not that her passing mattered, but it was a senseless, useless thing, lacking purpose or motive, unless it was something he could twist to use in his favor.

Finding her killer might return him to Lowell's good graces. It might not be enough to counteract Jonni's death, but if Quentin maintained his innocence, so long as the mage was out of the picture, he might be able to undo every unraveling knot.

If he could bring Fort Hamilton's treasure to Lowell, the fences between them might begin to mend too.

If not, if Lowell would not permit him the chance to restart at the beginning and work to regain his trust, Quentin could use what he acquired at the fort against the Laedan. He could take his due by force.

In the back of the greasy, dingy, near-empty tav where he eventually sought refuge, confident he was beyond the immediate reach of the Channon Guards, Quentin pulled out the crude hand-drawn map and studied it. Getting there would take time, would take supplies he could not easily acquire without the Laedan's resources, but he was confident he could do it. Lay low for a couple of days, let the firestorm of Yiva's death burn out and formulate a new plan, gather a crew, collect what he needed.

He knew just the man for the job.

His first order of business, however, was to find a temporary place to call home.

❧*❧

The pinking of the clouds over the sea heralded the encroaching dawn of a night without sleep. The snow had stopped falling and the water was calm, its rhythmic pulse against the Fortress's foundation lulling Oasis into the first moments of stillness she had felt in hours. Her eyes stung, her damaged ear continued to ring with that annoying, grating buzz, and the sole glass of whiskey she had consumed was proving to be a poor substitute for a meal she did not want.

She should close the window.

She should not think about the last time she had been in this room.

Yiva could not protect her any longer. Oasis would have to solve the matter of her too-violent husband on her own.

Licking her lips, finding the taste of whiskey lingering there, she tightened her grip on the unsteady railing. She could not blame Lowell for his silence, his distance, his distraction. Whatever the state of his marriage had been, whatever Oasis was to him, his grief was an expected thing. As was the guilt she read in his eyes, heard in his voice, that she tried to take away after coaxing him out of the basement and away from the dead woman's side.

He had not drawn back the shroud. He had not looked at her face. It was as if he was afraid of what he would see.

Was Yiva bruised? Bloody? Beaten? Disfigured?

Oasis had not looked either.

She had tried to offer Lowell a distraction with a half-hearted attempt to lure him to bed. His guilt had coldly expelled her from his side. Hers, she realized, would have prevented her from following through with her offer if Lowell had accepted.

Now she was here, at the place where Yiva had considered taking her life, wondering what it would feel like to fall and fall and fall…and crash against the rocks before being swept out to sea.

It was only wondering. Such an act was not the sort of thing Oasis, or any Hallister, would earnestly consider. She would find an answer, a way to knock the fangs out of her husband's bite, a way to survive. All while mourning the loss of the only ally she had in LaGuardia.

An ally she had betrayed.

Yiva's death was, she relented, as much her fault as it was anyone's. Hers, Donn's, and Lowell's. They were each to blame in their own ways. Nothing Oasis could do would atone for that. Even if she had the strength and courage to try.

∾*∾

"I don't trust him."

Addi wiped his hands on his stained shirt as Vance pulled his sweater back down, the bandaging on both his hand and shoulder changed after a thorough cleaning. The survivors from the lab had already been examined. Suffering from malnourishment, cold, and a general wasting that came with the disuse of their muscles, there was little Addi could do for them. They were given blankets and a meal of thin soup already bubbling over the fire, made more hearty with the addition of dried rations from the pantry and bits of meat brought from the Flushing Pack's stores. Most already slept in a huddle near the woodstove or stared blankly into the shadows of the dim room.

Liam remained awake, diligence etched into his face that spoke of days spent caring for those less fortunate than he had been.

Having made a thorough search of both upstairs and down, finding no rear door but a window they could exit through if necessary, Jia sat between her brother and Liam and accepted her best friend's hand when he offered it, smiling at him with affectionate relief in return.

There had been many moments after his capture when Jia feared she would not see him again. Moments she feared the loss of his steadfast companionship. She pulled his hand to her lips and kissed his knuckles.

Though his physical expression did not change, Liam's eyes smiled and he squeezed her hand.

"He gave us shelter," she murmured dubiously. "We'd be hard-pressed to find better."

"Damn convenient he showed up when he did." Kato stood at the pantry entrance, smoothing his hand over the blood stains on his thighs where Addi had already removed shrapnel and cleaned and bandaged the cuts. None of the injuries were serious. None would hamper him, so long as he kept the wounds clean. He kept watch over Beren and Wist as they pried broken glass from the shuttered window of their potential exit, glowering at the unfamiliar man who too-intimately held Jia's hand. He had heard the words 'Laedan Hallister' muttered by others and connected them to their unfamiliar benefactor, but he knew nothing about the man with which to judge him.

Leaning with his back against the door, Vance nodded. He felt no animosity towards Liam despite wishing, fruitlessly, to be where the thin man was. As frayed as his nerves were tonight, as raw as he felt without a drink, with the remnants of the plasm's effects still sparking through his blood, that sort of intimacy would be additional agony. He had endured it in the wagon because her hand in his had given him something to focus on besides Laedan Hallister.

Vance was relieved Addison was no longer touching him. Tucking unused supplies back into his bag, Addi muttered, "Too convenient…but in our favor, whatever his motives."

"Agreed." The timing of Hallister's arrival was too coincidental to be chance, but if the mage knew something specific, he was not saying.

"He's been there before." The mage pushed his hair out of his eyes as his head bumped against the door behind him.

"At the lab?" Vance's claim made Jia frown, made her hand tighten around Liam's as she felt his tension rise.

She faced Liam's profile as his head swayed side to side enough to be noticeable, seeking any confirmation he could give. Liam, however, shrugged without looking away. "I never saw him…but maybe Roland…" When Jia's gaze fell, the corners of his mouth fell too. "He didn't make it?"

"As far as the Fortress…but then…"

"Quentin killed him," hissed Addi as he closed the pack he had finished stuffing.

"We don't know that." She believed it, but saying the words would, she hoped, snuff out further conversation about that night.

"We know enough. Same person who killed Jonni…"

"Jonni too?" Liam choked on the words and shifted his head from his sister's shoulder to Jia's. Liam had grown up beside the Marrocks and the Channons. He knew them as well as anyone. While he did not think any of the Channons viewed him as a friend, he liked Jonni and Nik well enough to regret Jonni was gone.

"Wasn't me."

Jia nodded at Kato. She knew what she had seen when entering the room. Both she and Kato had been there as her father's life seeped from his lungs in blood-pink bubbles. Both had been there when Quentin had thrown Jonni against the cabinet.

It had not been Kato. It had to be Quentin.

"He's Fela," she whispered. There was no prejudice, no bigotry, only a statement of fact. "Quentin, that is. All along, he's been…" Maybe her father had known. Jia had never been around Quentin enough to detect it though she knew his face and scent.

Liam whistled between his teeth and wiped gathered tears from her eyes with his thumb. "I'm sorry, Jee…Jonni was a good one…and Roland…" He sighed as words failed him and he squeezed her hand, communicating his support without needing to voice the words.

Jonni had pushed for a marriage between the Channon and Marrock families, a union between him and Jia, that would have united the co-laedenship into a single ruling family. Perhaps the knowledge had contributed to her steadfast rebuff. She had known what such a marriage would create if her dual life, the Marrock secret, were exposed. Liam had expected it to happen anyhow, for the political alliance it would form.

As solid as their relationship had always been, Liam endured the knowledge that one day politics might come between them.

Then the world was upended and things like marriage and political alliances fell to the sideline as survival became the priority.

Jonni's death was unfortunate. The loss of Roland, who had taken so much risk to escape and return to the Pack was, for Jia, unquestionably worse.

"He gave enough for us to find you," Vance offered as if following Liam's unspoken thoughts. "Between him and Nik…"

"Now we know what Lowell's after."

Addi covered his sister's knee with his hand. "That's enough for tonight. Liam needs rest. We all do."

Outside, the day was brightening, pushing in around the cracks of the boards used to cover the windows as the sounds of early morning foot traffic began to pass by the door. If anyone out there wondered about the men standing guard, they did not ask questions anyone inside could hear.

Hand over his mouth to cover the yawn inspired by the doctor's words, Vance nodded and said, "Hallister'll be here soon." He reached for his pack and the gun lying upon it. Thankfully there had been no need yet to fire it. "Not gonna get past me…"

"If they try…" Kato bobbled an unused orb in his hand with a narrow-eyed stare at the door. He was not going to allow Vance to be the only one on guard. He would prefer to shift, to take a perch on the upper edge of the building's exterior to watch the people in the street, but he did not trust the mage, or the newcomer, to be alone with Jia, no matter how injured or weak either of them appeared to be.

"Once I hear what he wants, what he says…" Jia had to be the one to speak to him. Laedan. Alpha. Roland's chosen successor in both aspects of his life, public and personal. If anyone was to negotiate with Laedan Hallister, it had to be the one Roland had trained to do so.

The only one in the group Hallister was likely to listen to.

"Time enough to plan our move," Vance murmured. Time enough to rest, eat, to look at the world with clearer heads.

It might be time enough to learn the secret of this place and expose why Hallister had brought them here and what his true intentions were.

➷*➹

The dark amber liquid tasted bitter and stale on his tongue, the remnants of the glass he had filled hours before…before being summoned to the scene of a crime he had thought he would never see. Memories paved the way for a second glass, and a third, after Ernest sank into his uneven chair behind his too-cluttered desk. It was not enough to erase those images, however. His office was unlit but the glaring flicker of generator-fueled lights from the main room kept his eyes squinted, kept him from looking up as he tossed the empty bottle into the bin at the side of his desk.

His Protectors had their assignments. They would go about the business of hunting a killer, two killers, without him. They would question every person near the scene of the crime, resident or tav patron, passerby, employee, or addict, until someone, anyone, found something they could use to catch the guilty.

Having seen the alley, having left Protectors to pick up every piece of discarded waste when he had led the miserable procession to the Fortress, Ernest did not expect any evidence to remain. To be fair, with the tav's nightly din and the snow melted into mud, any visible, audible, or tangible evidence had probably been unheard, unseen, trampled, blown or washed away.

Beacons had been lit. Messages sent. Soon every Protectorate in the borough would be hunting too.

"Damn you, Segara."

Only a tracker-mage would find the necessary evidence now. Only Segara could tell them what they needed to know.

"Damn fine time you picked to go hunting."

He was not ready for another run. He was only ready for another drink.

He fumbled in the desk drawer for a second bottle, opened the first one he grabbed, and poured another glass without looking. If anyone in the main office saw him, he did not care.

Yiva Channon had been murdered.

They did not need to know his personal feelings to understand his reaction, his remorse, for this tragedy.

Finding a stolen med-shipment, finding the source of plasm, finding where Roland Marrock had been held, why he had been murdered, were important too. Segara was doing the right thing.

To Ernest, however, nothing felt as important as wrapping his hands around the neck of the man, or men, who had executed this atrocity, and squeezing the life out of them as they had done to Yiva…trial or not.

Chapter 4

It was not the first time Donnovan awoke with the bitter burn of alcohol lingering in his mouth or a sick feeling in his head and belly. This time, however, he could not attribute either solely to drunkenness. Rather, the feelings were the persistent shadow of things he had imbibed to forget, unfaded flashes less real than the stench of mold and the steady dripping of water assaulting his ears before he dared open his eyes and focus on the world.

Where the shart was he?

Where he lay could not be considered a mattress, but it was a crude attempt at one, several layers of hemp fabric and feathers and other materials sewn together and spread to make the sagging plank of wood less uncomfortable. It was a wasted effort, as his hips, his back, his shoulders screamed their protest at the abuse of lying here too long. With the faint scents of sweat, urine, and other bodily odors permeating the unwashed covering, the bedding aggravated the sick feeling waking failed to soothe.

He closed his eyes and rubbed his hands over his face.

Without opening them, he swung his booted feet to the floor and pushed to sit up with one aching arm.

He could feel the abraded scratches there, where nails had gouged through his shirt and ripped into his bicep. From the way the cloth stuck and pulled against his skin, he knew blood had been drawn. He had slept on that arm, exposing the open wounds to any contagions calling the mattress home.

He would need to tend to those gashes before infection set in.

His stomach lurched and rolled. Not hunger. The sensation was recognized in time to enable the swallowing of the bile the retching pushed into his throat.

Water. He needed water.

As he faced the single source of light, where the late day sun pushed through a vertical-slatted window, he made a quick assessment of the room, hoping he had the foresight when coming here to bring water. Eight feet by ten feet at most. The bed was sturdy enough, despite the sagging, but the empty table beside it tilted cockeyed towards the wall, one leg shorter than the others. There was a bucket in the corner serving as a bodily waste receptacle buzzing with enough insects to attest to how long it had been since the container had been emptied or cleaned. The candle sconce on the table held no candle nor any hint one had been in it recently beyond the cold drippings on the tabletop around it.

An empty sconce…but no water.

How had he ended up in a sharthole like this?

The taunting shadow returned.

Donn snarled his defiance at the air and fumbled for the coat hung over the scarred wooden post at the foot of the bed.

She should not have betrayed him. Thinking back on it, perhaps memory was wrong. Perhaps she had not betrayed him as he had feared. Perhaps he had overreacted to something he knew nothing about. Wrestling with a rare impulse to apologize, he began to rise, coat in hand, only to stagger back onto the mattress, assaulted by that damned dizziness and a splitting pain between his eyes, between his ears, that were worse than he thought they should be. He groaned, conscious only long enough to drop his arm over his face, blocking the light of day from his eyes.

The light, the stench, the buzz and hum of bugs, and the sway of the decaying room ceased and he slept once more.

ঙ*ঙ

"Any change?"

It had been an unbearable day of meetings with his father's governing staff, with advisors and household servants, trying to explain what little he knew about his mother's death. More than one person scoffed, thinking the tale no more than a fabrication of his addiction-addled brain, and took their concerns…that his son was spreading malicious rumors, to the Laedan. Each was met with outrage and swells of wailing grief accompanied by orders to take their business to his son, to get out of his sight and never return, commands that brought them groveling back to Nik with mumbled apologies and feeble, inadequate efforts to express remorse, shock, and condolences. What business many had come for was set aside for another time, when the Laedan would be better equipped in mind and body to see to the running of the borough few trusted Nik to manage.

Why would they?

There were some, those with the least experience with Nik and the wild tales of his addictive lifestyle, who laid matters of taxation and law and petty grievances at his feet in the hopes the Laedan's now eldest son would sort them out and solve them more favorably than his father might have.

It had been a long time since Nik's head had been clear enough to solve anyone else's problems or his own. It had been just as long since he had studied statistical reports, census records, taxation rolls, or changes to the law the Laedans had made. Those issues he felt capable enough to address and solve were handled. Those requiring further study were met with promises to meet after his mother's burial.

It was a passable, frank excuse for delays, a truthful way of masking his fumbling deficiencies, but it would not work forever.

The nearness of the dinner hour, a meal no one in the Fortress felt capable of eating, meant the end of meetings with the gradual dimming of daylight, permitting Nik his first opportunity to come to the basement where his mother lay alone in the dark, in the cold, behind a locked door meant as much to keep her in as to keep the unwanted out. Nik had sent his father's message to the chief, the command to call off the hunt for Jia and the Fela some claimed had abducted her. Though Nik worried that public perception would settle on Jia no longer being important without a trial or a burial to bring the matter to an end, he was satisfied it meant the innocent pair would be left alone.

How the cutting off of the hunt reflected on the official Channon position on the deaths of Roland and Jonni was a matter for his father to address. Nik trusted that, within the Protectorate, Chief Ernest had told his force what they needed to know, none of what they did not, and would continue to soothe the qualms of the suspicious.

Ernest, glancing up at the approaching footsteps from where he stood near the door's small, dirty window, several feet back from it so he was disallowed any sort of clear view of the woman inside, shrugged wearily, his expression bearing evidence of a haunting lack of sleep and a hint of too much alcohol.

It was the same expression Nik's father wore.

"No. I just…I had to…I was in the area and wanted to see…to be sure she hadn't…"

With a LaGuardia Guard, hand-picked by Captain Ortega, posted on each side of the door, if there had been any change inside, if the woman had moved, Nik would have known. Ernest would have known too. Silence meant no change.

Nik nodded with a frown. "Any news? Any evidence?"

"Everything we're gathering's at the Protectorate." Waiting for Segara or for some other mage to be brought in. "Gonna take time to question witnesses, find who was there, who might've seen or heard...only been about…"

He shuddered. It had been roughly twenty-four hours since Yiva had been in his office. A day she had been gone.

What had occurred in the brief time after that meeting, before her death, remained unclear.

Again Nik nodded, his gaze moving beyond Ernest to the window. From where he stood, he could see nothing. "You know we need to…"

Ernest blanched. "I know." They could get lucky and Yiva would not turn. Not everyone did. At most, they had two more days to find out her fate and Ernest did not want his final memory of her face to be of a twisted thing animated by whatever it was that turned corpses into monsters. "He's never gonna let us…"

"Leave it to me." If Nik had to go behind his father's back to see this done, he would. His biggest obstacle was going to be getting her body out of the room and past the guards at the front door.

But Captain Ortega was a reasonable man. Nik believed he would understand. Even if his father did not.

❦*❧

The increased Protectorate activity in LaGuardia's streets prompted Nepo to delay his foray into Kennedy rather than risk a confrontation he was reluctant to have. The search for the Marrock girl and the Fela said to have kidnapped her was none of his concern, and as no one had offered a bounty on either of them, Nepo opted to leave the hunt in the hands of others. Little by little, the number of Protectors on patrol, particularly around the tav he normally frequented, grew to be a hindrance preventing him from reaching the leased room where his traveling gear was stored. It was another reason to delay his trip.

He could barter for more gear. He had the currency and goods on hand, in safe stashes around the borough, to replenish his supplies many times over. But he had never been a spendthrift. Why waste resources on more when he only had to wait for the Protectors to retreat to other business to access what he already owned?

For a good part of the day, he watched the Protectors scour the alley between the dripping baker's awning where he had lunched on a stool and the tav where he wanted to be. Every person who entered either establishment or came out of them was accosted by one or more uniformed officers. Passersby were pulled to the side and questioned. Every face peering from surrounding structures, residents, business folk, and squatters, were likewise interrogated.

Nepo heard the questions. Had they been in the area the evening before? Had they seen anyone in the alley? Had they noticed any unusual activity? Had they seen anyone or anything suspicious? Where had they been after sunset?

They were the typical questions of a typical investigation that could have covered assault, theft, or murder. They were questions

Nepo often asked when on the prowl for a particularly worthwhile quarry. Questions he was often asked when found in the wrong place at the wrong time.

It was the Protectors' thoroughness, their intent, their severe demeanors that intrigued Nepo and prompted him to loiter longer than he should have, hoping to glean a tidbit of information and possibly an offer of payment if he chose to lend his skills to their search. He realized he had lingered too long when one of those Protectors, a face recently come on shift as the day turned towards night, fixated on him and gathered the fortitude to approach the broad, bulky, hulk of a man whose interest in their proceedings seemed more than casual.

He elbowed through the street traffic not with the intent of hiring Nepo's services but with the intent to ask him questions no one else had bothered to put forth.

"You from around here?"

Marginally surprised he had not been accosted sooner, Nepo studied the man, paunchy in the middle, pushing towards middle age but with a full head of black hair and a wry twisting at the corner of his mouth perceived to be a taunt. Nepo shrugged but held his gaze, unintimidated. "Not really."

"Then why are you…?"

"Got a room inside…and I'm curious." Nepo was not the only person who loitered to watch the Protectorate at work. He was, however, the only one who stayed from shortly after dawn until the setting of the sun.

"Shouldn't be. Not your business unless you know something."

There was the taunt again, as if the Protector was looking for a fight, daring Nepo to give him an excuse to incarcerate him. Despite the impulse to return the smirk, he shrugged and replied, "Wasn't here last night…business…places to be and all that…"

"What places?"

"Northside docks."

The spit of land serving as 'docks' for this portion of LaGuardia was situated between the Fortress and the Plant. A handful of boats moored there, used to ferry people and some goods along the coast when the weather permitted, and bring in a daily supply of fish to the Fortress staff and some of the local tavs. In his long, waterproofed coat, dry now from having sheltered beneath this awning as the sun absorbed the last of the falling snow, Nepo's wide face and gnarled hands were battle-scarred evidence supporting the life of a fisherman.

It was the sort of fringe-of-society work a mutani with lavender eyes and course, thick skin could get without many questions asked or prejudices shown.

What could be gleaned by looking at him was not, however, enough to prevent this particular Protector from trudging across town to the docks to verify the evidence. A man like this would stand out and be remembered by anyone working there the night before. If his story was false, a man like this should also not be difficult to find.

"Didn't see her? Laedan's wife?"

Nepo cocked one brow but it was the only part of his expression that changed. If the woman was missing, or dead, it was the sort of job to fill his purse better than any other. Better, he suspected than digging up dirt on Thomas Quentin for Donnovan Channon.

He shrugged. "Never seen her, 'cept at rallies and such." Those spectacles were the only public appearances the Channon wife made as a show of solidarity with her husband. Marrock's wife had been more involved with the people of the borough, as her husband had, but Nepo could not recall having seen her either.

He had never been allowed to get close enough to the ruling families to get a good look at any of them…except Donnovan and Nik.

The Protector grunted, unable to refute that claim, unable to know anything more than what the fellow was willing to say. Having Segara on hand at times like this would make the work so much simpler.

"Stand up."

Nepo did so without argument and endured the brusque pat-down that produced a knife, a handful of mismatched currencies, and a wrapped bundle of flat biscuits purchased from the baker cowering behind his window who had been interrogated earlier in the day. None of those items were questionable or illegal, none bore traces of blood or looked as if they would have belonged to Yiva Channon. The

Protector turned the man's large hands front and back, inspecting his nails and forearms for evidence of a struggle, but the only damage there was months-old scars and weeks-old yellow and brown bruises.

"Don't go far," the Protector muttered. "Chief might want to ask questions when he's back."

"Course." Though he had considered hiding in his room as soon as the way was clear and scurrying off to Kennedy before dawn came, it might be worth waiting for a chat with Chief Ernest. It might net him a job.

He suspected he would fare much better in gaining such a job from Donnovan. What boy wouldn't want to avenge his mother? Donnovan had already promised him gold.

What was another brick to the richest family in LaGuardia?

❧*❧

Aromas from the bubbling pot Helena fussed over filled their shelter as Zen and Addi offered further care to the weak and injured. At some time while Jia slept, Kato, ignoring the discomfort of his injuries, left the shelter through the rear window, scouting, Wist said before he and Beren found their way to the roof to spy on the pair of Kennedy guards loitering at the front door. Aman had come, as arranged, with food, blankets, and medical supplies, and left the same way…without a word.

His arrival was the only time Vance moved from his guarding stance at the door. Like many of the others, he too still slept, or gave the appearance of sleep, as the day waned and Jia waited for the promised arrival of an escort to the meeting with Laedan Hallister.

She did not want to linger here any longer than necessary. The building was clean, lacking the common smells of mildew and rot so many empty structures bore, and it contained the fire's warmth better as well, but those things did not reassure her of their safety. She did not want to be beholden to Hallister and as long as they tarried, they risked never being allowed to leave. She wanted to get her family home, return to the security of the Pack, to share what little she had learned about Roland, plasm, and HOPE's apparent involvement with both. Perhaps it would be enough to settle the Pack and permit them to return to more peaceful days. Perhaps afterward she could put this behind her and life could be normal.

Facing HOPE, finding the source of plasm, was not her responsibility. How could the Flushing Pack be expected to bring an end to the production and trade in plasm and anthro blood if not even the Laedans or Protectorate could do so? How could they be expected to do anything more than survive and live their lives far removed from the Fortress and the long history of borough leadership that had abruptly ended with her father's murder?

How could she bring Quentin to justice for killing him?

Perched near the top of the staircase where she listened to the sounds of Beren and Wist's movement above, awaited Kato's return, and watched over everyone in the room below, Jia twisted her brown locks around her fingers, scowling as those thoughts built pressure behind her eyes…until Liam's pained, stiff movements brought him to sit on the step below her. He rested his elbows on her knees and caught her hand in his to still her nervous fidgeting with a gentle, apologetic expression.

"I should have gone with him…I tried, but…maybe he would still be here. We couldn't leave them…" his gaze passed over the sleeping forms gathered around the fire. "And I was too weak. I knew he'd come back, or try to…or he'd send…"

"We almost couldn't. Find you that is. Between what he'd seen…what Vance learned from one of Nik's syringes…we were able to track the trail back." Her free hand rested on his shoulder, where her thumb stroked his neck in a gesture meant to reassure and soothe them both.

Liam smiled and pressed his cheek to her wrist. "You and the mage seem tight…"

"It's not…he's been a huge help…"

Liam nodded, accepting the incomplete statements despite the evidence he had perceived earlier. Jia and Vance in the wagon. Jia seated with the mage at the door, back against the only entrance to keep those inside secure. Her head was on the mage's shoulder when she had finally fallen asleep. Little things, perhaps, but enough to push Kato out of their haven in what Liam perceived to be a pique of jealous grumbling. Liam had noticed that too.

"The Fela?"

The movement of Jia's thumb paused as she swallowed, and then resumed after a long, low, hissing sigh. "Turned up injured…after the Pack relocated to Queen's College Library where Father…it was him and his sister. He helped the Pack when Pain challenged me for alpha. His sister's still there so he'll come back with us; we've accepted them but whether they stay…" She shrugged. "Not sure what his stake is in any of this," she waved her hand over the tableau below them, "but we need all of the allies we can get."

Kato's stake, Liam guessed, was Jia. "You don't think it's over?"

Again Jia shook her head.

"Then yeah…we need him."

In a time of limited interactions with outsiders, when the options of life partners were slim, it was little surprise to Liam that Jia would attract the interest of the variety of eligible outsiders they came across. It was the same for everyone. Maybe she would choose none of them. Maybe she would choose several. Eventually, for the benefit of the Pack, and their continuing survival, they would each select partners for the act of procreation. If Jia claimed her father's place as Laedan, that position would influence her choices too.

Liam trusted her to do what was right by the Pack, what was right by LaGuardia…but he wanted to be a part of it at his best friend's side.

"Father made it as far as the Bunker," Jia continued in a low voice, changing the subject from a direction, a future, she did not want to contemplate. "I was there when he came over but I didn't know you…I wanted to take him to the Pack, but he insisted on going to the Fortress…"

"Why would he…?"

"I dunno. He blamed Lowell, I know…I think he wanted to confront him about something to do with the map…"

"It's real then? Did he give it to you?"

"I haven't seen it…but it's real. Nik hid it for him…got it to Vance…then someone stole it." Shrugging, choking on the emotion that surged in her throat, she pressed her lips to the back of his thin hand. He smelled of the weakness of malnutrition, of captivity, and the scents of this room, but he also smelled like the boy she had always known, the man she considered her best friend. She had missed this smell. She had missed his hands. His smile. His voice.

"Long story, tangled with the ones of Jonni and Thomas and…"

Her words were interrupted by Vance scrambling to his feet out of specious sleep, an action followed by the stomping of boots on the steps outside, a knock, and the slow opening of the door with Vance's hand on the inner knob and the visitor's on the outer.

Aman lowered the hood of his rain cloak, shaking off the water and wiping it out of his eyes as he did so, and said tersely, "The Laedan will see you now."

Chapter 5

The scatter of rabbits when they stopped brought the urge for a hunt suppressed since the last pack hunt so many days ago that Jia had lost track of the exact day and time. Her father's funerary hunt. Yes, that was it, a memory drifting in on the prevailing scent of wood fires permeating the evening from nearby dwellings and the checkpoint before them. Not so long ago then. Why, she mused as Aman stepped away to speak to the sentries, did she feel like that had been a lifetime ago?

She had hunted since, to find Liam, to bring him home, but it was not the same. As crucial and satisfying as it was to find him, it did not fulfill Cana instinct in the same way.

The checkpoint at the outer rim of the Kennedy complex had once been a fueling station, the autos abandoned at the pumps having been pushed into a line at the edge of the lot to form a barrier to deter trespassers. Kennedy did not have the same stone walls around their Fortress as LaGuardia utilized to keep the public out. Instead, the Hallisters employed a series of checkpoints, razor fences, traps, and patrols to keep the unwanted away from the doors, to keep the Laedan's family safe. The system seemed inadequate to Jia, but judging by the family's continued dominance of Kennedy, it worked for the Hallisters.

The third of four sentries at the checkpoint returned to a table of scattered mechanical equipment under repair and Aman rejoined her, motioning Jia to follow as he began walking. The safehouse was not far from the Fortress, a twenty-minute journey to reach this checkpoint with the main structure looming in the distance, lit by an array of lamps so anyone in the vicinity could see it and know where they were. Its proximity also meant, she thought with a scowl, that Kennedy Fortress was less than two hours, on foot, from the laboratory where Liam had been found and her father had been held.

"Be careful," Vance had murmured as she prepared to leave, taking her hands as if to imprint on her or to imprint her onto his senses should her visit to the Laedan turn out to be a trap. She thought he might kiss her towards the same end, as he had before. Her stomach knotted with disappointment when he did not.

"Be vigilant," she whispered in reply, pressing her forehead to his so only he could hear her, not considering how the gesture would look to others. She trusted the mage. She liked him. She did not want to lose anyone else. "If I'm not back by midnight…"

He nodded grimly. Six hours would be adequate time for Laedan Hallister to have his say, to learn what he hoped to gain from Jia. Enough time for Jia to likewise probe the man's intent and decide whether he was trustworthy or not. Vance did not need to repeat his gut instinct of distrust, for he could tell Jia did not completely trust Kennedy's Laedan either.

After the way Laedan Channon had betrayed her father, betrayed her, Vance suspected Jia's trust would be a rare commodity for some time to come. He was still surprised she, as anthro, trusted him.

If she did not return or send a message within that six-hour window, it would be up to him to get everyone to LaGuardia, to safety.

"I'll take care of them."

If it was necessary to depart sooner, he would make sure to leave a trail she could follow. No more of the Flushing Pack would be lost if Vance could prevent it.

If she did not come back, he would return for her.

"Miss Marrock…if you please."

Aman gestured. Jia blinked, not realizing she had stopped to stare at a large metal sign emblazoned with multiple colored lanterns.

Welcome to Kennedy.

She nodded and followed.

She had been here with her father. She could not remember seeing that sign before.

The black panther made numerous circles of the safehouse during the long hours of daylight spent waiting for Hallister's man to arrive. He slunk through the shadows and found rooftop perches that allowed views of side streets and alleys, where the daily life of Kennedy's population could be scrutinized without anyone knowing he was there. Scavs and street corner merchants, men and women with hand carts or carts pulled by dogs, goats, or an occasional mule, taking their wares up one worn path and down another in the hopes of bartering their goods. Trades of food, clothing, cookware, herbs, poultices, and anything else a family could produce were made for items they could not. A daily sort of existence allowing little leeway for future planning, a life not part of Kato's path since he and Vanya had been forced to flee home.

Not even the Flushing Pack, with the upheaval presented by the Channons, by the flux of familial power as they strove to come to terms with the loss of their patriarch and alpha, had been able to offer the routine, the stability, he witnessed in the streets beneath him.

The Pack offered other things, enough to allow Vanya to feel safe, enough to ensure Kato she would be protected until he returned.

Having seen as much of the interactions between first Jia and Vance, and then Jia and Liam, as he cared to, Kato was not sure the stability and security of the Pack were enough to convince him to stay. Not even for Vanya's sake.

He had watched the silver-haired, icy-natured man arrive on horseback…the animal a rare commodity anywhere in the post-Undoing world…with the supplies the Laedan had promised. The sentries at the door helped unload them, helped carry them inside, but no one from within had come out and the sentries returned to their posts when the messenger closed the door and rode away.

There was no click of a lock. The guards were armed with batons and shockers but there were no guns or knives Kato could see or smell. The two could be easily overpowered by those inside, or by attackers from the outside. If it came to it, Kato was confident he could kill them both. Only understanding Jia's desire to meet with the one in charge, the one responsible for coming to their aid the night before, to know what he knew, deterred Kato from action though he, like many of those inside, preferred to leave this place.

Killing the pair would not be conducive to continued favor.

For a time, he considered backtracking to the lab, investigating more thoroughly in the light of day than they had been able to do the night before. It was likely the facility teemed with Kennedy soldiers, a danger Kato would rather not face alone, and he had a different duty he felt liable for undertaking to keep him close.

When Aman came to the safehouse, on foot this time rather than horseback, Jia left with him.

Kato followed.

Fenway might be alone with her, an opponent Jia could overpower if she had to, but Kato did not trust him. She might trust Laedan Hallister, trust Aman, but Kato did not. He remained at the fringes of her human form's perceptions. She was not nervous or anxious. She was not afraid. She was unperturbed about the winding path through the busy streets they took to Kennedy Fortress' door.

The nearer they came to the Fortress, the more certain Kato was that, though he might not be invited inside, if Jia needed him, he would be there for her.

The room she was escorted into was wide and uncluttered, with a scatter of seating of various types dotting the expanse surrounded by glass panels on the walls and ceilings giving the large room a much different feel than the almost claustrophobic meeting rooms Lowell preferred and more like the main level entrance lobby she had grown up playing in. Some of the panels were replaced with sheets of lumber or metal, some smooth, some corrugated, as the original glass had broken or fallen out over time. The presence of pails and other containers dotting the room to catch dripping moisture and the puddles she could see heralded the imminent collapse and eventual replacement of other panels if their seals were not repaired. Eventually, the chamber would lose its view of the sky and southern sea. Now the choppy surf gave Jia something to focus on when Aman left her alone.

There were no books, no objects to use as weapons except for the legs or arms of chairs and Aman knew she was unarmed. There was nothing to steal and since he did not lock the double sliding door on his way out, she gauged he judged her trustworthy or at least curious enough to stay where she was and wait for the Laedan to join her.

This was not the room where her father had once done business. That room, and others she assumed, were meant for the Laedans alone. She might be Roland's heir but she was not yet a Laedan. She was here as a guest, but not in the way her father had been.

The squeak and rattle of unoiled, unsteady cart wheels announced someone's arrival shortly before the double doors slid open, allowing two sets of footsteps to enter. Jia turned from the window to face Geary Hallister, the man dressed in a gray, high-necked sweater and trousers the color of the churning sea, and a serving boy dressed in black, like a shadow following behind, pushing a refreshment cart.

"Jia. May I call you that?" He continued speaking without waiting for her to reply. "It is good of you to be here. I'm sorry to hear about your father. Please, sit. Tell me why you have come to Kennedy."

He had come halfway into the room and stopped next to a pair of padded benches on either side of one of the few tables. The servant, his eyes downcast, set a pitcher, two cups, a tray of crackers, morsels of warm meat, and a collection of cut fruit at the center, the food intended, Jia determined, to generate a favorable opinion of her host and what he might ask of her. She left the window to join him, meeting the boy's eyes once when he dared to peer up from beneath lowered lashes before bowing and scurrying away, leaving the cart behind.

Though she could not be certain, she suspected Laedan Hallister was his father.

"Thank you," she murmured respectfully as she accepted the offered seat. Once she sat, Geary did so as well.

"How are the others?" He filled the glasses with water from the pitcher and offered one to her. After the trek to reach the Fortress, refreshment was welcome.

"Resting." He sounded genuinely concerned but she did not want to reveal more. "Thank you for last night."

"Yes, well…nasty business. I'd been hearing for weeks that HOPE had set up some sort of facility in Kennedy…but you know HOPE. It's never easy to trace their business, their movements. I'd received a tip about that place, abandoned the last I knew…I wasn't expecting to find anyone there except…"

"You brought a lot of forces to investigate an empty…"

Pushing the food tray towards her after picking up a slice of orange melon, he said, "One never knows, with HOPE, what you're going to find." The statement was spoken as the fact it was, giving nothing away of his actual reason for being there. "I must say, I was not expecting to find you here."

She took a plump, crimson berry from the collection and bit it in half. It was sweet and tart and the juices required the use of one of the hemp cloths left beside the tray to wipe her fingers and mouth upon.

"A friend's gone missing; I'd heard he was taken there. Do you know what it is? What it was? What HOPE was doing there?" She deliberately gave no hint of who that friend was or whether or not they had been found. Whether or not they were alive to answer questions.

Nibbling on a cracker between well-manicured fingers, clean the way Lowell's typically were, not worn the way Roland's had been, Geary shrugged. "I can't say. I'd heard about human experiments, some sort of viral studies. Possibly anthro and mutani testing. I thought I'd find the makings of biological warfare…or find the place filled with grubbers with tubes and such coming out of them." Finding ways to understand, prevent, or weaponize grubbers had been the talk of many since their emergence after the Undoing. "As you can imagine, the rumors are wild and many of them absurd. Recon proved activity there and we intended a raid but," he shrugged, "I'm glad we arrived when we did. It would be a travesty to lose you too after…"

He shook his head and set down the glass without drinking, his features and tone oozing the sort of remorse and regret expected from another leader, sincere on the surface but impossible to trace deeper. "You may be the only one who can keep Lowell in check."

"He needs to be checked?" she asked, leaning back as much as the hard bench permitted. Her father had said the same thing about Lowell. Jia had enough experience with the man to know it was true.

"You grew up in LaGuardia. You know he does, just as Roland did. He's up to something and I think we need to know what it is." Seeing her skepticism, Geary leaned forward, elbows on his knees, with an expression both charming and earnest. "How much did your father tell you? About the goings on in the…"

"Enough," she replied cagily without asking what he referred to.

"You know about the map? About Fort Hamilton?" He leaned back and stretched his arm across the bench back but read no reaction to his question on her face. "It fell into my hands by chance. I'm not good with such things, but Roland…he was a scholar as much as a get-his-hands-dirty sort of man." The note of respect and admiration in his voice was unmistakably sincere. "I had suspicions about what it was…what it might mean for the boroughs…and I hoped we could work together, the three of us, to find Fort Hamilton and share its contents."

Surprised he would discuss the fort without verifying Jia was privy to the matter, she took a piece of meat from the plate with a wooden skewer and replied, "Weapons in the hands of…"

"We don't know that there's weapons…but yes. A fort implies that they're there. If there's anything there, better we find it, control it, than let such a collection fall into the hands of those who would use it for chaos."

Chaos or control, Jia thought grimly. "There's no reason to think there are weapons there, no way to know what the fort could contain…that it's real."

"The map's no forgery, I'm certain. That means it was there…before the Undoing. It means the fort is real. Could've been raided since, but you know as well as I do, as well as Roland did, what a place like that would mean to the boroughs. I believe a shared interest in it would aid in the management of the boroughs…and in keeping HOPE in check."

The last, at least, was a benefit to any collection of weapons Jia could concede.

Geary continued. "I don't know what Lowell knows, if he's seen the map. I'd hoped Roland and I could work for the betterment of the boroughs…equip our Protectors to do their jobs. We knew Lowell has a scheme…I'd thought a marriage between our children would make us allies and remove the need for such secrets." Again, he shrugged. "Now he's got Roland out of the way, Jonni's gone, and there's only me to prevent him from getting his hands on those weapons. I'd rather see them destroyed than have them end up in Lowell's possession."

Hiding her suspicions, she bobbed her head and asked, "What has any of this to do with the lab? Did you find something there?" Bemused he considered destroying a weapons cache rather than using it, his roundabout dialogue seemed to hint there was a connection Jia did not see. The corners of his eyes and mouth twitched when she called the facility a lab but his face immediately calmed into a neutral, flat expression. He got up and crossed to the window where he stood with his hands clasped behind his back, staring at some point on the horizon where Jia saw nothing.

She did not move from her seat but watched and waited for him to speak. The delayed answer troubled her, suggesting something in the air was off, something that strained the set of his shoulders in the long pause before he answered.

"Perhaps nothing," he finally said in a quiet tone that prompted Jia to join him at the window to hear him better. "But if Oasis is right, if Lowell's in league with HOPE and whatever was going on there…if it's combined with an unknown supply of guns and explosives…I hate to think what such an amalgamation would mean to our futures. It would be the Undoing all over. The world…we've seen enough death. There was balance before, with Roland. Now the future is tipped and I fear it cannot be saved, repaired, unless you help me."

"I'm not Laedan…"

"You're Roland's chosen successor, are you not? His eldest?"

"That doesn't matter," she frowned. "Lowell thinks I killed my father…and Jonni…"

"That's preposterous."

From his tone, she deduced that, though he knew about Jonni's death, he had not heard the circumstances surrounding either men's ends. For all Geary knew, Roland could still be missing, only presumed dead. There was no reason for him to know Roland had been held in the same place he had intended to raid since Jia had not mentioned it. No reason for him to know Lowell may have had a hand in Roland's abduction. Geary might suspect it, but he could not know the truth…unless he had been part of the plan.

Jia pressed her hand to the glass, feeling the cold beyond the smooth surface, feeling the vibrations as the wind pushed against it. "There's been no ascension…no appointment…and so long as he believes I'm…" Deciding not to express her beliefs that Lowell was behind everything that had happened, she finished, "If his goal is sole leadership of LaGuardia…of the boroughs…as some believe, he's not going to allow me to…"

"There are laws? About the laedanship?" He was sure there were, laws and customs and expectations just as there were in Kennedy.

"Laws he can circumvent if I'm accused of murder." Or if, she thought, I'm dead or believed to be.

"Even so, there are other ways. You know people, your father's people. You have allies." The word faded with unspoken implications. "His supporters. His friends. Reach out to them. They'll help you, won't they? Bring the map to me and we'll…"

Ruffled by the reference to her father's people but refusing to show an unsettled mien, Jia shrugged and said, "I don't have it. I haven't seen it."

Geary scowled.

Jia was satisfied with his reaction. "He talked about a map; he was researching something connected to it when he…but he never told me what he was looking for…what the map was for…what it meant. He never showed it to me."

"That's unfortunate." He turned his head as if catching movement on the horizon outside. "I've seen it. I can replicate it enough that we could get a team there ahead of Lowell…if you're willing to help."

Jia's expression did not change. What aid did Geary think she could offer? There was a hint he suspected a connection between Roland and the anthro, so perhaps he thought that was an exploitable resource. Perhaps he expected her to recruit others, bring them together into a trap. As he said, the bulk of LaGuardia's denser population had supported Roland. If Lowell raised an army to seek out Fort Hamilton's treasure, especially if he was supported by HOPE's well-funded resources, Kennedy would need to raise an army equal in size and force to counter it. Kennedy did not have the manpower for that. What people they had were far-flung across the vastness of their more extensive territory and would not be easy to gather.

Maybe Geary wanted the alliance between Hallister and Marrock he had cultivated. Jia wondered if there had ever been a discussion of marriage between her brother and Oasis Hallister.

She smelled dishonesty, felt it prick across her skin so the hairs stood on end, but without Vance to read the room, to read Hallister's intent, she could not be certain what that feeling meant.

"I know you have injured among you. Stay on as my guests, and I'll see to their care while we make plans to find and take Fort Hamilton together."

The glass beneath her hand creaked as it vibrated. She allowed several moments of focus on the sensation before she eventually replied, addressing him as an equal in leadership for the first time. "It is a generous offer." If he regarded her as her father's successor, she was determined to capitalize on that. "But I cannot accept. Those people have homes…families…and I owe it to them to see them escorted safely back and reunited with those they lost."

Geary looked about to protest but after a pause and noticeable swallowing of his initial words, he nodded diplomatically. "Of course. Fort Hamilton can wait…but not long. Allow me to send an escort…"

"We don't need that." Hoping to sound equally diplomatic, she added, "After last night, if HOPE is aware of what has happened, you're likely to need all of your Guards here." She offered him the same respectful smile she had seen her father often use to disarm and diffuse awkward negotiations. "If you'd allow us the use of a wagon long enough for me to see them home, I'll consider your proposition." She paused to take a breath but not long enough to allow him to respond. "You're right, after all. If there's a chance the fort…that a store of weapons exists…Lowell, or HOPE, or any other single entity or individual cannot be allowed to find and control it."

Including Kennedy Borough.

"I will be happy to divide what we find, fifty-fifty, with you and LaGuardia, keep the scales between our boroughs balanced," he said amicably as if the offer would sway her choice.

"As I said…I'm not Laedan yet. I need time to consider this, talk to my brother, make arrangements."

Outwardly satisfied with her words, his expression suggesting the assumption of an agreement she had not given, Geary returned the consular smile and offered his hand. "I'll see to a wagon and food for your journey. You'll have use of the safehouse as long as you require it. If we don't see each other before your departure, know that I look forward to our partnership…as I did with Roland's."

"A working relationship between boroughs is better for everyone," she agreed, returning the firm handshake before he sauntered out of the room, leaving her alone.

She accepted, in the contact, his sincere desire to work with her. Perhaps he and her father had a similar arrangement. Jia did not, however, accept the honesty of the reasons behind it.

Chapter 6

Weary of the nerve-grating suspicions, bored of watching the in and out waves of Protectors inundating the tav, and concluding that waiting for the suggested arrival of Chief Ernest, who might recognize his face from innumerable reports over the last two decades, Nepo decided it was to his advantage to find somewhere else to waste time until he could regain entrance to his room and access to his belongings. With no particular plan to his wandering, he flitted from one drinking establishment to the next, picking up a drink here, a smoke there, a handful of pills he could trade for information or something more exciting elsewhere, until he stumbled into a tav in the middle of a brawl he was delighted to break up. Fists flew, blood was shed, and the two combatants were unceremoniously expelled into the street at the darkening edge of day.

Nepo's reward from the owner for solving the problem was a flagon of beer, the promise of another, and a portion of the evening's profit if he agreed to stand at the door to prevent the pair from returning and stem any further trouble.

The beer was gone, the flagon used to club a drunkard over the head for harassing a trio of too-high working girls, and the flux of patrons had thinned as a chill wafted in from the northern sea. There seemed no use in enduring the cold when he could monitor the door as easily from the counter, but Nepo made it no more than a handful of steps from the door when he heard it.

A familiar voice he had not expected in this place.

Thomas Quentin.

The man, taller than Nepo but slighter of build and taller than most in the room, ducked through the curtained doorway and hesitated there long enough for his eyes to adjust to the dim lighting, long enough for his gaze to sweep the room with the anxious darting of a person seeking someone, or hoping to avoid someone he knew.

It was the sort of anxiety Nepo liked to see, liked to capitalize on.

Donn Channon wanted information. He did not say he wanted the Laedan's hand harmed or hunted. Nepo would not cause a scene in the tav and risk his evening's cut, but a shakedown would be a fitting, amusing end to a frustrating day, and so he snagged someone's unattended drink from the nearest table, not caring what it was or who it belonged to, and altered his trajectory to return to the door, half intending to throw Quentin back into the street for some fabricated excuse no one in the tav would be inclined to contest.

He could challenge him outside, find something Donn could use.

A white-haired gentleman with craggy, handsome features and a once expensive but now tattered blue wool cloak, lifted his fingers in an offhanded wave from the front corner table nearest the door. Nepo had not seen the fellow come in, thus he must have been here before Nepo arrived or else had a room here or had come in through some secret entrance Nepo did not know about.

He scowled to realize anyone could have approached him, threatened him, from such an entrance without his knowledge.

Quentin waved back at the man and started over, his furtive demeanor and steps shed for something straighter, as if shedding his nervousness would lend an authoritative air to his face.

Nepo turned and after a brief hesitation to empty the drink down his throat and drop the empty glass onto another table where a motley assembly of dirty-handed, unshaven fellows huddled over a collection of wooden dice and pills. He waited long enough to be sure of Quentin's intent before pulling out a chair as if he would join the game, putting him near enough to hear the conversation Quentin was about to have.

Information it was.

"Lose it," slurred the twitchiest of the fellows at the table. "This is our game. No room for…"

Someone else caught the speaker's hand reaching across the sticky round table as if he would push Nepo away and yanked his attention back to the game with a crunchy-voiced, "Your turn, Dram."

"He ain't wantin' to play," said another, scooping up his winnings from the previous round.

"Can't sit unless he puts something in…"

Nepo glowered without a word and tossed the pills he had collected onto the table. It was enough to buy their tolerance.

"Told you nowhere public." Quentin scooted along the bench until he was pressed against the wall, finding comfort in its hard security as he continued to study the evening's patrons. He did not like places like this, filthy, wretched places, cold places with the stench of urine and alcohol where addicts slumped across tables and sat on the floor with their backs to walls waiting for someone to drag them into the street for sobering. Places like those Nik Channon favored.

The older man across from him shrugged and rubbed his finger around the rim of his glass. "You said private…not suspicious…away from your business. No one's gonna notice us here. No one's gonna recognize you. No one's gonna care."

"Better not." He waved the approaching bar girl away gruffly, having no interest in the sort of piss-swill they were likely to serve, and instead leaned his elbows on the table with a grunt. "Couple of things I need you to do."

The stranger held out an open palm. "Not without…"

"You know I'm good for it, just not now. Besides," Quentin's eyes narrowed, "You owe me, Uzzi."

Uzzi frowned, balled his open hand into a fist, and slowly withdrew it. "Not indefinitely…"

Ignoring the rebuttal, Quentin said, "This is different. One more mark…then we go after the fort."

"Know where it is?" Uzzi sounded skeptical as he leaned back and stretched his legs so his feet were propped on the opposite bench, trapping Quentin between his legs and the wall. "You have the map?"

"I don't, but I know…"

"You've said that before."

"I've seen it. Long enough to know I can get us there…if you can get some men together."

"Can't black 'em like you do me. Gonna want to be paid…"

"It's not blackmail. It's a mutually beneficial arrangement. It's a job. I've bought their loyalties. Paid enough. Once we get there, there'll be plenty for everyone. You'll be paid more than you're worth. Them too. Enough to take care of your price at least."

It was Uzzi's turn to narrow his eyes, but rather than argue, he asked, "Who's the mark?"

A folded scrap of paper was slid across the table, sticking and scuffing as it moved, the moisture of spilled drinks and more bleeding through to smear the ink and mar the word written there.

It was legible enough.

"That's gonna be extra…"

"He'll show up at one of these places sooner or later…the ones closer in…where he frequents. Should be easy for a man like you to find him…easy to do the job."

"It's not the difficulty." Uzzi stuffed the paper into his glass so it absorbed the last of his drink, the clear liquid turning murky gray as it sucked the ink from the paper. "Higher profile, more cost…and if I have to pay the others…"

"Told you, you'll get it, more than this is worth…more than…"

"I'll take it to my people."

"They'll do what you tell them," Quentin growled.

"I'll discuss it," Uzzi stressed, "If they agree, we'll send…"

Although he was unhappy with the concession, Quentin nodded. "Not there. Hinton. By the Change."

Uzzi nodded relieved Quentin had relented to his demand. He knew the place. The twisted wreckage of ancient roadways jutting up from the rising sea made it an easy landmark to find…and one far enough from the Fortress it was unlikely anyone would follow Quentin there. There were enough places around the Change to stash messages, hide goods and money, and enough people to offer cover if one was careful. Uzzi had used it before. Quentin had too. Uzzi knew where to look for further instructions…and where to leave word of his decision for Quentin to find.

He also knew the answer he would give, despite his effort to stonewall the other man.

"Better be there." His boots thudded on the floor as he pulled his feet down and slid out of the bench.

"You'd better be," Quentin snorted, emphasizing the first word. "Tomorrow evening. I need to know if you're in. When it's done."

Uzzi did not respond. He had already reached the door and pushed the curtain aside to disappear into the street.

Quentin was certain he had been heard. The other man would do what he needed.

The large man at the nearby table, arms folded over his chest, head drooping as if drunk or asleep when Quentin left the tav, intended to be there too. Whatever the plan, whoever this mark was, Nepo was too intrigued not to be there to learn more.

He might even gain payment out of it…whichever side he played.

❧*❧

At a different window, in a dark room where he was confident he could not be seen by anyone outside, Geary watched the woman escorted along the path she had been brought here on, back to the watchpoint where Aman had been instructed to leave her so she could make her way alone to her friends. If the rumors about the Marrocks were true, or if she was lucky, she would reach the safehouse without incident.

If she did not, in the grand scheme of things, with Roland already dead, his daughter's demise would not matter. Both Marrocks and Channons, at least most of the Channons, needed to be out of his way if he was to unite the boroughs under one banner. Jia's brother, the doctor, would not be a problem. Nor would the addict Channon. Jia would be a useful ally in his hunt for Fort Hamilton, and perhaps even in the long run to control LaGuardia, but she was not an integral part of his plan.

Pawns were, in the scheme of power and control, irrelevant.

Footsteps entered the room, heavy, steady, and stopped beside him. The tall man called Norse, his dark hair combed back, his equally dark beard cropped close to his long, narrow face, mimicked Geary's hands-behind-his-back stance and said nothing as he too watched the pair of retreating figures.

"I apologize," Geary muttered, feeling compelled to explain his actions to the impetuous, often rash man he employed. "I didn't know she'd be there."

Of course, she might have eventually tracked Roland to that place, but he had not thought it would happen so soon. Any report Roland made would have brought someone poking around. With Roland dead, there had been no reason to think a Marrock would be part of any team sent to investigate. Protectors, even LaGuardia Guard, he had anticipated, had been ready to kill with forces clothed in the garb of HOPE mercs. A Marrock, however…that was an opportunity Geary had been compelled to take advantage of, regardless of the detriment to his forces.

Norse nodded. "I understand." The lives lost in that fake HOPE raid meant nothing to him, so long as it wasn't his own. They had followed orders and been killed by their commanders…except for Norse, to hide the work Geary intended to protect. Now it was done. The expendable were no longer in the way and there was no risk of exposure of the Laedan's plans. Norse was satisfied.

He was silent until the weaving specks disappeared beyond their line of sight, the girl and the one man whose rank came between Norse and the Laedan, and then he asked, "What now?"

"There will be a wagon for them at daybreak." Leaning nearer to the window, Geary watched his breath form on the glass to hide the missing figures, and wiped it away with the side of his hand as if to erase them from his thoughts as well. "Follow it. Follow them. Learn where they go…if they'll be a problem."

He turned and stalked from the room. Completing the thought was unnecessary and unwise. He could disavow intent of the implication of meanings he knew Norse heard and understood. Such duties were an integral part of Norse's nature.

It was that nature, that understanding between them, keeping the man employed.

Without watching the Laedan depart, eyes on the distant lights at the perimeter of Kennedy's Fortress, Norse smiled.

❧*❧

"Could have moved them all. Could have saved them."

Doctor Gail Torrens removed the glove from one hand, its leather rough and cracked with age and too much exposure to the damp, to push aside strands of wet hair from her face, strands the wind had kept free of the cloak hood meant to shield them. Her horse stamped and snorted and the two men with her, bulky enough beneath their protective leather gear and waxed canvas cloaks to suggest mutani, moved closer, the nearness of their horses serving to calm the woman's more nervous mount.

Arriving unannounced, it was a serendipitous chance that placed Fenway here to greet her. Gail suspected his being here had something to do with the furtive figure she had passed scurrying into the shadows, but who it was, spy, messenger, lover, or plaything, did not concern her. What Geary did when she was not here never had.

"We took what we needed," she said to his words. "What was necessary. The rest wouldn't survive transport." Noting his frown, she snorted, "You know what they are. What are they to you?"

Another man might have shrugged or feigned offense at the question and its tone. Aman's face and posture did not change. As always, it was impossible to know what the stern-demeanored man was thinking. As always, Gail found the barrier to be an annoyance.

"Waste of commodities," was all he said, falling into step beside her as the checkpoint guards motioned for them to continue towards the main door. He did not know the details of the relationship between the doctor and the Laedan, but he could guess. He knew enough to know she would be one of the few visitors Hallister would want to see regardless of the late hour. If Geary did not have time for her tonight, was already in bed, she would be given rooms until morning.

"They're dead anyhow."

Gail thought she saw a slight twitching of the man's shoulders, his jaw, as if he disagreed or knew something she did not. It might have been no more than the wind pulling at the collar exposed beneath his leather shortcoat or an effect of the light of the lantern they passed beneath, one of many such light posts lining the path.

She said no more about those left in the abandoned lab. Whatever Geary's plans for that place, not knowing of the evening's earlier events, she knew cold and starvation would kill the weakest within hours, the rest within a few days at most. Their fate did not matter. Only the work did.

Aman did not speak until they reached the Fortress door where figures skittered out of the shadows to take the horses to shelter as he offered the doctor his hand to assist Gail from her horse. With a smirk of relenting disdain, she accepted the gesture and swung down, grateful they both wore gloves so she did not have to touch him.

"I will tell the Laedan you're here." The staff would see to the needs of her and her men. Perhaps Aman would see her briefly again if Hallister sent him back to her. Otherwise, he was relieved to be free of her company, free to see to his given duties, free to wrestle with thoughts he never let anyone else know.

There was only duty, as she posited. But duty, he understood, came with a price, a cost. What the doctor's duties were, to the Laedan, to the work, to the dead, should not be Aman's business. Tonight it felt as if they were.

☙*❧

Though it seemed likely the claims were true, that he had other business to conduct for Kennedy's Laedan despite the late hour, the instruction to allow her to make her way back to the safehouse unescorted, in the dead of night, made Jia suspicious enough to duck into the first secure hiding place she found to wait for any threat sent after her. If they were there, she did not want to lead them to the others.

In her hiding place, she opted to take advantage of Cana senses and so, after stripping to her skin and tying her clothes in a secure bundle she could carry, she claimed the wolf as her own. She sniffed the icy air, listened to the buildings creak around her, listened to the shuffling of grubbers in some other part of the building where she hid, the chatter and clatter of families in rooms within the periphery of her senses. Other than the grubbers, there were no threats here, no hunters, no stealthy footsteps or the expected tang of gunpowder, shockers, or the taint of metal and conductive components that comprised a stinger.

She was safe.

What she did smell on the wind, moments after concluding she was safe, was the feral scent of Fela, not a marking scent but wet skin and fur that moved out of the shadows into the circle of her senses. The instinctive raising of hackles, the territorial growl rising in her throat, was squashed as soon as she recognized the individual, as soon as the black panther leaped onto the sill of the open window from the street outside.

They stared at one another, swiping tails and flicking ears and tongues, small sounds in their throats the only forms of communication they could share. Jia did not need his words to know why he had followed her, waited outside of Kennedy's perimeter for her to emerge, and joined her. Was he the reason she had been sent out alone? Had Fenway or Hallister known she was followed and were hoping to spring a trap for him, either to offer to Lowell in exchange for a favor or else to hold as blackmail to force Jia into the pursuit of Fort Hamilton?

She crouched, belly to the ground, growling a warning before listening to the night again, expecting some small clue to support her fears. Kato, interpreting her gesture as anger or a threat, flattened his ears to his head and likewise crouched, lips curled into a snarl, his fangs bared.

Other than Kato's proximity, nothing changed. No one else was near. If he had been followed, if she had been, the hunters had remained far out of the reach of her senses. Unless they were using a night scope, it meant she and Kato were beyond the reach of human senses too. So long as they kept to the shadows, to the rooftops and littered alleys too difficult for Normals to pass through, they could reach the safehouse without interference.

She tilted her head, swished her tail, and beckoned him to follow.

As wolf and panther, her bundle of clothes carried in her jaws, the distance to safety was quickly covered, their matching sprint bringing them in sight of the safehouse door beyond the range of detection by the guards still stationed there. Their continued position suggested they might not have been placed or left there as protection against the attackers of the night before.

If Geary was right, those assailants were HOPE. If any remained alive, if any continued to pursue them, they could have found and raided the safehouse by now. Two guards would not have stopped them. Since no one had done so, there was no need for Geary's guards to still be here except to report their movements back to him.

Behind the decaying wall of a structure that provided enough covering from the partially collapsed floor above their head to keep them dry and out of sight, Jia dropped her bundle and shifted back to Normal form, noting as she did so that Kato kept his back to her, refused to look at her as she dressed, refused to likewise shift. She scowled, unaccustomed to such behavior, not sure if it was modesty or something else that turned his attention away.

"Shouldn't go in together," she murmured. "They don't know you're out…and I left alone…but thanks for the escort." He protected her as he protected Vanya, as she imagined he had once protected his mother, an endearing trait that made her smile in gratitude as she pulled her long blouse over her head and sat to pull on her boots. His head bumped against her leg, an action that prompted her to put a hand affectionately between the cat's ears.

Startled by the gesture, Kato took several steps back, putting enough distance between them that she could no longer reach him.

She sighed, stood, and pulled on her jacket. "We'll have a wagon tomorrow. Oughta come in, get something to eat, get some sleep."

There was a thump and skitter, the sound of weight borne on padded paws, and when she looked up, she was alone.

❧*❧

"Hear you've got the Protectorate in line?"

The hourly chime had rung the last hour of a too-long, too-tedious, melancholy day, an hour when most within LaGuardia's Fortress were already asleep or preparing to do so. Lowell had left Oasis in the sitting room, having found a small degree of comfort in her silent, distant company as they shared a bottle of wine and watched the wind in the branches outside, thankfully without any suggestion of sexuality. Lowell did not understand why the thought of something that had made him giddy only days before now filled him with a strangling sensation he could not shake whenever he looked at his son's wife.

His son's wife. Not his. He would never see his wife again. Her death was on his head.

Seeming sober and clean…how many days did that make, Lowell wondered…it was little surprise to find Nik hunched over the table with a variety of food scattered around him. As a small boy, before the medicating had begun to help him sleep when he should, Nik's eating habits had been voracious, his sleeping patterns unpredictable. Lowell had never made an effort to determine what normal had become for Nik during his years as an addict, but this late-night mountain of food and his bright-eyed, sad, and troubled gaze brought back those long-ago memories with an unexpected twisting stab.

What would Yiva have thought to see Nik like this again?

What did it matter?

Nik lay the half-eaten sandwich on the plate and nodded. "Chief's got everyone he can spare looking for Thomas…or else scouring the…place…where she was found…questioning everyone…"

"Donn? Have you seen Donn?"

It was not like his brother to be away from the Fortress for long stretches unless he was at the far borders of the borough conducting business. Nik was unaware of pressing matters anywhere in LaGuardia that needed attention. If there were, Lowell would know and have requested messengers to bring Donn home.

Then again, his father's distracted gaze and his penchant, at least today, for trudging soundlessly from room to room or to sit and stare morosely into a fireplace with a drink in his hand, might mean he had forgotten business altogether.

"Still looking, but I can manage til he's back. Until you're ready."

The hand that had picked up a slice of bread absently put it down.

"Yes, you will," Lowell murmured. "You're a good boy, Nik…a good boy…"

Nik frowned. While the words were a welcome thing to hear, Lowell had not said them in so long Nik could not remember when they had last been spoken. Their peculiarity worried him.

It did not worry him enough to prevent him from saying, "We need to plan her ceremony…her rights…"

With a sick expression and an avoidance of his gaze, Lowell muttered, "Niki…"

"We can't leave her there. It's been more than twenty-four…"

Interpreting the low-chested growl that followed and Lowell's abrupt stumbling back from the table as another hint his father wanted to continue to ignore the matter, Nik scrunched his hand in his lap and stared at the plate in front of him. Death did not trouble him. This one only did because it was his mother…and because it followed so hard upon the loss of Jonni. He could see to the arrangements for her sposal, for her burial, and the service that should accompany it, but he suspected if he did so, sooner or later his father would express his regret and anger for being denied the right.

They could wait a little longer. Twelve hours perhaps, but no more. If by mid-day Lowell had not picked up the reins, Nik would do so. Even if it meant the echo of his father's praise turning angry.

Nik's silence interpreted as acquiescence, Lowell bobbed his head once and trudged out of the barely lit room, the thing he had come into the dining hall for forgotten.

"Good boy," he mumbled on his way. "You're a good boy."

Nik's balled fists clenched tighter.

Chapter 7

The creaking of wooden wheels stopping in the street and the pounding of a fist on the door announced the arrival of the promised wagon, the sounds jarring awake those within the safehouse. Liam lifted his head to eye Jia with an expression of relief to see she was there but only Vance had moved when she returned, needing to do so to allow the opening of the door.

Kato had not come back inside.

That had been four hours ago, four hours during which Jia was unable to sleep despite her efforts to do so. Things Hallister had said, had not said, circled through her head until she was no longer sure how much she was reading into his words and how many of the details were fact. It would have been helpful to discuss her thoughts and concerns with the others, with Vance and Addi, Kato and Liam, and she hoped to do so once they were on their way north.

Until then, she continued to fret.

It was dark outside but the sun would be over the horizon by the time everyone had eaten, dressed in the warm clothing Hallister provided, and piled into the wagon's bed. A glance outside to let the sentries know they would be leaving revealed a smaller wagon than expected and, to her surprise, the absence of anyone, guards, wagon driver, or passersby, in the vicinity.

Their absence made her frown, but the Fela sitting on his haunches across the uneven street offered reassurance that, wherever they had gone, Kato felt safe enough to emerge into the open.

The wagon would not be stolen so long as he was there.

Standing to one side of the room where she could watch everyone gather the blankets they would take for additional warmth and comfort, Jia cocked her head when Beren stopped beside her while Vance, seated on the stairs in sight of the door, checked his gun.

"We're grateful to you all...but we're not going north," Beren murmured. His sisters were stuffing as much of the safehouse's store of food allotted to them into their packs as they could fit. Cocking his head towards Liam, he continued, "I asked about the others...one fits our father's description. If he's still there...if they have him...we've got to go for him. We need to get him free."

Jia frowned, her focus falling on the sister so far into her pregnancy that it looked as if she might give birth any day. "There's only...it won't be safe..."

Her small group had been barely enough to succeed. They had been lucky to have a mage leading them, lucky to find the facility mostly empty, luckier still to have had the orbs and the explosive powder and to have had Laedan Hallister arrive when they might have otherwise been killed. If the siblings found a fully staffed laboratory, it would be no easy feat to infiltrate it and rescue their father.

"We've got ways." Beren threw Vance a smirk the mage did not see. He had issued a warning about returning Below, but Beren believed it needed to be done. He could get to those orbs. He could take enough to give him and his sisters a chance at success.

"We know where there might be others to help. We know the direction they traveled." His voice cracked and grew softer as his gaze swept over the handful of people they had rescued. "We have to try...if what they told us is true. They'll kill him if we don't do something. You've got enough, taking care of your own. We need to do the same. You did what you came for; now it's our turn."

Jia sighed. She had no hold over the Fela siblings. They were not Pack and she barely knew them. Their intent to find their father was noble, the same choice she had faced not so long ago, and though all four were young, traveling without their mother's guidance for the first time, by now they had gleaned some experience to have a chance to survive the hazards of daily life.

Expecting an argument, Beren added, "We'll be fine."

"Travel with us for a bit, in case anyone is watching, so they don't suspect anything, and then…travel safe," she finally said, clasping his hand between hers. The door opened and Zen, Addi, and Wist began to help the weak down the steps and into the wagon.

Nodding, adjusting the weapons and tools he could use as such across his shoulders and hips, accepting the wisdom of her suggestion even though it meant the delay of time moving in the opposite direction, Beren said, "Good idea. We will…and thank you."

"Yes. Thank you." The three sisters reiterated their gratitude as they shook Jia's hand in passing.

They did not climb into the wagon but chose to walk beside it.

Inside the safehouse, Vance was the last to rise, the last to sweep the room for evidence they might be inadvertently leaving, as Jia waited at the threshold.

"That everything?"

Kato paced back and forth across the street, either agitated by danger or eager to be away. Or irritated that Vance stopped beside her with his mouth near enough to her ear she could feel his breath in her hair as he spoke.

"Everything we could take…everything we can use." He shoved the gun into his belt. "You trust him?"

Shivering, she nodded, assuming he meant Hallister and the gift of the wagon and not the Fela across the street or young Beren. "Much as I dare…we either take the wagon or we walk them home." A trip that would typically take about a day's travel might take them three or four with the condition many were in if they walked. The wagon meant fewer stops and meant, if they were fortunate, they might make Queen's College before midnight came.

"Agreed." The mage looked as if he might say more but chose not to. Something was on his mind as he climbed onto the driver's seat, unfamiliar with driving a wagon but preferring that higher vantage point as they traveled.

Jia closed the safehouse door after one last glance to be certain the stove fire was out and climbed onto the seat beside him, scooping up the single ox's reins in her hands.

She was not the only one to hear the Fela snarl before the cat darted forward to lead the way, intending to sweep their path to keep the wagon's occupants safe. Seated directly behind her, Liam clasped Jia's shoulder and she covered his hand with one of hers before snapping the ox into motion.

Vance stared straight ahead without speaking.

❧*❧

"Long night?"

Geary smiled at the woman at his breakfast table, the only acknowledgment, beyond the brush of his fingers across her shoulders the serving woman on the other side, pouring steaming tea into the Laedan's cup, did not see, that expressed his fondness for this particular visitor. As far as anyone knew, Doctor Torrens had come on business and it was a business breakfast they appeared to be sharing as he sat across from her and spread his cloth napkin on his lap. He felt no need to elaborate on the previous night's meeting with Marrock's daughter and knew Gail was not expecting details about his business matters.

It was the sort of question expected when a guest arrived late in the evening and was forced to wait until morning to be seen.

"You slept well?"

"Well enough." The Fortress beds were the finest to be found in Kennedy and garnered no complaints from her. Her rest would only have been better if they had shared a before-sleep rendezvous, but that would never happen here.

Geary was too careful.

"It's done, by the way. No one's going to go looking for you…or connect any of that to what's happened before." He spread jam on his toast with a casual glance at her through his lashes. "Dead were tended. There's no one left capable of drawing details together."

Choosing to believe him because he had always been honest, if politically coy at times, Gail sipped her tea and watched him, allowing him the decency of a few bites of breakfast before speaking.

"There is one."

Geary raised a brow, bidding her to continue.

"Fenway's suspicious."

"Of course, he is," Geary chortled. "That's what I pay him for."

"Not to be suspicious of me, of you, of our business." Her absent toying with her napkin revealed her agitation.

"He's been loyal." He was the closest thing Geary had to a best friend, a companion since childhood. He felt no reason to distrust him. "He's not a gossip. He's not going to talk…and if he's got concerns he'll bring them to me."

"I don't trust him."

"You never have." He had been aware of some animosity between Aman and Gail since the two were introduced more than a decade ago, but Geary had never pried about the reason. The two rarely crossed paths, rarely worked in the same vicinity for more than brief periods, and when they had, they conducted themselves professionally, giving Geary no reason to worry.

Despite her voiced concerns, he was not worried now.

Gail's expression, however, darker than before, spoke of a difference in the air he might not be able to brush aside this time.

"He's asking questions about the project, about those left behind."

"Not surprising." While a capable and skilled combatant, Aman did not savor unnecessary violence and bloodshed, especially unnecessary death, if it could be avoided. His craftiness, his observant nature, and his dependability were things Geary relied on. Less delicate duties were assigned to Norse.

It was why Norse had led the lab ambush and Aman had led, alongside Geary, the raid that had thwarted it. Aman undoubtedly had qualms after discovering the men ordered killed were some of their own. But it was done, and eventually, Aman would see the Laedan's actions and choices were in the borough's best interest.

"I want him gone."

Eyes narrowed, perturbed Gail would deign to give him such an ultimatum about how he ruled Kennedy, how he managed his staff, he scowled and set his cup down with a teeth-rattling clatter. "I don't tell you how to conduct your…"

"You don't have to," she huffed.

"Are you questioning my competence?"

They stared at one another across the table, the room quiet except for footsteps passing outside the door, the hum of the heating system, and muted voices from a nearby room where staff members were likewise dining. No one, not his daughter, not his late wife, not Aman or Norse, dared to challenge Geary Hallister without suffering the consequences. In his years as Laedan, only those few had questioned his choices, presented options and opinions, but never as a challenge. The results were his word, his rule, his law.

If anyone considered him incompetent, they never expressed that to his face. After a rash of executions for treason shortly after the transition of power from his father to Geary, most feared the outcome if they spoke out of turn.

Though Gail's unbending expression did not change, though her voice did not soften its frustrated edge, she did eventually say, "You know that's not what I mean."

Geary huffed, accepting the words as the only surrender he would get from her. He did not want to taint and sour their relationship. He would not, however, stand for insubordination.

"Aman stays. I'll talk to him, address any concerns he has." Voice lowering in timbre and sharpness, he added, "I'll address yours. You don't have to worry about him, G…Doctor." His tone and the term of title changed as the servant returned to pour more tea, take away empty plates, and add bread to the platter. Geary said nothing more until the young woman was gone. "He'll not be a problem."

"I hope you're right." She did not need to voice a threat. Geary knew the dangers, to her, to the project, to Kennedy or himself, if Aman or anyone else took their suspicions to HOPE or to someone outside of Kennedy. Fortunately, Aman hated HOPE more fervently than Geary did.

Geary had never learned why.

⁊*⁊

Since the nightmare had begun, Ernest's hours consisted of scouring the vicinity where Yiva's body was found for clues or else drinking at his desk until he dropped off into the only manner of sleep he could find. He dared not go home, afraid of the dreams he would have, afraid if he was not here, at his desk, at the Protectorate, he would miss something of vital importance.

He knew the men and women beneath him. They were the only family he had. For the most part, they were a good team, good people. Efficient. Thorough. Loyal. Some were born into the life, serving as part of a familial tradition that had existed since before the Undoing. Some did the job for the power it gave them over others. Some were here with a genuine desire to make order out of the chaos the world had become.

In Ernest's opinion, that sort of order was never going to be achieved. Not when people lived their lives in fear of what was different. Not when acts such as the one against Yiva remained unsolved, unpunished…and far too common.

If it was not for who she was, who her husband was, who her family was, and what she meant to Ernest, this crime would be the same as many others. Brutal, sadistic, entirely without justification, and likely unresolved.

He was not asleep, though his head was on his arms, on his desk, and his eyes were closed to block out the dim Protectorate lighting. The whiskey failed to mute the ongoing rumble of the Protectors at work in the outer room, the too-frequent opening and closing of the front door, the voices and shuffling papers, and the unending stream of footsteps. Always footsteps. He was thankful his staff perceived him to be asleep and left him undisturbed, while simultaneously wishing someone would come and give him a reason not to linger on the thoughts and doubts inside of his head that fueled the desire for the contents of his empty stash of alcohol.

He should go out. Buy more. He should get out of this chair, out of this office, have a meal, a bath, a real sleep. He should go home.

Still, he remained.

His circling thoughts had turned the office sounds into white noise, indistinct and unnoticed, and thus he was startled and jolted upright by the curt rapping on the frame of his door.

"Chief?"

Ernest rubbed his eyes, clearing them of the crust of sleep, and blinked at the shadow silhouetted by the glow in the other room. The soft light was like a halo, but Pubby was no saint, no manner of divinity. He was, rather, one of the better Protectors in Ernest's division and the one Ernest suspected would take his place one day since he knew Segara would never accept the office.

No mage had ever held the position of Chief. Ernest could not make it happen no matter how much faith he had in Vance. But Pubby…he had what it took to lead the Protectorate, to get things done, the most important detail of which was the respect of the other officers with whom he served.

"What?"

"We might have something."

"Something?" Ernest went rigid in his seat.

"A witness…someone who saw someone come out of the alley around the time we think she…" Pubby cleared his throat. "We're following up; if we find whoever…"

"I want to know immediately."

Pubby nodded his agreement but said, "With respect, Chief, you need to get out of that chair for a while. Go get some breakfast, change your uniform. Have a shave. Nothing you can do here…rotting in your chair's a bad precedent." He smirked. "Soon as we have anything, we'll get you in here."

The spark of potentially good news gave Ernest hope. Finding the murderer would not change the act, but it would make him feel better. Might make the Laedan and his sons feel better too. He was about to protest the suggestion to go home, but a glance across his desk to the can at his feet full of three empty whiskey bottles, and the rumbling knot in his belly begging for something more solid than liquor, as well as the stale pungent aroma of sweat in his too-long-unwashed uniform, gave credence to Pubby's admonition and reminded Ernest of what he already knew. He could not stay at his desk indefinitely.

If an arrest was made, he wanted to present a professional mien to the guilty when he met the scum face to face. He wanted the murderer to know fear the way Yiva undoubtedly had.

"If you make an arrest, no one's to touch him, talk to him, til I'm here. Lock him in holding til I get in."

"Will do," Pubby agreed. "Probably be a few hours while we track him down…but you'll know the moment we have him."

Wobbling as he stood, hoisting his coat from the back of his chair, Ernest grunted. "See that I do, Pubby…and not a word to the Laedan until we know the truth."

"Of course." Pubby knew as well as anyone that the last thing the Protectorate needed was the Laedan's interference.

❧Burn the Sea❦

Chapter 8

The slow plodding of the ox made the morning hours interminable, holding their progress to a creeping pace toward the checkpoint at Kennedy's border and the neutral sector between boroughs. Thankfully, Kennedy's main thoroughfare was clear of debris and dangers to allow a straight route north without detours. No one stopped them. Not a single person asked questions or gave more than a curious glance at the cart and ox that represented more wealth than most would ever have and might, if one was brazen enough to steal it, offer a family food for many weeks.

That sort of wealth suggested the animal belonged to the Laedan and few were willing to risk Hallister's wrath to claim it. They let the wagon and its pathetic-looking passengers pass with no more than looks of curiosity, pity, or occasional scorn.

Few people lived this far out from the Kennedy Fortress. As in LaGuardia, the further one traveled from the hub, the closer one got to the unincorporated streets, the wilder the world became. Hallister kept his primary roads up as well as his resources permitted, but the wagon was gradually forced to go slower as the path grew more cracked and rutted. Kato's assistance, running ahead to scout routes and returning to lead them, was beneficial in avoiding the worst pitfalls, but beyond the checkpoint, through the territory ungoverned, unmaintained by either Kennedy or LaGuardia, it would grow worse. Faces watching from the shadows, from haphazard dwellings and shoddy shelters pieced together from wood, glass, metal, and thatch, curious about the travelers as the wagon bumped onto an easterly street to avoid a manmade roadblock of broken concrete and stone, might not be hindered by the threat of a Laedan's retaliation if they chose to claim the ox as their payment for passage.

Every set of eyes in the wagon watched those faces, watched the shadows, for threats they were sure would come. There were no reassurances of safety Jia could offer. She did not try.

Beren and his sisters had left long ago, turning back to the south on a quest Jia could not undertake.

She wished them success.

"We're being followed." It was more than the paranoia the others with her struggled with. It was a feeling, a sense in the air rippling across her skin, tickling her nose, and pricking her ears despite the continuing lack of unusual daily sounds around them. The final checkpoint was several blocks ahead, beyond a westerly turn in the path Kato was helping them avoid. None of them wanted to face the checkpoint and the risk of being disallowed to pass. Better they took their chances on some other route.

Whoever was behind them would know the checkpoint was there too; if they were going to strike, they would do so before there was the potential for interference or they would steer the wagon towards it despite her effort to diverge from it.

If they were Kennedy soldiers, Jia did not want to be trapped between them and the border guards who might have advance orders to arrest them, prevent them from passing, or kill them on sight.

The healthy in the wagon grew more alert as they approached the edge of Kennedy's relative security. With Jia, Vance, and Kato focused ahead, the others focused behind and on side streets that might or might not be passable. If someone had followed since leaving the safehouse, none of them had noticed.

It seemed more likely, Jia thought with a frown as she made her glance behind appear as a casual exchange with Liam, the wagon had picked up a tail as they neared the in-between place, scavs hoping to pick off the wagon's occupants to steal the vehicle, the ox, and any supplies it contained as soon as they were beyond Kennedy's jurisdiction. Such a tail was no less threatening than Kennedy Guards or HOPE soldiers.

Even without using the ox for food, it was a valuable commodity for the same purpose it was being used for. The occupants of the wagon were less valuable…unless those following were Cana hoping to poach new pack members too weak to fight back or HOPE looking for anthro subjects for testing, for labor…for blood.

At the rear of the wagon, Helena sniffed the air before glancing at Jia, the alpha's concern easily read.

Not Cana.

Vance glanced sideways as Jia thrust the reins into his good hand. "Keep going? Or stand and fight?"

"We're in no condition to fight," muttered Addi.

"We don't know who they are…or what they want." She shrugged out of her jacket and removed her boots, stuffing both under the wagon seat as she said, "Zen…Helena…with me."

"I'm coming too…" started Liam, turning onto his knees.

Jia shook her head, ignoring his disheartened expression. "You, Wist, and Addi protect the others; Vance'll keep us moving."

"Flush 'em out," Wist eagerly offered, rummaging in the nearest pack for the remaining orbs, "we'll take care of 'em."

Jia had seen three of the orbs used during their escape and understood them to be explosives, but she had never seen the fist-sized, handled orbs before.

"What's…?"

"Found a stash of them Below on the way through, enough to bring down a building, enough to need a wagon to carry them," Vance muttered, keeping his eyes on the road and the Fela zigzagging from one curb to the other in front of them. "Been there a while, I'd say. Wasn't a trace left to track, but I'd wager whoever put them there did so for Hallister…or one of his predecessors."

Geary might not even know they were there.

"Relieved 'em of a few," Wist grinned. "Might as well use 'em."

"Think he knows they're missing? That he's following to…"

"Not likely." Vance shook his head and resisted looking at the woman undressing beside him. She had no right to be so damned distracting, but focusing on the street kept his gaze away. "Not unless someone's taken stock, sent another mage in there."

After blowing up the lab wall and fence during the escape, someone might have been suspicious enough to take inventory, if they knew the orbs were there. They might be able to connect the two things without much effort.

"If we do that," he continued, head tilted in Wist's direction, "everyone's gonna need to hold on." An explosion was likely to scare the ox. If Vance could not control the beast, they were in for a rough, erratic run through the furrowed streets.

"How far can you throw it?"

"Far enough that we're not gonna be hurt by the blast," Wist assured her cockily.

"Then watch for us…be ready…listen to our calls."

Such a hunt would be better with more than three participants, particularly since they did not know how many were in pursuit, or who they were, but three would have to suffice. Jia would not leave the wagon's occupants unprotected.

Fumbling one-handed at his hip, Vance removed the handgun and tendered it over his shoulder to Liam. "Take this; comes to it, you're gonna need it."

Testing the weight of the unfamiliar weapon in his thin hand, Liam nodded once. He had never held a gun, never fired one, but in a pinch, he was confident enough to think he could do so. To protect the others, to protect Jia, he would try.

One by one, the women leaped from the moving wagon and angled away into the buildings at the sides of the road, hoping anyone pursuing them would have no inkling of what lay in store and were too far away to notice the scattering of women.

The wagon bumped along as if nothing had changed. Jia took the left side of the street, Zen and Helena took the right, pausing when hidden to assume their Cana forms before racing through abandoned corridors, empty rooms and alleys, over disintegrating walls and under fences twisted with age and wild flora tangled into places where nature had gained a hold. They continuously sniffed the air for the traces of those who thought to make the wagon's occupants prey, listened for clues as to who their hunters were, until somewhere ahead of Jia's position, Zen's warning yip rang out at nearly the same moment Jia spotted a creeping figure dressed in indistinguishable black. Then another. Not scavs, as their movements were too synchronized, too militaristic, to suggest that. Their attire, their weapons, looked too sophisticated to make them a collection of residents from this quarter of the city, and they did not wear the markings of HOPE nor the uniforms of Kennedy Guards.

Ruffs then, working on behalf of someone else. Possibly HOPE. Possibly Hallister.

Jia yipped. Helena answered.

The hunters, recognizing the sounds as wolves, wild dogs, or Cana, began to sift out of the shadows into a cohesive group in the center of the road for security against the shifting feral sounds. The woven nature of the canine calls gave the appearance of numerous animals closing in, a threat requiring solidarity if they were to fight back and survive.

Stragglers were dealt with as any prey would that strayed too far from the herd. Jia heard evidence of first one kill, then another, sounds that turned the black-clad forms at the back of the group to protect their flank, forced to move backward as the group of hunters continued more slowly ahead.

The hunters no longer had the advantage of cover. Forced to slow because of it, they were exposed to the wagon's occupants with no chance of catching their prey unaware…and every chance of being picked off by the animals closing in around and behind them.

The leader gestured. Five men peeled off to the right, five to the left, and five held their position in the center of the road. Guns and shockers and netters were readied as the remaining eight, along with the leader, began to charge after the wagon.

Windows and shutters banged closed as people in nearby buildings took cover.

"Keep going," Wist shouted as he leaped to the ground, an orb in each hand, pins pulled with his teeth in preparation for throwing.

"What are you…?" started Addi. Vance, after a quick look over his shoulder, snapped the leads and prompted the ox to move faster.

The hunters with guns hoped to hold the hidden wolves at bay to either side of the road. From her vantage point on a precarious wooden beam above where the five on her side of the road were creeping, Jia judged Wist's intentions, the desperate act of the young who so often considered themselves impervious to death. As those he faced aimed at the foolhardy single individual, Jia too made a choice. She leaped into the heart of the nearest cluster with a howl that prompted the two Cana on the other side of the road to similarly act.

It also prompted Wist to abruptly stop his charge and throw his first orb at those taking aim.

They expected a rock or piece of fruit.

The throw curved left but landed near enough that the explosion threw the nine men off their feet, scattered the living, the maimed, the dead in every direction but not without one of them getting off a shot. Someone in the wagon screamed as the ox strained at the lead and propelled the wagon faster. Wist started running, confident the hunters were less of an obstacle now.

Assailed by Cana fangs and claws, and caught off guard by the exploding projectile, the remaining hunters were disoriented enough to make the subsequent battle a short one, particularly when Wist threw the second orb down the center of the road to toss the five huddled there off their feet as well. Through the dust and smoke, ears ringing, eyes stinging, Jia caught a glimpse of a limping wraith rising in the haze, gun aimed.

She jumped. Wist rolled to the ground beneath her weight as the crack of gunfire rang overhead and the lone panther launched from the other side of the road. The shooter fell.

With a snarl, Jia yanked Wist to his feet with her jaws around his forearm and propelled him towards the fast-bouncing wagon. Hoping the hunters were down, that no more followed, but not wanting to take time to investigate, she used the cover of chaos to get her people back to the safety of their transport. Kato fell into step beside her, herding

Wist along, as Helena took point to guide their way and Zen swept in from the rear.

As the young man scrambled into the wagon, Jia could not tell who was hit, but she did not think it was Liam or Vance. She would not take the time to look until they were far away from the bodies left behind, far enough away to be out of danger.

She did not know who those people were, but she felt certain they had been sent to kill her.

❧*❧

Pubby threw the disheveled, bedraggled, belligerent fellow with missing teeth and breath that stank of cheap alcohol, spliffs, and rot, into the dankest, filthiest holding cell the Protectorate had, a room barely used because its condition was so bad. Stagnant water puddled on the floor and vermin scattered as the boots invaded their scavenger hunt. The door's lock had been broken for as long as Pubby had been on the force, but a thick iron chain and the keyed padlock would hold it closed. Chief Ernest had the only key, was the only one who could open it now that it had been locked unless the chain was cut.

In this case, using this cell seemed particularly fitting to Pubby.

"Found that," the fellow repeated in a cough-heavy slur as he stretched his arm through the metal bars for the item dangling from Pubby's breast pocket.

"Bet you did," Pubby snorted, tucking the shiny strand of twisted gold chain out of sight. One of the two Protectors with him smacked the man's arm with a baton, adding to the accumulation of bruises mottling his pale, exposed skin. The prisoner had put up a hell of a fight; it had taken three officers to subdue him once he was located and he fought them all the way to the station. Fought as the witness was brought in to identify him, fought as Pubby dragged him into the basement to throw him into holding.

The witness was not sure if this was the one he had seen. It had been late. It had been dark. The figure witnessed leaving the alley had been wearing a cloak against the rain and this fellow currently had none. The voice was the same, however, he said, the stench of him in passing the same, the rancid belching sound the one he remembered.

And he had a necklace he could never afford.

It was not solid evidence but it would be up to the Chief to decide what to do with him, whether to take him to the Laedan or hand him over to the juds for processing and trial. But Pubby was satisfied. He had the evidence in his pocket. He was no tracker-mage but it was the only evidence of crime Pubby needed.

❧*❧

Only after crossing deep into familiar territory, when they had picked a path through the familiar southern Change that filled the narrow void between LaGuardia and Kennedy and the unclaimed territory to the east where the Flushing Pack had found refuge, did Vance bring the wagon to a halt at the southern edge of the Flushing Wilds. There had been no sign of anyone following them since the ambush and the familiarity of their location, as well as the potential of comforting, secure shelter in the Wilds, allowed the weary rabble the confidence to climb or stumble out of the wagon and build a fire in a lean-to sheltered by a still-standing stretch of ancient highway above.

The wagon bed was red with the blood of the dead man, the only Fela in the rescued group struck by the sole bullet the hunters had fired. The location of the hit had given Addi no hope of saving the man's life; even if the wagon had stopped there would have been nothing he could do. The hapless fellow died almost immediately, his blood, thinned by the chemical processes pumped into him for an unknown number of days, had seeped out too quickly, filling his lungs, for any doctor to stop.

They elected to bury him here at the edge of the Wilds.

None of those digging his grave knew if he had a family. If he did, they would never know what had happened to him.

No one knew his name.

Vance tipped his head towards the edge of the fire's glow, wanting words with Jia he thought best shared in private. The darkening clouds spoke of the waning of the day, and while others discussed whether they should camp once a meal was eaten and the dead was buried, or if they should press on towards the library, there was something else he needed to do.

Traveling with them further, identifying their dead, was not it.

"You're leaving."

Adjusting the collar of his coat, Vance noted the melancholy in her voice but did not look at her face to gauge how deep her regret was. The crackle of distant thunder on the heels of a lightning flash that drew his gaze to the sky, seeking the nearness of the storm, was a sufficient distraction to prevent it.

"Chief needs to know about that lab…where the plasm's coming from…the Laedan too…even if we're not sure." He felt confident in his assessment, but there was little tangible proof to support his claim.

"There's this." She squatted to rummage through the pack she had protected and pulled out the folder taken from the lab. "Don't know what it means; haven't had a chance to study it. But there are names, codes, diagrams. Might tell you something."

Accepting it in his good hand, thankful for the glove protecting him from images he was disinclined to experience, the only clue to the folder's importance and contents was the embossed symbol on its face.

"Seems conveniently left behind."

Vance nodded. A lab stripped of everything but the dead, the barely living, and a symbol-marked folder left conspicuously in the open seemed staged to him too. Any truths the file held would wait until he reached his long empty home.

"He wants me to help him find the fort."

With the folder secured in his bag, Vance pushed his hair from his eyes with his injured hand and looked up with a frown. He knew who she meant. "He knows about…?"

"He says he sent my father the map…wanted to work with him to split the find between the boroughs. Says he wants to keep it out of Lowell's hands, thinks it will be too dangerous if Lowell…"

"Given what we found Below, I'm not sure Hallister can be trusted with it either."

She nodded and glanced at her brother who moved from one person to another in the group, assessing their health and well-being. Kato brushed off the assistance in favor of poking at the fire he had built. "With so many knowing about the fort now, someone…Lowell, Geary, HOPE…someone's gonna find it and use whatever's there. Someone has to keep that from happening. I believe it's what my father intended…but I don't know how…"

"The Pack?"

"I don't know." Her voice faded as she faced another crackle of faraway lightning. "They won't all agree with me…and with so many pups now…I can't risk it. I don't even know where…"

"I've seen the map; I could get you there…if you decide to…"

Judging by her expression, his offer was as unexpected for her as it was for him. He had not considered the ramifications of seeking out the fort on his own, knew it was something few in the Protectorate would be interested in pursuing, but despite her reluctance and hesitation, he knew Jia did care, was interested, and wanted to follow through with her father's wishes regardless of the costs to herself.

He rubbed the back of his neck sheepishly, realizing his offer might have been an excuse to continue to see her. He suspected she knew it too when she replied, "You've got other responsibilities: the plasm trade to shut down…a stolen med shipment to find." Your own life to live. She reached for his hand but with a soft, sad smile drew back before making contact. "I…thank you for helping me with my father, helping me bring Liam home…for everything you've…"

"He's a good man." His gaze traveled over her shoulder, past her, to the side of the fire where Liam was aiding the lab survivors despite his exhaustion. It was obvious why she liked him.

"He's always been…if I'm gonna be alpha…" Her voice trailed off. She was not 'going to be'. She already was. "He keeps my head straight…keeps me from doing stupid things."

Swallowing past the knot in his chest trying to push into the back of his throat, Vance nodded. "Always good to have that."

He might have made many different choices in life if there had been anyone to likewise guide him.

Jia's melancholy nod was her response.

"Think you can make it to Queen's College? Need me to…?"

The impulse to express a continued need for his company, for his talents, his presence, was pushed down into her belly and held there by a determined force of will. He had things he needed to be free to accomplish. So did she.

Shaking her head, she sighed, "Like you said…we've both got things to do."

He nodded. "You know where to find me if you need anything, and I promise," he squeezed her hand, completing the gesture she had begun to make, "We'll see each other again. This isn't over."

"Come on you two…come eat," Xen called from the fire.

Jia looked at her hand in Vance's. Feeling his words carried more weight and meaning than what floated on the surface, she nodded and replied, "No…it isn't."

⌘*⌘

Elbows on the edge of the frigid metal table, Nik ignored the men outside of the tiny room in favor of staring at his mother's blue-gray face, the cold and cessation of bodily functions giving her features the sheen of carved, unpolished stone rather than the vibrant glow of the life that had birthed him, raised him, nurtured and loved him despite his trying flaws. He had long ago ceased blaming her or his father for their efforts to cope with differences they did not understand. Any other parent faced with a child with erratic sleeping and eating patterns would likewise have sought answers from every available source.

Had the doctors been to blame for their recommended remedies? Had his parents followed the best guidance or flawed advice? Had they settled on suggested solutions without considering the potential side effects and consequences?

It no longer mattered. That was in the past. Nik could choose to wallow in it or he could choose to fight and move forward and make his mother proud.

Wherever she was now.

He did not believe in an afterlife. Despite HOPE's assertions about an ultimate reward to be had after a life of duty, honor, and service, Nik had never seen proof of anything existing beyond the reach of his senses. All of his hours spent at the Plant, watching and aiding in the varying means of disposing of the dead, and not once had he seen a sign of something existing once the spark of life was extinguished. A body could be animated by the organisms that spawned grubbers, but no one called that an afterlife, despite the term technically applying.

His disbelief notwithstanding, he was not prevented from grasping on to the loitering hope of seeing his mother and brother, of the pair of them hearing him, watching him, from somewhere else he could not see, could never go.

They were better people than him. Wherever they were, Nik would not be welcome.

"Gonna find who did this," he promised, tucking her hair behind her ear, unafraid to touch her despite the loss of warmth. "Not gonna let this go. He'll pay for it…whoever it was…"

Two clipped raps on the door and it creaked open behind him. Captain Ortega's narrow, sun-browned face peered inside. His expression was neutral as he gave Nik a quick studying glance and asked, "Need anything, sirra?"

He had not been here when Nik arrived, but when the men at the door indicated how long the now oldest Channon son had been here, in the cold, with the dead, the captain had thought it wise to check in.

Though Nik appreciated that someone cared enough to see to his welfare, even if it was out of a sense of duty, he shook his head and replied, "No. I'm good."

"Not healthy to be around the dead so much."

Nik shrugged. "Cold as it is in here…anything living's gonna freeze. Not like she's gonna do anything."

"Maybe not." Ortega shrugged too. While there might not be physical dangers, being around the dead too much had to surely mess with a person's head. Every sposer he had ever met seemed off to the captain. Either they had been born peculiar and gravitated towards working with the dead or else the years spent with corpses had made them that way. Nik had enough idiosyncrasies without submitting to the detrimental effects of the dead. "Dinner will be soon. I was asked to draw you up to dine."

Unable to believe either Oasis or his father had made the effort to summon him, Nik assumed it was a member of the kitchen staff looking for him, seeing he was cared for and fed, as they had always been prone to do. He should eat, refocus energy and strength on fulfilling his promise to his mother, but he was not ready to leave her.

"Tell them thirty minutes."

Ortega started to speak, swallowed the first words that came into his head, and nodded. "Aye, sirra. I'll tell them."

He intended to return in thirty minutes to hold the Laedan's son to that promise.

❧*❦

"He came from the edge of the Wilds, mas…" the boy panted, stumbling into the cramped, drafty room his benefactor had chosen to occupy for the night. Lengths of dull, colorless fabric had been secured over the windows to reduce the wind's chill but it would do little to seal the cracks around the door and the crevices in the walls created by erosion and time.

"Was he alone?" Quentin tugged once on the square of leather he had finished hanging, the thickest fabric he had for the draftiest window, and stepped off the box used for a stool and wiped his hands on his shirt. He hated the state of his clothes but as he had yet to find anyone to clean them, nor the credits to pay someone to do so, he avoided the compulsion to change into something cleaner.

He had only brought so much with him when he fled the Fortress, what little he owned and could reasonably carry. He had to make due until his fortune turned.

"Don't think so…traced him back to the border and a wagon with a group of others. Dunno who they were…but they had a bull."

A bull meant money…or theft. Without seeing the travelers, Quentin would not assume which type they were.

❧91❦

His head bobbed and he moved to the center of the room, to the only piece of furnishing the shelter contained, a beaten, scratched, long wooden table someone had spread a moth-eaten mattress on to serve as a bed. The room was unoccupied when he found it, and since he had business in this part of town…business that had thrust this over-eager boy into his orbit…Quentin had opted to claim this place as his.

The pistol he removed from his waistband and lay on top of the mattress was within easy reach if anyone tried to evict him.

Or if the mage came looking.

The boy's eyes widened at the sight of the only gun he had seen.

That was Quentin's primary concern when he spied the mage moving past earlier. To his knowledge, LaGuardia's premier tracker-mage was still hunting the Fela accused of kidnapping Jia Marrock and of killing Jonni and Roland; the Laedan might have since sent him to find Quentin too. Find him and return him to the Fortress to face those same accusations. He could think of no other reason for the mage to be so far south in the borough. Quentin stayed out of sight, skulking from one hiding place to another to watch the mage after sending the boy to backtrack his path; if Segara had seen or sensed either of them, he had not turned aside from his business.

His focused actions might have been a ruse to keep Quentin off-guard but it appeared he had duty elsewhere, or was coming from it to return to the Protectorate where he was stationed.

"Anything suspicious? Hear anything? See anything?"

"Looked like they were burying someone. Think they were mostly Cana…some Fela…"

Quentin frowned. The youngster, a product of the harsh street environment without adult guidance or supervision, was one of the few to identify Quentin as Fela the moment they met. He announced himself as Ursa despite the dangers such an admission could create for one of anthro blood. He did not know who Quentin was and stubbornly clung to the belief that their shared secret and his willingness to be useful to the older man would guarantee food and protection.

Pepe was either brave or none-too-bright. Quentin had been in those shoes once, forced to trust others to survive but never revealing his secret to the adults in his world the way Pepe had done. He did not want a student, servant, or hanger-on, but since Pepe insisted on staying close, Quentin was not above taking advantage of his presence.

He had not asked for this. He did not owe the boy anything even after Pepe claimed he could track the mage's scent and had eagerly scampered off to do so. Quentin had not expected him to return.

"Only heard one name," Pepe continued, watching the older man adapt the room to his liking. "A girl called Jia…"

With that one name, Pepe earned his right to Quentin's protection. Within reason.

"Go back and follow her." It would be easy for a stranger to think Jia Marrock was a child, given her stature. "See where she goes. Come back and tell me. If I'm not here, go to the Hinton Change. Someone'll know where to find me. Can you do that?"

"I'm not stupid," Pepe snorted in offense. "Course I can."

Sending an eleven-year-old on such a mission was not the wisest thing he could ask, but it was Quentin's only option other than doing it himself. He could not guess why the tracker-mage, sent to find her and bring her to Lowell…along with the Fela who had been in her company, would come back without her. Perhaps, convinced Jia was safe if the Fela was no longer with her, the mage had let her go about her business if she would report to the Fortress later. She and the Fela were the only credible witnesses to Roland and Jonni's deaths, they were the only ones who could believably out him to the Laedan.

If Quentin found out where they were going, if he learned whom she was with, who was hiding her, he might be able to eliminate her. In doing so, he stood a better chance of eventually convincing Lowell of his innocence.

If she had told the mage anything, Quentin would have to eliminate him too.

That would be more difficult, but not impossible.

He would not do either tonight. There was a storm blowing in from the south, likely to hit within the hour judging by the taste of the wind, and Quentin had no desire to be out in it.

He assumed Pepe was street-smart enough not to be out in it either.

❧*❦

The stray bullet had skimmed past his head, grazing his scalp, causing a gush of blood down the side of his face. The force of it had thrown him off his feet and the cracking sound, in addition to the shockwave created by the explosion and the blood accumulating in his ear as he lay in the mud of the street, stunned him and dulled his hearing. By the time the smoke cleared and his vision along with it, the wagon was too far away for him to have a reasonable chance of catching it before it crossed the checkpoint. He could not risk the backlash it would cause if the guards recognized him. It was better to let them go. His head spun and rung as he staggered to his feet to assess those around him in the hopes there would be someone else to send, someone unrecognizable, in better condition and fleet of foot.

He was barely upright when the clouds opened and the rain gushed like blood from a severed artery.

Limbs scattered around dismembered torsos, bodies torn by the deep gashes of the fangs and claws of animals frightened off by the explosions. Most of his people were dead. The few who were not groaned in disoriented agony, in no condition to go any further. Even if there had been a doctor present, nothing could be done to spare them the slow path they traveled towards death.

Norse could not spare the bullets, nor the time to offer comfort and assurance. After gathering the usable weapons and assessing what he had to arm himself with for the trek back to the Fortress, he tucked what he could carry into his belt, into his pockets, through the multitude of straps crisscrossing his chest, back, and thighs. He straightened stiffly and stared north, trying to judge the wagon's path.

Odds were it was well on its way into LaGuardia. While the lawlessness of the world would offer adequate protection if he chose to continue the hunt alone, the potential for political blowback for his employer was not an acceptable risk. As frustrating as it was to fail his mission, it was better to abort and report the results to the Laedan.

Someone moaned as he turned towards Kennedy's Fortress. Norse paused and looked at the bloody mess of the man on the ground nearest him. With little thought to his action, he drove the butt of his baton into the man's skull, and then through another, until those still alive breathed no more.

The blood and brain pulp on the baton, on his hands, boots, and face, did not disgust him. Soon it would be washed away by the pouring rain.

❧*❧

He was not asleep but nor was he fully cognizant of his surroundings there in the cold with only the long sleeves of his wool sweater to protect him, his head resting on the woman's empty, immobile, cold-to-the-touch stomach. The canvas covering her, drawn back to expose her face, allowed for a degree of modesty he believed he owed his mother, though her nudity did not trouble him.

Nudity never had.

The canvas was not enough, however, to create a protective barrier between them. When, in his daze, he became aware something in the sense of the room, the smell of it, had changed, Nik lurched back in time to avoid the jerking motion that brought the woman's body into a sitting position. Her movement was attended by the gurgling, growling, ravenous sounds Nik had heard from many deliveries made to the Plant for final processing, grubbers trapped and transported by those who did not take the time, or did not have the stomach, to finish them off themselves.

Instinct took over. He flipped the table sideways, dumping the animated corpse on the floor. With the table between them, he kicked as hard as he could, pushing it towards the wall to trap her as the door began to open.

"Close it," Nik shouted. "Do it now!"

The shock sticks and clubs the guards carried might not be enough to incapacitate a grubber. He did not know if either carried a blade or something similar to separate the thing's head from its body.

It. Not her. This was no longer his mother. If he could not contain it, stop it, if it got loose in the Fortress basement or, heavens forbid, found a way up the stairs, there was no telling how many it might kill before it was stopped.

The door slammed closed as a baton was tossed inside. It clattered on the floor and slid within his reach.

His father, Nik believed, would never have the heart, or the stomach, to do what needed to be done.

The strength of his legs planted against the underside of the table was not enough. The grubber's thrashing, snarling efforts to be free, to reach the only source of heat in the room, meant it would eventually overcome his efforts to trap it. The baton might be enough to stop it if he bashed its skull into a fleshy pulp, but that would mean getting in reach of its gnashing mouth with the possibility of a bite that could kill him within a handful of hours.

Its pushback tipped the table and caused one of the lower legs to drag against the floor, revealing in that sound and movement that it was loose, rusted where it was bolted to the tabletop. Maneuvering sideways to push his shoulder against the table allowed the grubber the opportunity to get one flailing arm free enough to clutch at his shoulder with clawed fingers.

"Come on, Mama…you don't wanna do this," he muttered between gritted teeth as he kicked at the loose leg with one foot while bracing with the other and weaving his torso to and fro to stay out of the reach of the searching hand.

The sound of his voice meant nothing to the grubber beyond being a confirmation of a heat source it did not need.

Another kick.

He ducked, doubling forward so his nose was almost on his knee.

Another.

"Sirra!"

"Stay outta here, Captain! That's an order!"

It was an order Nik knew would not be obeyed. When the table leg gave way to his efforts, the lessened resistance meant a loss of balance. Without Nik's full weight pressed against the table, the grubber broke free of its pinning hold. The canvas encasement was scraped away, preserving the flesh on her legs as it came up and over the sideways table. Briefly, it was trapped there, its lower torso and legs pinned against the wall, its upper body and arms drooped over the metal. When Nik slithered backward, away from the flailing hands and snapping teeth, the table slid too. The grubber's efforts to reach and devour the heat freed it fully from the trap.

Nik rolled, swinging the baton hard enough the grubber snapped back with an inhuman, wheezing screech.

For a sickening moment, man and grubber stared at one another, one seeing nothing, the other seeing the disfigured side of the face that had once belonged to his mother.

"Mama…please," Nik croaked, his bravado, his surety in the face of a death he did not fear, cracking into his core. "Don't…"

The grubber made a staggering spring forward…

…and was met by the sharp metal edge of the broken table leg puncturing through the center of its face.

It fell, twitching. Nik rolled away, long blonde hair in his clenched fist, his retching, heaving stomach depositing its meager contents directly into the path of the door when it swung open and Captain Ortega barged in, a long, curved, cleaver-like blade in his hand.

He had disobeyed the command, as expected, but he had come too late. The deed was done.

"Torben…" Nik spat in a cracking voice. "Bring Torben…"

"Torben?" The captain shoved the blade through his belt.

"Sposer Moller…He'll know what to do…"

What to do for Yiva, what to do for Nik…to prevent him from falling into a hole he might not be able to crawl out of.

He had killed his mother…as surely as the man or men who had taken her life.

Nik retched again as his vision blurred.

Chapter 9

"Can't say who the target is," Nepo shrugged without looking at the slouched figure beneath the street lamp struggling to burn before the force of the storm that had raged throughout the night. It was early morning but it was impossible to verify the hour through the black billows belching fat drops of water and occasional forks of white light at the ground. Nepo was not surprised the youngest Channon had tracked him down but he was surprised Donn chose to converse with him in the street rather than getting out of the gale. Donn was more often the sort to summon someone to him, but there were some instances, some matters of business, that could not be conducted in the place the Channons called home.

Business such as the sort Nepo conducted.

"Who's the hunter?"

Again, Nepo shrugged. "Seen him around…small timer, I guess. Not up to my level. Don't think he's a mage. Just a ruff getting by. Want me to find out? Find his contract and…?"

His inquiry was aborted by a prickle at the back of his neck, a familiar sensation only people like him experienced, something he had not felt in quite some time. A turned head brought him eye to eye across the busy morning street with a face he had not seen in years.

The other man faltered in his steps and covered his hesitation with the adjustment of his coat around his neck against the wind as if the hesitation was intentional. The pause in Nepo's sentence was long enough to prompt Donn to turn his face inside the hood of his rain cloak, a movement that did not change the direction of the hood, to see what had distracted his companion.

He scowled.

As sobriety returned, aided by long periods of sleep, a robust meal, and hours of abstinence, Donn's memories had grown clearer, darker. Once his mother made it home, alone or with assistance, there was no way his father was going to allow such an assault to go unanswered. She would never betray her son to Lowell, not after so many years of shared secrets between them, but the demand for an investigation would be made. It would explain the hordes of Protectors Donn had dodged on his way to this rendezvous.

His mother might not betray him, but if the mage was called in, that would not matter.

Donn had to be careful not to be seen. No one else could identify him from that night or place him in the vicinity of the attack. But Segara, like Nepo, was one of a handful in LaGuardia who could undermine a lack of physical evidence and offer confirmation of guilt. One of a few who could take the woman's hand and know the truth without her uttering a word.

It was tempting to get out in front of the suspicion and hire Segara to go after Quentin, casting blame on his brother's killer, but as he knew his father had also employed the tracker-mage, intending him to locate a stolen shipment Donn could not afford Segara finding, he decided to drop the idea.

Better, he thought with a sneer, to do away with this problem before it grew larger.

"Know him?"

"We've met," Nepo said evasively, his tone hissing with what Donn interpreted as resentment.

Across the street, the dark-haired tracker shuffled on without any indication he recognized either of them. Neither man spoke until Segara was out of sight.

"Find out what Quentin's up to, who the ruff is, who they're targeting." Likely, Donn mused, one or all of the Channons. "I'll throw in an extra bar if you take care of Segara too."

There followed a long pause in which Donn assumed Nepo was weighing the pros and cons of the new request, deciding if the offered price was adequate for the job, and then, without needing a handshake or written agreement, there was a single word.

"Agreed."

His solitary trek north had been a miserable one, the rain and swirl of thoughts pounding through a head that had been too long without a drink doing their best to pull Vance back to those he had left behind. Back to Jia who would take his focus away from his private demons and make the lure of alcohol easier to resist. Back to the possibility of a life he did not often contemplate.

There was a cause for that. There were too many reasons why those like him, men and women who could read thoughts, impressions in a touch on people or objects…who could know the unknown and see the unseen in a room, in the air, in the world around them…opted for a solitary existence. Adding those details into the complicated familial and political path Jia traveled, Flushing Pack alpha and daughter of a LaGuardia Laedan…potentially Laedan herself…there was no chance of a future between them.

Those clues were obvious.

He could never give her what she needed.

She would never be able to get past the curse of a tracker to be what he needed either. No one could.

It took a determined effort to put her out of his thoughts and instead dwell on the vivid recollections of the lab, of Laedan Hallister, of Liam, and those they had rescued, the living and dead alike. He had not had the chance to study the sturdy folder Jia had given him, to glean what evidence it held, but as he pushed through LaGuardia, nearing his Protectorate, nearing home, he was beginning to develop a clearer picture of what it meant.

How the pieces fit, how they reflected off one another, had not yet become obvious.

When the noticeable presence of another tracker pressed against his thoughts, the sort of tingling trace impossible to deny or ignore, he lifted his head to search for it. The wind ripped the hood of his cloak away to expose his already-soaked hair more fully to the storm. He did not recognize one of the two figures standing beneath a street lantern in front of a tav on the opposite side of the road. But the other…he had hoped to never see that particular tracker again.

How many years had it been? Five? Ten? Maybe fifteen since their first meeting at least and a handful of times after as Vance hunted him to settle an ancient score that refused to die.

But he had gotten too busy…or perhaps apathetic…and the tracker called Nepo dropped off his radar. Vance had thought him dead.

Now he was back.

Memories of his aura and wide-legged stance brought with them the burn of unfinished business that could not be finished today. There were more vital matters to tend to, the most important of which was getting somewhere warm and dry, getting out of his soaked clothes, in a place containing the promise of whiskey to soothe his nerves.

Besides, what did Nepo matter now? Vance's father was long dead. No promise of revenge, no amount of blood spilled, no amount of death, was going to undo what had been done. It was, perhaps, time to let the past go.

Keeping aware of the tracker's aura until it could no longer be felt, Vance knew Nepo would not likewise be willing to move on now that they had seen each other again.

❮*❯

The rain dripped through the cracks in the ceiling of his shelter, gathering in pools on the floor, following the fractures in the tile like rivers drifting into a lake. Though the distracting sound of the seepage, the clap of occasional thunder, and the squealing of the wind through the gaps around the windows and doors deprived him of restful sleep and filled the air with a miserable dampness, it kept the night from freezing, a small blessing Quentin was marginally grateful for when he finally rolled off his table bed and out into the world.

Pepe had not come back last night but in the storm, Quentin did not expect him so soon. He would not wait here. He had somewhere to be and Pepe knew where to go.

Uzzi had a job to do, and Quentin intended to be certain he did it.

❧*❧

Portions of their shelter, wide wooden planks, sheets of metal, and flaps of canvas, were cobbled together to produce an awkward covering for those in the wagon bed when the decision was made not to wait for the storm to pass. There was still no evidence those who had attacked them were following through the storm, but the lack of evidence was not enough to verify they were not there, despite the watch of Fela and Cana alternating throughout the period of rest the group sought at the fringe of the Flushing Wilds.

For Jia, who drove the ox down the muddy streets, there was no cover. Only limited visibility and an innate sense of direction steering her towards the Pack. As close as they were to home and the promise of security from the storm, away from enemies with guns and shock sticks, the weather was deemed an acceptable inconvenience.

She looked over her shoulder and met Liam's gaze. He nodded his repeated agreement.

This was for the best.

The rain was not likely to kill them.

Whoever might be behind them likely would.

❧*❧

Nik stared at what had once been a human face, the center of it caved in by the metal table leg thrust through it, its eyes glazed with a milky gray sheen, its mouth twisted and slack, only recognizable as his mother in its overall shape and form. He refused to leave her despite Captain Ortega's prompting and efforts to move him. He refused to rise until he heard two sets of familiar footsteps, one heavier than the other, approaching quickly beyond the still-open door of the storage freezer.

Allowing Ortega to prop the door open so he was not locked inside with the dead was the only concession Nik had been willing to make.

"What is the meaning of…?" Lowell bellowed, his argument with the sposer and the guard sent to fetch him turned into an expression of outrage when he noted the open door. His tirade was aborted by the visage of the upturned table, Nik's torn and soiled clothes, blood, skin, and brain matter splattered across the floor, and the woman's twice-broken body twisted into a malformed heap on the cement tile.

He did not need to ask what had happened. The evidence of his eyes was answer enough. A host of protests, admonitions, retorts, and furious rebukes sparked and died across the surface of his blue eyes, pushed down into his center with each reflexive clenching of his fists.

If he had acted sooner, this might not have happened.

"Sent for Torben to…" Nik murmured, reluctant to say the words his father had previously forbidden. There was no avoiding a decision now. Just as the cold of the storage room had not prevented the transformation, it would not keep a body oozing fluids on the floor at their feet from decay. "He's the best…I trust him…"

"Well I don't," Lowell spat, his contrary tone a product of denial and disbelief.

"Who else?" ventured Ortega as Torben pushed into the room to offer Nik a hand to pull him to his feet. "You know someone who…?"

"Can't be just anyone! She deserves respect and…"

"I'll go with her, Fa…I'll see it's done right. No one else is gonna desecrate her. I swear it." Other than her killer. Nik felt he had done enough desecration to demand an eternity of atonement. Seeing his mother's body treated with dignity in her final moments, more than she had been afforded in the last moments of living, was the least he could do. "Torben took care of Jonni and Roland. I swear, you can trust him." There was no other, better way to explain, in this setting, how he knew the sposer well enough to entrust Yiva's corpse to him. Only his handling of Jonni and Roland might suffice in Lowell's eyes.

Lowell grabbed Nik's arm and yanked him out of the small room and with his other hand was about to slam the door shut between him and the memory forever emblazoned across his mind. He stopped, however, hesitating as his gaze swept over the stains on Nik's hand, his pants, the front of his shirt. He swallowed hard and lowered his trembling hand.

Nik had sacrificed enough.

"See that you do, Niki…only the best, you hear? Take Ortega with you, see it done…"

Nik nodded his promise with a resigned glance at the captain. "Only the best. I'll take care of everything."

❧*❧

Geary traced his fingers over the dustless ledge, watching the infernal storm that appeared, from his office window, to be slowing at last. The waves' chop had lessened, and the clouds above billowed with less fury across the gray horizon where the glow of the sun sank out of view. His brows were furrowed as he wiped his palms over the face of his uniform jacket, the impulse to wipe away invisible stains being impossible to ignore.

There was nothing there.

Norse had come to him bathed and recently changed, his injury bandaged beneath a fresh uniform, his hair tidy, his jaw neatly shaven, not a trace visible of the tale he relayed of explosive balls and an attack by wolves in the middle of the day. Wolves did not often hunt by day, but it was not unheard of. Geary was certain, however, he was not the only one to suspect those had been no ordinary wolves targeting Kennedy's undercover squad in a coordinated assault.

If Norse suspected the same truth, he did not voice it. Instead, he apologized for his failure in a growling fashion, accepted the rebuke and reprimand he expected to receive despite Geary's reluctance to give it, and stalked out of the chamber with the promise that he would atone for the failed assassination in any way the Laedan wished.

Including the newest task set to him.

Norse was no spy, was usually too brazen for covert errands, but for something like this, there was no one else Geary could utilize. He suspected it was a duty the man would undertake with relished zeal…so long as there was no more bloodshed.

Geary felt the imagined blood of the dead tainting Norse was on his hand still.

As those dead did not matter to Norse, however, those dead mattered little to Geary either. While it decreased the number of trained soldiers on hand for the upcoming mission and raid on the not-so-mythical fort he had planned, there were always men and women willing to be recruited for the promise of better food, decent clothing, possible shelter, and the Laedan's favor for their families.

Though he did not believe Jia knew anything she could twist to use against him, did not think she had any reason or inclination to do so when her primary interest was finding her father's killer and taking care of her family, Geary was a wise enough man to understand there was a chance he was wrong.

It would be simpler to be done with her. Since that was not immediately possible, his secondary plan of gaining her assistance in the quest for the fort had to be his focus. If the effort failed, he would need a third contingency. One he hoped, he grunted as he studied his open palm, would not result in blood directly on his hands.

If anyone was to bear the taint of spilled blood, it would be Norse.

∾*∾

Over the roaring wind and pummeling rain, with their attention on the respectful transport of the dead and the determined effort to prevent her exposure to the elements, there was no opportunity for discussion after the Fortress gates closed. Lowell remained at the front door, having followed the sposer, his son, and Captain Ortega that far but refusing to step into the storm with them even for his wife's sake. Nik was keenly aware of Oasis watching from the top of the stairs where Nik had stood with Jia not so long ago, on the night Oasis had married his twin.

He did not look at her. He did not care she was there. But by the time the gates opened and Nik glanced at his father before trudging through it, she stood at Lowell's side, her hand on his arm tenderly.

Their faces were unreadable through the ancient, mottled, distorted glass. Lowell needed the sympathy, the empathy, the support. The offer was not out of place and if he accepted her comfort where he did not accept Nik's, so be it.

The silence of the sojourn gave Nik time to debate options for disposal, the merits of each, so many choices and how those choices might benefit LaGuardia. In the end, however, he knew what his father expected. There were only two possible ends for a Channon. Either burial as an unaltered corpse beneath a fruit sapling in the courtyard or else incineration that for a few brief moments would provide power to the borough and leave ash remains for burial.

It was the customary end for grubbers, as no one wanted to risk the possibility of a decomposing grubber contaminating the water and food supply.

How many grubbers already lay decomposing throughout the borough, contaminating everything people breathed, ate, and drank? If the infection was present even in the living, what did it matter if one was buried before or after turning?

Nik still believed they should have sposed her sooner. They should not have waited for the turning. If not for her husband's refusal to accept her death, her beauty would be nourishing future fruit the way Jonni's was. There would still be a burial, a tree planted, as there had been for Roland.

But it would not be the same.

In the heat and stench of the Plant, where other sposers worked over vats of lye, over decomp cisterns and several dozen other furnaces, Nik helped Torben gently free the corpse from its canvas bag, lay her on the hemp mat that would go with her into the heat, and set to the task of washing her pasty grey skin, removing dirt and the remnants of her final battle under Ortega's watchful, uncomfortable gaze. Torben, meanwhile, set this particular furnace, intended for the burning of individual corpses when a family had means so the ashes for their dead could be returned to them.

No one else paid attention to their work. No one else made note of the dignitary about to give her final flame to their post-Undoing world.

Over his shoulder, Torben asked, "How you doin'?" There was no need to ask what had happened. The evidence on Nik's clothes and on his hands that came clean as he bathed his mother had been noted in the position Torben had found him in on the freezer room floor. The troubled flickering shifting of his eyes told Torben as much as he needed to know. He was not surprised Nik had the fortitude to act. He was only surprised that, thus far, Nik had not expressed any desperate desire for the crutches he was prone to seek to get him through the stresses of daily life.

Nik shrugged. "One minute at a time. Things to do." Finding focus outside of his thoughts, with duties piling up and no one else to shoulder them as had been the case most of his life, Nik found it easier not to dwell on the crawling itch in his skin, in his blood, that begged to be satiated. "Didn't expect it to be this though."

"We never do." Torben noticed the pre-mortem bruises, the abrasions, the evidence of assault on the woman's body but he knew better than to ask questions. That was not his job. His job was to treat each one as the person they had been one last time, regardless of their stations and circumstances. "Want me to do it?"

"No." Nik swallowed the lump in his throat and squared his shoulders, wondering if he would be so brave, so stoic, if Ortega was not here watching. Torben's offer wasn't the norm, as the public, the common families, rarely followed their dead to this step, but Nik had done it before, for others, when he had come here to watch Torben work and it made sense, to the two of them, for Nik to do it now.

He moved to the head of the roller platform, and bent to kiss his mother's cold forehead one final time, seeking words to say but not coming up with any that felt adequate except "I love you, Mama." He pressed the console button that started the rollers slowly spinning and took a step back. Feet first into the fire the corpse went, and with the first blast of the greasy burning flesh smell on the expelled air, Captain Ortega coughed, choked, and turned his face away.

"Torben'll see me home; it's okay if you go," Nik said gently, his gaze never leaving the woman's body as it moved into the flames.

The captain studied the sposer, making note of the scars of a dozen or more fights, the crook of his bent nose, the missing portion of an ear. He nodded. A man did not survive those types of scars without being the winner of numerous battles. The sposer was bulky enough, intimidating in stature and in girth, to make most people in the borough think twice about crossing him. With the sposer insignia on his outerwear and the respect most people held for those who disposed of the dead and fed the city what meager power could be generated, it was unlikely anyone would trouble him. If Nik trusted the sposer to escort him safely home, Ortega would rather resume the duty of weeding out the man or men beneath his leadership who had let this shameful thing come to pass.

He would rather do anything other than watch and smell a woman burn, a woman he had known and respected. He left Nik where he stood, directly across from the windowless furnace door, staring at it as if he could see the sizzling, crackling, charring flesh behind it. It was the sort of imagery Captain Ortega would be satisfied never to witness again.

Jia detected the sweet musk of her Pack's markings with a relieved grin as they crossed the boundaries of the new territory carved out for themselves beyond the borders of LaGuardia's borough. The other anthro in the wagon smelled it too and those familiar with familial scents sat up in anticipation of welcoming faces. Those unacquainted with it, the outsider Cana and the relatively new Fela member, shifted apprehensively or, in Kato's case, with the eager resolve to verify his sister had been cared for, as the Pack had agreed.

After Vance separated from the group, after the wagon had begun to move again, Kato returned, his Normal form dressed in damp, ratty clothes he had found, or stolen, at the onset of the storm. He refused to ride in the claustrophobically covered bed, preferred instead to sit on the weather-exposed steerage seat beside Jia where he could continue to look for danger through the rain ahead.

He found little comfort in her company. They were too miserable for conversation, wet, cold, and hungry for a hot meal. Things he wanted to say, questions he wanted to ask, dribbled away with the water trickling from his hair down his shoulders and back and he, like Jia, kept his eyes on the path.

Now that the library was close, the following yips and yodels and howls from the solo Cana trailing them unseen in the trees spread ahead like a fire towards the heart of the pack.

That it was Deuce there to welcome her, waiting for her, made Jia unexpectedly giddy. Kato could smell it.

How quickly she seemed to have accepted this strange, once-exiled, surrogate father figure.

Kato did not think he could have done the same if his father had ever come home after abandoning his family for so long. The only difference, of course, was Deuce had never abandoned her. He had stayed despite everything. Kato could not say the same about the man who had sired him.

When the wagon stopped its twists and turns through the passages between gradually decaying college buildings, it was to the greeting smiles and embraces of nearly every member of the Flushing Pack. Jia did not see Ilba or Trill, and Deuce was still watching from the shadows. She could feel Pain's presence and knew him to be close, though she could not see the Pack's new omega. There was no confrontation. There was no detectable hostility.

It was a relief to be met without violence and suspicion for the first time since being thrust into the role of alpha.

Behind the cluster of excited pups, Reif grinned wildly and waved at Wist as he wiggled free of the wagon bed. He waved back, started towards her, but when Addi clasped his shoulder, he turned instead to aid the weaker members of their company to the ground. People came forward to offer support and assistance and from the middle of the group, Vanya squealed and raced through the mud to throw her arms around her brother's neck.

Jia was relieved to see and feel Kato's demeanor change with their reunion. She doubted the siblings had been separated for long before and she was grateful her family had kept the young woman safe.

Maz met her at the side of the wagon, not needing to help her down but offering his hand in greeting with an expression of gratitude.

"You got him." Maz's head tilted towards where Zen escorted Liam into the library after his quick exchange of glances with Jia. While healthier than many of the others he had protected and helped bring to safety, the cramped nature of the wagon had stiffened his malnourished body and made his limping steps slow and awkward.

"We were lucky," she murmured, embracing the older man, finding comfort in his steadfast familiarity. "No trouble here?"

Knowing what she asked, Maz shook his head. "He's kept to himself. I've tried to engage him, draw him in." He sighed, shrugged, and steered her in the direction where the others were disappearing, through the door that promised a fire's warmth and hearty portions of the evening meal simmering over it. Though the Pack had already eaten, what remained, with additional ingredients added, had been set to warming as soon as Deuce's announcing call pierced the night.

"Maybe he will, in time," she said affectionately. Pain had been her father's friend. Was especially dear to Maz. Whether she could forgive him was something she would consider when that moment came. For now, she wanted a good night's rest, as close to her dearest childhood companion as she could arrange.

As if reading her thoughts, Liam looked up with a smile and caught her hand to pull her down beside him at the fire. She offered no resistance, despite Kato's dissatisfied scowl beside his sister on the other side of the fire.

Liam was home. Tonight, nothing else mattered.

The figure stopped far behind them when the first Cana call went up. Like those in the wagon, he too smelled the territorial markings of a Cana pack. Although he had not been certain before, he was certain now. The majority of those the Protector had traveled with were Cana. He could not see their destination through the overgrowth of trees and brush, could not tell at this distance where the scents of cooking meat came from, smells twisting his stomach into rumbling knots, but he guessed he had found what his new mentor wanted him to find.

There were also traces of Ursa in the vicinity, scratches on trees and a scent in the air, further reason not to go closer.

Claws came out. Deep gouges were scored into several trunks around where he stood, his mark left so he would be able to find his way back but would not interfere with the resident Ursa's claim on the territory. The Cana might find those marks, but as his were outside of the boundaries they had set, and he was Ursa, not Cana, he did not believe they would pursue him.

He hoped the Ursa did not.

With a light rain still falling, it seemed more likely his prey was seeking, and found, shelter and rest for the night.

Pepe, however, turned back along the trail he had left to report he had done as instructed. He had found the place Thomas Quentin was looking for.

Chapter 10

Seeing the tracker-mage in the street, dwelling on the troublesome possibility that he knew something…about Jonni's death, about the shipment Lowell had commissioned him to find, about the Marrocks, that might need to be shared with his father, Donn sauntered through the Fortress gates with arrogant, nonchalant ease, barely noticing the tension of the guards as he passed.

Of course they were tense. Jonni and Roland had been murdered. Yiva had been assaulted…which they must know by now. And if Nepo was right, Nik was missing.

His father needed him. There was a borough to govern and only one responsible mayor available to fill those shoes.

The niggling at the back of his head, terror-shades of memory trying to push to the forefront of his thoughts, was but one more reason he needed to be here. The longer he stayed away, the more terrifying those shades would become. The more likely they were to devour him.

He had a plan, an idea he could use to sway his father to side with him, a partnership that would set everything right.

"Fa!" It was an unexpected boon to find the hunch-shouldered man on one of the roomy foyer's benches, holding a wooden box between his hands. It was likewise a relief to see Nik squatting there before him, not missing as feared and, it was quickly noted when Nik turned towards him and got to his feet, seemingly sounder in mind and body than he had been in a long time.

His brush with death, surviving his last odose, might have scared him into trying to get clean.

It would not last. It never did. But for today, it was good to see.

"Where have you been?" barked Lowell, the eruption to his feet a sharp contrast to his previous lethargy, the thud of the box echoing and heavy on the tile.

"Making arrangements for LaGuardia's future," Donn began, neither surprised by his father's wrath nor by the way Nik took a step back to avoid a potential confrontation.

What did surprise him, as he reached them, was the hand that struck him across the face and the furious roar that followed. "You should have been here! None of this would have happened if you had been here!"

"Fa…" With a hand on Lowell's shoulder and the other catching the hand about to strike, an uncharacteristic intervention, Nik said softly, "You should see to Mama…she wouldn't want…"

Whatever words remained unsaid, whatever Nik's grim, steady tone implied, it was enough to erase Lowell's angry façade and replace it with the sort of despair Donn had never seen on his father's face before. The older man picked up the sealed box and cradled it as he trudged from the chamber without a word, as if his sons were forgotten, invisible to him.

Those peculiarities and details were swept aside. "I know where it is," Donn began, the voice trailing after his father hopeful of lightening his mood and restoring peace despite the irritation of the stinging flesh on his cheek and jaw. "Together we can…"

"Not here." Nik grasped Donn's arm and ushered him up the stairs in the opposite direction from where Lowell had gone. Captain Ortega and a handful of his guards passed through the room, on their way out the door, his expression dark and purposeful. When Ortega saw the Laedan, he motioned for the others to continue without him and hurried to fall into step beside Lowell, his head bowed, his hands behind his back, words spoken in quiet conversation.

Believing he understood the reason for what he witnessed, the meaning behind the air's pall, the only thing Donn could not explain was the business-like nod the captain gave to Nik, a nod Nik returned as he and Donn ascended the stairs.

"Why is Arlo…?"

Nik bristled at Donn's informal address of the Captain of the Guard but ignored the fleeting question of Ortega's loyalty. Donn expected respect and formality and titles from everyone who interacted with him, but he rarely returned it, as if to remind everyone he was more than they would ever be.

"Things have…happened…while you've been gone."

"I wasn't gone," Donn snorted. "You're a fine one to…making us track you down, drag you home, every time you…"

Elbowing Donn into the room, Nik closed the empty office's door and muttered, "Doesn't matter, Donni. Mama's gone."

"What do you mean gone?" Donn blinked, his entire body going rigid. "I just saw her the other…"

"Dead." The word was not easy to say, but after attending her cremation, the reality of it was more a fact for Nik than ever.

"How?" She had been in good health, fit enough to cross LaGuardia alone for some clandestine rendezvous with Chief Ernest or someone else at the Protectorate. The answer he expected to hear tugged the corners of his mouth and eyes into a condescending sneer despite his attempts to the contrary.

Nik was not looking at him, was instead staring out the window, and Donn was grateful Nik did not see his fleeting expression.

"Murdered. Out there." Nik's eyes scanned across the view of the borough through the rain-streaked glass.

"Murd…" Donn choked on the word, a strangled sound that prompted Nik to look at him. "How…who…?"

"Don't know." One shoulder twitched. "Fa thinks it was Thomas, revenge for being fired and expelled from the Fortress…"

Expression dark but uncomfortable, Donn snorted, "Should have done that a long time ago…before Jonni…"

"Think he believes me now…that Thomas did that…to Roland and Jonni…but this…the timing doesn't fit…"

Face pale, Donn sank onto the nearest dusty chair, his knees refusing to keep him upright, his hands refusing to stay steady. "Don't need to worry about Quentin," he forced another snort he hoped covered the uncomfortable tightness at the back of his throat. "He's being handled."

"Handled?"

"Doesn't matter. Took some work…but he's not going to be a problem much longer."

"So that's where you've been." Seeking retaliation for Jonni's death. It made sense. While the oldest and youngest Channon sons had never been close, their too-different personalities making any sort of friendship between them impossible, Donn was fiercely protective of the family name and those who bore it. A wrong done to any one of them, by anyone outside the family, was an affront Donn would not let stand. But it would have been helpful, Nik thought bitterly, if he had known so he could reassure their father that there had been no foul play involved in Donn's absence.

"Where else? Certainly not…I leave that shart to you."

The tone of the insult was ignored, despite its accuracy.

"When did she…?"

"Three nights? Four?" Nik had not been counting; as he had not slept during that time, day and night had bled seamlessly into one long period of wakefulness. "Long enough for her to turn…"

"Shart…." The monsters in Donn's head clawed free.

He remembered.

All of it.

He was too dazed by the evidence to consider the implications.

How could she have done this to him?

"Has she been…?" Had that been what remained of her? In the box Lowell carried out of the hall?

"Tomorrow, I think. Captain Ortega's seeing to the preparations."

"He's not family!"

"You weren't here! Fa's not…" Nik shook his head. "I've been busy seeing to…"

"I bet." Donn did not try to hide his sneer.

"Been a lot to do, with Jonni gone…without you being here and Fa not…someone's had to…"

"I'm here now."

Ignoring the condescension, studying Donn's face, looking for something he did not see, something to support the crawling sensation across the back of his neck, Nik continued, "Yeah…you are. Too much for one person. I can use the help."

"No need for you to do anything, Niki, to fret your little head over anything." Donn pushed to his feet, his posture enough off balance that Nik steadied him as Donn ruffled his brother's hair playfully. "I'll get it under control. You can get back to…whatever it is you do when you're not here. Just don't get lost."

Nik frowned. Donn knew he was capable. Not accustomed to sole responsibility for the borough, but capable enough. The perceived effort to push him out of the way was not unusual, however, and the last words were ones he understood. It was the expectation that so many had of him.

"I won't," he promised, determined, despite his brother's efforts to cast him aside, to prove everyone wrong.

❧*❧

His flat smelled the same as it had when he was last here, stale and damp with hints of sweat and whiskey that did little to mask the mildew traces lingering around the edges of his perceptions.

How long had it been?

It felt like weeks. Or months.

He hung his coat on the hook on the wall, where the continued dripping of water into the collection tray there, fashioned to keep the water from ruining the floor, added to the ambiance of the dwindling storm outside. He took enough time to open the liquor cabinet in search of the drink his nerves craved, only to remember as he did so that he had taken his last bottles to Queen's College. His cupboard was empty. He scowled as he lit a fire in the wood stove, removed his wet shirt, and collapsed onto the sofa to remove his boots, bundle in the blanket still hanging over the back, and sink to one side where he was asleep almost immediately.

The dreams that came, distorted, muted, discolored crimson, presented his consciousness, when he awoke later, with the latent remembrances of perceptions gleaned in the lab, traces of things felt in Laedan Hallister's presence hinting the man was not what he seemed. Hinting he could not be trusted. The same, in many ways, as the things Vance felt in Laedan Channon's company, the proof of political forces taught early to say anything to anyone if it afforded them what they wanted.

What did Kennedy's Laedan want with Jia?

The question, and the cold in the room now that the fire had burned out during his long slumber, prompted Vance to rise to relight it and fetch the protected folder from his bag. Without his gloves this time, he absorbed the details the exterior cover held, the narrow face of the man who had left it there at another's insistence, a military man, not a medical one, and not, Vance believed, part of HOPE's hierarchy.

But HOPE's far-reaching influence touched all strata of life, from the Grand Mas and his ilk to its proselytizers and soldiers, to political and economic puppets and the population of the boroughs' streets. The man who had left the journal might not be an inductee, but he could be a proponent easily enough.

What Vance read was not clear enough to tell.

The most troubling detail he detected as he opened the folder was that it had not been accidentally left on the counter. The sense of the place, the echoes of silence, the dimming of medicinal smells in the chilly dark, where the voices of the damned, the forgotten, were murmured echoes muted behind glass, abandonment. The passing of footsteps, the ghosts of those carrying equipment and supplies out of the building, shifting bodies housed in pod-like containers, evaporated like mist as time passed around them, until the abandoned, and this folder, were all that remained.

Left intentionally. Just as the handful of anthro had been.

He felt the passing of souls beyond the glass as lives seeped away one by one while his eyes scanned the pages, looking for clues in the code to tell him what the words, numbers, symbols, and diagrams meant. It was his fingers on the paper, more than the writing itself, that revealed its nature. Each victim was assigned a number. Each number was coded with their nature. Cana. Fela. Ursa. Mutani. Other. Details were provided for substances, supplements given to continue life and increase the production of blood. Test subjects who were given other things to note the effect on their blood, their lives. Poisons and contagions some were forced to endure. The number of units of blood extracted before each succumbed to their body's gradual weakness and were disposed of, empty husks with no humanity remaining and no purpose left to serve.

Roland and Liam had been fortunate to escape that fate. Having had no opportunity to touch Roland, to learn what he knew, to see what he had seen, either at his moment of death or in the days before it, and having no chance to shake Liam's hand or touch him in the chaos of their escape, Vance could not witness what they had endured. He did not know what they knew, how it connected to the coded details on the page beneath his fingertips.

He needed more detail. He should go to Queen's College. He should talk to Liam.

He should go back to Jia.

He clenched his injured hand so the pain shot up his arm from his severed finger and jolted his senses.

No.

That was the last place he needed to be.

He traced the ink diagrams, the details of blood processing equipment that separated plasma from the rest. While nothing on the page suggested how juice was made from anthro plasma, nor what became of the rest of what was stolen, it was obvious the process had begun there, in that lab. Perhaps it was the only one. Perhaps there were others elsewhere. He could not tell from the folder of data where the plasm went next, whether this facility generated juice or if they were, as Hallister had suggested to Jia, merely a facility for scientific blood study and experimentation.

No ethical facility, however, kidnapped its subjects…or routinely killed them. The recorded consent on the attached documents for some of the anthro was as false as the symbol on its cover.

Someone, perhaps HOPE, supplied those people. The facility, however, was not a HOPE operation. And it was not, despite what he read with his eyes or Laedan Hallister's suspicions, a purely medical and scientific research business. There had been profit made with the blood of anthro, in the production and sale of juice. There was the eradication of those who were different.

Whether Hallister knew about it, Vance could not be certain. Lowell Channon, he guessed, did not.

Vance needed details. He needed access to Laedan Hallister, to Mas Lord. He should go back to the lab.

But he needed to report to the chief first. He needed to report to Laedan Channon what he knew to clear Jia and Kato's names.

He closed the folder. At this late hour, he needed sleep, time to purge the ghosts of juice from his system, time to let the new puzzle pieces settle into place and, he hoped, add further form to the picture in his head.

He needed a drink.

That, however, had to wait.

⅌*↍

The bitter tang at the back of his throat, reminding him of his mother's betrayal, sent Donn barging out of the empty room in search of something to soothe his agitation. His father's melancholy fury, Nik's sobriety, the Fortress' hollow-shelled air, were because of her. If only she had stayed home. If only she had stayed away from the Protectorate Chief. If only she had lived.

Dying was her fault. There was no one else he could blame. It always came back to her betrayal. Or someone who had found her after he had abandoned her.

She had left him alone. How dare she abandon him. Who was he to turn to now, to purge his soul, to find solace in domination and some degree of peace without her there to satiate him?

Not entirely alone, he realized when his entry into the family sitting room revealed the spring-like visage of the wife he sometimes forgot he had. She had already revealed herself to be compliant to his needs and he supposed he owed her for succeeding in the expulsion of Quentin from the Fortress. She also owed him because she was his wife; it was reason enough to barge across the room, yank her up from the settee where she sat, bare feet curled beneath her, reading in front of the fire, and crush his mouth against hers in a bruising kiss.

For the briefest of moments, before their mouths met, there was a look of horror, of shock and alarm on her face, and though it was erased as abruptly as it appeared, it was there long enough for Donn to see it, long enough to fill his loins with a fire demanding to be fed. He spun her around, bending her awkwardly across the back of the settee, and yanked roughly at her robe to expose the flesh of her bare buttocks. He growled, held her down with a tight hand at the back of her neck, both pleased and disappointed she did not struggle, and fumbled with the front of his trousers.

"Her fault…" he hissed under a growling breath.

"D…husband?" Oasis caught herself and avoided speaking his name, knowing that using it would place them as equals and infuriate him. In this mood, subservience was the only hope of leniency she had. Not gentleness. Donn was never gentle. In matters of carnal satisfaction, Donn knew nothing of gentle. "You cannot do this."

The hand on her neck tightened. "I can do whatever I please." The sound at the back of his throat when she squawked in pain from the hold on her neck and his thrust into her unprepared body was one of supreme satisfaction and vindication.

"You can't…" she began.

His free hand cracked hard against her ass.

"Shut up!" He thrust again.

"I'm pregnant!" she managed to squeak. "You can't…"

The next blow cracked across the side of her head…and he froze.

The box of human ash was reluctantly relinquished to Ortega so the burial provisions could be completed but only after an oath was sworn that the captain would not let the box out of his sight until the moment it was placed in the ground. Numb, lost, Lowell stood at the top of the stairs staring in the direction Arlo had gone, making no effort to dig out of the mire of choking guilt.

They had grown steadily apart over the years, his wife becoming more sullen and withdrawn and silent, but was that entirely her fault? He should have done more, reached out to her, given her the honor, the protection, the love he had promised in marriage instead of drowning in work and mistresses and any other excuses he could find, or generate, to stay away. If he had upheld his vows to those he loved, Yiva, Jonni, and Roland would still be alive.

There was only himself, and Quentin, to hold accountable.

The punctuating sound of Oasis' voice from a nearby open doorway drew his focus long enough to identify the sounds and location. He should not go to her. The solace he had once found in her, the welcome relief of a woman who understood, accepted, and wanted him as he was, had been the final nail in his relationship with Yiva. Every time he encountered the young woman now he was overwhelmed with both longing and guilt to the point where staying away from her had become the only way he could endure Yiva's loss. But Donn's voice, the heat and brutality of sounds that came after, reminded him of what his son had previously done to his new bride, how he had hurt her. How Lowell had threatened him about respecting his wife and never hurting her again.

The way someone had hurt Yiva.

Having lost his wife, Lowell would not stand for the curdling of the Channon name by the malignancy of marriage violence. Furious that Donn would disobey him on the cusp of his mother's murder, Lowell charged towards the revolting evidence of another betrayal.

The door banged behind his brother on his retreat from the office, bouncing several times without latching until it ceased moving and remained open, causing Nik to scowl at the space as if there was a detail missing, obvious but hidden from view. His twin had been an angry young man since early childhood, since Nik's peculiarities demanded a significant share of their parents' focus. While Nik did not believe Donn blamed him, had never seen evidence of anger aimed at him because of differences Nik could not help, the anger blossomed and persisted nonetheless. Typically, Nik let those outbursts go, took solace in one substance or another while Donn sought his outlets somewhere else.

Now, believing they needed to be a unified front for the sake of their father and LaGuardia's future, Nik chose to follow the direction of Donn's footsteps, hoping he could do something to counteract whatever brutal impulses his twin followed this time.

That brutality, he realized as he faced his father's charge from the opposite end of the corridor, involved his newly taken wife.

For a moment, Nik hesitated, some small piece of him thinking Donn and Oasis' relationship was none of his business. But what he heard sickened and worried him and his father's barreling steps through the door prompted Nik's feet to move so that he burst into the room on Lowell's heels.

The slap across Oasis' face was not as hard as it was intended to be, barely grazed the back of her head, as Lowell caught Donn's arm and yanked him backward with enough force to propel him against the door jamb and into Nik's arms. The pain of his abrupt, sideways extraction made Oasis crumble onto the settee, and though Lowell was poised to launch into an attack against his youngest son, the force of Nik catching Donn turned them both so that Lowell's fist caught Nik in the jaw rather than Donn.

"I told you to never do that!"

"She's my…" Donn spat in outrage.

"She's a Channon and by the heavens, you'll treat her like one! It's bad enough your mother's…"

"It's her own damn fault!"

Nik pulled Donn into the hallway, ignoring the taste of blood in his mouth as he did his best to force an end to the dispute before it got worse. Having been unaware of any violent history between Donn and Oasis, though Lowell clearly knew about it, knew enough to have made some threat against Donn in the past, separating the two men seemed the wisest thing Nik could do.

"Lowell…don't…"

It was Oasis' plea, as much as Nik dragging his flailing brother away, that prevented Lowell from following his sons out of the room. It did not prevent him from roaring, "If this happens again, I'll kill you!" a cry that echoed beyond the door, into the corridor, and down the stairs into the entrance lobby.

Oasis, bleeding, in pain, and shaken by the abruptness of the last few moments, struggled to her feet and caught hold of Lowell's arm, offering a shaky, "No, you won't…" despite her predicament. Lowell, shaking beneath fury and desire and guilt, tried to jerk away from her. When she refused to release him, he reluctantly surrendered.

"I told him to never…you're better than this…he's better…no Channon should ever…"

"It's between him and me," she mumbled evasively.

"No, it isn't. Not anymore." He looked at her with wild, bloodshot eyes, a gaze intense enough to make her release him and step back to adjust her robe. "Are you pregnant?"

"I…" She swallowed hard. The lie had been Yiva's last piece of advice to her, the one chance Oasis had to temper Donn's brutality. When given, Oasis had known such a lie would mean Donn's continued brutality against his mother and she had been reluctant to make use of it. With Yiva's death, however, Oasis had struggled with whether or not she could use that advice, whether it would be moral or honorable or not?

With Donn's absence from the Fortress, the need to consider it too deeply had not existed. His sudden assault had prompted the lie unbidden and now, overheard by others, it could not be taken back. She had never meant for Lowell to hear it. She had not considered the ramifications of those words if they reached the Laedan's ears.

She thought about changing the subject but could think of nothing pressing that would not serve as an obvious mask. Instead, she sighed, swallowed, and nodded.

The lie would have to be played out.

"His? Or mine?"

"I…don't know." Even if she had been honestly pregnant, how could she know who the father was? She had slept with both men during the same period. There was no known way to determine the paternity of a child before its birth and no known way, even then, to distinguish traits between fathers of the same bloodline. "It…could be…either…"

"He'll not touch you." Lowell, interpreting her stammering and discomfort as pain and fear and despair, drew her into his embrace for the first time since Yiva's death.

"He is my husband."

"I will banish him from…"

"He is your son. One of LaGuardia's mayors. He should be here for his mother's…" She shivered at the thought, disgusted by the notion of Donn, having done the things he had done, standing at her side over his mother's resting place.

"I don't care." Lowell kissed the top of her head, inhaling her smell, soap and perfume, and her more personal scent, which made him tremble and tighten his embrace. She whimpered and shifted as if to melt into him. She felt so good. Soft, compliant, warm, alive…

He abruptly released her and retreated to the door. "He'll not touch you again. I swear it," he repeated before stopping out of the room.

Oasis wrapped her arms around herself and did not move.

"Shouldn't have done that…"

At the far end of the corridor, at the top of the lobby stairs, Donn finally pulled free of his brother's unexpectedly bruising hold and scowled as he adjusted his pants. "Not you too, Niki. She's my…"

Nik flexed his hands, his fingers aching from that grip and his brother's pulling free, and shook his head, "Fa's right. She's a Channon. She doesn't deserve…"

"It's none of your business! It's not anyone's business…"

"You can't abuse the mother of your child. It isn't right. You don't want to kill it…or her…"

Something dark flickered across Donn's face, prompting him to look away, or perhaps it was the opening of the lobby door where

Torben entered, hat in his hands, shoulders stooped and head bowed as if to appear polite and contrite when Nik suspected it was rather an expression of his discomfort in this place. He had not expected to see the sposer so soon, but the man had promised to look in on him, see how he was faring when he could. He might be here upholding their promise of friendship but Nik had not thought he would come back today.

"You don't know anything about me, Nik…"

"Don't I?" He leaned his elbows on the rail and nodded down at Torben to ask him to wait. "What did you mean 'she deserved it'? What did Oasis ever do to you to…"

"Chief Ernest isn't good enough for…I won't tolerate betrayal…"

Nik blinked, scowled, and stared at his brother. "Ernest?"

"Drop it, Niki." Donn started down the stairs.

Reluctant to pursue what Nik instinctively believed were answers he did not want, called, "Give Fa some space…be here for the burial but stay away from Fa, and Oasis, until…"

The only evidence Donn gave that he heard the admonitions was a dismissive wave of his hand to cut Nik off.

He had said too much but he could trust his brother. Nik relied on him to perform the duties of mayor. Nik was his twin. Nik, more than anyone in the family, could be trusted. Unlike Lowell, unlike Yiva, Niki had never let him down.

Now he was going to be a father.

If he could get his hands on the contents of Fort Hamilton, Donn could wrest control from his father and have his own heir to leave the borough to. He would have everything he had wanted, with Nik at his side and no troublesome Marrocks to contend with. After that, he would not need Oasis either. Or anyone else.

Chapter 11

"**W**hat has…?"

"Not here." There was no one near enough, with the doors of the lobby closed and the guards on the outside, to hear their discussion, but Nik would not take the risk that his wound-tight father would walk in and overhear them. Lowell was aware that Nik knew Torben but did not know how well, and for the moment, Nik believed it better if it remained that way. The pair went into the crisp air of the open courtyard, where the rain had ceased falling and the day's grey light was bending towards evening. He briefly considered heading to the nearest tav for a private conversation, but the compulsion to imbibe would be difficult to ignore in that setting, so Nik instead moved to the center of the courtyard, a distance he believed took them far enough from the guards for privacy.

Donn, it seemed, had left the premises.

Nik scowled. "Family stuff…between Donn and his wife and Fa…I dunno…but there's something he's not telling me."

"Your father?"

"Donn." He shrugged. There were a lot of things Donn never told him. Most people kept things from him because they thought he was not listening, would not understand, or would be unable to keep secret when under the influence. He was still surprised Roland had entrusted him with the Fort Hamilton map and notes. Most of the time he did not care to know more than necessary. But this was not the same; this instance felt different. Maybe the feeling was no more than the result of unfamiliar long-term sobriety. It might have felt different because for once Nik did care.

Torben nodded. He had no dealings with Donn, only knew what type of man he was through the tales Nik told and gossip overheard outside the Fortress walls. But it was easy to believe Nik's clear-headedness might allow for a shifting of sensitivities and might be perceived as a hazard to those used to the non-threatening nature of his addictions.

"Coming from a drop-off…thought I'd see if you need anything. Brought you this."

The pungent aroma of the pouch pressed into Nik's hand made him nod and smile gratefully. He did not know the ingredients of the tea Torben had provided during the hours of withdrawal, but he knew it would help with the shakes when they flared. While he did not want to use it, did not want to risk a psychological addiction to it in the place of long-standing physical ones, it was reassuring to know he had help on hand if it was needed.

"Thanks. Might need it to get through tomorrow." Burial day was going to be hell and he had few doubts he would need to be atypically strong and levelheaded if the Channons were to make it through the day intact. "Think you can come? Early, so the gates aren't closed?"

Torben nodded. They had reached the gates, which opened ahead of them as the sentries assumed Nik was leaving on a long overdue binge. Instead, he stopped when Torben did, when the man squeezed his shoulder and said, "You want me here, I'll be here." He was not one to socialize but for one of the few people he considered a friend, an almost son, Torben could do this.

He stiffened. His head cocked and he sniffed the air. Without warning, he thrust Nik against the gatepost with his body between Nik's and the whirring threat that rebounded off the stone with a ringing sound and ricocheted sideways. The redirect caught one of the sentries, a man barging forward in reaction to Torben's unexpected, apparent assault, in the side of the neck, grazing flesh and drawing blood before it landed several feet away in the middle of the yard.

Heads turned towards the borough streets but no assailant could be seen. There were only curious passersby who cried out in surprise or stopped to gawk at the unexpected turn of events.

Torben's unspoken question prompted Nik to nod once. "It was him…wasn't it?" Nik whispered.

It had to be the same one, the man who had come for him in Torben's brownstone, the one Donn claimed had been sent to bring Nik home.

No one else had ever made an attempt on Nik's life. This one had done so twice.

What if Donn was lying to him?

What if Donn wanted him dead, the only obstacle, albeit an unsteady one, to Donn's acquisition of complete power in LaGuardia?

"Let me see that." Torben snatched the metal-tipped arrow from the hand of the sentry who retrieved it, ignoring the man's offended snarl and corresponding defensiveness. While bows were common for hunting, a necessity for those who lacked the resources to raise livestock, chickens, ducks, or even dogs, cats or rats as the source of meat in their diets, most utilized stone or concrete tips, both being plentiful substances in the collapsing world around them.

Scrap metal was abundant, but few possessed the means to process it and turn it into something as precisely fashioned as this bolt.

"Should be easy to find where this came from," Torben grunted.

"Don't…I mean…I think I'd rather you stay…" stammered Nik.

"I'd do better finding…"

"We'll do that, Mr. Channon," said one of the sentries who was assessing the minor damage to the injured man's neck. "We'll get the bolt to the captain and he'll find who did this."

Thus far, Captain Ortega had not found evidence as to how or why Yiva had gone into LaGuardia alone, except that she had left the Fortress midday, insisting she did not need a chaperon and would be back shortly. The sentries who let her go without insisting on escorting her were enduring a harsh reprimand and demotion for their failure.

If he could not find the killers, how could he find an assassin based on a single arrow without a tracker's help?

Arguing, however, would be to offer Torben a way out of the request Nik had made. It was in his best interest to keep Torben close until the mutani with the peculiar eyes was caught.

"He's got lavender eyes," Nik stammered as he held tight to the sposer's arm with shaking hands. "If it's the same one…"

Torben sighed, gauging Nik's fear through the hold on his arm and the quaver in his voice, and grudgingly nodded. "I'm on shift, but I'll be back after. Stay here, don't go out without me. Wait till I'm back."

Nik's head bobbed, a jerky, nervous motion accompanied by the tense contraction of the hand around the pouch Torben had given him. "Find him; find Donn," he whispered. He would not voice his suspicions to the sentries. They would think him mad. But Nik believed if anyone knew why the lavender-eyed man was trying to kill him, or perhaps Torben, it would be Donn.

ຉ*ຌ

The craving for alcohol and the claustrophobic feeling of his flat propelled Vance into the street at an hour when most of the borough slept. But there were tavs open and secret corners where people congregated for the sale and sharing of a myriad of dubious substances, places Vance, as a Protector, knew about from his participation in raids, inquiries into murders or high-end thefts, as well as his purchases of whiskey to line his shelves for consumption in those moments when he would rather drink alone.

He knew he needed to break the cycle passed down from his father, and his father's father before him, his mother, and many others he had known. If he did not, Vance would end up like the man he both despised and loved, dead in an alley with a bullet in his head and a bottle in his hand.

Tonight there felt to be worse ways to die. Tonight he was losing the battle and at this moment, he did not care.

When he pushed through the dented, paper-thin metal sheets serving as a door into this back-alley squat, Thomas Quentin was the last person from the Fortress he expected to see.

Nik, perhaps. Maybe Donnovan. But never Quentin.

Thomas, an unopened bottle in his hand, was about to blurt something vulgar to the rude fellow who had hit him with the door, an act with little blame since there were no windows or ways to know who was on the other side. When he locked eyes with the tracker-mage, he blanched, froze, and tried to think of something more appropriate to say. Segara finding him here could be no coincidence. He had to be here on the Laedan's behalf, here to make an arrest, to drive him into the street where he suspected other Protectors waited.

The moment of surprise on Segara's face, however, gave Thomas hope the mage might not be here for him. He quickly considered his options, to leave after a polite nod or to endeavor to stay ahead of the snake-like noose gradually wrapping around his neck with well-intentioned words.

When Vance was the one to nod and speak first, muttering, "Mas Quentin," in a casual, if awkward greeting, Thomas made his choice.

"Been hoping to find you."

Vance fumbled in his pocket for the few coins he had to offer in exchange for a drink, drew them out, and clenched them in his palm as he cocked his head and muttered, "You have?"

"Lot has happened. Surely you've heard?"

"Just got in." He assumed Quentin was aware of the duties Lowell had thrust on him but would not know he had been out of the borough. His tone and question sounded as though he was fishing for information Vance was disinclined to give.

"Then you haven't." Thomas nonchalantly gestured away from the counter. "Sit…drink with me…"

Vance raked his hair from his face and glanced around the small room in which they stood. A few patrons were crammed into alcoves where they had chosen to enjoy the fruits they had come here to pluck. Others stood along the counter waiting for their requests to be filled. The line was long tonight, with at least a dozen crowded into the room; he could join the line, get what he had come for, but the press of so many others was already grating on his sober-frazzled nerves.

A single drink, or a portion of Quentin's bottle, was a better compromise, but not here in this hellhole. And he was curious, given what he already knew, to hear what the Laedan's aide had to say. Curious…and cautious.

"Got somewhere else we can go? Too stuffed in here for my taste."

Thomas too made a short visual inspection of the dimly lit arena and its host of patrons of the type he also found distasteful to mingle with. He had only chosen this place because no one here would recognize him. Straying out in public with the mage was little safer, but he did not want to be trapped in this dank stench any longer than he had to be either. He nodded towards the door.

"Not far," Thomas agreed. Though he pulled the door open for the mage to exit first, Vance caught the edge and bid him to go out instead. Thomas scowled, worrying about the potential for an ambush of Protectors. With the mage at his back, there would be no possibility of retreat or escape. Rather than express the fear as his thoughts scrambled for verbal defenses he could utilize, he nodded and went out as Segara indicated.

It made sense for him to lead. He had said he knew a place to talk.

In the empty street, they paused long enough to look up and down the path for potential hazards as the rumble of distant thunder far out to sea rolled over them.

"Gonna rain." Vance hated small talk, but it filled the strained void when Quentin turned to the left, away from the Fortress, and began walking with short, hasty steps.

"Always rains," snorted Thomas, his response one of equal discomfort with small talk, especially with a mage who could hear and read things in another person's voice, expression, inflection, and gestures intended to be kept hidden.

They trudged to the nearest intersection where those living in the area had erected a tin-roofed pavilion. It sported mismatched tables, chairs, and benches where the neighborhood residents could gather to allow their children to play on makeshift playground equipment carefully tended to prevent as many unintentional injuries as possible. There was no one there except for a bundled form curled on a long bench, asleep or dead or merely so well wrapped within the only warmth they had that they did not desire to move and be exposed to the cold. It could have been a pile of discarded blankets. Without getting closer, Vance could not be certain.

Thomas sat at a table as far from the lumpy form as he could get, the chair creaking under him as he settled. He uncorked the bottle as Vance perched on a backless stool across from him.

The mage eyed the bottle but said nothing as the other man took a long drink. He did not speak but waited to hear what the Laedan's aide wanted to tell him.

"Haven't caught the Fela yet, I take it. You know he struck again." He held the bottle across the table and waited.

Pepe had mentioned Fela in Jia's company, but it did not mean it was the same man. It was better Vance never know he had been spied on, that Quentin was watching the Marrock heir.

Vance's hand closed around the neck of the bottle. As Quentin wore gloves, there were few impressions to glean from the glass except what had been left by the sellers in the establishment they had come from. "Again?"

"Laedan Channon's fit to be…the entire Fortress is turned upside down over it. I know your boss stepped up the hunt since he was there when she was found…"

"She?" There were only two women of import in the Fortress now that no Marrocks lived or worked there. That either of those two might have fallen victim to some sort of violence made Vance feel so abruptly ill that the raised bottle never made it to his lips.

"Yiva. I didn't see her…Lowell wouldn't allow it…but I've heard it was terrible…beaten, raped, strangled…"

Again Vance shuddered. He closed his eyes. "When was this?"

"Few nights ago. Hasn't been a burial yet; think they're waiting to see if she'll…you know…or they're holding her for evidence…"

Waiting for her to turn. Why anyone would deliberately wait for that outcome came down to imprudence or a refusal to let the dead go, or else a suspicion that she, like Roland, could have been anthro.

Anthro never turned.

Not all Normals or mutani did either.

Waiting for a turn was impractical and inconclusive proof of anything. If the woman had been anthro, Lowell would have known a long time ago.

Perhaps he had.

"This happened…inside the Fortress?" To Vance's knowledge, there had been no murders inside the Fortress since the Channons and Marrocks had made it the seat of rule for the borough. No murders, that was, until Roland and Jonni.

Quentin snorted and took back the bottle Vance had yet to drink from. "Shart no…no one would dare after what happened to Laedan Marrock and Jonni. She was out here…" He gestured around them at the expanse of the borough.

"She was out alone? Why would…?"

"Dunno." Thomas shrugged. "Have to ask the Laedan…or the Chief." Not wanting to admit to a lack of details stemming from his current outcast status, he took a drink and set the bottle on the table, absently removing his gloves to rub his hands together for warmth.

"There's proof it's the same Fela?"

Thomas shrugged a second time. "I don't have any…but who else? He's picking them off one at a time; no one in the Fortress will be safe until he's found and brought to justice.

He did not look at Vance as he spoke but kept his gaze moving nervously about as if he expected trouble from the murderer of whom he spoke or someone else. Suspecting he was not used to being in this part of the borough at this hour of the night, as well as knowing that most people, even the innocent, were reluctant to be alone with a mage, his behavior was not atypical.

But Vance knew one thing. Kato had no motives for killing one Channon, let alone two, or Roland, unless Jia had put him up to it. That, Vance knew, was absurd. Kato had been nowhere near the Fortress in the past few days. Yiva's death could not be on his head.

Quentin, however, had every reason in the world to remove Roland and Jonni's influence on the Laedan. There was no obvious reason to turn on Yiva but that did not mean the man seated across from him was innocent. It only meant Vance did not yet know what he was looking at…or for.

Uncomfortable in the mage's intense silence, Thomas continued. "Might have something to do with that missing shipment Lowell's got you looking for."

"How so?" He was not expecting Quentin to know anything about that shipment, but as the Laedan's aide, it was not particularly surprising for him to know either.

"You do know it wasn't a med shipment, right?"

Vance frowned.

"You're not stupid" Such an accusation rarely held up about a mage. No matter how much Thomas might hope it was true, he knew better. Despite the rarity of mages, Segara would not have risen through the ranks to Primary Tracker in LaGuardia if he was stupid or bad at his job. By his age, a lot of tracker-mages were dead or driven mad. So far Vance was neither. "It was weapons…guns or…I'm not exactly sure…but I know it was…"

"How do you…?"

"Donn's doing. His father trusts him, of course…enough to never see he's the one who took them. Not sure what his plans are, but I do know he intends to use them against his father."

He took a third drink and wiped the back of his hand across his mouth. Seeing the raised brow, he added, "Told me himself…wanted my cooperation…"

"Why didn't you tell the Laedan?"

There was a soft, scoffing snort. "He was never going to believe me over his favorite son."

Vance picked out the past tense words from the sentence as well as the minute intonations suggesting Quentin had not spoken of this purported plot because he had been in on it with Donnovan from the start. Political intrigue was not unusual, nor was the revelation of a stash of weaponry a surprise given that Vance had been unable to locate any evidence of errant medical supplies or an influx of them into any of the borough's primary medical facilities.

Someone had murdered Sal to cover that shipment's contents and location. As valuable as medical supplies were, they were not valuable or benign enough to kill for.

Raised voices in a nearby side street, a short-lived exchange of insults and threats ending with the rattling slam of a window, its glass loose enough to vibrate in its ancient frame, distracted Quentin long enough for Vance to reach for the bottle and take a drink. The first gulp of alcohol he had consumed in days, the burn of the bitter swill as it slid down his throat and into his empty belly made Vance grimace and cough, both acts a cover for the evidence for details he read, had hoped to read, on the bottle's surface.

A needle in his hand. A child-like hand-drawn map with one destination prominently marked upon it. An argument with Lowell in the Fortress lobby, its words and contents obscured by the flaring anger that evaporated them. Ernest's footsteps and Yiva's hand hanging loose over the side of the makeshift pallet she was carried on. The Laedan's wail. Nik's entrance before Quentin slunk away. The voice of another, a napkin soaked in a glass of pungent liquid. A glimpse of himself and an order given to a skinny, dirty boy to find…

The revelation burst into a sparkle of interrupted color as Thomas snatched the bottle from his hand.

"I know where they are…or where they should be," Thomas' words, hastily spoken with a note of forceful distraction, drew Vance's focus from the clues he had gleaned from the bottle and those yet to make themselves clear.

Vance arched one brow and wiped his mouth on his sleeve while licking the liquor's burn from the roof of his mouth. Adept as he was, he kept any other expression of knowing off his face.

Before the mage could ask questions, Thomas cagily continued. "Not for certain, I mean, but I know where the mayors keep things, where goods are stored for each region where Donnovan segregates extra some for personal use. I can give you the addresses; you'll find everything in one of them, I'm sure, unless he's got new stash houses."

He hoped to profit, Vance guessed, by their removal from Donnovan's hands, perhaps even by the revelation to the Laedan of his son's duplicitous dealings and plotting.

"Don't have anything to write on," Vance admitted, patting his coat pockets as if to prove they were empty. "Unless you want to…"

His extended hand across the table was met with recoil and a glimmer of unsettled panic on Quentin's face as he hurriedly replaced his gloves. "Nor do I," Thomas stammered, "but I can send them to you. Look at them for yourself. You'll see I'm right."

Though Vance could not formulate a solid connection between a stolen weapons collection, Donn, and Kato, nor any connection between it and Roland or the Hallisters, he shrugged, stood up, and adjusted his coat as he said, "Leave them at the Protectorate. With the chief. Someone there'll get them to me."

For a moment, as he shoved the cork back into his bottle, Thomas frowned, leaving Vance to assume there would be no forthcoming list regardless of the promise. Finally, he shrugged as he stood, nodded, and crisply muttered, "It'll be there tomorrow. You'll see. You'll see I'm right. You'll do what Lowell's paying you to do…and you'll prove I'm right."

"If," Vance emphasized. "If you're right."

"I am."

Vance did not follow as Quentin marched away, nor watch him to see where he was going. He did not care. He did not expect the list to come but he did not need it to find what he was seeking.

He knew the mayors' primary storage houses.

The rest, he thought with a glance at his still-tingling hand, he could find without a written list. Quentin had given him that information without even trying.

Chapter 12

"Nik!"

Oasis was the last person Nik expected to call him from the top of the stairs as he sat, shaking, on one of the lobby benches forcing an inner calm now that Torben had returned to his primary job. Torben had asserted Nik was safe inside the Fortress so long as he did not leave alone. Nik wanted to believe it was true.

But the suspicion that two attempts on his life had come at his twin's command, or at least with Donn's knowledge, made Nik feel ill and unsafe even in his home. He had not voiced his suspicion to Torben as he did not want to prevent the man from fulfilling the one responsibility he had shouldered throughout his adult life. He had not revealed that fear to anyone.

Who would believe him?

The woman's descent on the stairs appeared awkward and uncomfortable, reminding him how unpredictable Donn could be when angry. If he could assault his wife, what was to prevent him from hiring assassins to murder his twin? Her makeup was flawless, her high-waisted pale orange dress impeccably in place, her hair coifed and coiled, perfectly fashioned between elegant and casual. If one did not know what had happened, nothing except her stiff gait and the bruising on the side of her face she tried to hide with her hair would indicate anything was wrong.

Though the polite thing to do would be to stand and greet her, his brother's wife, Nik did not trust his legs. He stayed where he was until she reached his side.

"Is he gone?"

"I guess. He went out." Nik sighed, cocked his head towards the door, but was unable to say whether Donn had gone into the borough or was somewhere on the Fortress grounds.

Shuddering, Oasis sat gingerly on the bench next to him and clenched her hands in her lap. Other than daily niceties, morning and evening greetings spoken in passing or across the dining table, she had rarely spoken to Nik, never sought him out or sat with him to know him better. Unlike Jia, Oasis seemed too sophisticated, too upper-class for Nik to approach and he could not imagine they had anything in common. He doubted she had anything in common with Donn, or with Jonni, either. Now she seemed small and fragile, lost and isolated in a place that should be home but had morphed into some sort of prison. She could not leave. She had nowhere to go except back to Kennedy. She had no one to take her there if she wished to go, and as a political pawn, she might not be welcome if she chose to go back.

He imagined she was looking for an ally. It was a position that, in conjunction with the growing belief that Donn wanted him dead, Nik found himself uncomfortable to be in.

"I think he did it." Her whisper cracked, awkward and fearful of being misunderstood, of not being taken seriously or believed.

Those were feelings Nik knew intimately.

"Did what?

"Before she…she told me…what he's done…to me…to her…I think he knew…I think he…" She swallowed hard amidst the stammering, her hands twisting so her knuckles turned white.

Nik shook his head without looking at her. He did not need to be a mage to read what she was not saying. "That's ridiculous."

Donn was a lot of things. A cruel, violent mayor. A bully. A tyrant of a man who ordered death without compunction when it suited him, for the pettiest of slights. He was a wife-beater. A wife rapist.

But a killer? His mother?

Nik pressed the back of his hand over his mouth to stifle the sickness rising in his throat.

Oasis stared through the panels at the front of the room, expecting to see her husband on the other side. "For a long time, I guess…"

He shook his head. Not just a killer. It was implausible, ridiculous. Insane. "She'd never let him…"

She snorted, a sick, disgusted sound that made Nik swallow hard. "You think anyone can stop him from anything? Only Lowell, maybe…and she never told…"

"No…that's absurd," he repeated the denial, lurching up, fighting to ignore the pounding in his ears, in the middle of his skull.

Grabbing his hand, Oasis prevented his immediate retreat, her expression wide-eyed and desperate. "You have to tell someone, your father, before he…"

Nik stepped back, stretching their arms out between them, tugging lightly but not yet breaking free of her grasp. "Nothing to…"

"Someone has to…" she begged.

"You tell him! Or go to the chief if you think you've got proof." He yanked away and stalked across the lobby, anger and disgust returning the use of his legs with the desperate need to hear no more.

There was nothing Nik could reveal to his father, nothing except his earlier suspicions, now given support by another who, as far as Nik knew, had no reason to lie.

Gods…

Donn was a lot of things, he argued, but he could not be the sort of monster who could have gotten away with anything so heinous for the period Oasis suggested. Not the sort who would treat his mother the way he had been caught treating his wife.

Nik charged up the stairs and away from the woman on the bench.

It was not possible.

It simply was not.

❧*❧

The boy, shaking, coughing, his exhausted muscles twitching as his body, pinched from dehydration and the audible churning of his hungry belly, collapsed at Quentin's feet muttering something about a college on the eastern side of the Flushing Wilds, a cluster of buildings where those he was sent to track had stopped. The directions he gave between choking breaths were vague enough not to be easily followed, should Quentin choose to send anyone there. But he had to alleviate the problem of those who could prove his involvement in the death of the Laedan's son…and the co-Laedan Lowell had too easily turned on when it suited him in his quest for domination of LaGuardia Borough. Segara, too, could be a problem, but Quentin did not believe the mage had any definitive proof against him yet.

Jia and the other Fela, however, certainly did.

Pepe knew the way, was the only one who had seen where she and her family had fled after the raid intended to capture them, so it was worth getting the boy on his feet. Begrudgingly, Quentin took the child to the nearest clinic, paid for his care with everything of value he had, and afterward had gone to the Change where Uzzi had agreed to meet.

He had a plan. He only needed the ruff to agree to it. And he needed Pepe to survive long enough to guide or direct Uzzi there. What happened to either of them afterward did not matter to Thomas, so long as they removed the witnesses to his crimes.

❧*❧

The bodies of the dead in this place, mutilated and made unrecognizable by the grubbers known to inhabit the Below, had been removed days ago, returned to their families for disposal in whatever manner the living saw fit. Such places, entrances into the ancient bowels of the world that had gone before, were known to be havens for grubbers and Unders, so such attacks, the deaths of those who got too close, were not unexpected.

Aman imagined, as he surveyed the broken grated gate no longer containing whatever had been behind it, the pair of men had been posted here to prevent such a threat from creeping out into Kennedy's streets. Or, as close to the neutral border as this opening was, perhaps Hallister had thought some enemy would take advantage of the Below to breech Kennedy.

There were more than a dozen such places Aman knew off. Likely more. No one with a shred of wisdom would risk the hazards of Below to cross into Kennedy when there were miles of safer streets and alleys to utilize for crossing, guarded only by debris and posted Hallister sentries. Nothing he could see made this particular passage stand out.

Whatever the cause, the Laedan had his reasons for stationing sentries here, men yet to be replaced.

Perhaps, Aman thought with a frown at the curdling cry of the huddled female figure not far from the passage opening, sentries were meant to catch ones such as this.

The girl and the boy squatting next to her trying to coax her to her feet, to offer her water, to scan the vicinity for threats her pain was going to draw to them were barely more than children. Bedraggled and dripping, muddy and disheveled, it was easy to imagine the unfortunate pair had thought to seek shelter in the tunnel opening when the pangs of birthing had come over the girl. But the remains of a grubber, a broken branch shoved through its face, lying between the pair and the tunnel opening, attested to the futility of their effort to shelter there. Another girl, younger still, lay twisted in the puddles in between, broken sobs punctuated by the agony of trying to hold her insides behind the bloody hands splayed against her side.

The identical gold of their hair announced them to be siblings.

The yellow eyes with their vertical pupils the young man turned on him, the fangs that broke through his gums, announced the trio's nature without any further change coming to the fore.

"Not here to hurt you." Aman presented open, empty hands to prove he wielded no weapon, and his cautious steps halted when the young man snarled. His hands might be empty but the baton on his hip and the cut of his uniform suggested he was far from helpless, far from innocent.

There was nothing Aman could do about that.

The heavily pregnant woman on the ground at the boy's feet cried out again as the child she carried pushed to be born.

"Should get out of this rain…out of the open…get to a clinic…"

The boy snarled.

Aman sighed. Clinics were risky. Medical oaths to offer aid did not guarantee fair treatment for anthro. Even those treated might end up arrested or separated from their child. These three looked to have had a rough time of it. From the boy's open hostility, trust was a luxury they did not have to spare.

"Least let me…

"Ber…" started the injured girl behind Aman.

"Wanna help…help her…" The boy pointed.

Aman turned his head. Where she had fallen, where the grubber lay, he assumed the youngest had given her life to protect the other two when the grubber attacked. The severity of her wound, the pumping blood seeping between her fingers, and the still twitching flesh of the grubber around the branch in its face suggested the confrontation had not happened long before his arrival, drawn as he had been by the other woman's birthing cries. He had not heard a skirmish. He had not heard the grubber's yowls.

He might have come faster if he had.

The other two appeared not to have been injured.

"Nothing I can do for her except…" He put his hand on his baton.

In his crouch, the boy hissed, "Touch her, you die," careful to protect the pack between his feet. It was stuffed full, probably of scavenged food and any personal items the trio owned, the only sack existing between the three.

Aman's hand dropped to his side. whatever else they had owned might have been lost in the tunnel, lost to the grubbers.

"At least…" He pointed at a cluster of nearby buildings, dark in the twilight, unremarkable and indistinguishable from any others. "You'll be safe enough there…out of the rain. I can help get you…"

"Not leaving her."

Uncertain if the boy meant the woman in labor or the dying girl nearby, Aman sighed and unhooked the baton from his belt with one hand as he unfastened the pack on his other hip with the other. The baton clattered at his feet when he dropped it and skittered through the mud as he kicked it over to the boy. The pouch, waterproof and fastened with both a buckle and leather ties, was tossed forward to land within the boy's reach.

"Not much…but it's something." Carrying something to eat when on patrol was standard practice for Kennedy guards and officers, as well as for anyone wandering far from their home. One never knew where or when anything edible might be found.

The boy snatched both items and hastily tucked them into the pack that rattled between his worn, muddy, handcrafted leather shoes, a peculiar sound that made Aman cock his head curiously. The boy narrowed his gaze.

Aman shrugged.

Whatever the bag contained, it was none of his business.

He was not here to search strangers for contraband.

He was not here to arrest anthro or expose them and turn them over to HOPE.

There was no need to tell them to be careful. No need to remind them of the dangers they were exposed to out here, where the sounds of the woman's labor as she struggled to her feet with a hand on her brother's shoulder, would be sure to draw grubbers, and worse. He could do no more for them than they allowed, than they would accept. He had given his food, his weapon, and pointed them to shelter.

Aman had done what he could.

On the off chance there was another threat in the tunnel, he lit the torch he carried, nodded to the boy, and left them there.

Ten yards down the crumbling cement steps. Twenty into the dripping cold where the smell of stagnant water and decaying organic matter grew stronger. Careful steps over three more disfigured grubbers defeated in a desperate scramble towards the freedom the staircase offered. Ten more feet to the lip of a waterway where a bloody hand print on the ledge gave evidence of a battle lost by the limp form floating amidst a cluster of bloated grubbers, distinguishable from them only by the golden hair and the still-fresh tint of pink skin in the glow of his torch. Here he lost what little light the outside world offered and ahead there was nothing except blackness and, he was sure, a certain death he chose to retreat from.

Back up on the street, where the misty rain fell heavier, he was greeted with silence. The boy and his pregnant sister were gone, far enough that her cries were no more than muted echoes he chose not to follow. The other girl stared blank-eyed into the distance, the only evidence of the direction her siblings had taken.

He closed her eyes with one hand, wondering if she had watched them go, watched them abandon her. He wondered if she had already been dead when they had.

Scanning the night, the streets, for threats, for help, for signs of the pair, Aman sighed and chose to drag the young woman's corpse into the tunnel, down the stairs, to the lip of the water's edge where her sister silently floated.

She was anthro. She would not turn. But he would not leave her in the street to become some scavenger's feast. Leaving her with her sister in this watery sepulcher was the best burial Aman could offer.

The sound her body made when it splashed into the water, when it bobbed to the surface with her sister's floating arm draped across her back, made Aman shudder and sigh.

If her siblings were lucky, his efforts would afford them a bit more protection from hunters until they got somewhere safe. It was not much but it was the best Aman could do.

The shadow slunk away. He should have gone after them. They would be easy targets, and an infant, if it survived, would fetch a hefty price. But they would not move far, and would still be there for many more hours if the process of birth continued normally. He was not here for them. He was here to observe. To report.

While not a crime, such an act was certainly something Hallister would want to know about…lest it undermined the plans, the future, the Laedan had in store for Kennedy Borough.

❧*❧

"Hold on."

Though disinclined to open the door to a stranger when the rapping on the wood first came, his recognition of the aura on the other side, a sense of the man gleaned after his sleepy eyes cracked open and his thoughts focused on the external rather than the soft haze of erotic dreams he rarely had, Vance pulled his shirt over his head, straightened it, and achingly rose from the sofa.

The rumpled shirt hid the collection of bruises and lacerations recently obtained. His bandaged hand, however, with its missing finger end, was impossible to hide.

"Pubby." Surprised to see him there, Vance motioned the other Protector inside and closed the door.

A cursory glance around the room revealed a small square table in a corner, littered with food containers not yet returned to their sources. The empty liquor cabinet was open and the lumpy sofa was adorned with a thin pillow, and a collection of faded, drab-colored blankets. Beside it, the adjacent coffee table was strewn with a folder and several pages spread for comparison. It was the sort of sparseness Pubby expected from a man who lived alone and was submerged night and day in his work. He could not see the rooms that should serve as a kitchen and toilet room, but Pubby did not think those rooms would look much different than this one.

"Glad to hear you're back; got your message."

"Message?"

Pubby drew a folded sheet of paper from the pocket of his ill-fitting Protector's coat, the coat he claimed had belonged to both his father and grandfather, and thrust the page into Vance's hand.

"These are all the stores on record…minus the ones that burned."

Vance nodded. That message. The one from Quentin. "More than one?"

"One more while you were gone. Nothing linking them except their emptiness…and the fact they're Laedan stores."

Reading no impressions from the page, suggesting that Pubby or whoever had written the information down had done so with gloves on, Vance unfolded the paper and scanned the contents. "District?"

"Three."

Donnovan's district. While it did not prove anything, as District 3 was the largest and thus contained more people and structures, that the fires had all occurred in a single district was hardly coincidental.

"Got the address of the last?"

"Sure." With a pencil from that same pocket, protected by a wooden case to prevent the precious commodity from breaking, Pubby took the page back and jotted down the additional location.

"Arson?" It was significant Quentin left both recently burned structures off the list, that he knew about both fires, but knowledge of them was not enough to implicate him in the burnings.

"Most likely." He glanced up as the pencil was returned to its case and to his pocket and gave the list back, all without removing his gloves. "Didn't have you here to give it a read-through, so, ya know…we might have missed something."

Ignoring the playful smirk but appreciating that Pubby did not find him intimidating, Vance shrugged. "Here now…I'll get to it soon as…I gotta stop by the Fortress first." He should have checked in with the chief, but the hour had been off. After his talk with Quentin, he had opted to return home to make himself presentable to the Laedan, thinking the Fortress was the best place to begin, to see if Quentin's claims were true, offer his condolences, offer his help if it was needed or desired. The little bit of consumed alcohol had prompted sleep as soon as he settled on the sofa to remove his boots and he was still there when Pubby arrived.

Pubby nodded and opened the door but did not ask the mage's business nor volunteer his own. He was a man known to gossip and speculate on cases inside the office when it suited him, but he was also one to know when to keep a secret, how to keep business inside the circle of the Protectorate he worked for. Whatever he thought Vance knew or did not know, he was not going to offer his opinion unless asked for it. Segara did not need his two cents to do his job.

What he did say, with his hand on the door, was, "Just…come by the office when you can. Chief could use your clear head."

The door clicked shut.

Vance understood.

If Quentin was right, based on Ernest's previous admissions, Vance knew where the chief would be today.

It was another reason to be there too.

❧*❧

The celebratory pack hunt lasted until the sun's ascent began. Its brightness was not yet coloring the sky as the boar and deer were cleaned and set to roasting over the fire spits prepared for the occasion, not far from the place where Roland was buried. Those able to participate in the hunt had done so. The less able aided in the preparation of other meal items or rested under Addie and Trill's care surrounded by curious pups. Kato's participation in the hunt was curtailed by Vanya's clinginess and perhaps because Jia, too, had remained behind.

Orliss and Maz led the hunt while Vanya dragged her brother by the hand to every special location and surprising find she had discovered during his absence, forcing him, despite his wishes, to leave Jia perched upon the highest point of the library's roof where she could attentively monitor the sounds of the hunt as they stretched and wove through the Wilds. She had been alone when he had first been pulled away. The next time he saw her, Liam was sprawled languidly beside her, not close enough to touch but too close, in Kato's opinion, for his proximity to be innocent.

Growling at his own behavior, Kato squeezed his sister's hand and allowed her to drag him off in another direction.

Liam, too, listened to the traveling howls and yips of the Pack's movement through the trees. Once, as pups themselves, they had enjoyed this same sort of vantage atop the structure they had called home. Roland had still been alive, had still led the Pack. He had led most of the hunts in those days, had made the Flushing Pack whole.

Jia did not need to express her fractured feelings for Liam to know they were there.

"You should be out there."

She smiled wistfully and offered her hand. Once, as best friends, it had been an innocent gesture. As he entwined his fingers through hers, she had the first spark of realization that his hand in hers was less innocent now.

"I've hunted enough."

She had hunted for her father. She had hunted for Liam. Soon she might be hunting again, a different sort of prey this time.

She longed to be out there but she was tired.

She wanted to rest.

He nodded without another word. They remained there, hand in hand, silent and observant, until the carcasses were cleaned and perfumed the air with their roasting aromas, drawing some of their mutani neighbors, led by their leaders Hacha and Zyair, to the fires with platters of baked goods and barrels of whiskey made from the fields of grain they tended within the boundary of the Zone. The arrival of Zone dignitaries prompted Jia to leave the rooftop, with Liam at her back, and join the cluster gathered around the fires.

The hunt was over.

It was time to feast.

Zyair offered her hand with a meek tilt of her head. The woman was tall, broad-shouldered, with wiry salt and pepper hair pulled into tiny braids bunched at the back of her head and tied there with a hemp cord. The graying in her hair did nothing to suggest her age, and beyond her physical size, nothing marked her as mutani. But not everyone inside the Zone was mutani. Some were there because of their love for another, family or friends banished to that place for their differences, while others retreated to the Zone for the security and protection community offered from the often intolerant outside world.

They had met before. Jia suspected the woman would continue to address her with the same deference no matter what Jia asked.

Hacha, her unmarried partner, was a mountain of a man with black dreadlocks framing his face, handed her the smoldering stick of rolled ivy and hemp held between thick fingers, and said, "Glad you're back." The rough surface of his skin, in addition to his mountainous size, explained his presence in the Zone, but despite his size, he seemed to be one of the gentlest, calmest people Jia had ever met.

Most outside the Zone, however, would never see beyond the external differences.

She accepted the spliff, took one drag as a token of respect, and handed it back to him with a smile, and said, "It's good to be back."

Being back, however, would not last long.

They ate together, sharing the day-to-day events that had passed during her absence, with the shadow of Pain at the perimeter of the group, conversational voices punctuated by the bright-toned interruptions of excited children until the meal drew to a close and the exhausted pups, having been awake all night, were escorted to bed. Liam deferred to his sister's desire for his company and sat beside her, while Kato, taking the opportunity of his absence, moved closer.

Not close enough, however, as Vanya's giggling affinity for the older children kept her near them and she insisted her brother not stray far from her. Deuce seated on Jia's other side, a peculiar position to most for the ex-omega to assume the right to sit at the alpha's side, kept Kato at bay.

She felt pulled in too many directions and wondered how often her father had felt the same.

There had been questions asked already about where they had been, what they had seen. Jia felt she should have spoken sooner, before exhaustion, food, alcohol, and spliff smoke dulled many to the important matters that needed to be addressed. But with the turmoil her life had been, the upheaval the Pack had recently endured, these moments of fragile peace were too important to interrupt with further darkness and danger. Now, fueled by the reassuring nod of the man beside her, her father but not, she told the tale of Liam's captivity, Roland's part in it, and the shadow of HOPE and Laedans Channon and Hallister hovering over it.

Some of those here knew slivers of the truth. None of them knew the contents of the conversation with Kennedy's Laedan.

"How could he not know about such a place right under his nose?" growled Xan. Scant details about the lab had circulated throughout the previous day and night, shared by those who had been captive there and by Liam who had been privy to much more than the rest. He filled the void of knowledge with details of Roland's escape and the days Liam had spent as a captive caring for the others. Liam detailed the extraction and processing of blood from hosts of anthro, people bled dry and discarded so no trace of them remained. To the Pack, the lab's location not far from the Kennedy Fortress made Hallister's ignorance unlikely, but when HOPE was involved, the unlikely was both possible and conceivable.

"I never saw him," Liam admitted with a shrug. "There was a doctor…never learned her name. At least I think she was a doctor. She seemed to be in charge, overseeing everything…arrivals and extraction and disposal. Tall…dark-skinned. Experienced. As much as she seemed to know…I'd say she has to be HOPE…"

HOPE hoarded knowledge and dispensed it to those they could use and manipulate, or to their acolytes and most steadfast adherents. Most with above-average learning were believed to be part of HOPE.

It was why even doctors of Addie's status often found it difficult to gain the trust of the common person.

"Doesn't mean Hallister didn't know," huffed Helena.

"Especially since he showed up just as we were getting out." Zen frowned and squeezed her brother's knee.

"Had to be HOPE…the first ones," mumbled one of the emaciated lab survivors, whose shaved head and pallid, almost gray skin made his age and heritage indeterminate. He, like the others, had not spoken much since their rescue, but as he sat at the front of their cluster, next to Liam and Zen, it seemed he had been designated the spokesman of those without home or family to shield them. "They looked like the ones who came for my pack…when we were…"

"Mine too," said someone else.

"The ones who took Roland, too?" murmured Maz. Liam nodded.

"Do you know where that was? Do you remember where you…any of you…?" started Uncle, adjusting his wool cap around his ears. The night was clear of rain, but the chill in the air promised more moisture before long.

"Kennedy Borough," said some.

"South LaGuardia," said others.

"Chased out of the Neutral into LaGuardia," said another.

There was no consensus. No connection to where they had been captured except none of them had been taken from the northernmost streets of LaGuardia. Since Roland and Liam had both been taken from southern LaGuardia, captured by men similarly dressed, it could only be determined that the hunters, the abductors were likely part of the same unit. Only HOPE was capable of moving between the boroughs without hindrance.

"So the Laedans are working with HOPE," muttered Ilba.

"As we suspected all along," Addi agreed, tightening his arm around his wife's shoulders.

Speaking for the first time, Kato grunted. "Doesn't explain how he showed up when we needed him…or what he wants with you." He met Jia's gaze, his eyes narrowed not with suspicion but with concern. There was still the possibility they had been followed by remnants of whoever had attacked them in Kennedy's fringe streets. If those people were connected to Laedan Hallister, or HOPE, if they were a threat to Vanya…or Jia…Kato wanted them gone.

How, his thoughts circled, had his life become so complicated?

Eyes turned to Jia with expectation, wanting answers, wanting the reassurance of her assessment. No one considered the alpha to be all-knowing, but they did expect her to present the Pack with the safety of answers they did not yet have.

Wishing Liam sat closer, wishing Vance was here to back up what she knew, what she had interpreted, what she had sensed, Jia replied, "Hallister says he heard rumors about a HOPE lab…happened to be there that night to conduct an investigative raid so that he could confront Mas Lord…"

"Sure," snorted Zen.

Jia shrugged sympathetically. "It could be true…or he's hiding his knowledge or involvement and was there for some other reason…but he couldn't have known we would be there…"

"Unless he's got spies and lookouts."

Jia met Deuce's gaze and nodded. "Maybe. We didn't sense them…and we were careful…but…" But there was a chance. "When we met, he wanted my help, our help, to find Fort Hamilton."

"Fort Hamilton?" asked Brie.

"The map," replied Maz. "The secret Roland was keeping."

Addi's eyes narrowed. "How does he know about the Fort?" Until recently, the Pack had not known the nature of the secrets Roland died to protect. It seemed the whole world knew those secrets.

"He claims he sent Father the map, the details…that he wanted the finding to be a joint effort…to split the spoils. Now he thinks Lowell is out to get everything…and he wants us to help stop that from happening."

"Wants to supplement his stash," Helena muttered. "Don't think he intends to share."

"He's got exploding orbs," Wist interjected. "A lot of them…"

"Orbs?" asked QiangXu, leaning forward with his elbows on his knees, more interested in the conversation now.

Wist balled his fist to indicate the size and made a pulling gesture at the top to signify the pulling of the containment pin.

QiangXu nodded. "Grenades."

"Probably more than that one stash," Jia reluctantly agreed.

"If he confiscates borough weapons like Channon, probably a lot more," Deuce offered.

While she did not know where LaGuardia's confiscated firearms were kept, or what was done with them, as her father had never shared that information with her, she was inclined to agree with Deuce's perception. Lowell was not the sort of man to destroy such things if he thought he could use them to his advantage. Nor was Geary Hallister.

"I'm not Laedan…but Geary seemed to think I have the resources or influence to supplement Kennedy's manpower…to help find the fort and go after whatever it holds."

Hacha stretched out his crossed legs. "He think you have the map?" Privy to enough of the evening's conversation, he knew there was a map involved, a map Roland Marrock had possessed.

"Told him I haven't seen it," Jia answered, "But Vance…"

"But he thinks you have the manpower…the Pack…?" Liam asked, voice tinted with the concern others in the circle shared.

"I don't know if he knows about the Pack…about any of you…if he knows about us. It wasn't obvious from what he said. I don't know how he could. But he does believe Father had a large base of influence and assumes I must…"

"I think it's a trap."

Heads around the bonfire bobbed in uncomfortable agreement with their former omega.

"Or at least he considers me…and anyone I can bring along…to be expendable," Jia agreed. "Why risk his people if he can risk someone else? Maybe he hopes he can curry favor and get me installed as Laedan…'cause he clearly doesn't trust Lowell…or Donn." While Hallister did not trust a large collection of weapons in Lowell's hands, no one trusted them in Donn's. Given Nik's known constant state of addiction, Hallister probably didn't trust weapons in his hands either.

Liam leaned back, his arms propping him up, as he stared at Jia as though seeking to read her thoughts. Finally, he voiced the opinion he knew she held but was reluctant to voice. "We can't let him have them. Either of them. If they're contributing to the production of juice…"

"But if Lowell…" Addi began. "Why else would Father have worked so hard to find the fort, to hide it from everyone? Keeping that knowledge, keeping weapons out of anyone else's hands…"

Candace shook her head, denying the direction she believed the conversation was taking. "There's too many pups. We can't uproot them to hunt for a mythical fort…"

"One that might not even be there anymore," agreed Trill.

Eddie eagerly waved his hand. "I'll go."

"You'll do no such thing," Candace scolded.

"We don't even know where to look," Ele reminded them.

"Vance has seen the map," Jia said. "He can find it…"

"You'd put your lives in the hand of a mage?" whispered Brie.

Kato snorted.

Reluctantly, Helena said, "He didn't steer us wrong." Despite the prevalent mistrust of mages, she had seen no indication Vance was a threat when they worked together to find Liam. If anything, his apparent bond with Jia made him a valuable ally. "He got us through the Beneath…got us across the Neutral and out of the lab…"

"We coulda done that without him," Wist countered with the haughty, snorting tone of youthful overconfidence.

"You would've blown your arm off with those grenades," Helena shot back, QiangXu's word for the orbs feeling foreign on her tongue.

"Or brought the Beneath down on our heads," Kato admitted. "We'd probably never have found them." As much as Vance rubbed him wrong, Kato had to admit the mage's participation in the rescue mission had been vital. Without him, they might not have found what they had been looking for so quickly…or at all…and might not have survived the extraction.

Not finding Liam, he thought with a reluctant hiss of air between his teeth, might have been preferable. For his sake at least. What failure would have meant to Jia, on the other hand, made their effort worthwhile. Kato had to admit it to himself if no one else.

"Without him," admitted Zen, "I don't think we'd ever have gotten Liam back…we'd have died in there."

"He can get us to the fort if it's there," Jia agreed. "And you're right…we can't bring the pups…"

"You thinking of joining Hallister?" asked Uncle.

She shook her head no. "I'm thinking we should find it on our own. A group of us…five or six…"

Orliss scowled. "If there's a stash, we won't be able to carry…"

Jia looked across the group at the lone Ursa among them who had been quiet thus far. "I think we take those grenades…what we've got left…and whatever you can give us…and blow it up."

"All of it? You think that's what Roland…?" began Maz.

In the glow of the fire, QiangXu nodded.

"All of it. I imagine anything else of value's been scavved by the locals. No reason it wouldn't have been. Anything hidden there should remain hidden…but Lowell and Geary aren't gonna let that happen. If Father wanted it kept out of Lowell's hands, we shouldn't let it fall into Geary's either. He'd want it kept away from both of them…from anyone likely to misuse it…keep it away from HOPE. The only way we can do that is to…"

"Blow it to hell!" exclaimed Wist.

"If you're going, I'm going," Reif said mulishly, staring at Wist, avoiding Jia's gaze, knowing the alpha had the final say.

"If we do this, I'll decide who's going." Not having the map, not having seen it, Jia had no idea how far away Fort Hamilton was nor how long it might take to find it. Traveling through uncharted regions and unknown dangers was risky. The security of the Pack, the security of those chosen to go with her, had to be carefully considered.

Only one person was a necessary inclusion.

Vance was the only one who could lead them.

"When do you plan to do this?" Ele asked, his gruff features mirroring the concern in his voice.

"I don't think we can wait too long. Got the impression Geary's planning on launching his expedition soon…and Lowell's likely to be right behind him. Whoever stole the map from Vance…they're going to use it. When one moves, they'll all move."

"Going to be a mad scramble," Orliss agreed.

"Whatever you decide, the Zone's got your back," Hacha said with a nod. His people relied on his guidance so he would not abandon them to march into a world that feared a face such as his, but he could aid in protecting anyone the Flushing Pack alpha left behind.

"Well, it won't be today." The sun was setting, the hunt and feasting bleeding into a need for a long, deep rest. She needed time to assess her options, to decide what was best for herself and her family.

She might not have time for much else.

She wished Roland was here to make the choice. The Pack had trusted his leadership. Though she had found Liam and brought him, and a host of others, home, Jia was less certain the Pack trusted her with a decision such as this.

And what, she wondered with a glimpse into the shadows where unseen eyes watched, would Pain have done? What would his choice now be? What would he do if she left the Pack again? Did she trust anyone enough to leave them as the acting alpha in her stead…in case she never made it home?

Chapter 13

One final blow, a bloody-knuckled fist into the mangled face of a man yanked to his knees on the crimson-wet floor by the matted hair on his head, and the body collapsed backward, colliding with the wall and slumping into an unmoving mass. There was no need to examine him for signs of life. If he was not dead, with the amount of blood gushing from the shapeless cavities of his mouth and nose, he would be soon.

Ernest looked dispassionately at the lump, feeling little about what he had done, only anger that, despite every torture, every punishment he had employed, the fellow had continued to claim innocence of the death of Yiva Channon, regardless of the evidence that put him at the scene at the estimated time of her death. The gold necklace he had tried to hock, a match for the one Ernest and others in the Protectorate had seen her wearing the last time she was seen alive, was the most damning evidence of all. His claim that he had found it but could not remember where, that he had never seen the dead woman, had never been in the alley, was as implausible to Ernest as his claims of finding the chain on the ground in the street had been.

Though the roles of judge and jury were not the Chief's to play, though the man had not been provided any manner of trial, Ernest felt justified in assuming the part of executioner.

He was confident the Laedan would agree.

Being here, seeing this duty done today of all days, was preferable to standing with the Channons beside a chasm in the ground which would be the last place any part of Yiva would ever be seen. Ernest did not want her grave to be his last memory of her. He wanted to remember her seated in his office, at his side, his hand covering hers…even if that memory brought with it the continual reminder that it had been her last act on earth, coming to him, calling out her son's abuse of his wife.

He wiped red smears down the front of his shirt so he could open the cell door without anointing it with blood. The guards outside the cell said nothing, not even when he grunted with a tilt of his head towards the corpse and sauntered towards the locker room where he would clean away the blood from his hands and face, change out of his ruined shirt, and put on his uniform. Then he would go to his office for a well-deserved drink.

His badge of office was untainted by this act. This death was entirely the act of a man off duty avenging the dead.

Ernest did not care who knew it.

❮*❯

There was no fanfare this time, no bleating horns or thundering of drums, no shots fired over the heads of LaGuardia's citizens, no speeches made from the parapet to the adoring borough masses. Most in LaGuardia were unaware of the funerary rights underway, save for those turned from the front gates and not allowed to pass or drawn to it by veiled, circulating rumors. Most had yet to hear the tragic tale of the loss of LaGuardia's First Lady.

Most would never know the truth. Barely a public figure, to the majority of those outside, Yiva's passing would make little difference.

That grim reality met Vance when he reached the gates. His position as the Primary Protectorate's leading mage allowed him access past the crowd and the guards who eyed him with recognition before allowing him to enter while turning everyone else away.

If the mage had arrived with news about the killer who plagued the Laedan's house, failure to permit him entry would result in punishment at the hand of the erratic, bewildered, unpredictable man holding the reins of power.

Captain Ortega made certain none of his men would take the risk.

It was a small gathering, Lowell, Nik, Oasis, Captain Ortega, and a collection of the Fortress's serving staff who had been closest to the woman, and a handful of others who thought it prudent to show their respects to the dead and to their Laedan. There were no Marrocks on hand as there should be, and Donnovan was notably absent.

Beside Nik, Torben stood with his hat in his hands, paying closer attention, it appeared to Vance, to the perimeter of the courtyard than to the burial service.

Undoubtedly, he had seen more than his share of death.

Wondering why the sposer was there, if he had come at Nik's request for moral support, Vance remained at a respectable distance, hands behind his back, head bowed, as the box containing the woman's ashes was lowered into the hole dug beside her son's burial tree after those who wished to speak, to honor her life and tragic passing, had done so. He had come too late to hear those words, too late to add anything to them though he would not have known what to say if he had been given the chance, and most of those gathered were already drifting away. Lowell, hollow-eyed and grief-stricken, appeared reluctant to leave but Oasis, with her hands gently on his shoulders, steered the Laedan inside with the man barely lifting his head or eyes to see where he was going.

The white bud he carried dropped to the ground beside the grave.

Nik picked it up as Vance, judging it a judicious moment to approach, came closer. Torben was the one to free the shovel from the mound of earth and begin to fill the hole; he looked at the mage and nodded once.

"I am sorry about this," Vance murmured thickly.

"Thanks." Nik studied the white bud before dropping it into the filling grave. He did not ask how much Vance knew. Odds were, the news had reached him directly from the chief…or else the mage had sensed the truth from the composition of the graveside gathering, who was there and who was not.

"How did it happen?"

The young man shook his head and Vance took that as his cue not to talk about the matter here. While Nik appeared sober, Vance knew from years of experience how tenuous the hold on sobriety could be when faced with something like this.

"Thought you'd want to know we got Liam back. Jia's okay. They're okay, except for strangers we found but couldn't save."

Some of the tension bled out of Nik's shoulders and eyes. "Thank goodness." His friend's troubles had been a constant burden in the back of his head, even after his mother's murder, and it was a relief to have that weight removed.

"We found an extraction lab…looked like there'd been hundreds of anthro processed through. Was the place Roland was held. Don't think they generated plasm there, but that facility would have to be pretty close. Don't think blood transports well. We came under fire by some ruffs…appeared to be HOPE but we're not sure. Got past them with a little help from Laedan Hallister."

Having set his mother's tree in the ground and patted down the soil Torben mounded around it as Vance talked, Nik leaned back on his haunches and wiped his hands on his knees. "What's Hallister got to do with this?"

"Wish I knew…but he's interested in that map…says he sent it to Roland…that he wants what's at the other end."

He did not need to be cautious with his words, as there was no one nearby to overhear what Nik and Torben already knew about, but Vance continued to feel the need for restraint.

"That's shart," Nik snorted. "Maybe he'd mentioned it to Geary in some meeting…maybe that's where Fa heard about it too…but Roland found the map, the Fort. I was there when he did…s'why he entrusted it to me, asked me to keep it out of Fa's hands." He shrugged as he staggered up. "He knew there's no way Fa would ever think I knew shart about anything."

Lowell was only beginning to see the competent side of his son.

"You're clean now," Torben grunted and shoved the head of the shovel into the soft, churned earth. One of the groundskeepers would retrieve it and put it away. For now, it served as a reminder of what, and who, lay beneath it.

"They don't expect me to stay that way." Again Nik shrugged. That perception was the only logical one anyone could have based on years of experience. "With Donn off gods' know where and Fa…someone has to keep things together until his head is on straight."

"Think he'll talk to me? Few things he should know…you too, I guess." If Nik was handling the borough's runnings in the Laedan's stead, he should have the details and conclusions Vance had to share.

Nik exchanged a nervous glance with Torben and cleared his constricted throat. "Maybe…but there's something else first…if you'd come up to my room?"

Curious, Vance nodded his agreement. After Nik made one last loving gesture to the earth covering his mother's remains, pressing his handprint into the soil, he led Vance inside and up the lobby stairs. Torben followed close enough behind that Vance deduced there was another reason for the sposer's presence beyond supporting Nik's sobriety and managing the details of Yiva's burial. Oasis' voice was heard behind a closed door as they moved through the corridors towards the private rooms where the family slept but Vance could not make out her words nor those of the person to whom she spoke.

He assumed it was Lowell or one of the servants. There was no one else.

"After…" Nik began, closing the door and moving to his dresser, "Fa wouldn't…Chief hasn't had much to go on without you here. Fa didn't want anyone defiling her…wouldn't even let her be sposed until she turned…so I took this."

The fistful of long blonde hair he offered was unmistakable. "Know her clothes woulda been better," Nik continued, "or her necklace…but by the time I saw her, she'd been stripped down. I dunno what happened to any of that. Maybe Chief's got it…or Fa. Just in case though, I've been hoping this would tell you something, anything, about who did this and why. I think Fa needs to hear the truth. I know…" He choked on the words before stammering, "I do."

Vance swallowed hard. Death images were easier to read in the eyes of the murdered, in their clothes or other personal objects, or by touching their skin. This was not ideal, but her hair should tell him something. It would have to be enough until he spoke to Ernest. Though accustomed to the final grizzly moments of so many victims that most bled into each other in his memory, this was one such set of impressions he was not looking forward to accessing.

He held out his hand and braced for what would follow.

The echo of whispered words shared with Ernest were fed by the stone-heavy burden of shame that weakened Vance's knees and made his breath rattle as though he was being choked. The prey-terror that followed, stalked, hunted by the unseen and nameless made his hands tremble and his knees knock. When Nik reached for his hand to take what seemed to be overwhelming evidence from him, Vance pulled back, still aware enough of the room to do so though what flashed in his mind's eye were the distorted borough streets. Their shadows were stabbed by the occasional light from windows and doorways. Raucous laughter and music, a tav, its sign broken, unreadable. The collection of faces gathered there as terrifying as what was behind, followed by fingers clawing into her arms, spinning her, pulling.

Clothes ripping. Bruising fists and hands at her throat. Hair caught in rusted chain fencing as she was thrust against it. And finally the piercing shock of defilement by one she had only ever wanted to love, cherish and care for as any mother would.

The last realization forced Vance to his knees as emotional pain outweighed overwhelming physical trauma and left him shaking his head from side to side, his arms so slack that the clutch of hair slid softly to the floor.

The moment, the memory, persisted.

He arched to the side and vomited, the vile nature of the act unlike anything he could recall experiencing. Less the act itself, he realized in the recesses of his spinning thoughts, as reality pushed to reassert itself over memory, than the persistence of knowing this act had not been isolated, had been but one of many.

Only this time, the rage, jealousy, and contempt of the other had come with a fatal price.

Nik's hand on his shoulder propped him up. Vance lifted his head and tried to focus on the other man's face. The moment their eyes met, he saw the horrors she had seen, smelled the stench of alcohol and fear, heard the grunting breaths and rattle of chain link, and tasted the copper of her own blood in her final fading moments. He barely managed to croak in a voice that did not sound like his own.

"Donn..."

"I'm not..." Nik's words choked to silence. His mother's voice, or a close approximation of it, the uttering not a failure of recognition or misidentification but a plea to the last person she had seen when alive. His grip on Vance's shoulder tightened, his fingers digging into the hidden injury there, making the mage wince.

He should be shocked. Horrified. Deep down in the buried places he did not want to uncover, he was. But the remaining traces of Oasis' private words to him and the fading echo of things Donn had said before storming out of the Fortress, reminded Nik he already had the truth, even if he did not want to hear or accept it.

In the touch of Nik's hand, through the one finger that made skin-to-skin contact near his throat, Vance heard Donn's words as well. And Oasis'. Again, he wretched.

"I know he's...but he's my...if he's...what does that make me?"

Torben pulled Nik back, breaking his hold on Vance, drawing him to the desk chair the sposer had pulled over behind him. That single word scratching out of the mage's throat had been enough for Torben too. "A good man," he grunted. "The best Channon we have."

Nik shook his head from side to side several times, his eyes squeezed shut. "Shoulda seen it...shoulda..."

"Not the sort of thing a woman talks about...not the sort of thing to be shared with her children..." Or her husband, Vance thought as he wiped his sleeve across his mouth. He was glad he had not eaten or drunk more than he had...but now he desperately needed a drink to burn those visions out of his brain. "You couldn't have...no one knew." The only person who might have ended the abuse once it had begun would have been her husband. She had not even told him.

"You think he's trying to kill you too."

Nik's response was a one-shouldered shrug. "First time," he whispered roughly, "he said he'd sent someone to bring me home. But he was brutal…attacked Torby…the second time…no one saw who took the shot.”

"Arrow," Torben interjected in the hopes the detail would help.

"You got it?"

"At home. Working on tracking down the maker."

"I can help with that if you want. As for…" His access to Nik's memories and his own recent passing of the man in the streets made Vance frown. "The one the first time…name's Nepo. I'd stay as far from him as you can." He did not share how he knew that detail. How he knew did not matter.

But Nepo was no bowman. Nepo preferred his hands, or guns when he had bullets, and was the sort of tracker who, instead of dreading the touch of death preferred to feel his opponents dying at the end of his fists. He had been known to sometimes use clubbing instruments too, but never, in Vance's experience with him, a bow.

Things might have changed in the years since they had last encountered one another. Perhaps Nepo's weapons preferences had changed too.

Torben grunted. "Why I'm here. He tries, he's gonna have to go through me."

"He will," Vance warned. "If he can."

"Like to see him try. Torben might not be a match for projectiles, but his mass would serve as a shield to give Nik a chance to escape. With his experience as a ring fighter, if he got a fist-to-fist fighting chance with the mutani mage, there would be no holding back. Torben would kill him without a care if the chance arose.

Vance hoped it would happen.

"Your father should know…"

"About Donn?" Nik shook his head violently. "He'd never believe…he still thinks Donn'll be the next…" Or did he? Nik would never be considered LaGuardia's heir; he had never done anything to be worthy of it, to prove he could carry the mantle. But to even consider Donn in a place of power, knowing what Nik now knew…

He shuddered.

If not Donn, who?

He groaned and doubled forward, clutching his stomach.

"He's not in a good head place, I know. I've been where he is. But if he's told…"

Maybe it would help him.

Maybe it would make the situation worse.

But there were other things Vance needed to share with the Laedan, promises made at the onset of this spiraling nightmare. These were the sort of details he believed a leader should know, things a man should know about his son, his wife, but rather than shoulder Nik with the burden of telling the truth, Vance continued, "I've got other things…I'll gauge him…and if I think he can handle it…I'll tell him. If not, I'll keep it to myself."

He did not want to be the one to offer this revelation, but better him, he knew, than Nik. If he had to keep the news private, he would do so until the moment he saw Ernest. The chief needed to know. The chief needed to find the youngest Channon before the District 3 mayor killed again…either Nik or his father.

Nik, glumly, bobbed his head without looking up.

ᴂ*ᴂ

She trusted the courier left at her disposal as much as she trusted anyone in LaGuardia now that her only female ally was dead and Lowell continued to push her away as he wrestled with his culpability and grief. Given her own, the change in their relationship was for the best, but it left Oasis isolated and out of place in her new home.

She would never plead to return to her father's house. No Hallister would do such a thing, would admit defeat in the face of what was a temporary obstacle and situation. In time, Lowell would regain his equilibrium, as would she. She would regain his favor by doing everything in her power to support him through his grief but for now, he preferred to wallow in it and she did not feel strong enough to help.

How could she blame him? He had only just laid his wife to rest.

Perhaps she should cultivate an alliance with Nik, whether he remained level-headed long enough to be of use or not. Even his addictions could be beneficial. Without Thomas to offer protection, Nik and Lowell were the only shields she could utilize against her husband should her feigned pregnancy fail to temper him.

If she was right about Yiva's death, Oasis would need every safeguard and ally she could obtain.

In the interim, her father, she was certain, would know what to do. He could be a shield. He would protect her. He would guide her as he always had. He would know what to do in this situation and find a way to be rid of a violent abuser before the alliance between Kennedy and LaGuardia, between Hallister and Channon, crumbled.

The sealed missive was dispatched. Within three days at the most, less if the weather remained favorable, her father would know her plight. Within a week she should have his advice in hand and have a recommendation for how to proceed.

Until that day, Oasis was on her own.

❧*❧

Retracing his steps out of Nik's room, regretting the mess he was leaving and the burden of knowledge deposited on Nik's shoulders with the hopes the young man was able to bear it without a relapse into chemical comfort, Vance reached the door where he had heard earlier voices to find it ajar with a light thumping sound emanating behind it. It appeared to be a library or study, a room with shelves of books and a multitude of padded chairs congregated around a dark furnace, a cold room whose heating ducts were closed as if the room was barely used.

Or unused, Vance mused with a glance at the wilted floral arrangements, needlepoint pillows, and the slightly opened window that allowed the wind to knock the weighted curtain against the frame, since its primary occupant had ceased coming. The realization brought bile back to his throat and when he coughed on the sensation to clear the burn, the room's sole occupant lifted his face from his hands, elbows on his knees, to look at whoever had entered.

"Apologies, Laedan. I don't mean to disturb you…"

"Yes…you do." Lowell was no more disturbed by the interruption than he had been by the burial of the dead, and though he did not feel competent to conduct business, Segara was one of the few he was willing to see. He beckoned him in with a gesture. "Ernest send you in his place?"

Vance shook his head and sat across from Lowell on a chair that groaned beneath him. "Just got back; I've not seen Chief yet."

"Then you didn't know…" Lowell, his face turned so he did not have to look at the mage as they talked, snorted, "Find the Fela? Jia?"

"Jia's safe with her brother."

"Good. Let it go. Safe's all anyone can be." His apathetic tone made Vance choose to leave the Fela unaddressed as Lowell wished.

"I want to report…while investigating the missing shipment, I found a lab where the primary ingredient of anitplas is collected…"

"You mean blood."

Trying to gauge what the Laedan was focused on upon the rows of books on the opposite shelf, Vance frowned. There were no family pictures, no art, no figurines or keepsakes. But Lowell's was not a vacant stare, as if he could see something Vance did not.

Perhaps it was the ghosts in his mind.

"Yes…blood. Lab was empty when I found it, recently vacated, but I've no doubt the juice that nearly killed Nik began its life there."

"Where?"

"Kennedy. Not far from the Fortress." Heading off the man's growing scowl, he continued, "Appeared to be a HOPE facility…but I can't say for sure without going back and getting a closer…"

"Do it."

"I've no jurisdiction in Kennedy…"

"I'll get you authorization."

The words, despite their weight, were flat and lifeless and Lowell's hands, twitching absently, clasped beneath his chin.

"And it wasn't a shipment of med supplies I've been looking for," Vance explained, mindful of the Laedan's body language when the older man tensed, the secrecy of that stolen shipment revealed at last.

Vance was not surprised Lowell chose not to deny the facts. "Haven't found it to know its composition, but I know who took it."

For the first time, Lowell looked at him. It was only a flickering, side-eyed glance, but it was enough to suggest his attention when his gaze returned to the empty spot in the air.

"Quentin and…"

"He killed her. Jonni…Roland…Yi…" Lowell choked on the word, swallowed, reached a hand towards the empty bottle on the low table in front of him, and returned to settle beneath his chin with the other. "I want his head. I want his…"

"That wasn't Quentin."

The Laedan's head slowly turned until he stared Vance full in the face. His blue eyes narrowed into a sharp expression warning the mage to be careful with what he said next. What Vance read in his expression was a focus so set on Quentin's guilt for everything that it troubled him Lowell had not considered there to be any other possible suspect. Nor did he want there to be one.

Rather than discuss the recent spate of deaths, Vance remained on the topic of the stolen shipment. "He aided in the theft of your…he and Donnovan…to aid in the location and the taking of Fort Hamilton…just as Laedan Hallister intends to do."

"They're not…?" Lowell's eyes narrowed further so their blue was barely visible through the slitted opening.

"Working with Laedan Hallister? I don't believe so."

"How do you know…?"

"About the fort?" Masking the truth with a well-practiced shrug and blank expression, Vance looked at his hands. He was a tracker-mage. He could have learned such details from anyone, from anywhere. Even from Lowell.

Lowell's eyes did not change but his scowl deepened so his jowls appeared as if they would slide from his face. He had done his utmost to hide knowledge of the fort's existence, once he got his hands on it, and his intent for that knowledge, out of everyone's hands. Now everyone around him, all of his rivals, knew about it. If anyone, particularly Quentin or HOPE, got their hands on the fruits of the research gleaned from Roland, LaGuardia was doomed. He was lost.

He had already lost enough.

"Who?"

Vance blinked. "No one," he began, believing the question to be an extension of how he knew about the fort.

"You know who took her from me," Lowell hissed with a note of exasperation. "I want his name."

For several moments, they stared at one another, demanding, daring, denying, until Vance swallowed his words and got to his feet. "No," he managed to murmur, "you don't."

Lowell did not move. "I have a right to know. How did you read her? How could you see…?"

"Nik kept a lock of hair…"

Staggering up, the anger of the action tainted by the amount of whiskey in his blood, he growled, "He wasn't supposed to…he already destroyed her…"

"So you wouldn't have to know. Protecting you." The air was silent and heavy. Lowell's expression demanded answers Vance was reluctant to give. Eventually, he couched his reply in the gentlest words he could muster. "For all of his years of using…what Nik did was far kinder than anything Donnovan ever did to her."

Lowell's roar of outrage came not with an argument of disbelief but with a charge out of the room at the head of a storm Vance was grateful he did not have to face.

Chapter 14

The perception of being followed persisted despite the detour he made to the first address on Pubby's list, the only Laedan warehouse between the Fortress and the Protectorate. It could have been anyone, Nik, Torben, one of the LaGuardia Guards sent on patrol, or merely someone curious to know what business the mage had with the Laedan and his family.

The ticking suspicion that it was Donnovan or Nepo, however, could not be shed.

Too-visceral images, memories that brought with them the tastes of blood, death, and fear, the scents of whiskey, sweat, and terror, and the bruising press of fingers around his neck, refused to diminish, and as they were evidence he did not want to share with Ernest while they were fresh in his mind, Vance decided a distraction was in order, a detour that might help either locate the missing weapons shipment or, if fate's twisted hand was against him, throw the youngest Channon directly in his path.

Instead, it brought him the chaotic cries of frantic people carried on the billows of overpowering black smoke. Men and women poured out of nearby and adjacent buildings or passed containers of salt to douse the source of the flames…a mountain of ancient, cracked rubber tires splashed with some oily substance to increase their flammability.

"Segara! Get over here and help!"

The unexpected voice, familiar despite the smoke distortion that cracked and choked it, came from a cluster of waving people doing their best with the resources available to contain the blaze before it spread to the walls, into the high-arched ceiling, and weakened the rafters enough to cause them to collapse. Fortunately, it appeared the blaze had been spotted before it had grown uncontrollable and threatened any nearby structures.

Joining his fellow Protectors, Vance pulled the collar of his high-necked sweater up over his mouth and nose. He took the first pail of salt thrust into his hands and spread it across the flames to absorb the oil and douse the burn.

People ran in and out in search of more salt, the only easily obtainable commodity that could be used on an oil fire, to win the battle against the flames. Eventually, they petered out, leaving only the dying gasps of smoke and the coughing and choking of those who staggered out of the charred building to gulp the fresh night air. Vance came out as far as the double doorway and squatted there to clasp the metal edge of one retracted door in one hand and splay his injured hand on the rutted tracks of innumerable wagons and carts that had passed here before.

Donkeys. Oxen. Goats. Horses. Wheels and boots and the voices of those who had worked here in the most recent days. But there were no distinct clues as to who had set the fire or why, only the lingering scent of something pungent and oily sloshing within metal containers no longer on the premises.

He could dig deeper, if allowed the time, the quiet, to do so, but for now, there were too many people here, too much anxiety, too many loud voices, too much smoke, to make a more thorough reading possible.

"Arson?" coughed Ernest, stopping next to him, doubled forward with a hand on one knee to wipe his sooty face with his other, equally blackened sleeve.

"Someone knew I'd come." Not today, perhaps, but after getting this tip from Quentin, another fire in another Laedan-owned facility was not a coincidence.

Quentin could have set this fire as a trap or distraction.

"Someone with a grudge against the Laedan?"

"Or the Channons themselves," remarked Pubby, coughing thickly as he moved into place on Ernest's other side. "Think they know about the list?"

"It's their stores," Vance answered with a shrug. Anyone could have compiled that list and given it to him. He could think of few logical reasons to burn down an empty warehouse, not when it would risk neighboring structures and remove one more usable building from the few available. It only made sense if there was proof left behind about what had once been stored here. So much rearranging of goods and materials and the efforts to erase what had been made little sense unless there was a need to consolidate or hide the contents.

"We'll find out what was here, what was in each of them, in the morning." Doing so meant going to the Laedan, a duty the twitching at the corners of the chief's weary, haunted eyes suggested he would delegate to someone else. "Until then, Pubby, make sure cleanup's in hand…no flare-ups…then go home and get some sleep. Segara?"

Ernest tilted his head in the direction of the Protectorate and Vance nodded. He knew what the chief wanted.

He knew what he did not want.

But they were words Vance had to share regardless of what either of them desired.

᎒*᎒

He did not drink often.

No matter the amount imbibed, it did not affect Aman as it did others. There was no fuzzy alcohol buzz, no inebriation, no stumbling blackout drunkenness.

There was only the sour burn of it in his mouth, in his belly, that sometimes made him feel sick but mostly left him with a heavy bloated knot inside that took hours to unravel. It was a useful sensation when food was scarce or he knew there would be too many hours before he could sit down to a meal, as the knot filled him and eased any sensation of hunger that would otherwise exist.

Today, he drank.

He drank to wash the sickening stickiness of bile from his mouth. He drank with the feeble hope it would erase the memories of a broken mother and child on a cracked tile floor, where moss and blades of grass pushed up between the crevices and brackish water dripped from the collapsing ceiling above.

Blood. So much blood. The evidence of strangulation, though the birth cord was no longer around the infant's neck, had been evident to Aman, from the bruised skin and bulging, bloodshot eyes, what end that girl child had met. It had been evident, from the spread of blood across the tile, still fluid as it mingled with the dripping water, what had become of the mother.

Evidence too, of another kind of violence, of a single bullet into the woman's head, into the infant's chest, bullets wasted on the dead but delivered to make a point.

Anthro deserved to die.

There was nothing about the dead to suggest that they were anthro. But the missing one…if the tufts of golden fur, if the claw scratches in decaying sheetrock, if the blood and indentations in those same walls spoke of a fight between man and Fela…that would have been suggestion enough to damn the others.

There was no evidence left behind to tell if the boy had gotten away. A Fela was no match for a bullet. Whether the shots had been left as a message for the boy, if he lived, or a message to anyone who might find them, it was a message Aman took to heart.

He had directed them to this place. He thought they should be safe. He had not stayed to ward off predators drawn by the woman's cries and the strangled screams of an infant. He was not responsible for anything that had come after the pair refused his help.

There was a knock on his door.

"Laedan wants you in the Hall."

"Coming."

He took another drink with the hopes it would calm him and erase everything else in its sharp, biting path. It burned all the way down.

He was not responsible.

But he sure as hell felt like it.

❧*❧

HOPE was his only ally.

Donn had known it the moment he passed through the gates of the Fortress he called home, the echoes of his father's tirade beating against his eardrums. Nik's suspicious gaze burned into his retinas as though a brand had seared it there. In the recesses of his twin's drug-fueled delusions, he was often suspicious and paranoid, but this time seemed different.

Nik was, surprisingly, unexpectedly, clean.

Nik might not remain that way, he never did, but for the time being, Donn thought it best not to tempt fate.

Unlike so many in his family, Donn believed in his twin, even when Nik failed to believe in himself. Drugs had prevented him from living up to his potential thus far, from gaining the experience necessary to rule as Laedan, but as a second, as co-Laedan at his brother's side in the place of a Marrock, Donn believed Nik would perform adequately. Perhaps more than adequately.

His compulsion towards fairness and the glimmers of wisdom that sometimes broke through even in Nik's most addle-minded moments proved to Donn it was true. Those things also proved, for now, that it was wisest to stay out of clear-headed Nik's company and seek an alliance in the only place he believed he would find it.

He did not need the alliance with Quentin. Quentin had killed his brother. It was for the best their stolen fruits were moved somewhere Quentin would never find them. If they crossed paths, Donn would make sure Quentin paid for his crimes.

Once he had his hands on Fort Hamilton's treasure, he would deal with his father, reclaim his wife, and convince his twin that the horrors he believed were fabrications generated by the tracker-mage Segara, the Protectorate, their father, the Marrocks, and everyone else.

The most direct route into the heart of the territory controlled by Grand Mas Lord and his holy militia required crossing the stretch of land ruled by no man and cutting across an equally narrow strip of Kennedy which served as an additional buffer between LaGuardia and the zealots of HOPE. Some long-intact agreement between the Hallisters and HOPE kept the road open, kept Kennedy from absorbing the easternmost parcel of reclaimed streets and likewise prevented HOPE from forcing their control over Kennedy. Since the immediate aftermath of the Undoing and humanity's struggle to reassert dominance over the world, each subsequent Grand Mas had contented themselves with eastward expansion and the continued dabbling in the politics of the Channons, Marrocks, and Hallisters.

It was that dabbling Donn intended to take advantage of.

He had not counted on being ambushed by ruffs, having a hood pulled over his head to prevent him from seeing where he was being taken, before enduring an arduous bumping ride over rutted streets on the back of the wet, stocky beast that smelled, to him, like a horse.

A horse meant someone of means directed these men. Someone of means meant Donn could reason with them, negotiate with them, bribe and intimidate them, and perhaps reach a mutually beneficial arrangement.

The final drag through antiseptic halls over what felt like a hard stone or concrete floor beneath his knees ended with a shove forward and the removal of the hempcloth sack from his face.

The man took a look at the trespasser dumped before him and rolled his eyes with an exasperated snarl. "Don't you know who this is?" he barked.

The man with the sack in his hand shrugged unapologetically. "Should I?"

Geary huffed and rose from the bench in the expansive room surrounded on three sides by glass windows. Rather than apologize, he smoothed the front of his tunic, cur of a more militaristic-looking gray cloth than anything Lowell favored, and offered the man on the floor his hand. "If you wanted an audience, Donnovan, you had only to request one at the checkpoint. Sneaking across the border suggests less than legitimate business, wouldn't you say?"

"Didn't think I needed permission," Donn snorted, though he accepted the offered hand to rise. "Now that we're family…"

"Family doesn't preclude courtesy or respect." With a haughty tilt of his head, he added, "You may go, Captain Norse."

Norse gave the Laedan the hood he gestured for and retreated from the room, passing Aman at the door with an unreadable neutral expression as the other man held it open.

Aman, ignoring the prickle that raced up and down his spine, went out behind him. Whatever Geary had summoned him for would wait.

Geary side-eyed his friend but stuffed his thoughts and feelings down where they would not interfere in the matter at hand. He knew Aman was not part of this travesty. Whatever faults the man might have, whatever had prompted the unusual lingering pungent aroma of alcohol on his breath today, Geary knew better than to think Aman would capture and drag Donn Channon to him like a criminal.

Once the two had left them alone, Geary motioned to the bench, an offer to sit comfortably to the man who smelled like a wet horse and bore traces of horse hair on the front of his clothes, evidence of how he had been brought here. "What brings you to Kennedy?"

"Summons from Grand Mas Lord." Such a summons was a safer excuse than admitting to a desired audience with HOPE. For anyone in power, or hoping to have it one day, a summons from the Grand Mas was something not to be ignored. Seeking an audience with him meant having an agenda, and an agenda would lead to questions.

His agenda was one he dared not mention.

Donn had no doubts his father-in-law would want Fort Hamilton if he knew about it. If he did not know of it already, or if he learned of it through careless mention, he would undoubtedly be interested and in the time it would take Donn to reach out to Grand Mas and solidify a treaty, Hallister would have the opportunity to find his own map and mobilize men to seek the Fort on his own.

"May I see it?" The black cloth hood was placed beside him on the bench as he sat and his now-empty hand asked for proof of the summons Donn did not have.

"He sent a courier," Donn shrugged with a callous, sneering expression. "Expect he didn't want Fa to see the summons."

There were many reasons the Grand Mas might choose to keep secrets from Laedan Channon, the primary one being a lack of trust in a man who had failed to notice his best friend and co-Laedan might have been Cana. Whether or not HOPE had proof of that, proof Geary had witnessed, it took only a whiff of doubt, a hint of scandal, to bring suspicion and mistrust from the Lord and his ilk. If there were suspicions, there would be questions for the Channon sons too, particularly the one destined to follow his father's path, to determine what Donn knew, to learn his stance on anthro and other topics important to HOPE. It was reason enough to summon the perceived heir of LaGuardia. It made more sense to summon Donn to them than for Lord to make an unwelcome visit to the northern Fortress.

"My daughter…how is she?"

Donn grinned at the change of topic, feeling vindicated and victorious his ruse had succeeded, feelings further fanned by the question and the answer he had to give. "With child."

The corners of Geary's eyes twitched. "So soon?"

"I'm a Channon," Donn retorted. "Of course so soon. Our combined bloodlines guarantee success…but you knew it would. This will be the first of many fine sons."

"You know it to be a son already?" It was the bragging right of a man of power, but the challenge had to be made.

"Channons only bear sons."

The burn of that boast, on the surface, appeared true, for the last three generations of Channons had only presented male heirs to the leadership of LaGuardia. That Geary's only son had died in infancy, leaving Oasis to carry the Hallister legacy, was a barb Donn expected to sting the other man. After Geary's death, the Hallister name would end. Donn anticipated any son shared with Oasis who would claim the title of Kennedy Laedan would bear the name Channon.

Rather than express any slight the claim made him feel, Geary smiled banally and said, "That is a blessing. Our futures will be secure because of it." Early conception in a marriage suggested the union might be a fruitful one, so long as the child lived and Oasis did not suffer in childbirth to be unable to have another. Channon-Hallister children were precisely what Geary had hoped for through this union of families. Sons or daughters mattered only in the continuation of power and blood. He expected Oasis to make certain at least one child carried the Hallister name, in any manner she could guarantee it, and that child would know its' heritage.

They might see the unification of the boroughs yet.

There was a knock at the door and Geary sighed, relieved to put the subject of children temporarily aside. "Business calls. You are welcome to take rest here tonight if you wish. It will be dark before you could reach the Hall, and there are dangers in the night, even here in Kennedy. Share a meal with me, tell me how things fare in LaGuardia…and what your plans are for my grandson."

Donn made his decision quickly. A meal, a bed, the avoidance of nocturnal anthro, and the borrowing of a horse for the remainder of his journey were temptations too great to resist. Buying time, forming another alliance, and perhaps sussing out what Hallister knew about Thomas Quentin or Fort Hamilton might also be to his benefit.

"Your offer is generous, Laedan. I accept."

The return of daylight would be soon enough to confront Grand Mas Lord.

The dampness of the pre-dawn fog had cleaned most of the soot from Vance's black duster by the time he and Ernest reached the Protectorate. He detoured to the locker room for a change of clothing and a quick washing of his hands and face, absently wondering when he would have the opportunity to clean those clothes, and joined the chief in his office. The older man had poured two large glasses of whiskey before removing his coat which hung dripping on the hook by the door. The morning gray pushed through the cracking seals of his office window as the first shift crew and the stragglers coming off of the night's duty flowed in and out of the front door. Some nodded at Vance as they passed, some eyed him with cautious curiosity before he closed the office door behind him.

As was most common, the majority viewed him with detached notice or with the distrust and contempt cast so often on those who saw into the thoughts of others when the opportunity arose.

This morning, Vance had less desire than usual to peek inside anyone's head. Especially not his own.

"Find what you were looking for?" Ernest asked, the night's bustle leaving him drained and wan-looking as he sank into his chair, automatically adjusting for the wobble he was accustomed to after so many years in this room.

"Should fix that," replied Vance with a shrug and nodded answer to the question. The sofa's lumpy embrace sucked the last of his energy so that he felt as deflated and weak as Ernest appeared.

"I'll leave that for Pubby."

Vance nodded. The smoky amber contents of the glass in his good hand begged for consumption, but instead, he stared into it, watching the liquid swirl within its hemplastic confines. "Found who we were looking for, where Laedan Marrock was held…a lab used to harvest anthro blood. Down in Kennedy. Don't think plasm's made there, just one step in the process, set up to look like HOPE's behind it…"

"You don't think they are?" If Ernest connected those details with the probability that the Marrocks were anthro, it did not show on his face. Nor did he inquire about the possibility.

"Not sure they're in it alone. Laedan Hallister might be in on it, or privy to what's happening at least."

The circumstantial possibility of Roland being in the wrong place at the wrong time was one of two explanations for his presence in that lab. The other involved his co-Laedan, but Lowell feeding the machine that had been poisoning his son, or having him hidden away there to get him out of the way, seemed a stretch to Vance.

Setting up the man's capture might not mean Channon had any inclination of what Roland's ultimate fate would be. There were HOPE work camps, and death squads used captives as training material. There was a myriad of other scientific research practices carried out in the name of eradicating anthro traits from the human gene pool. Vance believed at least some of those victims assigned to each place were Normals, criminals, and baseline test subjects. Lowell did not need to know the production of plasm by official channels was a possibility when, if, he had contracted someone to rid him of his governing partner, anthro or not.

"They were gone by the time we got there, tipped off maybe, but I don't think the work's shut down. Equipment was already moved. Didn't have the chance to get a good read on the place; gonna have to take a trip back down if I want to learn anything more definite."

"You know going up against HOPE's…?"

Vance nodded. "I know." Giving in to the temptation, hoping it would fuel the courage he needed for what came next, he drained the cup's contents and waited for the familiar alcohol blaze to burn through his body. "I heard about…I'm sorry…"

The glass in Ernest's trembling hand was set onto the desk with a too-heavy thump. "She was here…and I didn't give her an escort…"

"Not your fault. You couldn't know…"

"Couldn't I?"

Chasing back the fleeting images he had gotten from the woman's hair, Vance asked, "Did she say anything?"

"She was afraid…I thought she knew something about Jonni and Roland. But she'd come on behalf of Donnovan's wife…" Noting the mage's scowl, the sudden uncomfortable twisting at the edges of his mouth and his efforts to nurse a few more drops of whiskey from his empty cup, Ernest snorted. It was not his place to gossip about the relationships within the Laedan's household. There was nothing Vance could do about any of that.

"Least I got him. She can rest now."

Vance lifted his eyes to stare at him across the desk. "Got who?"

"The slag who killed her."

"You arrested…?"

"Got this off him." He opened his center drawer and pulled out the gold chain wrapped protectively in a gauze bag. "Several witnesses put him at the scene…"

"May I?"

Ernest hesitated. The sick sound in the back of Vance's throat, the way his reaching hand shook, made the chief unexpectedly reluctant to share the single piece of physical evidence he had. There was no body for Vance to read, no clothing or personal effects. Only the crime scene, which he had not yet been shown, and this single, delicate adornment Ernest should have returned to the Laedan but had, thus far, been unable to part with.

Keeping it in evidence, he argued, but for what purpose if the killer was dead? For what purpose if he did not allow the one man who could best examine it to do so?"

The guilty was punished. What did it matter if Vance read the evidence now?

The mage's shadowed expression made Ernest feel, not for the first time, that his assessment of guilt might have been premature.

"This is going back to the Laedan in the morning," Ernest grunted, dropping the cloth pouch into the drawer.

"Morning now." Vance's hand remained outstretched. "May I?"

Ernest grunted and shook his head. "Tomorrow then. Things to do today." It was impossible to hide anything from a mage for long, but he was sure as hell going to try.

Sighing, Vance set his glass on the edge of the desk and leaned back. He had known Ernest a long time. All of his professional career with the Protectorate. Even without being a mage, he knew the man was hiding something. "Nik has a lock of her hair."

The older man blanched and reached for the bottle to refill both cups. When he pushed Vance's back to him, however, the mage shook his head in refusal and stood up.

"Should go. Need a bath…and there's things to do."

"Glad you're back." The words were grateful but it was easy to interpret the mixed feelings behind them, Ernest's reluctance to reveal secrets and to know the ugly truth.

But there was a murderer at large and no matter how it could be done, it was the chief's job to see this through.

For Yiva's sake.

Ernest followed him as far as the front door as if chasing the demons of truth away. When Vance stopped with his hand on the edge of the open door, standing in the entry with a grim, sorrowful expression in the last place Ernest had seen Yiva alive, he was certain he could read her terror, her regret, in the mage's dark brown eyes.

Vance sidestepped to allow an arriving Protector to pass and waited until she was out of hearing range to speak. "Arresting Donn Channon's gonna be a helluva fight," he murmured without meeting Ernest's gaze. "Don't envy you on it. If you need me…?"

The door closed.

Inside, one man rushed to find the nearest waste bin to deposit the contents of his unexpectedly sour stomach.

On the outside, one man stared at his clenched hand and wished he could be spared the all-encompassing knowing of things. The wrong man was dead. The guilty remained free.

If he was the shade that continued to stalk Vance all the way home where he intended to clean up before checking the addresses on his list, a shade protecting his guilt, which of them stayed free and alive remained to be seen.

❧*❧

Torben made it his business, in the hours spent in the Fortress when off duty from the Plant and not pressed into the upkeep of his home, to memorize the names and faces of the staff who had access at any given hour to the Laedan and his son. The primary staff lived on-site, in a separate wing of the vast complex, making it easier to identify them and, to Torben, easier to keep track of the family's contact with outsiders. Deliveries of food and supplies not grown in the Fortress' greenhouses or livestock pens came every other day, but Captain Ortega, having witnessed one attempt on Nik's life and acutely aware of the deaths recently inflicted on the Channon and Marrock houses, had every incoming cart inspected, had every person passing through the gates searched for weapons or unidentified substances and questioned about their purpose for being there.

Those with business for the Laedan, who muttered and ranted as he paced the corridors, were directed to Nik and forced to wait until Torben was on hand to be at his side.

If another assassin came, Torben would be the one to thwart him.

The Fortress staff were afraid of Donn. If he was behind the attempts, as Nik feared, anyone Donn manipulated by that fear might be willing to carry out his wishes rather than face his volatile wrath.

No one in the Fortress was safe.

The man crisscrossing the rear of the meeting room, occasionally watching his son cope with the dwindling line of petitioners, was only safe from suspicion because, to Torben, there was no reason for the Laedan to want his only functioning, currently level-headed son, dead. Without Nik, without a Marrock co-Laedan in place, there was no one to carry on in Lowell's stead, now or in the future.

The pair of guards at the door nodded at another in the same uniform as he joined the queue. The fellow nodded back. At the end of the table, the Laedan stopped pacing to clutch the back of the nearest chair with both hands, the first time in several minutes he was not arguing with himself in illogical snippets of half-formed phrases or muttering inarticulate words beneath his breath. Nik glanced at the man silently staring at him as he dismissed a petitioner seeking compensation for a spoiled load of milk products that had not been allowed into the Fortress the day before. Nik's solution was a promise to inquire with Captain Ortega about the matter, to learn why the cart had been rejected. Nik assumed his father's sudden stillness came with a measure of disapproval for that decision and expected the silence to be followed by a berating outburst.

It was followed, instead, by the guard in the line charging around the two people in front of him.

Torben pushed aside those who stood between them and caught the man by his raised, extended arm. A yanking twist dislocated the fellow's shoulder and threw him to the ground with a yelp, causing him to drop the syringe he clutched in his outstretched hand. It shattered, its contents spilling on the floor while Nik, startled, skittered sideways so his chair tipped and deposited him on the floor too.

"Clear the room!"

It was the first sensical instruction heard from the Laedan in hours.

The guards rushed the remaining petitioners out of the chamber and closed the door, where one of them remained as the other ran in search of Captain Ortega. Torben, his foot on the downed man's chest, looked questioningly between father and son. Nik shook his head, his wide-eyed expression pleading with the sposer to stay, not to leave him alone with his father and this third would-be assassin.

The contents of the syringe could have been anything. Even a dose of one of Nik's favored recreational substances could have been lethal or at least sent him back into a spiral of abuse he was trying to stay free of. Addiction would have removed him from power and influence as surely as death would. It would have been enough, Nik suspected, for his brother.

"Who are you?"

"Doesn't…" began the frightened man on the floor.

"Not you," Lowell growled, his blue eyes not on the attacker but instead on Torben. He recognized the sposer from Yiva's graveside. He remembered him, barely, being the one, along with Nik, to take her mangled form away for sposal. He vaguely recalled seeing him after Roland and Jonni's deaths as well. None of those remembrances explained who he was and why he was here at his son's side.

"Torben's my bodyguard," Nik stammered. It was not an official post, and Torben had yet to receive compensation for being here, but it was, to Nik, the truth.

"You don't need a…"

"Third attempt on his life," grunted Torben. "Think he does."

"Third?"

"Ask Captain Ortega; Torby's saved me each time."

Lowell scowled at the figure on the floor trying to squirm free of the boot's weight, his efforts causing it to press harder. "Who would want…?"

"Dunno…but I think…Donn…"

The Laedan looked about to protest the absurdity of the idea, only to stare at Nik with a slack-jawed, disbelieving look of apologetic horror. The door flew open. Captain Ortega and four uniformed soldiers rushed in, aborting what Lowell might have said, erasing, temporarily, the fiery force of the thoughts in his head.

"Get Segara back here! Find out who he is, who sent him, what's in that." While the glass syringe was broken, the injection mechanism was intact and would possibly contain enough residue to make the contents identifiable.

Once Torben removed his foot from the man's chest, relieving the pressure and allowing him to breathe normally, he squawked, "Wasn't sirra Donnovan!" as Ortega's men yanked him to his feet and dragged him out of the room.

Of course he would say that, thought Nik with a shudder. Betraying his twin could be a costly, even fatal, mistake for anyone.

Though he did not know how he had betrayed Donn, Nik was learning that lesson the hard way.

"I'll get to the bottom of this," Ortega promised. "We'll know who's behind this, whoever it is. We'll find 'em."

The three left in the room wanted to believe the attacker's claim.

Not one of them did.

❞*❟

"Don't you have anyone who'll do what they're paid for?" snapped Quentin. The news of an arrest in the Fortress, of an agent attempting to poison the Laedan's son, spread like fire among the ranks of the Fortress guards and found its way to Quentin minutes before Uzzi arrived at the rendezvous spot at the Change.

Uzzi shrugged off the question as he ruffled the water out of his white hair. The evening breeze brought billowing fog and with it, the sort of dampness that permeated the fabric crevices at his wrists and neck, adding to the already uncomfortable cold. But it also provided cover for men like them to move about in the day's fading light, in a place known to be a haven for cutthroats and ruffs and the pirates who drifted along the choppy, rocky coast.

"You rather I go in myself?" He had considered the possibility, but tapping his inside man had seemed a wiser choice. He had not expected the fool to be so brazen as to act in the company of so many witnesses. The fellow might have detected Uzzi's reluctance to kill the Laedan's son without an adequate reason. Maybe he had been reluctant to do it on his own. Maybe he was an idiot.

"Want you to succeed! Two failed attempts mean they'll be all over him."

"If you want me to…"

"No." Quentin's furious pacing filled the night with the crunch of gravel beneath his boots, a sound that made Uzzi uncomfortable as it announced their location to anyone close enough to hear it. No use in seeking the shelter and anonymity of the Change if you were going to draw attention with unnecessary noise. "I've got something else, something more important."

Uzzi raised one brow and waited.

"Gather as many people as you can, promise them whatever you need to, and meet me here in three days." Three days, Thomas hoped, would be enough to find out if Pepe would live or die. "There's a college on the other side of the Wilds…"

"I know it."

Thomas stopped to stare at the older man in disbelief. "You do?"

"Just south of the Zone. Seen it when I've been there on business." Trade with the Zone could be a lucrative source of income if one was reliable and didn't double-cross the Zone residents. Uzzi did not often come up with anything the mutani needed but he had been there often enough to know the location Quentin spoke of.

"There's a pack there…" he began, Pepe's fate forgotten now.

"Wouldn't call them a pack," Uzzi snorted. "Four or five…"

"More of them now; I need them eliminated."

"Eliminated?" Uzzi scowled and absently swiped the moisture out of the traces of beard along his chin. "All of them?"

Thomas ignored the question. "If you know where it is, no need to meet me here. Get together those you need and get it done…"

Uzzi's frown deepened. He hated such work. "A pack isn't like…"

"Can you do it or not?" Quentin stopped pacing to lean in inches from Uzzi's face with a snarl. "They've threatened me for the last time. Take care of them or you can be damn sure I'll take care of you."

It was the same threat every time, but it was a trap Uzzi had yet to find his way out of. The sins of his past continued to act as a strangling noose he did not know how to escape.

"I do this…the whole pack…and we're done. I won't owe you anything else. You pay and the debts clear. And if HOPE comes after us, I'll rip your throat out myself."

Quentin laughed as he tightened the belt of his coat. "You can try."

"This job," he repeated, "and I'm done."

Going after a pack was insanity without the manpower and resources to support it, but if doing this bought freedom from beneath Quentin's thumb, what was a little more blood on his hands? Uzzi would not need to kill everyone, not the children at least, just enough people to weaken the pack and force them to relocate somewhere beyond Quentin's reach.

Quentin would never know the difference.

"This job…and the fort…and we're done."

Uzzi had forgotten about the fort.

That was a job worth doing and so Uzzi compromised with an offered hand and a stern glint in his eyes. "This job and the fort…and that's it."

Quentin's cold hand grasped his. "Agreed."

Chapter 15

"**S**hould have a medic with you…"

Liam's arm around her helped ease the anxious flurry in her belly as Jia watched QiangXu and Deuce inspect the collection of gathered supplies for the third time. The balcony offered a good view of every Pack member on the ground level and she found it a relief to sit on this spot and watch them. It was easier to keep everyone safe if she could see them. Most did not need such vigilance, but she felt better providing it, particularly knowing what lay ahead.

The debate over who should travel with her in search of Fort Hamilton, a journey through unfamiliar, possibly dangerous territory, had lasted for several hours, the pros and cons of each individual's participation weighed and judged before Jia made her decisions.

While her leadership would not guarantee unmolested passage through LaGuardia, not after Roland's death and the accusations of murder that were, as far as they knew, still swirling about, Jia was the logical choice of leader. She was also the only one who fully trusted Vance to guide them. The tracker-mage was their best chance of finding the fort. They needed him and thus the party needed Jia.

She would not send others into danger she was unwilling to face herself. And this was her father's mission, her father's quest. She had to do it for him. Only she would be likely to see the results through his unseeing eyes.

Wist, fleet of foot and fearless, had proven useful, if brazen and occasionally reckless, in the search for Liam, and thus was someone her team would benefit from. His inclusion made the former Queen's

College Pack feel as though they were part of the Flushing family, a political choice Jia felt confident in making.

Kato refused to be left out, despite Vanya's tearful pleading and begging for him to stay. Deuce refused to allow Jia to confront the unknown without him and had, in her experience, the most exposure to the sort of places they were likely to pass through. Pain's continuing distance from the Pack reduced the potential threat he represented, reducing Jia's lingering reliance on leaving someone to confront the omega if Maz could not. Pack cohesion had returned and she trusted that, if Pain proved to be a threat, others would put him down.

Maz did not need to oppose Pain alone. Jia would benefit from Deuce's endurance and survival skills, things that had helped keep the Flushing Pack safe for all of the years of her life. Having Deuce with her would make her feel safer.

With QiangXu on the team, a man of unproven strength but an Ursa with skills and expertise that would help them identify, transport, or destroy the fort's contents, it felt as if she had a team solid enough for what lay ahead.

Hallister would likely send an army. If Jia wanted to move fast, if she wanted to reach the fort before Kennedy, her unit needed to be small, streamlined, and fast. The five she selected, plus Vance and one or two more, would be enough.

"Addi needs to be here for Trill," Jia reminded Liam, leaning her head against his shoulder. With their child due soon, there was no way Jia was either risking Trill in the field or allowing her brother to make the trip away from his family. There were too many here still weak from the lab rescue. The Pack was large enough to need the full-time services of a doctor and soon there would be one more new pup to shelter. Despite Addi's protests, Jia insisted he remain at the library.

"Don't mean Addi."

Jia glanced at Liam and brushed his disheveled blonde hair from his face. "You're not a medic." He had experience, through Addi and Trill, through his service in the plasm lab, but he knew as she did it might not be enough for the sort of expedition she was undertaking. "QiangXu assures us he has someone…"

It would make a group of six, still small enough for Jia's comfort.

"In LaGuardia," Liam grunted, dissatisfied with the answer. "Who is this someone? You don't know them. What if you can't trust them? What if they don't want to…?"

"Someone he used to work with…and he trusts them." It was the only detail the Ursa had conveyed during the debate. While he could not guarantee the individual's help, he seemed confident the person in question could be depended on to accompany them and provide any medical care they required. "If they won't," she shrugged, "Vance might know…"

"Another Protector?"

Ignoring the unexpected note in his voice, assuming it stemmed from a mistrust of Protectors and mages more than a specific mistrust of Vance, Jia shrugged. "A healer-mage?"

"Not sure that's better." Healer-mages were rarer than trackers and in high demand, often drawn into the employ of HOPE or some powerful family with the promise of a secure life. Neither Jia nor Liam had ever met a healer, there had not been one at the Fortress since Roland and Lowell had been children, and only a few in the Pack had heard rumors of any in LaGuardia. If there were any out there, it seemed reasonable that someone in the Pack, or the Protectorate or Fortress, would have crossed paths with them.

"I should be there. With you."

Her fingers brushed back his blonde hair and this time trailed down his cheek and neck to the hollow of his throat. "You're not strong enough, Li…" she began.

Even if he was stronger and healthier, Jia would not have selected him for this expedition. She needed him here.

"It's Kato…and Vance…isn't it?"

He did not sound jealous, did not sound angry or bitter, only understanding and resigned. Having known him her whole life, she knew his moods and expressions well, however. There was little he could hide from her and he did not often try. She had expected he would remain a part of her life until the day one or both of them died, but with his capture, his rescue, something between them had changed.

She shook her head no but did not speak for several minutes as she searched for Kato below, finding him on the other side of the library, squatting at his sister's side, still trying to reassure her and explain what to expect in the days ahead. Leaving Liam with the Pack, while not directly connected to either Kato or Vance, meant she would not feel pulled in three directions. She needed to focus, not be distracted by the external male forces in her life.

"I need you to lead them while I cannot."

Liam's breath caught. His arm around her tightened. "You…want me to be your Second?"

He expected it would be Maz. Or Uncle. Or one of the newcomers, Orliss or Helena.

Never himself.

"Who better?" In her opinion, he had proven his leadership in the care of the test subjects at the abandoned lab, and many times over throughout their lives. He knew her opinions, her choices, her desires, and her thoughts better than anyone in the Pack and would lead accordingly, without blindly assuming her choices and his would be the same. As Maz had often been for her father, someone needed to be for the new Pack Alpha. Liam was liked and respected. Trusted. There was no one better suited. No one she trusted more.

"Maz? Uncle? Addi?"

"They were my father's arms…and Addi doesn't want it." The Pack elders would be respected, their council listened to and considered, but the initiation of a new alpha meant new blood in leadership. Her selection of a Second was expected. No one would be surprised to have Liam in that place.

Maz, rather than Roland's wife had been his Second. Liam understood what Jia's choice might mean for a future between them.

It was an honor, however, he would not reject.

"I'll do it…so long as you come back."

With Vanya's wail of discontent and the turning of Kato's head towards Jia, followed by the gazes of others towards the young woman, Jia suspected many believed she would one day elect Kato or

Deuce to the position of Second. But there was no one she wanted beside her at the head of her Pack more than her best friend.

She could not make it a promise, but she wholeheartedly replied, "I will."

Kato's hand covered Vanya's mouth as he glowered sternly, a look she had grown to recognize since leaving home, a look warning of danger if she was not silent. Her gaze darted about, seeking the threat amongst these safe people that her brother's act suggested was near, but there was only the growing number of those she had quickly adopted as her surrogate family in the absence of their mother.

He had feared she would forget him during his previous absence, or else she would have grown so inconsolable and unmanageable the Cana would be eager to be rid of her, and her brother, upon his return. Instead, Vanya had settled in as though she had always been part of these people and they welcomed Kato back as part of the Pack, although not with the same exuberance with which Vanya had greeted him. Both welcomes had been a relief but neither had eased the lingering unsettled feeling that came over him every time Jia and Liam were together.

This was a different threat than Vance. He did not know how it was different, only knew it was.

He had known the one they sought was dear to her, as dear as her father had been. He had no such childhood friends to draw experience from, only Vanya, and thus Liam's importance to Jia was unfathomable. The risks she had taken for him had announced his importance before Kato had any inkling of who the man was, so their closeness, once he was found, should not be a surprise.

But it did hurt.

Their gazes locked for a brief moment as Vanya stilled behind his hand. Jia seemed to nod at him before her attention returned to her conversation with Liam.

Kato sighed.

"I don't want you to go," Vanya hissed through the hand over her mouth, a frightened squeaking that mirrored the panic in her eyes,

"It's only for a little while…like the last time." He suspected this journey would take longer, but as Vanya exhibited little concept of the passing of time, he did not feel a need to elaborate.

"You just got back."

"I know; I'm sorry. But this is important. I have to keep you safe."

"You said everyone here will keep me…"

"They will…but they can only keep doing so if we do this. You remember the great castle?"

Vanya nodded eagerly as Kato's hand dropped. "Where Mama said we would live someday…safe from bad men…"

Kato forced a smile, relieved to have erased her initial distress. "Soon as we find it, as soon as I know it's safe, we can go there."

"Forever? All of us?"

"I…" He had gleaned his vision of what a fort should be from the collection of photo cards he had found over the years, the book Vanya continued to cherish and cling to, as she did Peppermint the bear, when Kato could not be with her. A fort was near enough to a castle that he expected Vanya would accept it as one when she saw it.

"Maybe…if they want to. This is their home…"

"My home. I want us all in the castle. It will be big enough for everyone, won't it?"

He nodded. "Castles are big," he agreed. He felt an anxious gnawing that suggested she no longer needed him as much as he needed her. He did not like that feeling.

Vanya's expression abruptly drooped. "Will Mama join us? Will she come to the castle when you find it?"

He could not voice the truth, not without a renewed onslaught of wailing. Quietly, he replied, "If she can. If we can find it, and it is safe.

That ray of hope made Vanya nod with a look of resolve. "Find the castle, Kato. Make it safe for Mama so we can be a family again."

It was the best permission he was going to get, the permission he had been hoping for. In a few hours, they would travel and he would leave Vanya in someone else's care, clinging to a pale thread of permission on the tails of a lie.

He hated lying to her.

This lie, he felt certain, was better than the truth.

❧*❧

"Aman…come in."

Though of the same age, Aman Fenway was grayer, his face more haggard than Geary's, a product of time spent in the elements in the employ of the man he had grown up with, schooled with, and stood beside since he was old enough to be of service. Even before Geary assumed the mantle of Laedan, when other children, less discerning of the role the boy would one day hold, harassed the short, scrawny child, Aman stood by his side to prevent harm from coming to his friend.

It made it more difficult to believe or accept the accusations made against him. Whatever actions Aman had taken, whatever he had said, surely came with legitimate reasons attached to them that served in the Laedan's, in Kennedy's, best interest.

Geary did not believe the man had a life beyond the duties required and asked of him. If he did, Geary had never seen any sign of it. To be fair, he had never asked. He had never cared to know.

Until now.

Aman's boyhood role of protector led to many rebellious, youthful fights as adulthood drew nigh until somewhere along the way he had set aside violence in favor of subtler, underhanded means of retribution and retaliation against Geary's detractors and enemies. Ways equally effective but less likely to be traced back to either him or Geary.

It had been a natural state of affairs for Geary to bring Aman up with him after his ascension. It had been natural to entrust him with the majority of details and tasks Geary's position demanded. There were times, however, when violence and bloodshed were the most efficient means to accomplish a particular goal.

That was Norse's function.

This, however, was not one of those times.

It would be, regardless of the outcome, a solution to a problem Geary did not want to dirty his hands with or think too deeply about.

Aman stopped in front of the Laedan, his hands hanging at his side the way he always stood, a posture of relaxed attention making him appear both at ease and alert. "Sirra?" he said with a nod of his head as he waited for the purpose of this summons to be made known, swallowing an uneasiness he was not accustomed to feeling.

It stemmed from that damned guilt over something he had no reason to feel guilty for.

"Have you heard the news?"

"News?"

Geary spoke without lifting his head. "Has Channon's wife been killed?"

Aman shrugged imperceptibly. So that was it. "I've heard it said," he admitted. In a world of verbal rumor, cut off from ancient forms of electronic and digital communication, news was often slow to arrive, often distorted and mixed with fanciful details not easily proven true. "I don't know if it's…"

"I must go to LaGuardia…see to Oasis."

Aman's gray head bobbed. "Indeed…you should." If there was any truth to the rumors, a tale Donnovan had not spoken of when he had been here, if the girl was both pregnant, as Aman had also heard from those eavesdropping on the Laedan, and in danger from the threat stalking the Channons, her father should see to her safety.

Aman would go if he thought he could get away from the Fortress long enough to make the journey.

"While I'm away, I want you to select thirty-six soldiers…anyone you trust to obey your orders without question…"

There was a pause, as if the Laedan was rethinking his request or strategy or was preoccupied with the scatter of documents across his desk and the one he rolled between his hands to stuff into a waterproof tube. Aman waited, silent for what felt to be a respectable amount of time for Hallister to continue, keeping his thoughts off his face. When the Laedan did not speak, Aman prompted, "Sirra?"

Geary looked up as if he had forgotten Aman was there, that he had left his instructions incomplete. He smiled, an expression, to

Aman, that appeared to be a mask for something darker behind the Laedan's eyes. "It is time…"

"Time?"

"No more to waste. If there's unrest in the north, we can't risk him getting there first."

Fort Hamilton. Aman nodded, understanding the nature of the task he was being given without explicit details, but there was a scowl on his face that Geary was quick to notice as he set the sealed tube aside and put the pen back in its ink well.

"There a problem?"

The suspicious note in Geary's voice prompted Aman to shake his head. "No, sirra, only…wouldn't Norse be better suited for something like this?" It was more natural to assume he would travel to LaGuardia at Geary's side as he had in the past. Taking Norse as an escort to LaGuardia was, in Aman's opinion, asking for trouble, if that was indeed what Geary intended. While Aman did not believe Norse was brash enough to make an attempt on either Laedans' life, Aman had suspected since Norse's first day in Kennedy's service that the man had an unspoken agenda that had nothing to do with the position he had been given. Aman was less certain than Geary of where Norse's loyalties lay.

It was both possible and likely Norse serving as escort to LaGuardia's Fortress was a front for some more sinister plan. Perhaps at Geary's request.

"Isn't going to be a fight," Geary responded with an offhanded chuckle. "This isn't war. It's exploration…extraction. If it's real…if there are munitions there…" He held out the tube for Aman to take, "do you want to trust them in Norse's hands? You think I would?"

Wasn't the possibility of turning Norse loose on the Channons a declaration of war itself?

"Want you to find them and report back. That's all. Besides," Geary continued, "I have something else I need him to see to. It ought to keep him placated and out of your way."

They stared at each other across the desk. The premonition of an unspoken motive behind the Laedan's choice to send him on this quest, to keep Norse close, intensified. But Aman agreed with the assessment that a cache of guns or other weapons in Norse's possession would be a disastrous thing. Norse might not steal them from the Laedan, beyond a handful he would undoubtedly claim as part of his pay, but he would have few compunctions using them…against civilians, against Aman, against the Laedan.

Aman was relieved to see Geary did not trust Norse with those weapons. But he had, for the first time, an inkling that Geary did not trust him either.

❮*❯

The opulence of HOPE Cathedral and Invocation Hall was unlike anything existing anywhere else in the lands reclaimed and rebuilt after the Undoing. Tile floors, polished to gleaming by the tireless hands of anthro and mutani slaves, reflected the colored glass of mosaic windows, each with lights positioned on the exterior to shine through and cast their glittering rainbow across the open central foyer even on the darkest of days or nights. White pillars supported the vaulted sky of painted frescos and the white walls, painted and cleaned to retain their unspoiled glow, displayed artwork scavenged from every corner of the controlled lands.

Some had been found by members of HOPE. Those seeking to curry HOPE's endorsement had donated others. Some had been confiscated from people unfortunate enough to end up out of favor, through disobedience, disrespect, or the unfortunate circumstances of poverty or genetics.

Donn had stood in this spot as a little boy of nine when his father had traveled here on business. He had been less awed or impressed by the display of beauty and the need to be still than his older twin and eldest brother had been, but he understood that with such wealth came power. Once he held that sort of power, he too would have displays like this. It would guarantee those seeing it understood what sort of man was behind the collection.

"Welcome to the Cathedral, Donnovan. It has been some time since you've been here."

Donn turned to face the man he had not expected to emerge from chambers to greet him. He expected the attendant at the foyer's central counter to return and beckon him to follow. He pondered the political choice of the greeting as he offered the Grand Mas a slight bow. "I have a proposition, Grand Mas, that I thought it best to deliver in person." He kissed the offered hand dutifully, skipping the niceties of small talk, hiding the displeasure of that acquiescent gesture from the man who expected it.

"Indeed?" Francis Lord smiled. "Please, follow me." He gestured down the corridor from where he had come and Donn fell into step beside him. "How is your father? Your mother? Your wife?"

"My wife is with child; we expect a son by late summer." That news expressed virility and power. Discussing his father's state of mind and health did not. As he could not report on how his father was faring, having been absent from the Fortress too much of late, Donn felt more confident addressing a topic he did feel confident of.

Talking about his mother was out of the question.

Lord smiled. "That is a blessing. The Channon line will continue. Your parents must be delighted. I'm pleased to hear it. After your brother's refusal to…well, it is good to know that one of you will continue to provide for LaGuardia. Your father? How is he coping with the loss of Roland and…?"

"He's not."

A hall sentry opened a door, allowing them to pass into a room more opulent, brighter and more ornate, than the entrance foyer of the Cathedral. Though not gilded white, instead being adorned with rich earthy wood tones of brown and grey and green, there were carvings and figurines on shelves and in nooks in the walls and illuminated paintings of ancient battles Donn knew nothing about. The history of the world pre-Undoing did not interest him except when he could find an application in it for his interests and endeavors. What came before no longer mattered. Only what was had value.

"He's fallen victim to the anthro influence as you suspected. He's a liability to LaGuardia."

Lord's frown deepened as he sank into his padded chair and steepled his hands beneath his chin, his elbows on his desk.

"I thought it was proven that Marrock…"

He did not believe that proof any more than Donn did. Despite the claim that Marrock had turned, a feat only possible if he was not anthro, Donn clung to the possibility that someone had made the claim for personal gain.

Marrock however, was not the problem. Marrock was dead, his daughter-heir scattered with the rest of her family. The dead could not hurt the living.

Only his mother was an exception.

"Thomas Quentin. You know how my father relies on him." Lord bobbed his head and Donn continued, "He's Fela."

Donn thought Lord's complexion greyed at the claim but he motioned for Donn to go on.

"He's stolen weapons from our stores and Fa does nothing. With Jonni's…he's become erratic, unstable, unpredictable…unsuitable for the duty he shoulders and I fear him giving Quentin too much authority. I have pleaded with him to unite with me, to strengthen LaGuardia before Quentin and Hallister undermine us. He's expelled Quentin from the Fortress but…"

"You say you fear him granting Quentin authority…"

"Quentin's been his right hand for a long time; who's to say he won't change his mind and take him back…especially in his current state of mind, with Jonni gone…"

"You think Laedan Hallister will undermine LaGuardia? With his daughter?"

Donn scowled. "My wife is not a threat." He had his wife under control, but their marriage did not mean Geary did not have other designs on the northern borough.

Lord leaned back in his chair, his elbows coming off his desk and his hands dropping into his lap. "So you seek assistance in removing your father…and strengthening LaGuardia…"

"It may come to that." Donn schooled his tone with the regret of a son reluctant to go against his father. He was confident the Grand Mas had few reservations about meddling in borough politics. HOPE had aided in the removal of at least one Laedan in recorded memory, had their hands in the manipulation of bloodlines and marriages and the creation of laws. There were ways to oust Lowell without tarnishing the Channon name or leaving evidence that might cast aspersions on his son or anyone else of import.

But Donn knew he was not yet a proven power in HOPE's eyes and he was, currently, the youngest Channon heir.

Proving more capable than Nik, however, would be easy.

If Lord continued to hear him and took what he offered, proving worthy could be done in a fashion that benefited them both.

"I'm seeking an alliance to find, access, and ransack Fort Hamilton's stores." The barely perceptible change of expression on Lord's face revealed he knew the mythos of Fort Hamilton. It was both an irritation, and no surprise, that HOPE could know about something so many had worked to keep secret. Donn suspected the information had passed to Lord through Quentin. It would not surprise him. "I have men, and I've studied the map, but without relying on my father's backing, I don't have the resources to go after it alone. His interest in the Fort has waned since Jonni's…but I think it's critical to locate it and confiscate whatever's there before Quentin or Hallister get to it."

"That would be unfortunate." Lord's clasped hands came up to steeple beneath his chin again, this time with his elbows on the arms of the chair. Once he had not feared Quentin's access to such secrets, as he had believed the younger man a strong and suitable ally. If this new claim was true, and not some slander designed by Donn to manipulate HOPE's favor, Quentin could not be allowed access to weapons that could be turned against HOPE and Normals alike. A man with such a secret would have followers, allies…perhaps enough to prove an irritation if not an outright threat.

Despite the longstanding arrangements between HOPE and Laedan Hallister, Lord was aware of the sort of man Geary was. Given the opportunity, Hallister would find and use a cache of weapons against anyone who stood in his way.

HOPE included.

Just as Donnovan would do if given the chance. Donn, however, was young enough to need the sort of political backing HOPE could provide to obtain the power he craved. He was smart enough to understand that need and be willing to work with HOPE instead of working against them. It was the sort of relationship worth cultivating in the hopes that, by the time Donnovan was in a position to move against HOPE's authority, he would be too entrenched in the doctrine, in the organization's politics, to choose to do so.

A loyal convert was a valuable thing.

"I will need to present this to the Council." When Donn frowned, Lord smiled disarmingly. "I could make a move without them, but it is best to have their support, don't you agree? We are talking men, commodities, weapons. Turning those things over to you without their approval and agreement just isn't done. Their support will mean more of what is needed. Success will be guaranteed."

There were never guarantees, of course. Lord knew it as well as Donn did. But their odds would be better if he had the resources to stand up to any resistance he met.

Donn schooled his face, his body's demeanor, and nodded with as much neutral agreement as he could express. He would prefer a secret agreement between him and the Grand Mas. A pact between them alone. One man was easier to manipulate than a council.

The support of HOPE would mean, when the time came, he could move against his father with the blessing of the most powerful entity in the land. No one would oppose him when he took control.

Complete this mission, bring back the wealth Fort Hamilton contained, and the seat of Laedan would be his.

❧*❧

"Am I interrupting?"

Lowell had stood silent in the doorway watching Oasis arrange flowers in the numerous vases in the room, as Yiva had done, for several minutes without moving. The practice of adorning the Fortress common areas with flowers from the greenhouse had continued every day since her death, as it had before it, and he had assumed one of the servants was upholding the practice. A memorial to the beloved woman they missed. Though he had thought to demand the practice cease, the simple comfort the flowers brought, the reminder of beauty amid guilt and pain, was something he clung to and cherished.

He had not thought it would be Oasis carrying on the tradition.

She was mistress of the Fortress now. It was fitting she did so.

Seeing her there, however, watching her hands organize the flowers into a pleasing display, filled him with a mix of feelings he did not know how to cope with.

He did not think she knew he was there as he watched, as she moved around the dining table positioning the arrangements in a fashion he believed Yiva would have enjoyed. When she lifted her face and smiled wanly at him, however, he knew she had sensed him there all along.

"Of course not. This is your home…"

Lowell grunted as he entered the room. The Fortress did not feel like home any longer. With his wife and best friend dead, one son as well, and another dead to him though still drawing breath somewhere, LaGuardia's Fortress felt like a prison to Lowell, a place of captivity whose walls he barely recognized, a trap he longed to escape.

Its walls were the bounds of guilt. If he could get free of the Fortress, he could be free of his guilt as well.

"I want to apologize…"

"You've nothing to apologize for." Oasis returned to the flower arrangements, an excuse not to look into the man's grief-dark eyes, an excuse to mask her own.

"I should have done more to protect you from Donnovan. I should never have allowed your marriage…"

"It was already arranged…"

"To Jonni."

"Who did not want me." She shrugged half-heartedly. Though she did not know the reasons for Jonni's rejection of the marriage, she understood it had nothing to do with her value as a person, with who she was. It had been, primarily, a rejection of a political treaty he had not chosen. If they had gotten to know one another beforehand, it might have made a difference. The marriage of Channon and Hallister heirs her father had pushed for was something she could not have pulled out of, a treaty she had believed in as strongly as her father had.

She had known little about Donn, about any of the Channons, before her marriage. Lowell had been the only Channon she knew.

Lowell had been her reason for coming to LaGuardia.

He nodded. He had known of Jonni's reluctance and resistance to the union long before that day, but he had believed his eldest would bow to tradition and familial responsibility and obey his father. It was Lowell's fault he had not understood until too late how stubborn his son could be.

Stubborn like his father.

It was his fault he had not seen earlier the sort of man Donnovan had become.

He caught her arm as she moved past and drew her against him impulsively, the first time he had held her since Yiva's death, the first time he had held any woman in weeks. Despite the surge of choking guilt and grief, he also felt a wash of longing and relief that overpowered those darker emotions and for the first time allowed him a small flicker of hope in a positive future. Nose and mouth pressed into her hair, he whispered, "He will not hurt you. I swear it. If you wish, I shall speak to your father, see your marriage dissolved so Donn has no hold over you. I'll raise your child as my own, protect you both if you are willing…"

"I…" she shivered in his embrace, likewise warring with conflicting feelings and a fight or flight or surrender battle that paralyzed her. "We can't…it is not safe…"

"I can make it…"

"He had the…if he gets his hands on…there are many who support him…if you try to keep me from him…he'll come for me, for you…and there's nowhere…LaGuardia hasn't the resources to…"

Lowell stiffened. She was right. With the stolen collection of weapons and who knew what else at his disposal, and a ruthlessness Lowell was uncertain he could match, Donnovan had an advantage. But it was only a short-term one. Lowell had the numbers, the whole of LaGuardia behind him. If Hallister learned what Donn had done to his daughter, if HOPE learned of the stain of matricide, Lowell believed Donn would, in the end, no longer be a threat except to the name of Channon.

To fight him, however, there was something Lowell needed.

"I will have…as soon as I reach Fort Hamilton."

Choking on a lump in her throat, Oasis muttered, "No one to send. Mas Quentin is…and Nik isn't…and we need Captain Ortega here."

"Don't need to send..." He kissed her head. "I will go myself."

Face tilting to stare at him with horrified surprise, she shook her head. "You can't, Lowell. LaGuardia needs you…"

"Don't fret." He caught her face between his hands to stare into her eyes and kissed her lips. It was chaste but a kiss that made her tremble in a way Lowell read as regretful or perhaps disgusted. His perception of her response, as well as the feel of her mouth against his, brought back a swell of conflicting memories, brought forth another bloom of guilt stronger than he had felt all day. His lips drew together into a steely, terse line and his eyes narrowed with determination.

"LaGuardia will be safe. You will be safe." He stepped away from her, attempted to straighten the rumpled clothes he had worn for the last several days, and squared his shoulders. It was the most like himself he had appeared since Jonni's death.

"Nothing like this will ever happen again."

He knew what had to be done. He had to see that the borough was in competent hands. He would find the fort. He would make his son, and Quentin, pay for the destruction they had caused.

He should never have doubted Roland.

He would see that LaGuardia had the strength to be the borough he had intended it to be. He would make Roland, and Yiva, proud.

Chapter 16

There was no need to take the Hallister wagon, despite the debate over what to do with it, whether to keep it for the Pack's use, dismantle it and use the wheels and lumber elsewhere, or drive it to a place where Kennedy's people would find and return it to Hallister. There were few good wagon paths through the Flushing Wilds, the most direct and shortest routes back to LaGuardia and no one wanted to travel south around the Wilds where Kennedy Guards, or whoever had hunted the survivors, might still be looking for them. Taking the wagon anywhere Hallister could retrieve it was to risk another confrontation.

The Pack could use the wagon for moving supplies around the college, however, and the ox would be useful to both pull it and maneuver other materials too heavy for most of the Pack to move.

If Hallister wanted the ox back, he would have said so. Or he would send someone for it.

With no hint of snow or rain in the crisp winter air, there was only the cold to slow the travelers, and so long as they kept moving, bundled in the warmest clothes they had, the group was confident they would make it across the Wilds by daybreak. The north borough bunker would provide shelter long enough to make contact with Vance and QiangXu's medical resource before they could be on their way.

Leaving the wagon and ox for the Pack made sense.

Without knowing Hallister's plans for Fort Hamilton, they had to assume Kennedy's Laedan had a headstart in the search for it. They had to assume they needed to move fast if they were to prevent him from reaching and confiscating any treasures the fort housed before they could find and destroy it.

As Deuce paced before the library door, stopping periodically to stare in the direction he sensed Pain to be, and QiangXu reexamined his pack's inventory as he had obsessively done multiple times, Wist and Reif shared whispered words and Vanya sleepily fussed over Kato's coat with a multitude of questions about what the castle he was going to find would be like. Most of the pups slept, but Eddie and his brothers squatted on the balcony where Jia had been earlier, watching the last-minute preparations with excitement.

They wanted to join this quest. They wanted to be part of the adventure like Wist. Candace, however, would not permit it, nor would Jia. They were too young, too inexperienced to take the risk. Even Eddie.

With Liam loitering nearby, the Pack aware he would be the acting alpha in Jia's absence, she returned her brother's embrace and kissed his cheek. "Don't worry. Keep Trill and that baby safe so I can meet her, or him, when I get back."

"I'd feel better if you would say when that would be." They had not known how long they would be gone when they had gone after Liam, but none of them had expected it to be more than a week or two. Addi had been at her side. The uncertainties surrounding the search for Fort Hamilton, even with a map in the tracker-mage's head, meant it was impossible to judge how long this would take. The Pack was safe, intact, beyond easy reach of the Laedans or HOPE, but the knowledge did not ease Addi's concerns.

"So would I…but we'll be careful." They would be beyond Hallister's reach at least and would stay clear of LaGuardia Guards and any Protectors who might turn them over to Lowell. So long as they remained vigilant against grubbers, HOPE, and the natural hazards of the post-Undoing world, Jia had no reason to think they were in additional danger.

Those dangers, however, were enough to be mindful of.

"You'd better be," Liam interjected, kissing the back of her head, his hands on her shoulders. "Don't stick me with alpha…and don't make me come after you…"

"The way we did for you?" snorted Addi with a chuckle.

"Not saying I wouldn't." Liam's smile was restrained but affectionate. "Only saying don't make me do it."

"I won't." Jia stepped away, nodded at those she had already bid farewells to, and joined Deuce at the door. The others followed.

It was not a promise she could legitimately make, or keep, but the intention to do so was there.

She looked back one more time at Liam, wishing, as she memorized the glint of the firelight in his blonde hair, the set of his shoulders, his warm but strained smile, that he was going with her. But he was not yet strong enough for what she suspected was ahead of her, and he was needed here. Nodding, she smiled despite the nervous tightening in her heart and stomach, and exited into the pre-dawn air. Her father wanted this. It had to be done.

But after getting Liam back alive, she was afraid she would never see him again.

❧*❧

Harris Warby was a squat, brutish fellow with thin sideburns encircling his face to create a bushy graying beard along his chin and jawline, the cut of which heightened the roundness of his battle-scarred head. The checkered cloth around his pate, held in place by a knit cap, hid his receding hairline and the additional scars collected throughout his service to Grand Mas Lord as HOPE's premier general. Nearly as broad and round as he was tall, some whispers pegged the man as Ursa, or at least mutani, for he had speed and a level of endurance in combat that made him more lethal than most, tougher, and kept him alive despite injuries that would have killed many others.

Lesser people, in Warby's opinion. His faith in his calling kept him alive. His service, his belief in HOPE's creed, the general weakness of constitution in the average man or woman, were what allowed him to win, to survive. Nothing more.

Rumors and whispers aside, it was said he was the best military mind HOPE had. Whatever genetics flowed through his veins, it was ignored in favor of what he offered the Council and the Grand Mas. What he was had not prevented him from taking oaths to serve, had not prevented him from killing in the name of his faith.

With such a man leading the thirty soldiers selected for this undertaking, men handpicked by Warby plus a couple of healers, grooms and horsemen and smiths, and various serving staff, Donn did not doubt they could succeed. Kennedy lacked the manpower and the sort of rigorous training provided to HOPE's forces. Even if these thirty, dressed in ceremonial black body armor many anthro and Normals alike would recognize, were matched in number, or even outnumbered, they would be victorious.

Donn did not have to like the prickly, gruff-voiced man barking orders that forced the troops into line and sent them marching through the Cathedral gates. He only had to work with him. Donn had been given command of the mission, the direction of its outcome, but Warby had the experience. If it came to a fight, if it came to tactics of actions for survival, Donn would have to defer to him if he wished to live. So long as the man spurring his chunky war pony towards the head of the column understood this was Donn's quest, that the ultimate achievement and spoils were his to divide as he and the Grand Mas had agreed, they were not going to have any problems.

Donn suspected Warby, at Grand Mas Lord's instruction, had been directed differently.

Any notion the man had of unseating his authority, however, was one Donn would quickly disavow him of.

At the end of a blade or a gun if necessary.

❧*❦

It seemed a peculiar request from Captain Ortega when he approached Nik with it in the lobby as the sun's light shifted slowly from dusk to dawn. Nik had never been able to talk his father into, or out of, anything. Addiction made him ill-equipped and averse to trying, and in matters of governance, in situations of borough business when he, as mayor of District 2, needed something, he had had Jonni or Donn to intervene with their father on his behalf.

Neither was there to do so any longer.

This was not a matter of mayoral business.

It was still a matter of political expedience, however, though not one, when Nik found his father packing a hempcanvas travel bag with neatly folded clothes, he believed he could influence.

He had promised the captain he would try.

"So he's right."

Lowell smiled but did not look up as his son entered the room. "Good, Nik. I was going to find you when I finished." Nik coming to him saved Lowell the trouble of looking for his business-busy son.

"You're not really thinking about…"

"I have to find the fort before Donnovan does."

Nik frowned. The tone of the matter-of-fact comment suggested his father believed Nik already knew about Fort Hamilton when there was no rational reason for him to know. Perhaps he believed he had already mentioned it. "LaGuardia needs…"

"LaGuardia has you. She'll be fine for a few days without…"

"I'm not Laedan!" Nik's palms began to itch and sweat, a stress response that brought with it the lure of seeking any substance he could find to smooth his agitation. "It's not gonna be a few days. They're not going to listen to me. I don't have the experience."

He had listened when others thought he was too deep in a stupor to hear. He had watched when others thought him too wasted to be aware. He had the same education as his brothers and better memory retention for information than either of them…so long as he was clear-headed enough to access the details and trivia inside his head.

None of those things made him a competent, confident leader, however, particularly after having lived in the shadows of derision, mistrust, and reservation for so long.

"Leave that to me. Just do what you've been doing…what you think I'd do or," Lowell snorted in self-loathing, "do what you think I'd not do. That might be smarter."

"Following bad advice from incompetent counselors doesn't make you…"

"Oh, he was competent. Too competent. But you're right; bad advice. Bad advice…and I didn't listen when Roland told me…"

Lowell sounded on the verge of incoherent rambling and Nik caught his arm, hoping to ground him, hoping to be the connection to reality he had often hoped others would be for him when he had spun out of control.

Jia and Addi and Liam had been that connection for him once, before they left the Fortress. Before the mistrust Quentin had sown in Lowell's ears.

Ultimately, that connection had to come from inside him.

Things had begun to change before, when the rumored cache of weapons at Fort Hamilton had bloomed in the boroughs. When Lowell's hunger for tighter control over LaGuardia turned at odds with Roland's desire for strengthened peace.

Now that rumor had grown into a thorny vine that could not be pruned or burned. Only digging it out from the roots would put an end to this madness. Nik had no idea how to accomplish that.

Lowell looked at the hand on his arm, tempted to jerk away as if angry at the restraint. His son's hand. Nik's hand, the only son he had left. He patted it twice, lingering each time in unusual, extended contact, and he closed his pack and slung it over his shoulder. "Keep doing what you're doing. They'll respect you…"

"Don't do this…"

"She's right, you know. It has to be done. You have to be safe. She has to be safe. She wasn't safe before and now she's…" Lowell's voice caught and he paused with his hand on the doorknob. "She wants me to do this. For all of you. Have to make it up to her."

Believing he was talking about Yiva, that he imagined he heard her voice, her wishes, the whispers of grief-voices Nik knew from moments of drug-addled delusion, he was kept from reaching out long enough for his father to slip beyond his reach.

His mother would never want this. For any of them. Safety should not come with the price tag of a fort full of weapons. It should only come at the hand of a son punished, or banished, for his sins against his family.

❧*❧

The office door banging against the wall as Ernest pushed it open more forcibly than intended with the toe of his boot, jolted Vance out of slumber found on the chief's lumpy sofa. He scrambled to his feet to take the hempfiber tray covered with steaming tea, honey rolls, and a plate of sausages out of the older man's hands. Ernest relinquished it and closed the door with one hand, his expression apologetic for the ruckus he had inadvertently caused.

"Need to get that damned thing fixed," he muttered, his chair groaning its protest as he sat and accepted the cup of tea Vance pushed in his direction. "Courtesy of Lavonia…and a few others," he added indicating the spread. Pubby's wife frequently sent breakfast goods for the Protectors so the offered tray was nothing unusual. After the arson call, she had taken it upon herself to see that everyone involved had hot food in their bellies.

"She's a good woman," Vance agreed, holding his cup between his hands to warm them. He had not intended to fall asleep in the man's office and did not know how long he had been there after his tour of a handful of Laedan storehouses. Long enough for his neck to feel stiff. Long enough for the chief to have hung his coat on the peg, gone out, and come back with the tray. Craning his neck from side to side to ease the ache, he asked, "Any news?"

"People skulking about, strange noises, a lot of activity during the preceding nights…the usual. Odds were, if you didn't pick up anything, there wasn't much to see."

Not taking the assertion as an affront, Vance shrugged. "Can get back later, after the smoke's cleared and there's less commotion."

"Laedan asked for you."

Vance cocked his head. "Say why? What'd he want?"

Ernest shrugged. "Don't know. Didn't sound urgent…don't think it had anything to do with the fire."

The fire was out and no one had been injured beyond breathing too much smoke. There did not appear to be any damaged goods, only the decaying tires. None of the nearby structures had suffered. If the Laedan had so little concern for his properties, was willing to burn them, or not seek answers afterward, there were other matters the Protectorate could address.

Rubbing his thumb over the lip of the cup pondering whether the Laedan's summons was a priority or not, Vance asked, "Did you go to the Fortress? Wanna go with me now?"

Shaking his head, Ernest pretended to ignore the hand splayed on the sofa where Yiva had last sat. "Didn't ask for me. Couldn't face them then…can't now," he mumbled around a mouthful of sausage speared on a fork. "Thought it better to honor her by dealing with…"

The peculiar note at the end of his words made Vance look at the hand rubbing over the adjacent cushion, his head silently sorting through the images, emotions, and voices resonating there, filling the room as though they were conversations still in progress. He pushed aside those he did not want to revisit in favor of those he did. Memories of long ago talks with Ernest, with Jia, orders and directions given, the faint shade of Sal's last time here, none of those things important any longer. It was tempting to linger on Sal's face, remember her support over the years, but those remembrances were not what he was hoping to find.

He already knew the truth.

Ernest did too.

"I said I'd take it back," Ernest muttered, peeping into the drawer to make certain Vance had not taken the necklace from it. "What you said before…"

"She was afraid…"

"She knew who had killed…"

"…of Donnovan…"

"…Marrock and Jonni…"

"…and he killed her for coming to you with the truth."

"That he had…Donnovan wasn't there when they…" Ernest's mouth snapped shut. He had heard what Vance had tried to tell him before but he had pushed the possibility out of his head in favor of the continuing arson investigation.

His hand at his mouth was the only thing to prevent the retching from producing results. With his other hand, he pulled a bottle from the drawer and filled his half-empty teacup to the brim.

It cooled the contents to lukewarm but it replaced the burn in his throat with a familiar one he preferred.

"No need to…do they know?"

Repeating the grim news, being more specific about the killer, was only necessary because Vance wanted to see the guilty punished…and that would only happen if the chief made finding Donnovan a priority.

"The Laedan? Nik?" Vance paused, eyeing the bottle and reconsidering his decision to continue to push back against the need for a drink. His head hurt, his hands trembled, and his vision and hearing felt distorted, his world off balance, but he could not say how much of that was due to the lack of alcohol in his blood and how much was rooted in the sickening truth of Yiva's death. "They do. Not sure Lowell believes it…but he knows."

"Shart. Where is he?"

"No one knows. No one's seen him since before her burial. Far as I know, no one's seen him since either." If Donn had gone back to the Fortress, no one had told him. It could have been the purpose of the Laedan's summons. If Vance could stay out of the Channon's business, however, he preferred to do so.

If the summons was a matter of importance, it would come on the heels of a demand.

"Quentin's missing too," Ernest muttered. "He was there when I took her home…but no one's seen him since…"

"Bumped into him the night before the burial, so he's around."

"Where? How'd he seem?" It was a relief to turn the discussion away from Yiva and the blood of an innocent man Ernest carried on his hands. Perhaps not innocent, he continued to argue to justify his actions, but innocent of the crimes of this particular rape and murder.

"Like a man hiding something…but he did confirm what I knew about that missing shipment." Settling for the tea, Vance swallowed the warmth and let it ease the discomfort in his belly. "Weapons, not medical supplies. Said Donnovan stole them…but I suspect he had his hand in the act…and the Laedan knows it wasn't medical supplies despite what he told me. Gave up some locations, some addresses. I was crossing the first off the list when I found you."

"Donnovan starting fires too?"

"Don't know. Would be a damn brazen thing to do." So was stealing weapons from his father and raping and killing his mother. At this point, Vance believed Donnovan was capable of anything.

"Either of them involved in the juice trade?"

"Don't think so…not as far as we could tell." Why, Vance wondered, did every mention of Thomas Quentin feel like driving a hot needle into the space behind his eyes?

"But? I hear a but."

"Long story, one I don't have details for yet. Gonna need time."

"To track down connections to the lab?"

Vance shrugged, his expression evasive. "That too."

Ernest put down his fork. "Not gonna give me details?"

"Better you don't know. Just something I need to do."

"Something to do with the Marrock girl?"

Vance shrugged and winced at another stabbing image flash behind his eyes as he met Ernest's gaze, an unrecognized face in the mist peering through the foliage at the Queen's College library façade.

He hated vague intuitions. Vague enough to lack meaning but menacing enough to leave a bad taste in the back of his throat.

Maybe it was the unquenched thirst for alcohol.

"Can't help you if I don't…"

"Isn't something you can help with. If you want to do something, find Brac. Find the source of the shart on the street. When I get back, we can go at them together."

As elusive as the one called Brac was, after having spent years and countless hours seeking the primary source of so much contraband in LaGuardia, the hunt would keep Ernest busy for as long as Vance had to be away. Finding Brac might also alleviate the man's conscience.

Not finding Brac would let Vance out of this particular agreement when he did make it back. Or if he did not.

"Tell Laedan you haven't seen me…if anyone but Nik comes asking. And if you really want to…" He stood, his appetite gone, his nerves rattled enough that he reached for Ernest's whiskey-laden tea and drank the small portion that remained.

"Nepo's back in town."

"Jeezus."

Neither needed to say more.

❧*❦

The library was silent. With the clarity of a dry day, most of the Pack had moved their daily routine outside. The final harvest of vegetables from the portable planter boxes was gleaned, the last of the fruit collected from the Queen's College orchard. Burnables for winter fires were gathered and stored out of the wet, used water from storage basins replaced with the clean water collected during the last storm. Cracks and split seams in the library's exterior were repaired to reduce the incursion of winter into their shelter and small animals caught during an early morning hunt were cleaned and prepared for salting so the meat would last throughout the days when hunting would be most difficult. The morning meal was complete and the pups too young for schooling or for helping the adults played in the empty fountain under Helena and Zen's watchful eyes. Those of school age were gathered around Ayla and Trill near the library fire for the daily lessons in numbers and reading that Roland had insisted was to be part of the Flushing Pack's priorities.

They were the only people indoors.

Every pup was accounted for…except Eddie.

Perhaps the women providing the lessons did not notice. Perhaps they assumed he had been, as an older pup, put to work with the adults or included in the hunt as Reif had been.

Candace, her arms full of the morning's first load of firewood as she stumbled through the library door, did notice.

Eddie was not with his brothers.

She dropped the wood haphazardly near the other collected pieces but did not take the time to stack it as she hurried back outside. The women with the school pups looked up.

Eddie was also not with Helena or with those returning from the pre-dawn hunt.

He was not with Reif nor working on the library roof to repair the places where the rain seeped in.

He was not with Brie and those gathering apples from the orchard trees or that had already fallen beneath the boughs.

He was not anywhere Candace could see him and his scent, despite lingering everywhere she turned, was faint enough to suggest that several hours had crept by since his last passing.

Sick with sinking panic, Candace tipped back her head and howled, "Eddie!"

Chapter 17

A mother's cry was a guaranteed means of drawing the Pack together from wherever they were. Liam, too unsteady for the physical exertions of roof repair, hunting, or harvest, had chosen instead to become familiar with the territory the Flushing Pack had claimed during his absence. He was near enough to Candace that her cry lent itself to a burst of speed that surprised him. He was the first to reach her, to find her crouched mid-shift, instinct prompting a reaction he understood despite having no children of his own.

His hand on her back, as he squatted beside her, made her jerk her focus around to look at him with a startled snarl.

"He's gone! Someone's taken…"

Liam sniffed the air as the others gathered. Those hearing her claim did likewise. The newcomers drew together, fear prompting the belief that they would be blamed or that someone, perhaps those who had held them captive or attacked the wagon on its journey north, were here to pick them off one by one.

There was no scent of intrusion in the air. No indicator that anyone had been in the vicinity who should not have been. That did not rule out the possibility, however, that Candace was right.

"Perimeter," Liam barked, a command Roland had often used and one the Pack understood. "Reif, you and Vanya take the pups inside, keep them there, search the library…anywhere Eddie could hide. Addi, Trill, Ayla, search the nearest buildings. The rest of you, spread out." Queen's College was an expansive place with many crevices, rooms, closets, basements, and rooftops where a curious or angry boy, or an enemy, could hide. If Eddie had been injured in any of them, if he had fallen or had something fall upon him, it would explain his failure to come to where he was supposed to be, his failure to heed his mother's call. Sending those with the most medical knowledge to find him might mean saving his life.

The other possibility made Liam scowl and he met the eyes of two men he had grown up respecting. "Find Pain," he demanded, holding his voice calm so as not to induce a panicked outrage before guilt or innocence was assessed. He did not believe Pain would harm the Pack pups, even if that pup was Fela and not Cana. But he had never considered that Pain would challenge Jia's right to her father's place as alpha either, when Roland had made his choice evident long ago. Those were tales of challenges and battles he was still coming to terms with, having not witnessed them himself, tales that made him worry for his safety as acting alpha.

If harming a pup was a challenge to Liam's leadership, sending men Pain had loved and respected to find and confront him was, he hoped, the wisest choice.

"What about the perimeter?"

"Let's rule out what's closest first," he murmured to Xan's question. "Ele, go to the Zone, make sure he hasn't gone there."

Eddie had expressed interest in the mutani before. He would not be able to enter the Zone without someone's permission, but he would be able to get close enough to watch the bridge, the gate, and watch the residents' comings and goings. Someone there might have given him access to explore the neighboring compound protected by walls and fences that made it one of the safest places to be.

The Pack scattered, some shifting to take advantage of Cana senses, but when Candace began to rise, Liam's hand on her shoulder held her back.

"I have to…"

"Up there." Liam pointed to the highest vantage point within their territory. The multistoried building was structurally sound, though the access to the parapet was less so. For a cautious, light-footed Cana, the rooftop was easily accessible. "You should be here when he's found…you can direct the search from there."

Inactivity went against every maternal instinct she possessed. Fear and frenzied panic, however, were clouding her senses, clouding her judgment. Liam knew it. She knew it. A wise alpha directed a pack in ways intended to benefit and protect them, individually and as a group. She understood he wanted what was best for her, for her son, and reluctantly, after a frustrated snarl, accepted his direction.

Sniffing the air as she bounded towards the rooftop lookout, raking his hand through his shaggy hair, Liam knew she would not accept it for long.

❧*❧

"What's the gig?"

The sprite of a woman next to him, her dark, shoulder-length hair windswept as it escaped the cord that tied her short braid at the nape of her neck, looked over the motley collection of scavs, mercs, ruffs, and ne'er-do-wells. Of those who most often came together under Uzzi's banner when there was some prize or payment to be gained, she picked out faces she recognized, those she trusted most, those she trusted least, those she did not know. The much older man was doing the same, although his expression seemed uncharacteristically distracted and pensive.

A product of age and fatigue, no doubt. The life of a ruff was never easy. He would not be the first to have finally had a belly-full of thieving, spying, or killing, to reach the day of wanting to settle into a peaceful life and leave this nonsense behind.

For people like them, however, retirement was rarely an option. Their daily survival did not permit it. Their lives were decided, directed, by need from the moment of their birth…or some later traumatic event, and continued to be manipulated by it until the day they gave up fighting…the day their paths stared back at them and devoured them as they devoured the lives of so many others.

Enola was not in it for the lives she could help. She did not care about the lives she took. No one before Uzzi had offered her so much as a morsel of kindness. Everything she owned, every day she survived, she had stolen for herself, most often at his side. She did not owe anyone anything.

Except for Uzzi.

"Eliminate a pack that's terrorizing the client."

"How many?" Most Cana, in her experience, left Normals alone. If a pack had taken to terrorizing someone, an individual, a family, or a neighborhood, it was best the matter was settled. Enola was not one to solve matters with diplomacy. She did not care what the root of the disagreement was. If the bloodshed paid, that was the path she followed. Most of the time.

The corners of Uzzi's mouth twitched. Her disregard for the lives of the targets was no surprise. Human, anthro, or mutani, it made no difference to Enola. She only drew the line at killing children and abandoning them to uncertain survival the way she had been abandoned. More than one orphan had been placed into the system by her anonymous tips. She might feel no remorse or guilt for killing their parents, but she would never leave a child to endure the sort of upbringing she had been forced to eke out. Not if she could help it.

"Don't know. When I was there before, only five or six. Am told the pack's bigger now."

"Hence the squad." Uzzi preferred small teams, solo jobs, or hit-and-run pairings with her as his primary partner. "Dink should be here with the gear within the hour. Where we headin'?"

"Cross the Wilds."

For the first time in the conversation, Enola frowned. Voice rough and low, she hissed, "You know I don't…"

"Quickest way." He wrapped an arm around her shoulders, one of the rare forms of physical contact she accepted from anyone, outside of combat, and one of the few he ever offered. "Dink and I'll have your back like always. Cross, in and out, and it's done."

Her expression barely changed, but the lines at the corners of her eyes creased more.

"If it'll make you feel better, I'll get you something to make the crossing easier…stretch one and paint it red…"

"Not hopping up just to cross," Enola grunted. "Slip me a bull tea and I'll have your balls in a crusher."

While having nothing against the use of mind and mood-altering substances for recreation, doing it on the job meant lowered reaction times and almost certain death when it came to a fight. She might not trust the Wilds, but she trusted the crew, and the threats out in the unknown, even less. "We do this, you owe me."

Uzzi smirked and dropped his arm as she pulled free. "Don't I always?"

Enola muttered beneath her breath and pointed to the far side of the bramble field where they were gathered. A figure in dark camo, his jacket hood pulled low, a black scarf pulled up to mask his face so only his eyes were visible, crossed the perimeter with a black and brown dog and its wagon clattering behind him. Dink's arrival made for an appreciated distraction from her anxiety.

No amount of fear was going to prevent her from doing a job. It never had before.

❧*❧

The day's light had warmed the clouds for a couple of hours before Jia and the others, having skirted Protector patrols and a funeral procession heading north towards the Plant with clanging metal bells and metal pot drums, reached the bunker safehouse at the outskirts of LaGuardia. Kato remembered this place, remembered the skeletal carcasses of abandoned vehicles blocking the street, remembered the maze of collapsed walls Jia had brought him to before.

The urine markers of Cana claim were fainter, as no one from the Pack had been here to renew them. Stale markers and the crisscrossing scents of others, anthro and not, meant anyone could be here. With the mission at stake and a need for a safe, familiar place to regroup, Jia nodded at Deuce, still in Cana form as he had been the entire way across the Wilds. Running ahead and circling from left to right on the lookout for danger, it primed him to be the one to investigate the security of potential shelter while the rest huddled impatiently beneath a precarious aluminum awning that squeaked and shuddered in the early day breeze.

Trusting Deuce's instincts and skills, Jia turned her eyes and senses back along the path they had come, seeking something in the mist that should not be there.

"He's been with us since we left Queens."

QiangXu's voice was soft, his eyes on the two younger men who had found opposing vantage points upon which they could crouch and stand watch over him and Jia. The Ursa had spoken little during the crossing, his overall discomfort in the company of others a product of both his personality, his genetic nature, and events in his life since his days at the Fortress he chose not to talk about.

Jia was marginally surprised he spoke to her.

"I know."

Her admission made her anxious, made her regret she had not acted sooner, and she had to agree with him when he added, "Should have sent him back."

The wind had been in their faces, blowing the boy's scent away from them for much of their journey. Secure in the embrace of the Wilds, Jia's focus had been on what lay ahead, the dangers, their primary goal, people she might soon see. Moving in front of them, it seemed Deuce had not noticed their tail either. During their brief stop to eat, drink, and rest their relentless pace, the one behind had sense enough to remain far enough away to mask his presence. The shifting of the wind as the morning began to warm and the Wilds gave way to decaying urban sprawl, however, and his inexperienced steps, had eventually announced his proximity.

QiangXu might have noticed him sooner, but he had not said so.

Perhaps he had presumed Jia was aware of him too.

By then, it was too late to order him home, to force him to go back alone. Seeing herself in the boy, Jia suspected Eddie would not obey her even if she did demand he go back. He would probably have loitered in the background, alone, where he could be picked off by predators and the dangers of the unfamiliar borough.

There was no one she felt she could spare to take him back.

Hopefully, someone in the Pack had noticed his absence and would follow to reclaim him and accompany him back to the library. If she lingered long enough in the bunker, one of them would find her, find Eddie, and return him to his mother.

"Think he'd listen?"

Despite her chuckle, QiangXu scowled. "How long'll you wait?"

"Until you're back, one of us will stay." She needed to reach out to Vance, wait for his arrival, seek supplies they had not been able to collect at the library. She did not think either Kato or Deuce would want her to travel through the borough alone, but someone needed to remain at the bunker, form the linchpin of their group, relay messages, and keep the unit intact until they were ready to move west. "How long do you need?"

"If she's where I last saw her…a day. Maybe two. If she isn't…" He shrugged and pulled his pack from his shoulder. "I should leave this with you."

"Four days. If you need more time…"

"I'll send word. I'll stop at the Protectorate, leave your message. If you haven't heard from me in four…"

Jia nodded at his grim tone. If no word was received within four days, something would have gone wrong for the Ursa. She did not know the doctor he was looking for, or his connection to her, but by his solitary nature, the ongoing threat of HOPE, and the increased movement of LaGuardia Guards and Protectors as they continued to hunt for a killer, there were dangers enough to detain him. She did not want to leave him behind, felt they needed his knowledge, but they both understood their priorities. "You'll catch up to us when you can. And if you can't…"

"I'll go back."

To the library. To the Pack.

She nodded. "Good luck."

"You too."

He hesitated at the edge of the street, glanced in Kato's hidden direction, in the direction of the boy whose presence here was a threat to all of them, and sauntered away as if he was any other borough man about his daily business. No one would know him. His face, his presence, meant nothing to anyone. Laedan guards were not likely to recognize a lowly scientist after so many years away from the Fortress, and he was not likely to cross paths with Lowell. Out of every member of their group, QiangXu was the most likely to move about anonymously. His glances towards those two individuals, however, were warnings Jia understood she should heed.

"Kato?"

The Fela leaped from his perch to stand beside her.

"Can you find him? Bring him to me?"

Thinking at first she meant the Ursa who had left, he frowned, nostrils flared, to test the air from the direction she was looking. His hope that she wanted him beside her, now that she was alone, fizzled like embers in the fog.

Reading his disquiet and disappointment, Jia threaded her hand through his and squeezed it apologetically. "You know he's there," she murmured.

He nodded.

"He'll listen to you. I don't think he'll run. He looks up to you…"

"He shouldn't."

"No reason he should know that." She did not know why Kato felt that way when she considered him to be trustworthy, but this was not the time or place to debate it.

He huffed and released her hand as Deuce's silhouette appeared in an upper-floor window of the building across from them. The former omega yipped once.

The bunker was clear.

"Bring him in, please. We'll decide what to do."

Kato reluctantly nodded and slid into the shadows to track the boy to where he had taken shelter further back along the street. Jia nodded to Wist as he left his vantage point to join her and together they crossed the soon-to-be waking street.

*

"Did you put him up to this?"

It was an irrational notion but nothing in Nik's life seemed rational anymore. The last conversation he had shared with his father had left a more unsettled swirl of bile and emotion in his belly. The nagging was stoked into a fire when he saw the man at the Fortress door, forehead pressed to that of the only other family they shared. It was a gesture followed by a kiss to that same place, perhaps familial but more affectionate and tender than Nik felt it should be. It might have been an innocent expression of compassion, such as one might share with a child, but it was followed by her long gaze following him into the courtyard. Lowell did not look back at her to see it.

There was no guilty start, no expression of surprise, and so innocent was what Nik chose to believe the kiss had been. That choice did not soften his clipped words or tone, however, and refused to dull the suspicious fire gnawing in his gut.

"There's no talking your father into anything," Oasis murmured with enough dismissive candor to make Nik frown.

"I use to think so…until Thomas came." Quentin had managed to maneuver Lowell into several questionable choices, many of which Nik believed had yet to be revealed. Once Roland had shouldered the power of talking reason into Lowell, had been the one to counter his sometimes erratic, grand intentions and make him see reason, but those more levelheaded days were gone. If anyone could manipulate the Laedan, a beautiful woman, wronged by an absent, violent husband capable of untold gruesome horrors stood a better chance of doing so than anyone else Nik could think of.

"I'm not Thomas."

"No…you're not."

When he did not speak for several tense moments, the pair watching through the mottled glass as two large dogs on thick chains pulled Captain Ortega across the courtyard, Oasis took a breath and said, "LaGuardia needs to be safe. There's been too much death. We need leadership, not…"

The sentence was left hanging, incomplete, words that neither supported Nik's suspicions that Oasis had been the one to prompt

Lowell to seek Fort Hamilton on his own nor indicated she had not. Without the Laedan in LaGuardia, both she and the borough were vulnerable to whatever Donn planned. So long as no public decree was made against his brother, no demand issued for his arrest, Donn was free to come and go from the Fortress as he pleased unless Ortega had set orders against it.

Lowell should be here. To protect her. To protect them all.

It made little sense, now that Nik thought about it, for Oasis to prompt Lowell to leave on this fool's errand.

Perhaps it was the ghosts of his past after all.

"Has he said anything to you?"

She shook her head. The words shared in private were not the sort she wanted to share with her brother-in-law. She was relieved Nik did not press her.

"Have you tried to talk him out of going?"

"He doesn't listen to me." He never had. Nik did not expect his father to start now.

"Maybe if we approach him together? Maybe a united front would work?"

The Fortress gates opened. The dogs were released from their restraints. The gates closed.

Nik frowned but agreed. "Together." The two of them, along with Torben, Captain Ortega, and Chief Ernest, might be able to prevent the Laedan's act of madness before anyone else died. "I'll see what I can do…but I can't promise anything."

"I'll try to talk to him again."

Something shifted in her eyes; the movement of her feet, the twitching of her hand as she tucked her hair behind her ear, made Nik believe her efforts would be the foreshadowing of disaster although he could think of no logical reason she might want Lowell to pursue the myth of Fort Hamilton.

Not even if she believed it was real, the rumors true.

If Lowell left the Fortress, nothing would likely protect them from Donnovan. Nothing would save LaGuardia from itself.

❧*❧

Pain said nothing and remained motionless as Liam circled taking a precautionary scenting that revealed no evidence of foul play. There was no trace of Eddie's scent on the stoic omega, no hint of recent bathing, and his submissive posture expressed no attempt to defend himself against the wary, angry glances Candace hurled as Xan held her back. The only traces of Eddie to be found in the surrounding buildings were days old, accompanied by the scents of his brothers, of Wist and Reif and other children, during the explorations they had taken to those places.

His trail had started towards the Zone but veered south, traveling along the wide, fast-moving creek separating the College territory from the Wilds where it had doubled back upon itself and been lost.

No one had yet crossed the creek to learn if he had risked going into the Wilds alone or had been taken there against his will.

If anyone had harmed the boy, it had occurred beyond the College boundaries. As those scouting the borders had not yet returned, their hunt for trespassers or evidence of Eddie's passing being as thorough it could be, Candace was not the only one refusing to offer the belligerent, glowering omega forgiveness for a crime he may not have committed.

Liam finally stopped in front of Pain and stood eye to eye, tempted to make the half-shift in reaction to the captive's agitation. They were of similar height, but aged experience and broad-shouldered health, despite his healing injuries, made Pain a likely winner against the thinner, weaker, less experienced acting alpha. Both men knew it, though neither expressed that knowledge in posture or expression.

Restrained by the men who held his arms, making a seemingly sincere effort to remain compliant, Pain was no threat. If Liam had been in his shoes, wrongly accused of a crime more severe than attempts to unseat an alpha, Liam would have likewise been as angry and stoically defiant.

He would also have been submissive and obeyed the rule of the one in charge, regardless of that anger.

❧231❧

He smelled no dishonesty, only anger, fear, and disbelief.

How often had Deuce been likewise accused of, and punished for, a multitude of pack crimes, ranging from the childish pranks of pups who blamed the outsider for the theft of food and supplies and damage caused to pack property? How often had his eventual innocence been passed over and shrugged off without apology?

It was a wonder Deuce was not hostile to all of them.

Liam did not think Jia would want that life for Pain.

He could not blame Pain for his feelings.

"We'll hold you til we find him…but you won't be punished without proof," he murmured, the only assurance he could give though not enough, he could tell, to appease those who felt the need for the spilling of blood. To the others, he said, "Keep looking."

The day was still early. Eddie might still turn up, having wandered too far and being unaware of the trouble he was causing. There was still time to learn the truth.

❧*❧

"Was told I'd find you here."

QiangXu casually studied the scruffy, shirtless man rubbing his temples as he opened the door. Neither were tall men, neither bore a fighting build, and both bore traces of injuries that gave testament to the years of hardship the borough had heaped upon them. It was evidence QiangXu had seen before when the mage had been at the College, but he had not paid particular attention to the details.

He was not sure why he noticed them now.

He had been surprised the unfamiliar Protector he had met earlier on the steps of the Protectorate had directed him here. He was a stranger, after all, someone who might or might not have sinister motives. The mage seemed unsurprised to see him despite the unsettled look creasing his face as he ushered the Ursa into the flat.

It was a look QiangXu did not understand but it was enough to solidify his hunch that the mage expected his arrival at the Protectorate, expected to be found here.

"Already?" If the Ursa was here, it was because Jia was close. Ongoing shadowy premonitions had prompted him to leave word with Pubby for the messenger who would come. It also compelled Vance to seek her out, to travel back to the Pack, fueling the longing to see her he argued was only to make certain she was safe. The likelihood of an impending search for Fort Hamilton meant he would see her again. He had known this moment would come.

He had not expected it to come so soon.

Eyes scanning the sparse, drab flat without knowing what he expected to see, QiangXu nodded. "Pack's in good hands; it was decided that staying ahead of Laedan Hallister is in everyone's best interest. Do this sooner rather than later."

Vance snorted. It was no longer simply staying ahead of Hallister. If his premonitions, if the clues Quentin had dropped were correct, there were also at least one Channon and LaGuardia's former adjunct to contend with.

The likelihood that HOPE was in the mix could not be dismissed.

Snatching a long-sleeved gray sweater from the back of the sofa, an article that smelled relatively clean to the Ursa's sensitive nose, Vance asked, "Where is she?" His movements nursed his injured shoulder, stretching the fresh bandages, and his grip on the fabric of the shirt was cautious as he favored his wrapped hand, but he moved like a man impervious to pain, a man used to pushing through it.

QiangXu nodded, satisfied. "Near the Wilds; family safe house." He offered his hand. With the haphazard existence of street names and sporadic recognizable landmarks among the host of decaying structures that looked more and more alike, it was easier to let the mage see his destination and the path to it rather than to try to provide directions.

"Not coming?" The assumption behind the question was confirmed in the clasping of hands Vance reluctantly accepted, a flurry of images and impressions passing from the uncomfortable Ursa into the mage in that touch.

The sizzle of expediency in the mage's voice made QiangXu scowl and reconsider his path as he pulled back his hand, flexing it as though it would erase the casual contact but refraining from wiping it on his jacket in distaste as so many people would have done. It seemed the mage knew something connected to details the Ursa's touch had revealed, a dangerous sort of secret driving Vance to action as he laced his worn boots.

Danger or not, QiangXu had his own mission. Vance would see to his path and QiangXu would tend to his. "We need a medic."

The other thoughts behind his words remained unspoken.

"Yeah…we might." Vance shook his head at the other man's concerned expression. "Don't know yet, just…find her…and hurry…"

None of the Ursa Vance had known were prone to hurried actions. They were more prone to meticulous, well-considered choices. When the need for it arose, however, they had never failed to surprise him. The ones to surprise him most, and rarely in good ways, were the men and women who called themselves 'Normals'. Everyone else was occupied with the struggle to survive.

He took QiangXu at his word when the Ursa nodded and grunted, "I will," before leaving Vance to finish dressing with the dream horrors pushing through his head that had forced him awake not long before.

Chapter 18

"I'm not going back!" Eddie barely refrained from stomping his foot, knowing the gesture would make him look like the petulant child he was trying not to be. "I'm fast too," he pointed at Wist as the example supporting his argument. "I'm old enough…"

"You're a cub." Kato had found the young Fela crouched in the branches of a wind-bullied tree, unaware of his elder's presence until the panther caught him from the back and knocked him to the ground.

"I am not!" Stung by the words, Eddie looked at Jia with pleading eyes. Not so long ago, she had been the one to treat him like an adult, or a budding one. Though she had not countered his mother's insistence on his remaining with the Pack, he believed the alpha had more faith in him than anyone else did. "You don't know me!"

A whistle from above, where Deuce kept watch from the jagged-edged opening that had once contained a glass window, followed by the crunch of footsteps that made no effort to mask themselves, interrupted both Jia's reply and Kato's intended argument meant to put the boy in his place. Their measure and the accompanying scent aborted the debate and Jia turned to greet the shadow that ducked beneath a splintered beam to enter the decay in which the group had found sanctuary.

"Didn't take long," snorted Kato.

"Know the area," Vance countered, assessing those he could see. It had been less than a week since he had seen Jia but the shortness of time did nothing to undercut his concern until he saw her. Healthy, robust…as striking as he had thought her at their first meeting. He hoped part of his visual inspection did not show on his face. "You can't stay here."

"Can't?" Deuce bristled and scrambled from the ledge to find a more advantageous lookout point, in case the mage had been followed.

"There's something…I've been seeing the library and thought you were…but you look…I think it's something else…"

Wist wiggled his way into the center of the group, his eyes wide and worried. "What sort of something? Is the Pack in danger?"

"Maybe." It was difficult enough to explain his premonitions to himself. Voicing them to others who might think him mad was an ongoing challenge. "Things have happened here, in LaGuardia…"

"What things?" Assuming he meant bad things, Jia sat on a length of a metal beam her father and other Pack elders had long ago dragged out of the reach of rain or cascading water to a dryer spot where it could be used as a bench, a table, or a place to sleep.

Reluctant to share the more sickening details, Vance shook his head. "Something's coming…hunting…"

HOPE.

It had to be. It had to be HOPE who had chased them out of Kennedy. It had to be HOPE who had followed the wagon north, exposing the den. No one else would presume to hunt a pack outside of the boroughs. No one else would know they were there except, perhaps, another pack.

"Let me go back to warn them," pleaded Wist.

"We don't…" began Jia, waiting for Vance to share more detail.

"Gonna start doubting him now?" Kato's scathing tone matched the narrowed gaze he leveled at the mage. He might not like Vance for the attention he stole from Jia, but the tracker had not been wrong in his guidance thus far. He had protected her, and Vanya, more than once. If Vanya was in danger, the mage's warning mattered.

Jia growled at the interruption. "I want to hear what he…"

"If there's trouble, each second we wait is lost," Wist countered. The type of danger, the details, mattered less to him than action. "Three days. I can make it there and back before you move out."

Hoping to subvert the argument, Vance started again. "I'm not sure of the nature or…"

"Doesn't matter. Kid's right. Warning's a warning."

This time when Jia growled, rising from the metal beam bench to glower and snarl in Kato's face, he fell silent. Wist likewise stilled after taking a jerking step away from the perturbed alpha.

Full picture or not, Jia concurred with their advisements. The Flushing Pack was larger, stronger than at any other time in her life, and they had the beginnings of a budding alliance with the Zone. But many were weak, injured, and unwell. They had barely settled into this new territory, their new home, and lacked enough prepared fortifications to withstand many external threats. She wanted to hear what else Vance had to say, but she was confident the threat was significant if it warranted his warning and fear for her safety.

"We should go back."

She raised her head to meet Deuce's gaze. To go back was to abandon Fort Hamilton and its contents to Laedan Hallister or someone else. Her only option was to trust Liam and the Pack to be resourceful enough to stay safe.

But only if they knew of the threat in time to act.

The strained sound beside her, as Vance held his breath, reminded her he had not yet been allowed to speak, reminded her he was an outsider to pack dynamics and might interpret the mood in the room as a hostile one despite her intent.

"HOPE?" she asked, refusing hasty action in favor of details.

Vance swallowed hard and shook his head. "Don't know…don't think so…it's a face…a voice…a smell."

"Voice?"

"Smell?" Kato asked simultaneously.

"Sweat…smoke…fear…"

"That's more than one…"

The mage ignored the Fela's sarcasm by adding, "Your sister's name."

"Then Vanya's in…?" began Wist.

"She's safe…as far as I can…"

Kato growled, "You don't know that."

The two men locked agitated gazes. "Know?" Vance countered, accustomed to being doubted, questioned, even ridiculed, but he was not in the mood to tolerate it when he was trying to help people he was beginning to view as family. He thumped his chest with his injured fist. "I feel it. Instinct. I trust what I feel…"

"Instinct isn't everything…"

"Isn't it?"

Clutching Kato's hand to still him, Jia murmured, "They'll protect her. Liam will…"

"He can't even protect himself!"

"The Pack then. Wist, take Eddie and…"

Despite her belief in Liam, in his wisdom and intelligence and cunning, she too was worried about his physical capacity to protect anyone if it came to a fight. Kato's grip tightened around her hand as tension raced up his arm, across his shoulders, into the other and back, the sort of physical response often the precursor to a shift, as Eddie whined, "But I want to help…"

Cutting him off, her gaze still locked with Kato's Jia added, "Go to her."

If Kato went, Eddie would be more inclined to go. She looked back and forth from him, to Deuce, and to Vance, with a barely perceptible nod to each. It would put them two men down, but Jia was confident she could do what needed to be done without them. "We can do this. Go to her."

She winced at the tightening of the hand in hers when she turned her eyes back to Kato and watched his thoughts race behind his eyes.

Vanya had the whole of the Flushing-Queens Pack to protect her. There was no reason to think any HOPE unit sent would be larger than the combined resources of the Pack and the Zone. Vanya would listen to Reif, to the Pack elders, when they directed her to safety…so long as Kato was not there, fighting for her, in the line of fire, where she could see him in danger.

Jia, on the other hand, faced the potential of a Hallister squad, whatever that looked like, with only a handful of people at her side, one of whom was twice injured and had Protectorate allegiances Kato did not fully trust. He barely knew the Ursa, did not know the medic being recruited, leaving only Deuce as a primary, but only marginally more trusted, source of protection.

That was not good enough for Kato.

He swallowed, let go of her hand, and instead gripped Eddie's shoulders, staring into his face with an intensity of command that made the boy shiver. "The two of you need to go back…to be sure your mother, Vanya, Reif, and the others are safe," he growled with gravel in his voice.

"And your brothers," began Wist to Eddie, bristling at Reif's name, having already accepted he would be the one to issue the warning and thinking he needed to further convince Eddie to join him.

"They need to be safe. I'm trusting you both." Jia's voice dropped into the low alpha command tone her father had often used, an instinctive reliance on command that brought a shadow over both young men's faces. Neither had known Roland, but they recognized the tone. Eddie cowered closer to Wist as if the other young man would shield him from both Jia and Kato, but he nervously nodded.

Wist's response was to bow his head, as Deuce did on his perch. Kato had made his choice. The alpha had spoken.

"Three days," she warned, "and you will stay there with the Pack." She stared sharply at Eddie, her gaze lingering until she was certain her point was understood. "And you will too…if they need your help to secure the den."

Wist opened his mouth to retort without lifting his head, but instead, he squared his shoulders and nodded. The Pack, the pups, his family, Reif…if the Pack would benefit by his remaining to fight, if HOPE was coming for them, he was going to obey the alpha and keep the Pack together.

Once satisfied with their responses, Jia nodded, giving them the command to go. As Wist scooped up his pack, Deuce scanned up and down the street, sniffing the air, looking for danger. The pair of young men looked as well, and seeing no one near who might notice their movement, they snuck into the street and ran to the east.

Holding her breath, forcing herself to be calm, Jia listened to the retreating steps until she could no longer hear them. She hoped she was doing the right thing by not taking the message herself or abandoning the mission in favor of the Pack. In three days, she could have made the run there and back.

She would be tempted to stay with the Pack, however, and it was three days she could not afford to wait for either outcome. If Vance's premonition turned out to be no more than a stray pack seeking dominance or a merc hoping for anthro pelts to adorn his belt, she would lose precious time in thwarting Hallister's quest for weapons no laedan should have. Going to Fort Hamilton, she believed, was what her father would have expected. The Pack would protect itself.

"You said things have happened?"

Only when the younger men were gone and Jia spoke, breathing easier now that a decision was made, did Vance too feel a small measure of tension bleed away. There was no easy way to answer her question. "Someone's tried to kill Nik a couple of times; Torben's been there each time to protect him, thankfully. And his mother…Yiva's been murdered." There was no need to explain how, or who, no reason for Jia to know those things. Speaking those disgusting truths would bring the rotten egg taste to the back of his throat and make him sick. "Donn's gone missing and Quentin's on the outs. Borough's in an uproar…Protectorate stretched thin…and I know at least two of them…Donn and Quentin…are interested in getting to Hamilton…"

"You think they're making a move…" Weak-kneed, Jia was tempted to sit again, but she locked her legs as she mulled over his words. Nik, the next in age lined up for his father's seat, was an expected, if absurd, target for anyone looking for power. Yiva's death, on the other hand, served no purpose except to influence Lowell, and the realization that the woman she had grown up knowing was dead, buried, and Nik facing this tumult alone, made Jia sad and sick.

Moving ahead of Hallister, staying in the shadows, would be difficult and risky. If she and her group were forced to contend with other factions led by Donn and Quentin, units likely to be better armed and larger than hers, the threat increased.

Hallister getting his hands on a cache of weapons was frightening enough. If Donn or Thomas Quentin reached it first, the future for all anthro became a tenuous, unsettled one.

"From what Nik says, from what I've seen in the last few days, stands to reason."

"We're gonna need more people to go against all of them…more resources…"

Believing he understood the pointed hint Kato was making, Vance grunted and shook his head. "Not going back for the grenades. There isn't time."

"Guns then. Bows. Something."

"Weapons aren't going to get us ahead of them." They had Cana blood on their side, Fela and Ursa too, but that blood was not going to protect them from the weapons the other players might utilize.

"More people then." They knew Hallister was going to send an army. No one knew what resources Donn or Quentin might have, but it was more, Deuce expected, than those standing in this room.

"I'm not risking the Pack," Jia said with a shaking head.

"I could call in a few favors…get us a Protector escort," offered Vance, already running down a list of individuals he thought he could trust with a situation like this.

Deuce snorted. "They're not going to work with us. We don't need to stand out that way." Normals working side by side with known anthro was a rare thing. Any Protectors brought along might not know they were in the company of anthro at the start, but before the trip was over, they certainly would.

The possibility of exposing any of them, outing the Marrocks as Cana, was both ugly and inevitable.

"Wouldn't pick just anyone…might be one or two we can trust…"

"One or two isn't going to be enough," Kato shot back.

Jia sighed. "Better than no backup. Smaller group…we can move faster than an army." She paused, wishing again, as she stared at Deuce as if she could see Roland there, as if she could hear his words and read his thoughts, his decision, that he was there to make this choice for her. The idea that came to her seemed both absurd and risky but also felt to be the right thing to do. Of all of the people in LaGuardia she could reach out to for help, there was only one who made any sense to her.

"I need to see him."

Vance side-eyed her, not sure at first who she meant. Slowly realizing what she intended, he nodded.

Kato knew too and hissed, "If you go back in there…it's suicide."

"I don't need to…" Jia began.

"I'll see what I can do, tell him you want to talk," offered Vance.

"Tell him I want to see him, need his help. Tell him I'm sorry."

Despite his reluctance to set foot in the Fortress, Vance nodded. "Give me time. Stay here, out of sight. I'll be back as soon as I can."

❧*❧

It was not real.

No matter what the mage claimed, what the others believed, what Kato feared, what they said, Eddie heard only excuses. Excuses meant to thrust him back into his mother's over-protective care, push him out of adventure and deny him the chance to prove to himself, to his family, to the Pack and to Reif, the way Wist had been allowed to do, that he could be a strong, productive member of the Pack. Eddie was younger than Reif by a year and a half, younger than Wist by three, with less experience with the complexities of his Fela blood than either of the Cana had with theirs, but he did not think he was weak.

Nor did he think he was stupid.

He could do this. He could help. He could protect his mother and brothers the way she, Helena, and Brie protected him.

It was time for him to be an adult.

Wist's pace back through the trees, once they exchanged the borough streets for the shadowy cover of dripping trees and the familiar scents of the forest, was unrelenting, spurred by the claim of threats he seemed to believe. Hours into the Wilds, hours of fleeing, in Eddie's opinion, in the wrong direction.

If he waited much longer, if he did not act soon, he would not have another chance.

A rocky outcropping, a mound that might have once been manmade but was now overgrown with earth and creeping vines, made an adequate place to pause. He gave up the Fela form assumed to keep up with Wist's earthy brown Cana and collapsed into a breathless heap where the wind at his back could no longer ruffle his cold, damp fur. Naked, his shed clothing stuffed into his pack as Wist's had been at the edge of the Wilds when both had made the change, Eddie pulled his knees to his chest and wrapped his arms around them as if for warmth. He silently observed Wist's continued press east, out of his line of sight, hoping he would not be noticed.

That push stopped as soon as the Cana realized he was alone.

Wist growled and turned back, quickly spotting the huddled boy through the winter-naked boughs of trees and glistening leaves of the underbrush. The wolf reached Eddie's side and butted him with his muzzle, encouraging him to rise, to move, to resume their run.

Eddie stubbornly shook his head. "Not used to this like you," he snapped with an angry whine. "I need a rest."

The wolf pushed his nose into Eddie's arm harder, knocking him into mounded damp leaves and twigs blown here by past winds. He eluded Eddie's slapping hand as the young man scooted away.

"Go on if you're in a hurry!" His shout was fed by forced tears and outrage as he rubbed his bleeding shoulder, cut on something rough and sharp in the debris he had been pushed into. "I'm tired!"

Sitting back on his haunches, the wolf became a man and Wist wiped his hand over his sweat-stung eyes. Eddie was adept enough to have followed from Queen's College to the safehouse without rest, but that crossing had been done hours ago, at a slower pace, without much opportunity to sleep, eat, or drink in between. Wist was tired too.

But he was mature enough to be bound by duty that pushed beyond the boundaries of fatigue. The warning they were compelled to deliver did not cease to be important because they could use a nap and a meal.

"Fifteen minutes," he snapped, his voice compassionate despite his annoyance and the underlying fear. Eddie was a pup. There was no way he was leaving him here to deliver the message on his own. They could wait a few minutes. "I'll see if I can find some water, something to eat…"

He turned.

Eddie's hand, splayed on the ground amidst the debris, balled into a fist. He had to act. He had to do this.

He was not going back.

With a large stone in his clenched hand, he swung and struck Wist across the back of the head. Wist spasmed, jerked forward, and fell face down on the muddy ground.

There was blood. Eddie stared. The rock tumbled from his hand as bile retched into his throat and forced its way onto the earth at his feet. Though Wist did not stir, did not rise, the movement of his ribs indicated breathing, indicated life. That was enough to prompt Eddie to snatch up his pack and break into a run along the path they had taken, back in the direction of LaGuardia without bothering to shift. He could not waste time doing so. He had to get as far from Wist as he could before the other young man woke up.

If he was right, Wist's sense of responsibility and belief in the unspecified, phantom threat would compel him to Queen's College instead of back to pursue him. There was time, still a chance, for Eddie to catch up with the alpha and the rest.

She would surely not send him away again. There were no other babysitters to send to make sure he made it home and stayed there. His resourcefulness would be rewarded and he would prove to everyone he could be valuable too.

◈*◈

The smells in LaGuardia were the same as when he had been here over a decade ago. Stale sweat and human waste, mold, mildew and rot, oil and wood smoke thinned by fog and sea wind. Food cooking, voices rumbling behind closed doors, creaking wheels and a muddled collection of animal sounds. The sporadic buzz from the barely maintained cables that delivered power from the Plant to a few of the borough's buildings burned and buzzed in his head, in his sensitive nose, and in the sinus cavity behind his eyes. People passed on their day's business, glancing at him to determine if he was a threat before they continued on, some with an acknowledging nod, others with the quick, shifting away of their eyes.

A small man, despite the layers of fabric worn to keep out the cold, there was nothing visually threatening about him. So long as he hid his private truth, no one would know who and what he was or have any reason to fear him.

It had been that way most of his life, as it was for most anthro, passing themselves as Normals as they scraped for whatever education was available, as they sought and maintained employment, as they married and raised families in a world that feared them. His had been the advantages of above-average medical and scientific training, learning, and the proximity to the LaGuardia Laedans that had afforded him food on his table, a decent roof over his head, and the opportunity to do good for the residents of the borough. He had enjoyed the benefit of Laedan Marrock's protection as they guarded one another's secrets.

His failure to affect a change in young Nik eventually eroded his welcome in the Fortress despite Marrock's efforts on his behalf. When his son was struck with a seizing sickness, the second seizure taking place in front of Nik and his mother, accompanied by a display of budding Ursa traits impossible to disguise or explain away, his tenure came to an end. Yiva had sworn to protect his secret if he would stay and help her son, but it was not an option. QiangXu refused to risk his family's security to the chance that the Laedan's wife or child would one day slip and reveal him to her husband.

He left his practice, his security, his life in LaGuardia, behind.

He had never come back…not even to see his son put to rest.

There was no reason she would want to see him. Too much time had passed. But he held to his belief in the immutability of truth and loyalty and the hope that protecting his family had earned him a sliver of forgiveness.

The place they had called home, once a place of learning where classrooms had been converted into a compound of small, cramped residences, stood there still. Only the faces within had changed, aging or being replaced by others he did not recognize. The laboratory room remained, filled with the end-of-the-day bustle of scientists and medics, biologists, chemists, and physicists tackling the needs of survival in the changes the Undoing had cast.

He knew few of the faces, but they knew her. She had not been in this place in several years, fleeing a raid, they said, that saw several other residents taken away on charges of dissidence, treason, or the sin of being anthro. He remembered that night of borough-wide raids, a night Laedan Marrock had tried to prevent, a night that, he later lamented to QiangXu when their paths crossed, spelled the start of the deterioration of the partnership between Laedans regardless of the public appearance to the contrary.

Of those arrested, some had gained their freedom but did not return to their former lives. Many were executed or were detained as indefinite prisoners in work camps or cells only Laedan Channon knew about.

Those who had fled and evaded capture never returned home. Trusting the link between their names, he was given directions to where he could look for her next and a chunk of goat cheese to munch on as he continued his trek across the borough.

They were rumors QiangXu followed as the day waned towards the cooling of the evening. Another school. Another clinic. A research facility maintained as much as the world allowed. Finally, with the setting of the sun, a chapel was found on the edge of St. Michael's Fields, a cemetery now used to grow food to feed LaGuardia's population…as so many other plots of empty land had become.

The foot and wagon traffic in the area made the facility a 'hiding in plain sight' location. It was not the sort of place QiangXu would have chosen to hide from the Laedan's forces, from HOPE, but it had become the refuge of many. The world needed to eat, needed men and women with expertise and passion for growing things, needed people who could oversee the grazing of sheep and goats for meat, milk, skin, and wool. Needed people who understood hemp and how and when to harvest it. Such people were generally unmolested because the service they provided was vital to so many.

It might be, he mused as he caught sight of a familiar shadow behind the billowing hemplastic that shielded a broken greenhouse panel, exactly the sort of place Yu would seek if she needed to hide.

"Hello, Yu."

No one questioned the small, non-descript visitor. He seemed neither nervous nor over-confident as he stopped in the greenhouse doorway and stared at the woman in a once-white lab coat turned yellowish gray with age and frequent use. Her black hair, braided in a single queue, hung over the front of her left shoulder; it was shorter than it had been the last morning he had seen her asleep on the pillow beside him. There were noticeable creases at the corners of her eyes and mouth when she looked up from the potted medicinal herbs she was tending and her shoulders seemed stooped, burdened by the life she had been forced to lead. They were not hopelessly stooped, however, as her inner strength bore her up, despite the scars along her left cheek gifted to her by their son during one of his seizures that had grown narrow and silver with age.

Despite those minor imperfections, she was, to QiangXu, the most exquisite woman he had ever had the honor of knowing.

He should not have left her in LaGuardia.

A familiar gesture bid him wait, but instead of doing so in the doorway, impeding the passage of others, QiangXu came to the rack where she worked, picked up the watering can, and began to dribble water onto those small plants that needed it. Careful not to overwater them, satisfied she trusted him to remember such details and be mindful of them, he followed her to the end of the row, watching her nimble fingers plucking offending weeds, pressing additional fertilized soil around stalks requiring it, until there were no more plants in the row to tend. Her lab coat was removed and hung upon a row of worn, rusted hooks along the wall opposite the door before she went outside, nodding at those she passed, bidding a few a pleasant evening, without once addressing the man who dogged her but silently accepting his presence at her back.

A collection of shelters was constructed along the northern edge of the fields, cobbled together materials scavenged from abandoned local buildings and made air and weather-tight with sealants manufactured from the plant waste their food production left behind. Metal and brick stacks ushered the smoke of heating and cooking fires into the sky and from within each home, boisterous, convivial voices followed. Wall to wall as the structures were, limiting the exterior exposure to reduce the heat loss to the outside, there was little privacy for any of them.

It was more privacy, he mused as he ducked through the low doorframe into the room Yu entered, than the Flushing Pack shared. How many of these people were anthro? Mutani? How many knew Yu's identity? How many cared?

"I did not think you had survived the purging." There was a note of relief in the otherwise cool statement made while she set a sloshing kettle onto the flat cooking surface of her stove and stoked the barely glowing embers inside. Frowning without looking at him, she shoved a handful of kindling into it and poked around in the ashy contents until the wood began to burn.

"I haven't been in the borough; I didn't know about it until after."

"You didn't think to find…?"

"Roland said you weren't among the captured…or the dead." Though he had not known if she had been caught in the raids that night, had not heard about them until long after, he had been relieved to hear those assurances from Roland and had chosen to believe them rather than risk both himself and her by drawing attention with a hunt to find her. "You were always the most resourceful…I knew you'd be safe."

Yu snorted but it was not the angry sound QiangXu expected.

They had mutually chosen to part ways long before that night, to protect their child from his father's compromised identity and potential further exposure to the Laedans. Despite his regrets and thoughts to the contrary, he had not technically abandoned her. She had made the choice.

He sat cross-legged before the low table she used as a desk, workbench, and dining space and quietly inspected the single room in which she lived. Her mother's handwoven blanket, its faded red and gold repaired in many places to combat the ravages of time, covered others on the narrow cot. The wide-brimmed leather hat her father had worn throughout his life hung by a dirty braided string from one cot post. A wooden chest that served as clothes storage was pushed beneath the cot and a metal box lined inside with hemplastic held what little food could be stored and protected from the assault of moisture and pests. One shelf attached haphazardly to the wall over the stove supported her meager cooking and eating necessities and there were water buckets on the floor. On the other side sat the small, ornately tooled metal chest he had given her the night they had committed themselves to one another and to the child they had conceived.

Few Ursa gave in to the lure of cohabitation. QiangXu had been surprised when Yu suggested it.

He had been equally dumbfounded when she later announced that, for the sake of their son's safety, they should part.

Doing so had benefited none of them.

She withdrew something from the tooled box without his realizing it; when she brought a cup of tea to the table, she put the cup into one of his hands and the contents of her other hand into his empty one.

The hempleather cord was brittle with age but did not appear worn or used. It was long enough not to require a clasp and from the metal pronged loop hung a single, yellowed bit of bone that brought tears to his eyes as he studied it.

"His first tooth…the only one he lost before…"

Before the tempest of his condition had taken him out of the world much too soon.

"I saved it for you…for the day you…"

He stretched his hand back to her. "You should keep it."

Yu shook her head. "I have my memories. That is enough." Time spent with their child without his father in their lives, time spent in quiet suffering strength as she fought to find a cure that would steady the boy's nerves and heart and give him as much of a normal life as the world permitted.

"xié xié," he murmured, pressing his closed fist to his heart and bowing his head.

Yu bowed her head in response too and set bread and cured meat on the table. With only a single plate, it was used as a platter between them and when she sat facing him with her legs crossed, it was with her own cup of tea.

Fleetingly, QiangXu wondered who else shared tea with her that two cups were required.

Just as fleetingly, he wondered if the second cup had belonged to their son and she had never had the heart to discard it.

"What brings you here?" She broke off a chunk of bread and pushed the plate towards him, encouraging him to share her meal.

"I have come with Marrock's daughter; we are on a mission and require a medic to travel with us."

"How is Jia?"

He was not surprised she remembered the girl. Yu had always been good with names and faces. "The head of the family now, caught in something Roland tried to avoid but could not complete before it took him. Both Laedans Channon and Hallister seek a store of weapons they believe to exist in a place called Fort Hamilton." He paused as Yu frowned before continuing. "Jia intends to keep whatever's there out of their hands; I am helping."

"Isn't her brother…Addison…isn't he a…?"

"He completed his studies." He did not know how much of borough business Yu was aware of since their parting of ways. "His wife is with child, due within days, so he remained with the family for her. We're a small group…"

"A small group against Laedan forces?"

Her skepticism was warranted. "We will move faster without so many…" he began, while simultaneously wondering if perhaps more people with them would be preferable.

"What's your interest in this? What's your part?" After his retreat from LaGuardia, something had drawn him back. They were questions he continued to ask.

"I offered my explosives expertise." That expertise had not been his primary reason for joining, but it gave him a logical purpose for his participation, one he could express. "Laedan Channon, Laedan Hallister…they cannot…after what has been…I owe it to Roland."

Yu's expression grew grave, her eyes narrow and sad. "The rumors are true then?"

"I don't know about rumors…but Roland is dead and I could not save him from that any more than I could save Hie."

Yu covered his hand where it lay on the table, still clenched around the tooth pendant. The news of Roland's death continued to spread like oil fire throughout the borough but the cause, the reason, were speculative rumors few agreed upon. "You could not save Hie. None of us could." If anyone should have had the knowledge to do so, it should have been her…and she had failed.

She doubted he would have been able to save Roland's life either if he had still been in the Fortress when death had come for him.

He stared at her hand on his, the dirt still beneath her nails from her day's work but the collected rainwater was too precious to waste until she cleaned the evening meal dishes. There were no words spoken for several minutes as they ate, their thoughts slogging through the mire of what-could-have-been until the plate between them was empty and their second cups of tea were tepid and bittersweet.

"Where is this fort you're looking for?"

Draining the dregs from his cup, QiangXu shrugged. "I have not seen the map. Only Roland and a few…only Protector Segara has seen it before it was taken and can lead us…"

"Protector?" Yu scowled.

"Mage," he corrected.

"That's no better."

"Jia trusts him. He helped find Roland after he was taken; he's on our side. He believes he can get us there. With him, a couple of pack members, a Fela they took in, some grenades the mage found…I think we can do this…so long as we get there first."

"Destroy it?" Yu leaned back and studied his face. "If it isn't there? If there isn't a threat?"

"All the better. With the way things are…though we're not expecting trouble, it makes sense to bring a medic…and I can't think of anyone better."

"You volunteered me?"

He shook his head, doing his best not to sound desperate for her assistance, her company. "Said I'd ask. Given who we have…anthro and mage…figure we need someone we can trust who's not going to…who can look past those things…"

"But a mage?"

"I trust him, much as I dare." Her trepidation was understandable. Not knowing if his faith in the mage, such as it was, would be enough to sway her, he continued, "You don't have to decide tonight just…think about it, Yu…for me…"

Leaning back as far as her cross-legged position allowed, she studied his neutral yet earnest features in silence, not yet debating his proposal but rather his sincerity and honesty. "When do you need…?"

"Told her I'd be back in three more days." That left a day or two for contemplation, but from her shadowed expression, QiangXu did not think it would be long enough. As well as he believed he knew her, he expected she already had her answer to give.

"If I decide not to go?"

He swallowed the emotion in his throat and shook his head. "You don't owe me. If anything, I owe you. But you've been further west than any of us…and outside of the Marrock boy, I wouldn't trust any doctor as much as I do you." He pushed back from the table, with a nod of gratitude for the meal, and stood up. "We're staying northeast…near the Flushing Wilds, near the Hinton Change. I only ask you to think about it."

Head tilted towards the sound of the whistling wind, Yu stood as well. "You're not going out tonight. Weather's foul and hunters roam these streets at night, mayor's men we think, looking for anthro. Those who're caught don't come back…" The corners of her eyes creased in response to his dour expression. "What do you know?"

He sighed. "HOPE's got people…or we think it's HOPE…taking anthro, mostly Cana, for their blood. They distill it down into a narcotic people call juice…"

"I've heard of it."

"Jia, Segara, a few others…they've seen the place it was done. You're not safe here if they're…" She might not be Cana, but that would not protect her from HOPE.

"Long as we stick to the fields and the perimeter here, they don't bother us…whoever they are. But out there…" She gestured to the streets beyond their agricultural borders. "Stay. Let me think about this until tomorrow evening."

There were no windows, no glimpses to be had of the outside world, but QiangXu looked towards the door as if he could see the threats waiting outside. He had made his argument, felt there was nothing more he could say to persuade her, and knowing her to be a meticulous planner, he had come expecting to wait for her answer.

He had not expected to be asked to remain with her while she pondered his request.

As if reading his perplexed musings, she smiled faintly and said, "If nothing else, I could use your help to prepare a kit from what we have on hand, so you won't be traveling unprepared."

"That would help." There was more to her request than she was saying, but gaining additional supplies was worth lingering for a day. The Flushing Pack possessed few spare medical supplies to send. There was some, Jia had said, in the safehouse, unless the stash had been raided, and she hoped she could gain more from the clinic where Addi had, until recently, plied his skills. Even that, QiangXu feared, might not be enough. A journey into the unknown demanded more. More preparation, more supplies. As much as they could carry.

He nodded and countered her smile with a matching one. "Tomorrow night." Anything Yu and the farmers could provide would be appreciated.

As would spending more time in her company.

Chapter 19

None of them were Wild trackers. Uzzi's most frequent playground was the borough streets. The people most often drawn to him or recruited for one job or another likewise tended to be more familiar with the decay of urban sprawl, with a preference for alleys, the Below, the often empty husks civilization had left behind. An experienced wildsman could travel the width of the Flushing Wilds in less than two days so long as the weather held, but without stars to guide them, with only Dink's large black and brown hound to track the overlapping trails of animals and people, Uzzi had to rely on the memories of previous trips to keep them pointed east.

In the fog and misty drizzle, that was no easy feat.

Nor did Enola's fear of the dangers lurking in the trees make forward progress as swift and steady as he had hoped. But he was not going to do this without her. Unless it was a solo job, she and Dink were the only two he trusted to have his back. The rest were along for the pay. A hit on a Cana pack of indeterminate size and strength demanded trust, people who could aid him in controlling the small army of ruffs pulled together for the job.

Hearing her rapid breathing, noting her jerky movements out of the corner of his eye as she reacted to some noise in the forest to their right, Uzzi chose to camp, to pull her down, to force her to settle and regain her calm.

"We'll rest here."

His memory of previous crossings and the rusted remnants of a huge metal sphere, fallen from its pedestal and partially overgrown with ivy and the forest bush meant they were nearing the border of the

Zone. They needed to turn south, find the lake, and push along the eastern shore before traveling east on the approach to the college's boundaries. There might be shorter, more direct routes, but Uzzi had few doubts those were paths taken by residents on both sides of the Wilds.

Stealth demanded staying out of sight of those people for as long as they could. Stealth demanded he avoid the Zone.

Enola understood the reasons for this path and understood his decision to stop despite the look of annoyance she threw at him. She dropped her pack beside his, hyper-vigilant to their surroundings. With a fallen tree to her right, a mossy mound that might have been a rock or some overgrown, manmade debris behind her, and Uzzi on her left, she made herself as secure as she could in a place of potentially hostile smells and noises.

The crew made camp around them, lighting portable cook stoves or building small fires behind makeshift windbreaks for warmth and the heating of rations they had brought. Any nearby predators already knew they were here. Refusing his followers such small comforts was not worth the dissent it would cause.

"Could do with a good stew right now. Maybe a little lights out and cry," Dink grunted as he dropped beside Uzzi. His dark skin glowed with the sheen of exertion, an ever-present physical characteristic noticeable even when he was relaxing by a hearth fire or asleep, and his natty beard glistened with the moisture accumulating from the air around them. He dabbed his dripping nose on a folded, tattered square of cloth before digging through his pack for a wrapped portion of dried liver he handed to the dog. As the animal sat with the tough morsel between his paws to gnaw at it, Dink pulled a cucumber wound in protective hemp gauze out next.

He always had a cucumber.

Uzzi never asked why.

The precious gift was offered to him as Uzzi wiped the stain of whiskey from his mouth and passed the bottle to Enola, but Uzzi shook his head, declining what he knew Dink was reluctant to share.

Despite the passing of his hands to dry his lips, the bitter taste of the homemade brew persisted.

"Plenty of that when this is done," he muttered. From the smell of it, someone already had onions on hand. If Dink had spared the liver he had given to the dog, his dinner request might have been fulfilled.

"No matter the size of this pack," Dink continued as he chewed the first bite of cucumber, "this is gonna be a tough one. Think we've got enough to do it?"

Uzzi both shrugged and nodded yes at the same time. "Has to be." It was the job and they were the only recruits he was able to secure in the time allotted. There were more than he felt comfortable working with, actually, a conspicuously large crew that would have gained unwanted attention in the borough if they had come together anywhere except the Change. "Should be border sentries, but we won't meet much resistance if we go in after dark and skirt around them. With a little recon, we hit 'em while they're asleep, contained in a single location, and disappear."

An owl screeched in the trees. Enola jerked, dagger in hand, ready to throw the blade at the bird who took to the sky in startled response to her movement. Uzzi's hand on her arm pacified her but Dink's soft chortle made her snarl and lunge her blade in his direction. He leaned to the side, avoiding what could have been a deadly thrust, and offered a friendly grin.

"Owl's on our side," he soothed. "I promise."

Enola's mouth moved, uttering unvoiced curses, and she shoved the blade back into her belt.

"Get some sleep, En. I've got this watch," Uzzi interjected, accustomed to this interplay between them. She trusted his eyes, his ears. She trusted Dink too. Only their watchfulness, and that of the gnawing dog at Dink's side, would permit her to rest.

Even though she lay back, wrapping herself in the tattered military blanket she had unrolled from her pack, the men knew it would be a long time before she slept.

❧*❧

An abnormal pounding at the back of his skull made Wist roll to stare at the boughs above, the action doing little to end the pain but instead, distributing it to other parts of his body, proving he had lain on the wet ground long enough for his muscles to grow stiff with cold.

"What the hell?" he mumbled as his field of vision tapered to his immediate surroundings, bringing with it the realization he was alone. It prompted him to scramble up, hoping to see Eddie nearby, hoping they had not been attacked and the other boy killed.

If anyone wanted to take or kill the boy, or him, they would have taken or killed them both.

There was no sign of struggle, no drag marks or scuffled leaves, no broken branches or torn fabric. If the threat to the Pack had caught up with them, Wist believed he would be dead, not left alone in the Wilds. There was only a dropped rock tinted muddy crimson that matched the area of impact at the back of his skull when his fingers probed there and came away with the stickiness of drying blood.

He had not been unconscious long enough for it to dry. It had been long enough, however, for Eddie to make his escape.

Not taken. Not killed. Possibly run off in fear if they had been ambushed, but the fact that Wist lived suggested no attackers and he did not recollect anyone else in the area before the darkness came.

Wist groaned. He should go after him. He should make sure the bullheaded pup was safe. But there was duty to the Pack to consider too. He suspected Eddie was well on his way back to Jia…and the unspecified threat would be closer to the Pack. They had not crossed paths with anyone or anything that might be a threat and had seen no trace of another living soul beyond the animals of the forest. But the Wilds was a big place, wide enough that avoiding others as they crossed was not out of the ordinary.

A threat might be encroaching from the south, from the lands HOPE controlled. Perhaps it was a threat from the far side of the college that no one would anticipate until it was too late.

Hoping the brash boy would be in safe hands before harm befell him, Wist pushed to his feet, steadied against the trunk of the nearest tree until the world stopped spinning, and ran.

Eddie's fate was in his own hands.

Wist was not going to let Eddie's choices put the Pack at risk.

❧*❧

"News?"

The haggard lines and dark circles of fatigue on Nik's face were enhanced by his body's ongoing battle with cravings he struggled to control, but to Vance, he looked healthier than he had in the whole time he had known the young man. Dressed in the dark gray jacket the Laedans most often wore when conducting business, sporting the epaulets of mayoral office, it suggested Nik had been otherwise engaged upon Vance's arrival. He was alone except for Torben's stalwart presence on the assembly platform behind him and Captain Ortega's square-shouldered stance on the other side, the man likewise looking drawn and weary.

The Ursa nodded his greeting but did not speak. The captain bobbed his head at the mage but likewise remained silent.

"I didn't mean to interrupt," Vance began.

"You're not." A small movement of Nik's trembling hand would have been judged a twitch of withdrawal by anyone else, but Vance interpreted it as an instruction to follow as Nik got to his feet and said, "You can go, Captain…let me know if you hear anything about Donn…if you talk to my father."

"Yes, sirra," Captain Ortega replied with a scrutinizing glance at the mage as he passed. Segara had been summoned days ago, should have arrived sooner; Ortega only forgave him for the delay because he knew the ongoing searches for missing medication and multiple killers had the Protectorate stretched to the breaking point.

They only knew each other in a professional capacity. To Vance's knowledge, Ortega did not hold any prejudice against mages, anthro, or mutani. With Nik serving as the only Channon in his right mind, without a Marrock to support and counterbalance his leadership, a disposition of increased caution was to be expected. Vance's reputation and position in the Protectorate afforded him the license to move about the borough largely unhindered but that did not remove the possibility that he could be a threat.

Ortega chose to trust his reputation, confident that if his trust was misplaced, Moller's presence would be enough to deter the mage from harming the young man holding the reins of borough leadership.

If he was here to seek Nik's would-be assassin, Ortega would leave him to do so.

Only when the door was closed and the three were alone in the room did Vance lower his voice and say, "Ms. Marrock's here."

It felt peculiar to call her that.

"Here?" Nik leaped to his feet. He too had assumed Vance was here to seek an assassin's guilt. This news was unexpected.

"In LaGuardia," Vance corrected. "She wants to see you…but I did not think it wise to bring her to the Fortress."

"Of course not." Despite his father's words, in the man's current scattered frame of mind, Nik could not count on Lowell's benevolence to stand. "You can take me to her?"

Torben caught Nik's shoulder, holding him back. "Not safe for you out there."

Snorting, shrugging away from the hand on his arm, Nik muttered, "Not safe in here either. She needs…"

"Doesn't matter. While I'm…"

"Come with me." Nik's pleading forced Vance's attention to his face. "Did you give her what Roland left? Is that why she's…?"

"Some of it. Someone waylaid me…stole the map…but she has the rest. I told her about your help…that's why she's come. She thinks you can…"

"Just in time too." Rocking on his heels, Nik grunted, "He's determined to go after it…we've tried to dissuade him but…she has to stop my father. She can't let this…"

"Think she has a better chance than you?" Torben muttered.

"Dunno…probably. He hasn't listened to me so far…and I have to do something. He shouldn't go…he can't have whatever's there…" Looking back to the silent mage, he mumbled, "He's going after the Fort, taking some men…but he's in no frame of mind to…"

"So's Laedan Hallister…and Quentin…and if I'm right, your brother too." The threats to the world, to Jia, had grown much broader and more severe.

"Shart." Nik raked both hands through his hair. "Without a map, she'll never…I don't think I could draw one that would do any good." He had only seen it long enough to know what it was. He had never studied the details as he had not wanted to bear the responsibility for speaking careless secrets in his less lucid moments.

That was before. It would be different if he could see the map.

"That's okay," Vance soothed, though his words calmed neither himself nor Nik. "I've seen it. I can get her there, and we've got a plan. But she's gonna need your help…"

"I can't go…LaGuardia needs me." Particularly while Donn was on the loose. Particularly while his father ran amok in search of something that might damn them all.

Knees knocking, Nik frowned and refrained from pacing by the tight grip he maintained on the chair arm. He did not know what assistance he could give but he had to do something. He could not allow one of his few, best allies to face his father, his brother, Hallister, the unknown west, alone. His father might consider Jia to be an ally too, but Nik doubted Donn would. Hallister was an unknown but Quentin, and Donn, were surely threats.

Maybe he could negotiate with Kennedy's Laedan through Oasis. Perhaps he could convince his father to see reason and work with the Marrock who should rule at his side where Roland had been.

Perhaps there were other options he did not yet see. He should talk to Jia, learn her intent, learn what she wanted from him before making rash, hasty decisions. But despite his stubborn insistence on seeing her, Torben was right. Leaving the security of the Fortress without a plan, without protection, was suicide.

"I'll go to her. Long as you're both with me…I think it'll be fine." He looked back and forth between them, expecting a protest.

Vance looked from Nik to Torben and back.

Torben swallowed his sigh and nodded with a grunt.

The mage bobbed his head. "Come. I'll take you to her."

⊱*⊰

Eddie ducked through the efflux of steam and compost smoke churning out of the hemp nursery at LaGuardia's border, taking the same path into the borough they had taken earlier, stopping at the top of the slippery sloped street to scent the air and gauge whether the group had remained where he had last seen them. The easterly wind should have carried their scents to him, despite the safehouse bunker being several blocks ahead, and yet nothing came except the overpowering hothouse smells and the variety of end-of-day sounds and scents created by families gathering for their evening meals as the sun set and the night grew colder. A pair of women in HOPE robes appeared at the edge of his line of sight, prompting him to scramble into the nearest vacant building and up to the rooftop as the duo came up the street, chatting quietly before ducking into the greenhouse.

He did not move, barely breathed, until they emerged later, each with a bundle of unknown content beneath one arm, and turned south where he could no longer watch them. Such transactions were common, he supposed, and he was not curious enough to investigate.

He wanted the security of those he had been forced to leave. He wanted food and drink he did not have. He wanted warmth and shelter.

None of those things, however, would be within reach until he revealed his return. Until now, he had not considered that going back could be met with punishment instead of welcome.

He needed to get out of the damp wind. With the HOPE agents gone, he crept back to the street, striving to appear as no one of importance as he slunk from one shadowed alcove to another. Others, too, shifted from shelter to shelter as the wind permitted, meaning his behavior was not overtly suspicious, and no one noticed when he finally followed someone into a tall building with several lights burning in windows and voices bleeding into the street. He climbed as high as the structure's integrity allowed, followed an unoccupied suite of rooms that had once been someone's home, and took a position at a window where he could watch the adjacent building.

She was still there. Cana and Fela scents pushed through the cracks and penetrations around the grimy window once pierced by an errant bullet but still otherwise intact. So long as she did not move from that place, Eddie did not need to move from this one. He could get the sleep his body craved, as long as his petulant belly allowed it.

❧*❧

"Shouldn't be you."

Aman side-eyed the sulking man beside him as he surveyed the men and women selected to undertake the Laedan's recon quest for Fort Hamilton. He did not believe Norse knew of the missive Aman had been given, the assignment he had been selected to undertake, but the leadership of so many suggested some action of importance. The men were equal in title but Aman was superior in his length of service and personal proximity to Laedan Hallister and this lack of knowledge, this secret kept from him and given to Fenway, was enough to make Norse feel overlooked and underappreciated.

He always did.

Or there could be some other reason behind his cagey, suspicious behavior and the dark eyes that followed Aman's movements as if Norse was looking for something.

The sneering gaze Norse cast over one of the female soldiers as they passed reminded Aman how much of a chauvinist the man could be, on top of his unpredictability, cruelty, and violence.

"Take it up with the Laedan when he's back," Aman grunted, refusing to be baited or to probe Norse's behavior too deeply.

The curve of the other man's lips and the arching of his brow indicated he intended to do that. Aman knew his comment, his tone, were read as apathy for the mission assigned, apathy Norse would attempt to twist in his favor. Despite agreeing this was not a mission for the likes of Norse, Aman would not be offended if another man was chosen to lead the field in his place.

His place had always been at Geary's side.

By the time the Laedan returned from his unexpected trip north, by the time Norse could argue his case for inclusion, Aman and his unit would likely already be gone.

At the end of the row of soldiers, standing at the base of a crumbling concrete and rebar arch that had once been a highway overpass, a man flanked by two Kennedy Guards waited with the confident posture of someone on business who was not intimidated by those he waited to address. Aman scowled, wondering which of them the stranger was here to see.

The closer they drew, the more he determined this was no stranger.

He had not seen the ruff in a long time but knew of him through his reputation and past jobs the Laedan had brought him in to pursue. Aman wished he did not know him. The fellow with the distinctive lavender eyes was nearly as distasteful of an individual to him as Norse was…for many of the same reasons.

"Nepo."

"You remember." Nepo offered his gloved hand and was relieved when the smaller, older man refused to accept the gesture. Norse, however, clasped it firmly, shaking it once in a perfunctory manner as if he likewise knew the man.

Aman assumed he did.

"Here on business?" Norse asked.

"Somewhere we can talk?"

Norse gestured to a side building used as a barracks and training facility for the Laedan's forces. "This way…"

"Both of you."

Aman scowled but nodded. Being included in the ruff's business, as distasteful as it might be, meant there would be fewer shady secrets woven behind his back between the ruff and Norse. He was the one to lead the way into the barrack house. The soldiers were left standing in the light drizzling rain blown in from the southern sea. They would remain there until he dismissed them.

He should have done so, taken the few extra moments to issue final commands but he did not want to miss a single word of Nepo's upcoming conversation.

"Can I trouble you for some tea? Been a long, cold ride…"

Neither captain had seen a horse and wondered where the ruff had stashed it before entering the Kennedy compound. Aman and Norse exchanged a glance, a challenge of command and leadership, until finally Norse growled and stomped off towards the barrack kitchen, losing the right to stay by the product of Aman's seniority.

"If it's business you've got here," Aman motioned to the nearest mess table and followed Nepo to it, "it's customary to correspond through official…"

"Nothing official, just questions I hope you can answer."

"Always questions and answers with you. You'll not get any secrets out of me."

Nepo chortled and nodded at Norse when the man reached the table and thrust one of two steaming cups of tea into the ruff's hands. The other he kept.

Aman refused to scowl or express notice of the affront.

"Thomas Quentin. You know him?"

"Laedan Channon's man?"

"Was," Nepo emphasized without offering details. "Served Hallister for a time, eh?"

"One of many adjuncts, I believe," started Norse.

"A clerk…more of an errand boy…" corrected Aman.

"How'd he end up in Channon's sphere? How'd he graduate from errand boy to a Laedan's right hand?"

"Damned if anyone knows," Norse muttered. His hands wrapped around the cup and he spoke over the lip of it, inhaling the spiced vapors but not drinking.

His lack of doing so made Nepo lower his cup without drinking too.

Norse grinned.

"What do you know about him? His family? Friends? History?"

Norse shrugged. There had never been a reason for him to dig into the background of an insignificant clerk, not even when the news came that the man had found a favorable position in Laedan Channon's cabinet and risen swiftly in rank and prominence.

By that time, he was Channon's problem. Not Hallister's. Not Norse's. He meant nothing to anyone in the southern borough.

"Mother was a clerk with enough pull to get her son into the work," Aman offered, his voice neutral as he picked silently at the threads of Nepo's interest in Quentin. It was a common enough thing, the systematic recruitment of family members of existing Fortress staff. Familial connections bred loyalty as each employee and servant knew a single wrong move could result in the punishment of others within the family. Quentin's employment by Geary was no more, no less, than business as usual in Kennedy Fortress.

Aman was, however, perhaps the only one who knew the reason Quentin had left Kennedy. The clandestine dance between the clerk and the Laedan's daughter had threatened both of their lives.

It had been a wise choice, leaving Kennedy as he had before Geary learned of the relationship.

The choice, years later, for Oasis to marry a Channon to unite the boroughs by blood had come with some suspicion, from Aman at least, about the young woman's desire to be in Quentin's sphere, but she had, when he had last seen her, appeared committed to the marriage and the alliance she had helped initiate. If there were any further connections between her and Quentin, Aman had not been privy to it or seen evidence of it.

Their involvement was a secret Aman would carry to his grave. For her sake if no other.

"Is it true he's Fela?"

Aman's face lost its neutrality and settled into a frown.

Norse, on the other hand, brightened as if he had received some new, deadly toy.

"Never heard it said if he was," the older man admitted with a slight rising shrug of one shoulder. Despite his penchant for easily identifying anthro, he had never paid enough attention to Quentin to judge him. He did not know who Quentin's father had been, had never heard mention of him or seen him within the Fortress. As it was not uncommon for Fortress employees to be married to others outside of the Laedan's direct employment, Quentin's sire could have been anyone. His mother might not have been married.

"No wonder he left. Shartin' hard to keep that sort of thing a secret." Norse gave in and drank his tea at last but the cup held to his lips did not hide his excited grin.

"Is it?" How many clerks and cleaners and cooks might be anthro? There was no easy proof of it most of the time and anthro had learned to be cautious. For those Aman was aware of, he kept their secrets to himself. How long had the rumors of the Marrocks being Cana persisted? Had it been true, regardless of the public proclamations to the contrary? Not that Aman, in his limited direct dealings with any of the Marrocks, had noticed. The Channons, at least, were clean. Their connections in HOPE affairs would have ended years ago otherwise.

Norse snorted. "Is if you want to keep your head."

"Mother alive? Siblings? Any idea where to find his father?"

"She died some years back, before he left Kennedy," Aman replied. "No siblings I know of…don't know his father." There were records for such things, births and paternity and death records meant to serve as a basic population census. But many parents never reported the birth of children, choosing anonymity instead, and it was easy to lie to hide a parent or claim one to be so who was not.

Her service in the Fortress at the time of Quentin's birth meant it was likely a matter of record, but it was a record Aman had never felt curious enough to investigate.

"Does it matter?" asked Norse.

"Who wants to know?" asked Aman.

Nepo shrugged a second time and set the empty cup on the table. "Client privilege. You know how it is."

Norse leaned forward, closing the distance between him and the ruff. "If he's a threat to Laedan Hallister…"

"No reason to think he is," Nepo countered evasively.

"Except you indicated he's lost his position in LaGuardia…"

The shrug that time was barely noticeable and Nepo chose not to confirm or deny anything as he got up from the table. "Thank you for the tea…and the chat."

"Is he coming here?"

Nepo cast a dispassionate glance at Norse but did not reply.

"If he's coming here, Laedan Hallister needs to know…"

"If he's coming here, you'll know soon enough."

Norse continued to hound the ruff out the door as Aman remained seated, staring absently across the dimly lit room. Through Thomas Quentin, Norse had found his purpose, his reason to stay behind, meaning Aman's assignment to find Fort Hamilton and confiscate its contents for the Laedan remained intact.

Danger to the Laedan, Aman suspected, would not come from any weapon in Quentin's hands.

If it came, it would come wound in the strings of perceived betrayal and accusation that Hallister might have sent Quentin to interfere in LaGuardia's politics. Even Aman suspected it, though since he could not prove it, he would never say it. With Geary away, Aman could not discover if the accusation was true. Neither could anyone else.

He did not want to believe it, but he knew Geary well enough to know it could be true. How such an assignment, and the ending of it, coincided with Oasis' marriage, was a thread he would not be able to unravel until his return from Fort Hamilton.

∾*∾

Wist tumbled into the library, panting, tripping over his steps to the surprise and alarm of those gathered around the evening fire. Pups who had been asleep lurched awake, some crying in fright, others rubbing their eyes and looking for the source of commotion that prompted Liam and Maz to their feet. Reif, however, was the first up and the first to reach Wist to hook her arm around him and draw him upright when his strength gave way.

"They're coming," he gasped, his arm tight around her shoulders. "They're coming…"

"Jia?" asked Liam, propping Wist up from the other side and guiding him to the fire. Wist's skin was flushed, damp with the sheen of exertion, and without the fire's warmth, as he stopped running, hypothermia might set in.

Wist shook his head as he gulped for air to further support speech. "The mage…says someone's coming for us…an attack on the college…the Pack…"

The agitated silence that followed, filled with someone offering a blanket, a cup of water, a bowl filled with the remnants of their evening meal, was eventually punctured by Liam voicing the question no one else would. "Who?"

"Dunno. He thinks maybe…HOPE."

"They followed us." Helena relinquished the bowl as soon as Wist was seated cross-legged on the floor.

"We can't hold off HOPE," hissed Xan.

Addi interjected, "Too many of us are too weak to run; we don't have enough wagons…"

"We can't run forever," Ilba groaned.

"Then we fight and die here," countered Uncle with a stoic growl.

"No one's dying." Liam squatted, adjusted the blanket wrapped around Wist's shoulders, and glanced at the still-ajar door.

Trill followed his gaze and got up to close it.

"How much time?"

Wist nodded gratefully at Liam and adjusted his shoulders beneath the blanket's warmth. It would not stay dry as it absorbed the moisture from his skin and clothes, but it made him feel warmer already. "He didn't say. Jia sent me back to warn you…just in case…"

Segara's warning was not overly suspicious, as most in the Pack barely knew the mage. If their alpha thought the warning was worth relaying, it would be foolish not to heed it and take precautions.

Liam's head lifted so his gaze could move between the three who had been the elders of the Queen's College Pack. They knew this territory best, its defensibility, its hiding places. Orliss shook his head in response to the unvoiced question. The campus was too sprawling, with no external walls. With no indication of which direction a threat could be coming from, spreading their numbers across the three undefended borders would leave too few to protect any who remained in the library, to protect the pups, the weak, the injured.

It was not a fight Liam was interested in. Sometimes a fight was necessary, and Jia might have opted for one, but Liam did not make that choice.

He met Ele's eyes last. "The Zone."

Ele nodded in agreement. "If they'll take us in."

"We can't abandon this place," Xan began.

"No one's abandoning anything," Liam retorted. "But the pups…"

Maz nodded too. "HOPE won't enter the Zone." For all of HOPE's interest in ridding the world of mutani and anthro, they had never attempted to subvert or eradicate the two regions where mutani banded together, where many had been banished to end their days. Out of the sight of the general population, with commodities and medical supplies provided in exchange for the food stock the Zones raised and harvested, anyone deemed mutani, and those who wanted to escape Laedan rule or be with their exiled loved ones had found unmolested asylum. Beyond the trade for food, the world ignored them.

Hacha and Zyair's friendly, accommodating gestures to their new neighbors thus far had birthed a mutually satisfactory alliance. If anyone could convince the pair to honor it by protecting the vulnerable members of the Pack, Liam believed Ele could.

"I'll go," he agreed, already on his feet. The hour was late but this matter could not wait for daybreak.

Liam nodded. "Candace, Brie, Trill…see to the pups. We gather everything worth anything and have it ready to move. The rest of us, we set traps and hope…"

"It won't be enough," Xan began again, his belligerence stemming not from anger but from fear.

Its root did not matter to Liam. "You want to complain or you want to do something to make this work? We're bigger now, but not in a state to fight. Doesn't look like we have a choice. Maybe they're not coming now…but eventually…we can't ignore the warning. We need an exit plan, a protective strategy, if we want to stay alive."

"And pray the mage is wrong," Maz added, a soothing hand on Xan's shoulder lingering long enough to hold him back from rash words and offer some of his calm strength.

"Eddie…have you seen Eddie?"

Wist's arrival had interrupted the discussion of what course of action to take to find her missing son, but Candace had not forgotten, even if the instruction to focus on pack security suggested Liam had done so. Her fear he was injured, poached by a passing pack, had metamorphosed into the belief that HOPE was already here and had gotten their hands on the boy, that he could be the reason HOPE had found them and intended to come for them now.

There was a glimmer of optimism, however, that her stubborn Fela son had done what he had been instructed not to do, following the alpha in the quest for adventure. Better disobedience than suffering at the hands of HOPE. Wist had been there. Only Wist could confirm or deny that tenuous possibility.

Wist's shoulders sagged. "I tried. He followed us. She sent him back with me but he…" He rubbed the back of his still throbbing head. "Imagine he's back with her, getting his ass handed to him…"

If he was lucky. If he had not run afoul of the enemy Wist had been sent to announce.

Candace leaped to her feet, Liam's instruction forgotten. "I have to go after him."

"If he's with Jia," Trill soothed, "he's safe. She'll watch out for him. We need you here…"

"He shouldn't be…" Candace protested, jerking away from the other woman's hand.

"No, he shouldn't…but he is," Wist sighed. "They'll protect…"

"What if HOPE's got him…?"

"They don't," Brie murmured, wrapping her arm around her sister's shoulders. "We'd know if they do…so they don't."

There was no way to be certain, but it was the truth they clung to. Helena took Candace's hand. "Help us set the perimeter, then we'll see. I'll help you bring him home." She looked at Liam, seeking permission for an action she was prepared to take alone if he denied Candace the right to retrieve her son.

"We'll help too, Mama," Petr said earnestly. "Neel and me, we'll help with the traps. It'll go faster…then we can bring Eddie home."

The boys were young, but not too young to help defend their new home. Liam reluctantly uttered a relenting sigh and nodded. Candace would act without his consent if he denied her the right to go after her son. Eddie was safe where he was, but might not remain so as Jia ventured into the unknown. It was as imperative to find him as it was to secure the Pack.

"We set the traps, get everyone safe…then you can go for him…but you go alone."

A lone mother Cana had a better chance of moving swiftly across the Wilds. There and back would not take long. The Pack needed Helena here.

"She shouldn't…"

"I'll be alright," Candace whispered, laying her head briefly on Helena's shoulder. "Protect the boys…protect Brie."

Helena growled her frustration but nodded with an affectionate glance at her blonde partner. Brie was no fighter. Protecting her was as important as protecting the boys, protecting the Pack.

Consensus reached, the acting alpha's decisions accepted, the able-bodied dispersed to tend to their assigned responsibilities despite the waning evening hour. Some border traps were already in place. They needed more, ones that could be hastily erected while those doing so kept watch for any threat that might rear its head tonight.

When Wist began to rise, Liam pushed him gently back down. "Stay put. Rest, catch your breath. You've done enough."

"I haven't…"

"If HOPE strikes we'll be ready. We'll need you then."

Reif kissed the top of Wist's head as she got to her feet too. "Rest a bit more, then you can help me here."

Her kiss had the power to cause Wist to sag back onto the floor, reluctantly defeated.

Chapter 20

Nik was not afraid of LaGuardia's desolate streets, not afraid of the dark. He had felt at home there, at peace, regardless of his state of inebriation or clear-headedness. His sense of security had changed now with the attempts made on his life but having Torben and Mage Segara with him as he slipped past Captain Ortega's men made him feel safe enough. He did not hide his departure, but he did not reveal his destination. With the mage as an escort, he could have been going anywhere, to the Protectorate, to a crime scene, on some important business no one except his father would be likely to question. The nature of his covert adventure replaced the fear with a bubble of excitement that continued to expand until they were greeted by a short alarm burst of Cana yips that made him shiver as his escorts came to a halt in the street.

In the open, there were no walls to shield him. There were only the Ursa's heightened senses and the mage's precognizant abilities to keep him safe. Another yipping trill rippled above them, originating high in the shadows of a seemingly abandoned structure; it prompted the grating sliding of a metal panel, a waving hand, and an unfamiliar voice beckoning them inside.

Vance led the way. Torben brought up the rear.

Anxiously, Nik held his breath until, within the seemingly empty room of musty shadows, a familiar figure emerged from a dark alcove and threw her arms around him.

"Niki!"

The Fela who had previously come to the Fortress with her maneuvered the panel back into place.

Until the night of his brother's death, Nik had not known the rumors of Cana Marrocks were true. He had not cared then; he did not care now.

"Thank the fates!" He held her too tight as days of remorse, stress, and fear bled into the tears dripping onto her shoulders, into her hair. Since the moment he had learned of his mother's death he had been forced to appear strong, forced to be something he had never been, forced to bury grief rather than bare any sense of himself to his father and those he was forced to serve and guide.

Torben remained near the door, a sentry against intruders, his face expressionless except for the intense focus of his eyes.

"Vance told me about…" Jia could not say it. Saying it made the tale more real, more horrifying, than the thoughts alone did.

"It was horrible." Nik sobbed and wiped his nose on his sleeve. "I had to put her down when she turned…Fa could not bear to…"

That had been a detail, one of many, Vance had not shared, and it prompted Jia to strengthen her embrace. Though Kato lingered in the space between Torben and Jia, the bristling energy in the air around him suggested not jealousy but rather the likelihood of a leaping attack if Nik made any threatening moves. Vance, trusting it would not happen, elected to give the two as much privacy as the gradually decaying room allowed. He pulled a rusted metal bucket to the entryway where Torben waited and sat upon it as if it was a stool, his face pressed to the narrow gap between panel and wall allowing for the entry of cold, whistling wind and a marginal view of the street.

Without visible moonlight, there was nothing to see except the silhouettes of the buildings across the street against the night-gray sky.

"Blames himself…we all blame ourselves…if we'd only seen the signs…paid more attention…"

"To what?" she whispered.

Nik stepped away and wiped his face again, shaking his head, refusing to speak such ugly truths in the company of so many others. Torben knew. Segara knew. That was enough.

"Liam's safe?"

"We found him and others in a facility used for the extraction of plasma. He's home. He's safe."

"You end it?"

His defiant, desperate question made her sigh. "It was empty except for a handful of test subjects and Liam. We were ambushed and might not have made it clear if not for Geary."

"Think he's involved?"

"It was meant to look like HOPE …but did he know?" She shrugged and glanced at Vance. If the Mage had studied the folder, if he had learned any details from it, he had not yet said. "Given its location, it wouldn't surprise me. He's hiding something…guilty of something…but I don't know if it's that."

"All guilty of something. S'why Fa's determined to do this…to go after the fort. He says…" He looked at the back of Vance's head to indicate who he was referring to, "Is Hallister going too? Donn and Quentin and…?"

"Doubt they're working together," Jia muttered. Before she left the Fortress, before Donn's wedding and Roland's disappearance, the animosity between Quentin and Donnovan had looked obvious. While Donn was now related to Geary via marriage, the long-standing rivalry between Kennedy and LaGuardia made it unlikely Donn would join forces with his father-in-law for such a venture.

As loyal as Donn was to his family name, Jia did not know if he would take action against his father. But Donn knew how to play political games to get what he wanted. Those perceptions could be lies. The one certainty she believed was his desire to be Laedan would prompt him to take any action he deemed necessary to further his chances of reaching his goal.

Even siding with an enemy or against his father.

"Segara says you have a plan?"

"Get there first, destroy it all." It was a barebones plan, but enough of one to get her on her way. Anything more specific would wait until they discovered what was at the other end of the journey.

Nik glanced at the few in the room around him, aware someone else was above, keeping watch. "Just the three of you? And Segara?"

"There's a few others. Smaller we are, the faster we move."

"Without a map?"

Jia's gaze drifted to the back of the mage's head. "Vance is our map…unless you have…"

Nik shook his head, wiping his face one more time now that the tears had stopped falling and his nose seemed to have come back under his control. "Didn't think to copy it…and my hand sucks." He looked at his hand splayed between them, the effects of nerves and fading withdrawal symptoms evident in the tremors that continued to make his fingers shake. "How are you planning to destroy…"

"We've got someone with the resources to help with that."

Vance looked past Nik to Jia. "Know someone who can identify the find, if he will, if you want him; he's pretty handy with that sort of thing too." He had not had the chance to ask if that help would be welcome and had not had the chance to bring it up with Jia before, but he had intended to do so after Nik was safely back at the Fortress. He might as well make the offer now and sort out the details later.

"I'd send men with you if I could." Unlike Donn, Quentin, or his father, Nik had never bothered to curry the sort of favors that would make men beholden to him. He could not draw from LaGuardia's Guards to provide support for a collection of Cana without drawing attention and putting himself, and those same Cana, at risk. Torben, Captain Ortega, and Mage Segara were the only men he could potentially ask. Segara was already going with her. Captain Ortega would either lead the Laedan's team or would be selected to stay and safeguard the Fortress. So long as someone wanted him dead and Torben had a duty to the Plant, Nik intended to keep the sposer close.

"We don't need men," Jia reassured him, masking the shiver of disappointment she felt. They did not need men, but having a few more would have made her feel more secure in her mission now that they had lost Wist's participation. "Is there anything else you can get us? Food? Tools? Medical supplies? We took what we could from home…"

"Weapons?" interrupted Kato, dwelling more on the endgame than on the pitfalls of the journey to get there. Food they could hunt.

Weapons and items to protect them from the weapons of others would be welcome.

Frowning in thought, Nik shrugged. "I'll see what I can do…maybe find another map." The possibility that his father had made a copy, or had found another, had not crossed his mind before. If Lowell had, Nik might be able to access it long enough to fashion a crude copy. "Out of all of them…be careful about Donn…if you see him. Don't trust him. Stay as far away from him as you can."

They had grown up together. Though they had never been close, had never shared anything in common, Jia had never considered Donn a threat. "Think he would…?"

Nik grasped her arms by the elbows and held tight. His eyes were wide and wild, more so than she had seen during any previous paranoid episode. "Never trust him. Ever."

Before she could speak, Vance murmured, "We'll be careful." His assurance, his tone, testified to some unsettling secret they shared that made Jia shiver.

"Got to get back before I'm missed…before everyone thinks I'm out scoring. Promise you'll be careful…and come back." Vance's promise held weight but it was Jia's promise Nik wanted. His brother had hurt every woman in his life. Nik did not want Jia to fall prey to Donnovan as well. "Promise me, and I'll get you what you need…everything I can."

The breath she held hissed out between her teeth. "I promise," Jia whispered with a nod, determined to pry that secret out of Vance later.

Relieved, Nik hugged her as tightly as before, a lingering embrace he was reluctant to end. "Thank you," he murmured against her ear. "That means a lot. If I don't see you before…please be careful. Take care of this if you can, come back…and I'll tell you everything. We'll fix this, you and me. Somehow."

He owed her. A Marrock needed to return to the seat of Laedan and he intended to make it happen, but it would not work if LaGuardia's secrets were withheld from her.

"Promise?" She could not promise a return to LaGuardia, but this promise between them would be a start.

He kissed her temple with a chuckle at the turning of the tables. "Promise. I'll still be clean when you're back. You'll see" Reluctantly he let her go and stepped back to Torben, his arms hanging limp and deflated at his sides. "Give me eighteen hours…less if I can manage it…and I'll send what I can get my hands on. Torby'll help."

Despite not being asked, the Ursa nodded his agreement.

Eighteen hours felt eternal to Jia, but as they were already waiting for QiangXu's return and Vance needed time to put things in order at the Protectorate, it was not much of a delay. She nodded and murmured, "You be careful too, Nik. Stay safe. Hold my chair."

It was not a premeditated request, but it suggested, without having given the matter much thought, she might one day take her father's place in LaGuardia.

That possibility gave Nik something to hang on to.

Kato drew back the panel. Nik nodded at Jia with a sad smile and followed Torben into the street.

Vance went behind. "Back in the morning," he promised. "With or without help."

"You be careful too," she murmured.

He nodded grimly and said, "Always."

Frustrated by her inability to do anything more than hide in the bunker, contemplating paths that might get her to the clinic unrecognized for supplies that might later be revealed to the Laedan, Jia watched him go.

The reverberating shudder of the metal panel returning to its place shivered through the night and the world fell silent.

„*‧

They talked for hours, as evening stretched towards midnight, of the years that had come between them. Of Yu's ongoing efforts to research the plethora of ailments the Undoing had unleashed that continued to multiply year after year. Only a fraction of those who came to her could be helped, but a fraction was better than letting each die without an effort made to save them. One formula after another was reconstructed to replace so many medicinal agents lost to the collapse of the world, and though none of those had saved Hie, Yu refused to give up the quest for something that might have been done if only she had worked harder, longer. If only Hie had lived long enough to see such a cure or stabilizing agent generated.

QiangXu's life had little to tell. His search for those same answers had come in the volumes stashed in the Queen's College library, with any potential details copied and sent to LaGuardia, to Yu, via the only man who continued to connect them until he no longer could.

Roland Marrock.

That those shared morsels of knowledge had come to her via the husband she had sent away drained some of the long-lingering resentment and hurt between them until they bid one another good night. She retreated to her cot to sleep and he, granted a place to spread his sleeping roll by her stove, had done so. After too many hours of tossing and turning, however, he rose and quietly slipped out of the hut to purge his thoughts between the rows of chaff and harvested stalks of grain, hemp, and corn to be mulched for animal fodder, building material, and fuel for fires.

At the eastern side of the compound, at the edge of the growing house, a cenotaph stood testimony to individuals lost in the days of the Undoing, men and women who had given their lives in a marathon effort to allow mankind to hold on to a veneer of dignity and humanity as the old world collapsed. He wrapped his gloved hands around the icy metal bar serving as a barrier between the memorial and humanity, staring at an oil flame kept burning at its base that struggled not to blow out in the dying gasps of an unfruitful snowstorm.

Would he have had the courage to do as these people had done? Strive for peace? Fight for what was right? Give his life for an unattainable ideal?

Was that what he was doing?

"Couldn't sleep?"

He had heard her approach but had been too absorbed in his thoughts to look at her. Yu had never been a threat, not even when they fought bitterly over their son's future and what had been the best for Hie. He had given in to what she wanted, what she believed was right. He had done what she decided was best. Any bitterness she felt over his leaving was hers; any he felt over being sent away, was his for refusing to stay. They both knew it.

It was behind them, forgiven.

"I didn't want to wake you."

"I know." Yu leaned her elbows on the barrier bar, staring at the same flames he watched burn. "What do they think about us…the ancestors?"

"That we continue to make a botch of things," he muttered. "That we haven't learned a damn thing the Undoing should have taught us."

"The Laedans?"

"Some."

Another wind gust tugged at the flames, threatened to extinguish them, but failed. Yu closed her eyes and focused on the wind on her cheeks. "Do you think the weapons are there? At this fort they seek?"

He shrugged, though she did not see it. "Doesn't matter what I think. It's what the Laedans believe. They believe because they want power. If it's true…I fear a second Undoing is inevitable. And if it happens, no one will live to see what becomes of the world after."

"Always inevitable," she sighed, "from the moment people like us came into the world."

"Always been that way…nothing to do with us." People always seemed to find someone, something, to hate. "Doesn't mean we should allow the greedy, the reckless, the insecure, to hasten the collapse."

"No…it doesn't." Yu's hand slid along the bar until her shoulder was pressed to his. He understood her hint as though they had never been separated and wrapped an arm around her. "In the morning, I'll speak to the others, let them know, gather some things, and we'll go."

He did not ask why she had changed her mind, what had prompted her choice. He simply accepted with a nod of relief that it was made. For Hie, for the world that was, for the world to come, they would do this thing together. There was nothing more he could ask for.

☙*☙

"Ever gonna return that?"

Ernest tried to shove the necklace clutched in his hand back into the open desk drawer but the fragile broken chain dangled over the lip and would not allow the drawer to close when he pushed it. The chief grunted with more annoyance than he felt, tucked the chain back into place, and after the drawer was closed, he resumed picking at the bowl of rice pudding perched near his elbow.

"Didn't think you'd be back tonight," he countered, changing the subject. He had already said he would return the necklace to the Channons…as soon as he felt strong enough to let it, let her, go.

"Surprised you're still here." Vance crumpled wearily onto the sofa, the place that seemed more and more of late to belong to him, avoiding touching the worn surface with his hands so as not to witness any further traces of the horrors of Yiva's life. He leaned forward, elbows on his knees, and swallowed the waiting yawn.

"Where else would I be?"

"Home?"

Ernest grunted. "Finding Brac's not gonna happen from there."

"Not gonna happen from here either if you don't get some sleep." At least the chief was consuming something other than whiskey.

"One to talk. Been home yet? Gotten any rest?"

"Before or after we talked?" Ernest's expression, frustrated and weary, was answer enough. "Came to ask a favor."

"Another one?"

Ignoring the strain in the other man's voice, Vance said, "Wanna borrow Pubby for a few days, maybe a few weeks…if he's willing."

Ernest eyed the mage, set the empty bowl aside, and leaned back; the uneven chair wobbled and creaked, mirroring the impressions of age and annoyance the chief's face expressed. "We have a choice?"

"Can do it without him…but if we find what we expect to find, he's one of the few who could tell us what it's worth…advise us what to do with it. If Sal was…" Vance shrugged off the trailing end of his sentence and started again. "Of everyone here, he's the one I trust with this." He could trust Ernest, but the chief's responsibilities to the

Protectorate would never permit him the freedom to leave LaGuardia. "It's risky…and he might not want to take the risk…but before I ask him I wanted to clear it with you."

Pubby had a family. A wife and children. Some risks weren't worth giving that up.

"He won't have a choice if it's an order…" He did not ask who 'we' might be. After the mage's most recent venture, Ernest assumed this one involved the Marrock girl as well.

"Don't need that. Like I said, we could do it without him. Give me the okay and I'll talk to him." That would be enough. Pubby would either agree or he would not.

"Could have talked to him without coming to me."

"I know. But you're the chief."

Ernest nodded. He understood professional courtesy. He understood keeping him informed, understood that to rob the Protectorate of the man most likely to fill the chief's shoes when he finally retired was something that deserved a formal request. Ernest turned the chair towards the shelves, rose enough to pull a ring-bound book from one of them, and turned back to the desk. With no need to write the details down, he found the desired page and turned the book so the mage could read what it said.

Pubby's home address.

Vance ran his finger over the entry of interest but shook his head. "Don't think I should invade his privacy."

"Thought you were in a hurry."

"Not going anywhere tonight. Tomorrow night or the morning after. Depends."

"On?"

"A lot of things."

Noting the shiver that passed through the mage, the uneasy rolling of his eyes and the clenching of his hand on his knees, Ernest held his breath, expecting another vision episode to come over the mage but instead, Vance swallowed and opened his eyes.

"Mind if I crash here? Wait for him to report in?" Few hours remained before the early day shift officers arrived. Pubby would be one of them. As much as Vance expected the sofa to fuel nightmares in a mind predisposed to such things, staying here would save time. It would save him having to face his empty flat and the temptation to seek alcohol he had yet to restock.

If the whiskey lure grew too strong, he knew, from the rattle of the contents when Ernest closed the desk drawer, the chief's stash had been recently refilled.

Scowling at the sofa where he, too, had spent many nights, pondering if he should sleep at his desk for the rest of the night or should trudge home for some sleep in a proper bed for a change, Ernest eventually offered a one-shouldered shrug and got up from his chair.

"Suit yourself."

"Thanks." Vance assumed, as Ernest left the office, that going home was exactly what he had forced the chief to do.

He did not remain awake long enough to learn if it was true.

❧*❧

The wedge of housing tracts known as the Zone was separated from the Queen's College territory by a long stretch of cracked and overgrown freeway and a fence and wall constructed near the end of the Undoing when the first mutani began to appear and fled denser population centers to avoid the prejudice and wrath of the Normals who had spawned them. Some of what had once been homes and businesses had been dismantled and used to create that protective shield and in doing so, a huge swath of agricultural land was cleared, spreading north to the borders of the Kissena Wilds. The north was bordered by old metal train rails and with it, the mutani could move people and material east and west from the edge of the flooded Flushing Creek and the Change to the remains of the Clearview Express in the east. Beyond there was nothing. East, where the Zone gradually expanded as newcomers arrived, and south, territory neither borough had yet claimed. Kennedy had run out of manpower, preferring instead to police their northern edge and tighten their grip on the lands they had already annexed, while LaGuardia turned their expansion to the west, spurred primarily by the Marrock vision of the great nation that had been before.

For now, the Zone was safe, and with the fear many felt about those forced to live in that bit of territory, there was no compulsion to intrude or attempt to drive them away. As long as they continued to trade the excess food they grew, the livestock they raised, with LaGuardia, the Normals let them be.

It was that isolation and the protection of the Zone walls the Flushing Pack chose to rely on. Anthro were welcome there, persecuted as they were on the outside, and Hacha and Zyair were happy to aid in protecting their new allies against the as-yet-unspecified threat.

"Here…this way…"

Hacha held open the gate with a glove-protected hand, a nearby electric hum suggesting a current running through the spiked wire overhead and on each side of them. Ele's petition to the mutani council brought several individuals from behind the safety of the Zone walls to aid in moving what little the Pack owned and those individuals not yet strong enough to make the short trip without aid. Others assisted in the construction of traps and pitfalls around the College boundaries, and a collection of more than a dozen volunteered to stand with the Pack, intending to keep an eye out for HOPE's inevitable incursion and to fight them off if necessary.

The anticipation was that none of this would be needed, that the threat would evaporate and the Pack could return home.

The Pack was nearly moved. The sounds of construction echoed still as trap-building continued.

This broad, single-level structure the Pack had moved in to, with doors that had once retracted with motion sensors in the ground and the edge of the roof but now slid on rollers, had been dubbed Ministry 12 with a hand-painted, white-washed sign on the left doorpost. Small round mirrors inside and out were angled so those in the interior watchman's booth could monitor those who came and went, those who took from the boxes of food and supplies stored here, and those who brought other goods in. Most of what was traded with LaGuardia was housed in heavily protected ministries in the north, where the ox-pulled carts continued to move along the maintained rail system with relative ease.

Loaning the Hallister ox for a provisional trade of shelter after using it to relocate seemed fair.

The off chance that forces from LaGuardia would raid them long ago prompted the choice to distribute and house supplies throughout the Zone, in fortified areas difficult for invasion forces to find or reach.

The Ministry, the council overseeing the sharing of commodities to Zone residents, had learned their lesson the hard way before the walls and gates were completed. They would not make the mistake of keeping their supplies within thieving distance of the Normals again.

The contents of Ministry 12 were pushed to the sides of the single, vast storeroom to make room for their guests. Much of what had been brought here already, along with the pups and the infirm, was gathered around an oil-burning furnace at the center of the room, where its metal stacks directed the combustion fumes and smoke out through the roof.

Zyair pointed, directing Liam with his last armload of books, those the Pack deemed too important to lose and those Roland had left with them for safekeeping and instruction, to where the others gathered. The scar on her shoulder, a HOPE brand gained long ago, was a visible indicator, beneath the sleeveless vest she wore, of her past service in a HOPE work detail. There were other scars up and down her arms, across her neck and face. It was rumored she had escaped the camp while others claimed she had been discarded as no longer useful, left for dead for someone else to find, use, heal, or kill. Beyond her size, and the fact she never spoke, communicating only through hand gestures and a complex series of clicks, grunts, growls, and hissing whines, there was no outward indicator of whether she was mutani or anthro. Whether she had been born without speech, had never learned how to, or had lost the ability at the hands of HOPE, her differences were enough for Normals to shun her. Hacha had found her, nursed her back to health, given her a place.

In the Zone, she was at peace.

"Thank you for this," Liam said as she took the box of books from him and stacked it with the others. He had struggled to carry it this far, refused to give the burden to someone else, yet Zyair made the box look no heavier than a pillow.

"You're welcome, Mr. Bardeau."

"Liam, please."

"Liam," corrected Hacha with a nod. His speech patterns were stilted and slow as if it took time to form the words he wanted to say. His voice was loud, however, deep and commanding, and when he spoke, most other mutani in the room stopped what they were doing to heed him. "We need to have our backs, no? Such as HOPE…they do not belong in this world. We must turn them out, bind their hands, protect the children." Zyair interrupted with a short burst of hand gestures and vocalizations, to which Hacha again nodded. "We go, take our places with those who fight…"

"You don't need to…" Liam began. They had only asked for shelter. Assistance with the traps, with moving, had been welcome too, but they had never asked, or expected, the Zone residents to fight their battles for them, with them.

"Too many are lost. It is necessary. Not your fight alone." Hacha looked Liam over, not with pity or derision but with understanding and sympathy. "You cannot fight. Laedan Marrock cannot fight. We," he gestured to himself and Zyair, "can fight. Do this for him and are happy for it. He was a good man. You rest…and be ready."

Liam nodded once. The walls kept the Zone safe and the presence of so many mutani should keep HOPE out of the Zone.

That did not mean this time it would.

The Zone gates were closed. Her family and pack were either safe behind them or had chosen to remain on the outside to fight for everyone's security.

Candace had not been selected to fight. Nor was she secure with her sons and her sister behind the Zone gates.

He had not voiced his final permission, but she was taking Liam at his word, clinging to his earlier promise, and acting on it.

She would find Eddie and bring him home.

If there was anything left of home, family, and pack to return to.

❧*❧

Arms thrown around the man who entered the lobby as she happened to pass through it with the hopes of watching the rising sun, Oasis murmured, "You did not tell me you were coming," to the one person she had never felt so relieved to see. His arms around her, hugging her the way he had when she had been a frightened little girl afraid of the raging storms that blew in from the sea, grounded her with a sense of relief and security she felt desperately in need of.

He was cold, his coat covered in a thin dusting of snow, his nose and cheeks red from exposure, and his eyes looked weary and creased with the weight of many burdens, but her father had come and that was all she cared about.

For the first time in memory, Aman Fenway was not with him.

"When I heard what happened, when your letter arrived, of course, I had to come." She did not bear the glow of pregnancy, but the chaos of recent weeks had undoubtedly worn on her. It was difficult to glow, he knew, if she endured the same morning sickness he remembered her mother suffering too.

"There is so much to tell you…"

"And I will hear it, but not now." He pulled back to look at her with an affectionate smile and smoothed back her hair from her face with both hands. The shadows of the dim hall dulled the obvious bruising on the side of her face; with his focus on her eyes, he did not notice. "Is Lowell here? I must express my condolences."

Despite the disappointment she had long ago learned to hide, his propensity to see to business and duty first was no surprise. There was a burn of bitterness in her breast, however, that this time he would put business before her, that his coming to LaGuardia might have less to do with her letter than it did with the news of Yiva's death. Lowell was suffering and Geary smelled blood in the water.

She nodded, matching his expression of affection, and walked with him to the stairs with an arm hooked through his.

"How are you? I've heard so many tales and rumors coming out of LaGuardia…"

His concern prompted a faint smile and the well-practiced, reassuring response of "I'm fine," even though she did not feel fine. She wanted him to believe her strong, wanted him not to worry when he had so many other matters to concern him. Despite desperately wanting his advice, the long corridor they traversed at the top of the stairs, leading towards the open conference room door where Lowell had, of late, spent most of his waking hours, was not the best place for a personal conversation.

Both could hear the rambling voice within that room, a steady flow of dialogue making little sense to anyone except Lowell, and Oasis considered whether allowing her father to see LaGuardia's Laedan in such a state was a wise decision.

It was too late, however, for Lowell pulled back the door and stepped into the opening before they reached it. He hesitated at seeing them, and then approached with an outstretched hand, his demeanor shifting quickly from madness to business-like with every step he took as if the distraction of a guest was what he needed to escape the ghosts in his head.

"Geary. How good of you to come. Please, won't you come in? Share a drink? It is too cold out…you should warm yourself."

He had already clasped Geary's hand and was pulling him into the room he had exited, giving his guest no opportunity to refuse. If he noticed Oasis there, he did not acknowledge or look at her.

"You will not leave without…?" Oasis began as her father disappeared into the room, the ghosts of being shut out of the Laedans' world slithering across her face, behind her eyes.

"Of course," he began.

The door closed, cutting off whatever else he meant to say.

Lowell pushed aside the collection of packs, boxes, and leather-bound packets so there was room on the conference table for the pair of glasses and bottle he brought from the liquor tray at the end of the room. "I apologize for the mess," he chuckled.

It was too early to drink, Geary thought as he watched the clattering glasses set down before him. He had not eaten his morning meal yet as he had traveled through the day and night to reach LaGuardia's Fortress as swiftly as possible. Whiskey would warm his blood, however, and diplomacy demanded acceptance, so he nodded at the offer and waited to be served. "You are planning a trip?"

Despite the casual, cordial tone of the question, Lowell read a dark underlying curiosity that made him frown, an expression his downturned face hid from view as he filled the cups. "I…" He used the resealing of the bottle to cover his hesitation. "I need to be away from here for a time. There are too many…"

Geary nodded sympathetically. So the stories were true. "Ghosts. I understand." He too had lost a wife, although his loss had come many years ago and he had moved beyond it as much as any man could. "She was a good woman. I'm sorry for your losses. Have the perpetrators been found? Punished?"

"Not yet." With an unexpected growl and a too-heavy fist slamming into the table, Lowell added, "I will see to his hanging myself when he's found." He had not expected the news of Yiva's death to have passed as far south as Kennedy's Fortress but he was not surprised it had.

Bad news traveled fastest.

"As it should be." Geary took the offered glass and sat in the nearest chair, across the table from where his counterpart sagged onto a backless stool. Lowell's mien was bitter, resentful, and dangerous, undercut by another quality Geary could not classify or explain. He found it uncharacteristically unsettling and so he changed the subject to something not involving Yiva.

He absently gestured to the collection on the table. "Where are you going?"

"I…" Lowell drained his glass and reached for the bottle. "Jonni's sector needs tending; I'm due there."

The words were evasive, the scattered packs and papers excessive for the duty he referred to. Wondering what Lowell had intended to say but left unfinished, Geary nodded. "Business is the best way of getting our minds off of unpleasant things," he agreed.

"Indeed." Sipping from his second glass this time, Lowell stared at Geary for several moments before lowering the glass and clutching it between his hands. "It's good you've come. My staff has brought disturbing news…"

"What sort of news?" Geary's voice was both curious and nonchalant at the same time.

"HOPE has plasm labs in Kennedy…"

Well-schooled in diplomacy, having a lifetime of practice hiding negative emotions, Geary nodded once. "It is so or was." Few knew about the lab's discovery, only the Marrock girl and her companions and a handful of individuals in Geary's employ. Who the traitor could be, who might have leaked the news to LaGuardia's Laedan, would need to be sorted eventually. He did not believe that leak had been Jia, not with the way the relationship between Lowell and Roland had ended and there being a price on her head. There would eventually be an inquest but for now Geary could not spare the manpower.

He hoped the leak had not come from Aman the way Gail feared.

"I recently discovered it myself. I assure you, the facility has been dismantled and related plasm production locations are being sought. I'm scheduled for a summit with Grand Mas Lord and the Council within a fortnight. If they think they can do what they wish in Kennedy or anywhere else outside of their…"

"Of course, they can." They were HOPE. Treaties and territorial covenants aside, members of the Holy Order of the Pristine Elect were prone to believing their affiliation with that body meant they could do anything they wished, wherever and whenever they chose, without consequence. They were assured of HOPE's backing should their work be discovered.

Whether directly commissioned by HOPE's hierarchy or acting on their own on HOPE's behalf, the results would be the same. The blame would be covered over, empty promises made, and the matter swept aside in favor of politics.

Lowell's concern was whether Geary was involved or had known about the lab, the plasm production, before.

"That shart nearly cost me my son. If I learn who did this…if you enabled them…allowed them…"

"I've no desire to poison my own people either," Geary scoffed with a growl. "Using's as much of a problem in Kennedy as here. As you know, I've made it one of my cabinet's primary projects to eradicate the manufacture and distribution of…"

"And how is that working?"

Lowell knew it was difficult to label the manufacture and distribution of addictive substances as unlawful when their use was permitted without consequence. In the grand scheme of daily borough life since the Undoing, such usage, such substances, were less important to address than daily survival was. The Laedans, the boroughs, faced the same challenges. Despite Nik's propensity towards addiction, Lowell had made no serious efforts to counter the manufacture of such substances either, until the one called juice had nearly claimed Nik's life the last time.

Given everything that had occurred in LaGuardia since that day, murders and betrayals, Lowell had not made any effort to accomplish anything beyond bringing two of those closest to him to justice.

Passing the responsibility of combatting plasm to Geary might, he hoped, keep the other man busy and out of his way.

Geary shrugged. "These things take time. Shutting down the lab should have an impact on production, but it will take time to do more." With his drink empty, assessing that both of them needed a distraction from the tension of their dialogue, he stood up from their brief summit and gestured to the items on the table.

"I'll let you return to your preparations. I must speak to my daughter, seek out my son-in-law…" Hiding that he had recently seen Donn in Kennedy seemed prudent, particularly after noting the angry shadow that settled over Lowell's face at Donn's mention. "We shall speak this afternoon, yes?"

Swallowing the thoughts begging to be said, about his son, about Oasis, Lowell swayed as he stood and nodded. "You will join us for dinner." He had not eaten a full meal since losing Yiva but he could put on the semblance of hospitality and entice Geary to remain a little longer. He did not think the other Laedan had traveled here merely for this brief, jabbing, probing exchange. He wanted something.

Lowell intended to learn what over dinner.

"Of course," Geary replied with a bowed head and hand offered across the table. The men stared at each other briefly before the offer was accepted. When the handshake ended, Geary made note of the way Lowell wiped his sweaty palm on the front of his suit jacket.

He could not tell if the gesture was intended to smooth the rumpled fabric, to belatedly dry his hand, or to wipe the physical contact away. But he did know Lowell was anxious, was hiding something. Like Lowell, Geary planned to learn those truths over dinner and not leave LaGuardia until he knew them.

⮞*⮜

Whether the chief had gone home to sleep as Vance prompted, when he eventually opened his eyes, it was to an empty office lit only by the glow of lights in the Protectorate's main room where a multitude of overlapping steps and voices muffled by the closed door announced the shift change hour's arrival. Vance sat slowly, dehydration causing his head to swim, and glanced through the glass. There was no sign of his quarry so he took his time rising, rubbing feeling back into his numb buttocks and pushing his hair out of his face and into some degree of tidiness with his good hand.

His shoulder hurt today. His hand less so. He wondered if the infirmary had anything they could give him to dull the ache, if they would be able to clean the wounds and change his bandages before he went out.

He should make sure it was done. Gods knew when he would have the opportunity to change the dressings once he started west with Jia. He could not afford to lose the use of his arm.

Boisterous calls of greeting announced Pubby's eventual arrival as the whole of the Protectorate welcomed him, another reminder of his popularity and a precursor to the future many believed was before him. It was comforting to see his cheery smile as Vance rapped on the glass to attract the other man's attention. He flipped on the light in the room as he made eye contact with Pubby and got up with a stretch. Pubby came into the office without taking the time to remove his coat or drop his lunch sack on his desk.

"Back from your adventures for a while?" Pubby asked with an offered hand.

Evading the effort to glean details from the other man, Vance accepted the shake, grateful for the barrier Pubby's glove provided. "Heading back out tonight, maybe tomorrow."

"We could use you more 'round here, ya know." He did not doubt the mage's business, wherever it had taken him or would take him next, was important. A mage's skillset meant a lot of solitary work across the borough, work for the Protectorate, for the Laedan, and for private citizens as well. The teasing twist of Pubby's lips suggested the desire to have Vance around for as many personal, friendly reasons as business ones and Vance bobbed his head in acknowledgment of the token of camaraderie.

It reminded him of Sal.

He missed her.

"Been busy. You know how it is."

"Yeah, I do, 'specially with everything going down lately." He did not speak details he knew Vance likely already had. "Where's Chief?"

"Home sleeping…I hope."

"So you've been waiting here for me?"

It was a logical assumption to make since Vance had summoned him into the office, and Vance nodded. "Got a job, if you're interested. Could use your help."

Pubby's eyes lit up as he removed his gloves and stuffed them into his pocket. As one of so many other Protectors in the borough, even though he was considered at the top of his job, he was not often selected for special assignments with the borough's primary tracker-mage.

"Depends," he hedged, despite his visible excitement.

"Already cleared it with Chief…if you're wondering. Got a group going a few days west of here…"

"Beyond the borders?"

Vance nodded. "Heard talk of a cache of weapons and…"

Face brightening more, Pubby interjected, "What sort?"

"Remains to be seen. Don't know if it's there but we need to find it, keep anything we find off the streets. Thought you might want a crack at the stash, identifying what's there, inspecting it, getting anything worthwhile into custody before we destroy the rest."

It was the exact lure Vance had expected would ensnare the other man. "When do we leave? You said today?"

"It'll require discretion," Vance warned. "Keeping our mouths shut and…"

"Understood," Pubby eagerly nodded. "When are we going?"

"Could be gone several days…a week or more…and it's gonna be dangerous if anyone else is out there looking for the same thing…"

About to ask when the mage intended to leave, Pubby's mouth snapped shut and he nodded grimly, understanding the seriousness of the situation, understanding what Vance implied. Duty was duty, and his family knew his life was at risk every time he left the house. In the post-Undoing world, every life was at risk every day, but it was even more dangerous for the men and women who worked to subdue chaos into order.

No matter how soon they were to leave, if he was to be gone for an extended period, Pubby owed it to his wife and children to let them know so they would not worry about an unexpected absence.

He did not want the epilogue of his life to be regret for leaving his family without a warning; he appreciated Vance's reminder of it.

Pubby offered his hand to seal their agreement. "Tell me when…and I'll tell them." He would go home right now if it was necessary.

Vance accepted the handshake with a nod. "Tonight if everything else is in place…else tomorrow morning. We could come by here, give you the day to wrap up business…"

"And give me the details then, right?"

"Much as I can," Vance promised, relieved he did not need to coerce Pubby into helping. He was also relieved to recognize, in that second handshake that there would be no cause for concern when the man learned the other participants in the quest were anthro.

"Fair enough. Let me get the unit set…talk to Lavonia about keeping them in line, talk to the chief about a release from dailies…and I'll meet you back here at the end of the day."

"End of day," Vance agreed. The less scurrying about he had to do to pull their quest together, the better.

He would meet Pubby here and take him to where the others were. It was better he did not bring a host of anthro into the Protectorate.

That would raise too many questions.

Chapter 21

"I hear you're to be a mother."

Oasis' face lost color and she looked away from her father, choosing instead to focus on the preserves she spread on her toast. The meal set on the table was more substantial than usual and she assumed Lowell intended some sort of breakfast summit to take advantage of her father's visit. Lowell did not join them, however, and she had yet to see Nik as the light of the new day brought a glow through the foggy Fortress windows. She was left to dine alone with her father, the same as she had dined with him for most of her life. No matter what else transpired in Kennedy, those morning ritual meals had been the one moment of each day her father had carved out for her. She had always looked forward to breakfast.

Hands quaking, stomach contracting into a knot, she wished she could be anywhere else, that she could eat her breakfast alone.

"I…" She had not sent that news to him, having no desire to involve him in her deception. Few people had heard it. She did not think it was the sort of thing Lowell would have shared. "How…?"

"Donnovan told me." He might not have shared his meeting with Donn with Lowell, but he saw no reason to hide it from his daughter.

Oasis frowned and set the knife on the edge of her plate, careful not to soil the table with the sticky sweetness still on it. "You can't believe everything he…"

"Then you aren't?" He frowned too.

"He's an arrogant, abusive slag…"

"Abusive?" The frown grew deeper.

She turned her face so that he could see the fading bruise left by the blow that had robbed her of some of her hearing she had not yet regained, visible evidence she kept hidden from most others. "He's done worse," she murmured, twirling her hair between her fingers.

"Such things happen between husbands and wives," Geary mumbled around a mouthful of eggs.

Stricken, she stared at him, aghast, though she tried to temper her response. "It isn't just me," she protested. "He may have killed…"

"The responsibilities of mayors, of Laedans, sometimes require unfortunate…"

"This is not unfortunate," she hissed, as annoyed by his dismissive interruptions as she was by his apparent lack of empathy or concern for her wellbeing. "This is cruel and violent sport…"

Geary lowered his fork and stared at her. "You knew his reputation when you agreed to this arrangement…"

"Not like this. I'd heard things but…I was supposed to marry…"

"Plans changed. You could have refused."

"Could I?" They stared at one another but he did not rise to her challenge. "I did this for you…for Kennedy…but it's different now. I want out. I need out…" There was no need to annul the marriage, but there was also little need for her to live here as his wife.

Getting away from Lowell, too, was probably a wise choice.

"Treaties aren't something you can nullify because you're unhappy with…"

"I'm not talking about the treaty…and you do it all the time."

Geary's eyes shifted away from her face. "That's different."

"No, it isn't…"

"I'm Laedan!" he spat as if that made a difference and excused the prerogative of changing his mind on policy and treaty matters when it suited him. "You are my daughter! You will do as I say, as you agreed…"

"He's going to kill me!"

"Nonsense." There was a tense, expectant pause, leaving those words hanging between them, his too-abrupt response a stinging slap, her words a heavy burden he could not believe. Doing such a thing would ensure war between the boroughs. He did not believe Donnovan would be so foolish.

"He wouldn't dare unless you've lied to him or…is that why…?"

"Is that why Mother died?" Oasis challenged bitterly. "You killed her for lying to you?"

Forced up from his chair by memories and secrets hidden from all but one person for most of the years of Oasis' life, Geary struck her across the face with his open hand, directly over the bruise Donn had deposited there.

It was the first time, the only time, he had hit her. Her ear rang. Her eyes teared.

"You will stay and honor your marriage. Honor me. You will do what is necessary for Kennedy…and never defy me again."

"You're no different than he is!"

Geary tried to catch her arm as she lurched away and fled from the room, grateful he did not pursue, grateful she had not said anything more. Whatever Donn had said to her father, whatever agreement the men had struck, Oasis realized for the first time that her father might not be the bastion of support she believed him to be. For all of his professed love, he would sacrifice her for Kennedy, even to the point of letting her die at her husband's hands.

She was, she sobbed with frustration, as much of a prisoner in LaGuardia as Yiva had been, without even that woman for support.

There was no one she could trust but herself. And possibly Lowell.

It was more important than ever that he reach Fort Hamilton before Donn. When he did, with her help, she would see that LaGuardia and Kennedy were united and that her father and husband were no part of it.

The two boroughs would be one, but not as her father imagined.

The vision would be hers and hers alone.

❧*❧

The tense, uneventful hours of night came to an abrupt end when Deuce jumped from the rafters with a hand tight around Eddie's neck, dropping him brusquely at Jia's feet with a shove.

"A present," he snarled, and when Eddie tried to scramble back, to speak in his own defense, Deuce snapped at the boy with half-formed Cana jaws and glowered with the yellow eyes of a partial change. The bravado Eddie intended disappeared as he ducked his head and tried to shield it from potential blows with his arms.

"Where's Wist?"

Eddie's reply was a moan.

Though small of build, Jia towered over him with enough authority that he whimpered when she repeated, "Where is he? Why are you here?"

"Jia," Kato began, hoping to soothe her and intervene on the young Fela's behalf. He was no happier about this turn of events, concerned for Vanya's safety, but scaring the boy was not going to get the answers.

Jia snarled and glowered at him, a warning not to interfere, and though Kato uttered a low hiss like a cornered cat, he remained where he was and did not speak again.

Eddie's desire to prove his value was something Kato understood. So did Jia. They had both been youngsters seeking their elders' approval not so long ago. In some ways, Jia was still caught in that cycle with the pack she had been selected to lead.

Putting the Pack in danger, however, was an unsatisfactory way to learn a hard, valuable lesson.

"He…" Eddie stammered, "…he went to the college…"

"Why didn't you?"

There was a signal knock on the metal panel, a second incursion into the evening's serenity that prompted an uncontrolled rippling of muscles and fur beneath Jia's clothes. Deuce's hand on her arm held her back as Kato carefully pulled the panel far enough so QiangXu and a woman of Eastern descent could squeeze into the bunker.

"Yu…"

The dark-haired woman pushed her long braid over her shoulder and smiled warmly, taking Jia's outstretched arms without fear of what the Cana might do. There was strength in her grip, Ursa strength, and a healing peace that came from one who had dedicated her life to the care of others.

Despite how long it had been, Jia recognized her, just as Yu recognized the grown woman before her. "It has been a long time," Yu murmured. "How like Roland…"

"I didn't know you and QiangXu…" Jia started, the outrage at Eddie temporarily set aside.

Seeing an opening, Eddie began to slink towards a dark corner of the room where he might hide behind fallen rock, disintegrated wall paneling, and metal beams.

Deuce growled.

Eddie froze.

"Very few did," Yu said, her voice small and sorrowful. "We had to protect our son."

There was no reason for Jia, as a child, to have known the relationships of the adults coming in and out of her father's office, or to know their children or business there. Her father would have known, but such knowledge shared in a world that feared, mistrusted, and hated their kind was a risk Roland would not have taken…no matter how much he trusted his daughter, unless she needed to know.

"I'm told you need a doctor for your journey?"

"Having one with us would be wise," Jia agreed.

Yu glanced at QiangXu. He nodded and she looked at Jia before releasing her arms. "Then I offer my help so you can shoulder the burden Roland left you…"

"I don't blame him…"

Chuckling with maternal affection, Yu kissed Jia's forehead, a gesture Jia recalled from long ago. "I know you don't." No matter how much cause for blame Jia had, Yu understood why she would never blame her father. "Will my help be enough?"

"Maybe we should send her to the college," Kato suggested with a huff, his unaddressed concern for the Pack, for Vanya, aggravated by the presence of another Ursa. "They might need her more than…"

"Why? What has happened?" asked QiangXu.

Instead of providing answers she did not have, Jia turned to Eddie, her anger briefly tempered, and asked again, "Where's Wist?"

"We got separated in the mist…"

There had been no mist in the borough, but mists in the Wilds were not uncommon. There was a taint of falsehood in his voice, in his scent, and Deuce growled, "That's what your nose is for, cub."

"I know…I know…but he was too…I couldn't keep up…and I was afraid that whoever's out there…I thought it was safer to come back here…to you…"

His pleading eyes and obvious fear only half-masked the lies. Jia could smell them, could understand his fear of being in the Wilds alone, but it was too late to reverse his actions. With luck, Wist had either arrived at the college or was nearly there. The Pack would be warned. Liam would take action and the Pack would be safe.

Sending Yu to the college, as Kato suggested, might offer Eddie an escort home, but it would also mean sending QiangXu with her because he knew the way. Without knowing the nature of the threat, where it would strike, or if it had already done so, sending more of their group away made little sense.

Whatever lay ahead as she traveled east, her team would need someone like Yu with them.

"Join our fire," Jia offered with a gesture to Yu. "We'll wait…trust that Wist…" She sighed and shook her head, refusing eye contact with anyone. They would wait for the help Vance would bring, for Wist to return if he could, for the help Nik could provide. "And you," she scowled at Eddie, "will not move from that spot until I allow it."

The frantic, frightened bob of his head was Eddie's only reply.

∾*∾

"You have to tell him! You promised!"

It was a desperate plea, begging an unusual tool in Oasis' repertoire she was unaccustomed to utilizing but one she felt to be her only option. The voice in the corridor, Nik passing in conversation with Torben, inspired a flash of honest fear, as she was certain, at first, the voice was Donn's. She stood frozen, waiting for the echoing footsteps to recede, waiting for the flutter at the back of her throat to ease so she could breathe. From room to room she had fled, seeking assurance, seeking an ally to ease the nightmare since her father refused to do so.

Lowell had said he would protect her. He had promised.

He looked up from the books on his desk, passages of history that might direct him to the location he sought. He no longer had the map that had been stolen from him, but he had a good memory. He was confident he could direct his forces to the location, confident he could bring Fort Hamilton's contents home. The corners of his eyes creased, his head cocked as though he was unclear about what she was asking, but the meeting of their eyes answered his unvoiced query and made the corners of her lips droop.

"I said I would try," he murmured apologetically. "I will protect you, but I don't think he'll…"

"He will listen to you!" She had trusted and believed her father would hear her, heed her pleas, and keep her safe. Today, she no longer did.

"We need the treaty, Oasis. You know we do. All of us. I'll find another way to…"

Her expression melted into bitterness and her fists balled as the dynamics of her world collapsed more. Something Aman had once said about relying only on oneself in a world where no one could be trusted burrowed out of her memory and into the center of her soul. She had considered herself to be strong, strong enough to face Donnovan's demons and absorb his fury, to redirect it from the rest of the world. Yiva's death at his hands, a truth she believed but had yet to verify, had shaken the foundation of that strength, made her doubt her own fortitude, but as her two cornerstones retreated into the mire of political expediency, she understood Aman was right.

Perhaps she would reach out to him. Perhaps he would do what her father would not. In the interim, she could depend on no one else. To survive, she would need to be her own steward and lock everyone who could hurt her out.

Oasis squared her shoulders, tossed her head, exposing the new bruises on the side of her face, and stalked back out of the room. The change in posture, the gesture of defiance, the ice in her eyes, conveyed a message Lowell had not anticipated.

"Oasis…wait…"

His plea fell on deaf ears.

She would do this her way. She would be safe. No one else was going to suffer as she had.

Even if she had to kill Donnovan herself.

❧*❧

Nik leaned against the open Fortress gate, listening to the shivering chirps of the birds nesting in the crevices time had eroded into the walls, watching Torben and his sposer cart bump east away from the Fortress over the rutted parallel street. It had been the only plan Nik could concoct on short notice, providing enough compensation to the eldest member of the Fortress staff in exchange for ending his years of employment with feigned death. Nik would make sure the fellow lived comfortably somewhere far beyond the Laedan's reach, promised more resources when they were required, but it seemed the only choice Nik had. The fellow would do it for Roland. He would do it for Roland's daughter. He would do it for Nik because he believed in the threat put forth despite the vagueness of its description. Wrapping the fellow in beggar's rags, the man who had once been a staunch supporter of Laedan Marrock slunk away from the Fortress amidst the host of beggars who daily congregated at the gate for the generosity Yiva had been inclined to offer.

That giving had ended, but still, the beggars came.

Torben's arrival with the cart, and his eventual departure with the wrapped body-shaped bundle upon it, would cover both the servant's absence and the collections of goods and materials Nik had procured, covering as well what had been stashed underneath the bundle.

No one would look too closely at the dead.

No one was likely to notice the missing servant's absence for days and Torben would see to it the man had a job somewhere the Laedan was unlikely to look.

"What are you doing out in the cold?"

Startled, Nik jumped at his father's voice and gripped the grated gate tighter. There was no accumulation of snow on Lowell's head or shoulders, not like there was on Nik's, suggesting he had recently come outside, but the older man might have been standing there long enough to see more than Nik wanted him to see.

"Listening to the wind."

Lowell snorted but closed his eyes as if listening too. Nik held his breath, expecting his breathing, or his silence, would reveal what he had done, the theft of food, weapons, clothing, and more he thought would benefit a quest into the unknown west. When Lowell snorted, Nik believed an admonition and punishment were at hand.

"I'm nearly ready. I know you have Moller…that we haven't found…so I'm leaving Captain Ortega to…"

Nik frowned. "If you're going out there, you should take him. The men will…"

"I know what I'm doing, Niki. I've done this before."

Nik had grown up with stories of the expansion of the borough's borders, exploration and discovery, and conflict with those living on the fringes before those bits of the world were cleared and rebuilt as much as they could be and brought back into the confines of civilization. The stories Nik knew, however, were primarily those of Roland's outward reach, administrative and organization structuring that Lowell had generated and woven skillfully into place. Lowell was not a 'hands dirty' sort of leader.

Nik doubted his father had traveled to those border acquisitions until conquest and reclamation were complete.

Head bobbing in the direction Torben had gone, Lowell asked, "Who?"

Swallowing hard, only his grip on the gate and the cold disguising the tremors in his hand, Nik muttered, "Wilson."

He had hoped to hide the man's absence for a few more days.

Lowell frowned. "Didn't know he was ill. Seemed fine this morning."

Hoping his anxious swallowing came across as an expression of sorrow rather than anxiety, Nik said, "Don't think he was ill just…age, you know…or his heart…"

Lowell bobbed his head but his frown did not change. "Sure he wasn't…?"

The fading note and darkening tone of Lowell's face prompted Nik to shake his head. "He hasn't been back Fa. Donn's got nothing to do with this. He's still out there…"

Somewhere, Nik thought with his mirroring grim expression. Wherever his twin was, whether he was aware his father and brother and the Protectorate knew what he had done, Donn was smart enough not to come home. If Nik saw his brother again, he suspected it would be the day they put him into the ground with those Channons who had gone before.

If his father even permitted him to be buried in the Channon plot and did not leave him to rot in the street.

"Gonna need another jani chief. I'll see to that before…"

"I can do that, Fa," Nik hastened to assure him, not wanting his father to probe into Wilson's death. The Fortress cleaning staff would never know the truth to expose him, but a single wrong word might result in an unfortunate revelation. "No need for you to…"

"Good…very well…glad you're stepping up, Niki. Been hearing nothing but good things. She'd be proud of you…always thought you'd be…" Lowell's voice broke as his hand hovered over Nik's shoulder but in the end fell to his side without making contact. "Hallister's here."

"I know."

Of course he did. There would have been talk. They might have even passed in the corridor. "Be careful what you say to him, Niki. Be careful with the truth. He must not know…"

Lowell trudged away, muttering beneath his breath, words better left unheard or meant, Nik suspected, to have been shared with a wife and mother lost. Nik did not need to understand the reasons behind hiding certain truths from Hallister but instead chose to take his father's admonition to heart for reasons of his own.

The cause of Yiva's death had been kept from nearly everyone. This was for the best too.

❧*❧

Pine branch-covered pits of buried wood and metal spikes, chunks of metal and stone held weighted in trees for a trigger to drop, darts tainted with the venom of snakes, frogs, and wild plants. Round metal spring jaws beneath fallen autumn leaves and hills of debris with trip wires hidden to expel spears at any who passed. Wires buried beneath the creek's muddy banks that would result in the unfortunate falling into the icy water long enough for those they hunted to fall on them with protective wrath. Thin ice disguised with anything found that might prompt invaders to pass that way and fall through. A spray and spillage of water spread over the dull surface that had once been a parking area, frozen and slippery beneath falling snow that had disallowed its evaporation into cold air heavy with moisture.

The impending night's freeze would be a hazard on its own.

Cana and mutani perched on walls, in the shadowy branches of tall evergreens, beneath brush, and behind walls of wood, stone, and metal, in strategic positions around the south and west borders of the territory.

The north was protected by the Zone.

The east, also under watch, was deemed too far into uncharted lands for any army, merc or HOPE, to travel to, to stage an attack.

No enemy had yet to come. Sentries stationed at intervals beyond the boundaries had not yet sounded an alarm.

Perhaps the threat would not come.

Perhaps they would wait for days before the threat showed itself.

Perhaps the warnings had been false.

Liam, however, trusted Jia. If the mage thought a threat would come and she believed him, the Flushing Pack would wait.

So would he.

No one was looking. As others worked hour after hour to build things she was not allowed to touch, things she was not allowed to explore, few of the others noticed her. They were too busy moving boxes and bags, baskets, and carts, armloads of goods and food, to pay attention to one stray girl who chose to stay out of their way after multiple scoldings not to touch anything. After a while, she barely noticed she had been forgotten. Pretending to be a flyer in one of the great metal birds she had seen pictures of in the book of cards her brother collected, she zigzagged between the bushes and trees, between decaying walls of buildings and the shadows of those scurrying around her until the world grew still and the glow of the sun dimmed behind the ever-present veil of grey covering the sky.

The library, devoid of life's merriment, without a fire's glow at its heart to warm the room, made her stop at last in confusion, alone, staring at the ceiling with her arms wrapped around herself and the barely yellow Peppermint the bear.

The flight of metal birds was forgotten. The day's chaos was over.

Perplexed, Vanya cocked her head. She listened as she had been taught, for the black cat's soft-pawed return.

When she could not hear it, could hear nothing except the songs of evening birds as they went to nest, she uttered a single, small squeaking sound of a word.

"Kato?"

Chapter 22

From the shadow of a nearby building, a mother's lullaby warmed the snowy night as Deuce poked at the fire they managed to scav enough wood to build, keeping his watchful eye on the cub still cowering, cold and alone, in the corner. Eddie was offered a blanket, but with it had come another of Jia's stern glowers of warning and he had left the blanket on the floor where it had been dropped, afraid, it seemed, to pick it up and use it. He accepted the food, however, and the cup of water with it, but the cub seemed to equate suffering the cold with the punishment he deserved for his defiance, with the contrition he was meant to make to win back his alpha's favor.

Foolish boy that he was, Deuce imagined Jia would see to his warmth soon enough. If he fell ill because of further folly, he was only going to slow the group down when she decided it was time to move.

Torben's arrival with the clattering sposer cart of goods provided enough food to last another week if they were judicious, additional clothes and bedding for warmth, and a satchel stuffed with bandages and medical supplies to supplement what Yu had brought and what had come from the Pack. There was a working compass, a rare commodity since the Undoing, and a rarer still radiation reading module of the sort Laedan-sponsored exploration teams used when entering unfamiliar territory or investigating buildings in the borough where unexplained sickness was rife. There were several hempcanvas packs to distribute the weight evenly among them, packs with enough potential space for items they could scav along the way.

The news Torben delivered with the goods, however, their weight left in his wake as he returned the empty cart to the Plant for its next use, was less welcome but not a surprise.

"Now we've got Laedan Channon to contend with," grunted Kato as he examined the collection of knives, shock sticks, a weighted net, heavy batons, and two handguns Nik had included. None of them except Vance, and the Protector he intended to bring with them, would know how to effectively use the guns and Cana preferred to fight without them unless pressed to do so, but the rest of the weapons would come in handy if it came to combat none of them wanted.

QiangXu and Yu looked at one another as they endeavored to divide the supplies into logical, equitable bundles so no one had to carry too much, or more than they could handle, while they waited for Vance to return.

He had said tonight.

Tomorrow morning at the latest.

So far there was no sign of him and Jia's nervous pacing was beginning to grate on everyone.

"We expected he'd go after it," she murmured, marveling at the single bottle of wine Nik had stuffed within the bedding so it would not be broken. There had been a handwritten memorandum reading, "For luck and success," along with a charcoal pencil, a knife for sharpening it, and a small, ragged covered but blank inside notebook upon which was inscribed, "Dictionary of Random Things," in his elegant, swirling hand.

Nik had the best handwriting of any of the Channons, despite his claims to the contrary. The book, its play on a long-held private joke, made her smile.

How better to keep track of the adventure ahead, and what they found, than committing it to paper?

Footsteps in the street and a cheerily whistled tune made the nearby singer fall silent. The steps continued until they stopped outside of the safehouse entrance. The whistling stopped too.

Jia did not know the whistler, nor the heavier set of steps, but she knew the familiar scents beyond the door. That scent, and the cadence of his particular steps, were seared into her brain. "Let them in," she said with a breath of relief.

Outside, Vance watched up and down the path, noting the new silence brought on by the lullaby's end, the muted voices of families settling in for the night, the distant sounds of scavs skittering and sifting through debris a few alleys away. None of those sounds were threatening, none near enough to pay attention to two men taking shelter from the snowfall. When the panel was drawn back, he urged his companion to enter and followed, shaking the snow from his long coat and lowering its hood as soon as the panel blocked the room from the swirling wind and snow.

"That's it," he murmured, looking around the room at faces he knew and the one he did not. "That's all of us." When the man with him likewise lowered the hood of his Protector's coat, Vance added, "This is Pubby. We can trust him."

Pubby offered his hand to the only other person he recognized as he took in the rest with a cautiously measured gaze. "You're a Marrock." Vance had explained that those they would be working with could be trusted, but Pubby had been hesitant to believe him without taking stock of the team.

A Marrock in the mix made this different.

"Kato, Deuce, QiangXu, Yu, and Eddie," Jia said as she accepted the firm handshake, the last name said with reluctant inclusion.

"Makes you the one the Laedan's looking for." Pubby looked Kato up and down, nodding once before shrugging. Two he judged to be a couple, another too old, another too young, to be the Fela rumored to have abducted Jia and killed her father. Whatever this was, whatever she was, Pubby did not believe she would tolerate the company of her father's murderer. There was something behind those claims that Pubby did not care to explore. He was not here for that.

Kato's only reaction to the perceived accusation was a growl.

Pubby chuckled.

"Quite a stash." Vance squatted and rubbed his fingertips over one of the two handguns, reading the impressions left on it by the last three pairs of hands to touch it. "Nik's done good." He looked up at the closed hand Jia extended towards him.

"Long as nothing unexpected happens…no more surprises," began Deuce with a sideways glance thrown at Eddie.

"Know there will be." Vance knew as well as the others this would not be an easy stroll into the unknown. He reached to take the item Jia offered but Yu caught his wrist before he could take it.

Studying his bandaged hand, she asked, "What happened?"

"Accident." One accident with a gun, however, would not prevent him from using another.

"You take those," Pubby said, patting a shoulder holster protecting one pistol safe against his ribs, his movement providing evidence of others carried on both hips. "I got everything I need."

The mage glanced around the room, taking the pouch from Jia when Yu released his wrist, seeking permission he did not need before picking up the guns after Jia's head bobbed her agreement. The pouch, left with her by Torben, was stuffed in his pocket for later study and both guns were tucked into the waistband of his trousers, revealing the other on loan from the Protectorate in its thigh holster. He shifted to warm his hands in the fire once the additional weapons were secure. "What's the plan?" Eddie was here when he should not be and the mage did not see Wist. Something had transpired and he worried about the Pack, that there had been an unexpected change of plans.

If it was something bad, Jia's demeanor did not show it. Nor did she address it when she chose to answer his question instead.

"Might as well load up and move tonight…unless you two need a rest?" While she and those with her had been at rest as they waited, Vance and Pubby may have been on shift all day. The mage wore dark circles of determination beneath his eyes, expressing a weariness of spirit rather than body, while Pubby's showed eager anticipation and a readiness to get to work as soon as someone gave the word.

Agreeing with her unspoken assessment, Pubby said, "Morning's gonna fill the streets with Protectors and Laedan Guards hunting some killers. Might be some out tonight, but not so many…and Segara and I can get us past those if necessary."

"All of us out in the daylight will draw attention," Deuce agreed.

Also agreeing with the former omega, Kato nodded. "Sooner we get this done, sooner we get back." There was a part of him still torn, still wanting to return to the library, but he chose to believe the Pack would keep Vanya safe.

He knew the advantages of moving at night, in the shadows, even though his previous travels with his sister had necessitated moving during the day.

One by one, the others in the room nodded, reassuring her the choice was a sound one. Jia's eyes met Vance's last. "Pack up. Bundle up. We leave in thirty."

They would leave tracks in the accumulating snow, but it could not be helped. Hopefully, other foot traffic, and the fact that no one would suspect them or be hunting them, would keep them safe.

If they waited for the snow to melt into the muddy streets of midday, it might be too late.

❧*❧

The approach to Queen's College brought Uzzi and his force to the edge of an open field where a fountain bubbled weakly, the cold and snow struggling to turn the agitated water to slush. They paused to listen to the fading echo of distant loons somewhere within the Wilds, to smell the air for traces of fire or other people, before he divided his number to spread them out to the north and south.

They had standing instructions to avoid the Zone.

Having conducted a significant amount of trade with the mutani, it was a relationship bridge Uzzi did not want to burn.

The scent in the air around them was strong, feral, and musky, the unmistakable Cana smell not many Normals could detect or recognize. Uzzi had crashed in Cana dens before, been nursed back to health in a few after one or another brutal clash. While he could not tell one Cana from another by scent as they could do with their own, the overall smell of them was something Uzzi knew well.

They were here. He was sure of it, even if the quiet air was tainted with an eerie, nerve-tingling quality of emptiness. There was no haunting here. Despite the whistling wind, the falling snow muted every other sound. Not haunted, just another abandoned section of a once great world.

Another Cana stronghold.

The distant bird calls began as each set of ruffs took position.

Uzzi scanned the way forward again. There. Ahead of him. No fires glowed, no voices tinted the night with the warmth of settling chatter. From what he could see, from what he remembered from passing here before, he knew the most likely places for a lair to be. His hunting sense told him it was there.

He gestured to Enola, who gestured to Dink on her other side.

The birdcall command went up.

The net of ruffs began to tighten at the college border.

The birdcalls were too measured, too distinct and falsely discreet to belong to any local flocks the Pack was familiar with. Not like the loon cries that had announced the enemy's approach from the deep of the Wilds. Maz signaled the mutani with him and tensed in their crouches, waiting for the cracking of twigs that would give the hunters away. A wise leader would spread his number like a net, not spearhead them into place on a single thrusting point. The primary approach might be from the west, but he suspected there would be others approaching as well. Uncle, Xan, Orliss, Helena, and the others would know it too.

A cry, a single staccato sound carried on the wind from the north, from the direction of the Zone, punctured the night, followed by a second excruciating scream of pain and surprise from the south. Uzzi's hesitation was brief. Lookouts around a pack's border and traps set to ensnare the unwary were no surprise. He would have been more surprised if there were none. So some of his people had already fallen victim to one or the other.

It did not matter.

The wait was over. The opportunity for stealth, to get in and out unseen, was lost. With luck, there would still be time to finish the job before the bulk of the pack emerged from their sleeping places.

With Enola and Dink at his side, he ran.

"I should be out there…"

Liam could not see any of the clashes heard beyond the boundaries of Queen's College Campus from the wall of the Zone where he stood. Here and there, small bursts of flame sparked, but the dampness of the night and the wet fuel it tried to ignite meant the attempts to start fires were unsuccessful. Liam's breath misted before his face, blowing over cold fingers to warm them as he listened to the fighting begin, the screams and shouts and howls of men, mutani, and Cana.

Jia had been right.

She was usually right.

And she had been right to leave him to see to the Pack's defense.

But whether his choices had been enough would not be known until the world grew silent and the sun rose again.

Addi, standing beside him with his attention split to the cries from Ministry twelve and those before him, frowned at the audible evidence of injuries he would soon tend, so long as the injured lived for care. Unlike Liam, he felt no desire to be out in the fight, preferred the security of the Zone from where he would be able to help when it was over. He felt no guilt over what some would deem cowardice. He knew where he was needed. He had to be practical.

He knew where Liam was needed too.

"You're doing your part," Addi murmured as another pair of Cana howled to one another as though engaged in a hunt. Addi guessed it was exactly what they were doing…Helena and Xan…driving some poor soul into a trap or someone else's line of attack. "Someone needs to be here…at the gate…someone needs to keep things together."

Though Liam's head bobbed, he did not believe it should be him.

Though some were stopped at the fringes, crushed by swinging pendulums of stone, gored by spear and spike, left writhing on the snowy ground by poisons that burned the blood and incapacitated the brain and other organs, other shadows dashed into the heart of the campus, finding their way around some of the safeguards intended to protect the Pack. There were not as many as they had feared.

Many, but not too many, and not HOPE.

The black wolf dashed across the alley alone. He circled and broadsided a straggler, cutting him off from the others.

There was no reason to think a motley collection of ruffs, no matter how well organized or armed, would attack a pack. It was not often done.

The man screamed.

Went down.

Pain tore at the back of the man's neck with powerful fangs and leaped away before the arrow aimed in his direction found its mark.

Hacha struck first one invader then another with the heavy length of an etched pipe he preferred to use as a weapon whenever weapons were necessary. His size and strength meant those he hit were thrown aside like sacks of grain, crashing into trees, into walls, into their companions. His thick, rough skin prevented the arrows hurled at him, the blows he did not successfully parry, to produce no more than scratches or bruises that failed to slow him. He howled, he raged, weaving with the wolves and the woman who fought at his side, racing towards the west where the majority of the enemy seemed to be pushing into the college's heart.

Zyair, unable to match his bellowed war cry, simply charged with him, ignoring the flaming bottle thrown past her by the individual she pursued, her long-handled ax cutting through limbs and unprotected torsos of anyone who got in her way.

"Bite." The wooden stick, cleaned of bark, soft and malleable in its freshness, was thrust between Trill's jaws to stifle the cries of pain as Addi supported her weight and paced the width of the ministry with her. If the baby came now, it would be too early, and the inopportune timing, as the Pack fought for its survival, made those hiding here concerned for their future. He had given her everything he had at his disposal to ease the contractions, to force the pangs of labor to end as abruptly as they had begun with the closing of the Zone gates, but neither he nor Trill knew if it would be enough.

She squeezed his hand and nodded. The silencing measure, the shifting of body tension away from her womb, helped a little.

He squeezed back and listened to Cana howls in the night.

"Kato!"

Vanya hunkered in the center of the library where the fire pit had once warmed the meal pot and given its heat to the room. She was accustomed to silence and knew what it meant.

Stay still. Stay quiet.

Wait for the black cat.

Stay safe. Do not move.

But she was exposed here, not secluded in some narrow protected corner. In her previous hiding places, no matter how many nights she had been entrusted to that sort of solitary embrace, she had never been surrounded by the shouts and screams and whiffs of smoke that filled her ears and nose and would not be kept out even with her hands pressed over them. With no response to her plea, believing he was in danger, that the cries were his, Vanya threw open the library doors and burst into the street, looking wildly about, Peppermint clutched in one hand to scream again. "Kato!"

She could not see him but he had to be there.

"Kato!"

His hands, his arms, the front of his coat, were drenched with the blood of mutani, an unfortunate fact that made no sense as there was no logical reason for them to be allied with those Uzzi had been hired to eradicate. There was no opportunity to consider what that might mean for future trade. The only Cana he saw were shadows darting to and fro, beyond the reach of the pistol he had lost in a skirmish that had dowsed him in blood.

He would have lost his life in that fight if not for Enola who fought as a thing possessed beside him.

It was impossible to tell how many his team faced. A pack of a dozen he could have handled. But they seemed to have known he was coming, had formed an unexpected alliance with the Zone. There were more than the expected dozen Cana to fight.

Two dozen at least. Perhaps more.

They had known he was coming. Uzzi was certain he had been betrayed.

Quentin was going to pay for this.

Running from a pair of howls behind, running towards the thick of the fighting where he expected to find Dink and others making a stand, Uzzi drew up short as the door of the building in front of him crashed open, and a skinny figure, ill-clothed for the cold and the snow, stumbled out, screaming a name he had not heard in a lifetime.

Enola raised her bow.

A fight for a fight's sake, the spilling of blood, the lure of revenge even if not on those who had robbed him of his pack status, was itself a reward, a release of frustration and anger that had previously been denied an outlet. Pain tore through one victim after another, gradually realizing he was killing not for the initial revenge he expected but rather for the survival of his pack, his friends, his family.

Some would argue he owed them nothing. Instinct and the understanding at his core that he had done this to himself, however, were further prompts forcing him to act when he could have turned his back and left the others to their fate.

They were his family. They were the only family he had.

When the pup crashed out of the library into the direct aim of the enemy's bow, he could have left her to her fate too.

But there was no thought to his action, only a leap that threw him into the line of fire as the white-haired man shouted, "Enola! No!"

Too late, the arrow loosed.

Pain's weight brought Vanya crashing down into the snow. The arrow sizzled past his head, slicing through his fur to fly through the open library door. She screamed, crying and thrashing and pummeling the wolf with terrified fists, but as he rolled to his feet, he turned his back to her to face down the two on the other side of the square.

Another arrow was drawn.

"No, Enola…don't…"

The woman hesitated.

Uzzi, shaken, his thoughts scrambling over the boulders of 'what if' questions shifting within him, was forced to make a choice. It should not matter. A job was a job. He should complete what he was being paid to do, kill them all, down to the last man.

But the sounds in the night, shrieks of horror and agony, the suspicions of betrayal and certainty he was intended to die here to be out of Quentin's way…as well as the face of the girl before him, prompted Uzzi to a course of action he had never expected to take.

"Retreat."

"Sirra?"

The black wolf snarled and took a step towards them, away from the fists pelting his hairy sides. Red stained her gown, his claws, and the impact with the ground had left abrasions on her pale skin, but they were not marks of an attack or intended harm.

The Cana was protecting her.

"You heard me," he snapped. "Find Dink." If they were separated they would find each other at the Custard Cat, where they most often left messages and came together after any time apart. "And you…" He pointed at the wolf who crouched with ears pinned to his head at the threatening gesture. "Get her out of here."

Pain did not move as the pair retreated without turning their backs. If they wanted to kill him, or the pup, they could have. Or they would have tried. They might still do so. Once they moved far enough away, Pain turned around long enough to butt Vanya back into the library with his head, issuing a snarled command to stay there, and then he loped after the enemy as they withdrew.

The call to end the attack might have been issued, but others were slow to disengage. Pain wanted to be sure they left as they intended and were not retreating to regroup for another assault.

Trembling on her knees in the library doorway, Vanya cried and shouted in dismay, "Kato!"

Uzzi grabbed Enola's arm and ran.

Chapter 23

"**M**r. Moller."

Torben did not allow the Laedan to see his scowl when turning to face him. Despite the friendship with the man's son, Torben had little use for politics or a relationship with the Channons. He had never interacted with Lowell before recent events brought him here one time after another, though he had been familiar, even friendly with Roland. Even now, Lowell rarely spoke to him. When he did, it was about Nik.

Torben assumed that was the man's intent now.

He did not call him sirra. Formalities of title stuck in his throat like dry crumbs as he despised any man having power over him in any concrete way, but he did stop at the base of the stairs, his hand on the railing, and looked back with hesitation and respect.

"Have you considered coming on full-time? Niki will need you while I'm away."

"I've got a job." He studied Lowell's leather trousers, long leather coat and gloves, and heavy boots of the sort meant for extended foot travel. Torben tried not to scowl for the second time. "You're going?"

Laedan Hallister had left LaGuardia. Torben had passed his procession in the street on his way here. Lowell's boots were clean, so he did not think the man had been outside seeing Hallister off, although he could have waited in the doorway for the other man to finally be gone from his home.

Hallister's absence would ease a little of the Fortress' tension.

"Soon as the men are ready." Lowell cocked his head towards the glass panels at the front of the hall. In the courtyard, there were two wagons bearing crates and packs, boxes and sacks, pulled by two large oxen. The collection of people milling about, some in conversation, some double checking and securing the wagons' content, some tightening the trappings on the oxen and the few horses waiting with them, wore the uniforms of the LaGuardia Guard and appeared to be awaiting orders. "I have to speak with Niki first. Is he awake? Have you seen him?"

"I just arrived." Torben assumed the young man who rarely slept was awake, assumed his father would know, though neither had been to his room to check.

"Yes. Well…when you see him, send him down. And please," he clasped Torben's hand between his, the first contact made between them, and held it firm. "Swear to me you'll keep him safe. I've never been very good at it, I'm afraid…for any of them." The words sounded frail, weary, bitter, and sad but also resolute. "Do this for me and you'll be repaid tenfold for your time and duty."

"Not here for a reward. Here for him."

A friend. Odd, but Lowell had never been aware of Nik having friends beyond the Marrock children. "You should be rewarded. You got him clean…"

"He did that himself." Torben was damned proud of him for it too.

"Did he?" Lowell mused, turning as the Fortress door opened and Captain Ortega came in, stomping snow onto the tiled floor. "Doubt he did it alone…but I'm grateful. Keep him clean, keep him safe until I get home. That's all I ask."

"I will," Torben promised, doubting, as Lowell released his hand and strode towards his captain, that the Laedan had heard him.

Leading HOPE's forces on horseback was an enviable place to be, a place few men throughout the recovering world could ever expect to be as the unit left the barred gates of the complex on a quest for the might that would permit control over both Kennedy and LaGuardia. The bay gelding set him apart from those men marching behind, some leading mules laden with supplies they would need along the way. For all of his dreams and expectations of holding power in his hands, doing so with Grand Mas Lord's blessing, with the support of the Council's Invocation, had seemed beyond Donn's grasp.

Perseverance, however, had proven him worthy.

Not even his father could have foreseen where he was.

Not even his father-in-law had dared to cement an alliance that would grant him ultimate rank and privilege.

Grand Mas Lord thought those things were his to wield by the right of the Corpus.

Donnovan was determined to prove him wrong too.

Riding out with General Warby, the man's dusky gray draft horse larger than Donn's but slow and ponderous in its plodding steps, was an unfortunate, but necessary, temporary setback to his plans. Donn did not want to share leadership.

He wanted to own it.

Despite the thick, straight-falling snow blinding them as they began their push east, Donn believed he would.

General Warby did not stand a chance.

❧*❧

"Papa was here."

Most of the Pack, secure behind the walls of the Zone, remained huddled together, unable to sleep until long after the distant clash of combat had ended and the normal melody of night birds and wind took its place. The mutani brought a meal most were unable to eat, water many were unable to drink, as they waited for the outcome many feared to contemplate.

Only when Hacha, bedraggled and bloody with the life fluids of enemies, staggered across the walking path to bang on the south gate, did Liam help open it to let them in. Brie and a few others kept the children back but Addi and Trill, her contractions temporarily soothed, pushed to greet their returning comrades, anticipating dead among the wounded, expecting to be needed. The three, along with Ele and a handful of others, followed Zyair back towards the center of the carnage to seek out those who needed help.

Finding Vanya in the library doorway, protected by Helena's arm around her shoulders, was unexpected. Many assumed her absence from the Pack's cluster in Ministry 12 was a result of her frequent exploration of her surroundings. With no one specifically watching her, there had been no reason to think she could have found her way out of the Zone to return to the library where she had been caught in the night's fray.

"Are you okay?"

Bodies were dragged into the square before the library door, a few mutani and more than two dozen men and women wearing a haphazard assortment of protective gear with an equally haphazard collection of weapons. They wore no uniforms, no insignia identifying them as HOPE agents or members of either boroughs' militia. As Wist, Ele, and Hacha poked through the dead, removing hats and helmets to expose heads with shaved patterns, tattoos, and skin dying in ancient tribal-like designs, it seemed more likely they were mercs and ruffs than any sort of military formation. Addi began to tend the injuries of those who needed it while Maz, gripping Vanya's arms, sniffed up and down her neck, into the hair at her shoulders, seeking confirmation that his senses were mistaken, waiting for her to answer his question.

Vanya nodded, absently rubbing the bare shoulder bearing the muddy scraping evidence of a sliding fall. "He stopped Papa…and Papa stopped her…she had a shooter and he had…"

"Who?" Maz squatted down in front of her, hoping to make her less frightened by not looming over her.

"I don't know." She held Peppermint up to her ear as if sharing a whispered secret and then shook her head and murmured, "Where's Kato? You can't tell him. He's very mad. He'll be angry he was here…that he tried to hurt me…after so long." She squeezed Maz's hand with a wide-eyed, tearful expression. "He'll go after him if he knows. He won't care that he…then he'll never come back…promise you won't tell him."

Maz looked at Liam who picked his way through the bodies, living and dead, to assess the Pack's success or lack of it. Both men scowled, thinking the same thing, but only one of them had sniffed out the evidence of Pain's apparent assault on the young woman he had previously tried to kill. Pain's body was not among the dead, and though there was blood evidence around them, it was tainted by the scents of too many to easily evaluate if Pain had been injured and taken, if he had crawled off to nurse his wounds, if he had chased some of the invaders away or if he had been interrupted in the act of finishing what he had started weeks ago and had been chased off by the attacking swarm.

Why had the ruffs not done Pain's work for him and killed the defenseless young woman?

Had he been the one to lead the attackers here?

"Come, sweetie…let's get you and Peppermint back to the others, next to the fire for some breakfast…"

At first, Vanya refused to budge to Helena's prompting, staring instead at the blood the woman smeared across her face when she swept her hair away. With hesitant fingers, Vanya touched Helena's cheek and studied the crimson fluid that came away on her fingertips.

"She was like that too…"

"Who, sweetie?" Helena assumed Vanya had witnessed someone injured in the fight, but Vanya's only response was to clutch Peppermint more tightly to her chest with both arms, carefully avoiding getting blood on the bear's faded yellow fur.

"I want to go to Kato now," she finally whispered.

Helena bobbed her head, her smile comforting and warm, and steered Vanya away from the dead. "We'll get some breakfast and see what we can find." It would take effort to distract her from seeking out Kato, but once in the company of the children, Helena believed Vanya's focus would turn to safer, less complicated matters.

Maz did not move from where he crouched until the women had moved several steps away, following the winding path to the Zone. He rejoined the others and the collection of corpses to study one face after another with a look of both growing relief and trepidation.

"Not here," grunted Uncle, toeing a dead woman's arm wrapped in boiled leather that had not been enough to shield her from the crushing impact of stone and metal in one of the perimeter traps.

"He was. He did that…" Maz thumbed over his shoulder towards Vanya's retreating back.

"Saw him once, towards the end." Maz glanced at Wist who had dragged another corpse from the battlefield to add it to the others. "Chasing a group into the Wilds."

"Chasing?" asked Uncle.

"Wouldn't run from a fight." Maz stubbornly challenged Uncle's assertion. Pain had never been a man to run or back down from a fight. He could have used the chaos of battle to kill anyone in the Pack if he wanted to, but every Pack member, every mutani who had been out here was accounted for. Battered, torn, bloody, and weary, but most were alive. And none of them, except Vanya, had any tales to tell of the omega attacking them.

There was no reason for Pain to kill mutani and it could be seen at a glance that those who had fallen had done so to bullets, clubs, and knives, not the slashing, crushing, or tearing of Cana fangs and claws.

If any member of the Pack had encountered him, fought with him, killed him, they would admit it. Maz chose to believe Pain was alive and had fought for the Pack rather than against it.

He chose to believe Pain wanted redemption.

"They HOPE?" asked one of the mutani, a small fellow with thick, mottled hair over his face and hands as if he was an anthro child in a permanent change to mid-form. His lower teeth protruded over his upper lip like tusks, warping his speech, and his long-nailed fingers and his cheeks were red with the blood of those he had killed.

A fierce fighter, but one who had never encountered HOPE.

"Don't think so." Liam squatted next to the head of the biggest fellow with battle scars across his tattooed face, a crooked nose and jaw, and several missing teeth. "HOPE'd never be so haphazard…not if they wanted to take us…"

"They might come back," murmured Xan.

Liam shook his head. "Don't think they will." Their losses appeared too great. He believed the number who had fled was small though he had not seen the combat. He wanted to believe Pain intended to kill any left alive. "We'll reset the traps, just in case…and school the pups to stay clear of them."

"Who are they then? How could the mage…?"

"How does a mage know anything," snorted Uncle. His only experience with mages was his brief acquaintance with Vance while the tracker recovered from his injuries in the Pack's library shelter. But everyone knew the rumors, the myths, the stories told around fires to frighten and awe children and adults alike.

Not so different, Liam mused, from the stories Normals told their children about anthro. "Maybe something he learned at the Protectorate…or in a tav," Liam countered. The mage had been instrumental in saving his life, in trying to save Roland's. They owed him respect regardless of the peculiarities he had been born with…just as each of them had been born with their own.

"Ruffs looking for a bounty most likely." Orliss wiped his hands on the front of his long-sleeved, dingy blue sweater. "Probably stumbled on us, watched us…"

"But if they know we're here…" Addi murmured warily, helping a mutani with the broken arm to her feet.

"We're not leaving," grunted Liam with an obstinate shake of his head. "We shore the traps, the borders, after we take care of the dead."

"Could stay in the Zone," Hacha suggested, the invitation one he had already discussed with his council.

Still shaking his head, Liam said, "If it comes to it, maybe. Roland chose this. It's defensible, far from the Laedans…"

"Leave enough of these out there," proposed Uncle, indicating first the dead and then the borders of their college territory, "and no one's gonna want to mess with us."

It was not his call to make and the idea of displaying the dead as border markers as some did was distasteful to Liam. Some would call it disrespectful, but Liam understood it could be psychologically effective. Did the Flushing Pack want to utilize such brutality to protect themselves? Was it necessary?

"Not yet. We'd risk grubbers." The longer the dead lay unattended, the more likely they were to turn…or draw grubbers to the college. Until the defenses were reset, they were prepared for an influx of the infected. "We've got enough materials to fortify ourselves…we can scav more as we need it. In time, we can make the whole campus our home, but only when our borders are secure."

Xan toed the dead ruff at his feet. "And Pain?"

"We'll deal with him when he comes back."

"If he comes back," corrected Maz. The potential act of redemption-seeking, if that's what this had been, did not mean Pain would choose to return. Once an outcast, some omegas never rejoined their pack. Nor did the act suggest the other man was alive.

Liam clasped Maz's shoulder. "He will."

"Plant in the Zone…we can burn them there," Hacha offered, indicating the bodies around them.

"Xan, bring the wagon…we'll load 'em up and take 'em in…put 'em to use. Wist, Ele, take anything they have we can use." There was no point in burning usable clothes, shoes, weapons, and anything else they had of value. Such things were too hard to come by. Robbing the dead had become a standard practice necessary for survival…a practice that had led to too many cases of killing for what someone else had. If something could be cleaned, mended, reused, or repurposed, it was fair game for whoever found it.

Many made a living stealing such goods from others.

"And yours?" Liam asked Hacha. Burning the ruffs was one thing. What the mutani did with their dead would be up to Hacha.

"Same." Families and friends would mourn their dead before feeding them to the Plant for what power their burnings could afford. The community would benefit. There would be no new grubbers tonight.

Liam nodded, relieved the Pack was safe, relieved his voice was respected and listened to. There was no guarantee this was over, but for now, they could rest. Roland, he thought, would have been proud of him. Jia, he believed, would be too.

❧*❧

Perhaps he was right.

The angry sea threw billows against the seabreak, thrusting its might into the air with a force that splashed the wet ground and sprayed the trudging shades dressed to avoid the worst of the cold and damp. The water at their feet dribbled into the ditch on the north side of the stony path or back towards the sea, failing to join it before more splashed in. Although Aman had argued for taking steam barges west along Kennedy's coast, a mode of travel that would have quickened their progress, Geary had denied the request, citing the turbulent winter sea storms as too great a threat to risk the barges. There were numerous skilled sailors accustomed to traveling that coast, people who knew the tides and the shoreline well enough to avoid the dangers lurking there, but under these conditions, as this storm came in, Aman suspected they would have told him the same.

Better not to fight this losing battle with the sea.

But starting on foot in this weather was little better, and as he had listened to the wind's fury throughout the night, he had debated the wisdom of following orders. Surely Geary would understand.

Understanding was not the same as approving, and with Kennedy spies reporting the amassing of forces beyond HOPE's walled borders, led, it was said, by Donn Channon, even a day's delay might mean failure…or a confrontation with HOPE Geary would prefer to avoid. Kennedy would never submit.

Such a confrontation would be akin to announcing a war.

Unless, he mused, Hallister intended for Kennedy and HOPE to work together. To split any treasure with his son-in-law in a move against LaGuardia.

Aman did not believe Geary was foolish enough for that.

HOPE could never be trusted.

HOPE would not heed the weather. What little regard they held for humanity would not prevent them from sending as many people as they believed they could spare, conscripting more along the way to replace any who fell due to the storm or other causes, and pushing steadily west.

The goal was to reach the fort before the Channons. Before HOPE. Whatever the cost. But that cost would not come at the hands of the winter sea.

Aman ignored the face glowering within its rain hood at the Fortress gate and rode out at the rear of his column of guards with their wagon of supplies.

To hell with Norse.

Aman would lead the expedition…but only after he was certain Norse was not tagging along at the rear of his force to cause trouble. Only when he was certain Norse did not follow him at the Laedan's request or against it.

❧*❧

The gusting wind drove the snow sideways, blinding Jia as it thrust its fist down alleys and side streets. Only her familiarity with LaGuardia, gained in a lifetime of pack hunts and business excursions with her father, and the Protectors' similar familiarity, allowed any sense of direction, kept the group trudging west. Deuce took the initiative to run ahead, his graying wolf form erased from sight by the snowstorm, but his reassuring, unmistakable voice helped guide them until the pale light of morning began to color the sky at their backs.

They found shelter within a brick and wood shell that had once been someone's home, an empty, unfamiliar place looted by scavs and the previous people who had called the structure home. Moldering curtains, a handful of sticks and boards and other burnables picked up along their way, and a splintered chunk of rafter beam brought down from the unsteady upper floor where Pubby had found it provided a suitable fire around which they gathered to share warmth and food and the reassurance of the necessity of their mission.

"Gonna lose the roof soon," Pubby muttered between chattering teeth, nodding towards the ceiling stained with the evidence of water damage that had gone on for too long.

"Long as it holds one more day," grunted Kato, crouching close to Jia, finding comfort and warmth and assurance in the press of his thigh to hers. She accepted the morsel of bread he offered with a grateful smile and nod. "How far you think we've come?"

"Should be getting close to the border," Vance answered though he was not the one Kato had addressed. Rather than sit at Jia's other side and stir the possessive Fela to anger, he chose to sit across from her where he could watch her face and evaluate her mood and state of mind. Other than Eddie, she was the youngest one here, a young woman forced into making leadership decisions, carrying the weight of their quest on her small shoulders.

He did not envy her position. He did not want to make this trip more difficult than it had to be by prompting the Fela to jealous outbursts and actions.

He already understood that, regardless of his feelings, there was no future for him with her.

"How'd you recognize anything out there?" Eddie's effort to remain apart from the group, an outcast because of his disobedience, had been thwarted by Yu drawing him closer to the fire and pulling him down to sit between her and QiangXu.

Vance shrugged, absently pulling the pouch Jia had given him at the onset of this trip from his pocket. "Just do." It was a mixture of experience in the borough and mage senses, things difficult to explain.

His fingers absently explored the pouch's contents through the soft hemp fabric that encased it. The corners of his mouth twitched.

Chuckling, Pubby added, "Don't last long as a Protector if you can't find your way around."

"Think anyone's gonna follow our tracks?" It had been QiangXu's primary worry throughout the night, despite the heavy snow filling in most of the trail behind them. The worry prompted him, and the others, to do their best to walk in the prints of the person in front of them in the hopes that any hunters would interpret the trail as evidence of a few people instead of many, with a dog in their company.

"Anyone hunting in this would be desperate," Yu murmured.

"Or crazy," added Pubby.

"What's that say about us?"

Kato's question elicited several chuckles as Jia took out the bottle of wine Nik had provided, opened it, and said, "No one knows we're out here. No reason for anyone to look for us. Long as the snow slows down the others, we'll be okay."

There was no reason to save the wine. No reason to risk losing it without savoring the gift. She took the first drink and passed the bottle to Kato.

The soft sounds of a shared meal and the shared wine was punctuated by friendly questions and quips between people attempting to get to know one another. Several minutes passed before the crunching of footsteps in the snow outside drew their gazes towards the as-yet unsecured entrance. Jia got to her feet and pulled open the sticking door. They might not be hunted, but this individual finding them was still a surprised. There was no reason for alarm, caution, or fear. Most within the room recognized the scent of the individual on the other side though they had not expected her to come after them.

Eddie hung his head and pulled his knees to his chin with his arms wrapped around them protectively.

"You must have run like the wind," Jia said in greeting, accepting the woman's wool coat and shaking the snow from it before finding a place to hang it.

"I know I shouldn't have come" Candace began, her gaze sweeping the room before falling sternly on her huddled son. Her cheeks and nose were flushed, her breathing labored, evidence of what it had cost her to catch up to them. "When Wist said…"

Not wanting the woman to think she had intentionally put Eddie's life at risk, Jia said, "I sent him back…"

"I know you…"

Uncomfortable with being the subject of conversation, Eddie whispered, "I'm sorry, mama…but I can help. I know I can…"

Candace shook her head sternly. "In the morning, you're coming back with me."

"Mama…"

Jia beckoned her to sit at the fire. With Eddie situated between the Ursa who provided him with a marginal sense of security, Candace sat across from her son as QiangXu offered, "This is Yu…my wife…" in the hopes it would soothe a mother's concerns.

Candace nodded to the other woman but did not have the opportunity to speak before Jia changed the subject to one concerning them. "The Pack? They got the message?"

"Liam's moved everyone into the Zone. They're setting traps around the border. If anyone's coming, everyone should be safe."

"Zone's probably the safest place anyone can be," Vance agreed. There were reasons the mutani banded together in those places. There were reasons anthro went there too.

"Except Normie's like me," Pubby said with a lopsided grin.

Taking the water bag from Yu and offering it to Candace, Vance shrugged. The wine was beyond his reach. After a single swallow of the sweet, pungent berry nectar, it was better, he believed, the bottle remained far away. "You'd be safe there…if you wanted to be." There would be some initial mistrust and likely bias towards a stray Normal, but Pubby would not be the only Normal behind Zone walls.

"How are they?" asked Kato, leaning nearer to the fire to see around Jia. "Vanya? Did you see anyone?"

"We're looking after her," Candace assured him. "I didn't come across anyone in the Wilds."

Which only meant, Jia thought with a nod, that possible assailants were approaching along some other path, probably from the south. There were many miles of border streets that could be used to approach the college. If HOPE had pursued them from Kennedy, there would be no need to pass through the Wilds and no reason for Candace to encounter them.

Sensing the fleeting hope that there was no threat to the Flushing Pack, Vance grimly met Jia's gaze and shook his head. The enemy was there. He knew it.

"Anyone's there, mutani will grind them to dust," Deuce snorted.

"Hope so." With a thousand or more adult residents within the Zone capable of defending their territory, a HOPE militia would be outnumbered. The Zone fortifications would be difficult to surmount. The chances of losses for the Pack, however, remained. Jia sighed and looked at Candace. "No use in you going back...unless you want to." Odds were, Wist would not rejoin them. With a storm at their backs and no idea what Candace might find when she reached the college, keeping the woman and her son with them made more sense than sending them back into the unknown. Their company would make up for the lost manpower and Candace could keep her son in hand.

Candace chewed her lip as she weighed the offer against the alternatives. It was impossible to know what dangers lay ahead if she and Eddie remained with the alpha, but traveling through LaGuardia with him to face what might be HOPE's efforts to overthrow the Pack was terrifying.

Her other boys were there. They were safe with Brie, with Helena, but Candace would have preferred to have her sons together.

The world had been frightening enough for her when it had been three Cana women and three children struggling to survive without support. Facing similar unknowns without them was a nightmare Candace was not eager to face.

"I'll consider it. I have to do what's best for..."

"Mama," Eddie whined before lowering his gaze in chagrin over how juvenile his protests sounded. He would never win Kato's respect, or the alpha's, if he continued to behave like an impertinent cub.

Jia nodded her agreement.

"I'll take first watch," Deuce offered, his meager meal complete, already starting his climb to the second floor where he could access the roof and serve as lookout for the day.

"So'll we," Candace offered. While the group slept through the daylight hours, she would have the opportunity to speak with her son, and if Eddie insisted on participating in this quest, she would enforce him pulling his weight in responsibilities to the others. With Deuce up top and the two of them at the door, the others would be secure enough to rest as the world outside pushed through a stormy, winter day.

"Two hours. Two per watch after you."

"Second," said Vance with a glance at Pubby. The second Protector had already proven he could climb to the upper level with ease. Pubby nodded.

"We'll take last…and have something ready to eat before we start," offered Yu with an agreeing nod from QiangXu.

Jia nodded too, agreeing with the assignments. It would be good enough. As the snow continued to blow and whistle against the sides of their shelter, she did not expect there to be any dangers today.

It was better to keep watch and not risk it.

She curled up, head on her pack with Kato at her back. The need for more heat than the small fire and wine in their bellies provided brought them together to sleep, the shared body heat increasing their warmth and chances of survival. Even Pubby crawled into the most obvious sleeping arrangement. He was the first to drop into a deep, snoring sleep.

Those on the first watch were not part of it.

Nor was Vance…and Jia fell asleep staring at the back of the mage's head as he stood at the boarded window where the light of day poked through, watching the falling snow as if looking for something or, judging by his pensive expression, trying to remember something…or forget.

❧*❧

Uzzi did not recognize the bruised and battered man Enola dragged before him, her hand tight at the back of his neck in a hold he probably could have escaped from if he tried. Judging by the state of Enola's clothes, the mud and snow there, the torn gashes that exposed bleeding flesh, and the black eye and freshly split lip she sported, his choice to submit rather than die or kill her suggested he wanted something, perhaps only his life, in exchange for what he believed he had to offer. He was not the first such stranger, the first potential recruit, Enola had brought to Uzzi this way, having tested their mettle before agreeing to present them to the man in charge. Unless the next one bested her initiating efforts, this fellow would not be the last.

He did not wait for Uzzi to speak. Uzzi did not recognize his face but there was something familiar about him, primarily the grazing injury of an arrow's bite, suggesting to Uzzi who he was. He wondered why he was here. He wondered what the Cana wanted.

Pushed to the ground at the white-haired man's feet by the hand on his neck, the captive held back the scathing look he felt the woman deserved and instead hissed, "Who is she to you?"

"Enola's my…." Uzzi began.

"Not her," the dark-haired man spat. "Vanya."

Uzzi blinked and sat still despite his racing thoughts. So this was the Cana who had intervened as he suspected. When he hissed, "Answer me!" and Enola cuffed him on the back of his head, Uzzi lifted a hand to prevent another strike and turned on his foldable three-legged stool to see the man kneeling at an eye-to-eye level with him.

Enola grunted and stepped back.

There were only three of them, Uzzi, Enola, and Dink…and the dog padding through the snow at the periphery of the fire's dying light. Perhaps others survived, scattered on the stormy wind, who would reach out at the Custard Cat or the Change when they felt safe. Some would expect their cut for risking their lives, even if they had not succeeded at the job they had been sent to do. They would not necessarily blame Uzzi for their failure, or for saving himself and calling for retreat, but the next time they met there would be blame passed around for abandoning so many to their fates.

Uzzi intended to cast the blame on Quentin. Some of his surviving cohorts might then go after the man and pluck his thorniness from Uzzi's side for him.

The stranger made the fourth at the warmth of their campfire. Uzzi's interest in hearing what he had to say did not mean he was welcome there.

"Could ask the same of you," he said evasively.

"You came to kill us. You saw her…and stopped. Think that says more about you than it does me for stopping you."

"She's no Cana…"

"No," Pain spat, "but she and her brother have been taken in…and that makes them family."

The way Pain spoke the word brother, the emphasis and the shifting of his stance as he spoke, the changes in his expression, in his eyes, revealed his expectation of a response. He was not disappointed.

"Brother." Uzzi leaned back as much as the stool allowed without tipping and began to cross his arms over his chest. Instead, he put his elbows on his knees, balled fists beneath his chin, and leaned forward, bringing their faces nearer to each other. "Where is he?"

Pain snorted. "Not here."

"Was he there? Did we…?" Uzzi scowled. Since laying his eyes on a young woman he had never thought to see again, older but no less recognizable, he had questioned the fates, his own eyes, and the possibility that, of those who had assaulted the Cana pack with him, someone had killed the one man he had not seen.

"Hasn't been there in days." Pain paused, rocked back onto his heels, and rubbed the back of his neck where Enola's gloved fingers had dug into his skin. Of all of the injuries he sported, his neck seemed to trouble him the most, although his movement indicated a favoring of injured ribs as well. "Take me with you…I'll take you to him."

"Where is he?"

Pain shook his head. "Nuh uh…not how this is gonna work. You're short of people…" He smirked and side-eyed Dink but could not see the woman behind him without turning. "And I've got nowhere to be. Dunno where they're headed exactly…but I can lead you to him." He did not know what the man wanted with the Fela, nor did he care. Pain had his own desires and this ruff and his companions appeared to be his best shot at attaining them. "Take me with you, pay my way, and you'll have him."

He did not have a map to reach the rumored fort but there would be a trail he could follow, her scent, Deuce's, Kato's. He could find them, earn a few credits, and if this fellow intended to harm the Fela

Jia favored, Pain might be able to protect him and recover some of the favor he had lost. If they found Roland's fort, there was bound to be something there of value this small team could scav.

"We don't know you," Dink spat.

"And I don't know you," challenged Pain, expecting to be struck in the back of the head again. A shared glance between the older, bearded fellow and the woman, however, prevented that. "If we don't have a deal, let me go…and I'll find the fort myself."

It was a risk, but one he changed his mind about sharing.

"Fort?" What were the odds, Uzzi mused, flicking his burnt spliff stub into the fire?

Pain shrugged. "Dunno where it is, but it's where they're going."

They stared at one another, trying, unsatisfactorily, to read the other's thoughts and body language. Eventually, Uzzi straightened and asked, "What's your name?"

"Pain."

Enola snorted. Dink grunted. Uzzi smirked and nodded. It seemed aptly fitting.

"No reason to trust you, Pain, any more than you have to trust me…but I believe you." Uzzi knew an outcast when he saw one. He knew the hard eyes and sour, dour expression of someone with nothing and no one to lose. He knew the makings of a good ruff, a good ally. It was how he had stayed alive for so long, surrounded by people drawn to him.

"Enola's gonna keep an eye on you, but so long as you get me where you promise, you'll earn more than your keep." He should track down Quentin and demand payment for the botched death mission they were sent on…one he still believed Quentin had sabotaged to avoid the need to pay. He was eager to be done with that extorting slag. It would be better if Quentin thought him dead, killed with the rest, but there was one final agreement between them, one more job they had arranged which promised the biggest payout of Uzzi's life. It also promised the end of the hold the slag had over him. If Pain could help him accomplish both ends, it would be worth keeping him around. And a Cana's nose, those fangs and claws, might be the best protection from Quentin Uzzi was going to find. Next to Enola.

"Once the storm lets up, we head out. Deal?"

Pain offered his hand without hesitation. "Deal."

He had not even gotten the man's name. It did not matter.

❧*❧

Nik assumed from Oasis' teary-eyed expression and tightly clenched ungloved hands tucked beneath her armpits to keep them warm, that she too had failed, as he had, to talk sense into his father. He did not need her as evidence, as Captain Ortega had already passed through the Fortress gates with the soldiers selected to travel with them to Fort Hamilton. At least the stubborn man had seen the sense of taking Ortega. Lowell's horse skittered sideways where it stood, nickering, shaking its head, anxious to be away or out of the falling snow. Or perhaps, Nik thought as it calmed when Lowell removed his hand from its neck to cross towards those he was leaving behind, the animal was reacting to its rider's nervous energy.

His father was no horseman. Nik could count the number of times he had seen Lowell on a horse on two hands. Between the whirling snow, the icy surface beneath the accumulating drifts, and the nervous horse, Lowell would be lucky to make it out of the Fortress courtyard without being thrown.

It might be enough to convince him to give up his folly and allow Captain Ortega to make the journey in his stead.

"You've got full Laedan authority while I'm gone," Lowell said, clutching Nik's hand.

"I'm not…"

Lowell uttered a scolding sound and shook his head. "I've drawn up everything the council needs. They already know and will listen to you. Anything that needs doing, you've got permission to see it done. Whatever it is."

The hair at the back of Nik's neck prickled as the woman beside him dropped her hands, her fists tightening more in support of the grim pursing of her lips.

"Oasis will give you the support you need, your second as it were. Without…" Lowell choked on the words that might have come next and shook his head. "It's just the two of you…the three…" his gaze traveled to her still flat belly, "until I return."

"If you don't?"

"Hush girl," he scolded her too, though with a marked note of affection Nik had not heard directed at himself. "I'll be back." He let go of Nik's hand and lay a lingering kiss on her cheeks and forehead. "You've got nothing to fear. I made you a promise."

His reassurances did not ease her expression or her stance and his words did not ease Nik's.

"It'll be a few weeks at most. And Niki?"

Lowell's voice lowered as he pulled his son towards him into an embrace meant to mask the words he said next from his daughter-in-law and the nearby sentries, "I didn't find the…but if you see Donn…if he comes back…"

"I know." Nik had put down his mother. It had been necessary. If it came to having to do the same, or worse, to his monstrous twin, Nik did not foresee having strong qualms against doing so.

Only the taking of life would make it more difficult.

"If you see…if Jia comes back…make her stay. LaGuardia needs a Marrock here. I'm a fool for not understanding that before. If she comes…promise me…"

Nik swallowed hard. Odds were, Jia was already on her way to Fort Hamilton. His father was likely to see her before Nik did. But he nodded as Lowell returned to his horse, keeping his secrets.

The animal sidestepped and tugged at the reins in the man's hand as Lowell swung up into the saddle.

"Good luck, Lowell. Safe journey."

The tone of Oasis' words made Nik shiver. Or maybe it was the blast of wind blowing the snow sliding from the Fortress roof across the back of his neck and beneath the edge of his fur collar.

"I'll be back before you know it."

Lowell did not say goodbye. He had said that too many times in recent days. Nik was no more inclined to hear the word than his father was inclined to say it. Although he waved, Lowell did not see it; his gaze remained straight ahead, his posture on the horse rigid and tense, until he crossed beyond the walls into the white-covered streets.

The metal hinges of the gates groaned as they were pulled shut.

"You're pregnant." It was as much a question as a statement.

As Nik did not look at her as he said it, Oasis did not look at him as she said, "I am."

Nik did not find reassurance in her news. He found only the assurance that his twin would come back to the Fortress for his wife and child. When he did, Nik was going to be the one forced to confront him. Alone. He believed he could do it if he must, but he was not looking forward to that day.

Not even Torben would be able to change what must be done.

Chapter 24

Chance brought Nepo to the western streets of LaGuardia, a side job hunting a livestock thief as he waited for a shot at the Channon boy or for Quentin to cross his radar. Chance, as he perched in the dark second-story window, where glass shards raked at his gloved hands, his worn boots, and tore and snagged on the hem of his too-well-worn wool coat, watching the collection of goats, sheep, and cattle crammed into a small square of overgrown, snow-covered land that might have been someone's backyard before the Undoing. Chance that brought the faint exchange of voices from a nearby structure wafting to him on the midday wind.

Such interruptions were most often ignored, unimportant snippets of daily lives he cared nothing about.

One voice, recognizable over the others, peaked Nepo's interest enough to cause him to temporarily abandon the livestock he had been tasked to locate and bring in along with their poacher. The animals were not going anywhere without him knowing about it, the thief was not currently here, allowing Nepo the opportunity to get closer to that voice and investigate its presence.

Those people were not going anywhere either. He did not know who the other speaker was, but behind the two men, the sounds of sleeping bubbled over the whispers of a dwindling fire. Day sleepers meant night workers, night movement. If the Protectors were here to likewise keep an eye on the livestock in the nearby yard, visible from where they waited but difficult to see from the angles of the boarded windows, it meant the Protectors too were likely waiting for the poacher to return to move his treasures under the cover of darkness.

Waiting to make an arrest.

Nepo did not intend to share his bounty. Not with a random Protector, and certainly not with Segara, who seemed out of place here. There were too many inside the room with him to make a move against his nemesis, but the waiting, and a word spoken quietly between the two Protectors he could not see, gave Nepo another idea.

Channon had mentioned the place the Protectors discussed. Quentin too, once, when he hired Nepo for a job for which he had never been paid. Tip the local Protectors to this yard, collect his finder's bounty, and then he could fulfill, if he was lucky, a personal bounty that rubbed him in all the wrong ways.

Segara would not escape him for long.

❧*❧

The bottle made a hollow sound as Ernest set it on the desk and dragged the back of his other hand across his lips. Doing so did not remove the alcohol's lingering taste or perfume, and draining the bottle did not soothe his nerves as he hoped, but both acts provided the courage to square his shoulders and emerge from his office into the main room where his officers and staff milled about their duties. No one paid him any mind, other than to note he was there until his stationary position outside of his door lingered too long in one place.

He did not need to raise his voice. He did not need to ask for their attention. He only had to wait.

Years of familiarity made those working beneath him aware of his moods, his intents.

It was why he understood some of them questioned an execution meted out without a trial.

It was why he could never let them know he had been wrong.

They were looking for Donn Channon on the Laedan's behalf, nothing more. None of them knew why. By the time they learned the truth, he intended to be long retired.

Maybe the truth could be hidden so they would never know.

"Got a new assignment," he eventually said after clearing his throat and sweeping his gaze around the room, making eye contact with every individual he could see. "At the Laedan's request, we are going to find, and arrest, the dealer Brac…"

"That's like looking for a ghost," someone muttered.

"A dangerous ghost," snorted another.

"Nobody knows what he looks like…"

"Was said Sal did…"

"That's a rumor…"

"Sal's not here…"

"Nor's Segara."

Heads bobbed. The mage was their best chance of finding anyone. They did not know if he had ever been tasked with finding the elusive dealer, but since Brac had not yet been arrested, and Segara was out on another assignment, what chance did any one of the others have?

"Someone out there has," grunted Ernest. "Someone moves his product, moves his credit, handles his trades. Someone knows where he sleeps, who he sleeps with, who his family is, where he hangs his coat at the end of the day…"

"We haven't…"

"No, we haven't. We've never made a determined effort to pin him down. Too much other day-to-day. But someone is moving juice for him, for HOPE my sources say…and the Laedan's decided it's time to get that shart off the street. Targeting anthro has to end. The bounty on their blood has to stop. Ask around. Talk to everyone, no matter how disconnected they seem. Bring me that inked slag Asan and we'll make him…"

"If anyone knows who Brac is, it's gotta be him," an end-of-shift weary voice agreed.

"He's never gonna talk."

"He will," Ernest promised. He had killed one man. He was not above beating the truth out of another.

"Like the other one?"

"Made him talk alright."

"Squeal like a cat."

Several Protectors laughed and nodded their heads approvingly.

Ernest growled, thankful the room was dim enough, and he was far enough away from most of them, that they could not see the troubled shadows crossing his face. "Nothing to do with that; this is different."

"We cracking down on everything or just plasm?"

"Laedan's only interested in juice, so whatever you need to do to bring in Asan, find Brac. We're going to track this shart to where it comes from and burn it to the ground."

He did not mean literal fire, but he was not opposed to that prospect so long as lives and homes weren't lost.

"Lost my sister to juice…I'll pay to see it happen…"

"I'll pay to light the fire," offered another at the back of the room.

"Anyone got questions…you learn anything…bring it to me. There's still business as usual, and the Laedan's still looking for his son…and Marrock's killer…but otherwise Brac's our priority. Bonus to anyone who brings him in."

Murmurs of delight rippled through the room on the heels of a chorus of 'yes, sirra' and 'we're on it' that came behind.

They had not camped after that brief respite around the warming campfire that allowed Pain to catch up to them. Enola wanted to pass through the Wilds quickly and Uzzi was eager to avoid the possibility other Cana were in pursuit, despite Pain's assurance they were not. Dink, as was often the case, expressed no opinion and no rush to get back to LaGuardia but Pain did seem eager to put distance between him and the pack he was leaving behind, despite his claim the pack would not follow. Uzzi did not pry as they pushed towards civilization, regardless of the questions rolling about in the back of his mind, and Pain did not speak except to indicate an occasional change in direction. His initial curiosity about Uzzi's interest in Vanya seemed to have been replaced with the burning desire to find those they chased.

He had said 'them'.

Uzzi only cared about one.

At the Wild's edge, they paused with the rising of dawn, the trail Pain was following directing him straight ahead towards the often used Pack bunker he was familiar enough with that he did not require the alpha's scent to find it.

Uzzi's business however pushed them north, skirting civilization, following the border of the Wilds until they reached the collection of tents and lean-to shelters scattered around the Hinton Change. Pain's agitation and annoyance at being led away from his quarry did not deter the older man from seeking out, and finding, the hovel he sought.

Pain did not know the average-height, average-built man who emerged from it but he recognized him as the face connected to Roland's downfall. He had seen him in Roland's company, but he did not know him. He only knew his face his name, and the man's responsibility for a death that had changed Pain's world. He growled at Uzzi's side as Dink led the other man towards them.

He had no idea why Thomas Quentin was in this place but the rumpled, dirty condition of his clothes and the shadows on his unshaven face indicated he had been roughing it long enough. It was tempting to laugh at how far the man appeared to have fallen, but to avoid potential recognition, questions, or even draw Quentin's notice, Pain hung back, remaining partially hidden in the shadow of what remained of a highway pillar, to watch and listen without pulling attention to himself.

Roland had been as cautious with the identities of the Flushing Pack members as he had with their Cana truth. Pain refused to undo the late alpha's efforts to protect them.

"Is it done?" Quentin's voice behind the slight cough that cleared his throat, carried a small hint of a whine that made the corners of Pain's lips curl.

"Don't think there were survivors," Uzzi replied with a shrug, masking the lie about the pack he had been instructed to terminate with the truth about the men and women who had accompanied him. From the chaos he had heard behind him as he and Enola retreated and joined Dink in the Wilds, he doubted many of the Normal ruffs had survived.

"Good." Quentin's eyes raked over Enola, admiring her exotic face and noting the extensive evidence of combat she bore. Dink, likewise, displayed injuries congruent with the tale of a battle won but Uzzi appeared unscathed.

That he might have sent others to their death while holding back like a coward made Quentin smirk even though he would have done the same.

"Got enough people to go on?"

"Let 'em go," Uzzi shrugged, ignoring the fading of the man's smirk into a scowl. "Don't like to keep 'em obliged for long. Paid 'em out of pocket so you owe me that. Besides, you said you had a squad."

"Doesn't mean they'll listen to you…"

"They will if you tell them to." It was one thing he knew about Quentin. The man surrounded himself with sycophants and a host he could bully, bribe, or blackmail into doing what he needed. Why that put him out here in the Change, living like a ruff, was none of Uzzi's business. He guessed that the increase of occupied structures in the Change were a result of that gathering of men, but the gradually dying snowstorm had kept most indoors so Uzzi could not evaluate them to decide if his guess was true. "Brought us a guide."

"Guide?" Quentin eyed the fellow slinking in the shadows. "You been to the fort?"

Before Pain could speak, forced to either lie or reveal his nature to a man who reportedly hated anthro…despite bearing the heady trace of Fela blood…Uzzi answered, "He'll get us there. I guarantee it."

If forced to go back on his promise, Uzzi could kill the Cana as easily as he could kill Quentin.

Quentin held his reply long enough to study the crouched shadow, seeking something he did not see, and nodded as if satisfied. "Let's get everyone up and get on with it," he grunted. Enola snarled.

"In this weather?" Dink grunted, holding out his hand to catch snowflakes on his gloved palm. Answering his own question, he shrugged and added, "What's a little more snow?"

❧*❧

❧348❧

"Drink this."

With shaking hands, ignoring the look Oasis cast from across the empty dining table, Nik accepted the cup of tea Torben pushed towards him. Not so long ago, the table had been full, brothers, parents, and Marrocks gathered around it, laughing, discussing politics and gossip, philosophy, and the daily doings those living closely together were prone to sharing with those they loved and trusted. But the love and trust were gone, eroded and replaced by absence, suspicion, and death.

So much death.

Now his father was gone too.

"Bad tonight?" Torben's voice was a whisper although, with the absence of familial chatter and the clattering of dinner dishes, it was likely Oasis could hear him.

Nik did not care. His demons were well known. There was little point in denying them to the woman whom his father intended to serve as his second in matters of politics during his absence.

It took a strong man, Yiva once said, to face his faults and failings.

If only, Nik thought bitterly, his mother had done likewise. Not that what had happened had been her fault or failure, but if she had been strong enough to call out Donn's flaws, those in the Fortress might have been detoured from this spiraling path of self-destruction.

He nodded. Hoisting the burden of Laedanship onto his shoulders after a lifetime of avoiding more than a whiff of responsibility filled his belly and blood with a flight or fight response he did not know how to counter. The first drug he could lay his hands on had been his solution to that feeling before.

He chose not to go down that path, though angels help him, the temptation to do so was strong.

The spiced aroma of the tea reminded him Torben was here to help him face temptation. The sposer offered him the one thing that could ease those burning longings without filling him with something shadowy and addictive to blind him for days.

"Maybe you should get some sleep," Oasis offered.

Her concern sounded genuine. Nik was not convinced.

"I don't wanna sleep." There was no need for it, not for his body, not for his head. What he needed was something to keep busy. Looking at Torben and cocking his head towards the window and the dark sky beyond, he asked, "What's it like out there?" He had not been outside, nor near a window, since his father's departure. The snow made him worry about Lowell's travels, about whether he had given Jia enough to succeed, and being near the windows, knowing there was someone out there who wanted him dead, made him feel uncomfortably vulnerable. "Think they've enough…?"

Torben grunted as if to remind him Oasis must not know about Lowell's competition for Fort Hamilton's resources. On the off chance she could warn Lowell, Torben thought it better such information not be shared.

Nik agreed.

Thankfully, the aborted question could apply to his father as well.

"He's got everything he needs," Torben replied. "He's Laedan. Of course he's prepared."

"I suppose." Nik sipped the steaming tea, his eyes closed, detecting the hint of peppermint amidst the blend of whatever Torben used for this particular soothing taste. The sposer returned to his meal but Nik could feel the woman's eyes on him, picking him apart the way Torben picked apart the roast fowl on his plate with his knife and fork. Soon Torben would leave for the Plant. Nik was tempted to go with him to escape the ghosts haunting the Fortress and the shades trying to kill him.

Leaving Oasis alone, however, at Donn's mercy if he chose to return, was a possibility Nik could not stomach.

Why did he have to be the strong one?

There was also an uneasy consideration plaguing him that leaving her alone for any length of time might prompt her to lay claim to the right of rule over LaGuardia in his stead. Other than something in her demeanor when Lowell left the Fortress, there was no evidence she had such a motive.

As Nik was a Channon, however, Oasis was a Hallister.

Why would she not want to rule if presented with the opportunity? No Laedan had ever been a woman, but with Jia poised for the same position, why would Oasis not likewise wish to pursue it?

Shaking off the uneasiness, Nik finally stammered, "I'll be in the office." The empty teacup clattered on the saucer as he set it down. "Not my office…his," he corrected. The mountain of unread missives, requests, and pending fiscal reports there would be more than enough to keep his head occupied until the sun rose and Torben returned.

At this hour, Oasis would soon be asleep. Nik would not have to worry about her for the rest of the night.

"I'll make more tea before I go."

Nik nodded, stood up, and with a slightly dizzy stagger, produced by the ache between his ears, he trudged towards the door. He paused with his hand on the frame and said, "Goodnight, Oasis," without looking back at her.

"Goodnight," she said, her tone as neutrally polite as his was.

He did not need to see her face to imagine her thoughts. Like a shark smelling blood, she smelled weakness in the political waters swirling around him…and he believed that, like his brother, she would move to take advantage of that as soon as an opening arose.

Perhaps she was more like her husband than any of them thought.

❧*❧

Though the snow stopped falling during their rest and the wind faded to a calm whisper, the frigid cold, and their overall reluctance to face it made for a slow start to the night's travels. The group was small enough to remain tightly packed as they moved, with Deuce on the lookout ahead for dangers they might not see until it was too late. Because Vance was the only one to have seen the map that should guide them, a map Nik had not been able to replace, he traveled at the front beside Jia, keeping them pointed in the right direction. They, too, pointed out prospective hazards to the others and tested the icy puddles, crumbled debris, and brittle planks sometimes set into place to cross over earthen holes and craters that opened into the Below.

Kato, feeling displaced and struggling to come to terms with a gradual shift away from the connection he had felt with her during their initial meeting, trailed far enough behind to guard the group's backs. Despite what had sparked between them that first night, something had changed since Liam's rescue and though he wanted to blame the mage who seemed to hover too close whenever Kato wanted a moment of Jia's company, he knew Segara was not to blame.

If anyone was at fault, it was the man who had taken her father's life and forced her into a role of responsibility for the lives of so many others. That sort of responsibility came with a price.

Kato saw himself as that price.

With the air silent and calm, with what little breeze there was pushing against their faces, and the sound of their breathing, the rustling of heavy clothes and packs, and the crunching of boots through frozen snow that showed fewer signs of disturbance the further they journeyed away from LaGuardia's borders, anything behind might pose as much of a threat as anything before them.

So far, there was nothing there.

Face coverings and the conservation of energy and breath kept them quiet. Awkward, worried thoughts undercut anything anyone might have said. This was only the beginning of what promised to be a long journey.

Jia had no idea how to build cohesiveness in the group, to unite them in their cause, rather than as individuals tacked onto her quest for closure, with the Channons, with her father, with herself. They weren't a pack. Few of them had anything in common. Roland could have done it the way he had united the borough.

Jia did not know how.

The movement of a varied group of livestock at midday had disturbed their rest and prompted Pubby to speak to the Protectors directing the herding so as not to expose those hiding nearby. Retrieving stolen property. Nothing more. He chatted with the officers, picking up gossip about this portion of LaGuardia's border but he learned little that might affect them. Details of the clearing of the streets west of the line for gradual assimilation into the borough.

Warnings about a roving band thought to be mutani ruffs stealing supplies from the assim crews and settlers being maneuvered in to occupy the secured structures. Cautionary advice about flooding and the icing of several locations after the last storm and the collapse of an overpass beneath the weight of wet snow that had killed the majority of one assim crew.

It remained to be seen if any of those hazards would be in the group's way. Without revealing plans, a direction of travel or interest in open paths leading west, what lay ahead remained unknown.

Some slept after the bleating of sheep and goats, the squealing of pigs, lowing of cattle, and the shouts of people settled. Others had not. Yu's offering of a hot meal greeted their eventual stirring, steaming tea and potato mash boiled with bits of sausage serving as hints of home and comfort that made them feel less isolated and more at ease.

But it was not enough. They were a splintered faction, Ursa, Cana, Fela, and Protectors, groups rarely known to cooperate beyond border treaties. Jia wanted to bridge the gaps, find common ground beyond the need to keep weapons out of the hands of those likely to misuse them against the whole of humanity.

If she did not, each night's travel would be the same.

If only her father was here.

He knew this game. He knew how to stalk, to hunt anthro, to avoid detection. He knew how to stay beyond another mage's senses. He would follow and he would wait. Sooner or later, he would catch Segara alone.

The rest of them did not matter.

Chapter 25

Despite Oasis' suspicious glower as she stalked from the library, Nik greeted Chief Ernest with an outstretched hand, expressing relief for an interruption that took him out of his head and away from the mountain of paperwork on his father's desk. At one time, Roland was the one to manage those mundane responsibilities, ones Quentin had gradually usurped as he wheedled his way into Lowell's confidence. With both men gone and Lowell's focus consumed by the loss of a friend, a son, a wife, the betrayals of those he trusted, and an expedition that had lured him out of LaGuardia for an indeterminate number of days, so many matters had been unaddressed, so many things left undone, Nik doubted he would catch up with any of it before Lowell returned from chasing fort phantoms.

Ernest's face was somber, with sleepless circles under his eyes and creases of pain etched there and at the corners of his mouth. He accepted the drink Nik poured, noting the young man poured none for himself before sitting in a faded, cushioned chair of teal green and motioning for Ernest to likewise sit. Ernest glanced at the chairs remaining, covered with the same dust-faded color, and sank into one directly opposite the acting Laedan.

"Been left holding the reins?" There were no other choices available, given the absence of the Marrocks and the implosion of the Channon family, but he was still surprised Lowell had chosen to trust the son with such a history of addiction. He could have put borough business on indefinite hold until his return or left some degree of power in the hands of his council. Nik looked clearheaded, however, and Ernest hoped it would stay that way, hoped his father's apparent trust and the chief's proposal would help.

Nik shrugged, reading the underlying thoughts behind the question but choosing not to address them. Anything he could say would only substantiate already existing opinions. "Did you find him? Do you have him?"

Ernest shook his head. "Borough's a big place…and I imagine he's got people willing to help him, places to go…"

Nik snorted. Such allies might have been gained through bribery and blackmail, and might not know what Donn was capable of. Or they knew and did not care. Or they knew and were too intimidated to resist. The power and prestige and favor to be gained by backing the Channon most likely to be Laedan one day, now that Jonni was gone, might make the risk of sheltering and protecting him worth taking.

Or Donn had not given the unfortunate souls any other choice.

"We're looking," the chief continued, "for Quentin too."

Finding Quentin seemed less important, though the man responsible for the deaths of Roland and Jonni needed to be found and punished too so LaGuardia, and Nik's remaining family, could begin to heal. Finding Quentin, however, did not feel as if it would suffice.

It would not be enough to heal Lowell.

"That why you're here?" Such updates were essential but tedious.

Ernest shook his head. "I'm building a task force to find the source of plasm so we can shut it down." He paused long enough to gauge Nik's surprise before continuing. "Without laws limiting distribution, manufacture, or the use of things like…"

"Addictive shart," Nik finished, prompting Ernest to go on.

"Yes, exactly. We don't…the Protectorate that is, have authority to take it too far. Hell, it isn't even illegal to abduct, enslave, or torture anthro. HOPE's seen to that…"

There were laws regarding abduction, but the common interpretations by the juds only applied those laws to Normals. When such cases involved anthro, rulings were twisted to fall in the favor of Normals or else tended to be dismissed for lack of evidence. Most such abductions, if reported, were invariably rumored to have HOPE connections. With so many juds affiliated or swayed by HOPE, most anthro and mutani alike were disinclined to bring the disappearances of their loved ones to the attention of the Protectorate or pursue a case before the juds.

Doing so increased the likelihood that they, too, would vanish.

"It is…it should be…in practice or not." Nik was familiar with those laws, forced to study such things as part of a Channon's education. He had studied them more closely when the rumors about the Marrocks first came to his attention, when he began to have suspicions about his own nature he had never discussed with anyone. "There are laws to prevent illegal experimentation…"

"For what good those do." Anthro and mutani were barely considered people by many, a position HOPE touted and a loophole in the law people consistently worked around.

"Thanks to Segara," Ernest began again, "I've a few leads…where product is entering the borough, and we're starting with some distributors who've been in our sights for a while. But I'm hoping…"

Nik shook his head. "Not going to be bait for a sting. Under other circumstances, maybe, but I have to consider LaGuardia's best interests until Fa's…"

"Wasn't thinking that. I came hoping you might have some names…people you knew...that you could point us to. Maybe even enact some sort of law to prohibit the sale of plasm in the borough."

Elbows on his knees, Nik leaned forward, his brow furrowed. The difficulty of prohibiting the use of a single substance would create a class of criminals LaGuardia was not prepared to manage. The Protectorate was not equipped to police the borough's borders to search everyone who crossed. There were too many avenues to guard, even if one ruled out the most impassible streets.

Making the manufacture of plasm illegal within the borough, however, prohibiting the sale, might make it possible for the Protectorate to hunt those responsible for it. It might make the product obsolete. Or it would drive the demand higher.

From experience, Nik knew there was a multitude of other substances to ingest, inject, and inhale. Get plasm off the street and most junkies would turn somewhere else. A drug manufactured from the blood of other people was not required. But he did not believe it would be as simple, as easy, as outlawing the manufacture of juice.

"Do what you have to, Chief," he decided with a nod. "I'll do what I can to back you. As for names…" His shoulders hitched and his gaze strayed with vacant distraction towards the window over Ernest's shoulder. "Was pretty worthless in those days…remembering names and shart like that…unless I had to…"

He remembered more details than others expected. It was why Roland had entrusted him with the map and documents about Fort Hamilton. But he had maintained the ruse of feigned oblivion for so long that falling back into it was a natural thing when questioned or threatened. His voice dropped, he swallowed a nervous breath and nodded. "I'll see what I can do…get you something by day's end. If the juds, if anyone, tries to impede what you're doing…if they try to come down on you or put up a fight…send them to me."

"Fair enough." Ernest stood, setting the empty glass on the low table as he did so, and offered his hand. "Thank you." Uncertain if he should call him Laedan, Mister Channon, or simply Nik, Ernest let the phrase of gratitude end there and was relieved Nik did not press him in either direction.

"Soon as we know anything, soon as we find…your brother…" he cleared his throat, "or Mr. Quentin…"

"Be careful with him…with them both. Hate to say it, but they're capable of anything. I don't want anyone else hurt." The two might have teamed up, Donn choosing to overlook the murder of his brother in favor of an otherwise like-minded ally. It would not surprise Nik in the least.

᷒*᷒

Liam dragged his hand down the edge of the busted library door, unsure when it had been torn from its hinges given the sequence of events Vanya described. The frame would be easy to repair, the hinges and the door requiring only a small amount of effort to remake into a suitable barricade or to be replaced by one of those found in some other campus building. Until it was done, the cold air and the occasional winter flurries and rain would push inside, leaving their residence an uncomfortable haven.

There were other buildings they could use but the Pack agreed.

The library was Roland's legacy. It was the building he would have chosen as home. None of them wanted to abandon it for something as inconvenient as a broken door. The door would be repaired. The books, the legacy, would be preserved.

Elsewhere around the campus, where the now-disposed of invaders had encroached, there were more broken doors, shattered windows, damaged walls. Places where the evidence of fires impotent under the assault of winter had left their mark. Those, too, would have to be addressed. Thankfully, there had been no time for the assailants to reach or decimate the orchard, no chance for them to assail the small flocks and herds secured inside the Zone, no chance to destroy the potted food too heavy to move to some place safer. The Pack's food supply was spared. They would not be hungry because of that.

The Pack concurred with Liam's assessment, a direction chosen he believed Jia and Roland would have likewise selected. Without knowing the origin of their attackers, unable to identify the dead they found and disposed of, the Pack chose to remain temporarily within the security of the Zone. The library would be repaired, the traps cleared and reset, new ones laid. Every adult pack member was encouraged to mark the perimeter so other Cana, other anthro, would know this territory was claimed.

They would remain in the Zone while the enemy was traced to their origin, if that was possible.

Until their alpha returned and advised them.

Too often now, the Flushing Pack had flirted with destruction.

None of them wanted to risk it again.

"Got one." Uncle and Orliss crossed the square with a replacement door carried between them, one that looked sturdy, undamaged, and likely to fit the opening in which Liam stood. It was laden with a collection of items gathered along their way, tools and usable materials for building and repair Liam was glad to see.

He stepped out of the doorway towards the pile of planks, saws, and mallets brought for the job and helped clear the door of what it carried. "Good…just in time."

The air smelled like rain. He wanted the door in place before the storm came in.

"Liam…come look…" Wist raced around the eastern corner of the library, waving his hand, beckoning the other man to follow. He called not in a tone of fright or dismay, but one of eager excitement.

Good news rather than bad, Liam hoped. He nodded at Orliss and said, "Be right back; let me know when it's done," before following in the direction Wist led. If there was some other resource the Pack could use, Liam was eager to see it.

❧*❧

The stub between her fingers was nearly burnt down, the end glowing a faint red-orange in the dimly lit room Geary was directed to as soon as he stumbled through the front door of Kennedy's Fortress. He was cold and miserable, and outside, his horse was taken to the stable to get it out of the icy mid-day drizzle that had caught them off-guard as they returned home.

His staff knew what to expect if his favorite horse was improperly cleaned, dried, fed, and made warm. He took less care, for the moment, of his own well-being.

He had sent no notice of his impending return. Gail's being here, long legs crossed, one exposed by the slit in a red kimono-like gown she rarely wore, should have been a coincidence. But Geary did not believe in coincidence and she looked as if she was expecting him, waiting long enough for the spliff to burn to the end of its life.

As pleased as he was to see her, the image of her in red, the line of her calf, knee, and thigh creating a tightening below his belt left too long unsatisfied, he was also suspicious.

"Shouldn't you be…?" he began, peeling off the constricting, tight blue sweater steeped with rain and sweat in the hopes the stifling feeling beneath would dissipate. His rain cloak and woolen undercoat had been left with the servants in the lobby, along with his gloves, his muddy boots, and damp socks. His feet were cold inside his slippers but that cold had been kept away from his torso by the layers of clothing he was forced to wear when he went out.

The soft fabric of the undershirt lifted as the sweater came free, exposing his stomach but making him feel no more comfortable.

Gail's gaze moved there from his face but she did not rise from the high-backed chair where she sat.

"Everything back to smooth; they don't need me to hover." She preferred to oversee each stage of extraction and processing, but her oversight was not required. Her staff knew what to do.

She paused to stub out the spliff in the metal tray on the table without looking at her hand. "Norse tells me Aman's…"

Geary bristled as he dropped the sweater over the back of another chair and adjusted his undershirt. "He's seeing to business."

Gail scowled but did not ask the nature of that business. The Laedan had his hands in many things, had control over the whole borough. She was not his wife nor adviser, was not his partner in anything outside of the lab. He did not owe her explanations or details. Still, she was curious and marginally concerned that whatever the business was, it could come back to reflect badly on her work.

"We need stock."

"Told you not to come to me with that…"

"Would you rather I go to HOPE?" The corners of her mouth twisted up at his sour expression. They both knew HOPE was the ultimate provider of anthro for the testing process, for the creation of potions, tonics, poisons, and plasm, and for the study of blood and life separating anthro and mutani from the Normals.

They also knew that removing HOPE from Kennedy's political doings was something they each wanted…but would not easily attain.

To shift the acquisition of anthro out of HOPE's hands was tricky and would expose Geary to both public backlash and the enmity of the Grand Mas.

Not that Geary was overly concerned with either.

"Norse can handle it," he grunted. "Just make damn sure it doesn't blow back on…"

"Of course." The spliff butt she had not yet released was fiddled between her fingers as she watched Geary move about the room, seeking a drink, turning up the heat, moving to stay warm. "How is your daughter?"

Geary snorted, swallowed the first drink intended to both cool his head and warm his blood, and then poured another before stretching out on the chaise next to her, his bare feet near her hips as he positioned himself to admire her dark-skinned leg without the temptation to touch her.

"With child."

"So soon?" Casually, Gail dropped an arm over the end of the chaise and rubbed his feet with one hand.

He nodded without speaking, watching her hand, wondering how much he dared say. She would know of Donn's visit to Kennedy now, either from Norse or one of the usual channels through which gossip flowed. Despite what he had said to Oasis, Donnovan was not the sort of man Geary wanted as a son-in-law. He was touchy, unpredictable, with a worrisome reputation for cruelty…but not the sort of thing Geary believed the young man would direct at his wife. It was not beyond expectation, however, to think Donn would seek ways to be in control or be rid of both wife and father-in-law in the hopes of seizing power in Kennedy if he could not gain it swiftly enough in LaGuardia.

It was competition Geary did not want.

"I should find Norse," he eventually mumbled. Norse could take care of this problem as he had taken care of so many others, without the details ever coming back to Geary. Supply product. Deal with Donn. For Norse, both ought to be simple duties.

He did not move away from the caressing hand until his gaze met Gail's and she smiled.

"Shall we take our business somewhere more private?" he grunted instead, voice abruptly hungry and husky. Babies and anthro and Donn Channon could wait. This was a matter of business more pressing for the weary Laedan than the others combined.

"That would be appropriate," Gail agreed with enough color to her neutral tone and expression to set a brighter fire alight in his belly.

❧*❧

It was not the discovery of new supplies or a previously unnoticed campus danger Wist had found but rather cries Liam could hear from a distance, cries within Ministry 12 heralding the arrival of the Pack's newest pup. Addi and Brie had done their best to keep Trill off her feet since the night of fighting, hoping to stave off the onset of premature labor and the too-early birth of their child.

The effort, however, was undermined by the futility of fighting against biology, and when labor came again, there was no aborting it. At early morning, when Hacha came with some of his people to resume securing the college territory and seek out materials from neighboring unincorporated streets to allow for the construction of a wall, Trill's contractions began.

Liam had been there then.

Swift and steady, the birthing progressed, and before Wist pushed open the Ministry door to allow Liam to enter first, the piercing cry that blasted through the crevices around windows and frames was followed by the most welcome sound Liam could imagine.

Addi's face turned to greet him after the sticky, slippery, dark pink mass of thrashing arms and legs was settled, still attached by the umbilical cord, in Trill's arms.

"A girl," Addi grinned as his son and the children adopted over the years scampered from around the room, pushing in to see.

"What's her name?" the little boy asked, his nose wrinkled in mild distaste at the filmy substance covering his new sister.

Addi and Trill looked at one another. Naming a child before birth was rarely done since the Undoing, as it was considered a bad omen in case the infant did not survive. This one, as far as Liam could see, was healthy, though prematurely small, a welcome gift into a family and pack who had lost so much.

That did not guarantee she would live.

"She'll tell us her name when it's time," Liam said to the boy, his hand on his head since Addi's were still soiled with the fluids of birth.

Liam's face, despite the brightness of his words, was melancholy.

Jia should be here for this.

Addi, judging by the nod of his head as Xan knelt on his sister's other side and pushed tendrils of damp hair out of her face, agreed. They should be together as a family.

Accepting Liam's presence in Jia's stead, however, felt right and comfortingly appropriate.

❧*❧

"What's up with the two of you?"

There were twenty others, mostly men compelled together by promises Quentin had made, hardened, weary faces Uzzi made an effort to know, to sway, to win to his charms as Quentin forced them into a quickstep march across LaGuardia through backstreets to keep away from Protectors and Laedan Guards. A few of the faces Uzzi recognized from past jobs but most he did not know. He refused to be in a position of risk with people he could not trust thus it behooved him to undertake the process of making nice without attracting the suspicious attention of the paranoid man who considered himself the leader of their expedition.

Far as Uzzi was concerned, Quentin was not the leader. Nor was he. Despite what they wanted to believe, despite the childlike map drawing Quentin presented as proof of a destination none of them had seen and few had heard of, they were in the hands of the one following an invisible trail only he could detect.

The rest knew, by the paths he followed, paths he marked, that Pain was anthro. It made some uncomfortable, but not enough to prompt anyone to move against him. He knew the way.

If Quentin trusted his lead, they would too, so long as he dangled the promise of pay before them. Given the opportunity, if they saw any hint of weakness or duplicity in Quentin or Pain, they would not hesitate to react accordingly.

Ruffs like these rarely did.

Pain knew it too. He kept his distance, leading at the head of the unit with frequent pauses and his nose in the air as if tracking a difficult trail through the snowy, busy streets. With the evening camp set in a dilapidated shopping center housing a handful of transients, he drew apart further with his attention split between their surroundings and Thomas Quentin.

He did not know Quentin had been the one to set Uzzi and his followers on the Pack. He did not ask why the attack had been made. He did not know if Quentin recognized him. Not recognizing was not mutual, however, as Uzzi continued to observe the Cana's hostility towards Quentin, and he wanted to understand why.

He wanted to know if it was something he could use or something that was going to be a problem.

"Nothing."

"Bullsh," Uzzi grunted back, dropping to the ground beside him, near enough for a conversation but not near enough to make the Cana uncomfortable. With Dink and the dog patrolling the perimeter of their campsite and Enola pacing in and out of the scattered groups of people with snarls and glares as if inviting someone to challenge her, it left Uzzi free to have this conversation. He handed one of the two slabs of meat, taken from the carcass turning on a spit, to Pain, its aroma sure to draw the attention of people outside, and ignored the grunt of reluctant gratitude.

"I see it, even if he doesn't."

"Don't trust him. He's a traitor. A liar. A killer."

Uzzi snorted. "Not the only one here." He believed they were each those things, to one degree or another. He ignored Pain's narrowed eyes and growl.

"You know nothing about…"

"Don't need to. Know the type. Wouldn't be an outsider like me if you weren't." He swallowed what was in his mouth before asking, "Have something to do with that?" as he pointed to the Cana's injuries.

Pain began to reply, shook his head, and shrugged. If not for Quentin, Roland would not be dead and the leadership of the Flushing Pack would never have come into question. Pain's actions were his own and he did not blame anyone else for them, but they had been spawned by the man he felt compelled to follow.

Not forced. He did not need Quentin or Uzzi or anyone else to find Jia. But leading them provided an excuse to follow her he had not had before. Taking Quentin to her as a gift so she could mete out justice to her father's killer away from the laws of the borough might improve his odds of redemption.

"Indirectly."

The answer was good enough. "He's an ass…and I'd rather be rid of him…but he's paying for all of this; figure I should keep him around long enough to benefit…"

"Think he's gonna pay you?" Pain asked skeptically.

Meat gone, fingers licked clean as he watched stragglers sneak in on the wafting scent of roasting flesh, Uzzi smirked. "Oh, he will…one way or another. You want in on that, I'll welcome the help."

More than welcome, Uzzi thought with a scoff. If he did not have to dirty his hands with the likes of Quentin, he would be satisfied.

"Don't need your help…or your permission."

Uzzi's smirk widened as he stood; Pain did not need to say those words for the older man to know they were true.

"Let's just say he owes me in more ways than one. We get our share of the spoils and after that, I don't care what you do with him…what happens to him…so long as I'm there to see it.

Pain grunted and did not watch him leave.

By morning, from the looks of things, their force would be larger still. Whatever they were going after, whatever they hoped to gain, Pain hoped it would be worth their while.

He intended to make it worth his.

Chapter 26

Her bare shoulder was cold where it was exposed to the air and he feared in that contact he had lost her. He knew the feeling of dead flesh and that memory made him jerk awake and turn his head to face her, his breath caught in the back of his throat on the tail of panicked suspense over what he expected to find.

Her eyes were closed, her lips slightly parted, and when one bare leg shifted against his and the soft snoring sound of exhaled breath escaped, Geary released his own as well.

This thing between them had never been serious. The arrangement had suited them over the years of their acquaintance as duties pulled them in directions where their knowledge of each other was best presented to the public as casual and businesslike. Why, he mused with a frustrated scowl as he pulled the blanket to cover her shoulder, did the fear of losing her rear its looming head now?

Realizing she was looking at him, he tore his gaze from the hand lingering on her shoulder.

"I know that look," she murmured sleepily. She knew him well enough to have seen it before but it was an expression she had never quantified or asked him to explain. Guilt? Fear? Memory traces?

He shook his head and rolled towards her, keeping distance between them so he could continue to hold her gaze.

"What I said…last night…"

"Which part?" she countered with a bemused chuckle.

His hair rustled against the pillow as he shook his head. "After one more batch…there'll be no new subjects. Not now. I'm shutting down the project until…"

Though Gail's expression darkened, she did not move. "You can't do that. It's not your decision…"

"The Channons know. About the labs, the plasm…about…"

"How could they…?"

"I don't know." There had been enough left at the lab to redirect anyone's belief of guilt onto HOPE. But he had not counted on that one individual being present. He had given those faces with the Marrock girl a lot of thought; only one possibility made sense. "I think one of them…seen him before but…he might be a Protector…could be a mage."

"You didn't say there'd be…" Mages looked normal, however, as anthro did before a change, and without a badge, identifying an off-duty Protector was no easier. Mages wore no identifier whether on or off duty. They were indistinguishable from anyone else. Suspecting someone was coming to the lab in search of a Marrock no longer held was one thing. She trusted the evidence Lowell had planted was as good as it could have been. When examined by a mage, however, the veracity of evidence was less certain.

She sat, turning to swing her feet over the edge of the bed. His bed. This was a first for them, her staying in the Fortress, overnight, in his room. The potential consequences of their choice had not been properly considered last night, but in the light of cloudy morning, Gail was beginning to believe this had been a bad decision.

"You've got what you wanted."

"You think I want this? The income keeps us safe, all of us…the research is…"

"Unethical?" she spat, snatching up the red kimono from where it had landed on the floor and pulling it on. It was the word some people used when referencing the ill-treatment of anthro…or would use if they knew how juice was generated.

"Necessary." Geary did not often debate ethics. Things were either necessary or they were not. Ethics was a weak man's game that prevented important decisions from being made.

Without bothering to dress, Geary rose too and came around the bed to stand in front of her, gripping her shoulders to hold her where they could speak eye to eye. "We didn't anticipate this…but it's done. We need to know what they know…how much…we need to understand the…"

"If the lab shuts down…"

"The extraction, the plasm production." Plasm was a byproduct of other processes, an accident enhanced over time. As much as Kennedy had come to rely on the under-the-table resource for financial gain, it was a resource he thought best put to rest long enough for suspicions to pass.

"Channon's preoccupied with the deaths of Roland, his son, and wife. He's looking for someone to blame and we can't afford that to be us. We halt production temporarily, let his anger run its course, and when the mood has cooled, when they find their killers, we'll pick up again."

Gail snorted and tried to pull away from his hands, but with the bed behind her, there was nowhere to retreat to.

"Give it time, Gail," he continued earnestly. "All I ask. Work with what you've got…liquidate what you can…shift to studying what you can get from the stock there is, and leave plasm alone. Shut it down. A week or two, maybe four, should be all we need."

The steel in her eyes made him release her and step back, allowing her to finish dressing in the silent room. He watched, trying to gauge her thoughts by the jerkiness of her movements, in the way she stalked out of his chamber without agreeing or disagreeing with his direction.

He trusted her, as much as he trusted anyone. She was smart. As soon as she calmed down and gave his argument consideration, she would understand the risks of continuing production in an atmosphere where discovery and the fallout from it were likely to destroy them.

It was only a few weeks. In time, something more important would distract LaGuardia's Protectorate, the investigating mage, the Channons. The spate of recent deaths, the shifts necessary in the governance of the northern borough, would force Channon's attention away from the trivial loss of a few anthro and the sale of just one more psychoactive substance to junkies on the street.

Gail would conclude the same by the time she returned to her new facility. She would do what they needed to do.

But a word with Norse on other matters remained in order. That, Geary decided as he dressed, was his first priority today…since breakfast with Gail, who stalked out of the bedroom and down the stairs, was out of the question.

⊷*⊷

The evidence of territory assimilation gleaned from the work crews could be seen in the partial clearing of several city blocks beyond LaGuardia's current western border. It was not always feasible or even desirable, to remove the evidence of collapsed structures from unending roadways, but where possible, fallen brick and stone were mounded at the sides of the streets. Piles of scrap metal were created beside them and collection crates dotted the landscape to hold glass and other potentially usable materials. Without Laedan Guards or Protectors to watch over it, with no authority established here, scavs were free to pick through the sorted debris for anything they could sell or use. Those people warily watched the passing group but as Jia showed no interest in them or their scavving efforts, they determined the strangers were no threat and resumed their work, allowing the travelers to pass unhindered.

How many others, she wondered as she held a hand down to assist Pubby to the top of the concrete mountain blocking the road, a barricade left to delineate the current edge of the reclamation project, had left LaGuardia to seek something better, something different, in the untamed lands to the west?

There was a whole world there, beyond what they could see, people surely, unbound by borough politics and the fear of HOPE, fighting to survive in whatever fashion suited them. She knew from history books and lessons her father had instilled in her that what lay beyond her line of sight was so vast she would never be able to see it. If they made it to Fort Hamilton, what might lie beyond?

Would guiding the Pack to these free lands be enough to save them? With Roland gone and the Laedan ties to the Fortress strained, nearly severed if Jia allowed them to be, was it time to consider moving the Pack along this same path or another like it?

Would they even want to go?

"Thanks," muttered Pubby breathlessly, wiping a sweaty hand on his trousers after balancing on the summit as others had already done. Near the back of the group, Candace tried to assist Eddie up but he stubbornly growled and insisted on making the climb on his own.

Kato came behind, protecting their flank, making sure no threat came at their backs.

As Cana, as Fela, as Ursa, the animal forms would have made the passage much easier. In deference to Pubby and Vance, the anthro resisted the temptation to make the change and take the easy path.

"Edge of the world," Vance mumbled as he scanned ahead for visible dangers barely discernable in the dark. Though no LaGuardia restoration crews had passed beyond this point, there was evidence of inhabitation. A path cleared through the street to allow unimpeded passage. The lights of fires glowed behind windows from ground to sky in the random pattern of starlight. There were large dogs tied to posts before a couple of doorways and wagons, some cobbled from wood, others fabricated from the piecemeal remnants of derelict autos. Some were parked on the roadsides, up against the walls of this structure or that, seemingly maintained for daily use but brought in tight to a residence's door to guard it against intrusion.

"But not the end of it," Jia added with a hopeful note. The moon's glow behind the clouds was sinking lower, the air warming a little as the not-yet-visible sun struggled to bring another day.

Deuce, who scampered to the base of the rubble, paced left and right to the sides of the street and then loped about twenty yards down the empty stretch before coming back to the debris' summit as a man. He squatted beside Jia, wiped his hands over his face with his eyes focused on the darkness ahead, and asked, "Go on or find shelter?"

She looked at him, at Vance, and to the faces around her, and down to Kato who had finally reached the base of the concrete pile to start his climb up it. They had not made as much progress tonight as she had hoped for. The need for caution, to avoid Protectors or assim crews who might recognize her, or Vance, or Pubby, as well as Eddie's dragging anchor, had slowed them too much. They should have passed out of LaGuardia sooner.

Reading her frustration, QiangXu offered, "Still a few hours before daylight."

"Not likely to be anyone who will know us out there," added Vance, the tilt of his head indicating the path in front of them.

No Protectors, no assim crews, no Laedan Guards, perhaps. But somewhere, behind or before them, to the north or the south, others followed the same beacon they were tracking. They should press on, use the last few hours of darkness to their advantage, but one final glance at Eddie, who slipped on the shifting concrete and snarled at Kato when the older Fela tried to steady him, made Jia scowl and sigh.

It was going to take time to descend the concrete mound without injury. No matter her desires, Eddie would not last much longer.

Seeing her scrutiny, Eddie hung his head and sidestepped towards his mother. Candace gave him a scolding hiss but accepted the hand he entwined in hers.

"Let's get down and see what's up there." She pointed ahead, to the barely visible edge of white in the dark, where a small fire appeared to designate the edge of a road or a fork in the path or some other sort of change guarded by someone.

"I'll take a look." Deuce barely finished the words when the wolf form returned and he leaped to the road.

"I'll scout us a camp." The irritable note in Kato's voice made Eddie's crestfallen expression deepen.

Pubby shook his empty flask. "Somewhere with water'd be good."

"Told you not to drink all that…"

Pubby shrugged at Vance with a little grin and tied the flask to his belt. "I was thirsty."

"And now ya gotta piss."

Yu chuckled, "He's not the only one…but not up here." She started to pick her way down, careful with her balance.

The others followed.

At the back of the group, with Kato having gone ahead to find shelter, Eddie mumbled, "I'm hungry."

"You'll have to wait," Candace scolded, looking back to be certain he was following and not in danger of falling.

From her belt pouch, Jia produced a small apple and held it out to him. "All I have until we camp."

Eddie met her gaze, hesitated in reaching for the apple, but gave in and accepted it with an embarrassed, reluctant, awkward nod.

⁊*⸙

General Warby's wide, gloved fist snagged Donn from his horse, yanking him to the ground at the edge of the road, forcing both to roll through the mud as the general's horse whinnied, reared, and jerked sideways to fall where the two men had landed. Donn's horse broke free, wrenching its rains out of his hand, and charged away in panic from the shouting and barrage of stones and arrows hailing down on them from both sides of the narrow street. A handful of HOPE men barged into the building on the opposite side without their general's explicit command while others leaped over their leaders and pushed into the building behind them.

The rest, those not nursing wounds, were either crawling out of the line of fire or attempting to return it.

In the pre-dawn light, with broken shutters to hide behind and the lips and side frames of windows to shield them, getting successful return shots at their assailants proved a futile waste of resources.

Someone screamed. Something fell from above and landed with a heavy, wet flour sack thud on the street nearby. A man, whose head split with the impact on the broken pavement, splattering blood and brain matter across the faces of the two huddled there.

Donn barely noticed. The corpse's hand clutched the barrel of a revolver that surprisingly had not discharged upon impact. The gun was all Donn saw. He lurched up, intending to grab it, only to be pulled back by the hand he had not realized still had hold of his arm. He turned and swung a fist at the offending hindrance, but the impact lost momentum with the whistle of another arrow that sizzled through the air and cut across his bicep. The unexpected pain and Warby's grip yanked him face down into the mud but it spared him the cut of a second arrow that might otherwise have found a deadlier mark.

More shouts. More bodies thrown from windows to the ground outside. Others behind shutters and cracked-open doorways retreated when they saw the uniforms of those in the street under attack.

Then there was silence except for the sucking of mud as men began to stand.

"I want every person in these buildings dragged out and…" Donn began, insulted more by the mud, the loss of his horse, and the loss of the revolver Warby had retrieved, than he was by the blood splatter and the travel delay the attack created.

"Not worth it," Warby grunted, wiping blood from his nose where Donn had struck him, assessing their losses with a sweeping gaze. Two dead he could see. Others were injured but not mortally so. Not enough, he decided, to keep them from moving on.

"Not worth it?" Donn bellowed.

"We're HOPE. It happens. Not here for them. We're here to…"

"Only the weak'd ignore this outrage, leave this unanswered…"

Warby glowered but did not respond. Donn stared back, square-shouldered and eventually frustrated when the general refused to be baited by his insult. Donn snorted and turned his attention to the nearest horse, claiming it as his since the one he had ridden could not be seen. Satisfied Donn was not going to be a problem at this moment, was not intending to further challenge his leadership in front of their men, Warby barked, "Put 'em down," he indicated their dead, "and leave the bodies. Mount up. We move in five."

Their deaths would have to be reported to their families but burials were a waste of time, a detraction from the mission.

His intent to make camp here was thwarted, but he was not discouraged. Not everyone in the boroughs welcomed the protection and power HOPE offered. In time, with persistence, he believed that would change. The Grand Mas would be told about the insolence of these people, this place, and HOPE would deal with them. Change would come, either willingly or at the end of a gun barrel.

It was not Warby's job. He had something else to do.

❧*❧

The stench of rot grew stronger the further along the path they traveled, carried on the wind and the barely rolling, largely stagnant drainage ditch that dribbled alongside the street before eventually disappearing through a series of debris-clogged grates into the murk of Below. The smell seeped in around the herb-soaked cloth Lowell had tied around his head to cover his mouth and nose and the alternating miasma of smells made him dizzy, made his stomach churn. Neither condition aided his ability to stay steady on his saddle.

A few hours at most. That was the longest he had ever sat on a horse when some business forced him to travel away from the Fortress. Roland had most often been the one to undertake those required duties. As those few hours had never been awkward or uncomfortable, Lowell had been confident that undertaking this journey west, an unspecified number of days' travel, would be an easy feat.

By the end of the first day, and during every ensuing hour spent in the saddle after an uncomfortable first night's sleep on the lumpy ground, the reality of his situation set in. He wished for a hasty return to the comfort of his bed, a heated room, and a warm meal spread on platters, in bowls and cups and plates of polished silver and china.

He could not go back. He could hear the sniggers of his detractors already. Yiva expected this of him. Expected him to keep LaGuardia, and their grandchild, safe.

Grandchild…or son.

There was no proof as to which it was. It did not matter. It was a Channon child.

Bringing back the glorious horde housed in Fort Hamilton was the only way Lowell could begin to make up for his multitude of failures, the only way he could redeem himself in the eyes of the woman he had betrayed too many times.

With the reins tight in one hand, he adjusted the cloth over his nose, squinting his burning eyes against the tears stinging them. When he swayed in the saddle without realizing it, the permeating odor of the sagging forms he could see making him dizzier, Captain Ortega steadied him with one hand.

"Plague," the word came back, spreading from those at the front of the column to those stretched out behind.

"We should go around."

"Nowhere to go for that," Ortega said grimly. Since setting off at daybreak, they had plodded down a twisting stretch of rarely used streets in this section of the borough where the side paths were barricaded in the fashion so often utilized to discourage roving grubbers. They could have bypassed more of the barricades after circumventing the first one in the push west, but they had chosen not to, to avoid lost time. They found themselves funneled into a fetid gathering of dirty, groaning wretches, their hands outstretched in supplication, who lacked the resources to treat what ailed them.

The few who tended the ailing in the twilight were little better off than those they cared for. Blankets covered the coughing huddles where they lay with no effort made to move them beyond the barred doors of nearby buildings. Heads lifted to watch the marching men and plodding horses pass, noting the clatter of wheels, boots, and hooves without the strength to beg for help. Some grabbed hold of passing ankles but the grip was not strong enough to stop them and the hands inevitably flopped into the mud.

By morning, most of these souls would be dead.

It had not occurred to Lowell, to Ortega, or to anyone else that the barricades passed were meant to keep people in, not out. It had not been obvious that the initial blockage had been erected with the intent of containing the sickness that had struck here.

There were deterrents for that, signs and symbols and protocols to carry out to warn people away from infected, infested buildings and streets. Ortega had seen none of that.

If the Laedan or anyone else had, they had either not recognized the markers or had not paid attention to them.

Perhaps the markers had not been set. Perhaps the plague had spread too fast.

"Single file," Ortega instructed those nearest him with a gesture directing the message to be passed to others. "Don't let them touch you. Keep your mouths and noses covered…and don't take anything they offer…anything you see."

"That bad?" Lowell hissed through clenched teeth, as if the closing of his mouth would inhibit the intake of putrid air.

It did nothing more than muffle his voice.

"Don't know what it is. Should send a rider back…warn your son and…"

"They'll be fine. Dying aren't going anywhere," Lowell said with a shaking head.

"No, but others could come here like we have and carry it back." He frowned, realizing that any messenger sent back would do the same thing. "Or it can spread in the air, the water, with rats and cats and…"

Lowell was about to speak again, finding the notion of losing even one man as a messenger, when they did not know what they would face ahead, to be an uncomfortable one. His head began to bob in reluctant agreement to the warning, but the turning of his face away from the rheumy eyes of a pleading child, the majority of its face and skin wrapped in layers of dirty bandage-like cloth, made him shutter and obscured the permission he thought to give. Only the child's eyes were visible, eyes full of suffering and pleading.

He could not bear to see it. He could not stomach the stench, the filth, the decay. But there was nothing he could do.

How, he wondered with another shudder, his focus shifting straight ahead, had Roland managed to be out in the midst of people such as these?

❧*❧

Rounding up a host of familiar junkies, faces well known to the District One Protectorate from prior arrests, thieves and brawlers, and those inclined to disturb the peace and harass innocent citizens, was a simple project as there were certain streets, drinking establishments, boarding hostels, and clinics, where they were known to frequent. Scattered as they were around the district, there was hope that picking those people up, shaking them down, would provide names, locations, or something else that might aid in finding the one called Brac.

But there were other districts, other places their prey could hide.

The five scattered around Ernest's office were as familiar with each other as any four people in their positions could be, weary faces lined with the weighted creases of death and trauma witnessed during their tenures as Protectorate leaders in LaGuardia. Four captains and one chief, Ernest, despite his impending retirement, being the youngest.

"'bout time we cracked down on this." John Bailey, the captain of West District 1, a grizzled, dark-skinned man with a thin line of white hair encircling his head like a partial halo and stretching down along his jawline and around his mouth in a way that made him look more distinguished than his manner of speaking portrayed, toyed with the glass of whiskey in his hand poured several minutes before. "They're gonna outnumber us if we don't do something."

"Improving shelters and giving them something worthwhile to do, making sure they eat, would go a long way towards prevention," began Patrice Corelli, the only woman in the room and a long-time proponent of welfare programs designed to help everyone in the borough live a better life. She had worked side by side with Jonni to improve conditions in East District 1. Life was better there, safer, less fraught with natural hazards than other areas, the people as well taken care of as the pair had been able to manage. She had been unable to stem the influx of plasma spidering through the streets, however. The oldest of the captains in the room, with piercing blue eyes and thinning pale red hair kept covered by a variety of colorful scarf wraps, Ernest did not foresee her stepping down from her post until someone was forced to carry her corpse out of her office.

She was, to Ernest, more dedicated to the work than any of them.

Andre Mallo, two years Ernest's senior in age and tenure, snorted and wiped his broad nose on his kerchief. Captain of District 3, his station covering the southern-most streets of the borough, he was the one to most frequently interact with Donnovan and many of the Protectors in his unit were prone to distrust him because of it. He ran his Protectorate, his district, with tight-fisted efficiency, intolerant of misconduct, leaving little leeway for lawlessness in the Protectorate or in his district. Even that had failed to thwart the sale and use of plasm or anything else. "Plenty of work to be done if they'd get off their asses to do it. Assim isn't going to happen without bodies."

There was often employment to be had in an assim crew. The grueling nature of the work and the fact that it took people from their families for long periods, meant many were reluctant to undertake it, even though the rewards for doing so were substantial.

"Some are doing their best just to survive." Everly Rahm, a small man with a reedy voice and a monocle he switched from eye to eye as it suited him, had been hand-picked by Nik Channon to serve as District 2's captain. His tenure had been, thus far, the shortest, and there had been unrest regarding his appointment at a time when there had been others seemingly better suited for the post. But Rahm, with Nik's often incoherent oversight, had arranged and maintained a stable relationship with the Zone, had secured trade along the coast, and had overseen a steady, if slow, expansion to the east without the usual unrest and violent pushback the other districts often faced when it came to their assim efforts. While Rahm faced the same issues his counterparts in other districts did, District 2 was more peaceful and less prone to problems, than elsewhere in LaGuardia.

Many argued its smaller size and population were the cause.

Ernest was not convinced it was true.

"Whatever the case," the chief grunted, hoping to prevent the inevitable descent into territorial squabbles these meetings often degenerated into, "we need the sellers…the pushers…if we're going to locate Brac and find the source…"

"You know how many sell fistfuls of pills and powders, homemade shart, just to…" began Patrice.

"There's hundreds of them," Bailey complained in a moment of rare agreement with the woman beside him on the sofa.

"Not talking about them…but even they're getting their shart…or the makings of it…from somewhere. Bring 'em in, shake 'em down. If they're small fish, let 'em loose…but keep an eye on them. Little fish can become bigger ones…and they will as we weed out the competition. If they're big enough, can 'em…or flip 'em to help us in exchange for a deal. Climb the ladder til we find the big hands in this. One of 'em knows Brac. One of 'em has seen his face, can lead to…"

Mallo sneered. "What if he's outside the borough?"

"What if he's based out of Kennedy?" asked Patrice.

"Or worse," Rahm muttered anxiously, "he's HOPE?"

"Wherever he is…when any of us get a lead…we're all in. No one acts alone. That clear?"

"But what if he's…?" Patrice began again.

"No one acts alone," Ernest reiterated. "We share everything. If we need to appoint liaisons to do that, we do it. No secrets. If it turns out he's from Kennedy…or HOPE…I'll take it to the Laedan…"

"Senior? Or Junior?" Mallo interrupted, still sneering.

Ernest shrugged off the attempt to bait him. "Either. Both. Their job is to play politics, not ours."

"What about the Fela killer?" interjected Bailey.

"That's no Fela," Patrice corrected with a deep frown. "That's Thomas Quentin."

Mallo shook his head. "There's no proof…"

"And whoever killed Yiva?" interrupted Rahm, his voice small and mournful.

Surprised to have one of the others bring it up when that news was relatively fresh and thus not prone to having spread far, Ernest swallowed his initial pained response and replied, "Segara's working on that." While not an entirely accurate statement, Ernest agreed with his mage. The threads were interconnected. Quentin, the Channons, the Marrocks, HOPE. Kennedy, stolen goods, burned warehouses, and plasm. It was all part of something bigger. Somehow, Segara would tie them all off if given enough slack to do so.

"I can send Queenie down if you want. She's worked with him before," Rahm offered.

Though Ernest scowled, reluctant to bring another mage into the twisted Channon drama and the deaths they were forced to bear, he did not think he could reject the use of the District 2 mage unless Segara refused to work with her. Nor did he want to tip Mallo's hand and risk word of a manhunt falling prematurely into Donn's ears.

"Segara's got this…for now. The Laedan's made this top priority. He thinks there's a connection between plasma and the murders…and we're only going to find it if we tap Brac. Keep all ears to the ground…if anything surfaces about the killers, we'll run with it…but Brac's the priority."

Mallo muttered his discontent but nodded in agreement, eager as usual for any excuse to crack down on dissidents, malcontents, and undesirables. Bailey and Patrice, after sharing a look between them, nodded simultaneously. Rahm was the unexpected holdout. The rapid shifting of his eyes, suggesting some sort of inner calculation or thought process, eventually steadied to allow him to meet Ernest's gaze with a somber, "Whatever it takes."

That was good enough for Ernest.

"Lunch in the commissary and back in thirty. Let's work this out and get this done. Let's show the Laedan we can work together on a joint agenda…"

'For once' remained unsaid.

"That'll be something," Rahm agreed. Working with the chief had always been easy for him.

Cooperating with his fellow captains for the good of the whole borough rather than the good of their districts was less so.

Ernest cared only about three things. Bringing in Brac and ending the plasm trade.

Finding Donn Channon and Thomas Quentin.

And redeeming his soul for the murder of a mostly innocent man.

❧*❧

"Doesn't smell right."

A lull in the storm had brought a cessation to rain and snow and though the night was cold, the exertion of travel kept the group warm as they pressed west through unfamiliar streets strewn with the expected debris of decay. The explosive forces of humanity's ancient clashes seemed not to have touched the streets through which they passed, but the collapse of society had bred its own brand of conflict and destruction. The struggle for resources, in addition to nature's efforts to reclaim land no longer frequented by humanity and the forms of transit they had once maintained, meant this region also endured the collapse of buildings, the rot of abandoned vehicles, and the litter of the bodies of grubbers left where they had fallen.

There were no Plants here to dispose of them.

There were no good places for the burial of so many in a world of cracked concrete and row after row of buildings.

When the dead grew to be too many in one location, often dragged into a compact area to decay out of sight, the people living around the powerful stench seemed to have gathered what little they possessed and moved somewhere else.

Night after night, the group felt the shadow of the curious, the hopeful, trailing behind them seeking the supplies the strangers carried. So far, none of those shadows dared emerge to confront them. If they came during the day, while the majority slept, those standing watch seemed deterrent enough to hold scavs at bay.

Eventually, someone would grow bold enough to try.

It was not the scent of scavs, nor the stench of the dead making Yu pace at the head of the group as the others caught up to her, her head cocked, her nostrils flared as she studied the corner of the building with the concave entrance they found. Its once neon tube lighting had been broken, stripped of usable metals, glass, and plastic parts, and the paper bills that had once been in place on either side of the intact double doors had faded and torn until the words were unreadable.

The last several blocks of their approach had been devoid of human life, silent except for the soft moaning wind and the barking of distant dogs weaving through the streets Grubbers banged against windows and doors of the places in which they were trapped, drawing the attention of crows that flapped their wings to keep balance on the perches where they watched for a potential meal and cawed to summon allies or warn their enemies away. The abandon set Jia's nerves on edge, as it did the others, as none had ever encountered an area like this except in places in the neutral region between boroughs where traps had been laid to ensnare the unwary and careless.

Deuce's continual side-to-side scouting at the head of their path revealed no traps, no threats, but the constant wrinkling of his nose suggested he concurred with Yu's assessment.

"It smells…" QiangXu sniffed the air too, "medicinal."

Candace looked at the façade of the multilevel building with a low whisper. "Hospital?"

"Might be supplies? A place to camp?" Eddie's teeth chattered and his arms wrapped around his torso. His eyes looked dejected above the edge of the scarf wrapped around his nose and mouth, but his mother's reassurance and Kato's glances of annoyance and challenge forced the youngster to keep moving with fewer complaints.

"If it is, probably already picked clean," snorted Pubby, wiping his red nose across the back of his glove.

Kato pointed. "Maybe not." A rust-red chain held the doors shut. The windows of the lower floors were boarded with weather-stained planks, old but not decrepit, an effort to keep out the rain and wind. If someone was using the building as a shelter, or had in the past, the doors would be locked from the inside, not the outside…unless the residents had journeyed elsewhere…or lived in the vicinity, unseen and undetected. It was possible the locals, if there were any, had locked it to protect their community's most valuable resource.

The chain appeared to have been undisturbed for a long time.

"I'll take a look." Vance removed his gloves and tucked them into the belt holding his coat closed around his waist.

"Got your back," grunted Pubby, his pistol in hand.

"Wait." If someone cared enough to guard the contents with a chain, there might be spotters keeping watch. Jia gestured to the others to take positions on the intersection corners, as the Pack had done when she and Kato had first met. Deuce ducked into the building behind her to find a higher vantage point to allow him to see up and down both cross streets.

Jia remained where she was, crouched in the shadows created by cracked and dented waste bins, where she could watch the Protectors cautiously cross the road and watch the street where they had traveled so no one would creep up on them from the rear.

With his back to Vance's and his gun aimed, sweeping back and forth, left to right and back, Pubby kept his eyes and ears open. Their protection made it safer for Vance to wrap one hand around the door handles and the other around the old key lock holding the chain together and kept the door closed.

Even with Cana vision, Jia could not see the things Vance saw, could not see his face, turned from her as he was. But she could feel the sizzling tension before he turned, nudged Pubby in the ribs, and muttered, "Spare a bullet?"

Pubby snorted. Bullets were scarce, but he knew how to make his own. If Fort Hamilton held to its promise, he might be able to pick up as many bullets as he could carry to bring back with him.

One shot. Those not watching, their attention focused on nearby threats, jumped, crouched, or fell flat to the ground to avoid an unanticipated attack. The crows in the branches and on window sills, building edges, and the leaning metal street poles and signs, screeched and took to the sky.

The splintered lock dropped to the ground. Vance yanked the chain free, pushed the bar lever, and released the stale air inside into the fresher wind of night.

He held it there, peering inside, while the others waited, alert for an assault by those who might want to stop their invasion of this place.

No one came. No one emerged from behind the opened doors. The echo of the gunshot, the clatter of the lock and chain, the creak of long-unused hinges, were swallowed by the night leaving nothing but the rustle of the crows as they settled back onto their perches.

The growl and shuffle of nearby grubbers did not change.

Pubby stepped into the doorway and held the door open with his body as Vance went inside. Despite the impulse to follow, to prevent the mage from facing potential danger alone, Jia remained still, anxious in her crouch, her inaction gesture enough to keep the others also in place.

If Vance needed them, needed her, she trusted they were near enough to offer help in time.

Eyes adjusting to the absence of the ambient moon, using only the pale fingers of light bleeding around cracks in window coverings and mage senses that allowed him a silhouette and shadow image of the layout of the lobby he entered, Vance found his way from the door to the front desk, noting that the chairs and benches remained, noting that the dust-covered terminal and keyboard had not been scavved and repurposed here as they had been in LaGuardia. Spiders had made their homes between the keys, weaving webs between it and the surrounding surfaces, webs undisturbed by anything except the flies that had left empty carcasses discarded around the wheels of the moldering chair.

A few buzzed still, caught in the sticky threads, hindered in the efforts to escape by the cold of night.

No footprints marred the dust except his, but a sense of panic, of sickness and confusion, lingered like perfume on the fringes of something else, a smell or something like it that his tracker gifts detected but could not identify, the way the air smelled after a lightning storm yet fainter, barely perceptible.

He had detected those traces before, in a grubber den, but there were no grubbers here. There were no signs of life, past or present, except for the spiders and the flies and the scattered droppings left by passing rats and mice.

Scowling, he left the building, tapped Pubby on the shoulder as he passed, and returned to Jia with a gesture in QiangXu's direction.

"Anything?"

Vance shrugged at the question, but to QiangXu he asked, "You have that reader?"

He nodded and squatted to open his pack and shuffled the contents until he removed what Vance required. "Want me to…?"

Vance nodded too but QiangXu was already crossing towards the building. A glance from the mage prompted Pubby to go with him.

"Looks untouched, probably since it was abandoned," Vance murmured, his eyes following the other pair rather than looking at Jia.

"Poisoned?"

She had never seen the effects of radiation poison but she recalled a debate between her father and Lowell about the subject when a group of assim workers came down sick after stripping a ship thrust onto LaGuardia's shore by a particularly strong storm. Those exposed to the dead with the materials unloaded and brought ashore, likewise suffered, until Lowell reluctantly agreed to break out one of the rare readers and scan the ship from top to bottom.

The elevated readings resulted in a tug towing the ship across the harbor to ground it on the already forbidden Riker's Island, with everything stripped from it returned. The dead, and some of those she infected, she carried, were left to rot where they had fallen.

Some of those exposed to the radiation recovered, though they had endured a host of health issues for the remainder of their lives. Others had passed within days or weeks. Fear of mutation banished exposed survivors to the Zone and their families with them, a better end, perhaps, despite Roland's reluctance to agree to the decision, than the execution or banishment to Riker's Lowell had argued for and initiated for the sickest individuals.

Jia did not know what that sickness looked like. But the possibility of it was explanation enough for the vacant surrounding streets and the boards and chains put in place to discourage entry into the hospital.

What had they released into the world by opening the doors?

From inside the building, the whirring screech of the reader's voice was the answer they were given.

A gesture and a whistle brought the others back together by the time QiangXu rejoined them, switching off the reader as he came. Its battery power was limited and precious. Out here, without a Plant, there would be no way to recharge it when the battery died.

"Faint, but it's there."

"What?" asked Kato.

"Radiation."

"Radiation?" From the way Kato spoke the foreign word, it was obvious he had never heard the term.

"Could have been a bomb on an upper floor…fallout bleeding in from somewhere nearby…a leak in equipment." QiangXu shrugged and turned the reader on long enough to measure the residual traces where they stood. The needle bobbed, the reader's voice chirped and squawked, and he shrugged.

"Here too…but fainter. Not by much though."

Jia frowned. "Enough to kill us?"

QiangXu frowned too. "I'm no expert…but I wouldn't chance it."

"Nor would I," Yu added. "I've seen radiation poisoning. It isn't pretty, isn't pleasant. Not worth the risk of staying, or taking anything from inside." She cocked her head towards the hospital with a sigh.

"We could use the medical…" began Candace.

"Not worth it," Yu repeated. "It'll be in the walls, in the dirt. Probably in the water. Might be safe but if it's not…"

"Are we poisoned?" whispered Eddie, horrified his actions could have brought him to this. "Are we gonna die?"

Yu patted his shoulder. "It isn't strong enough for that…and we haven't been exposed too long."

Jia heard something different in Yu's tone than in her words, however, something barely perceptible to an inexperienced boy who wanted only the reassurance they were safe. They did not know how long they might have been exposed. None of them could know how affected they might be or how far they would have to travel away from this place to be free of contamination.

Here in this unexplored region, they would have to be more cautious, not only for those who might assault them or natural hazards, but for manmade ones like this as well.

"How long can you run it?" she murmured.

QiangXu shrugged. "Assuming it was fully charged when we got it…long enough to get us to a clear zone, I think."

Without knowing the central source of the reading, the direction from which it originated, where they were headed might be into danger rather than away from it. With the reader running, they would have an answer soon enough.

Dawn was not far off and weariness was settling in after standing stationary for a little too long. But they could not stay here.

Perhaps in another ten years, any supplies that survived nature's entropy would be safe to use. For now, they were forced to leave them.

"Lead us out of here," she muttered to QiangXu. "Find us somewhere safe.

He nodded and they started west.

Chapter 27

The second winter gale was stronger than the first, the whipping rain driven sideways by wailing wind that blinded the oxen so they refused to take another step. The boxy wagon lurched and swayed as the wind shoved against it, and no amount of effort made to shout over the blowing or to whip the oxen into movement was creating the results Norse wanted.

Inside the wooden cart, the slats not sealed or close together enough to prevent the wind and rain from getting through, voices screamed in fear and fury.

A few more blocks. He had believed he would reach his destination before the black clouds pushing in from the sea reached landfall. He had not anticipated the speed of the prevailing wind and the wall of rain it brought with it.

Lightning crackled, its tongue biting into something ahead of them they could not see, causing a flash and explosion that made the oxen lurch. The wagon tipped onto its side. The wood splintered.

The oxen charged.

"Get them!" Norse shouted.

He might have meant the oxen. He might have meant something else.

There were snapping cracks. Perhaps gunfire, perhaps more lightning bites, perhaps the fracturing of the wagon's planked walls. But he could not see the things that had been right beside him moments before and he doubted the four men with him could either. If they could not see through the storm, he suspected those he had rounded up and shoved into the box could not either.

They might scatter like roaches out of the light but they would not get far. They would seek shelter in nearby buildings, as Norse and his men were forced to do. Once the gale subsided, he would gather his quarry and march them to their destination on foot if he had to.

A few more blocks was all it would take.

Beren climbed. He scrambled up decaying timber steps, clinging to the iron railing embedded in concrete when the planks gave out beneath his feet. With bloody fingers, he pulled over fallen blocks, pushed beneath a split log rafter, and burrowed into the first secure place he could find, the highest place, where the rain and wind could not reach him.

His sisters were gone. Childbirth and the grubbers from Below had taken them. It did not matter if he had been given up or if his turn of luck had been merely an unfortunate set of circumstances. He had to push on alone if he was going to survive.

The grenades they had confiscated from that place were likewise gone, taken by the brute who had knocked him out with the butt of a rifle against his temple. The quest to find his father was also gone and for many miles, many hours, many days, as other anthro were likewise captured and crammed into the holding cell, then into the wagon with him, he had lamented his lost freedom and the deaths of those he had left behind.

Freedom restored, ignoring the twisting in his belly that he had no food to appease, he turned his focus to the things he had left. Finding his father. Exacting revenge on the grubbers, the hunter, on anyone who got in his way.

They should have stayed with the Cana.

There was no point in regretting his choices. Survival would not permit that. The storm would pass and he would run again. He would spend his whole life running if that was what it took to find his father and stay alive.

৯*৶

The flooding of crashing storm waves over the eroding coastal road forced Aman to turn his team inland where the buildings there, as decayed and dilapidated as many were, would serve as a breakwater and shield, preventing men and animals and wagons from being swept out to sea. None of those structures, however, nor the portions of seawall built between them to inhibit the breeching tides, could halt the pelting rain or give back the visibility it stole. Though they departed the Fortress in a storm, they had been able to see through it. Now, each person could barely see the one in front of them and Aman, at the head of the force, could not make out the trail.

It was dangerous to push on.

The road should be clear. It was part of Laedan Hallister's mandate for Kennedy's upkeep that the primary thoroughfares were kept clean of debris and there were many employed to see to that responsibility. With the pushing force of the storm, however, wind with enough strength to kill two men beneath an uprooted tree, there was no telling what other hazards there might be.

Laedan be damned, Aman thought bitterly, He would not risk another life to these ravages.

They located a structure with a doorway wide enough to bring the animals and wagons inside. The doors strained against the force of the wind and rain and might have given way if not for the protection of the buildings between them and the sea. The building reeked of stale death and sewage from where water from the overtaxed, no longer maintained pipes in the Below splashed up through floor grates and then receded. They risked flooding if the pipes and tunnels under the building became too clogged to allow the wastewater to flow, but for the moment, Aman's party was secure. While some built fires for warmth in the single-level structure, as far from the puddling gates as they could be, others found what materials they could use to strengthen the doors against the storm.

The howling, the pelting of furious water drops that turned to hail against the walls of their shelter, and the uneasy chatter of people seeking distraction from the concerns for survival masked another unconsidered threat. The shouts of someone who had drawn apart to urinate in private reminded them that no haven, no matter how empty, could be deemed secure without sweeping it of lingering grubbers.

The storm had masked their moaning. The stench of the sewer had masked the scent of their putrefying flesh.

There was a scramble for weapons and a flurry of flailing limbs as the living fought to clear the threat from their shelter, two dozen grubbers once tightly packed in a back room who broke free of the door restraining them there, lured by the warmth of fire and life. The unfortunate man who released them was the first to fall, overwhelmed by their numbers and his own surprise. Another three endured bites that elicited screams of pain. When the last of the grubbers fell, those bites resulted in the requisite amputation of limbs which was often the only way to prevent the infection's spread and eventual death.

Three people. They would be sent back, sent home, to recover, to die, whatever fate had in store for them. Two arms lost and a hand and no guarantee that, by the storm's end, their lives would not be forfeit too. Limbs were burned in the fires that had cauterized the wounds, but the dead were left where they were.

There was nowhere to put them. Not while the storm trapped them.

Five men lost, Aman thought, wiping his arm across his brow and returning to the window slit where he had watched the storm when the screaming had begun. Five lost and so many more miles to go.

He wondered how many more would follow.

If he would be left to find Fort Hamilton alone or fall with them.

☙*☙

The arrival of dawn was swallowed by the onset of storm clouds and rain, forcing Jia to seek accommodation in the first promising shelter located that bore neither the scent of other anthro nor the lingering decay of grubbers. The windows of the strip of shops to the left and right had been removed, exposing the interiors to the elements as the rain began to fall. But the corner shop they chose, adorned on the outside by two long-rusted fuel pumps listing to one side as the ground buckled and cracked as though something was pushing up from beneath, had a backroom large enough for them, yet small enough to contain the warmth of the fire Kato built. Assured by the radiation reader that they had traveled far enough to be safe, an extra three hours of travel over debris-filled streets as the wind's intensity increased and brought the first hint of rain with it, most had fallen asleep without bothering with a meal.

Food would be there when they opened their eyes.

The Protectors took the first watch. Jia watched Vance squat in the inner doorway while Pubby stood at the outer, gun in hand, until her eyes grew too heavy to maintain her gaze. It was impossible to interpret the mage's thoughts as years of practice had taught him to hide the myriad of things his senses revealed, but she could tell something troubled him. She did not need to read his thoughts or ask him to know it. The evidence was there in the set of his pursed lips, his furrowed brow, and the way he would not look at her as she curled up to sleep with Kato's knees pressed to her back and Deuce sprawled next to her on the other side.

Deuce's relaxed position reassured her they were safe but perhaps it was her relationship with him, or with the Fela behind her, making the mage ill at ease.

It could have been anything else.

Looking beyond the man bundled in so much protective clothing he looked like a nondescript blob of gray stone against the darker gray of the outside winter storm, Vance nursed his throbbing hand, the hand used to push open the hospital door, against his lap, willing away the sensation while wishing he had a drink to numb him and erase it from his focus. Having intentionally not brought alcohol with him, forcing himself to be dry in the hopes he could remain clearheaded, he regretted his decision more at this moment than he had at any other since leaving home.

There was nothing obviously amiss. Deuce's relaxation reassured him. So why, he thought with a scowl that rolled in like the rumbling thunder growing closer with each hour, was he unable to shake the sense of pursuit, of being the prey, not the hunter?

"Expecting trouble?"

He could tell Pubby looked back at him by the shifting of his hood, but it was a brief glance, and by the dim interior lighting of the fire they were unable to make eye contact before Pubby returned his gaze to the outside world.

Vance got up, picked up his discarded coat and rain cloak, and pulled them back on. "Isn't that the purpose of keeping watch?"

"Purpose of a watch is to let your companions rest easy…not because we expect trouble. But I imagine," Pubby did make eye contact with him this time as Vance joined him in the doorway, "you're always expecting trouble."

The advantage, or disadvantage, of being a mage, Pubby surmised, was an ability to read things in the air, the atmosphere, the walls…everywhere…that revealed trouble when there was none obvious. Revealing secrets where others would never find them.

Vance shrugged. "Gonna do a once around…just to be sure."

A flicker and flash on the southern horizon brought a distant roll of thunder. Pubby counted the seconds and snorted. "No one would be stupid enough to be out there in this."

"We are."

Pubby grunted again.

"What's the point of standing here if…?"

"Make them feel safer, like I said."

"It'll make me feel safer if I have a look."

Pubby sighed. "Suit yourself. If you're not back in thirty, I'm sending out the cavalry."

"I'll be back before that." Visibility was decreasing, the rain falling harder, but Vance did not think it would take him more than ten or fifteen minutes to circle the building, reassure himself they were alone, and make it back to dry shelter before the storm got worse.

"Better be. I don't want to have to explain why you're not." Pubby cocked his head towards Jia. Vance huffed and stepped into the rain.

The same instinct prompting him to adjust his collar against the moisture when it was needed propelled Vance towards the northeast intersection where they had crossed before taking refuge in the service station. He wondered what the juncture had once been like, how many people had stopped here for a morning meal and beverage before going about their day. How many vehicles had passed, how many people had come from the surrounding apartments for a quick pick-me-up or emergency item their cupboards lacked? How much alcohol had been purchased from its shelves? How many accidents had occurred at this crossroad as the unwary met the careless?

How many lives had crashed the day the Undoing had begun…and every subsequent day in the protracted period after that had brought the world to the place it was now?

Would the world ever be that way again?

He turned along the edge of the building, keeping it in his peripheral vision as his focus stretched out into the storm.

Whatever the future of the world, men like him would not be around to witness it. With luck, the forces that had given rise to mages would dwindle and fade. But anthro and mutani were here to stay. They might even become the dominant, the future of humanity, if the Normals did not force mankind into extinction in their quest to eradicate such differences.

If the grubbers did not take them.

There were no scavs here. No one eking out a living he could see or hear through the rain, not a bird or dog, cat or rat. The animals, and most people, were too smart to be out in this weather. They were smarter, he mused as he found the back corner of the building and started along the next edge, than he was. He was alone out here, or should have been if not for the continuing trigger niggling against the nerves at the back of his neck to draw him, when he eventually reached the end of the long back of the building, to cross the street and continue moving beneath what remained of the ancient raised tracks once crisscrossing the vast city.

It was the symphony of hard-hitting rain on metal and the vibrating hum of the wind rushing over that same surface that attracted him, directing him to an overgrown oval of grass and thistles, with short evergreens and leafless maples edging it on this side against corroded aluminum risers. Such things had been stripped of their original purposes in LaGuardia, moved to political venues or cut to fashion smaller benches or crafted into tools needed to sustain daily life. Gone were the days of sports teams clashing for collegiate glory although he had often heard talk, in tavs and on street corners and over tea in the Protectorate, of formulating some sort of team system, some manner of sport, to channel the youth who roamed the borough streets, giving them the chance to best Kennedy, and each other, at something that would not kill them.

The discussions inevitably devolved into arguments about how to avoid the unfair advantages anthro and mutani presented, an argument that eventually made every discussion of team sports fail.

Still, the idea lingered.

There was a lot on the north edge filled with decaying vehicles, appearing as though they had been left when the world had ended or else moved there by those who remained for some unclear purpose, to clear the streets, perhaps, or serve as a testament of what the world had once been. It was between those stationary hulks that something moved, a shade too solid, too cumbersome in its movement to be a wraith or a figment of the mist. Moving against the wind, Vance did not think it was storm-blown debris. Thinking it was someone in need of aid, of shelter, something his companions could offer in exchange for information about the elusive fort, Vance shielded his eyes with a gloved hand and began a slow approach, calling, "Hello?"

A clatter of metal, like a car door closing, blown by the wind or pushed aside by the shape dashing between the rows, came at the head of a lightning flash that cut horizontally across the sky. The brightness made Vance wince and blink.

The shape was gone.

"You need help?"

What he would not give for a glower or a torch or anything to illuminate the area beyond the short perimeter of his field of vision permitted by the storm.

The last trajectory the shape moved in was towards the risers so Vance veered in that direction as well, scanning the nearby rooftops of the parked cars, expecting whoever was there to show themselves.

Or perhaps they were crawling away, unseen, or had fallen injured to the ground. He hesitated as he reached the first car, removed the glove of his injured hand, and pressed his palm to the dented, rain-slicked trunk. It was a long shot, but the only lead he had.

"Valentine."

"Ms. Marrock."

It was the hand on her shoulder that woke her rather than the words she had not been certain were spoken aloud. Pubby's hand. The others around her continued to sleep. Vance was no longer in the doorway where she had last seen him. From the grogginess, the fog and heaviness of exhaustion weighing inside her skull, she did not think she had been asleep for long.

Pubby tilted his head towards the door. She nodded, extracted herself gingerly from between Deuce and Kato without disturbing them, and followed the Protector to the outer room. The blowing rain was creating a puddle on the peeling linoleum at the base of the door.

"He's out there, hasn't come back." Pubby motioned into a world a darker shade of rain gray than when Jia had last seen it. "Told him if he wasn't back in thirty I'd go after him but…" he shrugged, "thought you'd have a better chance of finding him."

He had never seen her shift. So far, only Deuce and Kato had done so within his field of vision, one to a black Fela panther, the other to a graying black-brown Cana. Her proximity and relationship with both men were enough to give a smart man a judicious amount of suspicion. There had been rumors for ages about the Marrocks.

Whatever he knew or suspected, Pubby kept to himself, beyond a statement that expressed an acknowledgment of the truth.

"Which way?"

Pubby pointed in the direction from which they had traveled. "Said he was going to circle the building."

Though the storm would have slowed such a circle and Jia did not know how much time had passed since Vance had gone out, she assessed by Pubby's concern that the mage had been gone long enough for the other Protector to deem it too long. He was worried, afraid for his friend, and his anxiety made Jia nervous too.

Something had been on Vance's mind, something troublesome enough to lure him into the storm. That same something had, perhaps, prevented his return.

Her internal argument was swift and abrupt. Vance was the only one who had seen the Fort Hamilton map. He was the only one who could steer them in the direction they needed to go to find it. They needed him. His guidance. His skills as a tracker-mage.

More than that, she needed him. Without him, none of this made sense. Without Vance, she would not be able to put her father to rest.

She had to find him.

By now, the wind and rain would have swept away any trail the mage had left, but deciding the wolf would have the best chance of finding their lost companion, Jia stripped out of her clothes and made the shift without Pubby looking at her.

If he had not guessed the truth, he knew it now.

The Marrock secret was revealed one more time to an outsider.

The Pack might not forgive her for it if she failed to find Fort Hamilton and do as she had promised. If she failed to keep them safe.

With the rain matting her fur, she ran in a zig-zagging pattern to the edge of the block, around the side of the building, down the length of the rear wall which took her beneath the window of the room in which her companions slept. The thunder rumbles and the pelting rain made for restless slumber but thus far no one noticed she was not with them. By the time they did, she hoped she would be returning with Vance in tow.

He might have lost his way in the limited visibility of the stormy streets. He might have found something of interest or sought shelter elsewhere from the worst of the storm.

At the other end of the strip mall, she caught a faint trace of his passing, his hand pressed to the corner of the building as if to rest…or to subconsciously leave a mark for her and the others to follow. His voice, fainter still, a greeting call to someone, not as if he was lost but as if he was reaching out to someone who might be.

It offered his direction.

His path might have swerved around debris, foliage, and other hindrances, but Jia's remained true, the advantages of Cana allowing her to leap over, wiggle under, climb over every obstacle between her and his second call.

He was not alone.

She ran faster.

Another voice.

"Valentine."

"Long way from home," Vance grunted, backing away from the stalking form, the long-buried fear of a child watching his father die forcing him to react without thought for how his action might look. The corroded metal of the first riser bruised the back of his calves as he bumped into it, the jolt of pain and the momentary flash of a trapped feeling giving rise to a smirk on the other man's face.

"Don't seem surprised to see me."

"I'm not."

Nepo stopped his pursuit beyond arm's length of Vance, where neither could reach the other but either could lunge and strike if they chose. "You've gotten old."

"You've gotten fat."

Nepo did not frown, did not visibly react, but Vance felt the barb strike home as he intended. Nepo had always been a vain, stout fellow. Enough years had passed that Vance could not remember clearly how heavy the other mage had been. But his movements were the same, his stance, and his arrogance too, which made the remark about his weight the sort of thing Vance expected would rub him wrong.

Rather than challenge the assertion, Nepo came a step closer. Vance took a step back, up onto the first riser, an act that gave him the high ground in a fight and made Nepo pause. "Thought you'd come for me after…"

"Better things to do."

"Then kill me after what I…?" Nepo started with a chortle.

"You killed him." The blurted expletive had been long unsaid, the wounded accusation of a child once unable to confront the perpetrator.

"You know what business is like…"

"That wasn't business! That was…"

"Business," Nepo repeated with a smirk. "You're a tracker, like me…you know what we…"

"I'm a Protector! You're a thug who kills for pay, who torments children by haunting their nightmares with…"

"He shouldn't have put his credits on one fight and refuse to pay up…you know the trade. He shouldn't have dragged his kid along for pity. If I'd been him, I wouldn't have brought a weak boy to…"

It was not the words that stung but rather the memories of blood, his father falling, the other man's condolatory sneer, that made Vance roar and lash out. Childhood trauma turned to rage, unsatisfied after years of hunting, rage determined to find peace in the other man's execution. But Nepo, despite the advantage Vance had in that higher ground, stepped aside to avoid his leap with a dark laugh.

Vance, his jump unsteady from the rain on the slippery metal surface of worn ribs, rolled into the mud but not without grabbing hold of Nepo's arm and dragging him down. Furious to have failed the attempted evasion, Nepo swung. His larger, meatier fist caught Vance in the chest and pushed him back to slide away on the wet ground. Groundwater and mud sprayed in every direction, into Nepo's eyes; the moment it took him to wipe them clean allowed enough time for Vance to leap to his feet and charge.

The impact of his shoulders into Nepos' torso drove the larger man against the bleachers. The metal rungs struck his ribs to the thunder crack rolling across the fork-lit sky. His arms wrapped around Vance as he arched back and threw the smaller man up several steps where he landed face-first with a clatter.

An inhuman howl erupted nearby and the bleachers shook, this time with the impact of the wolf leaping into a protective position over Vance as he wiped blood from his eyes. At the bottom of the bleachers, Nepo staggered to his feet, facing them both with a gun in his hand.

The wolf snarled.

Nepo took his shot.

A malfunction caused by the rain, wet powder, or the hand of fate, prevented the discharge and wrenched Nepo's hand enough that he dropped the gun. Only the hand on the wolf's dripping side kept her from retaliating, kept her from following the lavender-eyed stranger when he eyed the gun, decided to leave it, and stumbled back with his injured hand clutching his ribs.

"Isn't over," he snarled. "You'll see me again."

The wolf growled and tensed to jump."

"Let him go."

The dazed fatigue in Vance's voice, the smell of blood from the gash across his forehead, and what dripped from his nose, prevented Jia from pursuing the stranger. She did not move but remained steady as Vance used his fingers in her fur to pull into a sitting position. She remained still until the stranger was far enough away she could neither see, hear, nor smell him through the storm. When Vance tried to stand, he stumbled, nearly falling between the metal slats. The wolf took his hand in her mouth and helped him to the ground.

Once there, his shaky legs gave out and he again collapsed, near enough to the dropped gun to retrieve it. He tested its weight in his hand and pulled out the cartridge. It was empty.

The chamber, however, contained the mangled remains of the bullet that should have killed her. Might have killed them both.

"Shouldn't be here," he muttered, as much to himself as to her. The wolf's scolding growl made his lips twist wryly. "Yeah…maybe I shouldn't be either," he admitted. She nudged his shoulder with her snout, urging him to rise, but he shook his head and wiped the bloody rain from his face one more time. Damn head wounds. Bled like crazy no matter how superficial. It did not even hurt at the moment.

"Give me a second. I'll be okay just…wait…then we'll go back."

The rain fell harder. The Cana tipped her nose into the wind and uttered an insistent yip. There were no seconds to wait. They had to go back. Now.

Reluctantly, Vance staggered up, using her height, as he trudged, to help him remain upright. Without her, he doubted he would make it back to camp.

Without her, he doubted he would be alive.

From the barely adequate shelter of a gutted minivan, its windows intact but splintered with numerous small impacts, Nepo tugged off his poncho to dig through the pack beneath it, looking for something with which he could bind his broken ribs, something to clean the sliced flesh on the meaty part of his hand where the gun had bitten into him. It happened sometimes, the misfiring of ancient equipment, no matter how well one tried to clean and maintain them. He could not blame the gun, or himself, but it did not prevent the uttered string of curses from spewing as the dregs in the alcohol bottle he carried were emptied over his bleeding hand.

So Segara had befriended a Cana bitch.

One of those he traveled with, Nepo assumed, which meant others were likely Cana too, a small pack on the hunt perhaps. They were not migrating, he could tell, but they did move with specific intent.

What was the chance they were interested, he wondered, in the fort Channon hoped to find? Or were they after something different? He would only know if he continued to follow them.

If he had killed Segara tonight, he might have lost the opportunity to know. But seeing him out there, alone, had been too tempting a chance to let pass. Now it would take him a day or two to get back on his feet, to be able to endure extended tracking without the constant throbbing stab of broken ribs. Thankfully, he healed quickly. Thankfully, he did not think Segara would be going anywhere soon.

At least not until the storm passed. That ought to be long enough to make it through the worst of his pain.

But Nepo could not stay where he was. If the storm lessened, the pack might come for him. He was too vulnerable here, too exposed. He needed better shelter, a more secure location to hide, to heal.

If the fates were with him, the tempest would sweep away his traces from the Cana's path. None would find him, see him, until it was too late to stop him.

Nepo did not want the others. They meant nothing. He only wanted whatever was important enough to drive their search west. He only wanted Segara.

❧*❧

Norse was not coming.

Forced to close the delivery doors against the heavier rain growing more biting as the minutes ticked past, Gail remained on the other side of the window, watching, expecting a delivery that would no longer arrive before Geary's promised visit in which he intended, she believed, to enforce the cessation of blood harvest and plasm production.

He had said one more batch. Gail was going to hold him to that.

New victims could be disguised as local patients, could be sedated and secured in ways other than the extraction pods. He would take an inventory of how many were on hand and expect fewer of them the next time he came, but he would not ask too many questions about the treatment of the local ill.

Gail did that sometimes. It offered blood samples to use for testing. It reduced the suspicions and wariness of those living nearby if she offered them something in return for turning a blind eye.

The more subjects she had on hand when he arrived, however she obtained them, the longer she could continue to work. He would not want her to kill them for expediency, surely.

There were numerous reasons why Norse might have been delayed, the storm being primary among them. It troubled her that she might not have the opportunity for one more harvest as she hoped, the collection of one more batch with which to experiment, study, process.

But if Norse could not reach her through the storm, neither could Geary. Norse was more likely to risk the storm's wrath than Geary was. The Laedan would stay safe, secure, dry, and unhampered by the fierce weather. With luck, his attention afterward would be consumed by the need for repairs throughout the borough, accounting for the dead, on the loss of resources.

Perhaps her request had been diverted and Norse would not come.

If so, Gail thought with a frown, if Geary had any inkling of her plan to bypass orders a little longer, he would have been here already.

"Close them," she repeated.

Norse would arrive, if he could, and bring the subjects he had been able to acquire on such short notice and go back out before Geary came. Or he would bring a trap meant to ensnare her.

He had promised one more shipment, but that had been before his change of heart. Gail was uncertain what to expect from Geary now. But she chose to believe Norse would arrive.

Norse believed in the work as staunchly as she did.

Tonight, as the tempest thrashed impotent and insistent against the metal bay doors, there was nothing for Gail to do except her job.

There were subjects to study. Dead to dispose of.

Work to be done.

❮*❯

"You're not dragging me out in that!" the bulky woman with ratty blonde hair yanked her arm to be free of the chief's hold on her bicep but despite his age, her effort proved futile. It was the flash of lightning outside, the crack of it loud enough to rattle the windows and jar the metal walls, and the barrage of hail it birthed, that prevented Ernest from throwing open the door and ejecting her into the street.

She was but one of many his Protectors had rounded up in the hours since the order had been given. He guessed she had no better answers for him than any of the others had provided, but the protocols were in place and a routine had begun to take shape.

Junkies gave the names of their sources. Those sources were found and, if deemed of interest, brought to the Protectorate to be held for questioning for as long as the chief or captains deemed it appropriate. The smaller 'fish' as Ernest called them, would be set free.

No one had been released yet, however, and the cells were growing crowded. The sources of shart on the street were gradually thinning. Bigger fish were either going to have to surface or the junkies, and the lack of revenue, would lure them out.

How long that would take was anyone's guess.

A ball of hail the size of a child's fist smashed through the window, prompting patrons to scatter deeper into the room or scramble to barricade the windows with upturned tables and the hammer and nails the tender provided from behind the bar. A woman, dark-complexioned and soaked to the skin, had the door ripped from her hand by the wind as she opened it. Someone grabbed her cloak and pulled her inside as someone else snatched the door and shoved it closed, locking it behind her.

"No one's goin' anywhere," shouted the tender, his voice frayed and frustrated. "Might as well get comfortable."

"So you can make extra creds?" someone sneered.

"To save your sorry ass from getting brained," chortled a drunken woman who picked up the ice ball and plopped it into her wide glass.

Ernest's hostage pulled her arm free with a sneering grunt. "Lemme go…unless you're gonna hold on to me until this is over. Gonna have to pay extra for that privilege if it's what ya want…"

Ernest grunted too, grumbling under his breath, and dropped onto the nearest stool. He did not need to worry about her slipping away. In this weather, there was nowhere to go. He side-eyed the newest arrival as she adjusted her raincoat around her shoulders and sauntered to the bar, giving him no more than a cursory once-over glance.

He did not recognize her…but there were many in the borough he did not know. Just another soul seeking refuge from the storm.

He raised his empty glass to the tender and gestured. Might as well have another drink while they waited.

Chapter 28

There was no privacy in the back room of the service station where they had found shelter. With Jia's help, Vance staggered through the front door where Pubby still waited, and would have collapsed when she moved away if not for the other Protector's support. The commotion of their return roused the others as Pubby accepted the discarded gun and helped Vance to the fire leaving Jia to resume normal form and dress in the other room. By the time she joined them, Vance had been lowered to the floor, where he leaned against the wall as Yu brought the medical kit to his side.

If not for her rain-drenched hair, and skin, no one would have realized Jia had been outside.

"Should suture this," Yu murmured, dabbing the gash on Vance's forehead clean with a bit of cloth steeped in witch-hazel. Over her shoulder to QiangXu, she said, "There's a bottle of whiskey in my…"

"No." The spike in his blood pressure at the mention of whiskey, the increased tremors in his hands, told Vance he was better off not accepting the bottle. If he got it into his hand, he was not going to stop drinking until it was empty. "Just do it." He absently reached for Jia's hand, knowing the distraction of someone else's thoughts and emotions would be enough to mute the physical discomfort of medical care. There was a jolt when she accepted his request, her concern washing over him, filling his senses, drowning his thoughts but leaving him enough presence of mind to mutter, "Do it."

"Check his shoulder too," Jia whispered. "And his hand." The bandages on his hand were too wet, filthy from the muddy fight, to tell if there was fresh blood and his coat hid his previous shoulder injury.

The punishment doled out by the lavender-eyed man could have reopened those wounds and Jia would not let him bleed to death or suffer in silence.

"I know."

She needed him. Vance heard the need, felt it as if it was his. But it wasn't. What he felt for her, a sting of longing, an appreciation of strength and beauty, was not the same as what she felt. Nor was it the same as what she felt for the nervously pacing Fela watching with narrowed eyes and a slightly sneering curve of his lips.

What she felt was not the same…but it was something.

The cut on his forehead was not long or deep and required only a few stitches to close. Lost in the vision of her thoughts, a swirling amalgamation of memories of her father, her brother, the Channons she had grown up with, injured friends and packmates, particularly Liam whose face bobbed to the surface of her mind more often than any other, Vance only knew the suturing was complete when Jia began to unbandage his hand.

"He's…" Vance swallowed the bitter taste of pain at the back of his throat and groaned. He would rather have this discussion privately, as sharing his history, his life, with a single person would be awkward enough. If Nepo continued to follow them as Vance suspected he would, those traveling with him deserved to know what they faced.

"You don't have to…" Jia began, a hand gently on his shoulder, her gaze straying to a leather string around his neck she had not seen before. Hanging from it, a small, polished, cured knuckle bone.

His, she suspected. The gift Torben had included in the supply kit Nik provided.

Vance followed her gaze, gave a half-shrug as he closed his good hand around it, and tucked the odd pendant beneath his gray sweater.

"Think I do." There was enough residual connection between them that she heard his reluctance to continue, or perhaps had seen his hesitancy on his face or heard it in the heaviness of his voice. He appreciated the offer to protect his privacy, but this needed to be done.

"He's a mutani tracker…goes by Nepo…a merc for hire. We've got history…going back to my father…"

"What'd he do to get a merc on his tail?" snorted Kato bitterly.

"Doesn't matter," scolded Jia. "A father's sins have nothing to do with…"

Kato's expression darkened.

"For all of this," Vance continued with an eye sweep over the others in the room, "my father doesn't matter. Only matters that I tracked Nepo for years afterward until he dropped off my radar and I eventually stopped looking. Saw him for the first time in probably ten years when I got back to LaGuardia after leaving you. Sighting in passing; he looked engaged in business and I had things to do. Didn't pursue him…didn't want to…but maybe I should have."

"He's been tracking us since LaGuardia?"

Vance nodded ad Deuce, wincing as Yu cleaned his hand. The place where his finger had been severed was not bleeding, but with it unwrapped, it was the best time to examine its healing and clean it. "Thought maybe it was Quentin…maybe one of the Channons. Didn't think Nepo'd come looking for me, especially out here."

"Is he dangerous?" whispered Candace, the corners of her eyes creased with concern.

"He's a tracker and a good shot; would give you a run," he replied with a side glance at Pubby. "Strong…with the endurance of an ox…"

"So you thought you'd take him in a fistfight in the rain," scolded Jia, pulling back Vance's coat to try to expose his shoulder. Unable to access the injury, however, Pubby helped Vance wiggle out of the coat and then Vance pulled his shirt off over his head.

"Logic didn't occur to me at the time," he admitted. "You're damn lucky the gun jammed…"

"Say we're both lucky. Shoulda let me kill him."

"You didn't?" She was no stranger to killing. Kato had seen it firsthand.

"I'll find him," offered Deuce, already getting to his feet. He had spent years as omega cleaning up threats at the periphery of the Flushing Pack. Mutani, other anthro, Normals…even HOPE agents. Who they had been did not matter. He would kill anyone without qualms to protect the Pack…protect his daughter.

"Not in this," Jia scolded him too, ignoring Kato's question.

"You won't find him…unless he wants you to." Vance could follow him, as a tracker himself, and maybe the Cana could track Nepo by the scent lingering on Vance's clothing. But the distraction of hunting Nepo would detract from their primary goal. "By now, he's gone to ground. Maybe gone back after…but if he wants me…"

"I'd say he does from the looks of you," Pubby commented.

"Who?" asked Jia.

Vance nodded and shrugged simultaneously. This was probably not the time to mention that Nepo had gone after Nik at least once. It was not like Nepo to contract out his work, but if he wanted Nik's life, he might have set someone to watch him during his absence from LaGuardia. As long as Nepo followed Vance, Nik was safe. As long as Vance did not mention it to Jia, her focus would not be split between the road ahead and what they had left behind any more than the split her family already created. "He'll come to us. He'll come to me."

Deuce snorted. "Shouldn't wait for that."

"We wait," Jia countered.

"How will we know him when we see him?" QiangXu asked.

"Scaly skinned, about as wide as he is tall…lavender eyes…"

"Think I've met him." Pubby shrugged at Vance's wary expression. "Loitering around a crime scene…thought he was a fisherman or a docker…hard to forget eyes like that."

"Probably trolling for side work," grunted Vance without asking which crime scene or when the meeting had occurred.

A reply was cut off by the Fela across the room whose posture had begun to relax now that Jia's hands were no longer on Vance.

"Should meet him on our terms, before he endangers everyone." Kato exchanged a glance with Deuce, marginally surprised the two of them were in agreement.

"Now that we know he's there," Yu began, cleaning the shoulder wound where old stitches had stretched in the flesh but not torn free, "we'll be ready. We protect our own."

Jia shifted on the floor to lean back against the wall next to Vance. "Yu's right. No one goes after him…and never off alone. We stick together and stick to the mission. We find the fort, keep what we find out of everyone's hands…and if Nepo gets in our way, we deal with him then. Otherwise, we wait until after…"

Kato glowered at Jia. "After's not our responsibility…"

"Kato's right," Vance nodded, also surprised to agree on anything with the Fela. "He's not your…"

"You're one of us," Yu smiled with a pat on Vance's injured hand, now cleaned and bandaged. "We take care of our own."

Pubby, testing the weight of the rain-slick gun in one hand, nodded. What came after they did what they had come to do, he and Vance were family now, more than they had ever been on the force. Family had each other's back. "We protect our own."

At least they would until they found Fort Hamilton. At least they would until they made it back to LaGuardia. What came after, none of them could say.

Kato's frowning scowl was an opposite reflection of Vance's reluctant sigh and bobbing head, a tightrope on which Jia would have to balance if she wanted to bring them each home alive.

❧*❦

The walls of Ministry 12 shook and shuddered with the wind's assault and every jolt of thunder that cracked the sky. The ferocity of the storm worried the adults but several did their best to soothe the crying, anxious children brought to huddle by the fire. Other members of the Pack, along with a dozen mutani, worked to secure the penetrations where the wind and rain forced their way inside, barricading windows and doors and trying to contain the water where it did come in. The paneled barricade was pieced together in the hopes the wind would not blow out the fire, but that, Liam thought with a groan as hail began to clatter on the metal roof, creating a disconcerting wobble seen by those inside, might be the least of their worries if the roof gave in.

"Xan back yet?"

"Where are you going?" Vanya piped, scrambling to her feet as Liam moved away. Carefully, he extracted Vanya's arms from around his waist and patted her on the head. The young woman had followed him about since the attack, watching everything he did, helping where she could, with Peppermint in hand, chattering constantly and inserting herself into his conversations with anyone who was not her. Reif and Ayla did their best to distract her but with the onset of the storm, their focus shifted to the children, leaving Vanya unattended to latch on to Liam with the persistence of a mosquito on a hot day.

"Vanya!" called Helena from the fire with a smile and wave, innocent to the girl but not, she knew, to Liam. "Come read us a story."

Vanya hesitated, frowning, her hand on her head where Liam had patted her, looking back and forth between him and the opportunity she was offered. Liam was not looking at her, was instead looking at the plank he held into place so Orliss could secure it. Helena, on the other hand, was smiling, friendly and motherly, cocking her head towards the younger, frightened children who needed to be settled.

Vanya was frightened too. The rain was loud and hurt her ears and the transition from rain to hail made her want to cry. She wanted Kato, wanted him to be safe with her. She wanted to be safe here.

Liam was not offering the security she wanted, although his work was meant to protect them. When a flash of lightning brought with it a too-close clap of thunder and he did not look at her to offer reassurance, Vanya fled back to the fire's warmth where Reif wrapped her arm around her shoulders with a welcoming smile. Helena thrust a book into her hands, one with more pictures than words to distract her, and Vanya felt immediately as calm as the pelting sound above them allowed.

She was afraid, but she was a big girl. A brave girl. Peppermint said so. So did Kato. She could help the youngest children not be afraid the way Kato and Peppermint helped her. Maybe then she would not feel afraid either.

Only when she was seated at the fire did Liam let out an exasperated sigh and answer the question. "If he's smart, he's in the library or somewhere else waiting this out."

As Uncle finished twisting hemp rope into place to bind several barricading boards together, he added, "Gonna have to think about ditches by then." Unlike much of LaGuardia, where concrete and pavement redirected the rain into the Below, the soft earth of overgrown lawn meant the growth of puddles and ponds that ate at the foundations of the college buildings. There was drainage into the Below here too, but the wide spreads of foliage meant accumulation that did not easily dissipate. Directing the water towards those drains or into ponds or away towards the Wilds might preserve their shelters and afford them water saved for other purposes.

"Wilds are gonna flood," muttered Orliss. "Orchards too."

Liam nodded with a frown. Some areas were prone to swampiness and the threat to the orchard, the drowning of younger trees, or the onset of mold in the mature ones, was something they would have to watch for.

Another jolt of thunder and another flash, close enough to rattle their shelter, made Liam look up, his frown deeper as some of the pups screamed and huddled closer to the adults seated with them.

Uncle patted Liam's back. "He'll be okay. We'll be okay." Xan was smart enough to find shelter. The Pack had survived worse storms. "So will she."

Jia.

Liam stooped to pick up another plank, hiding his flushed face from the other men. The reassurance of Uncle's words did not quite penetrate Liam's heart, but in his head, he knew the other man was right. Wherever she was, Jia would be safe. She had to be.

❧*❧

The glass walls of their shelter, safe from scavs because no one living in the building's vicinity had decided the glass was worth repurposing, rattled with each thrust of the storm's fury, prompting General Warby to move his soldiers towards the solid rear wall. Nose wrinkling at their unwashed stench, finding no comfort in the press of strangers he did not trust, Donn pressed his hand against the glass, remaining separate from them, and watched the torrent of water gush like river rapids through the street they had been forced to abandon at the head of the storm.

The delay irritated him.

Somewhere out there Hallister was making his move. Though Donn presumed whoever was leading that force would be wise enough to also get out of the storm likely to have swept across the whole of both boroughs, delaying them as well, the possibility of being the second, not the first, to reach Fort Hamilton was a grating source of frustration and irritation.

Donn did not do well with either emotion.

Frustration made him angry.

Irritation made him bitter.

Anger and bitterness made him violent. Those things made him long for the one person able to comfort and shield him from them.

Her final cries burrowed and wormed through his brain like gnawing maggots.

His hand balled into a fist, creating a squeaking, dragging sound of skin upon glass.

"Come away from there."

Warby's warning, gruff and insistent, the tone of command used for soldiers and subordinates, went unheeded. Donn did not obey commands. Not from his father, not from his mother, not from his wife or brothers, and certainly not from HOPE's general who lounged on the padded cushion brought with him, a thing of luxury no one else here could enjoy.

Not even Donn.

Warby showed no other penchant for luxury.

"Channon."

Again, Donn ignored him except to growl in the back of his throat.

Grunting, Warby closed his eyes and cross his arms over his chest. The others around the fires ignored both men after glances that gauged the power play between them; the dispute was none of their business.

The prattle of the rain on the glass echoed the rattle of chain link fencing behind her head. The squeak of a branch from the windswept floral bush as it grated against the window outside brought with it the sound made as blond hair snagged in rusted wire and tore free. The sound and feel of her quickening breath blasting back at him from the cold surface a few short inches away were like hers, a frightened bird's terror that both sickened him and filled him with unsatiated hunger. His lips parted and his tongue reflexively sought the remembered taste that had once lingered there.

It was an illusion shattered with the thunder snap that disgorged balls of ice from the sky, chunks that bounced in the rushing water and off of the pavement. Hurled by the fierce wind, it took only a few of the larger ones striking the panel of glass in front of him to produce cracks. Another strike and the glass was thrown into his face to shower the floor around him.

His arms came up as a shield, accompanied by an unexpected, undignified squawk. Donn lost his balance and fell beneath the barrage of glass shards, water, and bombarding chunks of ice. The violence of the sound, the thrust of rain, hail, and wind erupting into the room, brought Warby and others to their feet, some grabbing packs and weapons, some scrambling for animal harnesses to prevent the beasts from stampeding in alarm.

It was Warby who charged across the room, grabbed hold of Donn's flailing arm, and dragged him out of immediate harm's way.

"Can't stay here," someone shouted, the voice thin with fear and cut thinner by the whistling gale.

"Sit down!" Warby bellowed, shoving Donn down next to the only fire that had not succumbed to the tempestuous wind. His demand might have been meant for the soldiers or might have been intended for Donn. The rain did not penetrate this far into the room, only the spray of it pushed by the wind, and the hail that reached them did so only after bouncing off of the dusty, plank-covered concrete.

They had investigated the adjoining automotive garage upon their arrival. It had been stripped of everything they could have used, including the rolling metal doors that might have kept the weather out. The offices at the rear of the building had succumbed to structural collapse that made them unsuitable for shelter. This showroom had been their forced choice and with the worst of the storm upon them, they had nowhere else to go.

When the eye came, perhaps they could move.

Until then, they stayed.

A woman with a medical kit knelt on Donn's other side, smiling shyly as Warby pulled his arm down from his face so the damage to both could be assessed. Shards were stuck in his coat sleeve, a few in his still balled fist, and some had cut across his cheeks and forehead. While the general plucked them out of the leather, the medic removed the shards from Donn's hand and face.

"Lucky you didn't lose an eye," Warby muttered.

Donn snorted, wincing at the extraction of glass along his cheekbone. Any nearer to his eye, he realized, and Warby's words would have been much different. Only an eye, perhaps, instead of his life. "Don't believe in luck."

Warby snorted too.

"I can stitch these…"

Donn pushed the woman's hands away. "Don't want scars."

"They'll be worse if I don't," she murmured apologetically, her head bowed so tendrils of blond hair fell across her face.

He gulped. His hands shook. How much like her she looked, right down to the color of her eyes, her hair. Her contrite demeanor.

Coughing to cover what sounded to him like a nervous swallow, Donn looked away with a shrug and said, "Do it," accepting a liquor bottle from someone and drinking as she cleaned the cuts.

With no more to do on Donn's behalf, Warby got to his feet. "Next time, listen to me."

Donn's response was a sharp, sour glance hurled in the general's direction. There would not be a next time, he thought with another swallow of alcohol. Warby had saved his life, made him look weak, made him look like he needed the brutish man to survive.

He now held something over Donn's head, a favor he might call in at some inopportune time.

No, there would not be a next time because, before the next time, Warby would be dead.

•*•

"Here, sirra…drink this."

Wearily, Lowell lifted his head, focused on the man who stood over him, and accepted the steaming cup in one hand while holding the insulated canvas cloak closed at his chest with the other. The heat of the liquid in the pottery cup felt good on his fingers through the leather of his gloves and so, after adjusting the cloak around his shoulders to be sure it would not slip, he wrapped both hands around the cup. The steam smelled of herbal spices, cinnamon perhaps, cloves and anise surely, a common hemp or ivy tea mix for the less fortunate who labored in the cold or lived in too-drafty places without adequate heat. Lowell had smelled the aroma often in the guard barracks when he was there on business, in the camps of assim crews, and he recalled the same aroma, or something similar, wafting out of Roland's open office door.

He had never considered Roland to be more or less fortunate than him, than anyone else. Roland was co-Laedan. Roland had the perks and benefits the seat of power offered. That should have made him powerful enough. And still, he drank poor man's tea.

In the end, what had status and power gotten him?

The betrayal of his best friend.

And murder.

The shaking of his hands sloshed some of the tea onto his leather breaches, stained from the rain but not soaked through. Sipping the cup's contents, both to enjoy the warmth as it slid down his throat and into his belly and to lower the volume so it would not slosh again, Lowell tried to equate the taste with Roland as he side-eyed Captain Ortega when the man sat cross-legged beside him. Arlo's gaze focused on others gathered around them, taking advantage of portable fire kettles in the abandoned diner stripped clean of everything except the serving counter and a deep wash basin without pipes or fixtures to connect it.

There was still water there, dripping at random intervals, staining the basin and leaking out the bottom into an eternal pool on the floor.

"You okay, sirra? Arlo's gaze might have been attentive to his milling soldiers as they selected places to bed, ate, played cards, poked at the fires to keep them burning, and tended the animals and wagons brought in through rusted delivery doors at the back of the structure, but his primary focus was on the Laedan.

"Will be nice to be warm." Lowell's teeth chattered, taking some of the bitterness out of the complaint. None of them had stopped shivering since the icy wind first brought the rain across their path.

One of the oldest men in the force had warned of a severe storm in the air and advised seeking shelter before it arrived. Captain Ortega had expected the Laedan to resist the delay, to insist on pressing on for as long as visibility held. When he had not, when he had been the one to point out this shelter and prompt everyone into it, Arlo had suspected something was off.

For a man unaccustomed to travel of this sort, particularly the prolonged exposure to the worst cold and weather nature could throw at them, such weariness and cold were understandable. The Laedan's surrender, however, was not.

The tea, laced with herbs conducive to sleep, would help. The hours they would be forced to spend sheltered here would give them a chance for rest, provided the chaos of the storm allowed it.

The Laedan needed it.

They had been here for hours already, settling in, milling about in anxious response to the raging weather, without the sun or moon to indicate day or night. No one was sure how long they had been here. It had been long enough to prompt some to cook something more than the travel rations from their packs.

Now their shelter was fragrant with the aroma of roasting meat and potatoes. Ortega had not asked where either commodity had been found. It did not matter. The Laedan would be happy with both.

"Need anything?"

Lowell shook his head, his eyes dull within the stern blankness of his expression. "See to the rest. Bring me something to eat…and get some sleep, Arlo. We'll move out soon as the weather clears…"

"Fort's not going anywhere," the captain assured him, noting the uncommon use of his name.

"We don't know that." Donn wanted the fort's contents. Thomas Quentin too. And Hallister. Gods knew who else, how many others, might be racing against them. No one knew if the passage of time since the Undoing would leave anything to find.

Perhaps this was a fool's errand. Perhaps the fort had already been ransacked, emptied, or destroyed.

The longer they lingered here, the more chance there was for time, or any of his opponents, to claim the phantom prize.

But gods he wanted to rest. Just a little. Just a little while.

"There's more tea if you want it," Arlo offered as he stood. "Food'll be ready soon. I'll bring some over."

"Thank you."

Neither Lowell, the drooping of his lids prompting him to set the cup down between his knees, nor Arlo who watched him, expected the Laedan to be awake when the meal was ready.

❧*❧

The barkeep's offer of free drinks to his patrons as the storm continued to lay siege to those trapped amidst sticky floors and tables had been a tempting one. But it was an offer Ernest reluctantly refused after the third glass of whiskey left him bleary-eyed and suffering a throbbing at the bridge of his nose each flash of lightning made worse. Some guests took the offer to heart and were already slumped, comatose, on benches, against the walls, across the tables where they sat, in the corner near the heating stove, or on the rickety steps leading upstairs to the rooms the proprietor called home.

Many of these people knew who Ernest was. Not personally, not by name, perhaps, but by his Protectorate rank. The moment his guard was down enough to fall into the same drunken stupor he would find a knife in his back or a bullet in his head.

He had not seen anyone with a gun, but it did not mean there were none here. A knife would be enough to do the job.

The woman he had come to arrest was one of those who had fallen to the siren lure of inebriation; she sat beside Ernest at the bar, her head on her arms on the counter, snoring loudly enough he could hear her over the ambient noise of the storm. If anyone else heard her, they ignored her as they ignored the snores of others, and the tender continued to intermittently swipe around her in a failing attempt to keep the counter clean.

Trays of roasted nuts, their hot spiced perfume having long ago dissipated, were nearly empty, yet to be refilled, and the two men who had offered their voices in entertainment near the stove were quiet, sipping from steaming cups with their heads bent towards one another in quiet conversation. Others likewise engaged in muted exchanges. Only the last woman to arrive sat alone, toying with the handle of her ale stein, staring through the window at the storm. Dressed in brocaded leather, thus of enough wealth or influence to have obtained such an article…or else had been one to steal it…she looked like someone Ernest should know.

Moving from the stool, however, required effort, and as her sour expression was the sort to discourage people from approaching, Ernest chose to stay where he was.

The storm would not relent any time soon.

There was plenty of time for conversation later.

≈*≈

"Whatya think?" Dink perched on the edge of the unused stage, his back to the emptiness where a movie screen had once hung. It had long ago been scavved, leaving the wide wall devoid of anything except the cracks of gradual decay where ivy roots tried to push through. The rows of fold-bottom cushioned seats, connected like barricading soldiers with their arms linked to block an enemy's passage, remained intact because it had been thus far too much trouble to cut them apart or unbolt them from the floor. Scavenged bones, abandoned eating instruments, bits of clothing, and other paraphernalia of living indicated they were not the first people to have sought shelter in this place. They would not be the last.

Enola sat behind Uzzi, her back to his, their position affording them a watchful view of the side doors with unlit exit signs while Dink, from his leg-swinging perch on the stage, could watch the door through which they had entered.

The theatre made for a dry, secure shelter to wait out the storm. Though the two other screen rooms, similar to this one in every way, the film booth, and the lobby offered an opportunity for the group to spread out and find a little semblance of privacy, it also made it impossible to keep an eye on everyone.

Only Quentin, who had laid claim to the film booth, could see most of those who had filtered into the slope-floored theatre halls. Uzzi did not appreciate the spied-upon feeling it fostered, but he did not feel he had anything to hide. So long as his face was turned away from the booth and he kept his voice small, he did not believe even the Fela's enhanced hearing would pick out their low voices across the distance between them in the sound-absorbent room.

Only a paranoid, or overly cautious, person, or a guilty one, would worry about such things.

"'bout?" Uzzi picked at the half loaf of bread Enola had given him, curious about where she had acquired it but not curious enough to ask.

"Quentin. The Cana. All of this."

"Not paid to think," Uzzi muttered absently.

"Doesn't mean you don't." Enola felt Uzzi's shrug against her shoulder. "He's got an agenda."

"Course he does." They all did. It did not matter which man Enola meant. Dink agreed with them both and nodded at Uzzi's words.

"Least we know Quentin's…build up influence, cover his ass. Heard some of them talking. Rumor is he wants to be Laedan."

The thought made Uzzi chuckle. "Others have tried to unseat them and failed."

"Only one to unseat now," Dink reminded them. "With the state of things…maybe he's got a shot." There would be an appeal for many anthro to have one of their kind in a position of power.

"Never rule out a Channon."

Uzzi did not know any of the family personally. He had never met most of them. His only encounter had been with a wasted young man face down in vomit in a pub near the Fortress…the same young man he had been contracted to kill but had not. Odds were, that particular Channon was going to kill himself with his addictions. One son was already murdered. The other…and his father…were forces to be reckoned with.

Whatever had pushed Quentin out was not going to make it easy to get back in. Politics rarely worked that way. There was a reason Quentin was reluctant to return to the Fortress without an arsenal and the men to use it at his back. Uzzi did not plan to be one of them.

"I don't rule out anyone." The dog at Dink's feet stood and wagged his tail, its ears pricked towards the door at the back of the room. The man scowled at the silhouette there, silent, previously unnoticed. He had not likely overheard much of the short conversation, but the normally standoffish dog appeared to like their Cana sidekick, an irritation that shadowed Dink's face.

Uzzi glanced over his shoulder and waved Pain closer. To Enola, after a short look at Dink, he murmured, "Get me a drink, will ya? And something more than bread."

The pair were among the few he gave any trust to, who he asked to do things for him. If Pain wanted a private word, or was willing to give it to Uzzi, it was worth sending his companions out of the room. They would not go so far away as to be unreachable if he needed them and Uzzi was confident he stood a reasonable chance in a fight if that was what Pain had come for. Both Enola and Dink frowned but they reluctantly nodded and obeyed, scowling at Pain when the dog licked his hand as they passed in the center aisle.

If Uzzi learned anything from Pain they needed to know, he would tell them. Years of experience had verified that.

Pain hesitated at the end of the front row where Uzzi sat, listening to the others depart without looking at them. When they had taken shelter hours earlier, Pain was one of the few to remain in the lobby. Some had set to scavenging the abandoned debris for anything worthwhile. There had been a couple selected to stand watch at the entrance…where no one in their right head would come in as the weather worsened…and a sour-faced man who had exchanged harsh words with Quentin the day before and lagged at the back of the group ever since had made his bed upon the lobby counter where he could monitor the comings and goings of everyone else. Trusting none of them enough to sleep in their company, Pain eventually gravitated towards the distant companionship of Uzzi and his friends.

Pain trusted them enough to believe they would not slit his throat as he slept.

"The one you're after," Pain eventually began, refusing to sit in the fold-down chairs and not feeling secure enough to go to the stage and sit where Dink had been. "What's he to you?"

"Could ask the same of you."

"He's nothing to me." The pregnant pause that followed, both men waiting for the other to speak, waiting for private details neither wanted to share, ended with Pain leaning against the arm of the chair across the aisle and stretching his legs out in front of him.

"Looking for my alpha," Pain eventually added, eyes on his weathered leather shoes as if concentrating on the mud caked there. "I…owe her."

Uzzi cocked an eyebrow. "In a good way or bad?"

Pain shrugged.

"She's traveling with him?" Cana and Fela did not often mingle unless a relationship of some sort came about outside of the strictly anthro world and was supported by mutual interests. Uzzi could not conjure a scenario in which this might be an accurate course of events.

Pain nodded.

"Alone?"

"There were others, an Ursa, a mage." There were other pack members too, particularly the former omega, but none of them mattered to Pain in this. The Ursa only mattered because he was an unpredictable unknown, as Ursa often were. The mage mattered because he was a mage…and a Protector. The other scents picked up along the way as they followed southwest through the unincorporated parts of the city, were unfamiliar enough to be inconsequential.

"She wants him…I intend to see she gets him."

"Him? My…?"

"Quentin." The word was spat fast enough to cut Uzzi off and Pain regretted too late not allowing the other man to speak.

"Why?"

"Her father."

Despite waiting for him to say more, Pain did not continue until Uzzi prompted, "Same reason you want him?"

"Yes."

Uzzi nodded and put his feet on the floor. "Good enough." Offering the rest of the loaf of bread brought Pain reluctantly close enough to take it. As if taming a feral dog, Uzzi made no sudden movement as he brought his empty hand back, but said, "Someone I used to know…or think I did. Been a long time. If it's him…" he shrugged, "like the chance to catch up."

It seemed to Pain a lot of effort to catch up with a long-lost friend or acquaintance, but he did not question the explanation. He smelled honesty in the other man, heard no deception in the first tidbit of personal detail he had shared.

Trusting Uzzi with the shadowed edges of his purpose had paid off. "Quentin?"

Uzzi grunted. "Tired of owing him. Want my life back." He cocked his head towards the doorway where Enola and Dink were returning. "Theirs too. Tired of…all of it."

"Then we get what we want." Pain looked at Dink first, and then Enola and murmured, "All of us."

"All of us," Uzzi agreed.

꙰*꙰

The doctor had left the room hours before but the quickly building storm had likely trapped the woman in the Fortress, keeping her at the mercy of the hospitality the staff offered. Hunkered in this same dark room, without windows or access to the outside, where the lightning could not be seen and the thunder's fury was dampened, Oasis hoped that wherever the doctor had gone, she did not cross paths with Nik.

What did it matter? The Laedan's son already believed she was pregnant, a ruse carried out to protect her from Donn, a ruse she had considered ending now that it appeared Donn was unlikely to return to the Fortress, hunted as he was. A child lost before it could show was commonplace since the Undoing; no one would have been surprised. No one would have judged her or doubted her original claim.

A ruse no more.

Thunder rumbled above the Fortress and the hail began, shaking the walls of her hideout, rattling the roof above her head. She cowered as she always had, without her father to soothe her through the storms, without anyone else to turn to for distraction.

She wondered what Nik thought of the storm.

She considered looking for him. It would give her something to do and a conversation, as awkward as it might be, would ease her fears and focus as the storm raged.

Frustrated, she beat her stomach with an impotent fist and wiped away tears before they fell. She did not want this child. The possibility it was Donnovan's child sickened her. The chance it was Lowell's filled her with the guilt of something stolen from a dead woman. She had come to LaGuardia to forge alliances but not once had she considered or imagined the turn of events gradually devouring her like bog sand.

And her father had abandoned her.

Face upturned as if to allow the ice stones to pelt her cheeks, blind her eyes, she reminded herself her future was in her hands. Whoever returned with Fort Hamilton's spoils, she could not rely on them to provide the life she had envisioned for herself…and now this child. She could only work with what she had available. An unwanted child and Nik Channon.

When the storm ended, she would take her first step. Frustrated, she was not prepared to surrender to the despair that had devoured Yiva…that might have devoured her mother.

Oasis was stronger than that.

But she hated waiting, hated not knowing. She hated being alone.

Elsewhere in the Fortress, in the spacious room Laedans of the past had used for private ceremonies, Nik faced the storm with furious pacing, from one side of the room to the other, while the sea beyond the window churned and frothed. Boats strained at the ends of their moorings, a few had overturned, a few had broken free to be set adrift and ultimately dashed on LaGuardia's rocky coast. Torben watched it happen with dispassionate serenity, neither flinching nor otherwise reacting when the thunder clapped and the lightning lit up the stern lines of his broad face.

"How can you be calm?"

Torben shrugged without looking at Nik pacing behind him. "No use being otherwise. It's a storm. It'll pass. They always do."

"When it takes the Fortress down?"

"Think that's gonna happen?" Nik did not reply. "Fortress has stood for decades. It's well maintained, the stanchions kept up. Not gonna fall today. Fretting isn't gonna change if it happens or not."

Nik snorted. The wisdom of his words was true. Despite his fascination with storms, as with his fascination with death and the dark, the violence and uncertainty of this particular event felt to be the herald of something he did not feel strong enough to face.

"He's out there in it, you know. Jia too." Probably his brother as well, hunting an elusive treasure Nik hoped was never found. There was violence enough in the world. LaGuardia did not need a host of ancient weapons to compound the problem.

"They're smart enough to find shelter." Torben did not know the Cana alpha or the Laedan well, but anyone smart enough to be a leader should be smart enough to get out of a storm.

"What if they're not?"

"Didn't think you were a worrier."

Nik frowned and forced himself to stop pacing in the center of the room. Had he always been neurotic? He shook his head at his question. Having hidden behind a curtain of substances for so many years, seeking a balance robbed from him as a child, he could not say if he was prone to worrying or not. Facing storms, enduring responsibilities with a sober head, were as new to him as being clean.

"You're right. I'm better than this."

Smiling at the reflection in the glass as a jagged light bolt cut through the clouds over the sea, Torben nodded once. "Course you are. Never thought different."

Nik smiled too. It was comforting to have someone express belief in him, to know someone was on his side. Someone other than a mother lost and a twin he doubted had ever meant a word of respect or support he had given.

Chapter 29

Pubby did not have bullets in his arsenal to fit the cartridge of the newly attained handgun and thus could not test whether its failure to fire had been a mechanical malfunction or a fault of the round in the chamber. While the group waited for the storm to wane, while they took turns sleeping, eating, or keeping watch, he used his waking hours to clean the gun, to file interior imperfections, to return it to as nearly pristine condition as he had the equipment available to manage.

If he were at home, in his shop, he would do a more detailed job. It was what he did in his off-duty hours…repairing, rebuilding, cleaning guns of every type for anyone in LaGuardia who brought them to him. He had handled more than a few for the Laedans over the years, considered himself one of the few experts left, which gave him a unique perspective at certain crime scenes making him as invaluable to the Protectorate as Segara was. Not having expected to need a workshop's worth of portable tools on this expedition, he had only brought the basics required to maintain his guns and Vance's, and perhaps a few he might confiscate from Fort Hamilton.

A day passed and the rest of another night with it. A new morning brought gray sunlight behind the clouds and the waking to a mud-drenched world that made their trek difficult, even for the Cana who led the way. No one questioned the decision to travel; the cramped quarters of their back room had grown confining, stifling, and generated an awkward restlessness compounded by the fear of a hunter few of them had seen.

Most were ready to move before the tracker ruff found them.

If Nepo found their shelter, he would learn more about each of them than anyone wanted to be known, in the same way Vance learned such things. While Vance was discreet, keeping his learnings private, none of them expected Nepo to be the same. It was wisest to get as far ahead of him as they could and hope the injuries he had endured in the fight with Vance were enough to slow him down.

The new gun was tucked safely into the pack slung over Pubby's shoulder and he moved in step with Vance as they picked their way through puddled streets.

The torrential rain had overwhelmed the barely adequate tunnels of the Below, creating puddles, ponds, and lakes in every low-level place it could reach. Water continued to drip from the higher places, creating little waterfalls in some places or a constant falling of droplets where an accumulation followed the pull of gravity. Uprooted trees lay across paths previously been clear, materials not weighted down had blown to form barricades, and soupy mud made every surface sticky or slick and difficult to walk through.

They endeavored to stay on the cracked pavement paths, but that was not always feasible, and sometimes even those were overlaid with mud washed in by the storm.

Such hindrances meant backtracking, meant climbing under and over obstacles, meant searching for detours through alleys and buildings rather than forging a straight path in the direction Vance assured them they needed to travel. Obstacles meant delays, delays meant a heightened probability the other tracker might catch up.

As much as they could, however, to undercut Nepo's ability to follow through those same obstacles, they obeyed Vance's instructions not to touch anything unless they had to. Wearing gloves meant those things they did touch would offer only a muted sense of them, of their direction, if it gave the other tracker clues at all. If they were lucky, Nepo would spend long enough finding, sorting, and identifying their trail he would fall further behind. It might create enough distance between them to provide increased safety.

The handful of blocks they traversed, however, was not far enough, and the coming of night, the weariness the storm damage had caused, forced them to stop.

This time, Vance suspected without looking to see if it was true, that none of them except Eddie slept.

❧*❧

He crept out of hiding while the rain still fell, as the tail of the wind dragged through the streets but no longer burst windows or pulled shallow-rooted or weakened plants from their moorings. The street was empty, the upturned wagon dragged to the roadside by the still tethered, bedraggled oxen tangled in their leads, their heads thrust awkwardly through a doorway and window. They had gotten their faces out of the storm but their eyes were wide with trapped panic. Their sides were scarred and bleeding from airborne debris and heaved in distress but there was no one available to free them.

Only Beren, who had no inclination to try and no experience with such animals to risk their powerful hooves and horns.

Eventually, someone would come. Either the captors would emerge from the shelter they had found or locals would come to claim the animals for themselves.

Beren did not intend to stay long enough to witness either.

Like a crab he scurried about in a crouched position, poking through the goods scattered on either side of the road the wind had not blown away. Lighter objects were gone, but what he sought, his own pack, proved heavy enough to have survived and remained wedged in the wagon's frame folded and warped when the vehicle tipped.

He pulled. He twisted. He pushed the wood with his feet, the seat of his pants soaking through with mud, until the sack came free. He peered inside, counted the contents, and grunted with a satisfied grin.

HOPE had not yet won. His father had not yet lost. They might have taken everything from him, but Beren was not ready to give up. Not while he possessed his pack and its precious contents.

❧*❧

"An Anakirist? Here?" Nik squeezed the arms of his breakfast chair until his knuckles turned white and forced his eyes not to dart around the room in search of an unfound escape. HOPE agents came to the Fortress regularly, conducting business with the Laedans on behalf of Grand Mas Lord. None had come since before Donnovan's wedding, a wedding the Grand Mas had attended, so it was inevitable one eventually would.

The rumors of death attached to the Channon name increased the odds of a visit.

Laedan in name only, Nik would have preferred such a visit to wait for his father's return.

"In the conference room." With the storm's thinning, Torben had been on his way out, both to see his home was secure and to take a long overdue shift at the Plant. There were likely to be many dead in the wake of damage done; the need for sposers, the need for collecting corpses before grubbers arose to stalk the streets, was always highest after such a storm. This one, the worst in Torben's memory, would be different only in the magnitude of the damage and the death he expected to see.

Descending into the lobby as the HOPE delegate and his staff arrived subverted Torben's intentions. The Plant would wait.

"I can stay." Not indefinitely, as a lifetime of duty beckoned, but he had a duty to Nik too, and judging by the loss of color from the young man's cheeks, Torben thought it wisest to remain here.

There were other sposers to begin the collection of the dead.

Nik had no one else.

Nik's head bobbed as he rose, smoothed the front of his shirt and trousers, and followed Torben from the room, leaving his partially eaten breakfast behind. He should have worn a dress jacket. He did not look like a Laedan.

Thankfully, he did not look like a junkie either.

The face of the man who turned from the conference room window to greet him was unyielding and sour, the set of his mouth and the narrowness of his eyes in his regal features suggesting an air of superiority Nik thought common in the HOPE leaders who had come and gone through the Fortress before. His short dark hair was neatly slicked back away from his forehead and temples, a crown framing a face darker than the crags at the corners of his eyes and mouth suggested it should be.

Vain, Nik thought, satisfied that the man's entourage had scattered to the room's periphery, a show of offered privacy for a meeting none would allow. Bejeweled hands tugged at the hem of the black longcoat HOPE agents typically wore, an act less of nerves than of boredom and annoyance for having been made to wait.

Nik had met this man before.

"Anakirist Gracen. Welcome."

"Sirra Channon." Gracen offered his hand, ring up, inviting not a handshake but the kissing of the insignia worn there.

Nik, accustomed to the gesture common to the Grand Mas but less so to those serving beneath him, swallowed his anxiety and gave the expected bow and kiss.

"You came through the storm? That must have been harrowing."

"It was nothing." His black eyes scanned the room as if reluctant to retain contact with Nik's but eventually, they returned to the young man's face before continuing, "I have business with the Laedan."

"My father is not here. I am the authority in his stead…"

Giles Gracen scowled, a look suggesting a haughty lift of his chin Nik did not see. Given Nik's history and reputation, the shift in Gracen's demeanor and judgment was not a surprise.

"Where has he gone? When will he return?"

His gravelly tone was irritating. Nik shrugged and decided to play enough into the Anakirist's opinion of him without undermining the mantle of authority his father had placed on his shoulders. "West, on business. He did not say when he would return."

There was no need to provide the man with details of his father's business. That was one lesson Nik had learned from watching the Laedans conduct their affairs. HOPE had only as much authority and influence as those in positions of power allowed them to have.

Nik refused to allow this man any influence.

Huffing with annoyance he did not try to hide, an overly exaggerated sound that might have pressured a weak man into providing more information, Gracen instead said, "There have been disturbing rumors…"

"Rumors?"

"Of anthro in the Laedans' staff…that Laedan Marrock…"

At Nik's side, Torben bristled. Gracen looked the mountainous man up and down with only the shifting of his eyes but his expression did not change or reveal his thoughts.

Taking the offered opening, Nik nodded. "There's some evidence that Thomas Quentin is Fela," he began casually. He had no reason to protect the man who had caused so much havoc for his family and no reason to indicate he had seen such evidence with his own eyes.

"Quentin?" Gracen's frown deepened. Like Donn, Thomas had courted HOPE's favor for as long as Nik had known him. How many times had Nik, high and harried, passed Thomas in secretive discussions with whichever HOPE delegate had come to call? How many shared drinks had Nik spoiled by staggering into a room to swipe a liquor bottle from the cabinet and stumble out again?

Sullying the traitor's repute with HOPE was the least Nik could do. He owed Jonni, and Roland, that much. Jia and his father too.

"There's mage evidence he killed Jonni and…"

"We were told a Fela…" Gracen's mouth snapped shut and his lips stretched into a thin, terse line. "Marrock too?" he asked after a moment of awkward silence.

"Put down after he turned…but killed by the hands that took my brother. The mage…"

"What mage?"

With so few mages in the known territories of the boroughs and those mages undoubtedly known to HOPE who made it their business to keep tabs on anyone out of the ordinary…anyone not Normal…Nik believed the Anakirist knew the answer to his question. Swallowing his distaste for dragging Vance further into the purview of HOPE's attention but seeing no other choice if he was to discredit Thomas and ensure the man faced justice, Nik shrugged and said, "The one from the main Protectorate office…Segara…my father hired…"

Tie the connection to Lowell. Hide what Nik knew and did not know. Don't give the Anakirist any more than he needed.

Don't draw attention.

Why did Gracen need to know if there were anthro in the Fortress…except to strangle their existence out of history? Wasn't the Laedans' choice of staff entirely up to them?

Gracen's head bobbed enough for the gesture to be seen. "Where's Quentin now?"

"There was an argument; Fa sent him away…before the details of his involvement in what happened were known. The Protectorate's looking for him. Everyone in LaGuardia is looking for him as it's thought he also…"

Nik swallowed, hoping the look of pain and grief which slid easily into place and the mournful note in his voice when he spoke would mask the false portions of his tale. As tempting as it was to out his twin to HOPE, there were personal family details involved he knew should not be revealed to insidious moles like Gracen. Besmirching the Channon name would expose a soft underbelly none of them must ever reveal.

Donn was a problem the remaining Channons had to address for themselves.

"He's killed my mother too," Nik said, the cracks in his voice laced with grief. "Or so it's said."

"Yiva is…?" There were audible cracks in Gracen's tone too, the cracks of a man's fondness filling with the sad, unexpected news. "When did she…?"

"Few weeks past. The news should've been…" Nik shrugged. "Fa's not been himself…"

"Yes…no…of course not. He wouldn't be. No wonder he's gone west…" Seeking an escape from grief was an understandable excuse, seeing to the border expansion a legitimate responsibility, even though Gracen's eyes continued to carry a hint of suspicion about where Lowell had gone and why.

Hoping to shrug off the grief rather than wallow in it, Nik said, "You must be hungry…weary after your travels. Let me give you rooms, see to drying your clothes, your comforts…then we can speak more…unless your duty here is…"

As expected, Gracen's business manner fell easily back into place; what he thought or felt about the passing of the Laedan's wife was tucked back behind the mask of perceived superiority and duty.

"There are levies, the rolls, the inventories…"

Nik nodded. He knew the things Gracen spoke of. Levies paid to HOPE to fund their charitable efforts…and to line the pockets of the institute. Rolls of anthro and mutani, mages and dissidents identified and cataloged…for eventual extermination, Nik was sure. Inventories of food and supplies stored on behalf of the borough residents of which HOPE expected a cut in exchange for services Nik did not understand.

"I don't know if they're ready…given everything that's happened, but I can show you what's available…show you the improvements to the Fortress…perhaps take a tour through the borough if you wish."

After the storm, the borough would be a disaster, but if the need was great enough, HOPE might willingly forego a portion of their collection to aid the people they hoped to influence in their favor.

"Yes…a tour. That would be grand." His distracted tone, however, suggested Anakirist Gracen had no interest in Fortress improvements or a tour of storm-torn LaGuardia. He would have witnessed some such damage on his way to the Fortress. He wanted only what he believed the Laedan owed, to him and to HOPE.

"You can go, Torben." Nik felt more confident after facing down his initial fear of the gruff man before him. He knew such men. He had made a study of them from the background as his father and brothers juggled borough politics. Anything he did not want the Anakirist to know, anything he felt they did not need to know, could be hidden behind a veil of inexperience and put off until he could hide those details so well that HOPE would never find them…

…or put them off until his father returned.

Given what Gracen and others expected of Nik Channon, or did not expect, the arrogant man would never know the difference.

❧*❧

Korma Miller was exactly his type. Tall and lean, with exotic pale eyes set into her flawless oval face encircled by the blonde locks of the angels that graced so much of the artwork throughout HOPE Cathedral and Invocation Hall. Geary did not know her face, did not think he had ever crossed paths with her on any of his visits there. Nor had he ever heard, or seen, a woman in the role of Anakirist.

But the cut of her black uniform was unmistakable, despite the uncharacteristically unbuttoned front drawing his gaze down her throat to the crest of her cleavage.

He caught the ghost of triumph that flickered across her face and forcibly steeled his features to hide his scowl and any further reaction to her femininity. Taking notice was exactly what she intended.

He would not let it happen again.

"Is it time already?" he asked easily, offering his hand without an introduction. She would know who he was from the style of his suit and the formality of his posture, the same as he knew, from his staff's announcement, who she was.

There was no need for introductions.

"You know it is, Laedan. I do hope I'm not wasting my time, that you've not failed Grand Mas…"

"Failed?" He chuckled to hide the insult he felt and motioned her into his office before nodding to the servant to close the door after his guest entered. "Have I ever…?"

"There's always a first time," she said with cool amusement, dropping gracefully into an empty chair opposite him at the desk without being asked to sit.

"For others; not for me. Would you care for a drink or…?"

"A drink would be lovely."

Ignoring her penchant for cutting him off, using the retrieval of a drink to mask his irritation, he poured an amber liquid from a carafe on a silver tray at the side of his desk into two glasses and offered one to her. He did not take the other until he sat down.

"We've heard there have been difficulties…"

"Difficulties?" It was his turn to cut her off. Given the nature of HOPE's spy network, she could be referring to anything Grand Mas and the Council did not like. Without being a betting man, however, Geary was confident he knew what the Anakirist referenced before she continued with an upturned smirk at the corner of her mouth.

"There's been a decrease in production."

"We had to relocate the facility; some of the stock had to be liquidated."

"We hope this isn't…"

"I assure you, the new facility will be more secure, more remote, and the stock will be replaced as soon as we manage the storm damage." Regardless of his instruction to Doctor Torrens, despite his intention to halt the harvesting of blood until he was confident the LaGuardia mage was not going to be a problem, the claim was what the Grand Mas and the Council wanted to hear. Both sides relied on the income of anthro labor and plasm too much. HOPE, Geary wagered, more so than Kennedy.

"Grand Mas will be pleased to hear it. The alliance?"

"With LaGuardia?" His shoulders twitched, an aborted shrug reflecting his casual downward glance towards the cup he returned to the desk and cradled casually in one hand. "My daughter is with child, so I'd say the alliance is in hand."

"Despite the unrest in LaGuardia?"

"If you mean Marrock's death and the murders of Jonatan and Yiva? Unfortunate business, but nothing to do with me." The remembrance of Lowell's expression shuffled through Geary's mind, the way the other Laedan had shambled around LaGuardia's hall when Geary had been there. "Channon's holding up…all things considered. I trust the alliance will hold."

He assumed the deaths of Marrock and the Channon boy had spread into the ears of HOPE's hierarchy some time ago, but the news of Yiva's murder was fresh enough, kept contained by the Channons, that Geary was not surprised by the startled expression on the

Anakirist's face. Odd, he thought, that Korma Miller reminded him of Yiva Channon.

Maybe it was her eyes. Maybe it was her hair.

If HOPE wanted to control Channon, all they needed to do was send Korma to seduce and marry Lowell based on nothing more than the similarities of face and body type.

"How did it happen?"

Geary's shrug was more obvious that time. "I couldn't say. Oasis only said she had been murdered." He should have harvested more details from his daughter, but after the exchange about marriage and duty and obligation, Oasis had refused to see him before his departure.

That had not been like her. She had never turned him away before.

"But you did not come to gossip about LaGuardia," Geary changed the subject in a brighter tone. "I can get you everything you've come for…"

"I want to inspect the facility."

"That's not possible." His head-shaking, hasty retort was met with a skeptical arching of Korma's perfectly manicured brow and he quickly continued. "The roads are impassable. The storm…"

"Has ended."

"It will take time to clear the roads. The work's begun, of course, but even if I redirect the crews, make that road priority, it'll take time."

Korma studied her polished nails as if bored and said, "I can wait."

Although he nodded in agreement, he said, "It could take days…a week or more…"

He knew she would not be put off, stubborn as any of her male Anakirist counterparts, and so he smiled and continued, "I can give you these now…" He slid a thick folder of reports across the desk, the details HOPE always requested, updated, and kept on hand for surprise inspections such as this. "While you study them, I will inquire about the roads to the facility. If they're passable, or can be made so quickly, I will see it done at once. We can share dinner, discuss the reports if you wish, and I will let you know when the trip will be safe enough for an inspection."

They held each other's gazes, expressions equally cool, neutral, and unrevealing, until Korma put her hand on the folder he offered and nodded one time. "That's fine," she agreed. "If I need other resources or have questions about…" Her gaze flicked down at the folder.

"I'll leave someone to get you what you need," Geary promised.

"Fenway?"

The corners of Geary's eyes twitched, a response to a peculiar note in the woman's voice that made him wary. "Aman's away on business," he replied, pretending the twitch had not been noticeable.

"Someone else then," Korma murmured offhandedly.

"Of course." There were other staff members familiar with his office, his files, his work. Aman did not need to be here. If the Anakirist was disappointed or relieved, Geary could not tell. He, however, was grateful Aman was not in Kennedy.

A few hours' delay still ought to allow a message to reach Gail. Ought to provide enough opportunity for the facility to at least give the appearance of normal function.

He doubted Korma Miller, or any other Anakirist, would have the technological expertise to recognize differently.

⁂*⁖

Anakirist Gracen's entrance into the primary Protectorate elicited the turning of heads he expected, the notice of respectful, fearful, or disdaining eyes that either returned to their work or else stared at him as he located the destination he sought and sauntered towards it, his entourage trailing behind, without speaking to anyone. Nor did he knock or announce himself when he opened the chief's door and stepped inside without being invited.

His staff waited outside the room.

This was a place of business. Protectorates were open to the public. There was no one he could see behind the glass except the man at the desk and thus, in Gracen's view, there was no such thing as a breach of privacy.

It was a HOPE tenet that they had access to anyone and anything at any time.

Ernest looked up at the opening of his door and shoved the report aside he had been working on for the last hour since staggering into the Protectorate, weary from too long spent in the tavern, unshaved and unbathed but eager to write down the details of his hours there before the memories were dulled by the passage of time and sleep. He wanted to record everything while his memory was fresh enough to do so. His prisoner had been dumped into a holding cell with the others to await her turn at interrogation.

That would not be Ernest's job. After beating a man to death, Ernest determined someone else should extract information from uncooperative captives, at least until Brac was found and arrested.

Half-asleep, it had taken too long to scribble down the nearly one page of notes he had managed. There was more to add, but the arrival of the arrogant shart on the other side of his desk meant finishing his report was not going to happen any faster.

"I am looking for Protector Segara."

Ernest set down his pen and leaned back, arms crossing over his chest as his legs shifted to counter the unsteady balance of the seat.

"Not here."

Gracen nodded. His frown might have darkened, but as a sour expression was already etched onto his face, it was difficult for Ernest to notice any visible change.

"I can see that."

"I'll tell him you stopped by, tell him you're looking for him." If the Anakirist was staying in LaGuardia, he would be staying at the Fortress. There were few reputable boarding houses available and Gracen did not look like the sort to room in any abandoned building without the comfort of a bed and bath. Even boarding houses, Ernest assumed, would be beneath this man.

"Where is he?"

"On assignment."

"I'll wait."

"Will be days before I see him…maybe weeks…and you're not camping out in my lobby." Not that the Anakirist would, but saying it allowed a hint of contempt in Ernest's voice to bleed through, to express his annoyance at the other man's presumptive interruption.

"Days? You let your…?"

"No one lets a mage do anything. He's his own man. He'll follow his leads and report back when he's…"

"What leads? Where is he?"

"Classified. Not," Ernest stressed the word, "HOPE's concern."

Gracen's chin tipped up and the corners of his lips curled. "Thomas Quentin? I've been to the Fortress. I know what he's done. Are you going to tell me that's not HOPE's concern either?"

"What he's accused of doing," the chief corrected.

"A mage's word is…"

"Good enough for an arrest. The rest is up to the juds. Until we find Quentin…"

"I want to be notified immediately when he's located."

"You?" There was no reason to notify HOPE of Quentin's arrest, and no reason, as far as Ernest knew, to report the details to the Anakirist.

Gracen cleared his throat. "As an Anakirist, on behalf of Grand Mas Lord and the Inquisition…"

As if he had misunderstood the man's meaning, Ernest felt he knew precisely what Gracen meant, but he nodded and said, "Of course. When he's found."

"The mage too. When he returns."

Through tight, pursed lips, Ernest said, "I'll let him know." Letting him know the Anakirist was looking for him was not the same as telling Segara to report to HOPE.

"See that you do." For a moment, Gracen stood silent, his eyes scanning the room as if seeking something else to say, some detail to pick apart or question, but eventually, he stalked out of the office, leaving the door open. He passed through his wall of attendants without shaking the chief's hand or touching anything. Nor did he touch any of the doors or anything else he passed, as if afraid that doing so would defile him or leave Segara some proof of his passage and intent.

Ernest stared after him for a long time, the murmurs and mutterings in the main room falling on deaf ears as he pondered what interest, beyond the deaths of Laedan Marrock and Jonni Channon, the Anakirist might have in his tracker-mage.

He was going to do his damnedest to find out.

❧*❧

"There's an Anakirist here?"

To Nik's eyes, Oasis looked wan, harried and worn, red eyes of mourning nested within dark circles hinting at a strain he felt intimately familiar with. Anyone seeing her might think she too suffered the pangs of withdrawal Nik was accustomed to, but to his knowledge, she was no junkie.

He had rarely even seen her drink though he knew she did.

"You okay?" he asked, motioning to the space on the bench beside him from which he watched the cleanup of the Fortress courtyard from the shelter of the dry lobby. Torben had gone to the Plant hours ago and the Anakirist had yet to return from his foray to the Protectorate. Nik had accompanied him as far as the lobby, where Gracen declined a borough tour, and then settled here beneath the bit of warm sunlight sprinkled through the glass panels above their heads.

He did not think he would have to wait long for Gracen's return. There seemed no point in resuming duties the Anakirist would disrupt as soon as he came back.

Oasis sagged onto the bench with a sigh and leaned against the post behind them, her entire body seemingly sapped of strength and muscle control. "Hate thunderstorms," she muttered, rubbing her eyes with the heels of her hands.

"Yeah…I understand." Nik did not share her apparent hate or fear, but this last storm had been the most intense in his memory, intense enough to have rattled him too.

"The Anakirist?"

"Gracen."

She nodded, her eyes still behind her hands. "He's been to Kennedy. I've met him. I don't like him…any of them."

"Been a long time since he's been here…but me too." He paused, jumping at the bang of someone's rake accidentally striking the window, making note of her stance on HOPE, or at least those the organization employed. "Never trusted HOPE…not sure why Donn does, why my father tolerates them."

"Power and greed." They were the same reasons HOPE curried favor with her father, the reasons her father curried favor with them. The same reasons Thomas had dared exposure of his secrets in the hope the Grand Mas and his minions would further his political agenda. It was a game Oasis felt weary of playing.

"You ever dealt with him?"

"That was my father's business."

The distaste in her voice was noted. Nik looked at his nails as he rubbed his thumb across his fingertips. "Mine too. He asked about Quentin…and he wants to know where Fa is."

"You tell him?"

Nik shook his head. "Isn't any of his business. Sure they want it too. If Fa finds what he's looking for, HOPE'll know soon enough. And Quentin…" His hands moved involuntarily as if to grasp something not there. "Only told him he's a suspect, that the mage has evidence."

"Does he?" She seemed more surprised than Nik thought she should, but it was not the sort of detail his father might have felt compelled to share with his son's wife, who held no position of power outside of being tasked to help Nik manage LaGuardia in his absence.

"Don't know what it is…something to do with plasm I think…which everyone knows is a HOPE thing…so if it's connected to them through Quentin, best to keep what he knows to himself. Mage Segara'll take what he has to the juds when he's sure." He side-eyed her, wondering if she could pick the tendrils of truth from among the bone-shards of lies, and asked, "There's mages in Kennedy?"

"I think so. I've never met them, but my father must have dealings with them." Not every Protectorate office had a mage. Given the prevalent mistrust of men and women who could read thoughts and images from objects, from a touch, from the air of a room, it was possible the Protectorates around Kennedy Fortress did not employ mages, that mages in Kennedy were freelancers.

Most of them were.

"Never seemed to have much need of one before." It felt to Nik that employing a full-time mage at the Fortress would be beneficial for everyone.

He did not believe Segara would accept such a job.

"You think…he's found it by now?" Oasis looked at him when he turned his face and added, "Lowell. The fort?"

The way she spoke his name struck Nik as odd, but as he did not know what else she should call him, he pushed the niggling sense away. "Don't know how far he has to go to get there…and the storm would have slowed them down."

"Maybe HOPE knows about the fort too…" Her expression, as she leaned her elbows on her knees and propped her chin on her fists, was pensive and thoughtful. "Maybe they're looking for details…want to know who already knows…maybe Gracen's a spy."

"'course he is." Even if Gracen was not seeking details about Fort Hamilton, anyone Grand Mas Lord sent into the world was a spy. Lord's efforts to know everything, to dig HOPE's fingers into every political pie and borough business venture, were not a secret.

Oasis bobbed her head in agreement.

Several minutes ticked by in a congenial sort of silence in which neither of them, for the first time of late, felt the need to put on a brave front, to present a show of feigned strength or try to hide unspoken thoughts. Nik felt that sort of security when Torben was around but most often the sposer was with him in moments of borough business when Nik had to wear a rigid mask for his father's people, his officers, his councilors.

Oasis, her world once revolving around how she could manipulate and twist those in her life to further her survival in this unfamiliar place, as well as on her father's behalf, had, until this moment, discounted Nik as someone she could trust. He had been yet another she could manipulate, a junkie without anything to offer. Noticeably clean now, or cleaner than when she had met him, calm except for the occasional tremors that shuddered through him as his body sought something external to soothe itself, she wondered if she, like everyone else, had misread this Channon.

"Donn?"

Conversations would always come back to Donn, at least until he was forcibly removed from their lives. Nik did not know if his father would have the heart to execute his son, but Nik believed if Donn was caught, he would never again see daylight or the outside world.

"Nothing yet. With luck…" With luck, his twin had been caught in the storm, wherever he was, and lost in it. He did not wish his twin dead, but at least such an end would mean Nik would not have to face, to witness, whatever punishment their father intended to bestow. Nik would never have to decide on a path of punishment.

"I know." Oasis paused as they watched the opening of the Fortress gate and the gaggle of people who entered the courtyard through it. There was only one person it could be, two if the group heralded Lowell's return. It was too soon, however. She knew it. Nik knew it. Oasis lowered her head and got shakily to her feet. "If the Anakirist says anything…asks anything…"

Nik nodded. "Yeah…you too." Sooner or later Gracen would corner her. Extortion and isolation were tools HOPE often used.

"I will," she promised. If HOPE was fishing for details to undermine Channon authority in LaGuardia, they both needed to guard against his prying. They had to share what they learned between them, on their own behalf if nothing else. Against HOPE, they needed to be a united front. They had to be allies.

Whether they were in any other arena or not.

⇗*⇖

The woman was doing an admirable job of hiding her discomfort from the people around her as she rode beside the driver of the supply wagon. With the storm behind them, their dead left where they had fallen for collection or the scavenging efforts of rodents, birds, insects, and other small creatures, Donn had been the one to insist they leave their shelter before the rising of the sun.

General Warby had not disagreed with him.

The general had not said anything.

Perhaps he knew. But like the beautiful medic who reminded Donn so much of Yiva that the image of her on the wagon in front of him clouded his judgment, Warby kept any knowing to himself.

She squirmed, the uncushioned plank on which she sat aggravating tender buttocks and the searing burn of more secret places. Her discomfort, knowing he was responsible for it, knowing she would endure him again because his power over her kept her silent, produced a tightening in his trousers that the saddle's pressure rubbed in a deliciously frustrating way.

As if feeling his gaze, she peered over her shoulder only to quickly look away. The moment of eye contact was enough.

Yes, she would be back for more. If not willingly, he would take what he wanted.

Not even Warby would dare to stop him.

❧*❧

"He's not here, sirra."

Geary's scowl made the officer sidestep as though he expected to be struck for the offering of the bad news he brought.

But Geary did not blame him. The death and destruction left in the wake of the storm needed tending. Aman was not here to see to it. When his orders to clear the streets around the Fortress, to remove the debris around the perimeter and evaluate the number of deaths the gale had caused had gone out with the first light of day, it had been with the back-of-his-mind knowledge that Norse would have to be the one to follow through. Aman was more efficient at such duties, more organized and level-headed.

Geary had not foreseen needing him when he sent Aman away.

He imagined Norse was out there, bouncing from one crisis point to another in whatever random fashion seemed most important without organizing the follow-through on any of them.

"Make sure Old South is clear to Nassau."

"Sirra? That's not…"

"Unless you want to explain why it isn't to Anakirist Miller."

The threat of answering to an Anakirist had the expected effect. The officer began to quake.

"Deliver this to Doctor Torrens." Geary presented a large envelope, sealed with string, an ink stamp over the folded end, and a wax seal pressed with the Laedan's sigil. Though he trusted Gail to be prepared for unexpected reviews, it would be necessary to reverse his recent order and ramp up the work enough to appease HOPE's envoi and provide the Grand Mas with a glowing report of prosperity.

He expected she had the means to accomplish it on short notice.

"Return when it's done. I want to know she gets it. No excuses. And find me Norse."

"Yes, sirra. No excuses." He saluted and hurried off, leaving Geary to locate Norse on his own. It was a diversion from the Anakirist who had requisitioned his office. It gave him something to do.

❧*❧

From the outside, there was no indicator of what the unmarked, windowless building had once been. Situated on a sloped hill, the crumbling pavement of an ancient expressway and an overgrowth of trees shielded the sea from view and provided a natural windbreak to limit the storm's damage. It looked abandoned, unremarkable.

Except for the plume of smoke darkening the sky and the wires stretching from the stack at the corner of the building back into Kennedy borough to feed some portion of it with power.

It seemed an odd, out-of-the-way place to construct a Plant.

When Beren found it there had been no trace of foot or sposer wagon traffic, no signs of life except for the billows filling the air with the stink of burning flesh.

It was the stench more than anything else that hinted at the building's purpose. The building looked so much like the one he had raided with the Cana, minus the wire fence and mountain of metal container boxes accumulated around the outside, that Beren felt confident of the nature of what he had found.

But he heard nothing. Not the electric hum of Plant machinery, not the cries of captives, of the dying, not the voices of those who must surely work here, draining anthro of their lives, discarding them as so much inedible meat.

He selected a small building on the periphery, a public toilet whose systems no longer functioned as the encroaching sea eroded the underground pipes and the collapse of the city water system meant water no longer flowed in or out. The smell of waste was fresh, renewed by the gases forced to the surface by the storm, but no water had bubbled up here. There was no heat, no easily accessible food, but the shelter was dry and free of the wind. It also offered a clear view of the north and east sides of the building, where wagons might enter and people might pass in and out.

He only needed to see a delivery wagon to know the truth, to prompt him to action. He was determined to wait until that happened.

Chapter 30

Vance's bruised limbs and concussion, as well as the obstacles the storm had thrown into their path, resulted in more stops than the group wished to make. Until the mage was steadier, they would travel at his pace, his weight supported by Jia, Pubby, or anyone else as needed. The slow stride was more agreeable to Eddie but less so to Kato who often joined Deuce in running ahead or sweeping the path behind them to find paths with the least obstacles and to prevent Nepo from sneaking up on them.

The short stretch of wilds they crossed after passing between rows of abandoned homes with collapsing roofs and overgrown lawns emerged adjacent to an intact stretch of raised tracks extending as far to the east and west as they could see. A sign posted on the ancient concrete announced the place as Atlantic Avenue.

Without a map, without knowledge of the region, the sign meant nothing.

The length of crumbling street beneath the tracks was unremarkable, with the ivy-cracked walls of empty buildings and the passages between littered with abandoned rusty hulks. Doors were open on some, as if the owners had fled on foot leaving the buildings and vehicles to be ransacked in the decades since. As there were no noticeable hazards, no stretched wire or visible traps, and no people with weapons standing sentry to protect what waited on the other side, Jia led the way beneath the tracks until they reached the intact storefront of a large structure that had yet to give way to collapse like so many others around it. Faded as it was, the word 'sawkill' across its front was barely legible, the door missing from its hinges as though broken off rather than removed with tools. Deuce and Pubby took point to rule out external threats, and though Deuce was forced to backtrack east to the end of the block to make the circle, no hint of danger was found.

Jia and Vance exchanged glances. From the outside, it appeared large enough, sound enough, to shelter them from the frigid air of encroaching night. With luck, there would be something left inside they could use.

"We got lucky," Deuce grunted as, one by one, they entered to an array of shelves stocked with lumber, tools, and an unpilfered host of building materials covered with layers of dust and debris blown in through the broken doors.

A radiation test revealed there was none.

Inside was quiet except for the squeaks of skittering rats and mice and the rattle of the wind through the rafters. The location was empty. It appeared secure.

They had seen few people this day, and though the lack might have been attributed to the aftermath of the storm and people's reluctance to venture out, the lack might also have meant any humanity remaining this far west had chosen to relocate, to band together with others somewhere else where water or food was more plentiful. There was enough building material here, Jia believed, to have built or repaired many homes or at least provide fires.

Shelter and fire were of little use without food and water.

No one had tried, as far as they had seen, to grow food in the wilds behind them. What fruits or tubers or other edible plants were available would take scavenging to find, more effort, perhaps, than the residents here had wanted to make. Perhaps they had thought to have an easier chance for survival somewhere else, somewhere that might have survived the Undoing better than this region had.

The trees and shrubs had overgrown many areas and pushed in every direction to overtake the abandoned world of men but it had not encroached on this street, nor overtaken the rails.

Ultimately, it would. In time, the wilds would claim this place too.

"We could use the supplies." Kato paced the width of the opening, guarding the door where they entered, peering back into the wilds as if he expected something there they could not see. No one detected a presence, not even the looming possibility of Nepo's lingering threat. Jia suspected Kato's mood was less a product of the threat behind them than it was of Vance's drag on their progress and her ongoing effort to support the mage and help him keep up.

"Looks like we've got enough to choose from," Pubby grunted, helping Vance sit and remove his pack before dropping his with a groan and an arching of his back that resulted in a popping sound. The high ceiling above was unpaneled, its bare metal trusses exposed to the elements seeping through the gradually failing roof, damage he studied as he craned his neck from side to side. It would take a large fire, burning for a long time, to heat the entire room, but there was more than enough flammable material here to accomplish that. They did not need to heat the entire room. They only needed to stay close to the fire to enjoy its warmth. By morning, they might even be warm enough to feel in no hurry to leave this place and face the cold.

Candace too put her pack down and helped Eddie remove his despite his protests of not needing help. "Not unless you want to eat wood," she murmured. The storm and the delays in their progress afterward had resulted in a diminished food supply. It had been supplemented by berries, fruits, mushrooms, and other edibles foraged along the way but none was enough to fill their bellies.

"Eatery at the end of the block…and one behind," Deuce offered. "I can go and…"

"No one's going anywhere alone." The mutani tracker was not the only potential threat in this unfamiliar territory, despite them not having seen anyone else. Jia studied each of her companions until her gaze fell on the top of the mage's bowed head. His face rested in his hands, his shaggy, dark hair a curtain to hide his frustration and, she guessed, likely the overpowering drain of thoughts and feelings he had pulled from her and the others as they traveled, and any this place piled atop of his burden.

He never spoke of those things. He rarely visibly reacted to the ongoing blanket of stimuli the world wrapped around him. Though she had fought to avoid skin-to-skin contact to reduce the likelihood of unwanted sharing as they traveled, she doubted it was enough to spare him. His entire life was lived this way.

So much input and the lack of alcohol were undoubtedly an ever-present burden.

"Pubby, you, Eddie, and Vance stay here…see what you can find that we can use. Anything portable…canvas, tools, weapons. Build a fire. Yu, QiangXu, find the eatery Deuce saw, take what you can carry. Candace, you and Deuce take the one at the end of the block, bring back anything worthwhile. Keep your eyes open…"

"I don't want to stay here," Eddie groused. As dark as the circles were beneath his eyes, as slumped as his shoulders were, as dragging as his steps had become, sending him out to help would only slow the search parties down. Though he knew it, he did not want to admit to his visible exhaustion.

"You'll do as you're told," Candace scolded. "Look at this. There's too much to waste something because we miss it."

"Besides, kid," Pubby added with a fatherly smile. "You gonna make us old men climb up there and do this alone?" Neither he nor Vance was old, but such a claim was enough, coupled with his mother's scolding, to permit Eddie to nod in agreement without feeling as if he was being punished by staying behind.

"And me?"

Kato expected to be left on patrol. He expected to be appointed to guard the perimeter, to pace out his frustration alone. Jia's request, therefore, was a surprise.

"There was a hospital symbol on the overtracks. If it's close enough, might be something we can scav." Tending Vance's injuries had depleted their collection of bandages and antiseptic cleaners. Those things, at least, would be worth taking.

QiangXu and Yu might have been better choices to send to the hospital, but without knowing how far away it was, what obstacles might exist between them, Jia did not want to risk the group's medic by sending her into the unknown. The building behind their location was unknown enough. Jia had enough medical knowledge, thanks to Addi, to believe she could recognize the usable from the unnecessary. She and Kato could collect what they found, as much as they could carry, and if there was more to be had, the group could go back for more when the world turned toward daylight.

Vance grabbed Jia's gloved hand in his as she passed him, holding it with unexpected ferocity. He met her gaze, his somnolent and troubled, hers determined and weary and wary at the way he held her back. "Be careful." He repeated her words with an intensity that made her bob her head.

Nepo was out there, even if they had not seen him. Vance did not want her to face the lavender-eyed mage alone.

But she would not be alone. Kato's grunted, "Let's go," from the broken doorway, where the cold would continue to push in against a fire they had not yet made, reminded them both of that.

Vance hoped that, against Nepo, the Fela's presence would be enough to save her life.

ᴥ*ᴥ

"The Laedan will contact me when he returns."

The Anakirist's comment, as he adjusted his coat and tucked in the ends of his thick black scarf was not a question. The tone of it prompted Nik to raise an eyebrow and made Oasis frown.

"You?" Nik asked. "Or Grand Mas Lord?"

Gracen bristled at being cornered with those words a second time and hid his scowl with a turned head as he accepted his wide-brimmed hat from one of his attendants. "He may contact Grand Mas directly, of course," he replied smoothly, "but he is a busy man, as you know. It would behoove your father to come to me first…and not to trouble the Grand Mas with these petty formalities."

"I doubt Grand Mas sees any of this as petty," Oasis said lightly.

"No…of course not, you're right. Lesser then. Routine, if you will." After snugging his gloves over his fingers, Gracen offered his hand first to Oasis, the lady in their midst, and then to Nik, whom he gave the barest of bows as if both it, and the handshake, were repugnant duties performed out of necessity but otherwise unwanted. "Everything looks in order. Once the reports are assessed, the Collector will be in touch. I'm sure," he added with a sniff, "the Laedan will want to be certain everything is in order before that."

To prevent Nik from saying something snippy at the offense, Oasis gave a gracious smile and said, "I'm sure he will. Your concern for LaGuardia is admirable and appreciated."

The Anakirist appeared about to say something in rebuttal but instead inclined his head politely and muttered, "Condolences again; if there is anything we can do…"

Voice more clipped than intended, Nik said, "We'll let the Grand Mas know. Thank you. Safe travels, sirra."

Gracen nodded, muttered, "Good day," and stalked from the Fortress with the snapping, stiff steps of offense Nik expected to see.

"My figures don't need…" Nik began under his breath.

"I'm sure they don't…but sometimes agreeing with them is the fastest way to be rid of them. We'll tell Lowell Gracen wants a word then it's out of our hands."

Nik nodded, understanding she was right but feeling, in the uncertain corners of his soul where he had never lived up to his parents' expectations, that he was not about to do so now. He had done his best, to make the reports, calculate the borough's resources, to hold back…as he knew the Laedans always had…some extra portion for the benefit of LaGuardia where HOPE would never find it.

He hoped it would prove to be enough to garner comments of praise from his father. He hoped it would be enough to benefit the borough the way a Laedan's actions should.

❧*❧

"Not much."

It had taken Norse more hours than he was happy with to turn the wagon upright, free the oxen from their storm-panicked quandary, and untangle and repair the leads and harnesses so his journey could continue. Most of the work was left to three of his underlings while he and another had found and retrieved four of the captives the wagon had carried. Another was found dead, crushed beneath the fallen debris of a collapsed wall. The last two he failed to find, only the hiding place of one and the shoe of the other stuck in the soupy mud through which she had fled.

Refusing to arrive empty-handed, or nearly so, having promised the doctor at least a half dozen subjects, Norse spent several subsequent hours rounding up as many suspected anthro as he could in the four-block radius of his location.

He ended up with a dozen individuals. Only testing their blood would prove their fitness for the doctor's purposes.

"Lost a few in the storm…had to find replacements."

"They'll do," Gail said with a smile made plastic by a sniffing sound of annoyance as she waved the wagon through the open cargo bay doors. As she always did when she stood there, she scanned the horizon, looking for something she was unsure she would see.

She knew what to expect. Yet the messenger and delivery had not come.

Fresh specimens might anger Geary, as it would suggest she had not obeyed his demand as he expected. Given the new message, however, forgiveness for disobedience, and the explanative excuse she had already developed, should come easily. This new delivery would lend credence to ongoing research, harvest, and production HOPE expected to see. That would help.

If any of these subjects proved to be Normal rather than anthro, she had explanations for their presence as well.

Geary finding Norse here, however, would not work in anyone's favor. "Get them unloaded," she instructed, "and get me more."

It was the only way to get Norse out of Geary's sight.

Through the opening between dented, corroded metal slats covered with peeling paint, Beren watched the wagon disappear into the building, the doors closing behind it sealing the fate of anyone locked inside of the death box.

He did not know how many had been recaptured. Their voices, their cries and whimpers and moans, had carried on the steady blowing gentle wind, but he could not separate one from another. Some might have been those caught before him. Some might have come after. He should have stayed to help them. He should try to help them now.

But he had no plan yet for how to get inside, how to find those held captive, how to find his father…if his father was even here. The weight of the orbs in his sack gave him a weapon, but he was only one man. How to use so many of them efficiently against such a large building, against an unknown number of adversaries he never saw, was a puzzle he still had to sort out.

Perhaps he would wait for the wagon to leave. Perhaps the woman in the white medical coat and the brute who had caught him and led the wagon would be there when he did.

Killing them both with a single orb might be good enough to avenge the dead. It would not, however, be enough to satisfy him.

❧*❧

"They're close."

Quentin was hunched at a nearby fire, his back to the one Dink was stoking where Uzzi, Pain, and Enola had segregated themselves from the rest of those recruited for this venture. It was their typical camp formation, four fires with five to eight men and women gathered around each, Quentin often alone at a fire of his own. Despite the normalcy of the arrangement, he glowered suspiciously at Uzzi and his companions, his mistrust obvious in the sporadic, jerky movement of his hands and the creases at the corners of his eyes and mouth.

He was particularly wary of the Cana guiding them supposedly to Fort Hamilton along a path Quentin could not see.

Only his occasional perusal of a document he never allowed others to view and a daily evaluation of the sun's position behind the dull clouds kept him satisfied with their course, but it did nothing to reassure him of the Cana's guidance or motives.

Enola tried once to look at the page over their leader's shoulder.

Quentin threatened to remove her hands if she spied on him again.

Uzzi's marginal focus turned from Quentin, the man brewing a pot of tea as he stuffed the tattered document between the pages of a book and back into his pack. He looked warily, instead, at the Cana as he returned to the fire from his routine nightly circle of their campsites.

To Quentin, Pain claimed the circle around camp each night was intended to find, or ward off, any trouble lurking in the dark.

Uzzi, however, knew it was the pursuit of the people whose scents he followed prompting Pain to search every time they camped. The storm had made the search harder, having washed away much of the evidence of passage, and had made progress slower for the entire group, but it had not kept Pain from seeking his destiny.

Uzzi questioned him with a glance. Pain shrugged. Someone in the Alpha's group was injured enough to have dragged the group's progress. It was the only justification to explain their slower movement. It was an injury without blood or else the storm had washed that blood away or diluted it enough that Pain could not find it, but he was sure injury was the cause.

"How close?"

"Close."

"A day? An hour?"

Pain narrowed his eyes and shrugged. He could not gauge or express the distance in a matter of time. The distance was determined by the flow of the wafting wind and the strength of the scent. Tonight neither presented enough accuracy to make a guess.

"Strong enough to…" He tipped his head and sniffed the air. "Think if we head off there, we'd reach them before daybreak."

Uzzi glanced east but saw nothing in the darkness but shadow. Then he glanced at Quentin, who had spread his bedroll and was settling into it, seeming to have given up his sour staring. None had shelter over their heads tonight, but the air was dry, if cold and cloudy, and there were enough people awake at the edges of camp for the rest to afford a few hours of sleep before the watch changed.

It was the best opening Uzzi was going to get. After a few minutes of consideration, rubbing his hands over the fire, he made up his mind and began to pull his gloves back on. "I'll take a look."

"You'll never find…" growled Pain.

"Shouldn't go alone," hissed Enola.

Dink rubbed the dog's head. "Want me to…?"

"Give me some credit," Uzzi scoffed in a soft voice. "Not gonna be gone long. Just wanna take a look."

The scuffling on the gravel as he got up brought with it a muttered, "Where you off to?" asked without Quentin turning his head.

"Gotta shart…you wanna watch?" Uzzi asked wryly.

Quentin snorted. His lids parted enough to judge the direction Uzzi was facing, evaluating the veracity of his claim before closing his eyes.

"Watch him," Uzzi grunted in a whisper to Dink, the man chosen among the four of them for the night's first watch at the fire. With the dog lounging at his feet, no one was going to sneak up on them without them knowing about it, but Uzzi preferred to keep a pair of human eyes open at all times. Human…or anthro. "And you," he nodded at Pain, "keep that nose working…I'll tell you what I find…if they're too far away we'll…"

"We'll find a way to reach them in the morning…try to get closer." Pain did not want Quentin to get too close, not until he could be certain Jia was there, be certain his efforts to find them were worth the risk of a confrontation. He should be the one to face them, the one to make first contact, but there was no reason not to allow Uzzi his shot.

He could not stop him without a fight he did not want and could not afford in this crowd of Normal ruffs armed with a wide array of weapons Pain had not cataloged. He did not think Uzzi would find anything tonight. Not without him.

❧*❧

"You're too good for him."

Accepting Kato's hand so he could help her climb over the collapsed rubble of a wall to reach the room behind it, Jia ignored his tone and focused on the climb. Leaping over as Cana and Fela would have been easier, but collecting anything useful would have been difficult without hands, packs, or pockets to carry it. She moved quickly down the other side of the collapse into a room promisingly labeled *Pharmacy* and began to look through the shelves' contents before addressing the muttered comment.

They had not spoken since leaving the supply store, had moved stealthily through the streets wary of Nepo's potential appearance.

The timing of Kato's remark felt like the popping of a cork from a liquor bottle.

"There isn't anything…" she began. He had to be talking about Vance. Kato's bitterness had bubbled constantly since the mage's fight with the other tracker though she did not think the men had spoken to one another or argued in any fashion that might have contributed to the Fela's behavior and mood.

"Don't tell me you don't see it. I've seen it since the lab…and before that."

"He's a mage…and I'm Cana. It would never work." Jia swept bottles and small boxes into one of the canvas sacks she carried. When the adrenalin of the lab rescue subsided, there had been plenty of opportunities to consider that stolen kiss, a kiss Vance claimed would bind them in a way that would allow him to track her through the Below. Time to analyze whether it had meant something more, to analyze his gaze every time their eyes met. Time to grow more familiar with his scent, the way his heart beat and blood pounded when he was at rest, when in action, when interacting with her.

They were clues Jia had seen often enough in others, between Addi and Trill, between her parents before their deaths. While she had never applied such a study to herself and those with whom she regularly interacted, it had grown easier, particularly since the clash with Nepo, to read Vance.

As easy as it was to read the spike in Kato's body heat and heart rate as he kicked through the room's debris seeking what might be buried there. He was not Cana but she recognized the heightened level of pheromones that had peaked and waned since their first meeting.

"Why give him hope?" he grunted, swearing softly when his next kick sent a jolt of pain up his leg.

"Kindness isn't hope." She looked back to verify he was not seriously injured before opening the next metal cabinet on the wall. Its door creaked on unused hinges, the sound enough to cover her momentary silence before she started, "We need him. We'll never make it to the fort without…"

"I can…"

With her hand on the open cabinet door, she half turned towards him with skeptical surprise. "Have you been there? Seen the map?"

"No," he growled, "but I…"

"This isn't you versus him. It's us versus Hallister, Lowell, Donn. HOPE. Anyone else who wants those weapons to use against us. I'm not going to abandon…"

"Not asking you to. Just asking…"

"What then? What do you want from me, Kato?"

"Nothing. It's not…"

Exasperated, she slammed the empty cabinet door. "This isn't the time or place for this. I'm not looking for…not doing this…not until this is over…maybe not even then…"

The words felt bitter and foul in her mouth as if her future seemed forced to come down to a lottery between rivals when there was too much else at stake. Finding Fort Hamilton would not be the end of her responsibilities as Flushing Pack's alpha…or as Laedan Marrock's daughter. With so much ahead to sort out, she was not ready to consider the possibilities of family, children, a settled, tranquil life.

There was too much to be done.

The clatter of stones behind her made her turn, her statement unfinished. "Kato," she snapped, frustration and regret heavy in the back of her throat. She did not want to hurt him. She did not want to hurt anyone. She wanted to do what her father expected of her before LaGuardia imploded and took her Pack with it.

Kato was not behind her.

She looked at the broken window and the rubble they had climbed over, seeking the path he had taken, but she assumed, by the time she investigated either, he would be out of sight.

"Fifteen minutes," she shouted, assuming he was close enough to hear her. "Then we head back!"

She was not going to chase him as he threw a tantrum. There were more important things to do.

Trusting he could take care of himself, something he had been doing long before she met him, she sighed, grumbled and muttered beneath her breath, and resumed clearing the pharmacy of everything useful she could fit in her sacks. The room was large enough to contain an array of supplies they could make use of, and still reasonably well-stocked despite the gradual decaying collapse and the potential for scavs. There was more than she expected Addi had ever seen in any single delivery the clinics accepted.

She wondered why no one had ransacked the stores before.

Expecting Kato to return in the allotted time, her mood softening as the silence grew heavier, she decided an apology and explanation were due in place of the anger she cast at him out of frustration.

She did not expect he would believe or forgive her. Given his feelings for Vance, her words would likely mean nothing. But saying the words was the only way she was going to forgive herself for the unnecessary outburst.

❧*❧

With the initial greetings and introductions behind them, Geary kept his expression casually stern and his thoughts private as Gail led him and Anakirist Miller through the halls of the newly occupied research facility where everything ran as though it had been active for much longer than it had been.

Anakirist Miller asked few questions. Geary could not tell from her expression if she understood the process of blood collection and processing that Gail and her staff took the time to explain. Nearly three dozen subjects, male and female of varying ages, were suspended in stasis collection pods, tubes of nourishment flowing in, tubes of blood running out at scheduled intervals, other tubes of waste draining elsewhere to be collected and processed for other uses. Geary had seen this set up enough times to tell from their physical conditions which were older subjects, which were the newest, and he could guess from their bodily changes approximately how long each had been in place.

Some, he determined, were less than a week in process. Days at most. Hours perhaps. That should not be, he thought with irritation, but he was reluctantly grateful it was so.

"What happens to the blood? Once it is collected?" Korma ran her fingers delicately over the body of one male victim, a young man once handsome and vibrant but now losing the color of life from his skin, from the hollow of his throat to his bare groin, her gaze following her manicured nails until they stopped moving and her touch drew away.

"The components are separated," Gail clarified, the reprise of the process sounding as if it was being broken into terms and tones a child could grasp. "Some of it is transported elsewhere. The rest is retained for as long as it is viable, for research, of course. Same with waste and other body fluids. What is not needed or used is discarded."

"How long do they last? What do you do with them after?"

Geary did not miss Miller's dispassionate, detached tone. If she cared about the fate of these people, he did not hear it.

"A few weeks at most. We keep them in production for as long as possible, but the process only sustains them for so long. It is why," Gail glanced beyond the Anakirist to meet Geary's gaze, "we need a constant incoming rotation of hosts."

Korma nodded. "I will see you get them. Grand Mas Lord wants the work to continue. You will have what you need." Her expression did not reveal if she knew what the components were used for, if she knew about the production of plasm and the other genetic and physical studies undertaken on captured anthro.

Gail smiled.

Geary frowned, the first change of expression he had made since his arrival at the lab.

"Come, it is time for the night cycle. We have to conserve power where we can. Will you join me for dinner?"

"Of course," Korma said cordially.

Gail's invitation was directed at both of them but Geary believed she would have been satisfied if he refused and the Anakirist stayed.

It made him more determined to remain.

"We would be delighted," Geary agreed, even though he would rather do anything other than share another meal with the Anakirist.

Until the sun rose, however, he would not go anywhere. Night travel was perilous. One night allowed time to sort out a means with which to wheedle Kennedy out of a project that would turn Channon against Hallister and undo the coalition he was trying to forge.

❧*❧

Fuming, hands clenching and flexing, Kato jumped from the ground-level window to the street, troubled by the presence of a distant scent haunting him like the remnants of a dream, intangible, hazy, but not entirely forgotten. It aggravated his already ruffled nerves, prompting him to turn towards it, to seek it out. His internal battle swung between leaving Jia to her business and the possibility of tracking down what he suspected was the ruff tracker Nepo. If the other tracker had found them, if he was creeping up to capture Jia and use her as bait to lure Segara away, Kato would never let that happen.

Luring the mage to his potential death would not cost Kato sleep or cause disappointment. Jia used as bait, however, with the possibility of being killed, was something he would never be able to live with.

She was right. There were too many duties pulling at her for her to give serious thought to the men vying for her attention. Demanding a decision would guarantee he stood no chance with her. He had to be patient, he had to be kind and understanding, as he was with Vanya. But affairs of the heart were new and he had no idea how to work through them. He had no models to draw examples from, save for the relationships in the Flushing Pack he had barely begun to know. He did not know what to expect, or what was expected of him.

Across the street at the rear of the hospital, through an empty parking area where winter grasses and young trees had pushed up and taken root in the cracked pavement, between two large structures dark and uninhabited, towards the earth and water smells of the wilds. Kato had barely reached the second street, his view left and right obscured by the vehicles parked on each curb, when a lone shadow emerged from around the front of a long, broken-windowed bus.

The smell he had been chasing had a name.

Had a face.

When it spoke to him, it had a voice as well.

"Kato? Is it you?"

❧*❧

Beren judged the distances. How far could he throw? How fast could he run? How long would it take to pull an orb pin and throw it before drawing another and repeating the process? How many could he expect to throw before someone saw him, caught him…shot him?

How long had his father been held captive? Was he here? What was the likelihood he was alive if, as Liam said, most victims only endured draining for a few weeks?

He remembered those gaunt faces, men and women rescued from the other facility, others abandoned, broken, and discarded, dead already. The talk afterward, in the wagon, at the breach of the wall.

A few weeks at most.

It had been more than that now.

Long enough for his mother to die. Long enough for his sisters to die. Long enough to be captured, to find his way here.

Too long for his father to survive.

Beren was alone.

Staring at the orb he bounced in his open palm, he weighed his options as he weighed its mass. He was not yet ready to die, and yet he could think of not a single thing he had to live for. Only the purpose of helping those trapped here. Freeing them if he could. Killing them to end their torment if he could not.

Killing those responsible.

Maybe he would live to see another day.

Maybe he would not.

But this was what his father would do if he was here.

This was what Beren chose.

He eased open the door of his shelter enough to squeeze out and emerge into the world. Look left. Look right. No one he could see. With four orbs fastened to his belt so that pulling them free would pull their pins, and one orb in each hand, the pins already pulled, he took a breath, steeled his nerves, and began to run.

One orb struck the northeast edge of the building. Another struck a few yards away as he raced towards the northwest corner. One explosion. A second. And each subsequent explosion in turn, the fourth and fifth, ripping the cargo door open like peeling the lid of a food tin away. People screaming as they burned. Shouting and smoke and fire.

A single gunshot.

The last orb, its pin pulled, rolled free of the hand that flopped onto the pavement like a fish without breath.

One more explosion.

Nothing.

❧*❧

The collection of goods piled near the fire would require a wagon to carry when they left, but fortunately, with Eddie's help, they had replaced a broken handle on a wheelbarrow they found and fashioned another workable wagon from two heavy hand trucks, some rope, and some metal sheeting used as the sides and bottom. The two of them had done the majority of the scavving while Vance built a fire, started a meager meal cooking, and began sorting through the items they deposited next to him, sifting out those they were most likely to need or use from the rest.

"How come you're not mad at me?" Eddie asked Pubby as the man helped him down from the tall metal shelves they had located at the rear of the building where he had climbed to make sure there was nothing of value stashed high out of the sight and reach of most people.

The only thing Eddie found there was another coil of nylon rope he dropped into Pubby's hands before beginning his descent.

"They're not mad at you." Mad was a relative state of being and a mood Pubby did not find productive. "Got kids your age…younger too. Old enough to want to be included but not old enough to do the things adults can do…not old enough to know their limits." He ruffled Eddie's hair and coiled the rope around his arm.

"But I'm here. I'm keeping up. I'm carrying my own…"

"What do you think you're going to do when you get where we're going? What you gonna do if we get into a fight?"

"I can fight," the boy said petulantly.

Pubby chuckled. "Fighting your brothers isn't the same thing." Hoisting the latest collection in the clattering sack over his shoulder, Pubby gestured and started back towards the fire. "Being grown is more than going along, more than being included just because we want to be. It's helping without being asked to. It's doing what you can, stepping up, even when you don't feel like it."

"Even when I'm tired?"

"Especially when you're tired. We're all tired. It's been a long road. It's also about listening to those who know more than you, who have more experience, and doing what they say."

"He doesn't always listen…"

"Who?" They had reached the fire where Vance was adjusting a grated sheet they had found to make cooking easier, hoping the others would find something more substantial than fruit and the dregs of hard bread, harder cheese, and collected mushrooms they carried.

Thinking about what Pubby had said as he put down the armload of supplies he carried, Eddie murmured, "Could do with a rabbit…"

"Might have to hunt one…or several," Pubby said, noting his question had not been answered but at least the boy appeared to be thinking about the details of their dialogue.

"We'll have to wait for the rest to come back before we…"

Vance paused, stiffened, and cocked his head, listening. Pubby froze too. The floor beneath them cracked, buckled…and collapsed.

Chapter 31

Mud and dust and stagnant water erupted into Eddie's face as the men in front of him, the fire they had built, and a significant portion of the materials he and Pubby had gathered, disappeared before his eyes, swallowed by the maw that opened in the center of the floor.

"Sirra Segara! Sirra Pubinger!"

The gurgle of rushing water, and the fading rumble of the earth as the floor shifted and the edges crumbled were the only things he heard.

"Pubby?"

Eddie breathed an anxious gulp of air, relieved to have one voice echo up from the hole.

Coughing. Spluttering. Splashing.

"Here."

"Don't see you."

Vance could not see Eddie either from the angle he was in, clinging to a metal beam that had once been part of the floor support. Eddie was behind him, above him, but he could not crane his neck far enough to locate him. Pubby's voice came from somewhere below, nearer the bottom, Vance judged, as it was accompanied by the splash of flailing limbs trying to find purchase on something solid.

"Can't reach you…" Eddie could see them both, far below him. He thought if he lay on the edge and reached down he might be able to grasp the mage's hand, but he did not have the strength to pull him up. Nor did he trust the floor on which he knelt, knees bruised, hands scraped raw from being thrown to the ground. Pulling the fashioned wagon back so no more materials were lost, he called, "I'll get help. Stay there."

"Not much choice," Pubby grunted, continuing to shift his weight to find a sturdier hold.

Wincing from the renewed pain at the sites of old injuries, Vance added, "QiangXu…they're closest…"

"On it." Eddie's voice was already fainter as he ran.

Without the fire, the area above and around them was black.

The flow of water rushed beneath their feet.

❦*❧

One explosion after another, each piercing the northern edge of the building, weakened the supports and collapsed portions of the wall and the cargo doors. Dust and smoke and flame licked upward as men and women within the facility raced to extinguish the blaze. Others struggled to extract equipment, blood samples, the already harvested stock, and some of their newest subjects, out of harm's way in a desperate attempt not to lose the work they were doing.

That was where Geary, dragging Anakirist Korma through the murky haze, found Gail as he stumbled in search of a clear exit. He remembered one on the opposite side of the building from the cargo doors but finding it through the smoke was not easy.

"Gail! Leave it!"

"The work…"

There was another explosion, another flash of flame from somewhere they could not see as the heated air blasted through the corridor and pushed past Geary like a dragon's breath.

"Leave it."

He found her hand and clenched it tight.

"We need…"

"Leave it!"

❦*❧

Heedless of any threats lurking in the darkness, thinking only of the men he had left stranded, Eddie raced around the corner of the building in the direction the Ursa had gone, following their scents towards the deli they were to raid.

"Help!" he shouted. "We need help!"

The shaking of the earth and building had already prompted Yu and QiangXu to come at a run, their arms laden with the meager pickings they had scavenged, the sound of collapse drawing them back to camp. They met the horror-stricken young Fela partway; breathless and frightened, all Eddie could do was turn in his panicked run and point the way.

The Ursa raced past him.

At the other end of the block-long structure, Deuce dropped the items Candace had been thrusting into his arms the moment he detected the tremor beneath his feet. The worst of the shaking brought with it the scents of old dirt and stagnant water, the acrid stench of Below, and though they were running when the worst of the tremor hit, when Eddie's cry bled around the sounds of destruction, Candace fled passed Deuce driven by fear for her son.

They saw him in the distance, bursting out of the building, running in the other direction and disappearing around the edge. Candace ran after him.

Deuce aimed for their camp where the dust of the collapse billowed out through the open double doors.

In the medical center, the tremor was made less noticeable by the distance between the buildings and Jia's location on the second floor of the hospital. The sound of it, however, and Eddie's plea, perforated the quiet night like a spiked fist. Jia, slinging the straps of her sacks over her shoulder, scrambled through a hole long ago blasted through an old wall when a support beam buckled from the weight of the floors above it and called, "Kato!"

There was no reply and no time to look for him.

The explosive reverberations of collapse and the shout had come from the direction of their camp. That was where she needed to be.

Wherever Kato was, she assumed he would rejoin the group. Surely he heard it too. Surely he smelled the stink of fear and the fetid air of the Below and heard Eddie's cry for help.

Kato snarled at the man in front of him, the onslaught of memory and childhood fury resulting in a burst of energy and the leap of the half-form black Fela that pinned the older man against the bus and held him there with fangs inches from his face. His anger was underscored by a boy's cry of fear and Jia calling his name, but neither was enough to pull him away from this particular prey.

"Aren't you going to…?"

Kato snarled.

Uzzi fell silent.

It was disruption enough to bleed the full change away and permit Kato to resume Normal form, his clothing torn in several places, seams split or straining as his muscles shifted. "What are you doing here?" In a world full of people he could have found out here, invisible threats hunting them, he had never imagined it could have been this one.

"Could ask you the same…"

"You killed her!"

❧*❧

He was not supposed to be here.

The favor for the doctor had turned into one delay after another as the storm, the wagon accident, the tangled oxen, the hunt for escaped captives and newer stock to fill the wagon in place of those not found, kept Norse from the Fortress and the Laedan longer than he expected it too. Intending to use the storm and the state of the roads to explain his extended absence, intending to grab a few troublemakers and use general lawlessness as an excuse as well, Norse had located a reasonably weather-secure room in which to pass the night when the news of the Laedan's visit had come. He needed to remain out of sight, out of the Laedan's way, if he was to avoid unfortunate questions and less than fortunate results but he also felt compelled to remain close, on guard, in case the Laedan, with an Anakirist in his company, needed him.

The explosion and accompanying screams drew him to the window; the fires dotting the face of the building he could see across the street from his position resulted in a quandary for the narrow-faced man…and a change in plans he did not pause to contemplate.

He was there to grab the edge of the cargo door when someone on the other side yanked it open. Two sets of hands caused the door to fly to the side on its rollers, pulling the flames with it that burst inside and ignited the clothes of the nearest unlucky individual.

Norse did not try to help. The Laedan's voice croaked out of the smoke beyond the glow of the flames, the lure that pulled Norse past the burning figure flopping and rolling in the puddles outside.

The effort might be enough to spare his life.

"Laedan! Here!"

"Norse?"

Following each other's voices, both men moved towards the other until their silhouettes were picked out of the fire shadows. Norse tried to grab the other man but instead found an unfamiliar woman in a HOPE Anakirist uniform shoved into his arms. He caught her, growled as he stumbled, but did not argue as he turned and led the way out of the building.

Others rushed past with equipment, with subjects in their pods, with containers and documents and tools. Someone shouted as they fought flames with wet blankets and buckets of water. People who lived nearby, fearing the spread of fire to their homes, came to assist without knowing the nature of the work underway here or the identity of the people they struggled alongside.

Several yards away, in a freshly pitted crater, smoke and flame billowed. Norse had passed it on the way in.

He had not taken the time to see what it was.

❧*❧

"Help Pubby!"

❧475❧

Vance's hold was precarious, the muscles in his throbbing shoulder burning outward from the point of the arrow's previous entry, but so long as no more of the structure above them gave out, he did not think the metal crossbeam he clung to would shift. The movement of the water beneath them, flowing through the Below, was running from east to west though he could not see it, a river between his position and Pubby's rather than moving north and south under his feet. Its path increased the odds of further structural collapse and getting Pubby to safety before it did was a necessity.

Clinging to the concrete rubble made slick by mud and the water he had fallen into, water filled with the potential of disease, grubbers, and other hazards, Pubby's purchase was more precarious. Vance believed he could last. He was stubborn enough to fight, to hang on, until those arriving above them could pull Pubby to safety.

On the lip of the sinkhole, QiangXu stripped away clothing that would impede a change of form. "I'll be the anchor," he growled as Yu tied a loop in the nylon rope snatched from the makeshift wagon Eddie had abandoned by the door. Secured around the massive brown bear's middle, her hand splayed briefly in reassurance against her husband's Ursine chest, Yu pulled the rope taut and edged nearer the broken rim of flooring and concrete to peer down into the darkness.

"Need light…" she started.

"Here."

Wiggling free of his mother's unforeseen embrace when she caught him mid-run, Eddie raced to the wagon, rummaged through it, and produced an old flare, an item he and his family were familiar with from scavving efforts in the long weeks when they had fended for themselves. By the time the flare was ignited, his mother's arms circled him with a whimper of fear and relief and Deuce barreled past towards the dark stain of the chasm the flare's glow revealed.

"Mom," Eddie whined, wresting free to move the flare's light closer. Candace, however, took the flare, scooted him behind her where he would be protected, and approached the hole to see what manner of death trap their haven had become.

"If you hold this, I can climb down." Yu thrust the rope into Deuce's hands.

Deuce did not argue. He took the shift to half form, rending his clothes, using the wolf's hairy hide to protect his arms and hands as he looped the rope, and the wolf's strength and claws to gain traction as he lent his might to QiangXu's so Yu could safely descend.

Concrete shifted. Stones and rubble showered Pubby's head.

"Easy there…"

"Sorry."

Yu could not see the arrival of another set of steps but identified Jia by their weight and cadence. She looked up at the smaller woman from her precarious perch but no one spoke until Jia joined them at the rim of the sinkhole.

"Vance…"

The mage raised his eyes but his line of sight was poor. "Pubby…" he began, guessing, from Jia's tone that she would insist on rescuing him first. "I'm okay."

Jia heard pain in his voice, strain and a hint of fear but for the moment, he was calm. There was discomfort etched into the creases at the corners of his eyes and the edge of his mouth, the only facial expression she could see from where she stood. Despite those things, she did not think he could cling to the beam much longer, although she agreed Pubby's position was more precarious. The others were endeavoring to rescue Pubby. Her presence there would contribute nothing to their efforts.

Vance needed her here.

"Hold this." She circled the sinkhole to stand above Vance's position, trusting the other three to pull Pubby up without her. She peeled off the pack, slick from the night's mist and the shimmer-glisten of snowfall that had begun as she raced back to the lumber house, and thrust it into Candace's free hand before dropping to her hands and knees to crawl to the edge of the crumbled floor.

"You can't get to…" Candace whined softly.

"I can help," offered Eddie, eager despite the anxiety in his voice.

"You're not getting near…"

"I'm light enough! I can do it!"

"Here." Candace, swallowing enough anxiety to act, handed him the pack and flare and began the shift to half-form. She lay down on the cold floor and held Jia's ankles, allowing the smaller woman to creep forward and reach into the pit.

"Take my hand," Jia called, wiggling her fingers as if the action would summon Vance's hand to hers.

Half-form was stronger, allowing for a grasping hand and wolf claws. But even with Candace's grip around Jia's ankles, the young woman's reaching hand, when Jia lay on the lip of the hole, was not enough to reach the one stretching shakily back to her.

"Move forward," Jia said over her shoulder. A few more inches should be all it would take.

Candace growled her protest. Her body refused to move to the command of her brain.

Jia shifted sideways, pulling forward as much as she dared without pulling Candace off balance. "Take my hand…"

"I…" Vance wiggled on the metal rail, trying to support his weight with his injured arm and twisted to reach for her but his outstretched hand failed to meet hers."

"Use the other…" Jia instructed before looking back at Candace, "I need a few more inches…"

Candace growled a second time, fear making her shake her head.

On the other side of the chasm, Deuce loosed the last of the length of rope. The Ursa behind him grunted and dug his claws into the ground and Yu continued down.

The ground shifted.

Pubby yelped.

Concrete splashed into the churning water.

❧*❧

"What in the name of…?"

Geary's question was never completed as the flames devoured his words along with a portion of the building he had been inside not long before. The efforts of staff and locals and the lightly falling snow were gaining the upper hand but he was a practical man, a thinking man.

A man who could be honest despite the presence of the woman at his side.

None of their efforts would be enough to save this facility. There were anthro to round up, new subjects to harvest, but regardless of what equipment the staff managed to save, regardless of what might remain undamaged inside, it would not be enough for production to continue at the level it had before. His intent to put the work on hold long enough to throw off LaGuardia's mage, and anyone else prying into Kennedy's affairs, had been granted at the cost of future efforts.

New pods would need to be constructed. New equipment gathered, built, and assembled. That was going to take time.

Gail's bitter side-eyeing expression made his scowl deepen. He knew what she was thinking. She thought he had done this.

But this was not his fault. He would never have gone this far…at least not while he was in the building. He would never risk his life that way. He would have been reluctant to risk hers.

For as long as it lasted, he was offered a reason to suppress the business in a way not even Anakirist Korma could refute.

Word would be taken to Grand Mas Lord and that would be that…until HOPE presented a solution. If they wanted to rebuild, they could foot the expense.

Kennedy's purse was going to sting from the loss, a loss Geary had anticipated, but better that loss than the loss of alliances.

"I want to know who…" Geary began.

"Probably this one." Norse, whom Geary had not expected to be here, was circling the charred, smoking remains of what had once been a person. Limbs and burnt pieces of flesh were scattered from the proximity of the detonation of the last orb, leaving barely enough to identify the remains as a person. Only the blackened, bloody skull Norse poked with the toe of his boot spoke the truth.

"Who is it?"

Geary threw the Anakirist an incredulous sour look as Norse, barely managing to maintain a neutral expression, muttered, "Got a mage handy? Don't think there's enough left to know otherwise."

Narrow eyes looking away from the grizzly sight to watch the fire, Korma hissed, "No one should have gotten close enough to…"

"No," Geary agreed, "they shouldn't have." But there were no watchtowers or fences here. The openness of the facility required more security agents than were assigned, but the facility had not been functioning long enough to deploy more guards…or to build the sort of barricades that should have been in place. The Anakirist, however, did not need to know those details.

"Grand Mas Lord will hear about this," the woman snorted.

"By all means, tell him. Tell him we need supplies…building materials…people…if he wants this back up and running."

The wheels of that specific bureaucratic wagon would take time to spin, time that would allow Geary to weave a convincing tale of subterfuge and sabotage with facts to support either or both. Even if he had to produce the witnesses and bodies of the innocent to prove it.

❧*❧

Clawed hands unexpectedly encircled Candace's ankles. Her startled lurch caused Jia to slip, to brace herself to prevent falling and the younger woman threw a perturbed glance over her shoulder. Candace, too, looked back…to find the small Fela half-form straining to hold her with all of his young might. The flare lay on the ground, sputtering and popping, threatening to go out. Though frightened for her son's safety, she felt enough strength in his grasp, enough determination in his growling effort, to give her the courage to inch forward a little further as Jia asked.

It was far enough.

Vance twisted sideways, supporting his body's weight on the beam with his good arm, and in doing so was able to stretch the injured one enough to form a tight, if pained, grip on Jia's hand and wrist. The strain as he found a foothold and gave his strength to the effort to climb out of the chasm, made him hiss, wince, and grimace, but eventually, after an illusionary eternity of struggle, he collapsed on the ground at Jia's side, panting, trembling, his eyes closed to shove down both the physical pain and the lingering effects of her fears that spread through the contact.

A slight tremoring, as if the floor would fracture more, made Candace and Eddie pull both of the others far enough back to remain safe. With Candace's attention turned to assessing the condition of the pair, Eddie picked up the flare and circled the hole to stand beside Deuce, holding the crackling red light source out for Yu to have a better view of what was below her.

She had climbed low enough so that Pubby could wrap his weary, bleeding arms around her torso. It was an awkward position to climb in, made more difficult by the water-soaked earth that continued to shift and send concrete, rocks, and mud into the water. With the pulling power of both Ursa and Cana, the two large forms maintaining the tension of the rope as they pulled gradually backward, and Yu's strength, Pubby was eventually near enough to the top for Eddie to drop the flare and grab one arm.

The joint efforts drew Pubby to safety.

"The supplies…" Pubby gasped, the focus on material items allowing him to turn his attention from the spinning world and the lacerations on his body stinging with sweat and exertion.

The majority of what they owned, minus a few packs and some of the scavenged goods stowed in the makeshift wagon, had been lost into the maw.

They had few weapons left. No more food.

"Not all of it," Yu murmured, offering reassurance for a situation that was not Pubby's fault.

"We'll find more," QiangXu agreed, retrieving his clothes after his shift back to Normal. They could scavenge food along the way and from the two eateries they had been distracted from searching. Pubby's guns were still in their holsters, though there were no more bullets to feed them and if the packs Jia dropped inside of the doorway and had given to Candace held promise, they had enough medical supplies to tide them over.

The hospital Jia decided, would offer a more secure roof over their head for tonight. They could not remain here.

"Where's Kato?" murmured Eddie, the adrenalin of their situation beginning to catch up to him at last.

It was a question Jia could not answer.

He had not come to her aid when she called for him.

Odds were, she thought bitterly, as Vance's hand covered hers where they continued to lay, panting, side by side, staring at the trusses above their head, Kato was not coming back.

Chapter 32

"Killed a lot of people," Uzzi shrugged, unperturbed by either Kato's angry threat of violence or the eruption of fangs now receding with Kato's return to Normal form.

"You left us with her…you killed her…"

Only then did Uzzi's expression falter. "Winnie? She's…?"

"Think I'd have abandoned her like you did if she wasn't?" Kato snapped. "What did you think would happen when you left us?"

Uzzi shook his head as if to deny the truth. "Thought it was for the best…when did she…how…?"

"How could leaving your wife and two little…?"

"Wasn't my wife…"

"Doesn't matter!" In most corners of humanity, as Kato understood things, the formality of marriage existed only for those with the wealth and means for such things…or for members of Cana packs who considered the mating of partners to be a binding commitment. For nearly everyone else, partnerships were made, relationships built out of the need to survive, for companionship, for the rearing of children. But marriage?

It was no longer a legally viable or necessary institution, regardless of humanity clinging to the terms of husband and wife.

"You left us…"

"Because of you…"

Kato stumbled back, dumbstruck, ears ringing, head spinning, anger and fright morphing into a sort of disgusted verification that everything in his life had been his fault. Vanya…his mother…his father leaving…it had been the fault of one five-year-old boy.

As if hearing his thoughts, reading them in Kato's eyes, Uzzi clutched his shoulders with an attention-grabbing shake. "That's not what I mean! Wasn't your fault. You didn't do anything, you just…"

"Let go." Kato's abrupt turn as he pulled free yanked Uzzi to the left, and threw him to the ground.

"I've got history…history Winnie never knew," Uzzi grunted, wiping mud from his bruised shoulder. "Thought I could have a life…keep a family safe…little house by the sea with a garden, kids on a swing…all of that. But you turned…and I knew if they came looking for me, they'd find you…and I'd never be able to protect you. I had to get away before they found me, to keep you safe. It was the only way…"

Kato growled as Uzzi began to rise; the older man settled where he was and brushed the falling snow from his lashes.

"Who are they?"

"Made too many enemies in my youth…doing what I do best…"

"That is? Who are they?"

"Mercing mostly, scavving if I could, staying ahead of HOPE."

Eyes narrowed, Kato drew lower into a crouch. "Are you Fela?"

He did not smell like it. Nor did he smell like any other anthro Kato had met. But the world had become an ever-stranger place since the Undoing. Perhaps Uzziah Orr was mutani or something the world had never seen, something HOPE wanted to exterminate the way they wanted to destroy everything deemed not Normal.

Whatever Uzzi was had not presented in either Kato or Vanya.

"Worse." Uzzi rubbed the back of his neck and got to his feet. "Took out the last Grand Mas." Kato's frown bid him go on. "Long story. Doesn't matter. Everyone else who knows the truth, except me, the one who hired me, and one other, is dead." His tone was bitter, his expression grim. "Maybe most think I am too…given the life I've led…but at the time, when I knew Winnie, when you were born, it was fresh. I couldn't risk them getting you."

Kato took a few steps away from Uzzi as the man spoke, thoughts racing as he tried to file the man's story between the pages of his memory. "She always believed they'd…that HOPE's why you didn't come back…" In a way, his mother's belief had been right, more accurate than a little boy's anger and resentment and belief that either it was his fault his father had left or else his father had been a bastard of the worst sort.

Still a bastard, a murderer, but not the worst man Kato had ever met. At the moment, Thomas Quentin held that rank.

Looking at Uzzi, with his gray-white hair and beard, blue eyes mirroring Vanya's, and the weathered lines of his face, Kato assessed that the actual truth of Uzzi's actions had been a product of all of those things. It had been more, and less, complicated than a boy of five could easily understand.

"When did she…how…?"

"Been less than a year. She was gardening when the grubbers…" His shoulders sagged and the corners of his mouth and eyes twitched as Kato struggled to contain emotions he had hidden from Vanya to protect her, emotions he had been given no opportunity to face and accept in the daily push to survive. "Vanya and I ran. Only way to…"

"I saw her…Vanya. She looks so much like Winnie…"

"I know." The melancholy in Uzzi's voice brought the first shift in Kato's evaluation of him. Whatever else the man was or had been, he had loved Kato's mother. "Is that how you…?"

"Knew you were alive?" Uzzi shrugged and nodded at the same time. "Didn't think I'd see you though. If it wasn't for Pain…"

"Pain?" It took Kato a moment to realize Pain was an individual, not a state of being, and the growling snarl returned with the readiness to fight. "He's here?" His head cocked, he sniffed the air that brought with it sudden thought that Jia's cry for him, the events of minutes past that had shaken the earth, the air, and brought silence on its heels, had come at the expense of her life.

And he had ignored her.

Uzzi brought his hands up in a submissive posture of surrender. "Isn't like that. He's using her trail…your trail…to lead us to some fort Quentin wants…"

"Thomas Quentin?" That explained the faint Fela scent lingering on Uzzi's skin, not the smell of physical contact but the dregs of loitering too long in someone's company.

His snarl that time cemented Uzzi's belief about the connection between the alpha Cana they followed and Quentin, but he was unclear about how Kato and Pain fit into the picture.

"Doesn't know what trail we're following…whose…at least I don't think he does. He thinks Pain knows the way to the fort…and Pain's following you. Says your leader's got a score to settle with Quentin…and I'm happy to see the score settled if it gets Quentin off my back. We're not far behind…"

"How many?"

"'Bout two dozen of us; we lost a few some ways back…"

"Anthro?"

"Just Pain…and Quentin."

Still too many, Kato thought, suppressing the urge to pace. He did not think their little collection of people would be enough to face so many mercs and ruffs.

"Join us," Uzzi offered. "Between the three of us, with Dink and Enola, Quentin won't stand a chance."

"Not joining you," Kato spat. Uzzi might be his father, and finding him might have raked up a plethora of unresolved feelings, memories, and thoughts Kato had no interest in exploring, but it was not enough for him to abandon Jia. Quentin knew his face. If Kato revealed his presence, Jia would be at risk from both Pain and Quentin. As well as the tracker Nepo.

"Don't think you've got enough people to…" Uzzi did not know how many were traveling with Kato, but he knew the aptitudes of those in Quentin's orbit. It would take more than a handful of Cana to undermine them.

Kato shook his head, his gaze shifting warily. He needed to return to Jia, to make sure Pain or Quentin had not gotten to her. Make sure Nepo had not found them. He needed to warn her. "Don't trust him, either of them, or you," he huffed.

"Fair enough," Uzzi sighed. "But he won't let anyone get in his way. If he finds you, he won't hesitate to…"

It was unclear if he referred to Quentin or Pain. Kato did not care.

"Comes near me…near her…I'll eat his heart," he growled. "Stay away from her…stay away from me."

The younger man turned. The great black cat took his place. Before Uzzi could speak, could reach for him, before he knew what to say to prevent him from leaving, Kato was gone.

❧*❧

Of the supplies that survived the collapse, they were left with the radiation counter, the bundle of bedding wrapped around it to keep it safe, one of the fire building kits, the weighted net, and a wax wrapping of fruit Yu had packed into the same bag. As Deuce's pack was on his back when he had gone scavving with Candace, his extra clothing was intact and Yu and QiangXu had likewise retained theirs when they had gone in search of food, intending to use the additional bag space for anything edible they found. Candace and Eddie lost their clothing and bedding, but the pack of food they carried between them had survived in the wagon. Everything the rest owned, except for the book Nik had given Jia for luck, in which she had mapped their journey west every time they camped and had carried with her to the hospital, had also been lost to the devouring earth.

As they regrouped, they collected what they could from the shops on either end of their block but it was not enough. Their losses soured every face as they hobbled, supporting the wounded between them, carrying what they could, dragging the wagon behind. Progress was slow as they took time to investigate each structure along the way for anything they could use, clothing, bedding, food, goods to trade, until they were able to collapse, exhausted, on the ground level of the hospital. Using their newly scavenged resources and what little they had not lost, QiangXu built a fire, this time mindful of the possibility that warming the floor might result in another collapse of the storm-softened soil beneath them. Yu, Candace, and Eddie searched the level for additional goods, the abundance of medicinals enough to bolster their mood even though they were lacking other supplies. Functional clothing could be fashioned from hospital scrubs to supplement what had been found on their way here. Bedding stored in protective packaging was brought to the fire for examination. Pubby and Vance, suffering their newest collections of injuries, sorted through the inventory and endeavored to divide it into sacks fashioned from the recovered hospital bedding and the packing it had been stored in.

Both men would be able to carry less, at least for the next handful of days, but there was less for everyone to carry. The wagon could make dragging what they could less cumbersome but its rattling wheels would attract attention and the quiet debate about taking it or leaving it was left for Jia's decision. They would have to be frugal with their stores, with water and food in particular, until they discovered something else they could scav.

"Not leaving anyone behind," Jia muttered as she listened to Deuce's reporting yips from his maintained watch around the perimeter of the hospital. Pubby had offered to stay put so his injuries were not a drag on the company's travels and Jia knew Vance was considering the same possibility. She would not permit it. She needed the mage's guidance and Pubby had proven his worth to the team more than once. If they needed to camp here until the pair could travel, she would reluctantly do so despite the risks.

Movement in the doorway, a shadow who had gotten past Deuce's watch, caused her to leap, startled, to her feet. The only thing in her agitated state preventing her from attacking the presence was the familiar scent of one she was both relieved to see and angry at for failing to be there for the group when they needed him.

"Pain's here," Kato panted, diverting her anger with news she needed to hear and the evidence of his exertion. The news might buy forgiveness for his absence or at least temper her anger long enough to allow him to continue. He had not expected to find everyone at the hospital. He had run to the warehouse to discover the sinkhole, had hunted around the edges of it for evidence of the fates of his companions, and then chased their retreating scents back along the street to the hospital where they were now. Though he judged the Protectors to be injured, no one else appeared to be. He was relieved no one had been lost due to his failure to act, that Pain, Quentin, or Nepo had not been the cause of their injuries or their relocation. He was relieved Jia was alive and unharmed.

"Quentin's with him."

Jia marched to him and sniffed around his face and neck, seeking proof of his claims or an indicator he was lying. There was another smell on his skin and clothes, masculine, Normal, not the scent of either Pain or Quentin she knew from exposure to both. From the disarray of his clothes, the sweat sheen on his skin, she assumed there had been a fight or a chase, but there were no injuries. "Where?" she demanded. "What did you see?"

"Northwest…maybe six hours walking back on foot I'd say…maybe closer." Uzzi had not said, and Kato had not pursued him to verify the group's nearness, but it seemed a reasonable guess based on Uzzi's presence. "If they start at daybreak…"

"They're going to catch us here," Vance grunted as Jia swore under her breath. "You should reconsider…"

It did not make sense for Pain to be in league with the man who had killed her father, his friend, the previous Flushing Pack Alpha. Even if he was hunting her, doing so in cooperation with Quentin would gain him the permanent enmity of the Flushing Pack. Cooperating with the enemy, regardless of what Pain felt about her, struck her as impossible for the sort of man she had known him to be. The man her father had respected.

"We could move out now." Even as Pubby said it, however, he understood it was out of the question. He and Vance were in no condition to move without at least a night's rest. The others were exhausted too and they had supplies to reorganize, a meal to prepare and eat. They would never move fast enough to get far enough ahead for Quentin and Pain to cease being a threat.

"We could make a diversion?" Vance did not have any solid ideas in mind, but a deterring diversion seemed the only choice they had.

"Like what?" Eddie asked sullenly as he entered the lobby with another armload of blankets stored in plastic sheathing. The plastic had cracked and crumbled, but the bins they had been stored in had kept out the insects and natural elements. The blankets were stiff and smelled stale, but wrapping them around their shoulders would provide warmth they had not had before and replace more of the lost packs and bedding. "We don't have any more explosives."

"Some of this could make some," QiangXu waved his hand over the collection of bottles, tubes, and containers he and his wife had gathered. "If it's not too old…"

"Unless we kill them, explosions will attract a lot of attention," Pubby reminded him. "They'll know we're here…and Nepo…"

"Every grubber in radius will too, Candace offered.

"If they don't already. Maybe I should talk to him."

Jia shook her head at Vance's suggestion before he finished making it. His status as Protector Mage might buy a momentary reprieve of favor from Thomas Quentin, but they could not count on it. Not if Quentin suspected Vance knew the truth. Not if he assumed the mage's presence so far from LaGuardia meant the pursuit of the same goal…and meant Jia was nearby.

"They wouldn't know me," Yu offered.

"Or me," added Pubby with a stiff groan.

"We're not risking it. We keep our fire small…stay alert…put it out at daybreak…lay low…"

"And pray Pain doesn't bring them right to us," Kato grunted. Without revealing what he knew, it was a thought worth voicing. He did not think catching them, destroying them, was Pain's intent, based on what Uzzi had said, and a detour would look suspect. Quentin, however, annoyed by a detour or not, would not hesitate to kill them if he found them.

Kato felt certain of that.

"I'll watch the door."

"So will I," Kato offered.

Jia noted Vance's scowl as she motioned Kato aside and leaned against the doorframe with her arms crossed over her chest. This was not the time to question what the mage sensed or knew, but she, too, felt something she could not see was missing from the equation. Across the street, atop the building with the highest vantage point, Deuce peered down with an attentive, curious demeanor.

"Where were…?"

Cutting off the question he thought she was going to ask, Kato began, "I smelled them…thought I should…"

"No, you didn't." If anyone from Pain's party had been near enough to scent, Jia was confident she would have detected them as well. Kato had not had the opportunity to run far when he left her unless he had been in full Fela form. The condition of his clothing suggested a partial shift, but not a full one. If the party was as far away as he suggested, he could only have detected them by traveling towards them. On foot.

Away from her.

A six-hour march for a Normal, over storm terrain, was much less for an anthro. Kato could have made it that far in a short amount of time, but he would have needed the time to make it back.

There was something he was not telling her.

"Saw the hole. What happened?" Kato cocked his head towards Vance and Pubby without looking at them, ignoring Jia's unspoken question, avoiding a discussion he did not want to have.

His avoidance made Jia frown. "Sinkhole. Storm washed through the Below, eroded the underside of the floor. Got everyone out but lost most of our gear." Including anything Kato had carried before.

"That's good…about getting everyone safe, not…" he added hastily, not considering what he had lost. Her frown of disappointment ruffled his nerves, made him defensive, but he forced himself to ask, "Want me to scav some food? Hunt something?" There had to be something he could do to make up for his inaction, for the truth he was hiding, for his insensitivity.

"I want you here. Keeping watch. With us." If he left again, she believed he would not come back. He had returned to warn her about Pain, about Quentin, offered to keep watch, but the nervous shuffling of his feet and the shiftiness of his gaze convinced her that as soon as most of them slept, Kato would be gone.

Only Deuce's position on the opposite roof might prevent him from leaving. Even that might not be enough.

Kato sighed and nodded once. "I'll stay."

He would not say for how long. Not with Vance's gaze cutting across his skin like a razor. Not with his father out there somewhere.

The father, he thought bitterly, who was in league with the enemy.

❧*❧

He had not slept.

Knowing she was there, not so far away, knowing the sort of reception he was likely to face when he saw her next, on top of his concern about what Uzzi was doing, made him toss and turn on the bedroll he reluctantly moved beneath the overhang shelter Enola and Dink had chosen when the snow had begun to fall.

The soft flakes had turned to a gentle, misty rain that felt like the prick of fire ash on his skin as the nervous energy continued to build.

He could not blame her for such a response, any more than he blamed himself for his doubts about her readiness to lead the Pack. It was what it was. He could not change it. He could only go forward and perhaps regain the rank and respect he had given away by giving those things back to her in turn.

He rolled again.

Enola growled without opening her eyes.

The dog raised its head at the same moment Pain did.

Scowling, Dink too lifted his from the sharpening of his knives as the crunching of gravel brought a shadow out of the rain.

Uzzi nodded at them with a pensive, thoughtful expression before sitting at the fire. Pain sniffed the air and watched him plop another bit of wood onto the dwindling glow.

He had found the Fela.

There was no trace of any of the others, not Jia or anyone else, in the mud and damp on his clothes.

The Fela's scent was enough.

Hopefully, across the distance between them, Quentin, deep in slumber, would not smell it too.

The older man's return did not bring the relief Pain had expected it to and so he rolled to face the fire's warmth and watched Uzzi through barely parted lids. Something was on the other man's mind; perhaps he was replaying the apparent encounter with Kato, or contemplating his next action. Perhaps he was thinking about something said, something seen. Minutes ticked by on the echoes of the falling rain, the sound gradually lulling Pain towards the sleep that had eluded him throughout the evening.

The telltale intake of breath before speech made his eyes snap open.

"We need a distraction."

"What sort?" That was Enola's voice, an indicator she had not been asleep despite the relaxed rhythm of her breathing.

Uzzi shrugged. "Dunno…but something to keep us here another day or so."

Dink nodded and sheathed his knife. He leaned forward, elbows on his knees, and joined Uzzi deep in thought.

Not knowing what Uzzi had in mind, what he intended or why, not knowing him as well as the other two did, Pain waited.

❧*❧

He could not see in the direction from where his father had emerged. Their hospital shelter stood in the way. The snow had turned to rain but would not yet be enough to wash the trail away. If Kato left now, he believed he would be able to track the other man back to wherever he was camped. To where Pain and Quentin were.

What would he do, however, when he found them? He did not think he would have the nerve to kill them unless provoked.

Frowning, fidgeting with the edge of his coat sleeve, Kato stared into the shadows at the edge of the building barely visible beneath the ambient glow of the cloud-shrouded moon.

The rain fell harder. He could smell the burn of ozone that always brought a storm with it. Not a storm like the one past, perhaps, but enough of a storm to wash away the trail of one Kato had believed, had hoped, had feared to be dead. He wanted to speak to him again. He never wanted to see him again.

Quentin's threat lingered too.

A storm would hinder those behind Kato as it would Quentin's followers. Perhaps it would wash their trail from the air, from the muddy ground, but they could not count on that being enough to keep them safe.

He needed to go. To wait meant losing Uzzi a second time.

And Jia needed time.

He could buy her that. Somehow.

It was an unexpected shadow darting from across the street to crouch at the bottom of the steps in front of him, keeping him from moving, a man rather than a wolf, naked and vulnerable…although Kato knew, as he had every other time in the man's company, Deuce was less vulnerable than he appeared, naked or not.

"Which way?"

Kato stared, shivering off the nervous energy that slithered up his spine and across his shoulders. The resistance to a reply was brief, however, and he pointed as if forced to do so against his will. Into the hospital. Behind it. Back to the east but a more northerly route than they had traveled.

Deuce nodded once, sniffed up and down Kato's body for the scent he needed, and nodded.

"Stay here. Watch. I'll deal with this."

Behind him, Jia murmured in her sleep. Kato turned his head to look at her before speaking and watched her roll and flop one arm across the mage's waist. He growled, swallowing the impulse to argue with Deuce or to storm off into the night, to leave his post to do what he should have done when Uzzi had made his offer.

He had promised Jia he would stay.

When he turned to nod his agreement, Deuce was already gone.

⁂

The staircase to the raised-level shelter wobbled and shook as Norse led them to the room where he had witnessed the first explosion. Voices of command and obedience, the bang and clatter of equipment carried or dragged out of the structure, the creaking of cart wheels hauling the surviving test subjects into one of the smaller, metal-sided huts at the property's northern edge, created a constant underpinning drone that blended with the dripping rain the three of them were ill-equipped to resist. By the time Norse closed the door, Laedan Hallister and the two women were soaked to the skin, bedraggled and frazzled looking in addition to the varying degrees of anger, frustration, annoyance, confusion, and suspicion on their faces.

"I should be…"

"Norse'll go in, bring any salvageable clothes…get you set up here for tonight," grunted Geary as he stoked the fire in the pot Norse had left burning when he had run to aid those in the lab. "Food too, if you find any. Daylight will be here soon."

"Yes, sirra," Norse said, backing towards the door, grateful to be given something to do instead of being trapped in this tense room.

Simultaneously, Gail began, "There should be…"

"Daylight's soon enough. You'll have dry clothes. You're not dressed for…"

A crackle of distant thunder rumbled from the south, a sound mirroring Gail's bitter annoyance.

"Norse?"

"Sirra?"

"You have a horse?"

The younger man scowled but since the Laedan was involved in tending the fire, he did not see it.

The other animals, the horses the Laedan, Anakirist, and her attendants had arrived on, the doctor's horse, and the oxen used to draw the box cart, had been released at the start of the fire. Eventually, they would be found, but not tonight.

"Yes."

"I'll take it in the morning."

"I must report to Grand Mas Lord," Korma began.

Geary's cool glance made the Anakirist frown and abort her complaint. He continued, "I'll take Anakirist Miller to the Fortress, send aid for cleanup and rebuilding." Rebuilding might not be possible, but until the fire stopped burning and daylight revealed the extent of the damage, he could plan for the possibility.

If necessary, another suitable location would be found. The lab could be relocated one more time.

That would take time.

HOPE would hate it. Gail would hate it too.

It could not be helped.

Korma swallowed her protest and nodded in reluctant acceptance. She did not want to share a horse with him, but doing so was preferable to returning to the Fortress, rain or no rain, or waiting in this hellish room for him to send more horses…or for hers to be found.

Her staff, however, would be forced to either march with her or remain behind.

"You'll stay on here as security until I return, oversee the cleanup…find out who did this.

Norse pursed his lips. "Sirra…" Without Aman, there was no one else to oversee the Laedan's security. He had already been away from duty for several days and though the Laedan had remained safe, he could have died in that fire. If assassination had been the intent, Norse had been lucky to thwart it.

It seemed to him this duty shift was some sort of demotion.

"You'll do what Doctor Torrens needs," Geary continued, expressing no indicator he recognized or understood Norse's aborted protest. "You'll report the ongoing status to me every day. If she needs to come to the Fortress, you'll accompany her."

Regardless of Gail's anger, Geary would not take chances with her safety. Perhaps the terrorist had come for him. Perhaps the Anakirist had been the target or the act had been meant to destroy the lab. If Gail was in danger, Geary would not forgive himself for leaving her alone, leaving her vulnerable to another attack. For his own travel, his own safety, the Anakirist's entourage would have to be enough.

Despite Gail's scowl and the slight flashing of her eyes that expressed suspicion that the Laedan already suspected she and Norse to be in league with each other, Norse nodded and muttered. "Yes, sirra," before escaping out the door.

The outside was cooler. Clearer. Cleaner.

He was thankful to be out of that room.

❧*❧

It was a simple plan that involved backtracking to the lumber store and rummaging through the shelves for the things to fulfill the purpose he intended. Though he did not know what the effects would be of the substance in the small metal jug, he knew the faded cross-skull symbol on the side and what it meant.

With the jug and some wadded soiled rags, brittle with age, in hand, he ran in half form along the path the stranger's scent presented. Despite the rain, he found the point of confrontation, picked up the trail retreating north, and followed it with the hope that the harder falling rain would not erase it before he found where he wanted to go.

As the trail grew fainter, Deuce relied on instinct to guide him.

In time, the air brought with it the faint taste of rain-extinguished fires, and the splat of droplets on canvas announced an encampment. It was there, as he circled the fringes of the gathered collection of humanity, he found what he was looking for.

Deuce had never met Thomas Quentin. As Flushing Pack omega, he had never been invited into the Fortress, to the places Roland frequented. There had been no desire on his part to see those things or be part of that world. There had been numerous opportunities, however, to shadow the alpha, to follow him to meetings outside the Fortress held in the company of Laedan Channon, his aide Quentin, and a variety of other family members and LaGuardia elite.

Having watched from secret places, sometimes with Roland's knowledge but most often without it, Deuce knew Quentin's scent. He knew his face. He knew the sound, the rhythm, and tone of his breath.

There was another at his fire, facing the darkness in which Deuce crouched, a club-like branch in one hand. The Cana sniffed the air.

Normal.

Despite the club, he was no threat.

Deuce did not want a fight. He had not come for any confrontation that would attract everyone else in the camp.

With the wind at his back, he hesitated. Waiting.

Uzzi motioned his orders to Dink and Enola and the pair peeled off, Enola towards the north edge of the camp, Dink and the dog to the west, away from their southernmost fire. The only other sentry was posted to the east, and Uzzi chose to see to the man himself.

There was one other individual awake, the man seated with his back to them at Quentin's fire. Uzzi nodded at Pain and grunted.

"Whatever you're gonna do, be quiet about it." He hoped Pain would take the opportunity to kill Quentin and they could be done with this charade. Maybe he would temporarily incapacitate him. Uzzi did not particularly care. His goal was fixated on keeping his son safe.

Pain nodded and waited until he was alone at the fire, stirring it as if there was nothing unusual about the other three leaving him alone. He had not expected them to agree to leave Quentin in his hands. Now that they had, he needed an impromptu plan to serve them all. When he stood, it was with a casual stretch that gave way to cautious, creeping steps towards Quentin's fire without a solid idea of what he intended to do when he reached it.

He had the advantage of Cana stealth and Quentin was asleep. The chunk of concrete he scooped up as he rose, crumbly around the edges, would be enough to knock the Fela out, or perhaps kill him. The scuffing of his feet in the gravel made the other man at Quentin's fire look at him, but all he saw was the Cana picking up sticks to fuel his fire. He grunted and faced his own fire's dying glow.

Pain straightened, the kindling set quietly down, the piece of concrete again retrieved in its place. Two more steps and he hesitated, his nose tilted into the air, a familiar scent making him squint into the darkness on the other side of Quentin's camp.

It could not be.

It would not be enough to stop him.

Deuce's eyes narrowed. His lips curled into a silent snarl.

When Pain's hand came down with a snapping crack of stone against the sentry's head so the man slumped to the side, Deuce emerged from the darkness.

Quentin muttered something in his disturbed slumber and rolled away to face the emergent threat. No one else was awake to react to the stone's blow.

For several heartbeats, two men who had known each other most of their lives, former and current omegas of the Flushing Pack, stared at each other, assessing the threat the other posed, focus split between each other and the hated target.

The man who had killed Roland.

Neither spoke. Neither moved.

Pain's gaze strayed to the items in Deuce's hands. Deuce made a sniffling, huffing snort.

There was no nod of agreement. No questions asked. Deuce would do as he had always done, protect the Marrocks.

If it meant he might eventually come for Pain, Pain would be ready. Now, he understood the other man's intent and slunk back, blending into the shadows, allowing Deuce to uphold his oaths. Maybe he would kill Quentin. As Roland's contemporary, as the new alpha's biological father, it would be his right. Pain did not care what Deuce did…though if he did not kill Quentin now, Pain would do so.

As long as his actions provided the delay Uzzi intended, as long as his actions kept Jia safe and gave her the chance to proceed unhindered, Pain was content with allowing Deuce to make his choice.

The contents of the jug Deuce carried were poured onto the rags. On padded half-Cana feet, he crept close to press the rag over Quentin's nose and mouth. The man thrashed impotently for several seconds, held down by Deuce's weight on his chest, breathing in the pungent fumes. His erratic movements caused those sleeping nearby to stir from their slumber but the thrashing ended quickly.

Deuce moved away.

Most settled back into sleep.

One person stirred. Rubbed his eyes. Sat up.

The open jug was tossed into the fire, the rags with it, as the Cana leaped away into the darkness. The explosion of chemicals splashed into the flames as a flash of lightning crackled across the sky and a deluge burst onto the encampment with a deafening roar of thunder.

Thomas Quentin did not stir.

Chapter 33

The lightning, the thunder, the explosion of a chemical fire, roused the camp and scattered people in every direction, some in panic, some in haste to douse the flames the deluge failed to affect, some to discover comrades on watch struck down by unseen hands.

The natural impulse to turn to their leader for guidance proved the man to be unresponsive, alive but unmoving, with a faint chemical smell lingering around his mouth and nose.

It was the same smell given off by the fumes billowing from the uncontrolled fire.

The team's doctor was called, a round fellow who huffed and puffed as he waddled across the camp, and others, continuing to seek guidance against the erratic effort to take control, turned to the one man they had worked with, worked for, before.

No one noticed or questioned Uzzi's rush from the eastern side of camp or paid heed to the Cana crouched at his warming fire, watching the commotion without becoming involved in it. Uzzi shooed onlookers away to give the doctor room to work, spotting the silhouette of the metal canister glowing hot in the flames. He did not take time to piece together details that did not instantly make sense.

"Trench it! Let it burn!" They had little on hand to put out a chemical fire and if not contained, the rain would carry the seemingly oily compound outward and spread the flames through their camp. If they could contain the spread, the fire would be contained too. He looked at the doctor who was struggling to drag Quentin beyond the fire's reach and shouted, "What's wrong with him?"

"Not waking up, sirra," said the woman who had picked up Quentin's feet to help the doctor move him. With the rain stinging his eyes and dripping down his face too furiously to be wiped away, Uzzi could not tell who she was.

"Mori's not either." added someone else, dragging a man with a bloody gash on the side of his head out of the fire's reach as well.

"Been attacked!" shouted someone over another crack of thunder.

"Nonsense," snorted Dink, holding his barking, snarling dog back from the direction it wanted to charge. Dink could not see anything there. He had been part of that 'attack' against some of their people, but he had not been near the fire, near Quentin, to see what had happened. He assumed Uzzi had been part of it.

Thinking better of his choice, however, knowing others would expect the dog to capture or chase off any threat, Dink let the dog go.

The straining beast lurched forward and charged into the night.

"Someone did this," protested another voice of one of those helping move the man Mori from the fire.

Someone kicked the empty liquor bottle away from where Mori had been sitting and chortled grimly, "Maybe did it to himself."

"Keep your eyes and ears open and get this trench dug," Uzzi instructed, silencing the debate, dropping to his knees to aid in digging the muddy ditch. To the doctor, he added, "Get them on their feet…so we know what happened." For the moment, for as long as the rain encumbered them and the two unconscious men failed to wake, there was nothing else any of them could do except contain the flames.

Nature, it seemed had presented them with its own problem, one likely to also delay Kato and his companions. Nobody gained from the rain and the delay might, he feared, present their incapacitated leader enough time to recover without permitting Kato an escape.

For now, as he dug faster, it looked as if no gain had been made.

⤜*⤛

Without the need to carry anything, the half-form Cana took on the wolf skin and ran in a zigzagging pattern away from the enemy's camp, taking advantage of every pool of water, every running rivulet, every fence or wall he could leap onto, or over, to deter any who chose to follow him. The chemical fire would keep most of them busy and he did not believe anyone except Pain had seen him.

Pain might be threat enough.

From the interaction across the fire, Deuce believed differently.

The dog baying on his trail, let loose before he could put much distance between him and the fire, was closer than he liked.

His erratic route, his human knowledge of obstacles that would impede a hunting dog, eventually meant the animal gave up its pursuit to return to its master. Deuce continued his unpredictable run for nearly an hour, until his chest ached and his nose burned, before circling back to the hospital where his daughter sheltered.

Kato was still at the door, neither giving the watch to another nor following Deuce. In appreciation, the Cana howled.

Kato slid down the doorframe until he was crouched on the top step, relaxing but not prepared to forsake his post. Anything Deuce had intended to do was done.

The rain was gradually subsiding. Dawn was not far off. Behind him, sensing the coming sun, hearing the familiar note of Deuce's Cana call, others began to awaken.

Whatever Deuce had done, Kato hoped it would keep Quentin and Pain off their trail long enough for them to reach another night's shelter. Long enough for Kato to decide what his future should be.

❧*❧

Despite Geary's urging to take advantage of their night's shelter, none of them slept. Through the room's only window, they had, instead, watched the ongoing efforts to secure equipment while the rain extinguished the last of the fire. They had seen Norse crisscross their field of vision multiple times, once with one of the errant horses someone on the southern border of the lot had captured, and when he finally came back to the center of the commotion with two animals on leads, it came with the realization that the dwindling storm had brought with it the arrival of a new day.

Eager for the comforts of home, eager to be rid of the Anakirist and out of Gail's peevish company, Geary stomped through the muddy street to join the man with the horses.

Korma was right behind him.

Geary did not care.

He barely noticed her as his marching steps faltered and forced him to stop, to stare in disbelief at the eastern sky.

Others, gradually, did likewise.

The sun was still buried behind the perpetual veil of gray clouds, shedding enough light to lend a sparkle to the world where the raindrops clung to the edges of plants and buildings. And yet there, for the first time in anyone's memory, young or old, was a stretch of cornflower blue as wide as Geary's hand when he raised it to shield his eyes and as long as his arm from fingertip to elbow.

Innocent, unmasked, blue sky.

Korma's hand tightened on his elbow.

Norse uttered a croaking sound of disbelief punctuated by the cries and gasps of surprise from others around them.

Like everyone else, Geary swallowed his disbelieving breath. He pressed one hand above his hammering heart and wondered what trick the storm and a night without sleep were playing on his eyes.

৯*৯

He was breathing easier, a development Uzzi noted with both regret and relief. Mori had died from his head wound without waking. It would have been best, Uzzi thought, if Quentin had died as well from whatever Pain had done, but seeing the man suffer as the skin around his mouth and nose reddened and blistered, knowing it might yet deliver his chance to exact revenge, provided satisfaction enough.

Quentin retched several times in his sleep, bile and the night's meal soiling the front of his clothing, and now he lay in a tight ball as if his stomach muscles had contracted and drawn him into a knot.

Efforts to pull him out of that position produced agonizing groans and growls until the doctor decided to let him be. As long as he was breathing, the doctor believed he would survive.

Having never seen that container before, unable to identify the charred metal after it was retrieved from the eye of the fire, Uzzi had no idea where Pain had acquired it. Nor did he care.

Until Quentin woke, until their drenched gear was dried out and the injured sentries recovered from the incapacitating blows, Uzzi decided they would remain where they were.

It was not safe to move Quentin, he argued.

The delay should be enough for Kato and his friends to get away, even if it meant never seeing his son again.

Dink had eavesdropped on the muttered, grousing tales the night's sentries told of blows landed out of the dark that had knocked them unconscious before the explosion. Enola oversaw a camp-wide inventory but nothing had been taken. No other harm had been done. Only Mori had died and only Quentin suffered.

From what, neither the doctor nor anyone else could say.

Inhalation of the fire fumes, the doctor claimed, lacking any better explanation. Sparks and sprayed chemicals from the explosion had burned his lips, nose, and cheeks. No one could identify the burned container nor the explosion, though someone postulated Mori might have thrown it into the fire to dispose of it without being aware of the damage it would cause.

That did not explain the three unconscious sentries or the blow to the back of Mori's head.

"Scavs hoping to rob us; explosion scared 'em off before they could," Enola said with a shrug, staring at the knife she used to clean her nails rather than at anyone gathered around the single community fire built to keep the group together.

Someone whistled low and pointed at the sky. "Maybe something fell…from there…"

"Just happened to hit only three of us?" scoffed one of the sentries, rubbing his aching head as he turned on his rickety crate seat to see what the other was looking at.

One by one, heads turned.

Uzzi looked at Enola when she turned to gape at him with one of the few expressions of surprise he had ever seen on her face. Dink wrapped his trembling fingers in the fur at the nape of the dog's neck. Pain, who crouched on the edges of the congregation, listening but not participating in the community debate, craned his head and curled his lips in an anxious snarl.

If he had been in half or full form, Uzzi was sure his ears would have been pinned to his head.

The firmament was blue.

It had never been blue.

Blue sky was a rumor uttered in childhood fairytales.

And yet a small portion of the sky, to their surprise, was blue.

❧*❧

"Nik! Nik! Come! Come see!"

Having never heard his sister-in-law raise her voice, expecting to find Donn in the sitting room at the eastern end of the second-floor corridor or else find the woman in a pool of the blood of a lost unborn child, Nik flew into the room with Torben pounding along behind him. His abrupt stop allowed the bigger man to plow, unprepared, into him, pushing him against the long plate window that surveyed the harbor and the lands east of the Fortress.

The panel rattled but did not crack.

"What is it?" Torben grunted with unusual anxiety. He could see the same amazing vision they did but his question still stood.

The clouds had never parted to show blue before.

Oasis' voice remained shrill and excited as she asked "What does it mean?" over top of the sposer's question.

Nik shook his head, slack-jawed and silent. No one knew why the blue had vanished after the Undoing. Nothing he had read in the books Roland had found and brought to the Fortress or those the Marrocks and Channons collected over the years explained it. No speculation shared in fireside discussions or on the Fortress rooftop with Jia, Jonni, and Addi on sleepless nights had provided explanations, only speculation and rumor. Scientists had come and gone, debating how it had happened and how the change could be undone.

No one knew if the world would ever know the blue and black of day and night that had been part of the world since the dawn of time.

No man or woman alive, Nik was confident, had ever thought they would see this day. Such a little bit of blue, but a miracle none had believed in. How many of those still asleep would refuse to believe the exuberant tales of this stupefying moment that would fill the days and weeks ahead with excited talk?

Would he ever, Nik thought with his hand to the glass, as the movement of the clouds slowly overtook the blue and swallowed it, pushing the vision into memory, see such a sight again?

"I don't know," he whispered, blinking away unexpected tears that welled with the swelling of his heart "But it has to be a good sign."

Though Torben continued to look unsettled when Nik side-eyed him, Oasis, her face alight with childlike wonder, seemed inclined to agree. This had to be a good sign. She appeared to believe it.

Nik wanted to believe it too.

❧*❧

"We're not going anywhere," General Warby grunted, unpacking his horse after a gesture to the men around him instructed them to do the same. Confident they were nearing their destination and satiated by the woman softly sobbing somewhere beyond the edge of the camp, Donn had roused everyone not already awakened by the night's storm determined to press on.

He was going to find that fort before Hallister. Hallister was the only opponent he expected; any others had either yet to undertake the journey or would be too far behind them to be a threat.

Donn had not counted on a patch of blue sky to be enough to undermine his efforts to depart early. He had not counted on the general's insistence on wasting time with ritual and ceremony to honor something that, while never seen before, was only a physical manifestation of the natural world Donn cared little about.

"It's only…" he began, still sitting on his horse. A few of those closest to him likewise remained mounted, wary of angering the Laedan's temperamental son.

Warby wrapped his horse's reins around the branch where he had previously been tied and patted its side. "It is an omen. A portent. A tiding. Sacrifices must be made, atonement…"

"Superstitious shart…"

The general scowled at the young man's sneer. "It is the way of…"

"Didn't think you're gullible or delusional."

"It is doctrine. It is written." Warby grabbed the reins of Donn's horse and glowered, daring further challenge.

Frustrated, Donn fought for something to say, something he could use to refute Warby's claims and countermand his orders. Some of HOPE's men were already building another fire on the bones of a previous one and someone else pulled the saddle off the general's horse. Likewise indoctrinated, the history of Channon participation in HOPE ritual and study foisted on Donn from the moment he could speak, read, and understand, Donn could not recall a single mention of blue sky in the tomes he had been given or forced to study, nor in any of the lessons spoken by itinerant HOPE pastors.

There were secrets in the halls, however, known only to the initiated, with which Donn was not familiar. Knowledge shared by only a few. Mysteries denied to outsiders. Donn could not refute the general's claims and the soldiers of HOPE had already accepted their leader's assessment and decree and his commanded choice of action.

Unable to counter him, Donn hissed, muttered beneath his breath as he slid off the horse, keeping the animal's body between him and Warby, and stomped away in search of soothing. The blue of his mother's eyes overhead was gone, no longer watching him. No longer judging. She was not there to witness what he chose to do next.

He would not have cared if she was, despite the anxious gnawing in his center the blue patch instilled.

It was only blue sky. Nothing more.

❧*❧

The string of soldiers behind him, cut to ten by the ravages of the storm and ailments brought on by the damp cold continued to trudge dutifully in his wake. They had abandoned the coastal road, eroded in many places, blocked by the debris of collapsed structures, or washed-up fragments of boats and buildings from elsewhere along the coast. Instead, they traveled a more sheltered route, with roads and edifices between them and the sea, struggling to remain diligent despite the demoralized pall that enveloped them.

The second storm, brief as it had been, was a melancholy reminder of the friends and comrades so recently lost and for what?

A fort without proof of existence, a fort few of them expected they would find.

Aman was not the only one beginning to feel like this mission had become a death march intended to kill them. Especially him.

He searched his memory for anything he might have done or said to create such a chasm between himself and the Laedan but failed to find anything of value that would warrant his ordered death. There was only the possibility that the man who wanted his job had somehow poisoned Geary's ear and mind against one he had trusted most of his life. Though the possibility sparked an indignant fire within him, it also caused nearly overwhelming dismay that Geary might believe another's lies over a lifetime of service and loyalty.

Did the Laedan expect them not to return? Had he selected those men to come in lieu of some other form of punishment for wrongs they were unaware of committing? What would Hallister do if they gave up the quest and returned empty-handed?

Only his belief that, should the fort exist, its contents were best controlled by someone in no position to wage war with it, kept Aman moving. Only his conviction made those with him continue to obey.

He stopped his horse at the crest of a rise and turned to watch those with him climb the hill they were on and begin to march down the other side. Doing so made him the sole witness to the kiss of blue the sky offered.

He thought about alerting the rest, offering them the same swelling hope and wonderment he felt, bolstering their faith and belief in the mission the hint of blue birthed in his breast.

In the end, after a moment's consideration, he opted not to say anything. Most were a superstitious lot, and it struck him as likely this unexpected vision would, instead, be interpreted as a threatening omen. It might prompt his dwindling force to surrender to fear and abandon the cause, sworn duty or not.

For Aman, the vision lifted his flagging spirits. He tilted his head. He squared his shoulders.

The gods were with him, whoever they were. He was not superstitious but the feeling of encouragement he felt was strong enough for him to move his horse forward. So long as Aman held to the course, the world would be right. Whatever right was.

❧*❧

His energy and drive had waned more each day since before the great storm, but the compulsion to locate Fort Hamilton and procure the contents of its vaults for Yiva's sake continued to propel Lowell forward, even when it meant Captain Ortega was forced to secure him to the saddle so he did not inadvertently slip off when fatigue overtook him during a grueling day's travel. He hid his fever, the sweats, the chills, and the shortness of breath, by avoiding contact with anyone. Since he carried no responsibility for setting camp or tending to his horse when they stopped each evening, for doing anything more than riding and directing their journey, the symptoms of illness had been easy to hide.

When the cough first set in, Lowell chalked it up to a seasonal winter cold and insisted their habit of camping at sundown and setting off with the rising of the sun continue.

The brief, unexpected storm during the night, snow had turned to lightning, thunder, and rain, spooking some of the horses and necessitating a search for the errant animals at daybreak, prevented the host from starting as intended.

It was a long enough delay to gift Lowell with much-needed, extended sleep. The sharp pain beneath his ribs when he coughed or tried to take a deep breath, was beginning to make restful sleep difficult. One by one, others in the company had begun to cough as well, but none as bad as their stubborn Laedan.

Propped against the side of the building where they had found shelter from the storm, facing the direction of home as he tried to swallow another coughing fit and winced at the pressure it created in his ribs, Lowell believed he was the only person in the world to witness the sliver of blue the parting rain clouds gifted him with this morning. There were stories about such a blue, artwork and book images depicting what the sky had looked like before the Undoing. But in those images, he had never before noticed how much like Yiva's eyes that blue could be.

He could not remember the last words she had said to him…or he to her. Something mundane and ordinary, he suspected, a compliment on the floral arrangements she had last made, left to wither and wilt in their vases because he had not had the heart to discard them. Perhaps he had said something about one of their sons, or the morning meal, or an agreement made for a family dinner that had never been.

Yes. That was it. The family dinner Nik had been expected to attend. A dinner Lowell had missed for some petty reason, a dinner she had never come home to enjoy. An agreement given in passing as he had gone about his business the same as any other day. If he had gone to dinner, he might have notices she was gone in time to save her. When had he last told her she was beautiful? When had he last told her he loved her? When had she, in her hidden fear of the monster they had birthed, last said the same to him?

Lowell could not remember.

The gray clouds rolled in.

The blue sky was lost.

In time, he would not remember the magic of this moment either.

Not remembering, he thought with his fist to his mouth to abort the rising cough, was the worst part of it all.

⟡*⟡

The cessation of rain prompted most of the Pack's children to scamper into the early morning air in the hopes of splashing in puddles prone to accumulate between the Ministry's door and the bridge leading back to Queen's College Campus. Too much time had been spent cooped up within their temporary home since the last major storm had damaged the bridge and deposited broken debris in the open where the younger children might hurt themselves. Much of that had been cleaned up, relocated into usable and unusable collections, and the children were eager to run and scream and play. Likewise restless and eager to find Wist, who had taken the early morning watch at the bridge, Reif herded the impatient pups out the door and followed immediately behind them, adjusting her coat against the cold.

Despite the protection of the Zone walls, she was no less cautious here than she had been on the outside. Caution was a trait drilled into pups at an early age.

"Jack…Bruce…hush," she scolded, her hands on their backs as she guided them through the door. Some of the adults still slept, having been up late working on the last of the debris clearance. The newborn infant had recently settled in Trill's arms, allowing her parents to sleep too. The pair of boisterous boys did not need to wake them with their sniggers and yelps as they playfully poked and slapped each other.

At the front of the group, little Tori, Dora, and Estella squealed in mock horror at something they found on the ground.

None of them got any further out the door. The squeals and laughter fell abruptly silent as the children, instead of scattering to play, gaped at the display in the eastern sky.

From the direction of the bridge, Wist came at a run, his arms flailing and gesturing at the sky. "Do you see it? Tell me you see it."

His excitement brought several sleepy, irritated, or anxious adults out of the Ministry, expecting trouble or to issue rebukes to the children and young man for failing to respect their elders. Instead, they too arrived in time to witness the tail end of the miracle.

"Roland was right," Liam murmured beneath his breath as he absently patted Vanya's head when she crouched at his side to cling to his leg and point at the sky in awe and wonder.

"Was there any doubt?" Amused as he was at his statement, Addi was no less amazed by the moment. His father's belief in a day when the natural world would revert to what it had been was a hope the Pack clung to, but not something most believed. Addi wished Trill was at his side to see it. He wished Jia was here to see it too. Wherever she was, he hoped she did. He hoped it gave her the same sense of optimism it provided him.

Unaware he had spoken her name, he gave a slight smile when Liam whispered, "She sees it. I know she does."

Vanya's arms dropped to her side. "The angels have come," she whispered. "Mama said they would…when the sky came back."

Liam patted her head. Perhaps Vanya was right.

Maybe angels had come back.

❮*❯

The piece of driftwood bobbled like a boat on the lake-like puddle blocking the road in front of them, where Jia and the others waited as QiangXu tested the water's depth with a long branch he had found. Knowing Quentin was on their heels, despite Deuce's assurance his team had been delayed by several hours at least, and the tracker Nepo as well, it had seemed prudent to leave the hospital while it was dark, not long after being roused by Deuce's returning howl. They shared a quick morning repast of the meager food they had left as they gathered as much as they could carry, the majority of their burden now medical supplies and bedding that could serve in trade for food or other goods, and started southwest.

The more distance put between them and the others, the better.

Deuce rubbed against Jia's leg upon her emergence from their shelter, a reassuring gesture meant to express no need for worry, but it was not enough. They would discuss later what he had done to buy them time.

At the edge of the puddle, Eddie jangled the pouch of coins he had found, mostly worn smooth or corroded with time, coins of an unknown origin with little value in the boroughs but which made a reassuring tinkling sound at his fidgeting. As harrowing as the previous day's misadventure had been, his ability to be of use, the chance he had been given to help, to prove himself, had bolstered his self-confidence and outlook. He had not complained about rising early, about starting in the cold before the sun, about not having a full breakfast before their day began. He scrambled to the front of the group initially but eventually settled back into the middle to offer Pubby his support so QiangXu could test the route before them.

Jia looked back. Everyone was here, everyone except Deuce and Kato. Deuce, as usual, secured their forward flanks and sought other paths forward around this puddle although none of them felt up to an extended detour if they could merely continue through the water.

She had not seen Kato since shortly after waking when he had avoided her gaze before disappearing into the street. She wanted to believe he was keeping watch behind them, but after more than an hour of not seeing a trace of him, she suspected, as she adjusted the found silk scarf of pastel paisley in gold, pink, and green around her throat, it would not be long before Kato left for good.

He might decide to go back to Queen's College for his sister. Maybe, she thought with a glance to the east, he had already done so.

Arm around her shoulder, hating to be the burden he was proving to be but understanding that the others depended on his memory of a map they had not seen, Vance turned his head to look where she was staring, the explosion of tension in Jia's body, her heart rate and breathing no longer in sync with his as it had been all morning. He blinked. He rubbed his eyes with his other hand.

"Blue sky…" he murmured aloud.

The others looked up and saw it too.

"I think," QiangXu said softly as he stopped next to Jia, "Roland's trying to tell us we're on the right path. Come…we can cross safely."

Jia, despite the way Kato's absence dragged at her, agreed. About her father. About their safety. About the path they had chosen.

None of them moved, however, until the patch of blue was no longer visible.

❧516❦

Chapter 34

Captain Ortega pushed the Laedan back with one hand, removing him from the trajectory of the rock hurled by one of the dirty, disheveled people crawling out of the nearby buildings. Lowell, his attention focused on remaining awake and not succumbing to another painful coughing fit, did not see the people, the rock, or the gesture, in time to tighten his hold on his horse with his knees or his hands on the reins. He slid sideways and fell into the mud with a yelp. The nearest horses skittered to avoid him or were pulled up short by riders caught off guard as he was.

Someone leaped down and pulled him up. A hasty survey of their surroundings showed nowhere to retreat to that was not blocked by children and a host of half-form and full-form Fela.

"What are they doing?" someone barked, holding off an attacker with the buzzing crackle of a shock stick.

"Don't they know who I am?"

"Protecting their territory," replied someone else over Lowell's disoriented snarling remark.

Arlo turned his horse to shield the fallen man and barked, "Hold!" Other than children throwing rocks and a single half-form male who dared to approach but was kept at bay by the shock stick, the adults had yet to act in violence against them. The Captain intended to keep it that way. To Lowell, as someone helped him back on his horse, Arlo muttered, "We're leagues from LaGuardia, sirra; they don't know us. I'd say they're encouraging us not to stay."

It was unusual for Fela to gather in a cluster. Unlike Cana with their familial packs, or Ursa who tended towards a solitary existence, the Fela Arlo knew of lived most often in small family groups. Out in the Waste, however, coming together for survival made sense.

They were people, not beasts, regardless of what HOPE boasted. They were people who wanted community and security like everyone else.

Muttering beneath his shallow breath, his right side caked with mud that dripped down the horse's neck and sides, Lowell said, "Ask them where the Fort is. Tell them we're passing through."

There was no need for the captain to repeat the words. The Fela heard everything but did not react.

It was impossible to tell from their expressions if they understood.

A hand motion started the group moving cautiously forward. The street was one of the clearest they had passed through since leaving LaGuardia's border behind. There appeared to be an ongoing effort by the residents to remove debris and the hulks of old cars, to maintain the structures on either side showing a noticeable lack of deterioration. The Fela drew together in the street behind them, blocking a retreat back the way they had come, and crept steadily forward to force the intruders to continue moving. More rocks, an occasional branch or chunk of wood, or other random items picked up from the debris at the edges of the street where the recent storm had clogged the storm grates, were propelled at them, sometimes striking the men at the rear of the column.

LaGuardia's troops obeyed Ortega's command. Nothing was thrown in return, no insults or angry words were uttered to prompt retaliation, no violence was exchanged. Glances of angry annoyance, however, continued, though were not enough to prompt the Fela to further action.

One block. Two blocks.

Arlo side-eyed the Laedan. He frowned. The man looked worse than yesterday. More tired. More distracted. Others among the group were coughing and suffering too.

They should stop. They should rest.

But not here.

To do so would benefit no one.

They could not turn back to seek treatment and Arlo was beginning to fear few of them would reach their destination alive.

∽*∽

"It has to be done."

Geary's voice held the dispassionate note of command, the carrying out of necessary business those who worked for him were accustomed to. He was a man confident in his choices, in his actions, and by remaining so assured his subordinates their orders and actions were always in Kennedy's best interest.

A lifetime of military instinct that made Norse alert to subtle cues which might reveal danger exposed the twitch at the corner of the Laedan's eyes as he spoke, belying the man's usual certainty.

Norse accepted that the Laedan was certain enough, however, to voice the order, regardless of any reluctance he felt.

It was an unfortunate command, but one Norse did not argue or contradict. Aman would have. Aman would have offered a counterproposal, something about political necessity or logistics or finances, things Norse cared nothing about.

Ordered to do what he did best, he bobbed his head and left the chamber. The Anakirist would not have left yet. She would still be here, waiting for a horse to be readied. Norse would follow, see her safe a long way away from the Fortress…

…and then there was duty.

Laedan Hallister had a plan.

It was Norse's pleasure to make sure it came to fruition.

What was going on behind the Laedan's calm but distracted eyes was none of Norse's concern.

∽*∽

Torben frowned and pressed his hand to Nik's forehead as he waved the bottle of smelling salts under his nose. His arrival from his Plant shift was met with a swarm of worried staff, men and women bemoaning the absence of the temporary Laedan, frantically reporting he would not awaken from slumber, quietly whispering rumors of a relapse into old habits that would leave LaGuardia without leadership until Lowell's return.

Reluctant to assume the worse despite fearing it, the sposer-turned-bodyguard followed an older woman up the stairs to Nik's bedroom, a room he could find without her, and entered it when she cautiously pushed the door open.

Slumped in the faded green easy chair pulled over to a window to have allowed a clear view of that little patch of blue sky if it returned in the same place, Nik looked to have been seated there for some time. Long enough for his slack expression to deposit trails of drying spittle down the side of his chin and over the shoulder of the loose sleeping robe open to the tie at his waist. No one had attempted to move him.

Torben frowned deeper.

"He was like this as a boy," whispered the woman at the door, propping it open with her shoulder as she wrung her hands. "Before the treatments."

Torben's glance over his shoulder encouraged her to explain.

She shrugged, her eyes never leaving Nik's face. "Little mite would be awake for weeks at a time…drove his mother frantic." The mention of Yiva made her look away morosely and clench her hands. "Then he would sleep…sometimes for days…a whole week once. Wasn't right…wasn't natural."

Natural for who, Torben asked the bitterly silent question as he lifted Nik from the chair. "Help me.," was all he said aloud as he carried the slighter man to the freshly made bed.

She bustled over and pulled back the bedding so Torben could settle Nik onto the mattress and took a quick step back as he pulled the blankets up to cover him. Torben remembered the story, Nik speaking of medications to sleep, medications to wake up, the precursor to a life of addiction to anything to help him focus or rest. As the addict Torben knew best, it had not been until the loss of his brother that Torben had seen Nik without any external substance in his blood. Since the day Jonni had been laid to rest, Nik had been clean as far as Torben knew.

How many weeks had that been?

Had Nik slept at all in that time?

To Torben's knowledge, no.

So this is the life Nik had been given to lead.

Footsteps in the corridor stopped outside the open door. Torben did not need to turn to recognize the young woman's scent. He could feel Oasis' gaze on the back of his head.

He stepped away from the bed. Oasis hesitated, unspeaking, before quietly stealing away. What did she see? What did she think? Torben had not thought to ask. For the moment, Nik was fine. Still clean. Likely the healthiest he had been in more than a decade.

But so long as he slept like the dead, he was vulnerable. So long as he slept, until the Laedan's return, LaGuardia was vulnerable too. Nik had chosen the worst time to sleep but, Torben thought grimly, some things could not be helped. Not the way Nik's parents had tried to help at least.

Until Nik opened his eyes, it would be Torben's duty to protect him…and LaGuardia too…though he had no idea how to accomplish either when responsibility drew him often away from the Fortress.

Perhaps it was time to change that. Perhaps it was time to let go of his past and look to a new future.

He did not think he was ready for that choice.

❧*❧

Stomach churning, lungs still struggling for air, Quentin wiped the back of his hand across his mouth, wincing at the stinging pain as he steadied in the saddle. The blisters around his lips and nose were diminishing but wiping the rough fabric of his hemp and leather gloves across them rubbed the healing skin, burst the remaining blisters, and reawakened the rawness there he could not explain.

Uzzi's man Dink called it an allergic reaction to something he must have eaten, something that twisted his stomach into knots, preventing him from eating and filling his lungs with a stuffed cotton sensation that made each breath feel inadequate and labored and left its mark along his lips, cheeks, and nose.

It was either that or else, as the doctor said, it was the result of something explosive in the fire that had sparked and fallen upon his skin. He had heard about the explosion. He had seen the containment trench dug around the fire.

He was not, however, convinced either explanation was true.

Reluctantly he accepted the bitter unguent the medic provided, a paste whose aroma eased his breathing and whose substance sped the healing of his skin. Dink, likewise, offered something to settle his stomach long enough for him to believe riding was possible. It impelled him to travel again, but neither curative eased his suspicions.

Uzzi had been gone too long that night. Who was to say the state he was in, the fire's explosion, and Mori's death were not Uzzi's doing? Others swore to his being in camp at the time, at his fire, that he was there when the shadows brought death and assault. Considering how many of those traveling with them had come at the merc's request, how many had worked with Uzzi and served him before, Quentin was certain some would lie to protect the older man.

Perhaps they all would.

There was only one reason to believe them. He only trusted Uzzi because he held the man's leash. As long as he knew a truth that would be damning if it was used, Quentin did not think Uzzi would be fool enough to act against him. Kill him, perhaps, but not dole out such an impotent attack as this one had been.

It was either a thwarted attack by outsiders it was thought the explosion had scared off, or there was a threat closer to home.

Someone he trusted less…such as the Cana still leading their way, perched atop a crumbling half-wall where he could see ahead of them and around the corner of the side street they were about to cross. Quentin did not speak wolf. He did not think Uzzi did either. But with a single yip and a leap from the wall that took the black-brown wolf out of sight, Uzzi nodded and said, "That way," with a gesture directing the company to turn the corner and follow the wolf.

"Better know where he's going," Quentin grunted, a sentiment he seemed to repeat too often since the onset of their journey, before turning on his saddle to retch.

Uzzi did not look at him as he said, "He knows. Trust me, he…"

"I don't trust anyone."

Heels dug into his horse's flanks, Uzzi trotted ahead to hide the faint smirk twisting his lips. Nor should you, he thought. I wouldn't trust me either.

❧*❧

"Any idea who she is?"

The sketch artist turned the image she had drawn around so Ernest could see it more clearly in the flickering glow of the portable lamps used to illuminate the Protectorate since the storm. Many of the lines linking some borough structures to the power grid fueled by the Plant had been damaged. While supplies were scavved for repairs and the replacement of damaged wire continued, many throughout the borough were forced to resort to more ancient, common methods of lighting and heating. What caused suffering for some was a boon for those who provided such substitutes.

For Ernest, it was one more frustration atop so many others that he barely thought about it except in moments like this when he was trying to study details his tired eyes found less easy to ascertain.

"None…but I think she's important."

The Protector at his elbow, a mid-grade officer who had been on the force for nearly six years and who had stepped in to fill the vacancy Pubby's absence created, retorted with a snort. "Someone come in out of the storm's hardly…"

"Don't think she planned to be there." Ernest felt damn sure the fellow wanted Pubby's place. He was also sure the fellow wanted his chair too. "Call it gut instinct. Wasn't watching me for nothing."

"Protector Chief in an addict's den…I'd say that's reason enough for anyone to watch you."

The man had a point. It did not ease Ernest's suspicions.

The user Ernest had brought in had not given them information they could use, not about Asan, not about Brac, not even about her usual source of supplies, most of whom had been picked up for questioning in the days before and after the storm and were detained to squeeze supply and draw out Asan or others from the underbelly.

"Maybe…maybe not." Ernest set the cold cup of tea aside. It smelled days old and tasted bitter, causing his stomach to churn. Better not finish it, he decided. It was a poor substitute for the empty bottles in his office anyhow. "But I want everyone to keep an eye out for her. Whoever she is…I think she knows something we can use. I want to know what. Find her, bring her in alive. No accidents, understood?"

A chorus of "Yes, Chief," "Yes, sirra," and bobbing heads followed him to his office. Too many of late, innocent and less so alike, had died in this hunt. Some from overdose and withdrawal, some from the actions of his Protectors.

Some from the hands of people like Quentin and Donnovan, men who appeared to have vanished from the borough. One at the hands of the Protectorate Chief.

Ernest intended no more to die until he got his hands on those two men…and on the ones who reaped blood from the streets and fed it plasm in return.

❧*❧

The brief periods spent with the group, watching Jia cater to Vance and Pubby, seeing to their injuries, aiding the slow progress along often empty or scarcely populated streets, gave Kato the internal excuse for falling further behind.

The external excuse was one he could not voice without suspicion.

"Watching your back," he had grunted the last time he had crouched at the campfire with her, sharing the succulent drippings and lightly seared meat of the wild boar QiangXu had caught. Some food had been gleaned and kept from the vicinity of the hospital camp, but much of it had proven too old, inedible, tainted by the metal or plastic in which it had been stored and the ravages of too many decades.

The boar was a welcome addition that could be stored in the cold and eaten for a handful of days ahead.

Kato averted his eyes when Jia looked at him, took the portion of meat he was offered, and retreated into the shadows of nightfall. She did not believe him.

The mage who refused to look at him did not believe him either.

But the lie, partial as it was, and the souring of jealousy fading a little as hours passed, were the only truths Kato could share. Who would believe his long-lost father was there in the company of the enemy? Who would not, with such knowledge in hand, question Kato's loyalty to the company and its mission?

It was not his mission. Fort Hamilton had never been his mission in the way it was for the others. He was here for Jia, to protect Vanya from the sort of people who would use a large collection of weapons against people like her, like Jia, like the pack who had taken him in. If not for them, he would likely not be here, would likely not care. He could avoid such threats and by now, if he had not found the Flushing Pack, would have been far across this section of Waste to somewhere men like Hallister, Channon, and the leaders of HOPE could not reach him and his sister.

If not for any of them, however, he and Uzziah might never have found each other.

Remaining always upwind, Kato drifted to within range of the group traveling far enough behind now at a slow enough pace he was unconcerned with his companions being caught unaware. Telling himself he wanted to be sure the group stayed together, be sure Pain had not left them to hunt Jia, be sure Quentin had not been left behind or gone ahead alone, Kato approached near enough to pick out individual scents but never near enough to see them or to be seen by them. He heard their discussions about the delay. He heard the muttered rumors in anxious, fearful voices.

Whatever had made Quentin sick enough to delay them had not prevented him from traveling for long. As soon as he found the strength to force himself into the saddle, they pressed on.

Another nightfall brought the panther to the flat rooftop of a strip mall once crowned with apartments but now empty except for a single huddled family with children crying in the cold. The arrival of strangers, men and women with horses the family had never seen before, with weapons they recognized in function if not form, made the family afraid to search for wood for an evening's fire.

They were suffering because of it.

Kato suspected most of the group, except for perhaps Pain and Quentin, did not know the family was there.

Quentin did not likely care.

Kato watched the ruffs build fires. Without rain for the past several days, finding burnable materials was easier than it had been and though it was cold, there was no need to take shelter in structures that might not be sound, within walls that would muffle the approach of enemies or spies. Quentin had learned a lesson from the last rainfall. Kato counted six people on watch around the camp's edge.

The children cried louder.

Quentin looked up at the broken windows of the building across the street and frowned.

"Someone shut them up."

Heads turned but no one moved.

No one except Kato, who growled, snapped off two thick limbs from an overhanging dead tree with his full weight as he jumped on them, and with the branches carried awkwardly in his mouth, not heeding any attention the sound might have reaped, found his way into the building. The branches clattered as they dropped against the door of the occupied apartment. The people within did their best to muffle the children's cries as if expecting an imminent attack.

Kato did not linger. Eventually, the residents would open the door and find the wood. They would know what to do. The branches might not burn long but what warmth they would give would help the children stop crying long enough to sleep. They would be more comfortable. They might stay safe from Quentin's threats.

৯*৯

"Of course, you have the right to question the legitimacy of the Chief's direction," Oasis said, her expression mirroring the queasiness in her stomach despite her efforts to portray calm, confidence, and poise to the parade of petitioners who had come to the Fortress today. Others waited in the anteroom, faces she did not know any better than she did the man with the captain's insignia on his Protectorate coat in front of her, but she assumed they, too, were people of status.

Lowell would know each one. Perhaps Nik too. But neither they nor Donnovan was available. Oasis had to rely on her perceptions of each, her judgment, to direct them, in the hopes that doing so would prove her to be a sounder and more reliable leader than the man Lowell had left in charge.

Her alliance with Nik was crucial. Stealing the Laedan's seat from him, however, was a path still on the table.

Her statement was interrupted by the recognizable echo of Torben's heavy boots and she frowned when Captain Mallo turned to see who had entered the chamber.

"Sposer Moller." The elderly captain of District 3 was visibly surprised to see the man in the Fortress, not dressed in the sposer coat and coveralls but rather in a set of dark trousers and dark, pressed, button shirt that gave him an uncustomarily formal appearance.

Oasis, too, scowled at the man's atypical attire, an expression that darkened when Torben gave a slightly awkward bow and said, "Laedan Channon is indisposed. If you will come back tomorrow…"

"He's returned?" began Oasis, standing from her chair in surprise.

"Not the elder Channon," Torben corrected. "The younger."

Captain Mallo's surprise turned into a presumptive sneer.

The shadows crossing the sposer's narrowed eyes made the captain shuffle awkwardly, the sneer abruptly falling away. He might have been a Protector all of his adult life, a man used to facing a rough and fierce world of violent threats, but he was also an old man who wanted to live to enjoy retirement. A fight with someone the size of Torben Moller was not worth the effort it took to consider it.

"He's sleeping," Oasis casually corrected Mallo, as if attending to daily business was her normal function in these abnormal times. "The loss of his brother and mother…"

Captain Mallo snorted, a sound conveying as much annoyance as disbelief in the explanation. While having daily petitions tended by the wife of the District 3 mayor was uncustomary, it was a shift he believed he could work in his favor in the Laedan's absence, a more favorable shift than petitioning Nik Channon might have been.

Donn would have agreed with his request, agreed that, though redirecting resources from general law-keeping to a hunt for plasm dealers, was laudable, leaving District 3 with a shortage of manpower in other areas was not. Mallo had come seeking an exemption he had not thought Nik would grant in the absence of his brother-mayor. Finding Donn's wife on the chair had given the captain hope she would be more amenable.

"Tomorrow?" Mallo said, his tone more a statement than a question. "I hope he will see me; this is a matter of urgency…" Donn's unexpected absence was a source of concern to everyone in his district. Mallo most of all.

"If he cannot, I will…" Oasis began.

"If he cannot," grunted Torben over her words, "it can wait."

Captain Mallo resisted the narrowing of his gaze at the sposer, as if he would challenge a man he thought had no place here. Instead, he squared his shoulders and started out of the room.

"Send the others away," Torben said after him. "There will be no more of this today."

The chamber door ricocheted closed.

Oasis, with her shoulders drawn back, stepped from the platform, hoping her steps and manner looked forceful despite being hampered by nausea and indignation. "You don't have the right to…"

Her contained fury did not faze Torben. "Nor do you."

"Lowell said…"

"He left Nik in charge.

"With me in support…"

"Support. Not usurp."

His choice of words made her blink as if the notion had never crossed her mind as she filed away the realization that the lowly, menial sposer was either smarter, more observant, or more paranoid than she had given him credit for.

Perhaps he was all three, or else had been feeding off any diet of conspiracies Nik had fed him. Perhaps he was the one doing the feeding.

Any of those things could be dangerous.

"I want what's best for LaGuardia," she countered with a sniff and uptilt of her chin that belied the congenial tone of her words.

"You want what is best for yourself…as any mother would. I won't let you hurt him. You or anyone else. He's been hurt enough."

Her chin dropped. "I don't want to hurt anyone." The only one she desired to hurt was Donn…and in the style of a petulant child, her father too.

Torben nodded once. "Good. Don't…and we won't have a problem. Leave LaGuardia to the Channons and…"

"I am a Channon."

Torben held his breath for a moment before exhaling with another nod. "Leave LaGuardia to Nik until the Laedan's return. Everything'll be fine."

They held each other's gazes for several moments, each trying to read the thoughts kept masked behind their eyes. It was the churning of her stomach that eventually made Oasis relent and mutter, "It better be," before stalking out of the room with steps she hoped appeared more defiant and determined than she felt.

Chapter 35

L ed by the incoherent ramblings of one of the users his officers dragged in for questioning, the low, single-story structure appeared unremarkable from the outside, something of brick and metal Ernest had passed hundreds of times during his tenure as a Protector. He would have likely passed a hundred more times before retiring without questioning the nature of the work underway inside. The daily business of LaGuardia's citizens was none of his concern as long as no laws were broken and the owners or employees did not attract negative attention.

The people occupying this place never had.

He could not guess what sort of place the structure had been before the Undoing. A store, an eatery, or some sort of service provider for the city's busy population. There were no signs, old or new, and the door and walls on either side of it were windowless, unassuming. Faint yellow light bled into the street around the sheets of hemp plastic used to cover where the previous glass of its single window had been broken out, but there were no other windows or entrances on the street façade and no escape exit on the side in case of fire. Without the hum of an oil generator to feed them, it was likely power from the Plant fed into the building, but Ernest could not see the lines for it from where he stood.

If there were other ways in or out through which their reported questionable product was moved, Ernest could not see them from the shadows on the side of the street where he and one of his officers waited. The building was surrounded by six Protectors in inconspicuous clothing on each of the other two sides and another four perched with bows or firearms on the surrounding rooftops. Ernest had not scouted those sides. Another officer had done so. If there were any paths of egress, his officers had them covered.

They had been there, in the chill, since before sunset, moved into place when their passing along the street blended in with the flow of others trudging home in the fading light of evening. There had been no rain or snow since the miraculous spread of blue had pierced the cloudy veil but winter's grip still held, its wind carrying with it the distant aromas of bubbling stews, baking bread, and roasting meats and potatoes the Protectors here were missing as they waited for the suspected activity. So far only one had gone in, someone with a key who unlocked the door and left it slightly ajar so that, minutes later, another, differentiated only by the differing cut of their weather-worn cloak, could go out.

The door closed with a click.

No silhouettes moved behind the window sheeting.

Two people, however, did not constitute illicit activity.

When the sun's glow left the cloud cover a dark, sooty gray, other cloaked figures began to sift out of the shadows, providing a syncopated four-knock pattern that prompted the door to open each time to allow them inside.

They never passed the window.

The officer next to Ernest looked at him questioningly.

Ernest shook his head and continued to watch.

Ten in all, with no sign of how many might already be inside. No one else had come out. The chief was not sure he liked the odds.

The eventual clatter of wagon wheels divided their attention between the door and the small donkey cart dodging potholes as it jostled through the pitted street. A wagon without a seat, with two figures on foot beside it, bundled against the frosty air. One led the donkey by the harness around its nose while the other had his hand on the crated contents in the bed as if to prevent it from spilling out.

They could be scavs. They could be deliverers from any other business in town. They could be anyone. But when they stopped at the door Ernest was watching and gave the same four-knock sequence, and the door opened to expel six individuals to unload the contents, Ernest decided it was the best chance he was going to be given.

Guilty or innocent, the Protectors had to act.

"Put it down!"

The wagon drivers ran in opposite directions. A whistle from the chief sent Protectors in pursuit. Three of the six attempted to get the crated cargo into the building, to close the door behind them, but the officer at Ernest's side made it to the door before it closed and muscled it open with a shove of his elbow and shoulder. Other officers pooled in behind him, dodging the gunfire two of the workers set off.

One of the rooftop snipers got one. Someone tackled the other shooter as Ernest grabbed the frightened donkey's lead and kept the animal from bolting and scattering the rest of the contents across the frozen road. The last worker stood dazed with a crate in his arms as if he expected to be invisible to the invading Protectors if he did not move or else did not have the will, or courage, to run or fight.

There were sounds of hostility inside, shouts and punches thrown, and the crash of breaking furniture, shattered glass. Ernest needed evidence, did not want it destroyed since he did not have Segara to investigate, but his people had a right to protect their lives.

He wanted people to arrest. He wanted people to answer questions. People who knew what the shart was going on here.

The curious from nearby buildings peeped through windows to watch. A few braver souls came into the street and stayed gawking as the ruckus inside ceased and one of the officers stuck her head out the door and called, "Chief… better see this."

The donkey's lead was handed to one of the Protectors who had run from the farthest side of the building to join the action. Another began to load unopened crates from the ground back onto the wagon while a third tied the arms of the unresisting worker and pushed him belly-first against the side of the cart.

Everything was secure outside. The officers who pursued those who fled would either return with them or return empty-handed. No need to follow them. Ernest preferred to see what his people had found inside.

Nine men and women, five dead and four sporting cuts and abrasions, bloody noses, split lips, and the purpling of broken limbs obtained in the fight to subdue them were gathered on one side of the room. Ernest recognized and understood what the injuries meant.

The faint hum of a refrigeration unit, a buzz not heard from the street, exposed pouches of a yellowish powdery material he had never seen before. Some pouches were scattered across long tables where their contents were being combined with other substances and powders into final forms most experienced Protectors in the room recognized from busts and confiscations and the personal effects of addicts and odose victims they encountered every day.

Ernest glanced at the refrigeration unit with a grimace. He would need a chemist, his forepath…or Segara…for verification but his gut instinct told him enough.

It sickened him that something like this, the poisoning of the borough, the trade in anthro blood, could have been going on under his nose all of this time. But no longer. Not if he could help it.

"All of this…all of them…back to the Protectorate. Want this place so empty it's spotless." It would make it more difficult for the mage to eventually read, but he wanted nothing left here that anyone else could use. "Want to know who's in charge…where we can find them…and you," he pointed to two of his officers, "stay here and wait for whoever comes next."

Someone would, at the shift change. He wanted officers in place to detain those people too. There would need to be more than two officers on hand to do so; Ernest would send additional resources as soon as he got back to the office.

At the other end of the hunt, he expected to find the elusive Brac or at least someone with the scientific knowledge to accomplish this, to direct it, who could lead Ernest to the boss. Shutting this location might be enough to bring Brac into the open.

Ernest expected to have the man's head as soon as it was exposed.

৯*৶

The pair of horses slowed in passing, their riders so swathed in layers of cloaks, scarves, gloves, and head coverings against the cold that neither could recognize the other. But they gauged one another from the edges of the wide road, detailing the way they sat in the saddle, the way they handled the reins, the boots and color of the horse and the relative size of the other, with the intent of knowing those details to identify each other if they ever crossed paths again.

Norse knew he was not the only supplier of anthro to the doctor's business. He was not even the primary one. But as neither rider pulled a wagon or drew captives in tow, he could not guess what business the other had conducted with the woman who stood with folded arms in front of the burned outer skin of the lab.

It was none of his concern. Or would not be for much longer.

Debris was collected in scattered piles, potentially usable, potentially burnable fuel for the Plant furnace that sounded to be running, and useless or hazardous materials that would need to be hauled away to somewhere else if this facility was to resume operations. On one end of the building, the burned façade and the charred, empty maw behind had been peeled away to be replaced with material scavved from nearby structures, brought in on one of the ox-drawn flat carts parked nearby. The oxen munched calmly on a bale of dried feed grass, still wearing their harnesses, the delivery having recently come; as hastily as the unloading was conducted, it appeared the wagons would shortly be away in search of more material.

The Laedan had specified finding a new location for the handful of test subjects remaining.

Though the wall repair was needed to keep the winter out, Doctor Torrens, in Norse's view, appeared to have another plan in mind.

"Need more?" Norse asked as he slid off his horse before the animal stopped.

"You offering or you here to shut me down?"

Norse drew back his hood to expose his face, having nothing to hide, and shrugged. "Sent to see how you are, if you need anything, bring you this." He produced a rolled paper in a hemplastic tube and handed it to her. "Haven't seen them to know if they're suitable."

Gail grunted and took his offering, interpreting his words to mean the scroll contained a list of other locations for the lab. No doubt Lowell had done his due diligence on the properties he was offering and would only recommend ones suitable for the project or that could easily be made suitable. But the offer did not undercut the stinging reminder that he intended to shut the work down, despite HOPE's wishes, and that he might have initiated the attack on the lab to prompt her to cooperate.

No product moved. What life fluids she could extract from her survivors were processed and stored for eventual distribution but her stock would not last. She had no room for others and lacked the infrastructure for processing more even if she could get them.

"I'll look at them," she promised cagily. The crash and clatter of falling siding that billowed smoky dust into the air startled them and the oxen alike. The animals were quickly subdued by their handlers. The doctor, Norse noted without a change of expression, was not.

"I'll wait." It was his instruction, or part of it, and he knew Lowell's desire for a prompt response did not surprise her. "Anything I can do while I'm here? Anything you need? Shall I lend a hand?"

"Suit yourself." Gail stalked inside, her quick, short, perturbed steps conveying frustration she did not voice. What Norse did to stay busy was his business. She had her own to address.

☙*❧

"I insist you give me authority to act when you can't!"
Nik rubbed his eyes and looked up from the cup of hot tea and plate of toast he had devoured. Three days, he had been told, and his stomach demanded the nourishment sleep had deprived it of. The last thing he remembered was sitting at his bedroom window, staring at the sky, lost in private musings and memories of days when he, his brothers, and the Marrock siblings had been much younger. He did not know when or how he had been moved to his bed, or by whom, but the stiffness in his neck was a reminder of where he had been when sleep overtook him.

This day was gray as usual and without looking outside he could not verify if it was morning or evening. No matter the hour, the staff happily obliged his request for tea and toast and he felt better, stronger, for it, though not yet clearheaded enough to counter Oasis' demand with anything more than a perplexed stare.

"Fa said…" he began to mumble.

"I was there! You may be acting Laedan, but I have the right to…"

Brows furrowed, he interrupted, "To what? What happened?"

"If this is a regular thing…you asleep for days…someone needs to have the authority to act when it's necessary."

Gradually, her insistent, high-edged tone cut through the remaining sleep fog and Nik slowly turned his chair to face her. "Was there an emergency? Has something happened…?

Oasis responded with an exasperated sigh. There had been no emergency and any claim of one would be challenged and upended by the sposer when he returned to the Fortress. It would be a lie she could not maintain and thus was one she was too wise to lay on the table.

"Not yet."

"Then what?"

"There could have been," she huffed. "Mr. Moller wouldn't permit me to address simple requests…"

Not having seen Torben since waking, Nik did not know what she meant. The most he could offer was shrugged shoulders and a gentle, "I'm sorry. This sort of thing…I'm readjusting. He's right though; simple requests could have waited for…"

"For how long?" her eyes narrowed. "What if they hadn't been simple requests…?"

"That would be different."

"He interfered when he had no right to."

"I'll talk to Torben." Though confident the sposer acted in Nik's best interest, without speaking to him, Nik could not condemn or defend his actions.

"You'll give me my due!"

"Your due?" he asked, wondering what she believed she was entitled to, as his brother's wife and the daughter of Geary Hallister.

"Or I'll tell everyone what you are!"

They stared at each other, Nik assessing her defiance as she tried to judge the neutral expression he had mastered and maintained in his most intoxicated moments. The look prevented anyone from knowing how much he heard, saw, or comprehended. It was a look providing an advantage even when he was in no physical or mental condition to use it.

He shrugged. "Tell them."

Oasis narrowed her eyes.

"If you think they'll side with a Hallister over a Channon…if you think they'll believe you…"

"I'm a Channon…"

"By marriage…and you haven't proven your loyalties yet." She had endured his brother, she carried his child, but it would take time for the territorial people of LaGuardia to accept an alliance forged between boroughs by the marriage of Channon to Hallister. It would take time for them to believe she cared more about them than she did the people of Kennedy.

From the darkening shadows in her eyes and the way her lips pulled down at the corners, Oasis knew it too.

Nik shrugged and the traces of challenge that countered her defiance bled off into a gentler tone. "I don't want to fight. You've got rights. You've been through it too…we've been thrown into this until Fa gets back. He left the little stuff to me…the big stuff I guess too if it comes to that. Didn't ask him to…it's just how it is." He sat back and reached for the empty teacup. "I can't help when I'm awake, when I'm asleep…but I promise, I'll talk to Torben. If this happens again before Fa's back, leave the dailies to me. I'll get to them when I can. Probably haven't done a good job of it so far but I'll include you, inform you, so you know what's happening, so you're aware of things. So people see they can trust you. If something comes up that needs doing, that can't wait, then I'm gonna have to trust you too, to do what's right for LaGuardia, not just for you, and not," he sighed with disgusted frustration clogging the back of his throat, "for Donn…"

"He's my…" began her self-protective retort before she sighed as well and offered her hand. Donn was legally her husband because she had been brokered to make an alliance. Jonni, her intended, had refused to follow through and Donn had elected to take his place. Donn had never been her choice. None of what had come after had been her choice, only a series of decisions designed to help her survive and uphold promises she had made long ago.

Donn had turned on her. Her father too, in her opinion. Lowell was absent, mired in grief and the delusion of Fort Hamilton, and Thomas had slithered beyond the boundaries of a reliable ally as soon as the ink on the marriage treaty had dried.

Maybe even before that.

"Free me from him and my allegiance is yours."

"Don't want your allegiance." Nik shook his head before clasping her hand. "Rather be able to call you friend…family…think we can do that?"

She looked at his hand. A steady hand, not shaking with addiction, not seeking to take advantage of her, not coiled to strike. The novelty made her slowly nod.

"Yes."

The word was certain, the tone resolute, her expression bemused as though she was earnestly surprised by his offer.

But as she released his hand and left the room, Nik was no more convinced of her sincerity than he was of anything else about her.

Chapter 36

From the wide, semi-coastal parkway they followed, with trees as windbreaks against the sea and the back of homes on the other side, there were no barriers, no walls, nothing that appeared impenetrable to Aman as they reached the coordinates the Laedan had provided. The remains of a change loomed in the distance above a row of tall evergreens but nothing looked the way he imagined a fort should. He halted his thin unit, allowing them to rest as he dug through the waterproof pack kept protected and checked the map again. While still many blocks from where he thought they should be, with the expected collection of shops and homes at their flank, he thought he should be able to see the walls of their destination, see anything that could be considered formidable and protected.

There was nothing of the sort.

There were people living here in adequately maintained homes, more than they encountered accumulated together since leaving Kennedy, beleaguered faces watching from windows and doorways, people pulling scav carts or conducting dailies with neighbors in a mutual quest for survival. There were small boats pulled up to the doors, tied down against theft or possible storm waters, but the last storm did not appear to have caused undue damage here. They were not under the leadership of the Laedans but still had the appearance of a peaceful coalition determined to assist one another and survive. Their apparent quality of life was a stark contrast to the feral lands between Kennedy and LaGuardia or in any of the territories immediately adjacent to the boroughs.

How much of the wildness was a result of the Laedan's efforts to force order and compliance on people who preferred to govern themselves, Aman mused as he witnessed the exchange of a full cloth sack for a loaf of bread.

"Excuse me," he called to the two women ahead of them. "We're looking for…"

Startled rabbit expressions preceded the pair scampering into nearby buildings. Windows and doors banged closed. Those with carts left them where they were and hurriedly disappeared inside.

Aman frowned. Was it his voice? His language? His words? The strangers had seen and heard the group's approach. They had occupied the street for nearly thirty minutes as Aman sought to orient his bearings following the provided map. These people had known they were there.

Perhaps, instead, it was the repeating heated crackle in the air that tickled along his skin and into his ears, the precursor to the rattling boom erupting somewhere beyond the coastal copse. The breath was sucked from his lungs and the ground trembled more violently beneath his feet. Loose bricks, shingles, and other debris shook free and tumbled to the ground. The still unexpected, unfamiliar sound made his people startle again and ready their weapons for an assault from an unknown enemy who did not come. The barrage of falling material caused several to duck and jump away to avoid being struck. A few, unable to elude the debris, yelped or shouted in pain and surprise.

A sea threat? A great wave?

No threat fell. The air and earth calmed and stilled as it had every time the sound had come, but the people living in the nearby structures, seemingly familiar with the sound, did not reemerge. The sea did not slam the coast with its wrath. The rise and retreat of the waves continued unchanged.

"We should take cover for the night." If the residents continued to shelter despite the evening's silence, following their example to protect his followers seemed a wise choice, even if he did not understand their fears. "Walker, scout us a camp. Nua, take Heise and

Scott and see what's ahead. The rest of you, get us off the street. Stay clear of the buildings and keep your eyes open."

"Yes, sirra."

His soldiers dispersed. Aman kept his ears tuned to the sea.

❧*❧

Someone pointed out the scurrying figures in the shadows of the wilds at the end of the street, furtive movement causing General Warby to raise a fist and bring his unit to a halt. The volatile force that shook the air minutes before as it had done multiple times over the past several hours, prompting their hesitation, was the only thing that seemed to clear the blockade of locals from their path.

"They're already here."

Warby snorted at Channon's unnecessarily voiced observation. He had interacted with Kennedy's troops, on both sides of fights more often than Channon had years of life. He had known from the outset that they were likely racing against Hallister's people and as Kennedy's reach extended along much of the already explored southwestern coast, Warby presumed they would have an easier road to travel to get this far, despite the foul weather that would have hindered them too.

He frowned as he watched the shadows, however, motioned a scout to the scene, and waited for a signal to be sent back.

No one was there.

Pathfinders. They could have moved further into the wilds. Crossing into them, into the glare of sunset and the darkness to follow, was not a risk Warby wanted to take, despite Donn's nervous fidgeting.

Assuming the Hallister scouts knew they were there as well, gauging the position of the sun with a hand at his eyes, he grunted and muttered, "We camp here." This spit of land, once manicured but now overgrown with no one available to see to its upkeep, would provide suitable shelter and nooks for rest, as well as trees for the night's watch to spy from in case Hallister's moles brought back trouble.

"But we're…"

"This look like a fort to you?" Warby snorted at Donn.

"Could be a small one, beyond the trees, beyond the wilds." An apparent lack of size did not reduce the importance of what it was rumored to contain. "If Hallister's got people here, we've got to…"

"When the sun's up…"

Donn snagged the halter of the general's horse and yanked the animal closer. Warby grabbed Donn's wrist with a grip that made the younger man wince but he did not release the halter.

"This is my mission," he hissed.

"I don't take orders from you." Warby took orders from only one man, or one collection of men. He might have been sent to serve at Donn's disposal, but he would not endanger his team on the whims of an untested Laedan's son.

"You wouldn't be here without me."

"You wouldn't be here without me," Warby threw back.

Donn sneered. Both avowals were accurate but he did not have to admit it. Instead, he countered, "They'll come for us. If we wait…"

"They won't be stupid enough to challenge us." Anyone Hallister had put in charge of his retrieval team would not be so foolish.

"They," Donn said with a wave at the buildings around them, "don't know who we are." They traveled without banners, without uniforms, so unless those scouts were lucky, they would not know who they had encountered. Donn had been willing to fight through any locals daring to challenge them when he had believed they were too far off from the fort for it to be in their grasp. With the possibility of a confrontation with Hallister, however, Donn thought it wiser to save their strength, their number, for that fight instead.

"What if we combine forces with Kennedy?" someone offered, someone unaware of the stakes of their game.

"No." Both Warby and Donn cut off the suggestion at the same time. Their gazes held for several more moments as they accepted that they agreed on that point though they agreed on nothing else. Warby released Donn's wrist.

Donn let go of the general's horse.

"Daybreak," Donn grunted, acquiescing only because it seemed temporarily prudent to do so.

"Whatever's there, we find it together…for the glory of HOPE."

The corners of Donn's lips twisted as he nodded.

HOPE's glory…and his own.

∻*∻

Squinting at the faded sign in the failing light of day, Lowell turned his horse in the direction Captain Ortega was staring. They had skirted the edges of the wilds to their left for the last few days unhindered since their brush with the Fela at the wilds' northern edge. Corroded street signs designated their overgrown path as 7th Avenue, a path the Laedan swore would take them directly to their destination. That path, however, came to an abrupt end.

The sign hanging above them, held to the street post by a rusting chain, supported the Laedan's claims. But nothing Ortega or anyone else could see, suggested the existence of a fort.

No walls. No fences. Only a portion of wilds to their right, surrounded by a cracked, paved oval, and the curve of the road to the left flanking the southern edges of the wilds they followed.

Streets and structures lay ahead, unknown, unexplored, providing LaGuardia's team little means to protect themselves if they pressed through the dark, little trustworthy shelter to shield them from an enemy's approach. At least at this intersection, where the view was unobstructed on each side far enough to form a defensible perimeter, with attentive men and women on watch, they might see any threat that came at them.

More than the setting sun, however, it was the Laedan's gradual slide from his horse that prompted Arlo to stop where they were. He quickly dismounted to catch the older man before his legs buckled and he fell to the ground.

"Good place to camp," the captain instructed those closest to him. Though exposed to the wilds on the east and the unknown ahead of them, the intersection was wide enough for hem and the pavement, splintered though it was by nature's efforts to reclaim the land, was relatively dry and retained enough of the day's heat to make for a reasonable degree of comfort.

"Need to get in there, see what's…" Lowell's hacking cough began again.

"We need sleep," Arlo murmured, expressing a need for the entire group rather than pin the weakness on the Laedan's ego. Others were coughing and swaying too. There was no dishonesty in his assertion. He wiped bloody spittle from the corners of the man's mouth and though Lowell frowned at the fussing, he did not pull away from it. He was too weary for that. "Hot tea and a night's rest will give us a clear day to investigate. If anyone's there, it's best if we can see them."

Lowell snorted and sagged into a cross-legged position against his horse's leg. The animal remained still. "She'll be there. She promised. I have to get back; I promised her…I promised…"

Arlo pushed Lowell's pack, handed to him by another, into place behind the man's head and helped him lay down upon it. "You'll keep that promise, Laedan. In the morning."

Lowell mumbled something, a name or words of vows long past, and drifted into a slack-jawed, raspy-breathed slumber before the people around him finished unburdening their horses.

࿐*࿐

Despite Uzzi's argument against continuing south through the wilds to spare Enola the discomfort of the path through overgrown vegetation, despite Pain's warning of an impassable marshland in their way, Quentin insisted on pressing forward along the straightest path. His certainty of a conspiracy, that they were being tailed by LaGuardia's forces…likely led by Donnovan, for who else could it be…kept him focused on avoiding detours that might delay them and permit someone else to reach Fort Hamilton first. Not even the fetid stench in the air that caused his nose to wrinkle in distaste deterred him. They rode with their mouths and noses covered, ignoring swamp flies and the cawing cackle of crows in the trees.

Pain knew that smell. He refused to lead along a path he advised against and instead did his best to remain as far to the eastern side of the party as he could. The wilds' edge was not so far away. They could travel there and be free of what awaited them if they continued through this forsaken stretch of vaporous bog. The cover of mossy trees stripped the evening of light too early, and despite the oil lamps and rag-wrapped torches some carried, there was not enough light to see the hazards around them.

The Cana's restlessness held Uzzi back too and with him, Enola and Dink. The dog whined and wove a zig-zag trail between the three slowing horses despite Dink's efforts to calm him.

The path narrowed for several dozen feet before opening into a black clearing of rotting, leaf-covered ground. Nothing grew at its center and the trees at its furthest edges tipped precariously inward as if being pulled towards the darkness. Some had already fallen so the topmost branches and portions of their trunks appeared submersed in the leafy accumulation where they had landed.

"Don't like this," Uzzi muttered.

Enola snorted and stopped her horse beside his. "Never did."

"You never do," teased Dink, though his pensive expression supported no mirth.

At the front of the column, determined to be the first to reach the fort, Quentin heeled his horse's flanks to urge it forward. It reluctantly started across what appeared to be a solid path, only to pitch forward and sink into the mud up to its front knees.

Quentin's tight-legged grip, his firm hold in the stirrups, and the reins wrapped around one hand and wrist were the only things that prevented him from being thrown into the muck.

The horse whinnied in alarm, a sound growing more panicked as it struggled but could not pull free. The harder it tried, the more frantic it became, the more powerful the suction of the mud around its hooves.

Enola, despite her fear of the wilds, was the first off her horse. She freed the coil of rope hanging on her saddle and formed one end into a loop. She might hate the wilds, but she knew horses. Judging by the inactivity of the others, no one else did or else they were too afraid and confused to try.

"That side," Enola shouted with a gesture. "Quentin, get down."

"I'm not getting into that," Thomas retorted in disgust.

"She means get out of the way," barked Dink, following Enola's orders without dismounting to create a second looped rope on Quentin's other side. Most watched, uncertain what the pair was doing or how they could help, while the Cana paced the swamp's perimeter, teeth bared, ears flat to its head.

Uzzi was sure he and Pain were thinking the same thing.

This would be an ideal time and place to be rid of Quentin.

"How am I supposed…?"

Enola threw the looped end of her rope. The twisting thrashing of the horse's head and Quentin's bent form hugging the animal's neck resulted in the loop slapping into the mud, splashing it in Quentin's face. He coughed and wiped the offensive-smelling goop from his blistered lips and nose, and despite the aborted protest he had been about to make, he understood.

Her second try, once Quentin leaned as far back as he was able without falling from the saddle, was better aimed. The loop slid around the horse's head and tightened, when Enola pulled, around its neck. Despite his warring expectations for this moment, Uzzi nudged his horse forward and used his weight and the strength of the horse to keep the struggling trapped one still. The effort enabled Dink to make a successful binding throw. Keeping both ropes taut, working in tandem to pull with encouraging words, they were gradually able to ease the stranded horse out of the mud, and back onto solid ground.

"Smells like death."

Quentin muttered back as he slid off his horse's heaving sides to stand, shaky-kneed, bent forward to catch his straining, frightened breath. Uzzi could have said more, could have pointed out the error made in following this wilds' path in the dark against the advice of their guide, but he decided to keep his thoughts quiet.

The sound he made was near enough to an 'I told you so,' for Thomas to look for something with which he could strike.

Uzzi was beyond his reach. There were no weapons available nor anything he could have used for one. Behind Uzzi, the Cana continued to snarl and growl. Thomas wanted to lash out at him too, lash out at anyone in his anger with his choices. He was younger than either of them, stronger he believed. More agile. As Fela, he could take Uzzi in a fight. The other Fela too.

With a host of witnesses who did not know his truth, however, he was not willing to take the chance.

Uzzi shrugged. "East?"

West was more wilds. The only way south was to go around the sucking swamp. East it had to be, unless Quentin wanted to return to LaGuardia empty-handed.

He reluctantly nodded without looking at anyone and climbed back onto his muddy, unsettled horse.

Uzzi nodded too.

The Cana growled.

East it was.

❧*❧

Finding the streets this far west of LaGuardia to be cleaner and less littered with destruction than those they were accustomed to, was surprising evidence that this corner of the world had either not been impacted by the Undoing in the same way or that the people here had made the upkeep of their surroundings a priority. People seemed fewer, grubbers too, as if the majority had fled or else been so severely impacted by the Undoing, despite their work to improve their living conditions, they had felt no reason to stay. The scent markings of anthro, however, particularly Cana, were frequent enough to prompt increased alertness. The higher-than-customary passage of mutani through these same streets prompted speculation that something had happened this far west to leave an imbalance in humanity, something that made Normals the minority and might have contributed to them abandoning this quarter of the ancient city.

Vance's steps were steadier, the slow pace of the first few days since leaving the hospital enough for him to push beyond the lingering boundaries of pain. Pubby, too, had set aside physical discomfort to move at the pace the group maintained. They made good time through the unhindered streets, untroubled by the people they passed, until the distant smell of the approaching sea intermingled with the faint scent of ozone suggesting the eventual onset of rain. There was a growing smell of oil fire too, but no evidence of such a thing brightened the sky and the swirl of the wind made it difficult to determine its origin. They traveled with an extended section of wilds somewhere to the west, the scents of trees and grass and feral things acting as a powerful lure to those in the group who had been too long without a run, a hunt, a giving in to their primal nature.

The mage saw it in Jia's straying eyes, in her restlessness, which often resulted in the turn of attention back along the path they had taken to get here.

Back in the direction of the Flushing Pack.

Or she sought the absent Fela who drifted further away for longer periods the further west they traveled. His absence was not enough to make her turn back to look for him, or to prompt her or anyone of the others to confront Kato when he did appear, but Vance was not the only one preparing for the inevitable.

Whatever that proved to be.

With the periodic explosive crackle of fire and a roaring sound growing louder the further they traveled, the street they followed dead-ended at a north-south intersection and a wall of trees and dense shrubs choking the path. To their left, as they crouched to listen to another booming blast in preparation for an attack that never came, was a children's playground overtaken by ivy vines and tall grass swaying to the push and pull of the gradually building gusts. The sun had set behind the trees, drawing a blanket of darkness with it, but the sound erupting out of the dark did not come from the clouds or the trees. Rather, it seemed to explode from the sea to the south where the sky was still bright.

When it came again, louder and more violent than before, the sound brought Deuce back to crouch, flat-eared and wary, at Jia's side. She looked at Vance and pressed her hand to the back of Deuce's head as she sniffed the air. With the wind blowing from the south, it was difficult to judge if they were being followed, if Nepo, Quentin, or Pain were on their heels but behind was not where the sound came from. She was forced to trust that if their enemies were there, Kato was far enough back to detect them and near enough to alert her.

"We need to know what that is," murmured Vance.

"There…up there."

Pubby pointed to a platform obscured in the branches of the trees on the opposite side of the playground. Jia expected to see the movement of someone watching them but there was only the sway of branches in the wind.

"I can climb it," Eddie offered eagerly. "I can see what's there."

Jia looked at Candace. The woman pouted, trusting her son's climbing skill but loath to thrust him into the path of unknown harm.

"I'll go with him." QiangXu offered his pack to Yu and after a permissive, if reluctant, nod from Candace, the man and boy slowly crossed through the grass of the playground, listening, watchful, with Deuce following behind them to watch from a protective distance when the boy scrambled up the trunk with QiangXu's help.

"A house!" Eddie exclaimed, his movement evident though obscured through the limbs. His exuberance was cut off with a yelp when another explosion shook the air.

"Can you see it?" QiangXu asked from the trunk's base. "Can you see what it is?" From the ground, the copse was too dense to see what was beyond it.

Yu, wrinkling her nose, murmured, "Smells like petroleum." She had not been able to identify the smell before, but the shifting wind blowing in from the sea, or perhaps their proximity to the source, made the scent more recognizable.

"Hold on…there's more platforms…a whole house…lemme see if I can look…"

Since the pitch and volume of the explosion had not changed from prior ones, did not draw closer or move away, and with no sense of anyone else in the tree with him, Eddie swallowed his trepidation and clambered from one platform to another until he reached the one on the farthest side of the cluster. By now, not even QiangXu could see him but his scent, though eager and excited, was unafraid.

"It's the sea," he finally called back with a note of disbelief. "The sea is burning!"

Looks passed among them, confused and wary, as a light rain began to dribble from the gray billows.

"Let's go up and look," Jia decided. The leafy branches would shield them from the rain, help mask their scents from anyone following them, and provide a vantage point to observe threats before they reached them.

She wanted to see the burning sea with her own eyes.

Chapter 37

Crouching at Eddie's previous vantage point, Jia pushed aside the branches so she and Vance could see the field beyond the trees and the ocean on the horizon. Another repercussive blast shook the air. Flames and black pluming smoke shot into the sky like a blossom of orange, white, and gold, erupting from the long stationary wreckage of a rusting, listing ship, setting the skyline aglow east and west and filling the glow with inky, greasy billows. The fire appeared to be contained to the ship, the burning fuel not yet spilled into the water. Jia winced and shrank back from the brightness, shielding her eyes with her free hand.

The shrieking wail accompanying the blinding glow this time, like a dying wild beast or a person in great physical distress, was more startling than the explosion. Those already in the tree, those climbing up, and Deuce, who elected to remain on patrol on the ground rather than go up because 'Cana do not belong in trees', sparked the night with their startled cries and frantic search for anything nearby that could produce such horrific squealing.

"Banshee," Pubby muttered through chattering teeth, wishing for the lost bullets so the guns he carried would no longer be useless.

"What's that?" whispered Eddie, unashamed to huddle against his mother with her protective arms around him and his around her.

"A female spirit left in pain," began Yu, her voice shaky despite her efforts to appear calm.

"A ghost," said QiangXu, more matter-of-factly than his wife.

"Ghosts aren't real," the boy snorted, trying to sound less fearful than he felt as if saying the words would make them true.

Vance swallowed his first thoughts and cocked his head to listen to the trailing echoes of the disembodied voice, a wail that diminished into a moan and then into silence. For a mage, the ghosts of those who had been, the afterimages of life left behind, were real. But this was different, something other, he had never heard before, and nothing in the air, in the pattern of droplets on leaves and the planks someone had installed in the treetops for children to play on or as an outlook post, suggested what it could be. "Sounds real."

"Maybe we shouldn't be here."

He glanced at Pubby. "Didn't think you the superstitious sort."

"Not superstitious…but I'm the first to admit there's a lot of crazy shart I don't understand. Whatever that is…it doesn't sound good."

"It's a long way off." The faded echo had come from far enough away that Jia did not believe it was a threat. "But we should stay alert. This is a good place for the night. We'll go on in the morning."

Vance's shaking head made her scowl but her decision was made. They seemed safe, safer than they would be on the damp ground, and more comfortable than being directly in the rain. There could be no fire but they had food in their pack to last them through the night. An attacker could trap them here, perhaps, but she believed in Deuce's ability to warn them and protect them.

Kato's too, if the Fela was nearby…and willing to fight with them.

The possibility the scream was a feline death cry of the sort her father had once talked about was a prospect she refused to think about.

Kato was alive. Somewhere.

Another explosion out to sea stabbed the low-hanging rainclouds with flame. The deluge began. The banshee cry did not come again.

∽*∽

Though the explosions made Kato wince and freeze in a crouch, the black cat's ears turned one towards the sound and the other towards the camp he continued to spy upon, it was the shrieking that made his lips curl into a bared-fang threat aimed at the unseen unknown. He could not recall ever hearing a similar sound except for his mother's shrieks as the grubbers tore at her flesh and stripped life from her bones. Though he had not seen or smelled any grubbers in days, and the thoughts of his mother and sister had been stuffed down where they could not interfere with this journey, the sound brought with it a flash of memory that made him feel hot and ill. The fear that Jia had stumbled into a grubbers' nest to fall victim to the same horror that had taken his mother briefly prompted him to look back.

He was too far away to help her. If he went to her now, he would arrive too late and be forced to see her bloody final moments as he had his mother's.

He should be there. He should be with her.

As he should have been there to protect his mother.

The tell-tale traces of her scent on the wind that erased the shrieking cry, faint though both were, brought with it the scents of the others too, others who could protect her if necessary.

She did not need him to be there.

She needed him here, where Quentin's face tilted into the wind as if he could detect her too. His expression, like that of every person camped, was rapt with the horror the unfamiliar shriek birthed. Held back by Dink's hand on the braided cord around his neck, the dog pulled and whined but could not break free. Only Uzzi did not look up from the knife he held, did not appear concerned about the sound. His hand, however, quickened the pace of the blade sliding across the sharpening stone and the corners of his mouth and eyes creased.

If Quentin or Pain detected Jia, the two groups only hours apart, this was the place Kato needed to be. If Quentin or Pain did something unexpected, Kato intended to stop them.

Any danger closer to her location would have to be confronted by Vance and the others. Kato growled at the thought, not liking the challenge that represented, and crouched lower to remain out of Quentin's sight.

❧*❧

The shadow frowned as the pair of frightening noises faded.

Not that he would ever be called afraid.

The last person who had made such an accusation had been left as carrion for the insects, rodents, and grubbers.

He was not afraid but he was not fond of the unknown, the unseen.

Lavender eyes blinked away the rain.

The shadow continued on.

∽*∽

The reports of HOPE soldiers in position a long city block to the north, brought by the scouts he had sent, were no surprise. Aman was only surprised he had not crossed paths with them sooner given the delay the storm had caused when pushing him from the coastal road he had initially followed. The possibility that Laedan Hallister had sanctioned HOPE's movement through Kennedy, the knowledge that there could be a confrontation between them, rankled him and made Aman wonder once more if Geary had sent him here to fail, to die.

Not before finding the fort, of course.

Why would he do such a thing?

There were barely enough people with him to secure the northern flank of his camp. Others built fires and began to prepare their evening meal under the corrugated overhang which flapped and rattled in the wind. The covering did not keep out the sea wind, but a couple of resourceful women who had joined his unit along the way rigged tent canvas across the southern edge of the enclosure to keep out most of the wind and light rain as it continued to fall.

They were good people. They did not deserve to be out in this weather on a mission he had less and less confidence in.

The fire filling the air with a thick, oily smell, belched out of a tanker stranded far enough out to sea that it would not be a threat. Now and then, the ground shook with the force of an explosion that brightened the sky and spread the glow a little higher into the clouds. How long had it burned? How long would it continue to do so? Would the fuel and flame eventually reach the shore…and what would happen when it did?

Hands clasped behind his back as he watched, Aman frowned and turned his focus to those behind him.

The screeching wail that followed turned him from the sea, turned his attention from his troops so fast that he slipped on the damp grass and slid down the hillock until the windbreak trees blocked the sea and fire from view. Those in the camp erupted from it, weapons ready, wild-eyed and frantic.

Other than their bedraggled captain, there was no one to see. The locals had not emerged from their homes and in many of the windows, the lights glowing were abruptly extinguished.

A person? An animal? Some previously unknown anthro or an unfortunate mutani condemned to forever wail alone in the night?

No one knew. The not knowing, combined with the sea-fire's roar and the knowledge that HOPE was not far away, was going to make for a long night.

❧*❧

"Nothing we need to worry about."

They were camped too far inland, the air-rocking explosions too distant, for Donn to do anything more than lift his head when the sound rolled through their camp like waves over a rocky coast. He sneered and shook out his blanket in the hopes of getting a few hours of rest before their daybreak charge. His restless nerves were too on edge to allow sleep, but it had nothing to do with the explosions.

Their medic had disappeared several nights past, her belongings and her medical supply bag with her. No one had seen her leave, but with the score of minor injuries, aches, and pains the men suffered from, her absence, and the lack of supplies, were keenly felt. When her absence was first noted at daybreak, Donn stood firm on pressing on without looking at her.

They were close. Minor medical needs should not prevent them from reaching their goal. He was certain that, along with weapons, there would be medical supplies available. It was logical to believe there would be.

No man could be spared to find her. They needed every person they had if they were to succeed. She would return on her own. If not, if she was foolish enough to brave these streets alone, let her.

If she was a thief, stealing their supplies as she fled, Donn argued, they were better off without her.

The braided bracelet he had taken from her was clenched in his hand as he adjusted his pack beneath his head.

Her choice to leave was a weakness. It had nothing to do with him.

Even the frightening echo of the female-like screech that followed his words, his sneer, and made Warby startle and draw the long machete knife he carried on his hip, did not prompt Donn to regret his actions. He regretted her absence, but he felt no responsibility for it.

What the cry did, as the moaning notes were swallowed by the wind and rain, was remind him of another moan of surrender, the sound of a final breath choked off at the end of a plea for life beneath his hands.

His fist clenched with the memory of how her heat and breath had felt as it ceased against his skin. The bracelet he held bit into his palm.

"And that?" snorted Warby as many around him genuflected and began to pray for salvation from whatever demon or monster uttered that cry. "Suppose you don't want to worry about that either."

Donn shrugged, refusing to show how rattled the shriek made him. "Only thing we need to worry about is Hallister's men…or do you think we can take them?"

They were smaller in number, many lost to the ravages of the preceding journey. Warby had not risked sending a spy to locate Hallister's camp, but Donn expected the Laedan's force to be legion. HOPE would have to rely on speed and stealth and an early start to outmaneuver Kennedy. Warby thought it would be enough.

Donn did not.

"Someone trying to scare us. An alarm to keep people away from the fort." Why try to scare people away if there was nothing to protect, Donn mused, the thought increasing his certainty that they would find what they were looking for at daybreak.

Warby snorted. Donn could be right. But he was not going to sleep well without knowing what beast roamed the night with a cry like that.

❧*❧

Equally startled by the ungodly screeching arising from the cluster of buildings to the south and the Laedan's abrupt, upright lurching shout of "Yiva!" Arlo was unprepared for Lowell's unexpected leap to his feet and frantic dash towards the trees at the edge of camp. A few not occupied with erecting shelters against the rain set off in pursuit. Someone grabbed the man's arms only to have him slither free and stumble in his effort to scramble up a leafy incline. The pitch of it was enough to slow him, enough to allow another pursuer to sling their arms around his waist and bring him crashing into the wet debris on the forest floor.

"She needs me!" Lowell wailed as he was dragged into camp.

"He's delirious," the medic muttered, mixing something into a flask grabbed out of someone's hand. "We shouldn't be out here."

Inclined to agree but having nowhere convenient to go, Arlo held the Laedan upright so the flask could be pressed to his lips. Forced to drink the concoction, struggling feebly and pleading to be released, Lowell only began to calm when someone nearby said, "I'll find her," in a reassuring tone as the sleep agent began to take effect.

In Arlo's arms, Lowell's tension bled away and the captain sighed with relief. "Should sleep til morning," the medic said with a nod. "Should get him indoors, out of the cold and rain…"

"Not moving until we know what that was," snorted Arlo. "And I'm not sending anyone out there until there's light enough to see what we're dealing with. Tonight we watch him. Tomorrow we move."

Chapter 38

Unable to sleep, Jia watched the treeline, her attention on the wilds to the west and everything to the north from where a threat looked most likely to come. The rain had not lasted long but the wet sheen sprinkled over the ground and left dripping from the decrepit playground equipment was turning to ice as the temperature dropped. From their tree camp, Pubby watched the field to the south and the shadows of the buildings in the distance. Other than the continuing boom and sizzle of the tanker, the night was quiet.

"You know, there's something like a million ants per person?" Jia eyed the woman who had climbed from the tree to replace her on watch but did not immediately speak. Candace watched something crawl across her hand with detached intensity, something Jia could not see from where she stood. "Probably more now…since the Undoing." Candace shook the creature on her hand to the ground where it could find its way back home, wondering why it was out in the cold.

"That's a lot of ants."

Candace nodded. "Eddie showed it to me in a book in the library…he's fascinated with bugs."

"Lots of kids are."

Before tipping her head to study the faint glow of the moon behind the clouds, Candace nodded once. "You think he turned on us?"

Jia cocked her head.

Without looking at her, sensing the gesture more than seeing it, Candace added, "Pain."

Though she did not believe it was the question Candace meant to ask, Jia shrugged. "He challenged me twice…I don't know." Killing the alpha out here, where no one could take legitimate proof of the means of her death back to the Pack, was a possibility, although not one she believed Pain would take advantage of. His challenges had been legitimate enough to prevent her from killing him, and since his demotion, he had followed the rules of pack etiquette. Did he resent her? Was he biding his time?

He had been loyal to her father and she wanted to believe, differences aside, he would not side with Roland's assassin simply to assume leadership of the Flushing Pack.

Finally, she shook her head. "I don't think so…no."

Head tilted to sniff the air, listening to the shuffling in the trees above as bodies moved in search of warmth and comfort, Candace whispered, "Eddie's asking questions…"

"I don't know that either…" Jia knew the youngster's questions revolved around the only other Fela he had ever known, the one more and more absent of late. He wanted to know why, as Jia did. She could not give him an answer.

"Thought you and he were…"

Again Jia shook her head, letting her guard down in a way she rarely did. "It was…I thought it could be…possible…but now…I dunno…" There had been initial sparks of interest between them at their first meeting, sparks that continued to smolder although it had taken her too long, perhaps, to recognize them. The timing of their meeting, the events that had thrown them together and continued to agitate Jia's life, precluded any serious consideration of relationships for the foreseeable future.

There was only the Pack, the state of LaGuardia, her father, and the things Roland had sought to achieve left for her to sort out.

"Maybe once this is over…" She said the words, but she did not believe they held merit.

"You think he's coming back?"

Gauging that Candace's curiosity was as much on her behalf as it was Eddie's, that she too harbored some interest in Kato though Jia had not seen evidence of it before, she bit her lip, shoved the irrational flash of possessiveness aside, and replied, "For Vanya, yeah. He has to." He would not abandon his sister. Whatever his plan for the future, whatever his relationship with Jia, he would not leave Vanya behind.

A small smile sifted across Candace's face but she did not say anything more about Kato, did not ask about Jia's plans for the only Fela, other than Eddie, to be adopted into the Flushing Pack. "What do you think we'll find out there tomorrow?"

"Maybe nothing." Just because something was called a fort did not mean what they thought they would find would be there. Roland had never told her what he believed would be inside Fort Hamilton and had never written his suspicions down. He had never even spoken about the fort. Everything he had known had been taken from her before he could share it. Everything she knew about Fort Hamilton came from Hallister and the Channons. "Might be something we can scav…but I don't know."

"But not guns…right?"

"Right." Pubby had a right to replace what had been lost in the sinkhole. Jia had promised him his pick of what they found for his joining them on this journey. There might be something rare and valuable he might want or something worth bringing back to the Protectorate, or what others in the group might consider worth saving. Even the use of what they might find, however, made Jia anxious. If Vance thought it a worthwhile risk, she would consider permitting it.

But she made no other promises.

"Think Sirra Quentin'll fight us for it?"

"Absolutely." That was one thing Jia was certain of. Sensing Candace's uneasy shift in demeanor, Jia covered her hand tenderly where it was wrapped around the rusted chain of a swing. "I'll do everything I can to keep you and Eddie safe. You've got my word."

"I know." It was not Jia's fault Eddie was here. Candace had decided to stay instead of remaining stranded in LaGuardia or attempting to rejoin the Pack on the other side of the Flushing Wilds. If anything happened to her oldest boy, she could only blame herself.

"Get some sleep…I've got the watch," she murmured with a half-smile., a look Jia returned.

"Gonna try."

Vance rolled to his other side so Jia would not see he was awake when she reached the platform where the group packed tightly together to stay warm in their sleep. Maybe she could tell he was awake from the sound of his breathing, the quickening of his heart when she slipped into place beside him. Her back was pressed to his as if they might merge into one body and when her inhaled breath caught, his did too, expecting she would speak.

She did not.

The words he had heard burned in his ears, an acknowledgment, to him, of a choice made. He had accepted the inevitable before and still it seared the back of his throat and made him long for a drink to ease the ache. He rolled. His hand rested lightly on her side, below her ribs, carefully situated with gloves, blankets, and clothing between them. She mumbled and her breathing lightened, relaxed beneath his hand into a steady rhythm as the last tension of waking bled out of her muscles.

Whatever the future held, in this shared moment between them, his tension did too.

Ȕ*ș

The guttural rise and fall of gentle sawing that seeped into Lowell's ears felt faint and far away, indistinct and unidentifiable, as he sat and rubbed first his eyes, then his ears, to clear away the stuffed cotton sensation. He felt hot and cold at the same time, shivering and sweating, and he had no recollection of where he was or how he had gotten there. Bodies scattered around him as if dead, some beneath canvas tents, some wrapped in bedrolls that shielded them from the rain like corpses waiting for the sposer, and there was a wisping burnt smell carried by the blowing wind that made his stomach churn as he struggled weakly to his feet.

He should not be here. Yiva needed him. He had to get to her.

Her name and a whisper of a voice that tickled golden threaded trails through his memory, instinctively turned his body to face north.

He did not know it was north, only knew the wind pushed against his back and propelled him towards the swaying arms of nearby trees. Darting to and fro between the branches, small lights, like the summer glow-flies, bobbed in the dark.

Lowell reached for the lights but they were beyond his reach.

With shuffling steps he followed them, continuing to grasp at the glow with trembling fingers coming up empty again and again.

"See you, Yiva…I'm coming."

❧*❧

Choosing to ignore those to the north, to believe moving his followers before the sun crested the horizon was wisest, Aman started west in the dark, following the coastal road he had skirted since the start of his journey. The shattered pavement was slippery, encrusted with ice, the mud frozen so it crunched beneath their boots. A stealthy approach was impossible, made more difficult by labored breathing in the cold that misted in the frosty air and the annoyed nickers of the horses as they struggled to remain steady on their feet.

Along the edge of the overgrown expanse, following the curve of the ancient roadway that trees and the sea were gradually reclaiming, appeared to be a housing tract where no lights glimmered, where no traces of life arose to greet them. Not a fort, but he supposed any fort would require workers, serving staff, and soldiers as Kennedy's Fortress did, people to perform maintenance and clerical duties or fulfill other needs of those in charge. Such people would require housing and he assumed that was what they saw now.

There might not be light and there might not be detectable warmth, but it did not mean people were absent.

The fort had to be beyond the tract. Perhaps the walls had been breached before, during, or after the Undoing and dismantled for use somewhere else.

He would not know until he arrived.

"Be watchful."

Those behind him nodded and relayed the command to the rest.

HOPE was nearby. In true HOPE fashion, it would be impossible to know if they were friends or foes until they faced one another.

They had to be prepared for either possibility.

∾*∾

"There." Warby pointed across the low wilds between their camp and the structures on the horizon. The foliage seemed to end abruptly, giving way to either water or something manmade that could not be identified from where they stood. There were smaller structures to the left and something several stories taller on the right. Beneath the relative silence of morning, punctuated by gulls and the ongoing tanker burn on the rim of the world, there was the distant rumble of sound Warby identified as the movement of men. Possibly scavs. Possibly locals beginning their day.

Or else Hallister's team had gotten the jump on daybreak. The slight glow in the air hinted at the arrival of the sun but it was taking too long to sort his forces into units Donnovan was satisfied with.

They were all skilled men but the Laedan's son was infuriatingly picky.

Donn had no one else to blame if Hallister reached the fort first.

Donn understood, as he squinted against the light refracting off the ice on the ground and listened to those distant sounds. "Looks like the fort…I'll go…"

"Not without clearing whatever's…"

"You do that. I'm going…"

"You want my men, we start there," the general pointed mulishly. "We don't want an ambush…and we'll have a better survey point where we can evaluate the fort and make a plan."

Though he snorted his frustration, Donn reluctantly nodded. He listened to the movement of men to the south and wanted to breach the fort before Hallister's men could reach it. But there was wisdom in assessing the strengths and weaknesses of the fort, of those who might reside there, as well as the unit sent on Hallister's behalf.

The only reassurance he had was that Hallister's team was too far south to reach the fort without crossing them. He and Warby had time to arrive first if they moved now.

Maneuvering his horse to the front of the column he was to lead, Donn grunted, "Let's get in and get this over with."

&*&

Captain Ortega pulled his gloves on with a ferocity that would have ripped the leather if his fingers had been knives. "Thought you said he'd sleep?" he snarled at the doctor's anxiously wringing hands.

"He should have! In his condition, that much…"

Arlo snorted, cutting the doctor's justification off. There was no need to argue the obvious. Lowell had been weak, so disoriented that even unmedicated he should not have been able to wander from the camp unnoticed. Those on watch should have seen him leave. A hasty search of every tent and sleeping bundle revealed his absence as the others stirred with the cawing flight of ravens heralding the arrival of dawn. Someone found the Laedan's scarf on the ground between the camp and the wilds, the direction he had tried to flee the night before, with no trace of footsteps on the frosty ground and no signs of a skirmish. Arlo assumed the Laedan had wandered into the wilds towards home.

As thick as the trees and undergrowth were, in his delirious condition, the captain remained hopeful their leader had not gone far. In the frigid air, however, he also feared the worst.

"Esau, take the men ahead…building by building search. Don't engage any locals unless you have to. Find a staging point and wait for me. We'll join you soon as we can."

It had to be we. In Lowell's condition, Arlo would not leave him alone. He would not return to LaGuardia without the Laedan. If the day's perimeter search did not yield the promise of treasure Laedan Channon expected to find, it would be up to Captain Ortega to decide whether to press on or go home.

Esau, a wiry man all legs and arms, with a thin, craggy face, patchy graying hair, and sharp green eyes, nodded once and said, "Aye Captain. We'll find it for you."

They would find the treasure. Their captain would find the Laedan. Hopefully, both men thought with a handshake, both would be worth the effort and losses taken to succeed.

☙*☙

Vance was the last one out of the tree, having barely found the peace of slumber before Jia's hand on his shoulder brought him awake. Those gathered at the base of the trunk, bundled against the coldest day of their journey, passed around the last portion of bread. He accepted it from Pubby after adjusting his coat from the climb, broke off a stale piece, and passed it to Eddie who had finished tucking the ends of his scarf around his neck.

The creaking of wooden wheels rattled in the distance and eventually brought into view a hunched figure, stooped against the cold, pulling a two-wheeled cart with a loose wheel. Its contents rattled as it jostled over the frozen mud and cracked cement, the sound of glass containers bumping against one another. The individual stopped upon seeing them, seemed to assess whether the group was a threat, and as Jia murmured to the others, "Stay here," and left them, the figure started towards them as well.

"Hello," Jia called as brightly as the cold allowed, pulling down the cloth over her mouth and nose to reveal her face, hoping to use her deceptively youthful features to the group's advantage. There was no smell of anthro about the stranger, and bundled as they likewise were, it was impossible to tell the gender, age, or anything else.

"Not from around here, are you? Too cold to be out…"

It was a man's voice, raw and cracked with age and the effects of the cold. Jia chuckled and offered her hand when she got close enough to do so. "Cold out here for you too, I'd say."

"Man's gotta make a living. Wouldn't be interested in whiskey, would ya?"

"Hell yeah, we're interested," quipped Pubby who had followed behind Jia at a respectful distance with Eddie at his side, far enough back not to be a threat but near enough to hear the questions and appear protective of the smaller, more youthful figures as though he could be their father. "That'd warm us up for sure."

"Don't know what we've got for trade," she reminded him. There was the extensive array of medical supplies gleaned from the hospital, well worth their value for a trade, but she preferred to hold on to those as long as possible and to hear what the fellow needed instead.

"I can fix the wheel," Eddie offered, his voice hopeful, "if I can use the tools." There had not been much he felt able to offer before, but this was something he could do. He looked back at the others who gradually moved closer.

The old man hesitated thoughtfully but nodded and removed the divided crate of bottles from the cart. QiangXu delved through the pack for the tools saved from the lumber house and handed them to Eddie, who sat cross-legged on the hard ground and set to work.

"Maybe you could tell us the way to Fort Hamilton?" Vance asked, eyeing the bottle thrust into Pubby's hands as the other Protector uncorked it. The pungent smell of homemade brew guaranteed to have an excessive alcohol content made his heart race and his hands curl at his sides.

Gods, it had been too many days without a drink.

"You're in it," the stranger replied.

"We're…?" Candace looked around them, judging everything they could see. "There's no…"

"All the way from here to the sea…all along the road there and here…" The man gestured south and west, towards the roads t seen extending in every direction. "Out here's safe enough…but I wouldn't go to the heart. No one does. It's forbidden."

"Why's that?" Pubby wiped his hand across his mouth and handed the bottle to Deuce who had not yet changed to Cana form.

"Sickness in there…people go and don't come back…ghosts take 'em…and the monster."

"What sort of monster?" Ghosts Yu did not believe in, but since the Undoing, the world had become full of monsters.

Many said she and others like her, anthro and mutani, were monsters.

Many believed the Normals were the monsters.

"Is that what we heard last night? The screams?" QiangXu squatted next to Eddie and directed the fine-tuning of the cart wheel.

The bundled figure bobbed his head. "It's in there. No one's seen it…only shadows…but when it screams…someone dies."

Deuce snorted at the man's fearful, superstitious tone. "If no one's seen it, how'd you know…"

The bottle passed to Yu.

"What else can scream like that?" He shuddered. "Legend says there was a war…when Before ended…an accident. Water and the air got poisoned and the monster got loose. People got trapped." His shudder this time came with a shrug. "No one knows anymore, of course. All gone 'cept the screamer and the ones trapped underneath."

Vance took the offered bottle, his warring impulses causing his hands to shake. "Radiation?"

"Any sort of chemical disaster," Yu suggested. A military installation certainly contained many such deadly possibilities.

"That wouldn't explain screaming," Pubby pointed out.

"Some sort of grubber?" asked Jia.

QiangXu shook his head as Eddie righted the cart to test the wheel. "Any grubber from the Undoing wouldn't have lasted this long."

"Those going in, disappearing…could be them?" offered Candace as she helped Eddie to his feet.

"Think it's fixed." Eddie pushed the cart gently in the stranger's direction. The man pulled it back and forth and walked in a circle with it around his liquor crate. Though it still squeaked and chattered as it bumped over the pitted surface of the frozen road, the wheel no longer wobbled or threatened to come loose.

"Deserve another for that." He pulled out a second bottle and handed it to Jia. The first had ceased moving once it reached Vance's hand but he had not yet consumed any of its contents. "Dunno nothin' about grubbers…or radiation…"

She guessed from his pronunciation and use of the unfamiliar words that there was some other local name for the animated dead and the concept of radiation had died out with the educated population. His form of speech was simple, his manners plain, and despite his trust of strangers, she did not think survival out here, so far from the boroughs, could be any easier than hers had been.

"Only know no one goes there…beyond the fields…"

"We're looking for…" Jia began.

He shook his head fiercely as he put the crate of bottles back into the cart. "Nothing worth anything. Nothing at all. Whatever's there is best left alone." He turned the cart on its original trajectory and looked over his shoulder after a few steps. "Thanks for this…but I'm tellin' ya…only fools'd go in there."

"You're welcome," Jia called. To the others, after stashing the second bottle of alcohol in her bag for later use, she murmured, "We stay together across the fields; then, if it seems safe, we can split up to cover more ground. But stay careful…stay alert…"

"We'll be dead if we don't." Tools repacked in his satchel, QiangXu adjusted his gloves and head covering, meeting only Yu's gaze as he spoke.

Having given into the temptation of warmth in his belly, a burn that raced into his extremities and eased the shaking in his hands, Vance wiped his mouth and relinquished the half-empty bottle to Pubby, who sealed it and stuffed it into his pack. Vance met Jia's gaze with a nod, refusing to acknowledge the guilt of failure he already felt for having succumbed to the need for a drink.

"Shall we?" he muttered. The whiskey gave him courage. They had come this far. Turning back was no longer on the table.

Jia nodded.

"Guess that makes us the fools," Pubby chortled, gripping the strap of his pack over his shoulder.

"Not fools," Deuce countered, quickly stripping down for the change. He considered them cautiously determined. He clasped Jia's shoulder, entrusting what little he carried to her care, accepting any decisions she was forced to make, and then the Cana loped off in the direction the stranger had cautioned against.

Forbidden or not, it was where they needed to be.

❧*❧

From the rear, the primary building was imposing, sixteen levels that had not yet collapsed under the destructive weight of the Undoing. The other two buildings, the central one of seven stories and the northern one of five, appeared less sound, their structural integrity compromised by the overgrowth of ivy turning much of their façades a warm but frozen green. The tilt of their rooflines, where the ivy crept over like an invading army, suggested a crumbling that would have exposed the buildings' interiors. Many of the windows appeared intact, however, although the smaller structures at the eastern edge of the parking lot were littered with the abandoned relics of cars with windows shattered as though their occupants had endured combat. The combat did not appear to have spread to the buildings.

From the edge of the lot, Quentin studied the layout with a ponderous expression before asking, "Hear anything?"

His Fela hearing, muted as it was by his Normal ears, detected nothing except the pulse of the distant waves, the ongoing rumble that birthed sporadic explosions, and the labored breathing in the icy air of those nearest to him. Dink's dog sat at ease at the man's side, not agitated by potential threats, and their Cana guide had already disappeared, without undo concern in his movement, into the largest building in front of them.

If there was a threat there, a trap or ambush, Pain would be the first victim.

Quentin felt no remorse or guilt about the possibility only agitation that Pain might find the treasure first.

Uzzi shook his head. Having more experience in the world than Quentin would ever have, he was not surprised the man asked for his assessment. He was only amused that Quentin continued, in appearance at least, to trust his opinion, or to trust anyone after the sickness he had recently suffered. A more paranoid man would consider the episode to be an attack on his life and thus push everyone away. A more naïve one would write it off as an accident or the product of something he had eaten as the doctor had suggested. Quentin fell somewhere in between.

Or else he kept his suspicions and opinions to himself.

"Nothing out of the ordinary," Uzzi replied.

Quentin nodded, his expression still thoughtful. "You two," he pointed to Enola and Dink, "check those out." He gestured to the compromised, decaying buildings to the southeast. "Rogers, take a team of four north, there. Crandall, you and four take the center. Find anything…need backup…give the signal. If not, meet us in there."

In there. The largest building in front of them where Pain had gone. Quentin, Uzzi, and the two remaining men were heading there too. If this was Fort Hamilton, if the prize was in the largest, most dominant structure in the vicinity, it was no surprise Quentin wanted to be the one to find it with as few people at his side as possible to steal his glory. It made sense he wanted Uzzi near, to keep an eye on him, to prevent him from undermining his efforts or leading a coup against him, and, Uzzi thought with a frown, to take advantage of an opportunity to be rid of him when Enola and Dink, or anyone else, was nearby as witnesses or someone in the way to thwart him.

From the frown on Enola's face and Dink's pursed lips, Uzzi assumed they concluded the same.

"Yes, sirra," Crandall and Rogers responded, but not without side glances at Uzzi that Quentin, with his back to them as he continued to evaluate his destination, failed to see.

Uzzi expected they believed him to have the same motives in that small grouping as Quentin had.

He smirked and nodded to his friends.

They were right.

Chapter 39

Pants damp around the ankles from the melting moisture on the frozen grass they waded through, Jia halted at the paved intersection as a familiar figure emerged from the cluster of trees at the northern edge of the road. The mountainous structure across the vast lot bore the words Brooklyn VA Medical Center in faded lettering, evidence that made their eyes widen. Not the likely storage for a weapons cache, but the largest repository of medical supplies and equipment any of them had likely ever seen.

As if reading their thoughts, the emerging figure muttered, "Don't want to go there," before anyone could ask where he had been.

"You don't get to show up and tell us what to do," Jia growled petulantly. Somewhere to the south, dogs bayed and howled, drawing attention from Kato until the group judged the animals to be too far away to pose a threat.

Not Cana, Jia believed, and not wolves. But feral dogs could be a potential problem too. For now, they were not.

"Where've you been?" hissed Vance, moving defensively between the woman and a man he was no longer sure was an ally.

Kato had been too absent of late to be reliable. Allegedly scouting, supposedly protecting their flank, there was no actual evidence of him doing so, and he had been unnervingly quiet when he was with them. With Nepo suspected to be behind them and Quentin and Pain known to be on their heels, suspicion was tempered with possibility but the idea he had developed some other motive, that he was no longer on their side, had grown into a looming suspicion.

"They're there."

"Quentin?"

There could be no one else. Nepo was one man. Quentin and Pain and whoever they traveled with were the bigger threat. As angry as she was, as insulted and frustrated, Jia swallowed the bitter words she wanted to hurl and sidestepped around Vance to stand face-to-face with the much taller man.

She did not need the mage's defense. She was not afraid of Kato. "You've seen them?"

Her tone and the fact she did not scold Vance for his protectiveness, even though she had circumvented it, refusing to hide, refusing to let anyone shield her or block her anger, made Kato angry too. He thought she would trust him. He thought he had proven his loyalty. How many times had he helped her, fought at her side? Not enough, it seemed. He growled.

"Followed them; they split up in all the buildings." He tipped his head towards the array of medical structures and swept a hand through his waves of dark hair. "They're gonna be there awhile, I imagine."

As large as the primary building was, they could spend days searching room to room, even if they were forced to bypass damaged or inaccessible ones. Or they could recognize the facility was unlikely to hold weapons and abandon it in less than an hour.

"How many?"

"You're not thinking of going in there?" Candace asked.

"How many?" Jia repeated, ignoring the question.

"Just over a dozen…including Pain."

Jia nodded and studied the area around them. Quentin might have the advantage of numbers, but most of her allies were anthro. It seemed a fair fight so long as there were no guns involved. But she had not come to fight. They had come to avoid violence, in support of something her father had given his life to achieve and circumvent.

"Deuce, QiangXu, Yu…search the housing tract to the south. Watch for those dogs. Might be food we can use…but I don't want to have to fight for it. We need to be sure no one's there…or see if there's friendlies. The rest of us…" She looked toward the hospital, ignoring Deuce's displeasure with her order. "Once we get across," she pointed cattycorner from the hospital to a long, low building with a busted neon sign on which they could barely make out the letters BOW. "Candace, Eddie, and I will take that one. Vance, you and Pubby go left, see what's across from…"

"You shouldn't…"

Her narrow-eyed gaze dared Vance to challenge her again, a dominant look of power reminding him of their first meeting, a look that had both thrilled and intimidated him at the same time. Had that only been a few weeks ago? A few months at most? He swallowed his protest and nodded. He and Pubby were Protectors. He was a tracker. They could handle whatever they found.

Whether he wanted to take orders from someone younger or not, she was Cana alpha.

She could take care of herself too.

He chose to trust her instinct, regardless of the differences in their life experiences.

"And me?"

Eyes still narrowed, her face darkening in response to Kato's smirking tone, she grunted, "You're coming with me." Staying where she could see him. She left those words unsaid but the faltering of his prideful, hopeful, regretful expression told her he understood. She did not want him with her because she wanted his company. She wanted him there because she did not trust him out of her sight.

"Listen for the signals. We'll regroup at sunset so don't go far."

With the promise of another argument on the horizon and an explanation he was not comfortable giving to explain his absences, Kato nodded. The Ursa pair, with Deuce not far to their right, crept towards the south while the others, crouched low and moving quickly so as not to be noticed by spotters invading the hospital, raced across the lot seeking the shelter of their assigned destinations.

❧*❧

He knew she was there.

The dark wolf was aware of her on the wind that blew the smells of burning petroleum, salt, and fish in from the sea. They were near enough to each other, perhaps a half mile at the most, that he believed he would have detected her even without the breeze. The traces of her Fela companion, the outsider brought into the Pack, had been there too, closer but not near enough to be visible, likely spying to determine how much of a threat the omega was.

Pain had not pursued him then to demand answers or threaten him. He did not pursue him now.

Aware of the divisions in Quentin's force spreading his manpower between each of the towering buildings with their faint medicinal smells, Pain wound his way through the dark corridors, looking for a southern exit, hoping for one chance, one glimpse, and a decision to be made.

He did not expect to have his alpha's scent thrust more fully into his face when he wiggled through the hospital's ajar front door.

Two…the Ursa…and Flushing's original Omega, were retreating shadows between buildings to the south. The others, Normal, Cana, and Fela, had reached the opposite side of the parking field to separate without pausing. With the frequent turns of her head to stare at the hospital, the increased sense of wariness he detected, he knew she was aware of his proximity. No amount of stealth would surprise her, if that was what he wanted.

Kato's return to her company meant she had to know.

Maybe the wind gave him away as well.

Pain paused to listen to the far-off wild dogs, to watch the little human forms move away from him, to see them disappear out of his sight though he could still smell her scent on the air.

How much like Roland she seemed. Her movement, her scent, her actions.

She knew her omega was near…and chose to trust him rather than hunt him down.

Or perhaps she did not trust him any more than Roland had trusted Deuce. But Roland had valued Deuce enough to allow him to live. Jia, likewise, seemed to value Pain enough to keep him alive.

Why, he thought with a soft snarl before disappearing back into the building, did she have to make this so hard?

❧*❧

Arlo Ortega was a man of the borough. He knew streets and alleys, empty buildings, and the dimly lit entrances into regions of the Below where some people were daring enough to hide in the hopes of escaping justice. He had a passable knowledge of the dinghies permitted to travel along LaGuardia's dangerous coast and once he and a team had taken a skiff, on a calm summer day, to Riker's Island to deposit irredeemable criminals there at Laedan Channon's request.

Laedan Marrock had decried his choice. The island was inhospitable, not a place for even the worst offenders. Without food, without a means to grow any, anyone sentenced there was doomed to either survive by fishing or else be met with a slow, starving death.

But taking those criminals there had been Arlo's duty. Just as pushing into the wilds was a duty now.

He did not like the wilds. He did not know his way around them and was prone to losing his sense of direction. He did not know how anyone other than anthro could survive in a place of endless trees and wild beasts.

He did not need to be familiar with the wilds, however, to follow the trail of broken branches and torn bits of clothes, to follow the lost shoe and eventual echo of the tuberculosis cough that had plagued the Laedan for much of the journey. Coughing meant the man was not dead, and so long as he continued to cough, Arlo hoped he would survive to be found and brought back for treatment.

It was in a tangle of brambles, its branches devoid of berries in the winter cold, where Arlo found him, the Laedan face down with limbs twisted in the scrub, the sleeves of his coat and pant legs snagged on thorns that gouged long red lines on his bare hands and cheeks. On the leaves and ground beneath his earth-turned face, enough blood had been deposited from coughing to testify to how long he had been there without the physical strength or presence of mind to break free.

Between the coughing, he mumbled the same mostly incoherent words over and over.

"Come, sirra." Arlo looped his arms around the man's torso and worked him free of the thorns. New scratches, the tearing of clothes and flesh, seemed unnoticed as Lowell neither winced nor struggled against them or the one who moved him. "I'll take you to her myself."

"Good boy. I knew you'd never…what they said couldn't be…you love her as much as I do…"

Arlo did not know what the Laedan was talking about. He did not think Lowell did either. Cold-skinned, slightly blue around the lips and nose, the one thing the captain did know was he had to get the Laedan to the warmth of a fire before it was too late.

❧*❧

"Looks like a hospital."

Uzzi pushed the door open to allow Quentin to pass but the younger man motioned their companions through first. Those two, wearing the hard shell of boiled leather chest plates, carrying pointed metal-tipped poles, moved cautiously, crouched back to back, into the corridor their current path had brought them into. The room directly across from them bore an unbroken hall window and through it, they could see the stained, molding bed linens on a wheeled cot that looked to have been hastily abandoned, its sheeting unmade, its pillow sagging with an indentation made by the last head to have lain on it.

"Not likely to be any weapons…"

"Fort would need medical facilities," Quentin snorted, grabbing the door with one hand and cocking his head to prompt Uzzi through. "Few floors of medical doesn't mean it all is."

The first room they had entered was barren, picked clean of anything that could have explained the building's purpose, and the corridor to the stairwell had echoed its quiet taunt back at them. There was no sign of the Cana, but Quentin no longer cared. Pain had fulfilled his purpose in leading them here. If he had gone his way, or lost his life, it was one fewer division of treasure, or payment for it, Quentin had to dole out.

With the other two standing guard in the hall, Quentin pushed into the windowed room and began to rummage through the sagging cupboard drawers.

"Told you we shoulda gone down..." Uzzi started.

"Down wouldn't mean..."

"This isn't getting us anything. Too easy for scavs to pick the first few floors clean...and down tends to be easier to fortify..."

Or it meant Unders, but Uzzi was not afraid of those peculiar survivors. Unders would have kept scavs away from whatever had been stored there. A basement would have been Uzzi's choice of storage for anything important.

"Not in a fort."

Uzzi side-eyed him. "Look like a fort to you?" He doubted Quentin had any idea what a real fort was or looked like. The word had conjured images of LaGuardia and Kennedy and those images were the only possibilities Quentin could see.

Quentin banged the empty drawer closed; it shuddered and failed to latch. He did not want to admit Uzzi had a point, or admit it was fear of what might be beneath their feet, in the dark, where there were no windows to provide light or escape, that prompted him to avoid the subterranean level. "Has to be here! Has to be something!"

Hoping to avoid drawing attention as the man's volume grew, Uzzi shrugged. "First room we've been in; like I said, easiest to scav."

"We'll cover more ground if we split up." Quentin stomped into the corridor and snatched one of the torches from another man's hand. "You two, take the next two floors. Give a shout if you find anything good. You," he shoved his finger in Uzzi's face, making the older man snarl, "take this one."

"Where are you...?" started Uzzi.

"Shouldn't split up, sirra," the torchless man muttered. "If we're ambushed...if there's something in here..."

"It's empty. We're alone. No one's here." He was not convinced Uzzi's evaluation was accurate, but the man's certainty of belief was worth investigating. "Starting down…then I'll go up. Meet back here in two hours."

"How we gonna know when it's…?"

"I've got a pretty good sense of time," Uzzi offered, forcing down his scowl. "I'll give a shout?"

"Good." Quentin took the spear from the man still carrying a torch and marched down the corridor they were passing through. The pair looked at Uzzi as if for a different instruction. Uzzi shrugged.

They were unlikely to find weapons here, but there had to be something they could use, possibly medical supplies that were always valuable for trade.

There had to be something to enable him to be free of Quentin before the day was over. The man going into the basement alone, unadvised, might be enough to accomplish that end.

➮*➭

The trio ducked behind a rusted bus listing precariously on two slashed, deflated tires that had sunk into the earth some time before the ground had frozen. When the earth softened, the bus would likely tip onto its side, but for now, it offered a screening hedge between them and the uniformed soldiers who pushed into the nearest building.

"What are they doing here?" hissed Yu.

QiangXu, on his belly to peer through the narrow strip beneath the bus, counted the clipped marching boots as they passed. "Same thing we are…" Probably at Hallister's request as they knew Kennedy's Laedan had a similar interest in Fort Hamilton. Jia suspected Kennedy and HOPE were in league to manufacture juice; imagining them working together to get here made sense.

There were not as many as Deuce expected to see, but there were enough. A scouting party sent ahead of a larger reclamation and assim crew. The timing of their joint arrivals was unfortunate but HOPE could be avoided.

Deuce, shifting to normal as soon as they stopped behind the bus, peeped around the end of it and then looked in the direction Jia had gone. "Go…I'll take care of this and catch up."

"You can't go out there alone," Yu started.

"Dealt with HOPE before; trust me." He had lived evading HOPE after his earliest run-in with them. Distracting a handful of HOPE soldiers was nothing compared to Jia's safety. "Maybe you can herd those dogs up…give them something useful to do."

Giving the dogs a chase, distracting HOPE with them, would do the trick.

Yu and QiangXu looked at one another and nodded agreement to each other and to Deuce. When the half-form Cana leaped onto the roof of the bus and off the other side, the pair of Ursa ran southwest, away from the sounds of the crashing search HOPE made through the nearby building.

By the time HOPE finished with anything inside, there would be nothing left worth scavving.

❧*❧

Frustrated and certain what Warby had found was more promising than the vacancy he had, Donn yanked the chain of a weighted heavy sack hanging from the water-damaged ceiling and swore in fury at the barrage of moldy stained material that rained over him as the bag fell. Other men with him, likewise tipping weight equipment, exercise bikes and runners like those Marrock had once scavved, repaired, and installed in the Fortress when Donn had been a little boy, looked at one another but said nothing. While some of the metal bars and weighted disks would make suitable weapons if wielded by someone strong enough, nothing in the wide mirrored room hinted they were in, or near, a fort full of weapons.

The building itself looked no different than any of a multitude of others in LaGuardia. Outside, nothing nearby, except for that one tall building in the distance, looked potentially like a fort. But Donn begrudgingly admitted Warby was right. They had to make sure the area was clear of enemies before planning an assault on something that large. They did not have the numbers to risk an ambush, not even if they forged a tentative alliance with Hallister's team.

Duty here done, they rejoined their general in the lot outside to receive their next set of orders.

Everyone except Donnovan.

He stepped into the doorway, noting the brightening sky of morning, the growing rise of warmth in the air. The glint of light across the paved area between them and the presumed fort exposed a faded sign still readable despite the distance. Not a fort. Valuable, but not the source of wealth Donn hoped for. And not, he decided, worth considering an alliance with his father-in-law.

He ducked back into the building and pressed flat against the wall, collecting his thoughts as Warby's voice droned outside, undercut by baying dogs, wolves, or something equally savage and detestable.

He was tired of obeying Warby's directives. Tired of Warby being in charge. He had not come here to follow but rather to lead and decided it was time to do this his way. He did not need Warby or HOPE to find weapons. He was a Channon. He only needed instinct.

❧*❧

BOW turned out to have nothing to do with weapons. The room they found themselves in after Kato and Eddie pried open the mechanical doors contained rows of slick wooden aisles with shallow gutters on either side, dusty from decades of disuse, that fed into darkness at the end. At the heads of each aisle were grooved stands containing three-holed balls, heavy enough that picking one up made Candace give a surprised 'ooof' and drop it back down.

"Seen pictures of this," Kato murmured, offering his knowledge in the hopes it would ease Jia's silent, seething anger. She had not spoken as they crossed the parking area and skirted a long building in which they had heard muffled, barking voices. It was a wise silence, maintained until they entered this building and began to skulk about in the darkness, remaining mindful of the possibility that anyone could enter behind them. It did not appear anyone had been in this room in a long time, gauging by the layered dust and the damp, musty smell emanating from rows of deflated, discolored shoes lined up on shelves behind the counter.

Whoever those others were, residents, explorers, or some portion of Quentin's team, they dared not take any chance of being discovered. If necessary, they could create an ambush from here or hide and wait for the others to pass.

"It's for recreation…there would be white pins there. You roll the ball down the row to knock them over."

"You ever play?" asked Eddie, picking up a mottled red ball and testing its weight.

"Never had the…"

"Ssh."

Jia's warning was unnecessary as they heard the voices too, male voices passing the broken door. The baying of dogs heard before returned. The four ducked down where they were, hiding behind chairs and ball islands and the counter with the shoes. When Jia peeped over to see if she could identify the voices, the flashing sweep of a shock stick illuminated a long finger through the room and she dropped down with a sworn expletive under her breath.

"Who…?" Kato began.

She pressed her fingers to his lips. The door scratched open, dragging on the uneven ground, and though the beam made two more sweeps from one side of the room to the other, the owner seemed satisfied the location was empty and not what they were seeking.

Or, Jia thought with her head cocked, they departed in response to a far-off s whistle that caused each pair of boots to retreat at a run.

"LaGuardia," Jia whispered. She knew that signal. Laedan troops.

Most likely, she thought with a frown, it meant Donn was here.

"We need to get to the others." There was no time to wait for the scheduled rendezvous. This new information changed everything. They needed a new strategy in case the Channons found her.

With luck, Donn and Quentin would stumble across each other first, would face off, and only one would be left standing. Whichever one that would be, she would feel more confident facing down one of them instead of both.

⮑*⮐

The postal station contained fusty, deflated sacks of heavy canvas, stained cardboard boxes that had toppled as age weakened the integrity of those at the bottom, and bundles of catalogs, flyers, and envelopes with faded words molded into nearly solid blocks from decades of moisture or else rotting and crumbling in his fingers when Vance picked them up from the surfaces where they had been left. Despite the removal of his gloves to touch them, too much time had passed since their sending for there to be images or ghosts attached that might provide details about those who had come before, senders, workers, clerks, or curious scavs who might have rifled here looking for something useful. Food left in the breakroom was long past edible and the water jug atop an ancient plastic and metal dispenser had dribbled out, leaving evaporation rings in the bottle and on the floor where it had dripped. Dust had settled in the drip markings, forming circular patterns like tree rings on the cracked tile floor. The chains holding the doors closed had been cut, the locks stolen, proof that scavs had braved the tale of monsters and ghosts. Perhaps they had succeeded in their hunt. Perhaps they had fallen victim to the horrors rumored to lurk here.

There was fear, residual, barely discernable but once strong enough, left by the last person or multitude, to have allowed it to remain for a mage to bear witness to it.

"Segara."

Vance dropped the bundle of letters and followed Pubby's voice to a toilet room door held open by a boot. The angle of it, the dust and must and clawing scratched into the door, as well as the gnawing marks on the leather, told Vance enough that he pushed the door open without fear as Pubby kept his gun, with the last remaining bullets, aimed in case there was danger lurking inside.

The corpse within had been picked clean by rats, roaches, flies, and other vermin, the small window above its head open so such things, and the wind and rain, could push through without hindrance. Something, an animal or grubber, had separated the lower leg and foot from the rest of the skeleton and dragged it as far as the door, as if the door had been open when the fellow died and something had come in after him, disturbing him and causing it to close. A sawed-off shotgun lay haphazardly across his lap. One hand was tucked around the trigger; the condition of the fractured skull and the stain on the wall behind suggested an end neither man needed to touch to read.

"Shart."

"Musta gotten trapped," Vance murmured. Trapped with the belief he had no way out except death at his own hand or at the hands of something worse.

"Think he was a worker? Grubbers get him? Or the monster…?"

"There's no monster." Pubby's smirk at Vance's retort made the mage frown at the teasing and shrug. "Probably grubbers or an animal." Something scared off before it could finish its intended meal, so more likely an animal. Grubbers were not smart enough to flee.

"Something strong enough to pull him apart, for sure." Pubby picked up the shotgun and opened it to look in the chamber. It was empty, and though he suspected the poor fool had used his last round to take his own life, Pubby decided keeping the gun was a worthwhile precaution. "Should take a look; maybe there's more rounds."

"Be careful." The thing that had torn the dead man apart long ago was likely as dead as he was, its body serving as food for other scavengers as this soul's had done. With the presence of the baying dogs outside, it would not do to be careless.

Footsteps. The banging of the front door. "Someone's…" started Pubby, aiming the useless shotgun at whatever ran towards them.

But Vance knew that presence, that aura. "Put it down," he hissed, moments before Jia and those with her ran around the corridor into the hall where they were…to find a shotgun aimed at her head.

She said only two words.

"Channon's here."

☙*☙

When the basement proved fruitless, containing rooms of rusted laundry machines and bins of stained, brittle fabric, silent heating and cooling engines scavved for parts, spare gurneys, tables, chairs, and other objects Thomas could not identify, he opted for the topmost floor of the building instead. He had told the others he was going up, but not how far up. He did not want to tip his hand to the plans stirring in the back of his mind.

He did not expect to find guns or explosives at the top; the ever-growing-more-obvious medical nature of this facility precluded their existence as Uzzi had argued. What Thomas did hope to find was a clue as to where to look next. He stood at the window with his hands behind his back, surveying the surrounding world from the direction they had traveled to the western rise of an old change and out to the watery horizon to the south with its ever-burning tanker. He could not see north, into the wilds, but he could see enough.

He expected walls. He expected towers. He expected something akin to the fortresses in LaGuardia or Kennedy, except on a larger, more grandiose scale.

Instead, everything he could see looked much the same as everywhere else he had ever been. Buildings. Streets. Flat parking areas cracked by nature. Vegetation.

He had traveled all of those miles…for nothing. He had climbed all of those stairs just to gaze at an empty world.

Frustrated and weary, forced to reformulate a new strategy if he was to attain his goals…the governance of LaGuardia, Kennedy, and in time the rest of the known world, he leaned against the glass, feeling the vibration of the wind pressing and shuddering over the outside as it rumbled beneath his arm, watching the specks moving to the west.

He knew those uniforms.

Channon Guard.

Lowell or Donnovan, he mused sourly. Perhaps neither.

Perhaps both.

☙588☙

A flash to the south birthed another eruption of flame out to sea. Had any Laedan ever had such a view as this? Had they ever stood in a place such as where Thomas Quentin stood, a commanding vantage point where he could see everything? Had they ever basked in the feeling of power that came with this view?

He thought not.

Perhaps he could begin to build his empire here, from this room, suck the local resources dry, and take ownership of the streets reaching east to the boroughs' borders. There was a lot of it, unused, unclaimed territory, that might, in time, provide him the strength to push against the Channons, the Hallisters, the world, those who had belittled and spurned him. He could choose to embrace his nature and unite others like him under his banner, a borough of anthro to draw outcasts from everywhere else and feed his strength.

He would need people he could trust. People he could command. Uzzi might appreciate that sort of power and wield it well, as general of the Hamilton Borough.

He had the charisma for it. People listened to him. Uzzi would be the best sort of ally Thomas could ask for.

But not, he mused, at the end of a leash of blackmail.

His thoughts turned to the furtive movements on the ground. Lowell believed there were weapons here, believed it enough to kill for. Roland had believed there were weapons here too, enough to seek to hide the map, the knowledge. Lowell was a power monger, Roland a book-smart man with years of study behind him.

Hallister wanted to beat them both.

Thomas wanted to beat them all.

If each of the three believed there were weapons to be claimed, weapons had to be here. Given time, once he consolidated his hold, Thomas would locate them. Afterward, he would be unstoppable.

Here he would be beyond the reach of Channons, Hallisters, and HOPE until he was ready. He was safe from sins no one in this part of the world knew about...so long as he got rid of the Channon ants crawling around in his field of vision.

A sound. The sudden permeating reek of wet canine fur. The reflection of movement in the glass from the doorway behind him. He turned with a grin.

"Good. I have one more job for you."

It was easy to follow the Fela stench through the hospital corridors, to the end of the hall, up the stairs. Up and up and up, each set barely an obstacle for the half-form Cana on the hunt for one he knew to be alone. Others had moved elsewhere into the building, the man Uzzi and two more. Everyone else was occupied wherever they had been sent. Thomas Quentin was alone.

The fleeting thoughts he entertained as he climbed, of leading Jia here, leading Quentin to her, of being done with both of them and returning to the Pack as the unquestionable alpha, evaporated behind his eyes as he stopped in the doorway, chest heaving from the exertion of traversing so many stairs, and laid eyes on the man he had grown to despise and blamed for every one of his ills.

If not for Quentin, Roland would be alive. If not for Quentin, Pain would never have come to be at odds with his packmates, his family, his friends. He would never have made regrettable choices that had cost him everything he held dear.

If he had not lost those things, made the choices he had made, he would not be here, staring down the man with the spear whose initial imperious smile faltered and turned gradually stoic and snide when Pain refused to be baited by his charming, smiling offer.

The unspoken offer was revoked. Quentin could smell disdain, anger, hostility, although he did not know the intent behind it. It could have been anything, real or imagined, slight or weighty. From the curl of the Cana's lip, the root did not matter. Only what came next did.

"Uzziah's put you up to this?" Quentin grunted, stepping to the right, around the long conference table, keeping the table between them. It and the spear were the only weapons he had. He could drop the spear, use Fela speed and strength if it came to a fight, but the Cana was an ally he believed he could use if he could talk sense into him. All he had to do was drive a wedge of suspicion between the Cana and

Uzziah, turn the Cana against his keeper, and Pain would do for him what Quentin believed needed to be done.

"He's using you. It's what he does. He turns on everyone eventually; sooner or later he'll use your leash to choke you…"

Pain snarled and leaped onto the table, stalking its length towards the man attempting a casual retreat. He did not want to kill Quentin in one swoop. He wanted the Fela to come out to play, to reveal himself as the murderer he was. He wanted Quentin to suffer in death the way Jia claimed Roland had suffered. He wanted to see and smell the fear of it, the dying. He wanted Quentin to know who had bested him and why. Even if his name, ultimately, meant nothing.

"No leash."

Speaking was difficult in half-form but not impossible; the words came out enough for Quentin to understand them. His snorted chortle was cut short when he dashed for the second doorway at the other end of the long conference room, intending to reach the corridor. Pain jumped off the table.

In the hall, before he crossed the threshold, Pain was greeted first by the clatter of the spear that rattled the air and struck the edge of the doorframe near his shoulder, and then by a tawny panther whose leap broadsided him and bowled him backward. He snarled and with front limbs ending in clawed hands rather than wolf paws, grabbed the cat by the neck and hurled him away.

Pain's impact with the wall, his roll to his feet before tossing Quentin aside, made the spear skitter in the direction of an open door into a windowless room at the far end of the hall.

Blood smeared the walls, the floor, as claws and fangs lashed out for supremacy in a fight that left tufts of fur scattered from the conference room doors to the corridor's end. Unaccustomed to utilizing his anthro form after a lifetime of hiding and denying it, and being even more unaccustomed to the half-form he considered to be more of an abomination than the full cat form could ever be, Quentin quickly ascertained he needed the agility of half-form rather than full Fela if he was to have a fair chance of winning this fight. All he needed to do was subdue the Cana, not kill him, force him to capitulate and submit in exchange for his life.

Pain had no such agenda.

There was little attention to give to such a shift in the middle of combat, when Quentin's primary focus was on staying alive. The quest to force submission was ultimately abandoned. Killing Pain was his only option if he was to survive. There came a moment when he was able to thrust the bloody-mouthed Cana far enough back to allow him the shift of focus to change forms. When Pain launched again, the half-Fela came up with the spear in his hand and drove it through the Cana's thick-muscled shoulder. He aimed lower, hoping to drive it through Pain's chest, a blow that, even if it missed his heart, would leave the Cana drowning in his own blood.

Pain's leap thwarted his intent.

The injury did not stop Pain's forward momentum. Did not stop him from throwing Quentin backward into the small metal room. There was a lurch, the shudder of walls and floor, as his increased half-form mass and weight made impact, a quick scrambling as the Fela grabbed for the protruding spear end.

The room dropped.

Shoulder torn open by the pulled-free spear, spewing blood into his fur and over the hand trying to hold the injury closed as if it would keep the blood inside, Pain listened through the ringing in his ears as the metal room dropped and dropped…and crashed with such violence Pain could feel the vibration through his feet.

There was no other sound.

No way, he mused, had Thomas Quentin survived.

"That's," he hissed as he returned to his naked normal form, "for Roland."

Chapter 40

Grim faced, mouth turned in a frown, Uzzi gently pushed the man down by his good shoulder and hissed, "Lie still," as he resumed stitching up the gash below his collarbone in the light of the flare someone had produced. Uzzi had tended the exit wound as Enola held Pain still, but now she had gone in search of more gauze and antiseptic from any of the hospital rooms not previously raided by scavs.

The shudder that ran through the building was easy to track, a shiver punching from the bottom to the top. Instinct had driven Uzzi up the stairs rather than down, pulled him away from the echo of collapse and collision, until he discovered Pain in a pool of blood, covered in the evidence of unmistakable combat with another anthro.

Uzzi only knew of one other here but it did not mean there weren't more. Struggling to lift and carry Pain to the ground level, alert for an ambush by Pain's attacker, he found the other two men and many of those assigned to the search of the other buildings, and Dink and Enola as well, gathered for the intended rendezvous. By the time Dink helped lower Pain to the ground, Uzzi's shirt was soaked with blood. Uzzi felt certain the Cana would bleed to death.

But Pain continued to breathe, to moan, to sporadically mumble the name Roland. Uzzi took those things as positive signs.

None had yet to see Quentin but Uzzi believed the man would turn up in response to the commotion if he could. If he could not, it was better they find him first, better for Uzzi to control the search and avoid questions he could not answer.

"Search the upper levels," he instructed those drawn from other structures by the explosive sound erupting from the primary hospital building and the rendezvous their employer had set. "Go in twos; take some flares." He fussed over Pain's condition and did not look at any of them except Dink. He did not trust what his expression might reveal to anyone else. "Find Quentin. Whoever did this has to still be here. Find them…and keep your eyes open."

The people around him scattered, save for one older woman building a fire in a metal bedpan to contain its spread and Enola who was aiding in the Cana's care. With both women occupied, Uzzi focused on the slash of feline claws across Pain's naked skin, the press of fangs into flesh, the bruising of a hard-fought battle. He doubted anyone else knew what Quentin was, would equate Pain's injuries to the missing man and it was better, he thought grimly, that any conflict between the two was attributed to an unidentified third party.

"He…" Pain began, bleary-eyed and disoriented from the burn in his shoulder, his back, his chest, as consciousness pushed nearer to the surface and his memory began to return.

Uzzi shook his head. "Wherever he is, they'll find him." What came next was something they would deal with when it arose. Or they would not. If Quentin was dead, finding him did not matter to Uzzi. Finding him only mattered if the man lived. "You lost a lot of blood."

"The room…it fell…"

The older man bobbed his head but he said nothing as Enola returned with an armload of medical supplies. An elevator, he decided, ripping open a package of gauze, folding a few pieces into a thick mass, and dousing it with a pungent wound-cleaning solution. He had seen such rooms, though never a working one. Held by cables and gears that had likely suffered the same decay as the rest of the world, entering one, particularly at the top of such a towering structure, was taking one's life into their own hands. He did not believe Quentin's fate was entirely Pain's fault.

Even if Pain had intended to kill him. Even if he had tried.

"This is gonna burn."

Pain growled and winced, but with his jaw clenched, he allowed them to clean the injuries across his torso, arms, and legs.

"There's others out there," Enola murmured. "LaGuardia troops."

"Not a surprise," grunted Pain.

"We don't have enough…"

Uzzi glanced at Enola, cutting her off with a soft, "Don't need to fight them." He lay the blood-soaked gauze on the ground, rolled Pain onto his side, and began to form a wrap over his collarbone and under his armpit to cover the puncture and hold more gauze in place over it. "Not alone at least."

Pain side-eyed him.

Uzzi nodded.

"They'll never take us," the Cana muttered. Despite what Jia suspected about Pain's presence, he did not believe she would welcome him to fight beside her. He might be pack omega, she might be his alpha, but she had little reason to trust him. Even if she learned what he had done.

"Think they will." When they know who I am, if Kato vouches for me, Uzzi thought as he helped Pain roll back and settle his head on the pack used to elevate him slightly. "Just telling them what you've…"

Pain snorted. "You don't know the Marrocks," he muttered, drifting quickly to sleep.

Uzzi glanced at the door. Marrock. Was that who was out there? Not the murdered Laedan, but one of his children. That put an unexpected spin on the situation.

Sunset was approaching but their day was finished until they found Quentin, until the group made a new plan. If the man was dead, as Uzzi hoped, or nearly so, many of those who had come for this job would resort to bickering. Or they would choose to go their way to scav on their own if they believed there was no chance of receiving the promised recompense. It would be up to Uzzi to offer them an incentive to stay. To offer something better than scavved materials or a handful of credits.

With the threat of exposure to HOPE for the crimes of his past no longer on his shoulders, Uzzi considered himself free.

Such freedom did not matter without his son.

❧*❦

"We don't have a choice."

Captain Ortega did not know the purpose of the long building they were in, lined on two sides by streets with the mountainous medical facility to the east and the structures the LaGuardia forces had picked clean to the west. He knew there was a group roaming the hospital grounds but the reports gleaned were of people without uniforms, an unidentified collection who appeared to be scavs.

Scavs could be dangerous if armed, and if they were anthro they would be challenging to subdue in a fight. He hoped for peaceful negotiation. With the sun setting and the Laedan shivering and coughing under every covering the doctor was able to collect, it was best to avoid a fight with an unverified number of strangers.

"We're here to do a job," Arlo continued.

"If we don't get him home, get him…"

"Think he'll make it back?" It was an uncomfortable question, one Arlo already believed he knew the answer to, but it had to be asked.

The doctor frowned, the answer the captain expected.

He rubbed the back of his hand beneath his nose, hoping to wipe away the taint of sickness permeating their encampment. The enclosure of walls, even with the windows cracked open to allow for cross-drafts of fresh air, kept the stench contained so thickly it churned his stomach. Despite the cold, he believed sleeping in the open air would have been better, would have allowed the stink and sickness to dissipate, but with the possibility of enemies nearby and the Laedan's need for a shelter to contain enough warmth to aid in his care, this place was the option Arlo had chosen.

His gaze circled the cluster of subordinate officers who led the men beneath him and then returned to the doctor's face. "Tomorrow, when the scavs clear out, you'll take a couple of men and see if there's anything in the hospital we can use…anything that'll help him. I'll stay with him. The rest of you will fan out and find that fort."

"Don't see no fort out there," someone at the back of the gathering snorted derisively.

"Doesn't matter. You gonna tell him you gave up?" Arlo hesitated to allow his silence to drive the point home. "The Laedan says it's here. We'll find it and confiscate everything of value…unless you want to be the one to tell him differently when he's back on his feet."

Mutterings, groaning, and the coughing of those inflicted with the same ailment the Laedan suffered bombarded the captain but no one challenged him. He chose to ignore them, refused to punish men for questioning an order. He would not, however, fail to punish one who disobeyed those orders. These men had chosen this duty, this life, had agreed to this command. They would do as they were told.

Regardless of the Laedan's condition.

❧*❦

"They're close."

Yu glanced at QiangXu and nodded. The proximity of Kennedy's meager force was unsettling but with HOPE behind them, groups appearing to be acting independently from one another, the hungry violence in the scent of canines on the hunt was even more so.

Wherever Deuce was, he had not yet initiated his distraction. Or perhaps he had which was why HOPE had not yet found the pair of Ursa where they hid in the shadows.

They could allow the feral animals to rid them of their opponents but unless those few people ahead of them were also part of HOPE's force, both Ursa considered it inhumane to allow innocent people to die if they could prevent it.

Theirs had been lifetimes of helping others, of generosity for humanity regardless of the personal grief such kindness had brought them. Once the dogs were driven off, without engaging the strangers or drawing attention to themselves, they could rendezvous with their people as intended.

Everything they had scavved was stashed in a long abandoned cupboard. They understood each other without words, the separation of years not having dulled their knowledge of one another. They knew what they had to do.

❧*❦

"You found the juice lab?" Nik's excitement as he burst into the sitting room where Ernest paced from one window to another did not prevent him from noticing both Torben and Oasis were there. Nor did it prevent him from noticing the way the chief avoided looking at the floral arrangements around them, a curious choice Nik might question if the opportunity arose.

"Of sorts." Ernest wanted to sit, to cease pacing, but he felt trapped by the memories of this room. Sitting on the sofa where he had once sat beside Yiva would dredge up the collection of sick, helpless, guilty feelings threatening to overwhelm him multiple times each day.

It was hard enough to force his feet to be still when he spoke. "Not an extraction facility; there were no anthro there, no equipment for it, but there was enough dried plasma to…" He shuddered. "They were cutting it, prepping it. We're looking for a chemist to tell us with what, what they had, but the results were liquids, powders, and pills destined for distribution."

"I'll talk to 'em," snarled Torben, balling his fists.

"That's not necessary, Mr. Moller; we're questioning those we arrested and analyzing the scene." Still, the assistance could be useful, particularly if it kept him from killing another innocent person, so Ernest nodded and added, "But I'll keep your offer in mind.

"Can the mage tell you anything?" Oasis had no stakes in the business of plasm, in the capture and processing of anthro. Collectively, the anthro, like the majority in the boroughs, meant little to her. They were external faces, people who allowed her, as part of the Laedans' families, to have comfort and power and the amenities of day-to-day life…food and shelter, clothes and services, many on the outside struggled to obtain. Those on the outside mattered only in what they provided her.

But Nik, keeping to his promise of inclusion, would have brought her into this meeting if she had not been here already. Interjecting a solution to the matters at hand kept her participation pertinent and would, he hoped, discourage her from acting against him.

"Segara's not available," Ernest said with a sigh. The look he shared with Nik suggested Nik knew where the mage was, knew why he was unavailable, but the chief did not add further details.

"Then we find answers the old way," Torben growled.

Ernest nodded. "Someone'll talk. They always do. We'll find who controlled the building, who was responsible for oversight of the project, distribution. Those we grabbed seem to be grunts but one of them has to have a name we can go after. Thought I should let you know, keep you informed of our progress and…"

"Are they HOPE?" The facility Jia had found appeared to belong to HOPE, or so she believed. It was a fair question for Nik to ask.

"Don't think so," Ernest shook his head. "Might be employed by them, or influenced by their ideology, but they're not educated enough to be HOPE."

Oasis looked up from her fidgeting hands. "The Anakirist wasn't nosing around for nothing…"

"Maybe they know what happened to my mo…"

They looked at each other, not needing Nik to complete his painful sentence, gauging how much the others knew or did not know. That a Channon was responsible for the death of one of their own. That it was the last morsel of information they wanted to fall into HOPE's, or the public's hands.

The longer Donn was absent, unfound, hiding in the shadows, the more certain Nik felt that publicly outing his twin might be in the borough's best interest. It would drive Donn to the surface. Force him to act. The longer they waited for Donn to do something, the worse the damage to the Channon name, to the family, was likely to be.

"Working on that too," Ernest assured Oasis, his expression pained, distant, and dismayed. "No one's forgotten. We can do both at once. If we don't have answers before…we'll get them soon as Mage Segara gets back."

"Then bring him back," Oasis hissed. "It's not safe to be a Channon. We need answers."

Nik cut off Ernest's effort to speak with a hand on the chief's arm as Oasis stalked out of the room. With a nod from Nik, Torben followed her; there was nothing they could do to help her but make sure the woman he wanted to trust did not do anything rash. It allowed Nik to be alone with the chief.

"She's afraid," Ernest murmured.

"Every right to be," Nik sighed. "With my father…the longer Donn's out there…"

"No one's reported seeing him," the chief interjected defensively. "There's only so much…if I had more Protectors…or Segara…"

"Recruit more. Hire what you need." Somehow, Nik would make it work.

"Won't be easy…but I'll see what I can do, sirra. We want to track that plasm source and put it to rest."

Having put off his primary purpose in coming as long as the topic allowed, Ernest fished in the breast pocket of his coat and offered something in his open palm.

Nik recognized it without touching it and swallowed the jagged lump in his throat.

"Found it on a suspect," the chief began. "Said he found it at the scene. Maybe he stole it. Maybe it broke and fell off before she…kept it in evidence for a while but…I think you should have it back.

The gold chain was broken, snapped as if yanked free. Nik did not recall any evidence of such an injury on his mother's neck or any bruising where it could have been pulled away, but the evidence of strangulation and the discoloration of death might have masked that. Nik had not been looking for specific details, beyond the obvious, when he had seen her, and had not consciously realized the necklace his father had given her was absent.

"Fa will want…" She had worn it every day of Nik's life he could remember, since Lowell had given it to her when Nik had been a little boy. If the clasp and chain could be repaired, perhaps the return of this memento would bring his father peace.

Or it might drive him deeper into despair.

Reluctantly, he picked up the chain with trembling fingers and gently coiled it into his other palm. "Thank you," he whispered.

His arm dropped awkwardly, his hand was empty, and Ernest coughed to clear his throat of emotion, interrupting the need for Nik to express his. "This is where it belongs."

From the melancholy in his voice, Nik guessed parting with it was not an easy thing for the chief. He considered returning it, but it was not his to give.

That note in his voice explained why he avoided the flowers. Arranging flowers had been Yiva's doing. Ernest must have known.

"I want to know everything," Nik said, shifting the subject away from his mother onto matters easier for both of them. "If Donn shows up, I'll keep him long as I can…send for you…and hope he doesn't…"

"Be careful, sirra; you might be his brother but…"

But he was not sure kinship would keep Nik or Oasis safe.

Nik was not sure of it either. The blood of twins might not be enough to spare him, but he was willing to take the risk it would not if it meant stopping his brother from hurting anyone else.

❧*❧

Moving from one empty structure to another provided Aman and his band some passable bedding, an assortment of tools, jewelry, and semi-valuable objects for trade that made their venture this far west worthwhile even if they did not find the weapons they had been sent to locate and secure. HOPE's soldiers remained to the north, searching other structures, the occasional echo of their frustrated voices suggesting they were having no more luck than Aman was.

By splitting his force into smaller groups they could cover the area, move from one apartment building to another, more quickly. The apartments were eerie and empty, many appearing to have been abandoned in haste. Food, rotted, shriveled and unidentifiable, filled shelves and silent refrigeration units. Moth-eaten clothes were thrown from closets and drawers as the most important items were taken, and appliances and electronics sat idle without the power to function.

Where, when, and why had everyone gone?

Aman wondered if the night's unearthly screeching was to blame or if desertion had come with the eruption of fire upon the sea.

He and the two soldiers with him exited the second apartment structure on the north side of the split oval road, once a pleasant park with a cobbled path through its flower garden but now overgrown and as wild as every other open stretch of land had become. The soldiers waited for him at the street while Aman closed the apartment entrance door, a polite impulse despite the fact there was no one to appreciate or benefit from it. Shutting out the elements would preserve the living areas a little while longer. He signaled to the other groups in the complexes to the left and right, but the effort was interrupted by the baying, howling and snarling that erupted from the wilds and charged across the street to encircle Aman's ill-prepared companions.

One of the few in the unit to possess a gun, Aman took aim. Wolves rarely roamed or attacked people during daylight hours but feral dogs were less constrained. Though the sun was sinking lower, there was still enough light to consider the day not yet over. He had never encountered dogs prone to hunting people but these beasts, sleek with hunger, shaggy and matted with unkempt winter pelts, showed none of the expected fear of humanity. Protecting their territory or striking out of disease or hunger, it did not matter.

Aman only had two bullets.

The two men in harm's way, one armed with a club and one with a spear, had none. Cut off by the encircling dogs, they did their best to defend themselves and back towards the building but there was nowhere to retreat to, even if Aman opened the door. The dogs had them surrounded.

Two bullets were better than none. Two fewer of the roughly fifteen to twenty animals he could count might give his people a chance to retreat if the rest of his soldiers did not arrive in time to help.

Before the shots were made there was another roar that echoed from the space between buildings further down the block. Roars that came as the dogs closed on their prey, snapping fangs on arms and legs meant to drag their victims to the ground.

Startled by the unexpected sound, some of the dogs let go and spun to face the pair of dark-furred bears they had not scented, bears that charged into their midst without considering they were outnumbered. They scattered the pack with the force of their bodies and broad, swiping paws, creating a chaotic skirmish with the fallen men in the middle. A few of the dogs danced around the Ursa to drive them away from the meal they were attempting to overpower.

Aman considered shooting the newest threat instead of the dogs. If this was a fight over food, his people stood a better chance of beating back the dogs, he thought, than driving off the bears. As large as the pair were, their carcasses would offer enough of a meal that the dogs might leave the people alone. Aman had once witnessed a wolf pack chasing off a bear.

That these bears did not retreat suggested there was nothing ordinary about them.

The bears appeared to be protecting his people.

Bloody, overpowered by their unexpected opponents, most of the dogs chose to retreat into the twilight, limping, nursing injuries, knowing better than to continue a fight with this foe.

Choosing to conserve the precious bullets, Aman lowered the gun but kept it ready in case the bears chose to turn their precision against him and the injured men. They could do more damage than the dogs. But there were only two of them. One bullet for each.

The smaller of the pair reared onto its back feet and roared, lifting a dog clinging to its forearm off the ground. The other, as if in reply, roared too and lunged at the ungrounded offender.

Not bears, Aman decided.

Ursa.

That dog fell to the Ursa's mighty jaws and did not move. The others remaining finally lumbered off with their tails and heads drooping, looking back cautiously to be certain the bear who pursued them to the edge of the house across the street had stopped following. To see if their fallen companion would join them.

The men at the side of the road lay bloody and still, as did the dog beside them.

Aman could not tell if any of them were alive.

He waited, unmoving, as the first Ursa rejoined the second, standing over the injured one licking the wound on the other's foreleg as they looked from those at their feet to the man at the door. Perhaps evaluating whether a kill was worth the effort, whether they should complete what the dogs had started and take the spoils or move on. Perhaps this was their territory and they were contemplating driving the people away. Perhaps the Ursa were the cause of the previous night's wail, some sort of territorial cry meant to keep threats at bay.

Aman thought he knew Ursa. He thought he knew anthro. He had never heard such a sound from any anthro, but that did not mean his guess was incorrect.

With soldiers wearing Kennedy insignia on either side, having emerged from the apartments at the start of the chaos, the Ursa were outnumbered. Being outnumbered had not stopped them from attacking the dogs, nor did it seem to be the deciding factor prompting their retreat back the way they came. A distant howl, distinctly Cana, different from the sound of the retreating dogs, bled from the north. The Ursa looked at one another and lumbered silently away, ignoring the men, not looking back to see if they would be shot.

They had saved his life; Aman would not allow retaliation simply because they were anthro.

A few people ran towards him, some to offer aid to the fallen, some prepared to keep the dogs at bay if they returned, others began to head away as though considering the pursuit of the Ursa.

"Leave them." By now, Aman expected they were gone.

From the yelps and snarls of the retreating dogs, they were too.

Perhaps some of them would have survived the dogs without the Ursa's aid if they had barricaded themselves inside the buildings. Aman was the first to admit as he checked for the non-existent pulses on the bodies on the street, he would have lost more than two of the ten with him. Now there were only eight others and himself.

Whoever the Ursa were, Kennedy's people owed them their lives.

Letting them go was the only way Aman could repay them.

❧*❧

Aware of movement in the wide, multi-layered structure, knowing those others were far enough away on this ground level they would never detect him, Nepo leaned his forearm against the edge of the open door and looked into the chasm. His lavender eyes blinked as they adjusted to the darkness until he was eventually able to sift out the details of destruction at the bottom far below his reach.

Warped metal. Shattered glass. In the midst of it, buried, ruptured, and crushed by the impact, a man Nepo knew by scent.

So. Thomas Quentin was dead. Channon would be pleased to hear it. Unless Nepo chose to climb down, however, there would be no physical proof of the kill, no proof to garner the promised payment.

Channon would never pay him without proof.

Nor would there be payment forthcoming from Quentin if he managed to be rid of the other Channon boy, or the Fela and girl said to have killed Laedan Marrock. Free of those contracts, pockets empty, Nepo was no longer obligated to wander these forsaken wastes. He could go back to the familiar comforts of the boroughs, back to what he did best, in search of someone able to pay his fees.

There was one thing left to do, however. One thing if he was to be free of the only person who might someday stop him.

Segara was out there. Segara needed to die if Nepo was to be free.

He could find a way to the bottom and find the proof Channon would demand of Quentin's death. If not Donnovan, perhaps the Laedan would pay him for that too. He did not think it worth his time.

Another day or two of healing, he thought as he rubbed his aching ribs and slunk back into the shadows to avoid the gradually encroaching voices. Another day or two would make his success much more certain.

Chapter 41

General Warby stomped around the encampment, grabbing one person's shoulder after another, kicking awake those already asleep or trying to sleep, pulling aside bundles of supplies and materials collected in favor of locating the Channon boy. He counted and recounted his troops, finding none missing except for those lost along the way and Donn Channon.

"Anyone seen him?"

While he did not care about the arrogant dolt who had done nothing but counter him with contempt during the march west, he knew the Grand Mas had plans for this particular Channon. To lose him to an unseen trap or collapse, wild beasts or scavs, would strain relations with LaGuardia and impact the Grand Mas' intentions for the boroughs in ways Warby could not imagine.

He did not know what those plans entailed.

"Not since the fitness center," someone eventually replied. "He was with us inside."

But not outside. Donn could have come out with the rest, but the General's focus had been consumed by the movements of others to the north and he had paid little attention to those exiting the building. He had taken his portion of the team in one direction and instructed the rest to go another and meet in this place after, assuming the smart-ass Channon was among them.

The fact that Channon had not immediately challenged or contradicted the instruction, had not interjected some other action, should have alerted Warby to his absence.

After the cat and mouse tussle Warby and his unit had engaged in with a lone Cana who had picked off two of his followers and evaded their efforts to strike back, Donn's whereabouts had been the furthest thing from Warby's thoughts.

"You three, go back and find him." If he had been injured or trapped in the building, Warby wanted to know. If the lone Cana had picked him off too, dragged him away or gutted him and left him to rot in the open, it was also worth knowing. "You," he selected three others, "scout the perimeter of the hospital, see if he might be there…"

"But sirra…there's…"

"Scout, not engage. We need to know where he is. Maybe he went to talk to them…" Maybe those at the hospital were LaGuardia troops, though Warby had seen no indication of it. Those people might have captured Donnovan to use him as leverage or ransom. "The rest of you, look here. Could be he's up in one of the apartments."

They had made camp in this common room that ran from the front to the back of the building, where they could monitor everyone who came in and out of the main and rear doors. They built no fires close to the windows to minimize the exposure of their camp to those outside. There were enough rooms branched off from the commons and creaking stairs with loose railings leading to the upper floor, where a man could have wandered off to, to be alone. Channon considered himself better than the rest of them. The opportunity for privacy would be exactly the sort of chance he would have taken despite the risks.

Donn could be there. Warby was disinclined to believe it.

But nor did he believe Channon had the nerve to wander without another he could use as a shield, someone he could boss around and manipulate. He was a bully but he was, in Warby's opinion, a coward of a boy fighting to have control of the world around him through the exploitable weaknesses of others.

Channon had probably not gone far.

Not by choice.

⅌*∽

The dusty chapel made an adequate camp, far from the feral dogs' presumed territory, far enough from the sea that the tanker fire was muted and barely noticeable beyond the occasional belching explosion when the pressure inside of the tanker grew too great. The chapel also seemed a fitting place to dispose of the dead and Aman, as the leader, was the one tasked to say a few words in their memories.

What was there to say? He knew the two by name but not well.

Nor did he consider anything he could say to be inspirational enough to compel the rest to continue seeking a treasure he was less certain they would find.

They had crossed what appeared to be the center of the territory, halfway to the western change, and still, there was no visible indicator of a fort or any other structure that might house what Laedan Hallister was looking for. No doubt Norse would have found the stash already if he had been here. Norse had a nose for such things. Though Aman understood why sending Norse on this mission had been a bad idea, he was again struck by the belief that he had been sent to this place to be out of the way. Sent here to fail and die.

Aman rubbed the back of his neck. If not for those Ursa, he might already be dead. If HOPE got to the treasure first, or if he found it before they did and they learned of it, there was likely to be a fight. Outnumbered as Kennedy was, death might still come for him.

With so few men and women behind him, he bore little faith he would make it back to Kennedy. If he did so without something to show for his efforts, something the Laedan might deem worth the loss of so many lives, death might find him there, at Hallister's hand…no matter how long they had been friends.

☙*❧

He erupted through the unguarded door with a scornful, ugly expression of fury and horror, unfazed by the weapons pointed at him, seeing only the man he had spied through the dark windows. A man adjusting blankets around a prone figure, wasted, sunken in the firelight, a figure who looked both like his father and nothing like him.

Ortega hesitated, the edges of the blankets in his hands, staring at Donn with the same shock expressed by every other face in the room.

Why was he here? How in the name of anything sacred had he gotten past those who were supposed to be standing watch?

"Donno…" rasped Lowell, the word unfinished, recognizing the young man's presence though he was too far away for his bleary eyes to see clearly. His voice was reedy, cracked, and faint, pinched by something akin to panic as he squeezed Arlo's wrist and muttered, "Don't let him…he can't…"

His words remained unfinished as the younger Channon, charging unhindered, swung a fist and caught Arlo in the jaw. The captain sprawled to the side, landing across Lowell's chest, the impact and his weight creating a gasping, coughing fit that spewed blood over the back of Ortega's head and into Donn's face. The medic yanked Ortega away and tried to push Donn back with one hand, but the relief of pressure on Lowell's chest did nothing to end the coughing. The effort was met with a shove from Donnovan that knocked the doctor over as he shouted, "Leave him to…"

"Get away from my father!"

Lowell lurched weakly up with an outstretched hand. The cough intensified with one last, "Don't let him…"

What Ortega saw was an effort to propel his son away.

What the medic saw was an effort to pull his son close.

What Donnovan saw was the flailing of a delirious man who had threatened him with death, a man who went abruptly rigid, his eyes briefly wide before they rolled back and he collapsed onto the pack supporting his head. The rattling cough ceased with one long wheezing inhalation.

"Let me…" The doctor sprang forward to assist him.

"Stay away from him!"

Donn stared at his father for a long, deafening minute as that breath squeezed out of him in an extended hiss. Two minutes. No one moved or spoke, and if they breathed it was unheard over the pounding blood in his head, in his ears. When nothing changed, when his father failed to move or cough or breathe, Donn grabbed a nearby metal plate of food and swung it as hard as he could against the side of the doctor's head. The man toppled over, falling directly in front of Arlo.

Expression blank and unfeeling, Donn turned a slow circle to stare at everyone around him. There were fewer soldiers than he had hoped but they were LaGuardia Guard, the finest soldiers in the boroughs. Against HOPE, against Hallister's people to the south, they would be enough if he needed them to be.

"Tomorrow we find the cache…"

"We must see to the Laedan," Arlo began, fighting to mask the shock he felt for the son's disdain for the medic and his father, refusing to rub his bruised jaw or wipe the blood from his mouth away.

"I'm Laedan now. You'll do as I say, Captain or you'll join them."

The unit was without the one who had led them here. Without a doctor. Men and women who had followed Captain Ortega looked to him for guidance. Arlo had his doubts, having watched Donnovan allow his father to die unaided, having watched him kill the medic without thought, that any of the options before them were wise ones.

But what Donnovan said was true. Or partially so. Laedan or not, by right of succession or any decree Lowell had left, Donn was the only Channon here and thus was, by default, the leader of the expedition. Donn's eyes were on the same prize that had brought Lowell this far. Nothing else about their mission had changed.

"Aye, sirra…tomorrow," he agreed reluctantly.

But he would not abandon the dead. Lowell Channon would be offered the respect he deserved. Tonight Ortega would wrap the dead, order a hole dug in the icy earth outside, and hope for the chance to bury him at dawn.

Or that the body would keep, would not turn, long enough to return LaGuardia's Laedan to his wife's side, where Arlo had promised him he would be.

⬦*⬦

His hand trembled against the glass of the Fortress door as he stared into the dark at walls he could not see past, in the direction of something he did not expect to be there. Torben, dressed for his trek across the borough to the Plant for his evening shift, paused with a frown at the sudden grim pall that descended over the younger man.

"What?"

Nik shook his head. He shrugged. He pulled his hand away but immediately pressed it flat against the cold surface as if the glass was trying to reveal something without words he could hear.

"Something's…wrong…"

"Lot of things are wrong," Torben muttered with a deepening frown. "Want me to stay?"

Unhampered by the host of altering substances Nik had spent his life addicted to, Torben had begun to see in Nik a little of the same shadows the sposer had grown to recognize in Segara during their acquaintance. He would swear, if Segara asked, that the middle Channon bore a touch of the mage in him, but it was not a revelation he would speak out loud to anyone else.

Not even to Nik.

There were already whispers of 'mutani' amongst the Fortress staff. How else could Nik stay awake for days without a shadow of exhaustion, before collapsing into an indeterminate period of death-like sleep? A claim of mage too might be enough to condemn Nik and drive him out of his family's home, acting Laedan or not.

"Not necessary," Nik sighed before dropping his hand to pull the door open for him. "Whatever it is, it's far away. I hope she's alright."

"Marrock?" It seemed an odd person for Nik to be bound to by premonition, but Torben did not understand how being a mage worked and did not know the exact relationship between Nik and Laedan Marrock's daughter.

When Nik nodded, Torben nodded back. "Sure she's fine. They'll be back soon and we'll settle this…for all of us." His world was in upheaval too. Pulled between two jobs, rarely able to return home, Torben yearned for his former life, the simple life of a LaGuardia sposer. That was not going to happen, however, until Nik was safe.

"Stay in. I'll be back after shift."

Nik snorted. As if he had anywhere else he could go.

❧*❧

"Knew they'd be here."

The Ursa's return to the camp set up within the deserted post office had brought the news of Kennedy's small unit far to the south and HOPE's presence somewhere in the area. Talking about it as the hares Deuce had caught cooked over the fire, was easier than confronting Kato. There was no privacy to be had in this place for a personal dialogue likely to erupt into an argument. As each expected the smell of roasting meat to bring predators, human or animal or both, it had been decided they would remain together for the night.

Confronting Kato, his perceived disloyalty and disrespect, her personal complicated feelings, would have to happen later.

"HOPE's got more men…but not by a lot," Yu said, washing her face of blood with a section of cloth they had gathered when scavving. She had already cleaned QiangXu's arm, the dog bite seeming to be superficial after his return to Normal form. "We could smell them, hear them, but they're spread out. Impossible to get a good count."

"There are LaGuardia forces north of us, too," Candace added, the stress of their situation pulling at the corners of her mouth and eyes.

Looking up from the shotgun he was cleaning, Pubby muttered, "Sounds like a party." He had found a partial box of shotgun shells behind the main post office counter but he dared not test the gun or the condition of the shells until it was clean and in working order. If he wanted to use the munitions for defense, he was only going to get a single test.

If they did not want others to pinpoint their location by more than their fire and the aromas of dinner, choosing the time and place for a test shot mattered.

Squatting by the door, peering into the night, fidgeting as if to adjust to the wounds sustained in his game with HOPE's team, his eyes narrowed as he rocked restlessly side to side, Deuce grunted, "Not a party I want to attend. Don't trust any of them."

Pubby glanced at Jia who poked at the fire with a stick and indirectly watched Deuce's fidgeting. "You're a Marrock, right? Think the Channons would…?"

"After what they did to her father?" Kato shot, not looking up from the bedding he spread in one corner of the room.

"The Channons killed…?"

"That was Quentin," Jia interrupted Pubby's question, her mournful expression shifting to the back of Kato's head. They had shared the blame. "You know it." She had thought Pubby, as a Protector, would have been aware of the accusations against her and Kato for the death of her father and Jonni Channon, but if he did, he had never spoken of them or shown her distrust.

Without raising his head, Kato snorted, "Still think they put him up to it…just to blame you. Whoever's out there probably won't give us a pass…we can't give them the chance to…"

"So we shoot first, sort it out later." Vance was inclined to agree with Kato again. "If it comes to HOPE…only one of us has a guaranteed pass out of their crosshairs."

Only Pubby. The only Normal in the group.

"He's associating with us." QiangXu began to slice the sizzling, dripping flesh from one of the roasting rabbits. "Might be condemnation enough."

"Kennedy might be more forgiving…since we did save their lives…but if Hallister's there…" Yu added.

QiangXu shrugged. "We didn't see him. We don't know who's…" He had not recognized Aman. He had no idea who the man was.

It did not mean Hallister was not in the area. "But if he is," Yu continued, "and they're as eager to find what we're looking for…"

"I wouldn't count on them as allies," Vance agreed.

"So we're on our own."

At his mother's worried tone, Eddie pensively slid closer to her and wrapped his arms around her shoulders. "We don't have enough to fight them." He remembered what Pubby had said. Fighting with his brothers, in anger or mock combat, was not the same as fighting a borough army or HOPE. That truth was more real to Eddie than it had been before.

"We don't need to fight." She did not have a plan, did not know what her options were, but Jia would not commit to a fight they were unlikely to win. It would be suicide. "We have to be faster and smarter and…"

Deuce thumped the floor with one hand, interrupting her. "Someone's coming."

There was no point in dousing the fire. Whoever approached in the dark had already seen it. They could probably smell the rabbits from yards away.

Using one foot to toe open the door to allow the scent of the approaching shades inside, Deuce growled and crouched deeper, coiled and prepared for an attacking spring. He knew one of them.

It did not reassure him or change his stance.

Jia caught the scent too. Judging by Kato's sudden rise to his feet, he did as well. Her words still ringing in her ears, the reminder that they needed to be faster and smarter to avoid a fight, she stopped at the door with one calming hand on Deuce's shoulder, blocking Kato's exit, and carefully pushed it open further. Any of the three in the darkness might have guns or other hand weapons, might shoot her on sight, but she did not smell a threat. Two of the three who approached had their hands raised in capitulation and peace.

That did not mean they were not a threat.

Pain moved as low to the ground as his human body allowed, his head bowed, a familiar gesture of supplication and surrender. She smelled blood in the air, his blood, and there was evidence in his gate, in the way he favored his left shoulder, in the bruises and gashes across his face and the back of his hands and arms, of a fight. But not with the man or woman he was with, despite the blood evident on the visible portions of the older man's shirt.

A fight with another anthro.

"You don't belong…"

Jia's hand on Deuce's shoulder, as she wondered if his injuries meant the past and present omegas had clashed earlier in the day, prevented him from saying more. Her anxious trembling, however, kept him alert.

She believed he would have told her if that fight had occurred.

"We want to talk…" Pain began.

His tone supported his submission. Jia wanted to believe him. But it was not enough.

"Don't think you have anything to say," shot Candace from her protected place inside the room where her frightened defiant stance formed a shield in front of her son. Vance looked at her as she spoke but his gaze was drawn beyond her, drawn to the unsettled Fela whose wary, uncomfortable gaze seemed more intent on the silver-haired man beside Pain than on either Pain or Jia.

His mood and interest prompted Vance to rise too. Kato knew these people. If they made him uneasy, they might not be trustworthy.

It might be worth a Protector's efforts to keep the peace.

"Think we do."

The older man threw something forward, something small and metallic that rolled across the ground and stopped when it struck Jia's shoe. His gloved hand went back into the air over his head. Thinking it might be an explosive, Vance grabbed Jia's arm to pull her back as Deuce threw his body over it.

The woman with them, the only one of the three carrying a visible weapon, a long, wide cleaving blade hanging at her hip, a position easy enough to pull free if she chose, said nothing.

Jia pulled gently out of Vance's grasp but did not bend to pick up what had been thrown, not willing to put herself into a vulnerable position if Pain decided to jump. Instead, after a few tense moments when no explosion came and nothing else happened, she held her hand down so Deuce could put the object into it.

Not large enough to be a grenade or any other weapon.

A ring.

The seal Lowell had given Thomas Quentin when granting him authority to act on his behalf.

Not something Quentin would give up easily, or by choice, but possibly something he would part with long enough to double-cross her if he thought she would be baited into a parlay.

"That's yours…" Uzzi said, his tone neutral despite the effort to fish for details no one else had provided. If Pain was submitting to her, she was also Cana. If she was the Marrock mentioned before, it explained a lot of details in LaGuardia Uzzi had not had before.

They were details he would hide from others, however, for her sake as well as his own. He did not need that sort of trouble. Nor did his son.

"He's dead." Pain did not lift his head as he said the words. His posture and demeanor did not change.

Jia's eyes narrowed. Pain's behavior exposed her identity to these strangers in a way she did not like, but so far her name had not been spoken. Pain might have already told this stranger the truth. He must have for the older man to believe the ring should belong to her. Since Pain did not hide his Cana posturing, the stranger knew what Pain was.

She sniffed the air.

"He's telling the truth," started Uzzi. "I've seen…"

She hissed at his interruption and Uzzi shrugged, hands in the air. Enola's hand closed around the knife hilt.

Behind Jia, the echo of the prepped shotgun announced that Pubby had aimed at the armed woman, prepared for his test shot if the three outside forced it.

Kato struggled not to pace, not to react, nor give his knowledge of these people away. He should be there, at Jia's side, where Vance stood, to protect her, to assist her, but he was too conflicted to move, to take a stand.

Vance held out his hand to Jia. "Give it to me." He could have tried to read Pain, or either of the strangers, but the ring was easier to reach, easier to touch, and was less likely to incapacitate him or fight back for doing so. He could learn the truth by touching it and, he observed, after a nod of Pain's bowed head, that the omega assumed he would do that and was accepting the mage's assessment. He understood what Vance was; it would be foolish to lie with a tracker-mage on hand to peel back the truth.

Without looking away from Pain, Jia offered the ring in her open palm. Vance covered her hand, and the ring, with his.

Kato's lip curled.

"Elevator shaft," Vance murmured, stumbling with the momentary weightlessness of falling and the multitude of injuries across Quentin's body, wincing with the sudden impact and the shower and eruption of debris as the small room splintered on impact. There had been injuries, a moment of ceasing Quentin had not felt, had never known he was experiencing. One moment he fell and hit the floor of the elevator. The next…nothing."

"It's over."

Snorting, pulling her hand and the ring away, noting out of the corner of her eye that Eddie skirted his mother's protection to stand on Vance's other side, holding him up as he swayed beneath the sensory assault of witnessed memory, she muttered, "Over for him."

That did not mean it was over for her. Her primary adversary in LaGuardia, her accuser, her father's killer, the man who had Lowell's ear for so long, might be dead, but it did not mean Lowell would believe she was innocent. Lowell had turned on his best friend. It seemed likely he would remain against her as well.

Especially if he was here to get his hands on Fort Hamilton's weapons and thought she was an adversary.

Softly Pain said, "He came for the weapons…was going to come whether I was…"

"You were leading him to her," Deuce growled.

"I hoped she would end this…for…" He dared to lift his brown eyes to hers but quickly lowered them without speaking her father's name. Perhaps he had not revealed her identity to the stranger after all. "I wanted to be here when you…when he…I didn't expect the way things happened…"

"Vance?"

The mage nodded. The words were true. He had felt the longing to kill from the ring she had been given, Pain's thoughts glossing a thin sheen atop Quentin's. The older man had left little imprint upon the metal surface. Pain's longing to kill had not been aimed at, or intended for, Jia. He had wanted retribution for Roland.

The death had both been accidental and intentional; he was glad Quentin was dead. His thirst for death and blood ended there.

Jia weighed the admission against what she saw, what she scented, what she wanted to believe, and the fears she carried. If she was wrong, if she drove him from her in his innocence, she was no better than her father. If she let him join her as she assumed was his intent, and her perceptions of his purpose were wrong, she would deserve it the next time he rose against her.

"How many with you?"

"Now?" The older man was the one to reply, his shoulders tilting in an uncertain shrug. "One more I trust with my life…and yours." The words were directed at Jia but his blue-eyed stare had shifted towards Kato who was visible over her shoulder. "Ten more trustworthy enough…so long as they're paid…"

"Mercs," Pubby spat.

"We don't have…" started Jia.

The older man continued over top of both of the speaking voices, "People making a living the only way some of us can," he deflected unapologetically. "Not all of us have the good fortune to be born on the right side of Laedan Law."

"So you don't respect authority?" Pubby challenged.

"Anything that keeps me ahead of HOPE is a good path; all I'm saying. I'd wager," Uzzi looked from Kato back to Jia, "you understand that.'

Anthro were always born on the wrong side of Laedan Law, simply by the accident of what they were. They might follow the rules, but they were outside the natural order, and it made them as dangerous to order in some ways as any mercs or ruffs were.

She frowned.

"You want paid?" asked Pubby. "Revenge on HOPE?"

Uzzi's sideways smile was answer enough. "Believe me," he said, offering his hand, "I'd rather be as far from HOPE as possible. Name's

Uzziah…this is Enola. Dink's back with the rest. As for pay…" He shrugged. "Cut us in on what you're looking to bring back and we'll call it square."

"We're not bringing anything back," Yu said.

"If we find what they think's out there," QiangXu agreed, "We're blowing it up."

"Really?" Since Jia had not accepted the offered greeting gesture, Uzzi lowered his hand and looked at Kato. The claim was unexpected.

Their visual exchange again attracted Vance's attention, as did the twitching at the corners of the Fela's eyes and lips.

"It makes sense," was Jia's reply.

"This I gotta see," Uzzi nodded with a bemused expression. "Told me you were a force to reckon with…"

Pain shook his head in denial. He had never said those words. Kato turned his face away.

"We've got HOPE out there. LaGuardia and Kennedy. They outnumber us…and they're not going to give up easily." Even with Uzzi's fourteen people, the odds were stacked against them. "We're heading out at daybreak. If you're in…you'll be here before that. Not in here…out there."

She would not bring strangers into her camp, people who might murder them in their sleep. Inviting them to camp outside of the post office doors, where they could lay siege and prevent those inside from getting out, was a risk on its own.

"We'll be here, Alpha." Despite the physical discomfort of his injuries, the gesture Pain made was the closest to groveling she had ever seen Pain display, to her or to her father.

"With as many as we can sway…even if it's only four of us and a dog," Uzzi promised, beginning to retreat, unwilling to turn his back on a collection of anthro who could tear him to shreds.

He had led an attack against their pack. When they learned the truth, it would be enough for them to turn on him.

His gaze tried to lure Kato to follow.

Kato did not move.

Thankfully, thought Uzzi, Kato did not know the truth either.

"Deuce…see them away."

Deuce nodded, shed torn clothing, and the wolf followed the trio into the shadows. They might know he was there.

Pain certainly did.

"Don't like this," Vance muttered. There was no deception in Pain and he believed Quentin was dead. But there was something in the older man, a hint of deception he could not identify that made Vance less certain they should trust these people.

"You said he's trust…"

"Pain? He's telling the truth. They both are about Quentin but…I…" Kato made a snorting sound in the back of his throat cutting Vance off and prompting him to shrug. He had gotten mixed signals from the older man, making it difficult to judge how much he knew about them, about Jia, and to fathom his intentions. "Don't know what it is yet. But I say we watch him. Watch them both. Watch them all."

"We will," promised Pubby.

Out here, without the Pack behind her, a confrontation with Pain could spin off in directions she did not want to consider. Eyeing Kato too, assessing the sound he made and the shared look between Fela and mage who had been at odds since their first meeting that irritated the nerves at the back of her neck, Jia grunted and returned to the fire.

Kato took watch at the door in the place Deuce had vacated without meeting Jia's gaze.

She grunted and muttered, "I intend to."

⧫*⧫

"Storm drove the cod in," Gail said with a satisfied smile as her sole servant, a girl who cooked and cleaned so Gail could focus on her work, set the steaming bowl of stew on the table between them. The day had proven more productive than expected. Having convinced the local residents they were a medical facility and Plant, a host of strangers aided in the cleanup and reconstruction so the last of the burned portions of the exterior walls had been removed and replaced to keep the foul weather out. Materials were dragged in from nearby empty buildings to complete the work. The plant furnace was not yet operational, meaning the surviving stock of 'patients' continued to be barely maintained in the outer shed with a generator serving to keep the pods' temperature controlled and the stock fed through the IV tubes piercing their flesh. Gail's staff seemed confident the furnaces would be working by tomorrow evening.

Materials and corpses to burn in them were already being delivered.

Without Norse's help, his interface with the community that had prompted their aid, she did not think so much would have been accomplished so quickly.

It was almost a shame, she thought as the girl ladled soup into both bowls and Gail split a loaf of bread in half to offer him a portion, this needed to be done.

He was her best supplier of stock.

She did not blame him.

She blamed Geary.

"I imagine the shore is littered with the bounty." Such storms often brought kelp and mussels, stranded fish and octopus in tide pools for plundering by the residents along the sea's edge. Trade always brought that abundance inland so it was no surprise the doctor would take advantage of the opportunity to acquire something rare and share it with her guest.

Many people took similar advantage of the bounty.

"You aren't allergic, are you?"

"Not to seafood." Eyeing her skeptically, he added, "Not to anything."

"Good." She smiled. "I know some who are; it is never a pretty thing. I think it's the toxins from the mainland…things left by the Undoing that washes into the water."

Norse nodded. "There's a lot of that." Not just from the sea. The Undoing had poisoned so much. Those poisons, it was said, had given rise to the anthro and mutani. He did not see why it should be so, but he was a simple man. If not those poisons, what else could have created such abominations?

"You'll need more stock; if you want me to see what I can find, we could build a holding cell until you've got pods ready…"

Her spoonful of stew hovered between the bowl and her mouth as she stared at him. He ate with gusto, savoring the sweet and spicy flavor of the blended fish broth and onions. Her moment of reconsideration, however, was brief.

His lulling words, as sincere as the offer sounded, were only that. Words. Geary would never permit his efforts, no matter what he offered. If it was not him, it would be her. It was unfortunate she could see Geary's double-cross coming from so far off.

She had always been fond of Norse.

Of both of them, if she was honest.

The spoon touched her lips.

Norse began to choke.

"Are you…here…have some water…" She filled his glass from the table pitcher and slid it towards him, rising from her chair with alarm as one of his hands clutched at his chest, the other at his throat. "Norse…can you breathe? Tell me."

She knew how to save a man from choking. The effort was made as the servant returned to the room and dropped the tray of fruit she carried. "Don't stand there!" Gail ordered. "Get help!"

The door into the kitchen clattered and banged as the girl ran out.

There was nothing to be done. Frothing at the mouth, Norse continued to twitch and spasm in Gail's arms as she held him, smoothing his hair back with one hand. She thought she should apologize while he could hear her, before doing what he would have done if given the opportunity. The most comfort she could offer, however, was the stroking of his hair. By the time the servant returned with one of the nursing staff and the cook, Norse was limp in her arms, his eyes rolled up in their sockets.

"It must have been…he must have been…" stammered the serving girl, pale-faced, certain she would be blamed.

"Yes," Gail murmured. "He must have been."

It was the lie she would tell Geary.

She did not expect him to believe her. Without a mage, he would not be able to prove anything. Even with a mage, the details would be uncertain at best.

She would not believe her either…if she was him.

Chapter 42

It was with mixed feelings and the exhaustion of a night's lost sleep that Jia found Pain, Uzzi, Enola, and a gaggle of indistinguishable forms waiting in the pre-dawn chill outside of their post office shelter. Thankfully the ruffs had not camped there during the night but had instead remained in whatever shelter they had already claimed. Uzzi waited at the head of his followers as Jia emerged to greet them. Pain gave Deuce a wide berth as Deuce glowered and glared from Jia's side at every move the omega made and Kato did his best to avoid the newcomers from a safe distance behind.

Uzzi noted Kato's position, the posturing of Pain and Deuce, and offered his hand with a nod, again expecting she would reject the offer. "As promised."

She hesitated long enough to sweep her gaze over the rabble, men and women in mismatched attire with an array of weapons and tools to use as such. They wore the thin-faced shadows of hunger and weariness, the unwashed stench that enveloped much of humanity, but none appeared to be overly weak or suffering. Though they watched her, and those with her, with the same wariness, they appeared willing to serve, to fight for whatever Uzzi had promised. Jia nodded her approval of them, of him, giving her welcome, and accepted Uzzi's gesture and pledge of support with a returned, "As promised."

He tipped his head towards a point in the distance without asking for the name she had not yet given. "There's movement to the south…whoever they are, they're not very quiet." He had noticed them as he picked his way over ice and through tall weeds and had stood long enough in the cold to continue to monitor the movement as he waited for Jia to appear.

"Probably HOPE," Pubby snorted as he shouldered the newly acquired shotgun and double-checked that his pistols, empty though they were, were easily accessible on his hip and against his ribs. "Confident bastards; probably don't think they need caution."

"Might not know we're here," said QiangXu.

"We should keep it that way," Yu agreed.

"Did you see them? Where they were heading?" asked Jia.

Pain gestured towards a large structure to the west of their position, having scouted the area earlier when the anxiety of the upcoming day refused to allow him to sleep. It was not as dominant as the medical complex, but it was large enough to be noteworthy, another possibility for the mass storage of hidden weapons.

"Kennedy's that way somewhere too," Yu added. They would have sought refuge from the feral dogs, regrouped, made a new plan but no one expected them to leave.

"And we know LaGuardia's to the north; we saw the uniforms before." Uzzi felt slightly rankled and unsettled to give command to a girl with barely enough years to have significant life experience, one who would not introduce herself. Those around her appeared to trust her judgment, Kato did too, even if he did appear to be keeping his distance. It did little to derail Uzzi's compulsion to take control.

Jia studied the horizon in each direction, weighing options, the heaviness of their expectations pressing on her shoulders as if to make them sag. They were pinched between multiple adversaries with no clear indication where their objective might be located. The building in front of them seemed as promising as anything else, but a run-in with HOPE was something to be avoided. They might be able to talk their way through a diplomatic confrontation with the Channon and Hallister camps but they would never do so with HOPE.

"Deuce?"

Having spent his watch roaming the nearby streets with his Cana nose to the ground, to the wind, after making sure Pain and his companions returned to their hospital camp, Deuce shrugged.

"Offices…an abandoned education center I think. Don't think what you want is there." He could be wrong, if those of the ancient world had thought storing munitions beneath children was a good idea. Head tilting to the side, he added, "West to the change is pretty wild."

Yu pointed south, "Mostly old housing that way."

"Unless what we want is in the wilds," offered Candace hopefully, eager to leave the discomfort of unknown streets for the security and familiarity of the wilds.

"Then what we want," Vance finished, "is probably north." North to cross paths with whichever Channon was there, or perhaps, if they were lucky, with Captain Ortega. Ortega had always seemed neutral to the mage.

Arlo had seemed supportive of her father on the occasions when Jia had interacted with him. Finding him in command was the best they could hope for. To Uzzi and Pain, she asked, "You know where they were going?"

Pain shrugged. "No, but I can track them" He knew every pack signal. He could warn her, announce LaGuardia's movements, with a sound that would carry across the divide of the grounds between them.

"As can I," grunted Deuce, wanting to trust the man who had taken his place at the bottom of the pack's hierarchy, but after multiple attempts on Jia's life, he trusted Pain only as far as he could heave him. If Pain was going anywhere out of Jia's sight where he might double-cross her, he was not going to do it alone.

Jia agreed. "Both of you then…but keep your distance. Don't let them see you." A pair of wolves would not expose her and the others to LaGuardia, but it might put the two Cana in danger. Both nodded and stripped away clothing that would shred in the change.

If Uzzi and his followers did not suspect Jia's Cana nature before, they were likely to suspect it now.

"Pretty open out there," muttered Kato as though the observation was an afterthought.

"They'll be fine…" And so will we, Jia decided.

There were unexplored places at the opposite end of the bowling alley building and a large structure adjacent to it on the west.

LaGuardia's people were there. Beyond it, abandoned vehicles denoted another parking area surrounded by winter-bare maples. The gray walls of more buildings had been noted on the northwest side. It was where Jia intended to go next.

It would keep them far away from their competition, she hoped.

"Stay together; no wandering off." She addressed the warning primarily to Kato but also to the stranger who lead what was either a band of reinforcements or a threat. "Keep your eyes open, even in the wilds. Could be a hidden entrance anywhere."

"Underground?" whispered Eddie. He had left the library with visions of a mighty, castle-like structure in mind.

Having to go Below, into a realm of grubbers and Unders where he had never been, was a frightening idea.

Uzzi nodded. "Good place to hide something you don't want others to find," he agreed. He had found enough hidden underground rooms with supplies, goods and materials, in his years as a scav, a thief, a merc. Just because the hospital basement had not yielded what they were looking for did not mean it was the only structure with underground access. Anything kept above ground was too easy for outsiders to ransack. Basements and underground storerooms potentially connected by tunnels between these local structures came with the offering of Unders and grubbers who had fallen in and not been able to get out. They also came with the potential of water seeping in from the subterranean water table and burst pipes and ground collapses, but those hazards were good ways to protect what someone did not want to be found.

The two Cana scouts yipped in tandem and ran to the northeast after a flick of Jia's hand, Pain leading Deuce in the direction where he had last noted LaGuardia's force to be, each warily eyeing the other. Jia looked at Vance, who bobbed his head and fell into step beside her when she decided to move.

His knowledge of the map had gotten them here. Now in the right area, where the Fort was meant to be, he was as blind as the rest of them to what they needed to find and perhaps less useful if his skills failed to offer them warnings or insights they could use.

He fretted it was true.

Jia's hand unexpectedly squeezing his assured him she needed him there, wanted him there, regardless of what he believed.

Kato growled.

❧*❧

Irritated by the nightlong symphony of coughing that had kept him awake and the proximity of his father's corpse that prompted a parade of nightmares when he did sleep, nightmares about the man's grubber hands reaching for his throat to his mother's mournful wailing, Donn eventually gave in to necessity and permitted the man's burial here in the godforsaken ruins of what was meant to be a great fort. Thus far, the area was proving to be as worthless as any stretch of buildings in LaGuardia. There was no plant to spose of the man's corpse, no tree to plant in his honor, no fuel for cremation to provide ashes to take back to the Fortress for burial with their Channon ancestors.

This burial was the best Laedan Lowell Channon would have.

It was all Donnovan was willing to give him.

Propriety. The people of LaGuardia would demand some token ceremony when he returned. Donn would allow it because custom demanded it.

But he could not say he cared about the man who had threatened his life.

Men had been struggling to dig in the frozen earth throughout the night. As the sun crested the horizon, lending a pale pink glow to the perpetual gray clouds, LaGuardia's Laedan was given silent rest.

Donn had no words to say on his behalf.

Captain Ortega, the Laedan's badge of office in hand, his personal effects stuffed into his camp pack, stepped up to say, "You were a good man, sirra. LaGuardia will miss you. I will miss you. We all will. We will see to LaGuardia's future. Rest in eternal peace with your wife and son…and trust the borough is in secure hands."

Donn scowled.

He would have to do something about Ortega before they returned to the Fortress. Ortega was the one person who might topple Donn's plans if he could not be swayed to join him, but he was an obstacle Donn was confident he could overcome, one way or another.

With the urgency of finding the treasure before General Warby or the Hallister team, Donn demanded they set out as soon as a blank stone slab was set as a flat marker over his father's dirt-covered body. Camp needed to be taken down, however, the weary men stuffing uncooked food into their mouths as they did so to avoid being disallowed a meal. By the time they began to slog through the thawing mud towards the next building in their path, the sun was near its zenith.

Too much time wasted.

Since his father had given the Laedanship to him at last, the delay was a sacrifice Donn was forced to reluctantly abide.

❧*❦

The church was abandoned for a school, rooms of books and computers without power to run them, a supply closet and a library full of learning materials, and another of cleaning tools and chemicals, some of which had long ago corroded through their containers. Those which had not were bundled into packs to provide burning fuel, explosive fuel, in case Aman's much-dwindled team needed them.

They might no longer burn. The compounds within each container might have broken down to the point of uselessness.

The weakened state of his team, however, demanded invention if they were to complete their mission and make it home with news of what they found. If they succeeded, they did not need to transport everything back to Kennedy. They needed to protect it here long enough for a messenger to go back, for Laedan Hallister to send another team with the resources to move whatever they found.

Potential explosives might be a good start to holding off enemies in the event of a siege.

His followers were demoralized and weary, trudging through the building, poking through the rubble, stoop-shouldered and distracted.

Rather than pushing them into another forced march to yet another likely empty building, or risk running into HOPE and a fight they could not win, Aman opted for the slow but thorough search of this one, from top to bottom, and a raiding of cafeteria canned goods that allowed for a substantial, if slightly tasteless, warm meal with the setting of the sun.

An easy day, a full belly, a good night's rest.

It was the best Aman could give them.

If they had to fight tomorrow, if they had to march or die, one good day, and a message and crude map sent to Geary with the man Aman felt most likely to make the journey alive, was worth the delay.

⧫*⧫

"We camp here."

The suite of offices, a military hub with faded, printed resources worth preserving for HOPE's archives, was spacious enough to prompt Warby to spread his forces thin to explore every room, every closet, every storage nook in the hopes that directions, a map or memo or guidebook, something that would direct them to where weapons might be stored, could be found. Sturdily built and shielded by acres of buildings around them that had, to his trained eye, been relatively untouched by scavs since the Undoing, this complex had not suffered the degree of decay and destruction he was used to seeing. It would suffice as a warmer, drier overnight camp as the day came to an end.

He had not found what he was looking for yet, but a secure camp, the artifacts and historical documents gathered and stashed on one of the wagons, was adequate compensation for their efforts.

He decided it would also be a good base from which he could explore the entire area, where the wagons could be stored instead of dragging them from one vacant, worthless location to the next. A handful of people would be left to protect their supplies, the wagons, enough to deter Kennedy from raiding them.

The absent Channon remained Warby's primary concern.

No one had found him, or seen him, since the fitness center. His corpse had not been recovered. If death had come for him, if he had turned, his ambling grubber form could have meandered anywhere. The territory from the eastern border to the western change, from the sea to the distant wilds, was too vast, too populated with buildings, and dotted with patches of wild earth, each with its pitfalls, to allow a more extensive search or to allow such a search to be readily successful without clues to follow, without a tracker-mage to aid them.

Son of one Laedan, son-in-law of the other, both were going to have Warby's head if he failed to locate him. They would hold HOPE accountable if anything happened to Donnovan, and the Grand Mas would probably blame him too.

"Not my fault," Warby grumbled as he tossed a wooden table leg onto the fire someone had built. If the fool had gotten killed, it was not Warby's doing. He would have killed Donn himself if he had thought his death would be worthwhile.

On the off chance Donn had been taken by the circling enemy, Warby sent men as spies to discover if his concerns were true.

He had to say he tried to find the younger man. An honest fellow, he had to try to support his claim. He did not, however, have to look for Donn himself.

❧*❧

They skirted the perimeter, listening to the yips of their patrolling comrades, knowing when LaGuardia broke camp, knowing which direction they moved, where they eventually stopped. Something had delayed LaGuardia's progress, a boon enabling Jia's group to cross from one parking lot into another, to nose through the wilds, and make a circle of the most promising building they had encountered thus far.

A United States Army Garrison.

The entity known as the United States ceased to exist some time after the Undoing. Perhaps it had existed formally after the initial events ground the world to a stop, but having lost control of the majority of their territory almost immediately as communication was severed with the world, all cohesion had abruptly ended. For Jia, for the others with her, as they slipped into a broken-doored building to the north of the garrison, the world was reduced to the boroughs and the lands immediately surrounding them. The edge of the known world had stretched a little further, to Fort Hamilton and the rise of the elevated change they had seen to the west. For Kato, the world had begun further east.

But there was nothing united about the world any longer. Survival meant every individual, every family, fought for themselves…even those living under a Laedan's claimed control.

"A bank," murmured Vance, running his fingers over the dusty countertop, recognizing the area's function only by its layout. There were other external entrances, broken signs denoting a commissary and an identification office, but this room offered the clearest line of sight to the garrison they had jointly deemed to be their target when the sun came up.

What they sought could also be in the building they currently inhabited. Banks meant vaults, some larger than others, so Vance thought it worth investigating. Without adequate light, however, exploration was not going to be thorough tonight.

"Think there's anything valuable?"

Vance gave Uzzi a side-eyed, dubious look. The man shrugged.

"Fair question. I've got pockets out there to line…and I don't see any of you offering to do it." The people whose pockets he spoke of were building small fires around what had once been the bank lobby but Dink and Enola remained by the door, watching through the cracked glass into the growing darkness for either signs of trouble or the two Cana scouts. Across the empty parking area, beyond the wilds they had previously searched, they knew LaGuardia had taken shelter in the building adjacent to the bowling alley. The trees separating them, the walls at the back of the building, and another between, kept their presence in the bank hidden, even with the warming fires glowing. It would only take one LaGuardia scout, however, to note their camp and bring a middle-of-the-night raid.

No matter how evenly matched their numbers might be, according to Deuce and Pain's announced count, no one was looking for a fight.

Not even those who expected one to be inevitable.

"Someone's beaten us to it." Uzzi followed Candace's voice to a busted half-door and another beyond it blasted off the hinges. The room beyond was lined with small drawers, some open and empty, some beaten upon as if to force them open. Most remained sealed.

"Could there be a key?" piped Eddie. "A map to the weapons?"

"Could we blow them open?" asked Kato from the room's doorway, reluctant to enter in his father's footsteps but curious to see what had been found. The concept of a bank meant nothing to most of them and Kato had no idea what such drawers might contain, but Uzzi seemed excited by the find.

"Not unless you want to destroy everything in them," QiangXu said, tracing a lock with one finger before rummaging through the pouch at his hip. "Don't think they would have kept a key and map like that here…but there might be a master key for these on the premises…long as it hasn't been scavved."

The only other option was to try to pick them open, a task that would take many hours, perhaps many days, to complete if he was to open each drawer. He found the length of wire he had scavved elsewhere for bomb-making, a piece stiff enough he hoped it would work for this purpose. He bent it in half and began to poke and pry in the lock of the large drawer nearest to him.

"Keep at it," prompted Uzzi. "I'll look for something to help."

"Could Mage Segara find the key?" Candace offered hopefully. While not seeking treasure, she was curious about the drawers, eager for a distraction from the outside, and worried they might contain hidden threats as dangerous as those they were hiding from. The focus of her curiosity helped provide a diversion for her son as well.

"Maybe," Uzzi agreed though he made no effort to enlist the mage's help as he pushed past Kato. He did not want to remain near a man who could read his thoughts if he chose to. One of the last people to know his secrets was finally dead. The other likely believed he was.

As far as Uzzi was concerned, he was free. The mage did not need leverage over him too.

Uzzi also recognized the jealous enmity between Kato and the mage, something he did not want to be involved in. Best not to aggravate the situation. They could sort out their issues without his meddling.

In the lobby, Jia hoisted onto the counter Vance was examining, looking beneath for drawers, for buttons, for anything dropped and abandoned when the last people had been here. It was a high enough perch for her feet to swing without touching the ground. The glare of the fires reflected off the dark plate glass window-walls of the building's front façade so she could barely make out the outline of the nearest building.

"Think that's it?" she whispered in a low voice, wiping her nose to stifle the sneeze the dust was trying to elicit. Kato was preoccupied with the newcomer and though his distrust of the stranger was expected, she felt there was more to his mood than he was revealing. It had something to do with the stranger. Something to do with her.

She was relieved Vance was still speaking to her.

"Garrison sounds promising, but I don't expect we'll walk in and find weapons laying around. People took what was important…" he gestured to the drawers open before him, empty of cash, money that had, in the end, proven useless after the collapse of civilization. "I'd think it'll be the same there…but maybe…" He looked up from the drawer to see her face reflected in the glass across the room, her features burdened by too many worries for one so young, and wished he could hug her, shoulder some of her burdens. Hugging for a mage could be an incapacitating exchange, however, and he doubted the gesture would help or benefit her in any significant way. Not an embrace from him at least. "How are you doing?"

"I miss Liam." The words came out unexpectedly and she bit her lower lip when she realized what she had said. The longer she spent in this unfamiliar place, looking for something she was unsure she would find, separated from her friends and family, the more deeply Liam burrowed into her mind. Concerns about how he was doing, how he was managing the Pack, if he had survived the potential attack, if he thought about her, filled many of her waking moments, particularly as Kato pulled further away and Vance did his utmost to maintain a professional distance.

To cover the unnecessary revelation with a deeper admission she continued, "I miss Addie…I miss my father…" Her swinging foot struck the cabinet, creating an empty thump on the wood surface that caused others to startle, lurch to full attention, look at her, and return to what they had been doing. "I wonder how Nik's doing…"

Her first admission was not surprising but the words cut Vance more than he expected them to. They burned enough to make him yearn for the bottle in his pack he had thus far resisted. Having it on hand eased the longing since his last drink, but it did not relieve the longing for something he could not have.

It was no wonder so many mages brought their short, troubled lives to an abrupt end. Loneliness was a bastard.

"Sure they're fine," he murmured. "Liam's clearly a survivor," like you, "and Addi's got your brains." He could not guarantee his beliefs, but he was relieved when she nodded, accepting the sentiments without dispute. Sounds from the back of the building made them look towards the open security door, the personal exchange pushed aside.

Kato, watching from the doorway, looked away as if he was more interested in what was happening in the back room than in eavesdropping on their conversation.

Rather than express her thoughts out loud to prevent anyone from hearing them, Jia slid her hand, splayed on the countertop, until her fingertips pressed against Vance's.

The mage jumped. He nodded to her unspoken question and wondered if he should tell her what he knew.

It was a suspicion not his to reveal. But he believed someone had to do so.

☙*❧

It was not weapons found in one of the multitude of rooms this shopping area housed, but the crates of pouches brought into the main area where the disheartened LaGuardia force gathered were nearly as valuable. The find was more useful, in Arlo's opinion, to the people of LaGuardia than would be scores of guns, bullets, and explosives that would only be used against anyone deemed to be dissidents by the people who held power.

"Believe they're called emarees," he explained to the man whose sneering skepticism made him wary. "It's food meant to be taken into combat, stored to last, easy to carry…easy to prepare…nutritious. And there's a lot of it."

More, he mused as he rummaged through the box at his feet, than they would be easily able to transport to LaGuardia, particularly if their wagons were loaded with munitions. It was not an indefinite supply, not enough to feed the entire borough for more than a week or two, but it would be useful if properly rationed.

"We don't need food."

We don't need weapons, Arlo thought, swallowing his protests as he handed one pouch each to every hand that reached for one. "It'll stretch what we have, make the trip home less worrisome."

"You worried, Captain?"

Lips pursed to avoid frowning, Arlo responded, "You're not? We don't know who's out there…how many…what we're going to find."

"I know precisely who's out there." There was only one person Donn felt any concern about, and that was General Warby. So long as Captain Ortega and his soldiers obeyed orders, however, Donn felt confident they could best the threat, despite the ill health of the men coughing and snuffling around him.

"HOPE. Yes; so you've said." Arlo did not trust HOPE to work with them, share with them, if it came to munitions both sides wanted. He knew Donn had no interest in sharing. The desire for power would prevent HOPE from accepting LaGuardia's claim over anything they found that might, in turn, be used against HOPE…as the Laedan would refuse to accept it from the Grand Mas and his minions regardless of any past cooperation.

But Lowell was no longer here to take a stand and negotiate a truce with the Grand Mas and whomever he had sent to Fort Hamilton.

With Donnovan, there would be no negotiation. He was not the negotiating sort.

Their faltering dialogue was cut short by the blaring of music erupting from one of the other rooms. It filled the building and ruptured the night, shattering the silence and causing every person within the building to scramble to locate the source of the sound.

The snippet of tune did not last long. The source, as Arlo and Donn flew into the origination room with shouts and swearing, was being smashed by a heavy length of shelving pipe by another, as the hapless fellow who had inadvertently caused the chaos stared at the sound system with alarm.

"You've given away our…" started Donn, kept from throwing the poor man against the wall by Arlo and the others between them.

"Didn't try to!" the man protested. "All I did was lean on it…"

"Couldn't have known it was powered," Arlo retorted defensively as he grabbed the arm of the man smashing the unit so that sound could no longer announce their presence to the outside world. He likely had not even known what the machine was capable of.

That smashing was as much a giveaway of their location as the short blast of music had been.

Irrationally, Donn hissed, "He should have!" before Arlo's other hand clapped over his mouth to silence him too. Donn yanked the hand down angrily, prepared to retort, but the abrupt heavy silence of the night, punctuated by a pair of wolf howls, took his breath away.

Donn strained his ears to listen. For a threat, for the monster scream they had not heard since their first night here, for someone or something throwing themselves against the doors and windows of their hideout.

Nothing came.

The wolves stopped howling.

The silence remained.

Donn glowered at the guilty man and snarled, "It happens again, I'll have your hands," before stomping out of the room, throwing an accusatory glare at the captain who had dared to silence him.

Losing hands would be better than losing a life. The offender was safe for now. Arlo, however, expected that by morning Donn would have his retribution one way or another. He did not think he would be able to prevent either threat, or worse, from coming to pass.

❧*❧

Some of them froze.

Some erupted to their feet, grabbing weapons or burning timbers from their fires to use as such. Jia caught herself mid-involuntary change, the muscles of her limbs straining against the fabric to pop stitches and rip it in some places as the instinct to take half-form for an unexpected fight rose to the surface. She threw herself without thought between the glass windows and the mage, but the brief moment of unexpected blaring music ended as abruptly as it began, ending as soon as she stopped moving, poised for combat.

"The monster?" whimpered Eddie, cowering behind his mother.

"No." Kato remembered music like that, played on a hand-cranked player his mother had owned, a gift, she had said, from his father. He looked at Uzzi, perplexed.

Uzzi nodded. He remembered that gift too. He did not think, however, this was the same thing.

"Manmade," Pubby muttered, straining to listen to the outside world without opening the door. "Radio maybe."

Radios, after the Undoing, had lasted as long as there was power to operate them. As long as there were others available to send and receive signals. One by one they had fallen silent, but they had persisted long enough to remain in the verbal memory of humanity.

"Think someone…?" QiangXu began.

Jia nodded in agreement as the pair of howls was cast into the void the music left in its wake. They had known they were not alone. This further confirmed what they knew. Judging by Vance's expression and the faces of the others, no one knew anything more about the sound than she did. Until the pair of scouts returned, they could not know the origin of that sound either.

☙*❧

Aman was the first to the door, gun in hand, expecting a threat to follow the short-lived tune that rattled the schoolhouse windows and made his harried team brace for the inevitable conflict. A few shuddered at the howls that followed, the reminder of the feral dogs hunting the night bringing back remembrances of the dead.

No dogs followed. No eyes glimmering in the night, no monster scream or sound of running boots on the attack. Only silence and the proof they were not alone.

Crouched, waiting, not a single person was likely to move or sleep that night.

Aman's choice to give his people a day at ease had proven to be a wise one.

☙*❧

"General, think we found them…"
The scout only spoke when the night was silent again.
Warby's grin was feral and slightly malicious.
Yes, he thought. I think we have too.

Chapter 43

L eaving a handful of men to continue exploring the building selected as their camp, sending others west to investigate and secure the long building his scouts had spotted through the trees, Warby reluctantly took the rest in pursuit of the errant Channon heir, reportedly seen with another group bearing LaGuardia uniforms.

It was a logical place, if the Laedan was there, for Donn to go.

He had a plan, with several contingencies that would depend on what happened when he found the Channons. If the Laedan was in charge, Warby was confident of his chances to convince the man to join forces. There might even be an advantage if he could persuade both LaGuardia and Kennedy to work together with him. Which path he chose would revolve around the base belief in the strength of numbers. The more they worked together, so long as the Channons and Hallisters were willing, the better the chances they would find what they sought. The higher the likelihood of success.

They knew the location of the night's eruption of music.

Reaching it before LaGuardia left the area was Warby's goal.

Intermittent canine howls, distant but close enough to monitor, and the icy wind blowing off the sea, were the only things that could foil them.

Not the dark. Not fear.

Certainly not Donn Channon.

❧*❦

The others agreed. Approaching the two-story garrison under the cover of darkness made sense, despite the frigid temperatures and the wind that tugged hair and clothes to the side, into eyes, across exposed noses made red by the cold. Automotive garages and the lot east of them, once filled with military vehicles, were empty, looted or abandoned when the last soldiers stationed here had moved into the surrounding streets to restore peace that failed to hold. The tools contained behind sheet metal walls had been scavved, those metal walls as well, and the solar panels over the southern parking had been destroyed by wind and rain, snow, and hail. None of those things sheltered the swiftly moving hunched figures facing into the gale.

With the proximity of LaGuardia's force, they chose not to linger in the storm longer than necessary.

The locked garrison door, rusted and unused since the Undoing, required the force of a heavy mallet brought with them from the lumber house. The ringing crash of the impact when Deuce, the biggest and strongest among them, swung at the door, echoed across the compound. Eyes on the horizon, watching in the dark for threats, Jia hoped the wind's wail had swallowed the majority of the sound and swept what remained inland.

One blow caused the door to swing inward, pushed by a gust to clatter against something behind preventing it from opening further. Dink, after turning the dog loose to protect their flank, joined Deuce in forcing the door open far enough to permit entry.

The blocking object turned out to be a metal desk.

The musty reek of stale death spewed into their faces, making those at the front cough and gag.

The faded lobby, dimly lit and layered in the sheen of undisturbed dust, was littered with the molding, shriveled effects of the dead, bodies decayed to bones held together by the clothing they wore or else dispersed by the vermin that had picked them clean. This was the first significant evidence of mass death they had found since the warnings given by the man with the whiskey wagon. There were firearms amongst them, handguns, assault rifles, and ammunition Pubby, Uzzi, and a few others, were quick to collect.

"Careful," Pubby instructed. They had likely been in working order when the dead barricaded themselves behind windows blocked by bookshelves that kept out the sun and the desk at the door, but after being so long unused, collecting dust particles and moisture from the air, the guns would need cleaning before they were reliable.

Vance leaned on the frame of the doorway after everyone squeezed inside, grimacing at the force of imagery bombarding his mage senses. No one had entered here since the fall, when the dead had made their final stand. Though memories and images did not typically linger so long, perhaps, he mused as Jia's hand closed around his, the final traumatic thoughts and feelings of these people remained because no one had entered to disturb them.

Or their final days of terror had been so great the ghosts of it had seeped into the walls, the furnishings, the sagging ceiling tiles, and refused to dissipate.

He shook his head to her unspoken question, his eyes squeezed shut, a question he could not read directly without skin-to-skin contact but saw in her eyes when he peered out between his narrowed lids as Yu murmured, "I don't like it here."

QiangXu was already removing the radiation counter from his pack, thinking the uneasy prickle over his skin might be the unseen silent killer that had affected those around them.

"There was no violence here." Enola squatted to inspect the nearest scatter of bones, touching them without disgust, only a sense of reverence for the deceased many no longer displayed. "No blood." Her fingers traced through the dust and she brought it to her nose as if to smell it. "It's like they died where they stood."

The radiation counter buzzed.

"Moderate…not dangerous if we don't stay long."

"Was it higher when they…?" began Eddie with a sick note in his squeaking voice. "Did it kill them?"

"Poisoned air," Vance murmured, his hand pressed to his chest to alleviate the heavy sensation accumulating there. "They suffocated; it's dissipated now."

"They do it to themselves?" Uzzi shoved the handgun he picked up through his hip belt and tightened the leather to secure it.

"I don't think so."

A corridor ran off both sides of the lobby, barely discernable in the pre-dawn shadow. None of them carried light sources but soon the sun would rise and there would be light coming in around the objects used to bar windows. A placard on one wall, next to a door likewise blocked with an upturned desk denoted a stairwell; beside it, a door into a tiny paneled room was held ajar by the lack of power and a leather, metal, and plastic swivel chair wedged into its track. The entrance door, no longer closing due to the broken latch, clattered against the metal desk with every gust of wind sweeping inside to stir up the dust of the dead.

"We'll take the upper floor," volunteered Uzzi, already motioning to his people to follow him.

"Not without one of us," growled Kato. The narrow-eyed glower he shot at the older man made Vance scowl.

"We don't need all of you to…" started Jia, brow furrowed.

"And we need sentries." It was a duty Deuce was well suited for, one he was used to fulfilling, and though he protectively wanted to follow Jia as she poked through dangerous rooms, they needed to be diligent for hazards from the outside as well.

"Someone should stay here…a central hub…so no one sneaks in," Vance suggested.

"Fine." It was not acquiescence but rather an acknowledgment of the points each speaker made. "You two," she gestured to Enola and Dink, "take the south. Candace, go with them." She trusted her new Cana packmate more than she trusted the man and woman she barely knew. Though Candace nodded and shot a concerned glance at her son, her concern about being separated from him noted, there was little change of expression on any of the three faces.

"Kato, go upstairs with the others…"

A brief flashing scowl crossed Kato's face, despite his previous reluctance to let Uzzi and his cohorts go upstairs without someone from Jia's group with them. Once more he was being sent out of her company, but as it had been his idea, as he had side-handedly volunteered to go, he could not protest the direction. He could only glower at Vance with a nod.

But he did not move.

Uzzi, meanwhile, smiled at the welcome division of manpower as his ruffs gathered around him.

"Pain…"

Jia swallowed the tightness in her throat, the remembrances of betrayal warring with the steadfast obedience the man had always given her father. "You and Deuce are our sentries." They had served well together the night before, or at least both had returned to the Pack uninjured without a bad report about the other. The role of omega had always been to protect the Pack from the outside, from the fringes. She trusted current and former omegas to continue the tradition.

"No one'll get past," Pain swore with a bowed head. "For Roland."

"For Roland," Deuce agreed with a growl.

Some of the ruffs looked at one another, perplexed.

"Eddie, stay with Vance and Pubby…"

"But I want to help…"

Pubby slipped his arm around the boy's shoulders. "Who else is gonna run with messages if we need it," he said warmly. "You gotta be faster than an old man like me."

Eddie looked back and forth between the Protectors, his mother, and Jia. Pubby was hardly old, nor was Vance. Both, however, had been recently injured. It was easy to agree that Pubby was right. Eddie could run faster, particularly in Fela form. It was the first excuse he had ever had, the first reason, to assume the form his mother overprotectively tried to suppress.

Jia offered him the opportunity to use it. The chance to do something important.

"I'll stay," he said with an accepting nod as he began to peel off his warm clothes and stuff them into his pack or tie them to the straps.

Candace frowned with deeper worry but said nothing more than, "Be careful," when she kissed the side of her son's head. He was revealing his identity to the ruffs and mercs, a dangerous predicament for a cub, particularly if Uzzi lacked the control over them he claimed to have.

"QiangXu, Yu, and I will take the north hall. Note everything you find. If there's stairs, if you find anything worthwhile…or dangerous…let the rest of us know. Watch for soft spots in the floor and ceiling." It may have been an obvious warning but she felt better providing it.

"If anyone," Uzzi added, offering the acquired gun to Vance and motioning Enola and the others to do likewise, "comes through that door that shouldn't be here, blow them away." If the guns worked, it was better to use them against threats here than save them for an unknown, unforeseeable future.

Vance recoiled at the brush of the man's hand against his and stared at the Fela who dragged the desk away from the staircase door. The room shuttered with the squeal of metal against the tile.

He knew. He understood.

It did not mean anything specific at this moment, but it might mean everything in the end.

As if feeling the Protector-mage's eyes on him, Kato looked over his shoulder, but instead of meeting Vance's gaze, he sought for and met Jia's. Surrounded by the dead, something felt off in a way he could not name. It could be the radiation QiangXu measured. It could also be his imagination. Lit by the fingers of coming dawn that reached around the window barricades, it occurred to Kato that Jia was the most beautiful woman he knew. Brave. Strong. Direct. Capable. Solid.

Not that he knew many women.

Giving his autonomy to her direction had been a hard thing to do at first after so many weeks alone with Vanya, but doing so had brought him on this journey. Had brought him his father. He had believed he had done both to win her affection, but perhaps that had not been the intended purpose. Perhaps he had come seeking his own identity, away from his sister, for the first time in his life.

Perhaps Jia was merely a catalyst.

Perhaps he needed to let her go.

As he pulled open the stairwell door and allowed Uzzi to be the first into the vestibule that offered a path upward, he accepted he was taking yet another step away from her as he had been doing for so many days past.

This step, however, felt unexpectedly final.

"Be careful too," he said to her, his voice heavy. "Stay safe."

Jia nodded solemnly, feeling the weight of his tone, his words as if they would unexpectedly drown her. It was a weight she did not understand. "You too."

The stairwell door closed.

Vance nodded with a choking sigh, refusing to burden her with further oppressive emotion or the knowledge he had gleaned from Uzzi. "Go on. We've got this."

"I know you do." Her hand brushed over his, taking comfort from him as though he was an anchor, a tether, to bring her back as it had brought him to her from the Below. She had never thought to trust a mage. She was reminded, as she led the Ursa into the north corridor, that she trusted Valentine Segara completely.

❧*❧

The sound, faint as it was, gave Aman a sense of direction. HOPE was ahead of him, in a building he had thought to search next, and as he had no desire to join forces with them or the capacity to fight against them, he led his companions out of the church, northwest around the end of the open-aired parking structure and the building infested by HOPE, and pressed in the direction the sound had come from. It was unidentifiable as anything more than a crash, but it was a sound offering a peculiar rush of anticipation.

Soldiers crossed their path, five shades in HOPE longcoats of black flapping in the propelling wind. With a hand signal, Aman's team crouched and froze around him, some behind trees, behind shrubs, behind an abandoned vehicle, behind the tall grass that grew up past their knees and snapped with frozen crunches as they dropped. Such little sounds were propelled towards the HOPE agents as they stalked westward, weapons at the ready, but they were either not heard over the wind or the scouts ignored them as nothing more than the product of the gale.

Minutes passed. The cold of the earth seeped through every layer of clothing Aman wore. When he decided that waiting any longer would prevent him from rising, when the five HOPE soldiers were long out of their line of sight and hearing, he gestured, struggled to his feet, and started north again.

☙*☙

"If they'd found what we're after," Ortega muttered, voice low as he cinched his uniform coat around his waist and tucked his scarf in at the neck to fasten the buttons and buckles there as well, protection against the sea wind rattling the door of their shelter, "we'd know." He was not feeling argumentative and knew the risks of challenging Donnovan, but the statement felt to be a reasonable one, both to protect the people with them as well as to protect the self-proclaimed Laedan.

The booming crash precipitating Donn's order to move out before most of his unit was dressed sounded both near and far away. The whistling storm made it impossible to pinpoint its origin, but they knew there were people to the north and south. Dividing their force seemed foolish to the captain without knowing who those others were, where they were, what they were doing, but like his father, Donn was disinclined to hear arguments that did not coincide with his desires.

"I won't let HOPE outflank us. I won't let them take LaGuardia." He could not verify HOPE's presence without revealing he had come here with them but he intended to sound certain enough of his knowledge to thwart questions from the captain and anyone inclined to challenge him.

"If it's not HOPE?"

Donn snorted. "Not afraid of Hallister either." Those were the two sides he knew he was at odds with. The two he knew were here. He believed whatever was here belonged to him regardless of treaties forged through oaths, writs, and marriage. He would not let anyone else have what rightfully belonged to him. "This is what my father wanted. It's what LaGuardia needs…"

"LaGuardia needs you alive." As much as Arlo hated saying it, as much as the thought sickened him, having lost first one of the co-Laedans and then the other, having Donn at the helm would be better than not having a Laedan. He had no idea how Nik would fare as a leader if he could stay clean but he did know how LaGuardia would suffer if the oldest Channon twin lost his fight with his demons.

Perhaps the Marrock heir could be convinced to come back to the Fortress and take her father's place.

Even if she did, without her father's supporters, in the shadow of the man's murder and the accusations against her, and against Roland, Arlo did not think she stood much of a chance against Donnovan.

"I'm not dying here. Hurry up. Sun's rising. We have to move." They were losing the advantage of darkness. It was time to go.

❧*❧

The dark corridor offered one open chamber after another, offices and conference rooms, a dining area, and a storage closet, all with windows boarded or blocked as the entry windows had been. None of the rooms contained what they were seeking or offered clues as to where they might search next. Given the time to rummage more thoroughly, to pick apart brittle pages bound together by decades of mildew and dust, or to pull open every drawer and cupboard and shelf, there might be materials to scav, useable books and paper, pencils and pens, and furnishings and metal for repurposing. There could be numerous things the Pack could use or trade if there was a way to carry it home. But none of it was the treasure the small armies combing the territory were hoping for and the pressing encroachment of others meant there was no time to dawdle.

An end of the hall stairwell, its door held shut with rust that gave way to the force of two Ursas' shoulders thrust against it, offered access upstairs and down. While Yu held position at the junction, Jia crept up to the landing above where a door wedged open with a crisply deformed leather boot allowed the voices of the second-floor search party to bleed through. She could not see them in the dark and chose to leave them to their assignment and rejoined Yu.

The stairwell QiangXu descended dead-ended at another door, this one of burnished metal not easily penetrated. It had originally been sealed by a smashed digital keypad panel, and now the knob was broken off, removed to leave a gaping hole through which a heavy metal chain was looped and run to a metal spike jammed into the wall nearby. The lock holding the chain together required a key none of them had.

Nothing could be seen through the knob hole, only the black of the room behind, but the three were in agreement.

The measures taken to keep others out…or keep something in, made what was behind it worth exploring. After so many decades, any captives held here, any grubbers locked away, were no longer a threat.

There was no evidence on the walls, the floors, or the stairs, of grubbers dragged or herded here.

Behind the door, there was no noticeable stench of death.

While Jia sent the agreed-upon signal back, a message to the rest that they might have found something of interest, QiangXu applied an explosive mixture to break the lock. Time spent searching the dead for a key would be time wasted. After a sparking pop, the lock dropped off and he pulled the chain free, the rattle of it echoing up the stairwell as he slowly peeled the door open as the women crouched in wait for the emergence of some threat. The hinges squealed with disuse.

Yu lit a flare they had saved from the lumber house and extended it into the dark before them.

Nothing appeared, only a short set of concrete steps barely visible in the light of the sizzling orange glare. Again looks were exchanged, nods followed, and the three started slowly down, not knowing what they might find in the hidden Below.

There were no working lights in the wide, shelf-lined passage. Fixtures once containing lighting tubes were mostly broken and dangled from the ceiling on wires holding their weight only because no one had disturbed them. A few tubes remained but they too were broken, or else had ceased to operate without the electrical current to power them. Without windows, without foot traffic, the floor was cleaner than the level above and the material installed on the surfaces of the walls and ceiling deadened the sound of their footsteps echoes.

There was only the sound of their breathing, their shuffling steps, and an unnerving sort of silence that made each of them anxious.

The contents of the shelves, however, alleviated much of their anxiety when they paused to investigate. Boxes and crates of survival goods, some tipped and rummaged through, some set upon the floor and emptied by previous looters before someone had the foresight to chain the outer door closed.

"Panic room?" Jia murmured as she pulled open a crate containing unfamiliar food packets. "My father told me about such rooms, places meant to protect people inside from the outside…" Something about this room, about the memories of her father, or maybe the impending sense of dread and finality that came with the nearness of revelation, made her feel dwarfed by the older pair with her, inferior and inexperienced. Her hands shook and she was unable to look at either of them as she closed the crate.

Searching the shelves made hiding her apprehension easier.

"Didn't protect them from themselves," Yu sighed, indicating the almost black splatter on the wall near the end of the shelf unit she was perusing and two small holes at their centers. It appeared the theft had been thwarted. From the height of the bullet holes, they assessed that two of the looters had been stopped by fatal force but the bodies were not here.

Jia glanced where the other woman pointed and shivered. Death had never troubled her beyond the loss of loved ones. Why, she mused, did the holes and surrounding spray evidence make her feel sick?

"Turned on each other for the rights to it I'd guess," said QiangXu from the farthest end of the room where another electronic keypad guarded another door. To his right, a third metal door, held ajar by a crowbar on the floor, led into a corridor that stretched beyond the flare's glow.

He traced the display with one hand and jiggled the handle with the other, opting to examine the inaccessible first. The handle and the keypad remained intact although there was scratching evidence consistent with the abandoned crowbar, indicating someone had tried to get inside. Possibly the same individuals who had tried to steal from the shelves and had died for their efforts. "Might not be able to knock out this one so easily…it'll take more to blow open the panel then it did the lock…"

"There's something in there worth protecting…" Jia's softly murmured, her quavering words nearly a question. They were enough to make QiangXu nod.

"If we don't try…they will."

They. Hallister. Channon. HOPE.

Jia sensed they were waiting for an order, a decision or guidance they expected her to give. If Roland was here, he would know what to do. What to say. After coming so far, leading them here, she felt at a loss for how to proceed as she faced this obstacle.

A locked door.

But it was, she believed, a door of significance. Its significance could not be proven without opening it and though the risk of an explosion, even one contained at the door to this long room, might attract the attention of those outside, it was a risk they needed to take.

As QiangXu indicated, if they did not open it first, someone else would.

"I can rig it, try to blow the lock…"

"Is it safe?"

QiangXu shrugged. "Doesn't need a big charge…but if it's reinforced, if the locks rigged in some way or there's something back there that can explode…"

She swallowed and nodded. There could be money behind the door. The room could contain sensitive documents, ancient computers and data storage, none of which mattered anymore. Or it could be the hoard Roland had wanted to keep out of his best friend's hands. They would not know without opening it.

She looked through the other open door and wondered if they should look there first. How much time did they have?

Yu gave Jia the flare with a reassuring, motherly smile. "Give him some light. I'll tell the others, bring them down. Might as well get some of this out…take it with us before we go further. No sense in wasting it."

Jia nodded. They had lost most of their supplies. They were unlikely to find another collection of goods as large as this one. "Good idea." She should have suggested it. Should have given the order. The trepidation, however, about what waited behind the locked door and the potential repercussions of opening it strangled her effort to think.

The goods on the shelves were more survival-vital than anything the offices had contained. Potentially more valuable and important than anything behind the barred door or at the end of the exposed dark corridor. These were things the Pack, and others, could use to survive. Things that would allow her group to return home. Food, bedding, and clothing in particular were as valuable in the borough as weapons. They could replace what they had lost in the sinkhole and bring the rest home.

Providing for their Pack was what Roland would have wanted.

Listening to Yu's retreating steps, Jia forced her attention back onto QiangXu and turned with the flare held high to offer him enough light to work by. "Do your best," she squeaked.

"All we can do. Here…put that here and help the others," he encouraged, taking the flare and positioning it at his feet so he could empty the necessary components out of his bag. "I've got this."

"You sure?"

"It'll take some time, but make it fast. More we get out the better."

They had to get as much material out of the room as they could before anyone else arrived.

They had until the door opened to do so. QiangXu was right too. Jia helping to empty the stores was more valuable than holding a light.

If what they expected was not here, the other corridor beckoned.

❧*❦

Damp-smelling, frigid, empty office after empty office. A waste of time, but a methodical quest that needed to be undertaken to rule out dangers or suss out usable resources. He wanted weapons, not to use them but for the sort of accumulated wealth such rare commodities stood for. He understood the Cana girl's intent and the keeping of promises made to the dead, but he found it both irritating and short-sighted to wish to destroy something she, too, could benefit from.

Such things could protect her pack from people like Quentin. People like Channon. People like Uzzi.

From people like HOPE.

"You haven't told them."

Another office, vacant but intact except for layers of dust and a broken window that had allowed in enough moisture over the years to allow the decay of the sill, the wall beneath the window, and the floor below, was left unexplored behind the door Kato pulled shut with a disgruntled growl.

There was no use in entering, rummaging through shelves and drawers and cabinets for something they could use.

There would be no weapons here. Nothing of value.

Kato had never had to survive entirely on scavving for any significant length of time. The few weeks between his mother's death and meeting up with the Flushing Pack had only required the need for food and shelter. There had been no need to seek clothing, tools, medical supplies, or anything he could trade.

He had never had to barter for anything in his life. What his family had needed they fabricated, improvised, or did without.

"Don't need to know." Kato released the handle without looking at the older man, his mixed feelings about sharing this corridor, this task, with him choking his grousing tone.

"Ashamed of me." Uzzi shrugged, sighing, snagging a lifted corner of wallpaper and pealing it away as they moved towards the next door. With each room so far, Kato had made certain to reach them first, to be the one to open them. It was not clear if he wanted the credit for anything they found or if he meant to protect Uzzi from potential traps. "Can't say I blame you…but I did what I needed to…"

"To protect yourself." Kato pushed open another door far enough to poke his head inside. Over his shoulder, he muttered, "Doesn't matter. Don't think any of this changes anything."

His brooding arrogance reminded Uzzi of himself when he had been a younger man and he chuckled to hear it. "Get your hands on those weapons and it will."

"I don't need…" The door was closed. Uzzi and the others did not have the opportunity to see past Kato to note its contents.

"Of course you do. Can't be part of her world forever." He had seen it before, doomed relationships sparked by proximity the post-Undoing world rarely allowed to succeed. "It'll never work, Fela and Cana. You know it." The few instances Uzzi knew of where such relationships had seemingly worked were ones he had lost track of years ago. He was enough of a betting man to believe, appearances aside, those unions had failed within a handful of years.

"You don't know anything."

"Know more than you." Uzzi snorted. "Join me. Best way to survive. With what's gotta be here, once we find it…you and me…we could go anywhere we want. Gotta think of Vanya's future…"

Kato's spinning lunge was so abrupt, his forearm pressed beneath Uzzi's chin to hold him against the wall with choking force, that Uzzi had no opportunity to avoid it. The mercs in the corridor, those not inspecting rooms Kato had already closed, aimed, or lifted their weapons but Uzzi's slight gesture, even as he fought to breathe, kept them from moving in.

Narrow-eyed, nostrils flared, with the muscles of his shoulders rippling as if in a struggle to resist a change of form, Kato hissed, "All I've done since the day you left is think about Vanya. Everything I've done's been for her. You did this to her, to us. Joining you's the last thing I'd do. We get this done, you go your way, I go mine, and I, we, never see you again."

The words were spoken but the twitching at the corners of his mouth and eyes, the trembling of the fist aimed at the side of Uzzi's head, the tremors shaking the arm holding him captive, caused him to resist smiling. Kato growled, a disgusted sound followed by the fist dropping its aim from Uzzi's head to catch him beneath the ribs. Then he released the older man into a heap on the floor and stalked towards the next room.

∽*∽

The half-form Cana circled them, herding them closer and closer to a door that banged and rattled against the wind's assault. There were two of them, odds Aman thought he could potentially beat, but the emergence of a familiar figure in the doorway with one hand silencing the banging door gave Aman a peculiar sense of destiny when one of the Cana propelled him forward with his snout. The man in the doorway stiffened, frowned, and silently watched them approach until the Cana herding them forced them to stop.

"You."

Aman had stolen a map to Fort Hamilton from this man without knowing what information the map contained, only suspecting its value from a host of clues that had swirled around both Laedan courts for months. Had it only been a few weeks ago, before he decided to give it to the Laedan's daughter after a quick peek at it? A map he had not, at the time, thought would involve him in any way, until Geary opted to send him west.

It would not surprise him to learn the Protector-Mage had viewed the map before its theft. Any curious man would have looked, and a mage would have seen details in it before ever unrolling the page. A mage would have remembered its contents. Aman had never considered this mage would have an interest in the rumored treasure, however…any more than Aman had an interest in being here. Dragged along by forces outside of themselves, he mused, as one of the Cana butted him forward.

Being in the company of two Cana made it unlikely the mage was here as part of HOPE's or Channon's teams. But Aman knew Geary had made an effort to recruit the Marrock girl to aid in the search and retrieval…and the mage had been in her company the last time Aman had seen either of them after the offer was made.

The mage was likely here with her. It was the only sensible reason for him to be here. Refusing to take his eyes fully off the Protector, he glanced briefly at the two Cana with an arched brow and planted his feet. Another Protector appeared over the mage's shoulder. Fate had thrown him and the mage into this pot. It was, he mused, the logical culmination of irony.

"Far enough." Behind Vance, Pubby aimed the shotgun at Aman's head, but Vance was unarmed as he took another step outside of the structure.

Aman read the words above the door with visually dispassionate interest. The phrase held promise. The Protectors had no intention of letting Hallister's man inside.

"I'm not here to fight."

"Expect us to believe that?" Vance grunted. Despite the question, Vance did believe the other man's words. Laedan Hallister's right-hand man, despite his effort to stand square-shouldered and proud, looked beaten down, war-weary, and the small gaggle behind him exhibited only exhaustion and wariness of the circling Cana. They had no desire to fight either.

"Think we're here for the same thing…" Those with him did not know what that thing was, but Aman was confident the mage did.

"You're not taking it back to Hallister."

It was the only evidence of knowledge Aman needed. "You found it? The stockpile?"

Vance grunted, started to speak, but was cut off as Yu bounded into the room and said, "We need some hands…" before spotting the stranger on the other side of the door.

"Eddie," Pubby muttered under his breath. "Get the others." Whether it was for an extraction of weapons or something else, or to fight the group beyond the door, he and Vance were going to need backup. He did not see visible guns on any of them, only clubs, shock sticks, and knives, but even with the support of the guarding Cana,

Pubby was not confident it would be enough. Not if a fight attracted the attention of HOPE and the Channons.

The juvenile panther pacing the room with a whipping tail shot up the stairs. The others in the southern corridor were near enough to come running with a call.

"If they're here, better they stay put. No place out there for…"

Aman's head cocked, his expression one of mild surprise to find he agreed with the mage. This place and any weapons it contained were relics of a world, a time, a mindset that had led to the Undoing and brought civilized humanity low. The closer he had come to this moment, the more certain Aman had become of what he needed to do. He did not know what he could tell Geary when he saw the Laedan again, but bringing instruments of destruction back to Kennedy seemed a foolish thing to do.

Just as foolish as allowing the Channons to do likewise.

As foolish as it was to let HOPE sink their hooks in and drag death back to the boroughs.

Vance's assertion remained incomplete. A screeching wail of horror and agony shattered the peace and warbled on the stormy air. Normal and anthro alike dove for cover or else ducked into frozen crouches, ready for combat against a beast they could not see.

❧*❧

Jumping away from the panel of buttons, levers, and small points of faintly flickering lights, Enola crashed backward into Candace and both stumbled to the floor, barely avoiding the striking end of Dink's club as it swung and crashed repeatedly into the offending board generating such horror when Enola leaned across it to look out of the window at the group the Cana were herding towards the door. The wail sputtered, groaned, and died with a wheezing gasp.

❧*❧

The screech was piercing enough to reverberate into the passage where Jia maneuvered her armload of goods towards the stairs, enough to blow her off her feet as they tangled in fright beneath her. The sound flooded the corridor and enveloped QiangXu too with a shockwave of startled terror making him lurch…and then scream as the materials he was securing to the door's locking apparatus exploded in his hand.

❧*❧

Across the weed-infested cracks of the frozen parking area, the two groups spotted each other. "Let's be smart about this," Warby called in a cordial tone. His relief at finding the Channon boy alive, in the company of LaGuardia Guards, evaporated before the bluster and snarl in the other man's stance. He was surrounded by enough men and women that Warby did not doubt Donnovan's intent. "Let's do this together and split the…"

An alliance was the wisest choice. If Grand Mas Lord was here, or Laedan Channon, they would have agreed. Donnovan had already made promises to the Grand Mas. It was why he had made it across the ruins to Fort Hamilton.

Donnovan, however, did not agree. With a gun confiscated from one of LaGuardia's men, he had already taken aim at Warby's head.

Wailing shook the air.

The ground trembled.

Gunfire split the peace.

Chapter 44

"QiangXu!"

The simultaneous disjointed shriek above and the explosion behind made Jia push to her feet amidst the dropped contents of the crate. Bruises burned beneath her clothes and abrasions stretched with searing pain on her palms as she forced herself up, ignoring as she did so the long sliver of fractured wood wedged into the meat of her palm. Pulled in two directions but trusting those above could cope with what had emitted the banshee-scream, she opted to race to the Ursa's side. She was the only one here to help him.

The explosives he had set to blow the lock worked as intended, filling the air with a puff of dust and black smoke, throwing the door open with enough force to scatter items immediately inside across the floor. She saw them, brief flashes noted in her run, boxes and crates, open cases of handguns, rounds of munitions. Not the missiles and bombs her father had feared but enough other weaponry, and possibly grenades, dynamite, and other explosives too, to force both boroughs into compliance beneath the boot of whoever wielded it.

Those details were noted but given no deeper consideration as she focused on QiangXu…and the mangled stump of his left hand.

He stared blankly at her stunned, breathless, his cry having ended in a slack-jawed stare as he watched her, unable to move, as if he did not realize what had happened, what had thrown him against the other open door, unaware of the injured limb he cradled against his body. When she reached for him, he turned slightly to face her, looking as if he would speak, blood dripping at the end of his arm.

No sound came.

She caught him before he slumped to the side. "Dear god…"

❧*❧

He heard the young Fela, smelled the approach of sweat and anxiety before Eddie burst out of the stairwell with a warning roar catching the Normals, already startled by the piercing alien wail, off guard. They turned to aim their weapons at him at the same moment their ears made out the smattering of gunfire somewhere outside and the shouts of people engaging in combat.

Kato did not ask questions Eddie could not answer. There was trouble, and his thoughts, his fears, focused instantly on Jia. He shoved past Uzzi and through the others, without thought.

"Take care of that!" Uzzi yelled, breaking into a run behind Kato, following Eddie into the stairwell reverberating with the chilling squeal. The ruffs burst into the rooms nearest them on the eastern side of the building, where windows led onto a level of roofing for the first floor. Proficient with such dives and falls, they scrambled through the already open windows or over the broken glass of ones they did not take time to open properly, to roll down the incline and leap to the ground, most of them landing on their feet or rolling onto them without injury. The combatants in the distance could not be seen, the sound of the clash echoing from beyond the collapsing parking structure in the distance, but as the ruffs hit the ground, they joined the handful of people in Kennedy uniforms already running south on the wings of someone's battle cry.

The pair of Cana followed.

"For Kennedy!"

Pubby still had the shotgun pointed at Aman's face.

The exploding jolt shaking the floor made him drop it, however, and pulled Yu back into the hall at a run, her message barely delivered. On the other side of the lobby, Candace, Enola, and Dink stumbled over each other in shock and near-panic. From the stairwell, Eddie, Kato, and Uzzi burst into the lobby at a breathless speed.

"No time for this," Vance yelled, more to his fellow Protector than to the others.

Eddie did not stop running. He flew past the pair of Protectors and the stranger at the door, charging in the direction Deuce and Pain were already running.

"Eddie!" Candace dashed after him, shedding Normal for half-form, tearing her clothes in the process causing shreds of fabric to trail behind her as she ran, determined to catch up to her son and keep him out of harm's way.

Vance tried to grab the woman's arm when she passed but his hand came up empty, her flightpath being beyond his reach. Realizing he was in command whether the others granted it or not, he barked and pointed to the north corridor. "Get down there and help her!"

It's what Jia wanted. Help. Whatever had brought Yu to them, there was the subsequent explosion to consider and the threat of battle outside that would soon be upon them if the warring parties learned they were here. Not a fight for dominance, perhaps, but a fight to prevent others from finding them first.

He had not wanted this fight any more than Jia, but a fight was what they were dealt. With the others following Yu down the north hall, Vance stayed where he was, the shotgun Pubby had retrieved and shoved into his hands still warm to the touch. He took refuge behind the reception desk, the rifle muzzle supported on the upper lip, the barrel aimed at anyone who dared to come through the door before the others rejoined him.

In the scramble, he did not see where Aman had gone.

Kato smelled blood before he rounded the final corner, before he threw aside the broken first door the explosion had tried to close, before he leaped over the splintered crate of supplies behind it and wove through the boxes of food pouches, clothing, and bedding blown from the shelves when the explosion had hit. It had been a small explosion compared to those previously experienced, localized to the end of the room, but the shockwave had been enough to dislodge the lighter, more precariously perched objects from the shelves and be felt throughout the building. Fearing the blood to be Jia's though his nose detected Ursa, not Cana, afraid the explosion had killed her, Kato crashed over the last of the fallen mess to find Yu squatted beside QiangXu, frantically wrapping his bloody stump of a wrist with her scarf, his, and the dainty silk one Jia had worn.

Pubby had already pushed past the three squatting in the doorway into the previously barred room and was throwing open one box, one crate, after another, tucking a multitude of objects into his pockets and the makeshift sling fashioned from a blanket he had snagged from the shelves. No one tried to stop him.

"Kato…take this…" Pubby began to thrust boxes of munitions into the Fela's unprepared arms, reaching over the heads of the three crouched on the ground.

"Let me help."

Ignoring that he had been holding a shotgun to the speaker's head, Pubby gave items to Aman and Uzzi as well.

"There isn't time for…we need to get the rest of…" Jia began to protest…only to stumble over her words when she recognized Fenway standing above her, his arms bearing the spoils of their find.

Kennedy was here.

Aman looked at her without a hint of surprise. Any questions he might have about her being here would wait for some calmer moment.

She could protest, deny his offered assistance, but at the moment, as Pubby began speaking, there were more important concerns than a single Kennedy agent…even if that agent was well known as Hallister's right hand.

"Got a war outside…gonna need some of this to hold 'em off," Pubby grunted, ignoring the protest. He had been promised a portion of what they found for his aid. Uzzi had too. Pubby did not want to be greedy, but considering what lay ahead, up there, with people coming to claim what they had found, he deemed it important, at the moment, to arm themselves.

He was no anthro. When it came to a fight, guns and his knowledge of them were going to be all Pubby had.

Whether they had the time, materials, or ability to blow the place or not.

Voice strained, her movements frantic as she worked to staunch the bleeding, Yu murmured, "We'll get you out of here…"

QiangXu shook his head. "I can't…I need…to set the…"

"You're in no condition…"

"I can do it." The two speaking simultaneously looked at one another. Jia did not know what experience Uzzi had, nor did he know what she knew, but they nodded at each other in agreement. It was best, she felt with another glance at Fenway, they get Hallister's man as far from the storeroom as possible without tipping their hand to their intentions.

For the moment, Fenway, his arms full of the munitions Pubby had given him, did not appear to know their intent.

Jia brushed QiangXu's hair from his face. His forehead was cool and clammy, telling her shock was setting in. They needed to get him out for better treatment, but she needed his direction too. "Tell me what to do," she murmured to the injured man with a gentle squeeze on his uninjured shoulder. "Then I want you out of here."

"I'm not…" began Kato with a growl.

"Nonsense, boy. Do as you're told. Get that stuff topside…take the food and gear up…you too, Pubby. And you," Uzzi looked at the unfamiliar man, choosing to trust him because the others did so. "Load up. By the time you're back for more, we should be set."

Kato growled. Pubby chose not to argue but took everything he could carry to get it safely away from what was likely to be a great explosion when the munitions began to pop. Aman, who the others paid little attention to, followed. They could make one trip up with guns and munitions. One trip with food, clothing, and survival gear.

It was the best they were going to get now that HOPE and the Channons were here.

Vance, Kato guessed, was up top alone.

"You're coming with me when I get back."

Jia was not certain who Kato was talking to but nodded her head in agreement. Anything to get him out of the basement.

Kato, running with his arms full, was unsure who he meant either.

⮜*⮞

The instinct to take shelter at the deafening blast of sound howling out of the metal horn at the top of a nearby pole was the only thing that kept Warby alive. The bullet cracked past him, missing his head and turning shoulder as he jerked away from the sound.

The man behind him was not so fortunate. He screamed and toppled to one side, his hand clutching his neck where red flowed between his fingers.

A glance back as the rest of his unit surged to meet the oncoming marauders in LaGuardia uniforms revealed those Warby had left behind emerging from the building they had been instructed to explore, drawn by the wail, drawn by the gunfire.

Their insubordination meant General Warby had backup, small though the number was. The need for them circumvented any irritation their disobedience might have fostered.

It did not appear that Donn Channon had any more than the number of LaGuardia Guards the general could see.

Back on his feet, his soldiers surging past, Warby took his shot.

Across the short field, Captain Ortega threw Donn to the ground. "Get off!"

Arlo rolled, a shooting pain in his side announcing the short blade wedged there. He blinked, staring in surprise, at the man who had stabbed him. "It's HOPE!" he gasped, certain in his duty though uncertain if the blade in his side had been an accidental assault or not.

"I don't care!"

With an angry shout of pent-up, bloodthirsty frustration, Donn yanked the blade free and ran with his force, leaving their doubts on the frozen ground with their bleeding captain.

⮜*⮞

A sound. A premonition. A sense of things common to those blessed with, or cursed with, the gifts of a tracker-mage. Something pulled Vance cautiously from behind the reception desk moments before Pubby, Aman, and Kato erupted into the room to deposit their collection at his feet.

"How's…?" he began, his senses disrupted, his focus torn by the heady smell of copper wafting on the air the three trailed with them.

Blood on the floor, partial footprints tracked far enough to have brought their evidence with them.

"Watch this!" Pubby cried before dashing from the room.

Eyes narrowed in annoyance, wondering if he should follow to assist, Vance bent to open the nearest latched metal box.

Something flew overhead and clattered to the floor.

He lurched around, pulling the shotgun's trigger.

Nothing happened.

Nepo laughed as he charged from the shadows at the back of the room like an enraged beast, his expression menacing and amused as he pounced on Vance and knocked the other mage off his feet.

Why, Vance thought fleetingly as he drove the butt of the shotgun into the side of Nepo's head, pushing him away, had no one thought to look for other exits or make sure the one they had seen at the rear in their exterior circle of the building was secured?

Nepo might have been here all along and Vance had somehow failed to detect him.

Unable to roll away with the reception desk blocking him, Vance slithered back, favoring the shoulder that, while externally healed, continued to be sore, stiff, and prone to aching in the worst of the cold. Nepo grabbed for his wrist, caught the gun barrel instead, and, when he tried to wrest it away, sent it sliding across the dusty tile floor.

"No Cana bitch to protect you now," he sneered.

The scramble to avoid the man's grasp resulted in a turned position from which Vance was able to kick Nepo in the face hard enough to push them apart from one another.

"Don't need protecting!"

⬧*⬧

Frustrated in his assessment, Warby saw what he deemed to be unforeseen reinforcements close in at the rear of LaGuardia's ranks. Despite his miscalculation, he was not worried about being outmatched. HOPE's forces received the best combat training available and were better armed, overall, for conflict. LaGuardia's men and women, weak, slow, and coughing, fell before them at a rate he did not expect those reinforcements to replace.

The fury and ferocity of the three unexpected Cana and one Fela prompted a change in tactics and orders.

"Take them down."

He would deal with Channon. The anthro must be eliminated first.

Without nets, without sufficient shock sticks to subdue them, Warby understood that, if they were not removed from the field, the anthro were likely to kill them all.

But not only them.

The three looked to be targeting LaGuardia, as the handful of those in Kennedy uniforms were.

Warby swung at the nearest man without a HOPE insignia, paying little attention to which side the man might be fighting for. Brain matter and blood splattered across his face.

He did not understand the apparent coalition of anthro and Kennedy. He did not know if there was one, or if the specious cooperation was more a matter of a shared target rather than any previously agreed treaty. But it was a fortuitous turn of events for HOPE. Let the boroughs fight amongst themselves.

Warby had his own target to mark.

Ortega crouched, wincing, twitching, instinctively ducking away from the three Cana, one Fela, and a host of others, some wearing the ragtag attire of mercs and ruffs and a few wearing Kennedy uniforms. He did not know when or how Kennedy had flanked them to the north, why the anthro appeared to fight beside them, or whose side they were taking as they surged into the U-shaped bowl of men and women created as Donn led LaGuardia against HOPE. Screaming. Shouting. Barking orders. Cries of pain and horror. Sporadic gunfire punctuated by anthro howls and roars. Chaotic turns as people in uniform fought first one enemy and then another.

All the while, Donn stalked General Warby across the muddy field warming beneath the rising sun and soaked with hot blood.

Arlo should rise. He should be at his Laedan's side. But the Laedan he had sworn fealty to lay buried in a field a few hundred yards from where Arlo had fallen and Donnovan, despite his leadership claims, had not been named to the chair. There was another hope, two of them if either could be convinced to take up their fathers' dropped mantles. Two who Arlo was certain could rule in a more level-headed, even-handed manner than Donnovan ever could.

The man had committed patricide. A man who would watch his father die the way Donn had did not deserve to rule LaGuardia.

Inching back to a cluster of brush, hoping to use it for cover, to hide from the battle or pull to his feet, Ortega made his decision.

He had to return to LaGuardia. He had to warn Nikolaj of Donn's betrayal.

Donnovan could fend for himself in the war he had made.

❧*❧

Nepo's backward movement knocked over the crate Vance had begun to open, spilling bullets across the floor. "Well now…" the lavender-eyed man whistled, stuffing a handful into his breast pocket as he rolled to maneuver to his feet.

"No you don't!" Vance charged. Nepo crashed back and rolled sideways, the littered floor hindering his escape. The bullets he had tried to pocket fell amongst the rest. It was Nepo's turn to kick out at Vance; his boot struck the smaller man in the center of his chest hard enough to drive him away.

"I don't need you. All I need's down there…"

❧*❧

Quentin.
It had to be Quentin.

Donn had never seen a Fela, had never seen Quentin change. But he knew Quentin was here, somewhere, as the man was also in search of the one thing that might grant him the power and prestige the Channons had denied him. Despite his purported hatred of anthro, a lie told to protect himself or else uttered in self-loathing, Quentin having Cana allies made sense…even though he had accused Roland Marrock of the same fault and ultimately killed him for it.

In the end, Roland had proven to be Normal. Niki had said so.

Perhaps Quentin had turned on him, murdered him, because Roland had known the truth and refused to support his quest for power.

Donn neither knew nor cared.

Nor did he care the Fela was here. Surrounded by the dwindling number of HOPE soldiers who were fighting those in Kennedy uniforms or the ruffs Quentin had brought in support, Quentin would not outlive this fight.

Donn's primary target had been reached. Warby swung at Donn's head with a spike-gloved fist as soon as they were in range of one another. It was a blow Donn easily avoided.

The confiscated gun was empty but it made an adequate club to strike sharp blows low around Warby's broad frame and across his face and head when Donn could reach him there. The knife used against his fool of a captain was in his other hand.

Warby was a warrior. Donn was a scrapper.

It was easy enough, Donn thought bitterly, to dance out of the way of the older man's curved blade.

From the side of the field of battle came a howl.

They turned beneath the shadow of a half-form Cana's leap.

It was time enough for Donn to make one more swing at the side of Warby's neck.

❧*☙

"Only place you're going is to hell!"

Vance charged at the man's retreating back and brought him down in a full-bodied tackle at the head of the north corridor. Undisturbed dust blasted into their faces, into their eyes and open mouths. Bullets clattered in every direction.

Nepo roared.

❧*❧

The fuses were tied and set as QiangXu instructed, the charges secured in the places around the room the bleary-eyed Ursa indicated would do the most damage to the contents. The remaining grenades brought with them out of Kennedy's Below not lost to the swallowing earth were piled at the center of the room and now that Pubby had pushed past with one last selection of goods in his arms, there was only one thing left to do.

They could not hear the fighting above from where they stood.

They heard only Pubby's retreating steps, each other's breathing, and the hammerings of their hearts.

"Allow me." Aman held out his hand for the lighter in Jia's fist.

She did not know what he was thinking. She could not see his thoughts the way Vance could. She only knew Fenway as a silent presence always in the background whenever Laedan Hallister came to LaGuardia. It seemed he understood, and agreed with, what she planned to do, an obvious realization now that the explosive charges were set. Aman had stood at the blown-open door, watching the final preparations, with a resolute, stoic expression of understanding and, Jia believed, approval.

Had she been wrong about Geary's intent? Had Kennedy's Laedan sent his people to do precisely what Jia was determined to do? Or was Fenway acting on his own, choosing an opposing path…or was he destined to betray her too, the way Lowell had betrayed her father?

She did not believe it. The creases at the corners of his eyes, the set of his mouth, told a story of weariness and surrender.

"Tell him…"

Though not a mage, she believed she saw resignation and determination in the man's ice-blue eyes.

He shrugged. There was nothing to tell. Nothing, at any rate, Geary would want to hear or was likely to believe. Despite their long, well-trusted relationship, Geary had sent him here, outmanned, undersupplied, to die.

Whether it was true or not, it was what Aman believed.

Everything that needed to be said were words spoken before.

"He's not gonna do it…he's gonna keep it for himself," Kato spat, pacing the narrow room with the agitation of a cat swishing its angry tail with its ears flat to its head.

"Not if I stop him." Uzzi propelled the others to the storeroom door and blocked their way back. Those who could had grabbed packs, boxes, or crates from the shelves, but what they could carry was limited by their haste.

"You stay down here, you'll die…" Kato protested. His pacing had stopped when the older man spoke, but the tension and anxiety in his body remained.

"Should have time to make it out before it sparks, if you run," QiangXu offered in feeble reassurance, "but I can't promise it…"

Uzzi nodded, wiping the grime on his face away with the sleeve of his coat. "All we need."

"I'm not leaving you here…"

"Go on, son; I'm right behind you. Not leaving you again." He did not want to argue. It was time, he thought, to do something good with his life. Make up for lives he had taken, ruined. Prove himself, set his son free. He had no intention of dying here, but if he did…well, he thought wryly, at least HOPE would not be hunting for him any longer.

Not understanding the shifting dynamics in the room, Jia grabbed Kato's hand as Pubby led Yu and QiangXu with hurried, stumbling steps to the staircase. Kato hesitated long enough to stare at their joined hands before squeezing hers and letting her go.

"Go," he prompted, making a show of picking up another crate of food packets. "I'll get another. I'm coming."

Jia nodded, turned, and ran through the debris with the sizzle of the match, and the following crackle of the fuse hissing in her ears.

"Would you," Nepo shouted, thrusting his wide fist into Vance's face, "just die already?"

Behind him, from the darkness in the hall, came a Cana roar, followed by the impact of the half-form leaping onto Nepo's back. Vance, sputtering blood from his nose and mouth, fell and struck his head on one of the crates. Nepo dropped beneath the Cana's weight as others tumbled out of the corridor…

…and were thrown to the floor as the stretch of building behind them shook, expelled debris and hot air into the sky, and imploded in upon itself.

End Part 3

About the Author

With fantasy and sci-fi as her passions, Tamara has written multiple novels to date, including the Kestrel Harper Saga, The Scarecrow Trials, and the stand-alone novel Suspicion's Gate. Burn the Sea is the third book in the Blood Wild Chronicles.

When not indulging in her love of words, Tamara relaxes in the company of her pack of Papillions, her horde of cats, and an ever-growing collection of films.

Learn more about Tamara's work at www.agdhani.com